Utah Legislative Assembly

Indian Depredations in Utah

memorial of the legislative assembly of Utah Territory, praying for an appropriation

to pay for Indian depredations and expenses incurred in suppressing Indian

hostilities

Utah Legislative Assembly

Indian Depredations in Utah
memorial of the legislative assembly of Utah Territory, praying for an appropriation to pay for Indian depredations and expenses incurred in suppressing Indian hostilities

ISBN/EAN: 9783337284886

Printed in Europe, USA, Canada, Australia, Japan

Cover: Foto ©Andreas Hilbeck / pixelio.de

More available books at **www.hansebooks.com**

INDIAN DEPREDATIONS IN UTAH.

MEMORIAL

OF THE

LEGISLATIVE ASSEMBLY OF UTAH TERRITORY,

PRAYING

For an appropriation to pay for Indian depredations and expenses incurred in suppressing Indian hostilities.

MARCH 22, 1869.—Referred to the Committee on Military Affairs and ordered to be printed with the accompanying papers.

The honorable the Senate and House of Representatives of the United States in Congress assembled:

GENTLEMEN: Your memorialists, the governor and legislative assembly of the Territory of Utah, would most respectfully represent to your honorable body, that for the last three years we have had a vexatious Indian war on our hands, the seat of which has been in Sevier, Piute, and Sanpete counties, extending more or less to the counties of Wasatch, Utah, Millard, Beaver, Iron, Washington, and Kane, rendering a strong military force constantly necessary in the field. Colonel Irish, former superintendent of Indian affairs, called on General Conner to protect the settlements of this Territory from Indian depredations. The general replied that if those depredations were committed upon any settlements along the overland mail line he would protect them. But if on settlements remote from said line he could not do it.

Colonel Head, present superintendent of Indian affairs, called on Colonel Potter to protect the settlements of this Territory where Indian hostilities existed. Colonel Potter sent east for instructions in the case, and received answer from General Sherman that we must rely on the militia of the Territory. During this war Sevier and Piute counties were abandoned by six extensive and flourishing settlements, it being considered impracticable to defend them there; their removal was effected at the loss of nearly all they had, their stock and teams being mostly stolen and driven away by the Indians, and they were removed by the citizens of Sanpete county. Likewise four settlements on the borders of Sanpete county were broken up and removed at much expense and loss. Also fifteen settlements in Iron, Kane, and Washington counties, besides two or three small settlements in Wasatch county.

In this war we have furnished our own soldiers, arms, ammunition, transportation, cavalry horses, and supplies for the years 1865–'6 and '7. We have borne a heavy burden, and we ask for compensation and aid as most of our citizens at and near the seat of this war have become greatly reduced and impoverished thereby; and likewise the other settlements that have had to remove are more or less so.

We therefore ask your honorable body to appropriate one million five hundred thousand dollars to compensate the citizens for their services, transportation, and supplies, in suppressing Indian hostilities in the Territory of Utah during the years before named, or so much thereof as will cover these expenses, as per vouchers and testimonies now in the adjutant general's office, which will accompany this our memorial, or follow it at an early day. And your memorialists, as in duty bound, will ever pray.

GEORGE A. SMITH,
President of the Council.
JOHN TAYLOR,
Speaker of the House of Representatives.

Approved February 21, 1868.

CHARLES DURKEE,
Governor of Utah.

Recapitulation of expenses incurred by the Territory of Utah in the suppression of Indian hostilities in said Territory during the years 1865, 1866, and 1867.

1865.

Service rendered as per pay rolls	$21,194 76	
Commissary supplies as per vouchers	6,819 98	
Quartermaster's supplies as per vouchers	4,453 50	
Transportation as per vouchers	7,518 00	
		$39,986 24

1866.

Service rendered as per pay rolls	431,285 54	
Commissary supplies as per vouchers	130,545 86	
Quartermaster's supplies as per vouchers	30,832 43	
Transportation as per vouchers	39,795 00	
		632,458 83

1867.

Service rendered as per pay rolls	300,112 19	
Commissary supplies as per vouchers	102,198 42	
Quartermaster's supplies as per vouchers	23,637 30	
Transportation as per vouchers	22,644 40	
		448,592 31

	1,121,037 38

ADJUTANT GENERAL'S OFFICE, UTAH TERRITORY,
Salt Lake City, February 8, 1869.

I certify that the above accounts are correct.

H. B. CLAWSON,
Adjutant General Utah Territory.

I, Charles Durkee, governor of Utah Territory, do hereby certify that the military service rendered by the militia of this Territory comprised in the foregoing accounts was absolutely necessary, and was therefore sanctioned and authorized by me at the times specified, and that the accounts are just.

CHARLES DURKEE, *Governor.*

VOUCHERS FOR COMMISSARY SUPPLIES FOR 1865.

UTAH TERRITORY, *Fairview, September,* 10, 1865.

The United States to Andrew Peterson,   DR.

September 10 to 25.—To 491 pounds bacon, at 35 cents.......	$171 85
To 379 pounds beef, at 10 cents.........	37 90
To 1,200 pounds flour, at 6 cents........	72 00
To 135 pounds beans, at 11 cents.......	14 85
To 90 pounds rice, at 40 cents..........	36 00
To 90 pounds coffee, at 40 cents........	36 00
To 145 pounds sugar, at 40 cents.......	58 00
To 8 gallons vinegar, at $1.............	8 00
To 10½ pounds candles, at 50 cents......	5 25
To 33 pounds soap, at 50 cents..........	16 50
To 45 pounds salt, at 5 cents..........	2 25
To 4½ bushels potatoes, at $1..........	4 50
To 2½ gallons molasses, at $2..........	5 00
	468 10

2028698

GREAT SALT LAKE CITY, *October* 10, 1865.

I certify that the above account is correct and just, that the above bill of articles were purchased of Andrew Peterson and furnished to Captain John L. Ivie's company cavalry on expedition against the Indians in Sanpete and Sevier counties.

ALBERT P. ROCKWOOD,
Commissary General Nauvoo Legion.

Received, Great Salt Lake City, October 10, 1865, of Albert P. Rockwood, commissary general, Nauvoo Legion four hundred and sixty eight dollars and ten cents, in full of the above account.

ANDREW PETERSON.

UTAH TERRITORY, *Mount Pleasant City, July* 20, 1865.

The United States to William Seely,   DR.

July 20 to Aug. 4.—To 319 pounds of bacon, at 35 cents........	$111 65
To 271 pounds beef, at 10 cents............	27 10
To 900 pounds flour, at 6 cents........	54 00

July 20 to Aug. 4.—To 90 pounds beans, at 11 cents.............	89	90
To 67 pounds rice, at 40 cents..............	26	80
To 60 pounds coffee, at 40 cents.............	24	00
To 100 pounds sugar, at 40 cents.............	40	00
To 5 gallons vinegar, at $1................	5	00
To 15 pounds candles, at 50 cents...........	7	50
To 25 pounds soap, at 50 cents.............	12	50
To 35 pounds salt, at 5 cents..............	1	75
To 3 bushels potatoes, at $1..............	3	00
To 3 gallons molasses, at $2..............	6	00
	289	20

GREAT SALT LAKE CITY, *August 20, 1865.*

I certify that the above account is correct and just, that the above articles were purchased of William Seely and furnished to Captain John L. Ivie's company cavalry on expedition against the Indians in Sanpete and Sevier counties.

ALBERT P. ROCKWOOD,
Commissary General Nauvoo Legion.

Received, Great Salt Lake City, August 20, 1865, of Albert P. Rockwood, commissary general Nauvoo Legion, two hundred and eighty-nine dollars and twenty cents, in full of the above account.

WM. SEELY.

———

UTAH TERRITORY, *Manti City, June 1, 1865.*

The United States to Andrew Moffitt,   DR.

June 1 to 30.—To 513 pounds beef, at 10 cents................	$51	30
To 483 pounds bacon, at 35 cents..............	169	05
To 119 pounds dried beef, at 25 cents.........	29	75
To 1,700 pounds flour, at 6 cents..............	102	00
To 175 pounds beans, at 11 cents..............	19	25
To 127 pounds rice, at 40 cents...............	50	80
To 117 pounds coffee, at 40 cents.............	46	80
To 191 pounds sugar, at 40 cents.............	76	40
To 10 gallons vinegar, at $1.................	10	00
To 15 pounds candles, at 50 cents............	7	50
To 45 pounds soap, at 50 cents..............	22	50
To 54 pounds salt, at 5 cents...............	2	70
To 5 bushels potatoes, at $1.................	5	00
To 5 gallons molasses, at $2.................	10	00
	603	05

GREAT SALT LAKE CITY, *July 5, 1865.*

I certify that the above account is correct and just, that the above bill of articles were purchased of Andrew Moffitt and furnished to Captain George Sidwell's company cavalry while on expedition against the Indians in Sanpete and Sevier counties.

ALBERT P. ROCKWOOD,
Commissary General Nauvoo Legion.

Received, Great Salt Lake City, July 5, 1865, of Albert P. Rockwood, commissary general Nauvoo Legion, six hundred and three dollars and five cents, in full of the above account.

ANDREW MOFFITT.

UTAH TERRITORY, *Glenwood, June 1, 1865.*

The United States to James Wareham, DR.

June 1 to July 31.—To 372 pounds bacon, at 35 cents	$130	20
To 490 pounds beef, at 10 cents	49	00
To 1,100 pounds flour, at 6 cents	66	00
To 125 pounds beans, at 11 cents	13	75
To 75 pounds rice, at 40 cents	30	00
To 75 pounds coffee, at 40 cents	30	00
To 125 pounds sugar, at 40 cents	50	00
To 7 gallons vinegar, at $1	7	00
To 15 pounds candles, at 50 cents	7	50
To 40 pounds soap, at 50 cents	20	00
To 35 pounds salt, at 5 cents	1	75
To 9 bushels potatoes, at $1	9	00
To 4 gallons molasses, at $2	8	00
	422	20

GREAT SALT LAKE CITY, *August 9, 1865.*

I certify that the above account is correct and just, that the above bill of articles were purchased of James Wareham and furnished to Captain Artemas Millett's company cavalry while on expedition against the Indians in Sanpete and Sevier counties.

ALBERT P. ROCKWOOD,
Commissary General Nauvoo Legion.

Received, Great Salt Lake City, August 9, 1865, of Albert P. Rockwood, commissary general Nauvoo Legion, four hundred and twenty-two dollars and twenty cents, in full of the above account.

JAMES WAREHAM.

UTAH TERRITORY, *Fountain Green, July 20, 1865.*

The United States to R. L. Johnson, DR.

July 20 to Aug. 4.—To 330 pounds bacon, at 35 cents	$115	50
To 295 pounds beef, at 10 cents	29	50
To 1,000 pounds flour, at 6 cents	60	00
To 97 pounds beans, at 11 cents	10	07
To 67 pounds rice, at 40 cents	26	80
To 68 pounds coffee, at 40 cents	27	20
To 97 pounds sugar, at 40 cents	38	80
To 4½ gallons vinegar, at $1	4	50
To 17 pounds candles, at 50 cents	8	50
To 29 pounds soap, at 50 cents	14	50

July 20 to Aug. 4.—To 40 pound salt, at 5 cents $2 00
                     To 4 bushels potatoes, at $1 ....   4 00
                     To 3 gallons molasses, at $2 ....   6 00
                                                                 _____
                                                                  347 37
                                                                 ======

GREAT SALT LAKE CITY, *August* 20, 1865.

I certify that the above account is correct and just, that the above bill of articles were purchased of R. L. Johnson and furnished to Captain Abner Lowry's company cavalry on expedition against the Indians in Sanpete and Sevier counties.

                              ALBERT P. ROCKWOOD,
                            Commissary General Nauvoo Legion.

Received, Great Salt Lake City, August 20, 1865, of Albert P. Rockwood, commissary general Nauvoo Legion, three hundred and forty-seven dollars and thirty-seven cents, in full of the above account.

                                    R. L. JOHNSON.

_____

UTAH TERRITORY, *Manti, April 10, 1865.*

The United States to Andrew Moffitt,   DR.

April 10 to 29.—To 692 pounds bacon, at 35 cents $204 50
                 To 385 pounds dried beef, at 25 cents 96 25
                 To 2,000 pounds flour, at 6 cents 120 00
                 To 200 pounds beans, at 11 cents 22 00
                 To 150 pounds rice, at 40 cents' 60 00
                 To 160 pounds coffee, at 40 cents 64 00
                 To 200 pounds sugar, at 40 cents 80 00
                 To 12 gallons vinegar, at $1 ....   12 00
                 To 25 pounds candles, at 50 cents 12 50
                 To 35 pounds soap, at 50 cents 14 00
                 To 60 pounds salt, at 5 cents 3 00
                 To 4 gallons molasses at $2 ....   8 00
                                                                 _____
                                                                  696 25
                                                                 ======

GREAT SALT LAKE CITY, *May 10, 1865.*

I certify that the above account is correct and just; that the above articles were purchased of Andrew Moffitt and furnished to Captain N. S. Beach's company cavalry while on expedition against the Indians in Sanpete and Sevier counties.

                              ALBERT P. ROCKWOOD,
                            Commissary General Nauvoo Legion.

Received, Great Salt Lake City, May 10, 1865, of Albert P. Rockwood, commissary general Nauvoo Legion, six hundred and ninety-six dollars and twenty-five cents, in full of the above account.

                                    ANDREW MOFFITT.

UTAH TERRITORY, *Richfield, May* 1, 1865.

The United States to N. S. Higgins, DR.

May 1 to November 30.—To 9.333 pounds beef, at 10 cents...	$933	30
To 10,248 pounds flour, at 6 cents ..	614	88
To 1,098 pounds beans, at 11 cents.	120	78
To 732 pounds rice, at 40 cents.....	292	80
To 753 pounds coffee, at 40 cents ...	301	20
To 1,098 pounds sugar, at 40 cents..	439	20
To 54 gallons vinegar, at $1	54	00
To 91 pounds candles, at 50 cents...	45	50
To 275 pounds soap, at 50 cents	137	50
To 320 pounds salt, at 5 cents......	16	00
To 31½ bushels potatoes, at $1	31	50
To 21½ gallons molasses, at $2	43	00
	3,029	66

GREAT SALT LAKE CITY, *December* 10, 1865.

I certify that the above account is correct and just; that the above bill of articles were purchased of N. S. Higgins and furnished to Major Higgins's command while employed in the suppression of Indian hostilities in Sevier and Piute counties.

ALBERT P. ROCKWOOD,
Commissary General Nauvoo Legion.

Received, Great Salt Lake City, December 10, 1865, of Albert P. Rockwood, commissary general Nauvoo Legion, three thousand twenty-nine dollars and sixty-six cents, in full of the above account.

NELSON HIGGINS.

UTAH TERRITORY, *Moroni, April* 10, 1865.

The United States to George W. Bradley, DR.

April 10 to 29.—To 517 pounds beef, at 10 cents	$51	70
To 753 pounds bacon, at 35 cents.............	263	55
To 382 pounds dried beef, at 25 cents	95	50
To 2,740 pounds flour, at 6 cents..............	164	40
To 300 pounds beans, at 11 cents	33	00
To 215 pounds rice, at 40 cents	86	00
To 200 pounds coffee, at 40 cents	80	00
To 295 pounds sugar, at 40 cents..............	118	00
To 19 gallons vinegar, at $1..................	19	00
To 27 pounds candles, at 50 cents.............	13	50
To 31 pounds soap, at 50 cents	15	50
To 100 pounds salt, at 5 cents	5	00
To 9½ gallons molasses, at $2.................	19	00
	964	15

GREAT SALT LAKE CITY, *May* 20, 1865.

I certify that the above account is correct and just; that the above bill of articles were purchased of George W. Bradley and furnished to Captain Abner Lowry's company cavalry while on expedition against the Indians in Sanpete and Sevier counties.

ALBERT P. ROCKWOOD,
Commissary General Nauvoo Legion.

Received, Great Salt Lake City, May 20, 1865, of Albert P. Rockwood, commissary general Nauvoo Legion, nine hundred and sixty-four dollars and fifteen cents, in full of the above account.

GEORGE W. BRADLEY.

VOUCHERS FOR QUARTERMASTER'S SUPPLIES FOR 1865.

UTAH TERRITORY, *Fountain Green, July* 20, 1865.

The United States to R. L. Johnson,   DR.

July 20 to August 4.—To 217 bushels oats, at $1	$217 00
To 71 bushels barley, at $1 25	88 75
To 3,500 pounds hay, at 1 cent	35 00
	340 75

GREAT SALT LAKE CITY, *August* 20, 1865.

I certify that the above account is correct and just; that the above bill of articles were purchased of R. L. Johnson and furnished to Captain Abner Lowry's company cavalry, while on expedition against the Indians in Sanpete and Sevier counties.

LEWIS ROBISON,
Quartermaster General Nauvoo Legion.

Received, Great Salt Lake City, August 20, 1865, of Lewis Robison, quartermaster general Nauvoo Legion, three hundred and forty dollars and seventy-five cents, in full of the above account.

R. L. JOHNSON.

UTAH TERRITORY, *Mount Pleasant, July* 20, 1865.

The United States to William Seely,   DR.

July 20 to August 4.—To 178 bushels oats, at $1	$178 00
To 48 bushels barley, at $1 25	58 75
To 3,000 pounds hay, at 1 cent	30 00
	266 75

GREAT SALT LAKE CITY, *August* 20, 1865.

I certify that the above account is correct and just; that the above bill of articles were purchased of William Seely and furnished to Captain John L. Ivie's company cavalry, while on expedition against the Indians in Sanpete and Sevier counties.

LEWIS ROBISON,
Quartermaster General Nauvoo Legion.

Received, Great Salt Lake City, August 20, 1865, of Lewis Robison, quartermaster general Nauvoo Legion, two hundred and sixty-six dollars and seventy-five cents, in full of the above account.

WM. SEELY.

UTAH TERRITORY, *Fairview, September* 10, 1865.

The United States to Andrew Peterson,	DR.
September 10 to 25.—To 337 bushels oats, at $1	$337 00
To 27 bushels barley, at $1 25	33 75
To 7,000 pounds hay, at 1 cent	70 00
	440 75

GREAT SALT LAKE CITY, *October* 10, 1865.

I certify that the above account is correct and just, and that the above bill of articles were purchased of Andrew Peterson and furnished to Captain John L. Ivie's company cavalry, on expedition against the Indians in Sanpete and Sevier counties.

LEWIS ROBISON,
Quartermaster General Nauvoo Legion.

Received, Great Salt Lake City, October 10, 1865, of Lewis Robison, quartermaster general Nauvoo Legion, four hundred and forty dollars and seventy-five cents, in full of the above account.

ANDREW PETERSON.

UTAH TERRITORY, *Glenwood, June* 1, 1865.

The United States to James Wareham,	DR.
June 1 to July 31.—To 195 bushels oats, at $1	$195 00
To 79 bushels barley, at $1 25	98 75
To 7,000 pounds hay, at 1 cent	70 00
	363 75

GREAT SALT LAKE CITY, *August* 5, 1865.

I certify that the above account is correct and just, and that the above bill of articles were purchased of James Wareham and furnished to Captain Artemas Millett's company cavalry on expedition against the Indians in Sanpete and Sevier counties.

LEWIS ROBISON,
Quartermaster General Nauvoo Legion.

Received, Great Salt Lake City, August 5, 1865, of Lewis Robison, quartermaster general Nauvoo Legion, three hundred and sixty-three dollars and seventy-five cents, in full of the above account.

JAMES WAREHAM.

UTAH TERRITORY, *Manti City, June*, 1865.

The United States to George Peacock,	DR.	

`June 1 to 30.—To 487 bushels oats, at $1 .... $487 00
           To 15 bushels barley, at $1 25 ....   18 75
           To 29 bushels corn, at $1 50 ....   43 50
           To 5,000 pounds hay, at 1 cent................   50 00
                                                           ————
                                                           599 25`

GREAT SALT LAKE CITY, *July* 5, 1865.

I certify that the above account is correct and just, and that the above bill of articles were purchased of George Peacock and furnished to Captain George Sidwell's company cavalry, on expedition against the Indians in Sanpete and Sevier counties.

LEWIS ROBISON,
Quartermaster General Nauvoo Legion.

Received, Great Salt Lake City, July 5, 1865, of Lewis Robison, quartermaster general Nauvoo Legion, five hundred and ninety-nine dollars and twenty-five cents, in full of the above account.

GEORGE PEACOCK.

———

UTAH TERRITORY, *Richfield, May* 1, 1865.

The United States to N. S. Higgins,	DR.	

`May 1 to November 30.—To 840 bushels oats, at $1 .... $840 00
               To 15,000 pounds hay, at 1 cent.....   150 00
                                                       ————
                                                       990 00`

GREAT SALT LAKE CITY, *December* 10, 1865.

I certify that the above account is correct and just, and that the above bill of articles were purchased of N. S. Higgins and furnished to Major Higgins's command while employed in the suppression of Indian hostilities in Sevier and Piute counties.

LEWIS ROBISON,
Quartermaster General Nauvoo Legion.

Received, Great Salt Lake City, December 10, 1865, of Lewis Robison, quartermaster general Nauvoo Legion, nine hundred and ninety dollars, in full of the above account.

NELSON HIGGINS.

———

UTAH TERRITORY, *Manti City, April* 10, 1865.

The United States to F. C. Robinson,	DR.	

`April 10.—To 250 bushels oats, at $1........................ $250 00
        To 2,000 pounds hay, at 1 cent....................   20 00`

April 15.—To 200 bushels oats, at $1....................... $200 00
April 28.—To 50 bushels oats, at $1....................... 50 00
    To 1,500 pounds hay, at 1 cent.................... 15 00
                                                            535 00

GREAT SALT LAKE CITY, *May* 10, 1865.

I certify that the above account is correct and just; that the above bill of articles were purchased of F. C. Robinson and furnished to Captain N. S. Beach's company cavalry on expedition against the Indians in Sanpete and Sevier counties, and that they were necessary for that purpose.

LEWIS ROBISON,
Quartermaster General Nauvoo Legion.

Received, Great Salt Lake City, May 10, 1865, of Lewis Robison, quartermaster general Nauvoo Legion, five hundred and thirty-five dollars, in full of the above account.

F. C. ROBINSON.

UTAH TERRITORY, *Moroni City, April 10, 1865.*

The United States to George W. Bradley,   DR.

April 10.—To 536 bushels oats, at $1...................... $536 00
  17.—To 241 bushels barley, at $1 25.................. 361 25
  28.—To 2,000 pounds hay, at 1 cent.................. 20 00
                                              917 25

GREAT SALT LAKE CITY, *May* 20, 1865.

I certify that the above account is correct and just; that the above bill of articles were purchased of George W. Bradley and furnished to Captain Abner Lowry's command, on expedition against the Indians in Sanpete and Sevier counties, and that they were necessary for that purpose.

LEWIS ROBISON,
Quartermaster General Nauvoo Legion.

Received, Great Salt Lake City, May 20, 1865, of Lewis Robison, quartermaster general Nauvoo Legion, nine hundred and seventeen dollars and twenty-five cents, in full of the above account.

GEORGE W. BRADLEY.

VOUCHERS FOR TRANSPORTATION FOR 1865.

UTAH TERRITORY, *Mount Pleasant, July 20, 1865.*

The United States to William Seely,   DR.

For the use of horses, mules, and wagons, hauling baggage, provisions, and forage with Captain John L. Ivie's company cavalry while on expedition against the Indians in Sanpete and Sevier counties.

June 20 to August 4.—To five pack mules, 15 days, at 40 cents
            per day each........................ $30 00
          To 3 four-mule cams, 15 days, at $5 per
            day each......................... 225 00
                                                _____
                                                255 00
                                                =======

GREAT SALT LAKE CITY, *August* 20, 1865.

I certify that the above animals and wagons were engaged in and for
the service and time specified.

LEWIS ROBISON,
Quartermaster General Nauvoo Legion.

Received, Great Salt Lake City, August 20, 1865, of Lewis Robison,
quartermaster general Nauvoo Legion, two hundred and fifty-five dollars, in full of the above account.

WILLIAM SEELY.

————

UTAH TERRITORY, *Fountain Green, July* 20, 1865.

The United States to R. L. Johnson,   DR.

For the use of horses, mules, and wagons, hauling baggage, provisions,
and forage, with Captain Abner Lowry's company cavalry, on expedition against the Indians in Sampete and Sevier counties.
July 20 to August 4.—To 6 pack mules, 15 days, at 40 cents per
            day each........................... $36 00
          To 4 four mule teams, 15 days, at $5 per
            day each........................... 300 00
                                                _____
                                                336 00
                                                =======

GREAT SALT LAKE CITY, *August* 20, 1865.

I certify that the above animals and wagons were engaged in and for
the service and time specified.

LEWIS ROBISON,
Quartermaster General Nauvoo Legion.

Received, Great Salt Lake City, August 10, 1865, of Lewis Robison,
quartermaster general Nauvoo Legion, three hundred and thirty-six
dollars, in full of the above account.

R. L. JOHNSON.

————

UTAH TERRITORY, *Glenwood, June* 1, 1865.

The United States to James Wareham,   DR.

For the use of horses, mules, and wagons, hauling baggage, provisions,
and forage, with Captain Artemus Millett's company cavalry, on expedition against the Indians in Sampete and Sevier counties.

June 1 to July 1.—To 3 pack mules, 60 days, at 40 cents per day
each... $72 00
To 1 four-mule team, 60 days, at $5 per day
each..................................... 300 00

372 00

GREAT SALT LAKE CITY, *August 5, 1865.*

I certify that the above animals and wagon were engaged in and for the service and time specified.

LEWIS ROBISON,
Quartermaster General Nauvoo Legion.

Received, Great Salt Lake City, August 5, 1865, of Lewis Robison, quartermaster general Nauvoo Legion, three hundred and seventy-two dollars, in full of the above account.

JAMES WAREHAM.

UTAH TERRITORY, *Manti, June 1, 1865.*

The United States to Andrew Moffitt,   DR.

For the use of horses, mules, and wagons, hauling baggage, provisions, and forage, with Captain George Sidwell's company cavalry, while on expedition against the Indians in Sanpete and Sevier counties.

June 1 to June 30.—To 9 pack mules, 30 days, at 40 cents per
day each............................... $108 00
To 4 four-mule teams, 30 days, at $5 per
day each............................ 600 00

708 00

GREAT SALT LAKE CITY, *July 5, 1865.*

I certify that the above animals and wagons were engaged in and for the service and time specified.

LEWIS ROBISON,
Quartermaster General Nauvoo Legion.

Received, Great Salt Lake City, July 5, 1865, of Lewis Robison, quartermaster general Nauvoo Legion, seven hundred and eight dollars, in full of the above account.

ANDREW MOFFITT.

UTAH TERRITORY, *Richfield, May 1, 1865.*

The United States to N. S. Higgins,   DR.

For the use of horses, mules, and wagons, hauling baggage, provisions, and forage, with Major Higgins's command, while employed in the suppression of Indian hostilities in Sevier and Piute counties.

May 1 to November 30.—To 3 four-mule teams, 210 days, at
$5 per day each............... $4,150 00

GREAT SALT LAKE CITY, *December* 10, 1865.

I certify that the above animals and wagons were engaged in and for the service and time specified.

LEWIS ROBISON, .
Quartermaster General Nauvoo Legion.

Received, Great Salt Lake City, December 10, 1865, of Lewis Robison, quartermaster general Nauvoo Legion, four thousand one hundred and fifty dollars, in full of the above account.

NELSON HIGGINS.

UTAH TERRITORY, *Manti, April* 10, 1865.

The United States to Andrew Moffitt,   DR.

For the use of horses, mules, and wagons, hauling baggage, provisions, and forage, with Captain N. S. Beach's company cavalry, while on expedition against the Indians in Sanpete and Sevier counties.

April 10 to April 29.—To 12 pack mules, 20 days, at 40 cents per day each......................	$96 00
April 10 to April 15.—To 2 four-mule teams, 15 days, at $5 per day each..........................	150 00
April 15 to April 27.—To 2 four-mule teams, 12 days, at $5 per day each............................	120 00
April 21 to April 29.—To 2 four-mule teams, 9 days, at $5 per day each............................	90 00
	456 00

GREAT SALT LAKE CITY, *May* 10, 1865.

I certify that the above animals and wagons were engaged in and for the service and time specified above.

LEWIS ROBISON,
Quartermaster General Nauvoo Legion.

Received, Great Salt Lake City, May 10, 1865, of Lewis Robison, quartermaster general Nauvoo Legion, four hundred and fifty-six dollars, in full of the above account.

ANDREW MOFFITT.

UTAH TERRITORY, *Moroni City,* 1865.

The United States to George W. Bradley,   DR.

For use of horses, mules, and wagons, hauling baggage, provisions, and forage, with Captain Abner Lowry's company cavalry, on expedition against the Indians in Sanpete and Sevier counties.

April 10 to April 29.—To 15 pack mules, 20 days, at 40 cents per day each......................	$120 00
To 3 four-mule teams, 20 days, at $5 per day each...........................	300 00

April 17 to April 29.—To 2 four-mule teams, 12 days, at $5 per
To 2 four-mule teams, 12 days, at $5 per
day each............................. 120 00
day each............................. 120 00
To 1 two-horse team, 12 days, at $4 per
day.................................. 48 00
                                        _____
                                        708 00
                                        ========

I certify that the above animals and wagons were engaged in and for
the service and time specified above.

LEWIS ROBISON,
Quartermaster General Nauvoo Legion.

Received, Great Salt Lake City, ———, 1865, of Lewis Robison, quartermaster general Nauvoo Legion, seven hundred and eight dollars, in
full of the above account.

GEORGE W. BRADLEY.

UTAH TERRITORY, *Fairview, September* 10, 1865.

The United States to Andrew Peterson,   DR.

For use of horses, mules, and wagons, hauling baggage, provisions,
and forage, with Captain John L. Ivie's company cavalry, on expedition
against the Indians in Sanpete and Sevier counties.

Sept. 10 to Sept. 25.—To 13 pack mules, 15 days, at 40 cents per
day each........................... $78 00
To 5 four-mule teams, 15 days, at $5 per
day each........................... 375 00
Sept. 17 to Sept. 25.—To 2 four-mule teams, 8 days, at $5 per
day each........................... 80 00
                                      _____
                                      533 00
                                      ========

GREAT SALT LAKE CITY, *October* 10, 1865.

I certify that the above animals and wagons were engaged in and for
the service and time specified.

LEWIS ROBISON,
Quartermaster General Nauvoo Legion.

Received, Great Salt Lake City, October 10, 1865, of Lewis Robison,
quartermaster general Nauvoo Legion, five hundred and thirty-three
dollars, in full of the above account.

ANDREW PETERSON.

Recapitulation of expenses incurred by the Territory of Utah in the suppression of Indian hostilities in said Territory during the year 1865.

Names of commanding officers of companies.	Service rendered.	Commissary supplies.	Quartermaster supplies.	For transportation.	Total.
Nelson S. Higgins....................	$6,275 50				
Abner Lowry........................	2,265 76				
Nathaniel S. Beach.	1,653 20				
George Sidwell	1,320 83				
Artemas Millett....	1,658 98				
John L. Ivie	767 50				
Abner Lowry	783 50				
John L. Ivie.....	1,037 48				
Colonel Albred, field and staff........	398 01				
General Snow, field and staff........	5,034 00				
Total....	21,194 76	* $6,819 98	†$4,453 50	‡$7,518 00	$39,986 24

 * As per commissary general's vouchers.   † As per quartermaster general's vouchers.
     ‡ As per quartermaster general's vouchers.

I certify that the above account is correct.

H. B. CLAWSON,
Adjutant General Militia Utah Territory.

PAY-ROLLS FOR 1865.

Pay-roll of Captain Abner Lowry's company —— Utah militia cavalry, employed in the suppression of Indian hostilities in San-pete county, Utah Territory, in the month of April, 1865.

We, the undersigned, acknowledge to have received from James W. Cummings, paymaster Utah Territory militia, the sums set opposite to our names, in full payment for our services for the time specified.

Number	Names	Rank	Period of service — Commencement	Expiration	Days	Pay per month	Monthly allowance for clothing	Total monthly pay and allowance	40 cts. per day for use and risk of horse and equipments	Total pay and allowance	Signatures	Witnesses
1	Abner Lowry	Captain	April 10, 1865	April 29, 1865	20			129 50	$8 00	$91 31	Abner Lowry	John Kirkman.
2	Joseph Anderson Allred	1st lieut.	April 10, 1865	April 29, 1865	20			112 83	8 00	83 22	Joseph A. Allred	William Blain.
3	John Chester Hichcock	...do.	April 10, 1865	April 29, 1865	20			112 83	8 00	83 22	John C. Hichcock	David Candland.
4	Orange Seeley	2d lieut.	April 10, 1865	April 29, 1865	20			112 83	8 00	83 22	Orango Seely	John R. Winder.
5	Thomas Robertson	...do.	April 10, 1865	April 29, 1865	20			112 83	8 00	83 22	Thomas Robertson	William Blain.
6	James Martin Allred	...do.	April 10, 1865	April 29, 1865	20			112 83	8 00	83 22	James M. Allred	David Candland.
7	John F. Sanders	1st serg't.	April 10, 1865	April 29, 1865	20	20 00	3 50	23 50	8 00	23 67	John F. Sanders	William Blain.
8	Andrew Madsen	Sergeant.	April 10, 1865	April 29, 1865	20	17 00	3 50	20 50	8 00	21 67	Andrew Madsen	
9	Isaac Morley Allred	Private.	April 10, 1865	April 29, 1865	20	13 00	3 50	16 50	8 00	19 00	Isaac M. Allred	John Kirkman.
10	Rasmus Justesen	..do	April 10, 1865	April 29, 1865	20	13 00	3 50	16 50	8 00	19 00	Rasmus Justesen	Do.
11	James Harvey	..do	April 10, 1865	April 29, 1865	20	13 00	3 50	16 50	8 00	19 00	James Harvey	Do.
12	Andrew Leslie	..do	April 10, 1865	April 29, 1865	20	13 00	3 50	16 50	8 00	19 00	Andrew Lesley	Do.
13	Thomas Blackham	..do	April 10, 1865	April 29, 1865	20	13 00	3 50	16 50	8 00	19 00	Thomas Blackham	Do.
14	P. C. Anderson	..do	April 10, 1865	April 29, 1865	20	13 00	3 50	16 50	8 00	19 00	P. C. Anderson	Do.
15	J. C. Nelson	..do	April 10, 1865	April 29, 1865	20	13 00	3 50	16 50	8 00	19 00	J. C. Nelson	Do.
16	Parley Draper	..do	April 10, 1865	April 29, 1865	20	13 00	3 50	16 50	8 00	19 00	Parley Draper	Do.
17	Andrew Anderson	..do	April 10, 1865	April 29, 1865	20	13 00	3 50	16 50	8 00	19 00	Andrew Anderson	Do.
18	George T. Jackson	..do	April 10, 1865	April 29, 1865	20	13 00	3 50	16 50	8 00	19 00	George T. Jackson	Do.
19	Peter Yorgenson	..do	April 10, 1865	April 29, 1865	20	13 00	3 50	16 50	8 00	19 00	Peter Yorgenson	Do.
20	Laurs Christiansen	..do	April 10, 1865	April 29, 1865	20	13 00	3 50	16 50	8 00	19 00	Laurs Chrestesen	Do.
21	Peter Christiansen, 1st	..do	April 10, 1865	April 29, 1865	20	13 00	3 50	16 50	8 00	19 00	Peter Chrestesen, 1st	Do.
22	Andreas Jensen	..do	April 10, 1865	April 29, 1865	20	13 00	3 50	16 50	8 00	19 00	Andreas Jensen	Do.
23	Ola Olsen	..do	April 10, 1865	April 29, 1865	20	13 00	3 50	16 50	8 00	19 00	Ole Olsen	Do.
24	James Christensen	..do	April 10, 1865	April 29, 1865	20	13 00	3 50	16 50	8 00	19 00	James Christenson	Do.
25	G. H. Bradley	..do	April 10, 1865	April 29, 1865	20	13 00	3 50	16 50	8 00	19 00	G. H. Bradley	Do.
26	J. B. McCumber	..do	April 10, 1865	April 29, 1865	20	13 00	3 50	16 50	8 00	19 00	J. B. McCumber	Do.
27	Erasmus Curtis	..do	April 10, 1865	April 29, 1865	20	13 00	3 50	16 50	8 00	19 00	Erasmus Curtis	Do.
28	H. Langston	..do	April 10, 1865	April 29, 1865	20	13 00	3 50	16 50	8 00	19 00	H. Langson	Do.
29	Nathan Faux	..do	April 10, 1865	April 29, 1865	20	13 00	3 50	16 50	8 00	19 00	Nathan Faux	Do.
30	John Bailey	..do	April 10, 1865	April 29, 1865	20	13 00	3 50	16 50	8 00	19 00	John Bailey	Do.
31	John Blackham	..do	April 10, 1865	April 29, 1865	20	13 00	3 50	16 50	8 00	19 00	John Blackhorn	Do.

Pay-roll of Captain Abner Lowry's company —— Utah militia cavalry &c.—Continued.

Number.	Names.	Rank.	Period of Service — Commencement.	Expiration.	Days.	Pay per month.	Monthly allowance for clothing.	Total monthly pay and allowance.	40 cts. per day for use and risk of horse and horse equipments.	Total pay and allowances.	Signatures.	Witnesses.
24	Andrew Anderson	Private.	April 10, 1865	April 29, 1865	20	13 00	3 50	15 30	3 00	19 00	Andrew Anderson	John Kirkman.
25	John Nelson	do	April 10, 1865	April 29, 1865	20	13 00	3 50	16 50	2 00	19 00	John Olsten	Do.
26	John Olsten	do	April 10, 1865	April 29, 1865	20	13 00	3 50	16 50	2 00	19 00	J. H. Child	Do.
27	J. H. Child	do	April 10, 1865	April 29, 1865	20	13 00	3 50	16 50	2 00	19 00	Lars Yergesen	Do.
28	Lars Yorgensen	do	April 10, 1865	April 29, 1865	20	13 00	3 50	16 50	2 00	19 00	Peter Christensen	Do.
29	Peter Christiansen	do	April 10, 1865	April 29, 1865	20	13 00	3 50	16 50	2 00	19 00	Christian Cromer	Do.
30	Christian Cramer	do	April 10, 1865	April 29, 1865	20	13 00	3 50	16 50	2 00	19 00	Daniel Roads	Do.
31	Samuel Reads	do	April 10, 1865	April 29, 1865	20	13 00	3 50	16 50	2 00	19 00	Eli Asheroft	Do.
32	Eli Asheroft	do	April 10, 1865	April 29, 1865	20	13 00	3 50	16 50	2 00	19 00	S. Knott	Do.
33	Samuel Knott	do	April 10, 1865	April 29, 1865	20	13 00	3 50	16 50	2 00	19 00	C. A. Dani	Do.
34	C. Antone Dane	do	April 10, 1865	April 29, 1865	20	13 00	3 50	16 50	2 00	19 00	Rasmus Anderson	Do.
35	Rasmus Anderson	do	April 10, 1865	April 29, 1865	20	13 00	3 50	16 50	2 00	19 00	Lars Swensen	Do.
36	Lars Swensen	do	April 10, 1865	April 29, 1865	20	13 00	3 50	16 50	2 00	19 00	Robert Mallison	Do.
37	Robert Melcmsen	do	April 10, 1865	April 29, 1865	20	13 00	3 50	16 50	2 00	19 00	John Reese	Do.
38	John Reece	do	April 10, 1865	April 29, 1865	20	13 00	3 50	16 50	2 00	19 00	Jens Jensen	Do.
39	Jens Jensen, 2d.	do	April 10, 1865	April 29, 1865	20	13 00	3 50	16 50	2 00	19 00	Thomas B. Allred	William Blaic.
40	Thomas B. Allred	do	April 10, 1865	April 29, 1865	20	13 00	3 50	16 50	2 00	19 00	I. N. Allred	Do.
41	Isaac Newton Allred	do	April 10, 1865	April 29, 1865	20	13 00	3 50	16 50	2 00	19 00	Peter Land	Do.
42	Peter Land	do	April 10, 1865	April 29, 1865	20	13 00	3 50	16 50	2 00	19 00	Henry Eilertsen	Do.
43	Henry Eilertson	do	April 10, 1865	April 29, 1865	20	13 00	3 50	16 30	2 00	19 00	Joseph Fretwell	Do.
44	Joseph Fretwell	do	April 10, 1865	April 29, 1865	20	13 00	3 50	16 50	2 00	19 00	Harden Allred	Do.
45	Harden Allred	do	April 10, 1865	April 29, 1865	20	13 00	3 50	16 50	2 00	19 00	Sidney R. Allred	Do.
46	Sidney R. Allred	do	April 10, 1865	April 29, 1865	20	13 00	3 50	16 50	2 00	19 00	Niels Benson	Do.
47	Niels Benson	do	April 10, 1865	April 29, 1865	20	13 00	3 50	16 50	2 00	19 00	Sanford Allred	Do.
48	Sanford Allred	do	April 10, 1865	April 29, 1865	20	13 00	3 50	16 50	2 00	19 00	Wm. Scott	Do.
49	William Scott	do	April 10, 1865	April 29, 1865	20	13 00	3 50	16 50	2 00	19 00	Nickll Land	Do.
50	Nicholi Land	do	April 10, 1865	April 29, 1865	20	13 00	3 50	16 50	2 00	19 00	Rasmus Fransen	David Candland.
51	Rasmus Pransen	do	April 10, 1865	April 29, 1865	20	13 00	3 50	16 50	2 00	19 00	Peter Madsen	Do.
52	Peter Madsen	do	April 10, 1865	April 29, 1865	20	13 00	3 50	16 50	2 00	19 00	Martin Miller	Do.
53	Martin Miller	do	April 10, 1865	April 29, 1865	20	13 00	3 50	16 50	2 00	19 00	Peter Myller	Do.
54	Peter Miller	do	April 10, 1865	April 29, 1865	20	13 00	3 50	16 50	2 00	19 00	Nels Madson	Do.
55	Niels Madsen	do	April 10, 1865	April 29, 1865	20	13 00	3 50	16 50	2 00	19 00	Christian Jensen	Do.
56	Christian Jensen	do	April 10, 1865	April 29, 1865	20	13 00	3 50	16 50	2 00	19 00	John Johnson	Do.
57	John Johnson	do	April 10, 1865	April 29, 1865	20	13 00	3 50	16 50	2 00	19 00	Morton Johnson	Do.
58	Morten Rasmussen	do	April 10, 1865	April 29, 1865	20	13 00	3 50	16 50	2 00	19 00	Andrew Larsen	Do.
59	Andrew Larsen	do	April 10, 1865	April 29, 1865	20	13 00	3 50	16 50	2 00	19 00	Jacob Christensen	Do.
60	Jacob Christiansen	do	April 10, 1865	April 29, 1865	20	13 00	3 50	16 50	2 00	19 00	Jens C. Harbro	Do.
61	Jens C. Howbray	do	April 10, 1865	April 29, 1865	20	13 00	3 50	16 50	2 00	19 00	Frederick Petersen	Do.
62	Frederick Peterson	do	April 10, 1865	April 29, 1865	20	13 00	3 50	16 50	2 00	19 00		

No.	Name		When enrolled	When mustered out							Name	By whom mustered
63	Andrew Jensen	do	April 10, 1865	April 29, 1865	50	30	13 00	3 50	16 50	8 00	19 00	Andrew Jenson	Do.
64	Niels Johansen	do	April 10, 1865	April 29, 1865	50	30	13 00	3 50	16 50	8 00	19 00	Nick Johansen	Do.
65	H. Y. Simpson	do	April 10, 1865	April 29, 1865	50	30	13 00	3 50	16 50	8 00	19 00	H. Y. Simpson	Do.
66	Peter Devlin	do	April 10, 1865	April 29, 1865	50	30	13 00	3 50	16 50	8 00	19 00	Paul Dehlin	Do.
67	Peter Frederickson	do	April 10, 1865	April 29, 1865	50	30	13 00	3 50	16 50	8 00	19 00	Peter Fredeson	Do.
68	Peter Y. Jousen	do	April 10, 1865	April 29, 1865	50	30	13 00	3 50	16 50	8 00	19 00	Peter T. Yensen	Do.
69	W. G. Barton	do	April 10, 1865	April 29, 1865	50	30	13 00	3 50	16 50	8 00	19 00	W. G. Barton	Do.
70	Lyman Peters	do	April 10, 1865	April 29, 1865	50	30	13 00	3 50	16 50	8 00	19 00	Lyman Peters	Do.
71	John Reynolds	do	April 10, 1865	April 29, 1865	50	30	13 00	3 50	16 50	8 00	19 00	John Reynolds	William Blain
72	Sidney H. Allred	do	April 10, 1865	April 29, 1865	50	30	13 00	3 50	16 50	8 00	19 00	Sidney H. Allred	David Candland
73	William Scovill	do	April 10, 1865	April 29, 1865	50	30	13 00	3 50	16 50	8 00	19 00	William Scovil	Do.
74	H. Poulson	do	April 10, 1865	April 29, 1865	50	30	13 00	3 50	16 50	8 00	19 00	Hans Pelsen	Do.
75	Edward McArthur	do	April 10, 1865	April 29, 1865	50	30	13 00	3 50	16 50	8 00	19 00	Eward McArthur	Do.
76	Frederick Nelson	do	April 10, 1865	April 29, 1865	50	30	13 00	3 50	16 50	8 00	19 00	Frederick Neilson	Warren P. Brady
77	David W. Sanders	do	April 10, 1865	April 29, 1865	50	30	13 00	3 50	16 50	8 00	19 00	David W. Sanders	Do.
78	James Anderson	do	April 10, 1865	April 29, 1865	50	30	13 00	3 50	16 50	8 00	19 00	J. Anderson	David Candland
79	Thomas House-keeper	do	April 10, 1865	April 29, 1865	50	30	13 00	3 50	16 50	8 00	19 00	Thomas Housekeeper	Warren P. Brady
80	Orson M. Terry	do	April 10, 1865	April 29, 1865	50	30	13 00	3 50	16 50	8 00	19 00	Orson M. Terry	Do.
81	William Oliver	do	April 10, 1865	April 29, 1865	50	30	13 00	3 50	16 50	8 00	19 00	William Oliver	Do.
82	Alexander Gibson	do	April 10, 1865	April 29, 1865	50	30	13 00	3 50	16 50	8 00	19 00	Alex'r Gibson	Do.
83	Joseph M. Sanders	do	April 10, 1865	April 29, 1865	50	30	13 00	3 50	16 50	8 00	19 00	Joseph M. Sanders	Do.
84	Tholeton Humbrick	do	April 10, 1865	April 29, 1865	50	30	13 00	3 50	16 50	8 00	19 00	Jordan Brady	Do.
85	Jorden Brady	do	April 10, 1865	April 29, 1865	50	30	13 00	3 50	16 50	8 00	19 00	Thomas Robertson, jr.	John R. Winder
86	Thomas Robertson	do	April 10, 1865	April 29, 1865	50	30	13 00	3 50	16 50	8 00	19 00	James A. Holman	Do.
87	James A. Holman	do	April 10, 1865	April 29, 1865	50	30	13 00	3 50	16 50	8 00	19 00	R. H. Johnson	Do.
88	R. H. Johnson	do	April 10, 1865	April 29, 1865	50	30	13 00	3 50	16 50	8 00	19 00	Nephi Robertson	Do.
89	Nephi Robertson	do	April 10, 1865	April 29, 1865	50	30	13 00	3 50	16 50	8 00	19 00	Thomas H. Caldwell	Do.
90	Thomas H. Caldwell	do	April 10, 1865	April 29, 1865	50	30	13 00	3 50	16 50	8 00	19 00	James Collard	Do.
91	James Collard	do	April 10, 1865	April 29, 1865	50	30	13 00	3 50	16 50	8 00	19 00	Martin Lund	Do.
92	Martin Lund	do	April 10, 1865	April 29, 1865	50	30	13 00	3 50	16 50	8 00	19 00		

This company was mustered into service at Moroni City, April 10, 1865; marched to Selina, 65 miles, in time to re-enforce Captain N. S. Beach, and, with him, went in pursuit and overtook the Indians, gave them battle, killing and wounding several; returned with Captain Beach, and was mustered out at Moroni, 29th day of April, 1865.

I certify that the above account is correct.

H. B. CLAWSON,
Adjutant General Nauvoo Legion.

Pay-roll of regimental field officers commanding companies A and B Utah Territory militia cavalry, employed in the suppression of Indian hostilities in Sanpete County, Utah Territory, in the month of April, A. D., 1865.

We, the undersigned, acknowledge to have received from James W. Cummings, paymaster Utah Territory militia, the sums set opposite to our names, in full payment for our services for the time specified.

Number.	Names.	Rank.	Period of service. Commencement.	Expiration.	Days.	Total monthly pay and allowance.	40 cents per day for use and risk of horse and horse equipments.	Total pay and allowance.	Signatures.	Witnesses.
1	Redick Newton Allred	Colonel	April 10, 1865	April 29, 1865	20	$211 00	$8 00	$148 67	Redick Newton Allred	George Brough.
1	Joseph T. Ellis	Lieut.-colonel	April 10, 1865	April 29, 1865	20	187 00	8 00	132 67	Joseph T. Ellis	Do.
1	Daniel B. Funk	Major	April 10, 1865	April 29, 1865	20	163 00	8 00	116 67	D. B. Funk	W. S. Snow.

I certify that the above account is correct.

H. B. CLAWSON,
Adjutant General Nauvoo Legion.

Pay-roll of Captain N. S. Beach's company A Utah Territory militia cavalry, employed in the suppression of Indian hostilities in Sanpete county, Utah Territory, in the month of April, 1865.

We, the undersigned, acknowledge to have received from James W. Cummings, paymaster Utah Territory militia, the sums set opposite to our names, in full payment for our services for the time specified.

Number	Names	Rank	Commencement	Expiration	Days	Pay per month	Monthly allowance for clothing	Total monthly pay and allowance	40 cts. per day for use and risk of horse and horse equipments	Total pay and allowance	Signatures	Witnesses
1	N. S. Beach	Captain	April 10, 1865	April 29, 1865	20			129 50	$8 00	$94 34	N. S. Beach	Luther Tuttle.
1	Wm. Beach	1st lieut.	April 10, 1865	April 29, 1865	20			112 83	8 00	83 22	William Beach, Jr.	Do.
2	Ezra Shoemaker	2d lieut.	April 10, 1865	April 29, 1865	20			112 83	8 00	83 22	Ezra Shoemaker	W. B. Parr.
2	Lewis Larsen	do	April 10, 1865	April 29, 1865	20			112 83	8 00	83 22	Louis Larsen	William K. Barton.
2	Jorgen Hansen	do	April 10, 1865	April 29, 1865	20			112 83	8 00	83 22	Jorgen Hansen	Luther Tuttl.
1	Joseph Farmer	1st serg't	April 10, 1865	April 29, 1865	20	$20 00	$3 50	23 50	8 00	23 66	Joseph Farmer	W. B. Parr.
2	Andrew R. Anderson	Sergeant	April 10, 1865	April 29, 1865	20	17 00	3 50	20 50	8 00	21 66	A. R. Anderson	Do.
2	Louis Olsen	do	April 10, 1865	April 29, 1865	20	13 00	3 50	16 50	8 00	19 00	Lewis Olsen	John R. Winder.
3	William Kearns	Private	April 10, 1865	April 29, 1865	20	13 00	3 50	16 50	8 00	19 00	H. H. Kearnes*	Luther Tuttl.
1	Joseph S. Snow	do	April 10, 1865	April 29, 1865	20	13 00	3 50	16 50	8 00	19 00	Joseph S. Snow	Do.
2	Andrew Van Beuren	do	April 10, 1865	April 29, 1865	20	13 00	3 50	16 50	8 00	15 00	A. C. Van Buren	Do.
3	William Richi	do	April 10, 1865	April 29, 1865	20	13 00	3 50	16 50	8 00	19 00	William Richy	Do.
4	George Sidwell	do	April 10, 1865	April 29, 1865	20	13 00	3 50	16 50	8 00	19 00	George Sidwell	Do.
5	William A. Cox	do	April 10, 1865	April 29, 1865	20	13 00	3 50	16 50	8 00	19 00	W. A. Cox	Do.
6	Daniel B. Funk, jr.	do	April 10, 1865	April 29, 1865	20	13 00	3 50	16 50	8 00	19 00	D. B. Funk, jr.	Do.
7	Heber H. Petty	do	April 10, 1865	April 29, 1865	20	13 00	3 50	16 50	8 00	19 00	Heber K. Petey	Do.
8	George E. Bench	do	April 10, 1865	April 29, 1865	20	13 00	3 50	16 50	8 00	19 00	George E. Bench	Do.
9	Orson Taylor	do	April 10, 1865	April 29, 1865	20	13 00	3 50	16 50	8 00	19 00	Orson Taylor	Do.
10	Alma Brown	do	April 10, 1865	April 29, 1865	20	13 00	3 50	16 50	8 00	19 00	Alma Brown	Do.
11	David Lewis	do	April 10, 1865	April 29, 1865	20	13 00	3 50	16 50	8 00	19 00	David Lewis	Do.
12	John Lewis	do	April 10, 1865	April 29, 1865	20	13 00	3 50	16 50	8 00	19 00	John Lewis	Do.
13	Nathan Lewis	do	April 10, 1865	April 29, 1865	20	13 00	3 50	16 50	8 00	19 00	Nathan Lewis	Do.
14	Daniel Henry	do	April 10, 1865	April 29, 1865	20	13 00	3 50	16 50	8 00	19 00	Daniel Henrie	Do.
15	Harrison Edwards	do	April 10, 1865	April 29, 1865	20	13 00	3 50	16 50	8 00	19 00	Harrison Edwards	Do.
16	Fritz E. Nielsoul	do	April 10, 1865	April 29, 1865	20	13 00	3 50	16 50	8 00	19 00	Frist Nielsen	Do.
17	Joseph Tuttle	do	April 10, 1865	April 29, 1865	20	13 00	3 50	16 50	8 00	19 00	Joseph Tuttle	Do.
18	Christian Anderson	do	April 10, 1865	April 29, 1865	20	13 00	3 50	16 50	8 00	19 00	Christian Anderko	Do.
19	Albert Beach	do	April 10, 1865	April 29, 1865	20	13 00	3 50	16 50	8 00	19 00	Albert Beach	W. H. Parr.
20	Thomas A. Woolsey	do	April 10, 1865	April 29, 1865	20	13 00	3 50	16 50	8 00	19 00	Thomas A. Woolsey	Luther Tuttl.
21	Andrew Nielson	do	April 10, 1865	April 29, 1865	20	13 00	3 50	16 50	8 00	19 00	Andrew Nielsen	Do.
22	Don C. Mills	do	April 10, 1865	April 29, 1865	20	13 00	3 50	16 50	8 00	19 00	Don Mills	Do.
24	Christian Christopherson	do	April 10, 1865	April 29, 1865	20	13 00	3 50	16 50	8 00	19 00	Christian Christoffersen	Christian Christoffersen
25	John Williams	do	April 10, 1865	April 29, 1865	20	13 00	3 50	16 50	8 00	19 00	J. Williams	W. B. Parr.

Pay-roll of Captain N. S. Beach's company A Utah Territory militia cavalry, &c.—Continued.

Number.	Names.	Rank.	Commencement.	Expiration.	Days.	Pay per month.	Monthly allowance for clothing.	Total monthly pay and allowance.	40 cts. per day for use and risk of horse and horse equipments.	Total pay and allowance.	Signatures.	Witnesses.
26	Peter Taylor	Private	April 10, 1865	April 29, 1865	20	$13 00	$3 50	$16 50	$8 00	$19 00	Peter Taylor	W. B. Parr.
27	Peter Greaves	do	April 10, 1865	April 29, 1865	20	13 00	3 50	16 50	8 00	19 00	Peter Greaves	Do.
28	Peter Johnston	do	April 10, 1865	April 29, 1865	20	13 00	3 50	16 50	8 00	19 00	Peter Johnsten	Do.
29	Peter Anderson	do	April 10, 1865	April 29, 1865	20	13 00	3 50	16 50	8 00	19 00	Peter Anderson	Do.
30	Peter P. Thompson	do	April 10, 1865	April 29, 1865	20	13 00	3 50	16 50	8 00	19 00	P. P. Thomson	H. F. Peterson.
31	Peter Larson	do	April 10, 1865	April 29, 1865	20	13 00	3 50	16 50	8 00	19 00	Peter Larsen	W. B. Parr.
32	Henry Green	do	April 10, 1865	April 29, 1865	20	13 00	3 50	16 50	8 00	19 00	Henry Green	Do.
33	Louis Thompson	do	April 10, 1865	April 29, 1865	20	13 00	3 50	16 50	8 00	19 00	Louis Thomson	Do.
34	Niels Thompson	do	April 10, 1865	April 29, 1865	20	13 00	3 50	16 50	8 00	19 00	Nils Thomson	Do.
35	Thomas P. Peterson	do	April 10, 1865	April 29, 1865	20	13 00	3 50	16 50	8 00	19 00	Thomas P. Peterson	William K. Barton.
36	Powal Powalsen	do	April 10, 1865	April 29, 1865	20	13 00	3 50	16 50	8 00	19 00	Paul Poulsen	W. B. Parr.
37	Chris-tian Nielsen	do	April 10, 1865	April 29, 1865	20	13 00	3 50	16 50	8 00	19 00		
38	Erasmus Clowson	do	April 10, 1865	April 29, 1865	20	13 00	3 50	16 50	8 00	19 00	Rasmus Clowson	Do.
39	Henry Yensen	do	April 10, 1865	April 29, 1865	20	13 00	3 50	16 50	8 00	19 00	H. Jensen	Do.
40	Niels Rosengreen	do	April 10, 1865	April 29, 1865	20	13 00	3 50	16 50	8 00	19 00		
41	Tom P. Yensen	do	April 10, 1865	April 29, 1865	20	13 00	3 50	16 50	8 00	19 00	Soren P. Jensen	Do.
42	Niels Biergard	do	April 10, 1865	April 29, 1865	20	13 00	3 50	16 50	8 00	19 00		
43	James Hanson	do	April 10, 1865	April 29, 1865	20	13 00	3 50	16 50	8 00	19 00	James Hanson	Do.
44	Louis R. Larson	do	April 10, 1865	April 29, 1865	20	13 00	3 50	16 50	8 00	19 00	Louis R. Larsen	Do.
45	Andrew Whitlock	do	April 10, 1865	April 29, 1865	20	13 00	3 50	16 50	8 00	19 00	Andrew Whitlock	Do.
46	Thomas Williams	do	April 10, 1865	April 29, 1865	20	13 00	3 50	16 50	8 00	19 00	Tomas Williams	Do.
47	Jens Swensen	do	April 10, 1865	April 29, 1865	20	13 00	3 50	16 50	8 00	19 00		
48	Franklin Hyde	do	April 10, 1865	April 29, 1865	20	13 00	3 50	16 50	8 00	19 00	Franklin Hyde	Do.
49	Tom Nielson	do	April 10, 1865	April 29, 1865	20	13 00	3 50	16 50	8 00	19 00	Soren Nielsen	Do.
50	Erastus C. Nielson	do	April 10, 1865	April 29, 1865	20	13 00	3 50	16 50	8 00	19 00		
51	Austin Keams	do	April 10, 1865	April 29, 1865	20	13 00	3 50	16 50	8 00	19 00	Austin Keames	William K. Barton.
52	Andrew Nelson	do	April 10, 1865	April 29, 1865	20	13 00	3 50	16 50	8 00	19 00	Andru Nielsen	W. B. Parr.
53	John Sorensen	do	April 10, 1865	April 29, 1865	20	13 00	3 50	16 50	8 00	19 00	Johannes Sorensen	William K. Barton.
54	William Rudd	do	April 10, 1865	April 29, 1865	20	13 00	3 50	16 50	8 00	19 00	William Rudd	Do.
55	Joseph Bartholomew	do	April 10, 1865	April 29, 1865	20	13 00	3 50	16 50	8 00	19 00	Joseph Bartholomew	Do.
56	Albert Gay	do	April 10, 1865	April 29, 1865	20	13 00	3 50	16 50	8 00	19 00	Albert Gay	Do.
57	Niels Jensen	do	April 10, 1865	April 29, 1865	20	13 00	3 50	16 50	8 00	19 00	Niels Tucksen	Do.
58	James Doherty	do	April 10, 1865	April 29, 1865	20	13 00	3 50	16 50	8 00	19 00	James Doherty	Do.
59	Julius Christiansen	do	April 10, 1865	April 29, 1865	20	13 00	3 50	16 50	8 00	19 00	Julius Christensen	Do.
60	Theodore Christiansen	do	April 10, 1865	April 29, 1865	20	13 00	3 50	16 50	8 00	19 00	Theodor Christensen	Do.
61	Andrew C. Nielsen	do	April 10, 1865	April 29, 1865	20	13 00	3 50	16 50	8 00	19 00	Andra C. Nielsen	Do.
62	John Boshurt	do	April 10, 1865	April 29, 1865	20	13 00	3 50	16 50	8 00	19 00	John Boshard, his x mark	Do.
63	Peter Brown	do	April 10, 1865	April 29, 1865	20	13 00	3 50	16 50	8 00	19 00	Peter Brown	Do.

64	Morten Mortensen	do	April 10, 1865	April 29, 1865	20	13 00	3 50	16 50	8 00	19 00	Morten Mortensen	Do.
65	Jonathan Lancaster	do	April 10, 1865	April 29, 1865	20	13 00	3 50	16 50	8 01	19 00	Jonathan Lancaster	Do.
66	Heber Maxam	do	April 10, 1865	April 29, 1865	20	13 00	3 50	16 50	8 00	19 00	Heber Maxam	Do.

* H. H. Kearns is father to William, who was killed in battle, April, 1865.   † Wounded in battle, April 12, 1865.   ‡ Killed in battle, April 12, 1865.

April 10, 1865, the Indians killed Peter Ludweeksen near Manti, Barney Ward and Mr. Lambson near Salina, and drove off a large herd of cattle and horses. In consequence of these outrages, this detachment was mustered into service by Brigadier General Warren S. Snow, and on the evening of the 10th started in pursuit. Traveled forty miles to Salina, there discovered that the Indians had gone up this almost impassable cañon; they followed on, and when about eight miles up the Indians opened a deadly fire on them from behind the rocks. Two men were instantly killed, and one seriously wounded. In consequence of the superior numbers and strong position of the enemy the company retired. Re-enforcements came up, and they again pursued them. After several days' march came up with and gave them battle, killing and wounding several Indians. The stock had been driven ahead and could not be recovered. The detachment returned to Manti, and was mustered out on the 29th day of April, having performed twenty days' hard service.

I certify that the above account is correct.

H. B. CLAWSON,
Adjutant General Nauvoo Legion.

Pay-roll of Major Nelson Higgins's company —— infantry, Utah Territory militia, employed in the suppression of Indian hostilitits in Sanpete and Sevier counties, Utah Territory, from May 1 to November 30, 1865.

We, the undersigned, acknowledge to have received from James W. Cummings, paymaster Utah Territory militia, the sums set opposite to our names, in full payment for our services for the time specified.

Number.	Names.	Rank.	Commencement.	Expiration.	Months.	Pay per month.	Monthly allowance for cloth.	Total monthly pay and allowance.	Total pay and allowance.	Signatures.	Witnesses.
1	Nelson Higgins	Major	May 1, 1865	November 30, 1865	7			$151 00	$1,057 00	Nelson Higgins	John R. Winder.
1	Heber Higgins	Captain	May 1, 1865	November 30, 1865	7			118 50	829 50	Heber Higgins	Do.
1	Green Taylor	Private	May 1, 1865	November 30, 1865	7	$13 00	$3 50	16 50	115 50	Orson Taylor	H. F. Peterson.
2	N. L. Christiansen	do	May 1, 1865	November 30, 1865	7	13 00	3 50	16 50	115 50	L. N. Christiansen	Do.
3	C. P. Anderson	do	May 1, 1865	November 30, 1865	7	13 00	3 50	16 50	115 50	C. P. Anderson	Do.
4	August Nelson	do	May 1, 1865	November 30, 1865	7	13 00	3 50	16 50	115 50	August Nelson	David Candland.
5	John Peterson*	do	May 1, 1865	November 30, 1865	7	13 00	3 50	16 50	115 50	John Pederpin	H. F. Peterson.
6	Albert Lewis*	do	May 1, 1865	November 30, 1865	7	13 00	3 50	16 50	115 50		David Candland.
7	John Wilkinson	do	May 1, 1865	November 30, 1865	7	13 00	3 50	16 50	115 50	John Wilkinson	John R. Winder.
8	Carl Higgins	do	May 1, 1865	November 30, 1865	7	13 00	3 50	16 50	115 50	Carl Higgins	Do.
9	Marion York	do	May 1, 1865	November 30, 1865	7	13 00	3 50	16 50	115 50	Marion York	David Candland.
10	Peter Godfreson	do	May 1, 1865	November 30, 1865	7	13 00	3 50	16 50	115 50	Petter Godfreson	H. F. Petersen.
11	Hans Mortensen	do	May 1, 1865	November 30, 1865	7	13 00	3 50	16 50	115 50	Hans Martensen	John R. Winder.
12	Morten F. Mortensen	do	May 1, 1865	November 30, 1865	7	13 00	3 50	16 50	115 50	Morten F. Mortensen	Do.
13	Aaron Lewis	do	May 1, 1865	November 30, 1865	7	13 00	3 50	16 50	115 50	Aaron Lewis	Do.
14	J. F. Duxford	do	May 1, 1865	November 30, 1865	7	13 00	3 50	16 50	115 50		Do.
15	Nathaniel Hanchet	do	May 1, 1865	November 30, 1865	7	13 00	3 50	16 50	115 50	Nathaniel Hanchett	Do.
16	John Norton	do	May 1, 1865	November 30, 1865	7	13 00	3 50	16 50	115 50	John Norton	Do.
17	David Norton	do	May 1, 1865	November 30, 1865	7	13 00	3 50	16 50	115 50	David Norton	Do.
18	Hans P. Larsen	do	May 1, 1865	November 30, 1865	7	13 00	3 50	16 50	115 50	Hans P. Larsen	Do.
19	Ferdinand Oberhansley	do	May 1, 1865	November 30, 1865	7	13 00	3 50	16 50	115 50		
20	Angus Stocks	do	May 1, 1865	November 30, 1865	7	13 00	3 50	16 50	115 50	Angus Stocks	H. F. Peterson.
21	John Harper	do	May 1, 1865	November 30, 1865	7	13 00	3 50	16 50	115 50	John Harper	John R. Winder.
22	Jorgen Smith	do	May 1, 1865	November 30, 1865	7	13 00	3 50	16 50	115 50	Jorgen Smidt	Rees. R. Lewellyn.
23	James Mortensen*	do	May 1, 1865	November 30, 1865	7	13 00	3 50	16 50	115 50	Jens Mortensen	David Candland.
24	Nelson D. Higgins	do	May 1, 1865	November 30, 1865	7	13 00	3 50	16 50	115 50	Nelson D. Higgins	John R. Winder.
25	Peter Ball	do	May 1, 1865	November 30, 1865	7	13 00	3 50	16 50	115 50		
26	Andrew Angreen	do	May 1, 1865	November 30, 1865	7	13 00	3 50	16 50	115 50	Andrew Aagreen	H. F. Peterson.
27	A. M. Bearson	do	May 1, 1865	November 30, 1865	7	13 00	3 50	16 50	115 50	A. M. Berentsen	Rees. R. Lewellyn.
28	Andrew Christiansen	do	May 1, 1865	November 30, 1865	7	13 00	3 50	16 50	115 50	Andrew Christiansen	Inwid Candland.
29	Soren Thompson	do	May 1, 1865	November 30, 1865	7	13 00	3 50	16 50	115 50	Soren Tounsen	Soren Tounsen.
30	Christian Bertholsen	do	May 1, 1866	November 30, 1865	7	13 00	3 50	16 50	115 50	Christian Borthelsen	Do.
31	Thomas Hansen	do	May 1, 1865	November 30, 1865	7	13 00	3 50	16 50	115 50	Thomas Hansen	H. F. Peterson.

No.	Name		Enlisted	Mustered out						Name	Captain
32	William Morrison	do	May 1, 1865	November 30, 1865	7	13 00	3 50	16 50	115 50	William Morrison	David Candland.
33	Dedrick Mortensen	do	May 1, 1865	November 30, 1865	7	13 00	3 50	16 50	115 50	Dedrick Mortensen	A. Andersen.
34	Paul Poulson	do	May 1, 1865	November 30, 1865	7	13 00	3 50	16 50	115 50	Paul Poulson	Rees R. Lewellyn.
35	N. C. Christiansen	do	May 1, 1865	November 30, 1865	7	13 00	3 50	16 50	115 50	N. C. Christiansen	David Candland.
36	Peter Christiansen	do	May 1, 1865	November 30, 1865	7	13 00	3 50	16 50	115 50	Peter Christiansen	John R. Winder.
37	Hans Lewis Dastrop	do	May 1, 1865	November 30, 1865	7	13 00	3 50	16 50	115 50	H. L. Dastrop	H. F. Peterson.
38	Ulrick Winchler	do	May 1, 1865	November 30, 1865	7	13 00	3 50	16 50	115 50	Ulrick Winkler	David Candland.
39	John Readhead	do	May 1, 1865	November 30, 1865	7	13 00	3 50	16 50	115 50	John Readhead	John N. Larsen.
40	J. M. Jensen	do	May 1, 1865	November 30, 1865	7	13 00	3 50	16 50	115 50	J. M. Jensen	Rees R. Lewellyn.

*Wounded in battle. †Killed in battle.

This company was mustered into service at Richfield, Sevier County, on the 1st day of May, 1865, for the purpose of defending the settlements of Sevier and Piute counties. They were divided up in small squads, and performed service, both mounted and on foot, in the mountains and passes; took part in several engagements with the Indians. Some of them were with General Snow on both the Fish Lake expeditions and took part in the battles. They were in active service. They were mustered out at Richfield, having been in active service for seven months.

I certify that the above account is correct,

H. B. CLAWSON,
Adjutant General Nauvoo Legion.

Pay-roll of Captain George Sidwell's company —— cavalry, Utah Territory militia, employed in the suppression of Indian hostilities in Sanpete and Sevier counties, in the month of June, 1865.

We, the undersigned, acknowledge to have received from James W. Cummings, paymaster Utah Territory militia, the sums set opposite to our names, in full payment for our services for the time specified.

Number	Names	Rank	Commencement	Expiration	Months	Pay per month	Monthly allowance for clothing	Total monthly pay and allowance	40 cts. per day for use and risk of horse and horse equipments	Total pay and allowance	Signatures	Witnesses
1	George Sidwell	Captain	June 1, 1865	June 30, 1865	1			$129 50	$12 00	$141 50	George Sidwell	W. S. Reid.
1	Franklin Spencer	1st lieutenant	June 1, 1865	June 30, 1865	1			112 83	12 00	124 83	Franklin Spencer	Do.
1	William H. Peacock	Private	June 1, 1865	June 30, 1865	1	$13 00	$3 50	16 50	12 00	28 50	Wm. H. Peacock	Do.
2	Ezra Shomaker	do	June 1, 1865	June 30, 1865	1	13 00	3 50	16 50	12 00	28 50	Ezra Shomaker	Do.
3	Christopher Andersen	do	June 1, 1865	June 30, 1865	1	13 00	3 50	16 50	12 00	28 50	Christoffer Andersen	Do.
4	Joseph Tuttle	do	June 1, 1865	June 30, 1865	1	13 00	3 50	16 50	12 00	28 50	Joseph Tuttle	Do.
5	Joseph Smith	do	June 1, 1865	June 30, 1865	1	13 00	3 50	16 50	12 00	28 50	Joseph Smith	Do.
6	William Sarie	do	June 1, 1865	June 30, 1865	1	13 00	3 50	16 50	12 00	28 50	William Sarle	Do.
7	Henry Henderson	do	June 1, 1865	June 30, 1865	1	13 00	3 50	16 50	12 00	28 50	Henireh Henlrihsen	Do.
8	Samuel Rosengreen	do	June 1, 1865	June 30, 1865	1	13 00	3 50	16 50	12 00	28 50	Samuel Rosengreen	Do.
9	Soren Nielson	do	June 1, 1865	June 30, 1865	1	13 00	3 50	16 50	12 00	28 50	Soren Nielson	Do.
10	Christian Peterson	do	June 1, 1865	June 30, 1865	1	13 00	3 50	16 50	12 00	28 50	Christian Peterson	Do.
11	Thomas Bell	do	June 1, 1865	June 30, 1865	1	13 00	3 50	16 50	12 00	28 50	Thomas Bell	Do.
12	Adam Beal	do	June 1, 1865	June 30, 1865	1	13 00	3 50	16 50	12 00	28 50	Adam Beal	Do.
13	William Short	do	June 1, 1865	June 30, 1865	1	13 00	3 50	16 50	12 00	28 50	William Short	Do.
14	Isaac Herring	do	June 1, 1865	June 30, 1865	1	13 00	3 50	16 50	12 00	28 50	Isaac Hering	Do.
15	Major Hervin	do	June 1, 1865	June 30, 1865	1	13 00	3 50	16 50	12 00	28 50	Major Hervin	Do.
16	David Wilson	do	June 1, 1865	June 30, 1865	1	13 00	3 50	16 50	12 00	28 50	David Wilson	Do.
17	Henry Lamb	do	June 1, 1865	June 30, 1865	1	13 00	3 50	16 50	12 00	28 50	Henry Lamb	Do.
18	Isaac Bowren	do	June 1, 1865	June 30, 1865	1	13 00	3 50	16 50	12 00	28 50	Isaac Bowren	Do.
19	Peter Allen	do	June 1, 1865	June 30, 1865	1	13 00	3 50	16 50	12 00	28 50	Peter Allen	Do.
20	William Bench, jr	do	June 1, 1865	June 30, 1865	1	13 00	3 50	16 50	12 00	28 50	William Bench, jr	Do.
21	John Squires	do	June 1, 1865	June 30, 1865	1	13 00	3 50	16 50	12 00	28 50	John Squires	Do.
22	George Beach	do	June 1, 1865	June 30, 1865	1	13 00	3 50	16 50	12 00	28 50	George E. Beach	Do.
23	Ezra Funk	do	June 1, 1865	June 30, 1865	1	13 00	3 50	16 50	12 00	28 50	E. K. Funk	Do.
24	Frederick W. Cox	do	June 1, 1865	June 30, 1865	1	13 00	3 50	16 50	12 00	28 50	F. W. Cox	Do.
25	William A. Cox	do	June 1, 1865	June 30, 1865	1	13 00	3 50	16 50	12 00	28 50	W. A. Cox	Do.
26	Haslem Clark	do	June 1, 1865	June 30, 1865	1	13 00	3 50	16 50	12 00	28 50	Haslem Clark	Do.
27	John Hall	do	June 1, 1865	June 30, 1865	1	13 00	3 50	16 50	12 00	28 50	John Hall	Do.
28	Andrew Van Buren	do	June 1, 1865	June 30, 1865	1	13 00	3 50	16 50	12 00	28 50	A. C. Van Buren	Do.
29	William Richie	do	June 1, 1865	June 30, 1865	1	13 00	3 50	16 50	12 00	28 50	William Richey	Do.
30	David Lewis	do	June 1, 1865	June 30, 1865	1	13 00	3 50	16 50	12 00	28 50	David Lewis	Do.
31	Peter Rasmussen	do	June 1, 1865	June 30, 1865	1	13 00	3 50	16 50	12 00	28 50	Peter Rasmusson	Do.

32	Johnson Black	do	June 1, 1865	June 30, 1865	1	13 00	3 50	16 50	12 00	28 50	Johnson Black	Do.
33	Zenith Wingate	do	June 1, 1865	June 30, 1865	1	13 00	3 50	16 50	12 00	28 50	Zenith Wingate	Do.
34	Peter Hogard	do	June 1, 1865	June 30, 1865	1	13 00	3 50	16 50	12 00	28 50	Peter Hogard	Do.
35	Peter Mrockelsen	do	June 1, 1865	June 30, 1865	1	13 00	3 50	16 50	12 00	28 50	Peter Mukkelsen	Do.
36	Ole Nielson	do	June 1, 1865	June 30, 1865	1	13 00	3 50	16 50	12 00	28 50	Ole Nielsen	Do.
37	Frits Nelson	do	June 1, 1865	June 30, 1865	1	13 00	3 50	16 50	12 00	28 50	Fred Nielsen	Do.

May 24, 1865, John Given, wife, and four children were killed by Indians, in Thistle Valley, the same day Mr. Nielson, near North Bend, was killed; and also, on the 29th, David M. Jones, near the same settlement. Said Indians stole a large band of horses and some cattle. This company was mustered into service at Manti, June 1, and started on that day in pursuit of the Indians, and followed them to Thistle Valley, and by the head of Spanish Fork to Green River Ford; the company, having two days' start, could not be overtaken; the company fell back into the mountains and continued scouting and watching the mountain passes, which kept the Indians from committing further depredations in this vicinity. On June 30 this company was mustered out of service at Manti, having performed thirty days' active service.

I certify that the above account is correct.

H. B. CLAWSON,
Adjutant General Nauvoo Legion.

Pay-roll of Captain Artemus Millett's company —— cavalry, Utah Territory militia, employed in the suppression of Indian hostilities in Sanpete and Sevier counties, Utah Territory, in the months of June and July, 1865.

We, the undersigned, acknowledge to have received from James W. Cummings, paymaster Utah Territory militia, the sums set opposite to our names, in full payment for our services for the time specified.

Number.	Names.	Rank.	Commencement.	Expiration.	Months.	Pay per month.	Monthly allowance for clothing.	Total monthly pay and allowance.	40 cts. per day for use and risk of horse and horse equipments.	Total pay and allowance.	Signatures.	Witnesses.
1	Artemus Millett	Captain	June 1, 1865	July 31, 1865	2			$129 50	$24 00	$283 00	Artemus Millett	Luther Tuttle.
1	Joseph Herron	1st lieut	June 1, 1865	July 31, 1865	2			112 83	24 00	249 66	Joseph Hering	Do.
1	Moses Gifford	2d lieut	June 1, 1865	July 31, 1865	2			112 83	24 00	249 66	Moses Gifford	Do.
2	George Robins	...do	June 1, 1865	July 31, 1865	2			112 83	24 00	249 66	George Robbins	Do.
1	Charles Green	Private	June 1, 1865	July 31, 1865	2	$13 00	$3 50	16 50	24 00	57 00	Charles Green	Do.
1	Harmon Wilson	...do	June 1, 1865	July 31, 1865	2	13 00	3 50	16 50	24 00	57 00	Harmon Wilson	Do.
3	James McPherson	...do	June 1, 1865	July 31, 1865	2	13 00	3 50	16 50	24 00	57 00	James McPherson	Do.
4	Neils Christian-sen	...do	June 1, 1865	July 31, 1865	2	13 00	3 50	16 50	24 00	57 00	Neils Christiansen	Do.
5	Walter Barney	...do	June 1, 1865	July 31, 1865	2	13 00	3 50	16 50	24 00	57 00	Walter Barney	Do.
6	Andrew Allred	...do	June 1, 1865	July 31, 1865	2	13 00	3 50	16 50	24 00	57 00	Andrew J. Allred	Do.
7	Joseph Farmer	...do	June 1, 1865	July 31, 1865	2	13 00	3 50	16 50	24 00	57 00	Joseph Farmer	Do.
8	Alma Brown	...do	June 1, 1865	July 31, 1865	2	13 00	3 50	16 50	24 00	57 00	Alma Brown	Do.
9	John Richardson	...do	June 1, 1865	July 31, 1865	2	13 00	3 50	16 50	24 00	57 00	John Richardson	Do.
10	Hans Masten	...do	June 1, 1865	July 31, 1865	2	13 00	3 50	16 50	24 00	57 00	Hans Madsen	Do.
11	Andrew Yensen	...do	June 1, 1865	July 31, 1865	2	13 00	3 50	16 50	24 00	57 00	Andrew Jensen	Do.

I certify that the above account is correct.

H. B. CLAWSON,
Adjutant General Nauvoo Legion.

This company was mustered into service at Glenwood, for the protection of the frontier settlements in Sevier Valley, viz, Glenwood, Alma, and Mary's Vale. Their time was spent in scouting and guarding the mountain passes. On the 14th of July Robert Galespie and Mr. Robinson were killed, near Salina, and on the 20th this detachment accompanied Brigadier General Snow, in pursuit, to Fish Lake, overtook them, and had a desperate battle; fourteen Indians killed and several wounded; Moroni York seriously wounded. While on this expedition, another party of Indians attacked Glenwood, shot Mr. Staley, and drove off a large band of horses and cattle from the settlement. This company was in active service until the 31st day of July, when they were mustered out at Glenwood, having performed sixty days' active service.

Pay-roll of field and staff officers commanding the Utah Territory militia, employed in the suppression of Indian hostilities in Sanpete, Sevier, and Piute counties, from July 1, 1865, to November 1, 1865.

We, the undersigned, acknowledge to have received from James W. Cummings, paymaster Utah Territory militia, the sums set opposite to our names, in full payment for our services for the time specified.

Names.	Staff-appointment office.	Rank.	PERIOD OF SERVICE.		Months.	Total monthly pay and allowance.	40 cts. per day for use and risk of horse and equipments.	Total pay and allowance.	Signatures.	Witnesses.
			Commencement.	Expiration.						
Warren S. Snow	Brigade adjutant	Brigadier general	July 1, 1865	November 1, 1865	4	$399 50	$18 00	$1,246 00	W. S. Snow	John R. Winder.
George Peacock	Brigade adjutant	Lieutenant colonel	July 1, 1865	November 1, 1865	4	187 00	48 00	796 00	George Peacock	Do.
Frederick C. Robinson	Brigade quarterm'r	do	July 1, 1865	November 1, 1865	4	187 00	48 00	796 00	Frederick C. Robinson	Do.
Luther Tuttle	Brigade aide-de-c'p	do	July 1, 1865	November 1, 1865	4	187 00	48 00	796 00	Luther Tuttle	Do.
Madison D. Hambleton	Brigade aide-du-c'p	Major	July 1, 1865	November 1, 1865	4	163 00	48 00	700 00	Madison D. Hambleton	W. S. Snow.
Rural M. Rodgers	Surgeon	do	July 1, 1865	November 1, 1865	4	163 00	48 00	700 00	Rural M. Rogers	Wm. Clayton.

I certify that the above account is correct.

H. B. CLAWSON,
Adjutant General Nauvoo Legion.

Pay-roll of Captain John Lehi Ivie's company —— cavalry, Utah Territory militia, employed in the suppression of India nhostilities in Sanpete and Sevier counties, Utah Territory, in the months of July and August, 1865.

We, the undersigned, acknowledge to have received from James W Cummings, paymaster Utah Territory militia, the sums set opposite to our names, in full payment for our services for the time specified.

Number	Names	Rank	Commencement	Expiration	Days	Pay per month	Monthly allowance for clothing	Total monthly allowance	40 cts. per day for use and risk of horse and horse equipments	Total pay and allowance	Signatures	Witnesses
1	John Lehi Ivie	Captain	July 20, 1865	Aug. 4, 1865	15	$17 00		$129 50	$6 00	$70 75	John L. Ivie	David Candland
1	William Nelson Tidwell	1st lieut	July 20, 1865	Aug. 4, 1865	15	17 00		112 83	6 00	62 25	William N. Tidwell	Do.
2	Jefferson Tidwell	2d lieut	July 20, 1865	Aug. 4, 1865	15	17 00		112 83	6 00	62 25	J. Tidwell	Do.
2	George Coats	do	July 20, 1865	Aug. 4, 1865	15	13 00		112 83	6 00	62 25	George Coats	Do.
3	John Hitchcock	do	July 20, 1865	Aug. 4, 1865	15	13 00		112 83	6 00	62 25	John Hitchcock	Do.
3	William Warren Major	Sergeant	July 20, 1865	Aug. 4, 1865	15	13 00	$3 50	20 50	6 00	16 25	W. W. Major	John R. Winder.
4	Soren Jepson	do	July 20, 1865	Aug. 4, 1865	15	13 00	3 50	20 50	6 00	16 25	Soren Jepson	Do.
5	Cal-b Hartley	Private	July 21, 1865	Aug. 4, 1865	15	13 00	3 50	16 50	6 00	16 25	Caleb Hartley	David Candland.
6	Caretal C. Rowe	do	July 20, 1865	Aug. 4, 1865	15	13 00	3 50	16 50	6 00	14 25	C. C. Rowe	Do.
7	George Meryck	do	July 20, 1865	Aug. 4, 1865	15	13 00	3 50	14 50	6 00	14 25	George M. Meyrick	Do.
8	George Francom	do	July 20, 1865	Aug. 4, 1865	15	13 00	3 50	16 50	6 40	14 25	George Francom	Do.
9	Wilford W. Brandon	do	July 20, 1865	Aug. 4, 1865	15	13 00	3 50	16 50	6 00	14 25	Wilford W. Brandon	Do.
10	Alma Zabriskie	do	July 20, 1865	Aug. 4, 1865	15	13 00	3 50	16 50	6 00	14 25	Alma Gabri-kie	Do.
11	William Stephens	do	July 20, 1865	Aug. 4, 1865	15	13 00	3 50	16 50	6 00	14 25	William Stevens	Do.
12	Andrew Jacobson	do	July 20, 1865	Aug. 4, 1865	15	13 00	3 50	16 50	6 00	14 25		Do.
13	John Young	do	July 20, 1865	Aug. 4, 1865	15	13 00	3 50	16 50	6 00	14 25	John Young	Do.
14	Rasmus Fransen	do	July 20, 1865	Aug. 4, 1865	15	13 00	3 50	16 50	6 00	14 25	Rasmus Frandsen	Do.
15	Aaron Amon	do	July 20, 1865	Aug. 4, 1865	15	13 00	3 50	16 50	6 00	14 25	Aron Amurus	Do.
16	David Brown	do	July 20, 1865	Aug. 4, 1865	15	13 00	3 30	16 50	6 00	14 25	David Brown	Do.
17	Niels Jensen	do	July 20, 1865	Aug. 4, 1865	15	13 00	3 50	16 50	6 00	14 25	Nils Jensen	Do.
18	Rodolphus Bennett	do	July 20, 1865	Aug. 4, 1865	15	13 00	3 50	16 50	6 60	14 25	Rodolfus Bennet	Do.
19	Andrew Peterson	do	July 20, 1865	Aug. 4, 1865	15	13 00	3 50	16 50	6 00	14 25	Andru Petersen	Do.
20	Andrew L. Larsen	do	July 20, 1865	Aug. 4, 1865	15	13 00	3 50	16 50	6 00	14 25	Andru L. Larsen	Do.
21	Lewis B. Barney	do	July 20, 1865	Aug. 4, 1865	15	13 01	3 50	16 50	6 09	14 25	Lewis Barney	William Blain.
22	Isaac Newton Allred	do	July 20, 1865	Aug. 4, 1865	15	13 00	3 50	16 50	6 00	14 25	I. N. Allred	Do.
23	William Smith Barney	do	July 20, 1865	Aug. 4, 1865	15	13 00	3 50	16 50	6 00	14 25	Wm. S. Barney	Do.
	Henry G. Jensen	do	July 29, 1865	Aug. 4, 1865	15	13 00	3 50	16 50	6 00	14 25	Hen. G. Jansen	W. R. Parr.
	David H. Allred	do	July 30, 1865	Aug. 4, 1865	15	13 00	3 50	16 50	6 00	14 25	David H. Allred	William Blain.
	John Frantzen	do	July 29, 1865	Aug. 4, 1865	15	13 00	3 50	16 50	6 00	14 25	John Frantzen	Do.
	John H. Zabriskie	do	July 29, 1865	Aug. 4, 1865	15	13 00	3 50	16 50	6 00	14 25	John H. Zabrisky	Do.
	Thomas B. Allred	do	July 29, 1865	Aug. 4, 1865	15	13 00	3 50	16 50	6 00	14 25	T. B. Allred	Do

24	Peter Peterson	do	July 29, 1865	Aug. 4, 1865	15	13 00	3 50	16 50	6 00	14 25	Peter Peterson	W. B. Parr.
25	Andrew H. Whitlock	do	July 29, 1865	Aug. 4, 1865	15	13 00	3 50	16 50	6 00	14 25	Andre H. Whitlock	Do.
26	William Blain	do	July 29, 1865	Aug. 4, 1865	15	13 01	3 50	16 50	6 00	14 25	William Blain	William Blain.
27	John Neilu	do	July 29, 1865	Aug. 4, 1865	15	13 00	3 50	16 50	6 00	14 25	John Neild	Do.
28	Samuel B. Frost	do	July 29, 1865	Aug. 4, 1865	15	13 00	3 50	16 50	6 00	14 25	S. B. Frost	Do.
29	Harvey M. Rawlins	do	July 29, 1865	Aug. 4, 1865	15	13 03	3 50	16 50	6 00	14 25	Harvey M. Rolleus	Do.

In consequence of the recent outrages in the vicinity of Selina Rae, killing of Robert Galespie and Mr. Robinson, and a large herd of stock driven off, this company was mustered into service at Mount Pleasant, on the 20th day of July, and started on that day in pursuit; followed the Indians 150 miles, and overtook them near Fish Lake; gave them battle; 14 Indians killed and several wounded, Moroni York seriously wounded. Company returned and was mustered out at Mount Pleasant on the 4th day of August—15 days' active service.

I certify that the above account is correct.

H. B. CLAWSON,
Adjutant General Nauvoo Legion.

Pay-roll of Captain Abner Lowry's company —— cavalry, Utah Territory militia, employed in the suppression of Indian hostilities in Sanpete and Sevier counties, Utah Territory, in the months of July and August, 1865.

We, the undersigned, acknowledge to have received from James W. Cummings, paymaster Utah Territory militia, the sums set opposite to our names, in full payment for our services for the time specified.

Number.	Names.	Rank.	Commencement.	Expiration.	Days.	Pay per month.	Monthly allowance for clothing.	Total monthly pay and allowance.	40 cts. per day for use and risk of horse and horse equipments.	Total pay and allowance.	Signatures.	Witnesses.
1	Abner Lowry	Captain	July 20, 1865	Aug. 4, 1865	15			$129 50	$6 00	$70 75	Abner Lowry	John Kirkman.
1	Ruel M. Rogers	1st lieut.	July 20, 1865	Aug. 4, 1865	15			112 50	6 00	62 25	Ruel M. Rogers	Do.
1	John Reese	2d li-ut.	July 20, 1865	Aug. 4, 1865	15			112 50	6 00	62 25	John Reese	Do.
2	John Mott	Sergeant	July 20, 1865	Aug. 4, 1865	15	$17 00		20 50	6 00	16 25	John Mott	Do.
1	Jacob Cloward	Private	July 20, 1865	Aug. 4, 1865	15	17 00		20 50	6 00	16 25	Jacob Cloward	Do.
2	Joseph Jolley	do.	July 20, 1865	Aug. 4, 1865	15	13 00	$3 50	16 50	6 00	14 25	Joseph Jolley	Do.
3	Henry Rees	do.	July 20, 1865	Aug. 4, 1865	15	13 00	3 50	16 50	6 00	14 25	Henry Rees	Do.
3	John Kinder	do.	July 20, 1865	Aug. 4, 1865	15	13 00	3 50	16 50	6 00	14 25	John Kinder	Do.
4	James Christiansen	do.	July 20, 1865	Aug. 4, 1865	15	13 00	3 50	16 50	6 00	14 25	James Christenson	Do.
5	Lewis Hatch	do.	July 20, 1865	Aug. 4, 1865	15	13 00	3 50	16 50	6 00	14 25	Lewis Hatch	Do.
6	Orson Davis	do.	July 20, 1865	Aug. 4, 1865	15	13 00	3 50	16 50	6 00	14 25	Orson Davis	Do.
7	George Hatch	do.	July 20, 1865	Aug. 4, 1865	15	13 00	3 50	16 50	6 00	14 25	George Hatch	Do.
8	Ole Olsen	do.	July 20, 1865	Aug. 4, 1865	15	13 00	3 50	16 50	6 00	14 25	Ole Olsen	Do.
9	Albert Draper	do.	July 20, 1865	Aug. 4, 1865	15	13 00	3 50	16 50	6 00	14 25	Albert Draper	Do.
10	John Russell	do.	July 20, 1865	Aug. 4, 1865	15	13 00	3 50	16 50	6 00	14 25	John Russell	Do.
11	Samuel Rhodes	do.	July 20, 1865	Aug. 4, 1865	15	13 00	3 50	16 50	6 00	14 25	Samuel Ronds	Do.
12	Moroni Bradley	do.	July 20, 1865	Aug. 4, 1865	15	13 00	3 50	16 50	6 00	14 25	Moroni Bradley	Do.
13	John Eliason	do.	July 20, 1865	Aug. 4, 1865	15	13 00	3 50	16 50	6 00	14 25	John Eliason	Do.
14	James Guyman	do.	July 20, 1865	Aug. 4, 1865	15	13 00	3 50	16 50	6 00	14 25	James Guyman	Do.
16	Samuel Jewkes	do.	July 20, 1865	Aug. 4, 1865	15	13 00	3 50	16 50	6 00	14 25	Samuel Jewkes	Do.
16	George B. Maddison	do.	July 20, 1865	Aug. 4, 1865	15	13 00	3 50	16 50	6 00	14 25	George B. Maddison	Do.
17	Thomas J. Caldwell	do.	July 20, 1865	Aug. 4, 1865	15	13 00	3 50	16 50	6 00	14 25	Thomas J. Caldwell	John R. Winter.
18	Alonzo Nay	do.	July 20, 1865	Aug. 4, 1865	15	13 00	3 50	16 50	6 00	14 25	Alonzo Nay	Do.
19	James Woodward	do.	July 20, 1865	Aug. 4, 1865	15	13 00	3 50	16 50	6 00	14 25	James Woodward	Do.
20	John H. Robertson	do.	July 20, 1865	Aug. 4, 1865	15	13 00	3 50	16 50	6 00	14 25	John H. Robertson	Do.
21	Wm. H. Johnson	do.	July 20, 1865	Aug. 4, 1865	15	13 00	3 50	16 50	6 00	14 25	Wm. H. Johnson	Do.
22	Erastus S. Wakefield	do.	July 20, 1865	Aug. 4, 1865	15	13 00	3 50	16 50	6 00	14 25	Erastus Wakefield	Do.
23	James M. Allred	do.	July 20, 1865	Aug. 4, 1865	15	13 00	3 50	16 50	6 00	14 25	James M. Allred	James M. Allred.
24	John F. Sanders	do.	July 20, 1865	Aug. 4, 1865	15	13 00	3 50	16 50	6 00	14 25	John F. Sanders	Warren P. Brady.
26	Noah T. Guyman	do.	July 20, 1865	Aug. 4, 1865	15	13 00	3 50	16 50	6 00	14 25	Noah T. Guyman	Do.
	Eline Cox	do.	July 20, 1865	Aug. 4, 1865	15	13 00	3 50	16 50	6 00	14 25	Eline Cox	Do.
27	Jordan Brady	do.	July 20, 1865	Aug. 4, 1865	15	13 00	3 50	16 50	6 00	14 25	Jordan Brady	Do.
28	Moroni Turpin	do.	July 20, 1865	Aug. 4, 1865	15	13 00	3 50	16 50	6 00	14 25	Moroni Turpin	Do.

No.	Name		Mustered in	Mustered out							Signature	
29	John Romero	do.	July 20, 1865	Aug. 4, 1865	15	13 00	3 50	16 50	6 00	14 95	John Romero, his + mark	Do.
30	Erastus Mechem	do.	July 20, 1865	Aug. 4, 1865	15	13 00	3 50	16 50	6 00	14 95	Erastus Mechem	Do.
31	Joseph S. Wing	do.	July 20, 1865	Aug. 4, 1865	15	13 00	3 50	16 50	6 00	14 95		
32	Edward Stewart	do.	July 20, 1865	Aug. 4, 1865	15	13 00	3 50	16 50	6 00	14 25	Edward Stewart	Do.
33	John Cox	do.	July 20, 1865	Aug. 4, 1865	15	13 00	3 50	16 50	6 00	14 25	John Cox	Do.
34	Jacob Jones	do.	July 20, 1865	Aug. 4, 1865	15	13 00	3 50	16 50	6 00	14 25	Jacob Jones, his + mark	Do.
35	Henry Sanderson	do.	July 20, 1865	Aug. 4, 1865	15	13 00	3 50	16 50	6 00	14 25	Henry Sanderson	Do.
36	Alma Miner	do.	July 20, 1865	Aug. 4, 1865	15	13 00	3 50	16 50	6 00	14 25	Alma Miner	Do.
37	James Anderson	do.	July 20, 1865	Aug. 4, 1865	15	13 00	3 50	16 50	6 00	14 55	James Anderson	John R. Winder.
38	James Guyman	do.	July 20, 1865	Aug. 4, 1865	15	13 00	3 50	16 50	6 00	14 55	James Guyman	Do.
39	Samuel Jenkins	do.	July 20, 1865	Aug. 4, 1865	15	13 00	3 50	16 50	6 00	14 25	Samuel Jenkins	Do.
40	Thomas Caldwell	do.	July 20, 1865	Aug. 4, 1865	15	13 00	3 50	16 50	6 00	14 25	Thomas Caldwell	Do.

This company was mustered into service at Fountain Green, by Brigadier General Warren S. Snow, on the 20th day of July, 1865, and accompanied him to Fish Lake; was engaged in the battle, when fourteen Indians were killed and several wounded; returned with General Snow, and was mustered out at Fountain Green, on the 4th day of August, fifteen days' active service.

I certify that the above account is correct.

H. B. CLAWSON,
Adjutant General Nauvoo Legion.

Pay-roll of Captain John Lehi Ivie's company —— Utah Territory militia cavalry, employed in the suppression of Indian hostilities in Sanpete and Sevier counties, Utah Territory, in the month of September, 1865.

We, the undersigned, acknowledge to have received from James W. Cummings, paymaster Utah Territory militia, the sums set opposite to our names, in full payment for our services for the time specified.

Number.	Names.	Rank.	Commencement.	Expiration.	Days.	Pay per month.	Monthly allowance for clothing.	Total monthly pay and allowance.	40 cts. per day for horse and horse equipment use and risk of.	Total pay and allowance.	Signatures.	Witnesses.
1	John Lehi Ivie	Captain	Sept. 10, 1865	Sept. 25, 1865	15			129 50	6 00	$70 75	John L. Ivie	H. P. Miller.
1	Orange Seely	1st lieut	Sept. 10, 1865	Sept. 25, 1865	15			112 83	6 00	62 41	Orange Seely	Do.
1	William Stevens	2d lieut	Sept. 10, 1865	Sept. 25, 1865	15			112 83	6 00	62 41	William Stevens	Do.
2	Isaac Morley Allred	do	Sept. 10, 1865	Sept. 25, 1865	15			112 83	6 00	62 41	Isaac M. Allred	John R. Winder.
3	Fred-rick Neilson	Sergeant	Sept. 10, 1865	Sept. 25, 1865	15	$17 00	$3 50	20 50	6 00	16 25	Fred-rick Neilson	H. P. Miller.
4	James Gaymon	do	Sept. 10, 1865	Sept. 25, 1865	15	17 00	3 50	20 50	6 00	16 25	James Gaymon	John R. Winder.
5	Philip Hurst	do	Sept. 10, 1865	Sept. 25, 1865	15	17 00	3 50	20 50	6 00	16 25	Philip Hurt	H. P. Miller.
6	Peter J. Christopherson	do	Sept. 10, 1865	Sept. 25, 1865	15	17 00	3 50	20 50	6 10	16 25	Peter J. Christoffersn	Do.
7	William Street Barney	Private	Sept. 10, 1865	Sept. 25, 1865	15	13 00	3 50	16 50	6 00	14 25	Wm. S. Barney	John R. Winder.
8	Amasa Tucker	do	Sept. 10, 1865	Sept. 25, 1865	15	13 00	3 50	16 50	6 00	14 25	Amasa Tucker	H. P. Miller.
9	Joel H. Child	do	Sept. 10, 1865	Sept. 25, 1865	15	13 00	3 50	16 50	6 00	14 25	Joel H. Child	John Kirkman.
10	William Scovil	do	Sept. 10, 1865	Sept. 25, 1865	15	13 00	3 50	16 50	6 00	14 25	William Scovil	H. P. Miller.
11	Erick Erickson	do	Sept. 10, 1865	Sept. 25, 1865	15	13 00	3 50	16 50	6 00	14 25	Erick Erickson	Do.
12	Jeremiah Page	do	Sept. 10, 1865	Sept. 25, 1865	15	13 00	3 50	16 50	6 00	14 25	Jeremiah Page	Do.
13	Peter Miller	do	Sept. 10, 1865	Sept. 25, 1865	15	13 00	3 50	16 50	6 00	14 25	Peter Mylen	Do.
14	Neils Madson	do	Sept. 10, 1865	Sept. 25, 1865	15	13 00	3 50	16 50	6 00	14 25	Neils Madsen	Do.
15	John Carter	do	Sept. 10, 1865	Sept. 25, 1865	15	13 00	3 50	16 50	6 00	14 25	John Carter	Do.
16	Aaron Amann	do	Sept. 10, 1865	Sept. 25, 1865	15	13 00	3 50	16 30	6 00	14 25	Aron Annern	Do.
17	George Merrick	do	Sept. 10, 1865	Sept. 25, 1865	15	13 00	3 50	16 50	6 00	14 25	George Meyrick	Do.
18	Jefferson Tidwell	do	Sept. 10, 1865	Sept. 25, 1865	15	13 00	3 50	16 50	6 00	14 25	J. Tidwell	Do.
19	Jens C. Neblle	do	Sept. 10, 1865	Sept. 25, 1865	15	13 00	3 50	16 50	6 00	14 25	Jens C. Nelile	Do.
20	Niels P. Jensen	do	Sept. 10, 1865	Sept. 25, 1865	15	13 00	3 50	16 30	6 00	14 25	Nils P. Jensen	Do.
21	Andrew L. Larsen	do	Sept. 10, 1865	Sept. 25, 1865	15	13 00	3 50	16 50	6 00	14 25	Andrew L. Larsen	Do.
22	Christian Petersen	do	Sept. 10, 1865	Sept. 25, 1865	15	13 00	3 50	16 50	6 40	14 25	Christian Petersen	In.
23	Sidney H. Allred	do	Sept. 10, 1865	Sept. 25, 1865	15	13 00	3 50	16 50	6 40	14 25	Sidney H. Allred	John Kirkman.
24	W. ford W. Brandon	do	Sept. 10, 1865	Sept. 25, 1865	15	13 00	3 50	16 50	6 00	14 25	Willerd W. Brandon	H. P. Miller.
25	William G. Burton	do	Sept. 10, 1865	Sept. 25, 1865	15	13 10	3 50	16 50	6 00	14 25	William G. Burton	Do.
26	Adolphus N. Bennett	do	Sept. 10, 1865	Sept. 25, 1865	15	13 00	3 50	16 50	6 00	14 25	Rodolfus N. Bennet	Do.
27	Joseph Fretwell	do	Sept. 10, 1865	Sept. 25, 1865	15	13 00	3 50	16 50	6 00	14 25	Joseph Fretwell	George Brough.
28	Stephen Allred	do	Sept. 10, 1865	Sept. 25, 1865	15	13 00	3 50	16 50	6 00	14 25	Stephen H. Allred	Do.
29	Thomas G. Scroider	do	Sept. 10, 1865	Sept. 25, 1865	15	13 00	3 50	16 50	6 00	14 25	T. S. Scroder	Do.
30	Nickli Lund	do	Sept. 10, 1865	Sept. 25, 1865	15	13 00	3 50	16 50	6 00	14 25	Nickli Lund	Do.
31	Henry Eilertson	do	Sept. 10, 1865	Sept. 25, 1865	15	13 00	3 50	16 50	6 00	14 25	Henry Eilertson	Do.

No.	Name		Mustered in	Mustered out							Name	Remarks
25	Joseph S. Major	do.	Sept. 10, 1865	Sept. 25, 1865	15	13 00	3 50	16 50	6 00	14 25	J. S. Mazor	Do.
26	George Blain	do.	Sept. 10, 1865	Sept. 25, 1865	15	13 00	3 50	16 50	6 00	14 25	George Blain	Do.
27	Joseph L. Jolley	do.	Sept. 10, 1865	Sept. 25, 1865	15	13 00	3 50	16 50	6 00	14 25	Joseph L. Jolley	John Kirkman.
28	John Elrumsen	do.	Sept. 10, 1865	Sept. 25, 1865	15	13 00	3 50	16 50	6 00	14 35	John Elrumsen	Do.
29	Samuel Rhodes	do.	Sept. 10, 1865	Sept. 25, 1865	15	13 00	3 50	16 50	6 00	14 35	Samuel Rhodes	Do.
30	George Hatch	do.	Sept. 10, 1865	Sept. 25, 1865	15	13 00	3 50	16 50	6 00	14 25	George Hatch	Do.
31	Peter Christenson	do.	Sept. 10, 1865	Sept. 25, 1865	15	13 00	3 50	16 50	6 00	14 25	Peter Christensen	Do.
32	Herbert Loomgson	do.	Sept. 10, 1865	Sept. 25, 1865	15	13 00	3 50	16 50	6 00	14 55	H. Longson	Do.
33	John Lewellin	do.	Sept. 10, 1865	Sept. 25, 1865	15	13 00	3 50	16 50	6 00	14 55	John Lewellyn	H. P. Miller.
34	Olu Olsen	do.	Sept. 10, 1865	Sept. 25, 1865	15	13 00	3 50	16 50	6 00	14 25	Olu Olsen	Do.
35	Jordan Brady	do.	Sept. 10, 1865	Sept. 25, 1865	15	13 00	3 50	16 50	6 00	14 25	Jordan Brady	Do.
36	Isaac N. Wilson	do.	Sept. 10, 1865	Sept. 25, 1865	15	13 00	3 50	16 50	6 00	14 25	Isaac N. Wilson	Do.
37	Orson M. Terry	do.	Sept. 10, 1865	Sept. 25, 1865	15	13 00	3 50	16 50	6 00	14 25	Orson M. Terry	Do.
38	Alma Miner	do.	Sept. 10, 1865	Sept. 25, 1865	15	13 00	3 50	16 50	6 00	14 25	Alma Miner	Do.
39	James F. Knight	do.	Sept. 10, 1865	Sept. 25, 1865	15	13 00	3 50	16 50	6 00	14 25	James F. Kniltet	Do.
40	Thadius Hamblick	do.	Sept. 10, 1865	Sept. 25, 1865	15	13 00	3 55	16 50	6 00	14 55		W. B. Parr.
41	John Battise	do.	Sept. 10, 1865	Sept. 25, 1865	15	13 00	3 50	16 50	6 00	14 25	John Battise	Do.
42	Nephi Robertson	do.	Sept. 10, 1865	Sept. 25, 1865	15	13 00	3 50	16 50	6 00	14 25	Nephi Robertson	Do.
43	Alonzo Nay	do.	Sept. 10, 1865	Sept. 25, 1865	15	13 00	3 50	16 50	6 00	14 25	Alonzo Nay, his + mark	Do.
44	Albert Collard	do.	Sept. 10, 1865	Sept. 25, 1865	15	13 00	3 50	16 50	6 00	14 25	Albert Collard	Do.
45	Sanford Holman	do.	Sept. 10, 1865	Sept. 25, 1865	15	13 00	3 50	16 50	6 00	14 25	Sanford Holman	Do.
46	Albert Sherman	do.	Sept. 10, 1865	Sept. 25, 1865	15	13 00	3 50	16 50	6 00	14 25	Albert Sherman	Do.
47	Christian Otrson	do.	Sept. 10, 1865	Sept. 25, 1865	15	13 00	3 50	16 50	6 00	14 25	Christian Otrson	Do.
48	John Green	do.	Sept. 10, 1865	Sept. 25, 1865	15	13 00	3 50	16 50	6 00	14 25	John Green	Do.
49	Edward Koyle	do.	Sept. 10, 1865	Sept. 25, 1865	15	13 00	3 50	16 50	6 00	14 25	Edward Koyle	Do.
50	Thomas Morgan	do.	Sept. 10, 1865	Sept. 25, 1865	15	13 00	3 50	16 50	6 00	14 25	Thomas Morgan, his + mark	Do.

The Indians made a raid on the City of Fort Ephraim, killed five men and two women, and two men wounded; they drove off a large herd of horses and cattle.

This company was mustered into service on the 10th day of September, by Brigadier General W. S. Snow, and with him went in pursuit and followed the Indians for two hundred miles through the mountains, overtook and surprised them in the vicinity of Fish Lake, killed seven, and wounded several. General Snow and Orson Taylor, wounded. The company returned to Fairview, and was mustered out on the 25th day of September—15 days' active service.

I certify that the above account is correct.

H. B. CLAWSON,
Adjutant General Nauvoo Legion.

UTAH TERRITORY, *Moroni*, 1866.

The United States to George W. Bradley,　　　　DR.

May 1.—To 495 pounds rice, at 40 cents	$198	00
To 586 pounds soap, at 50 cents	293	00
To 75 bushels potatoes, at $1	75	00
10.—To 2,113 pounds beans, at 11 cents	232	43
June 1.—To 15,000 pounds beef, at 10 cents	1,500	00
To 997 pounds sugar, at 40 cents	398	80
To 1,397 pounds coffee, at 40 cents	558	80
To 280 pounds candles, at 50 cents	140	00
To 89 bushels potatoes, at $1	89	00
4.—To 15,000 pounds flour, at 6 cents	900	00
To 225 gallons vinegar, at $1	225	00
Aug 5.—To 781 pounds soap, at 50 cents	390	50
To 591 pounds sugar, at 40 cents	236	40
To 101 bushels potatoes, at $1	101	00
To 591 pounds salt, at 5 cents	29	55
To 37 gallons molasses, at $2	74	00
To 95 gallons vinegar, at $1	95	00
Sept. 1.—To 15,000 pounds flour, at 6 cents	900	00
To 785 pounds rice, at 40 cents	314	00
11.—To 1,481 pounds rice, at 40 cents	592	40
15.—To 17,830 pounds beef, at 10 cents	1,783	00
Oct. 5.—To 1,159 pounds beans, at 11 cents	127	49
14.—To 21,500 pounds flour, at 6 cents	1,290	00
	10,543	37

GREAT SALT LAKE CITY, *November* 30, 1866.

I certify that the above account is correct; that the above supplies were purchased of George W. Bradley, and issued to the Utah Territory militia while employed in the suppression of Indian hostilities in said Territory, in the year 1866, and that they were necessary for that purpose.

ALBERT P. ROCKWOOD,
Commissary General Nauvoo Legion.

Received, Great Salt Lake City, November 30, 1866, of Albert P. Rockwood, commissary general Nauvoo Legion, ten thousand five hundred and fifty-three dollars and thirty-seven cents, in full of the above account.

GEORGE W. BRADLEY.

UTAH TERRITORY, *Nephi*, 1866.

The United States to Charles Byran,　　　　DR.

June 15.—To 9,317 pounds beef, at 10 cents	$931	70
20.—To 16,000 pounds flour, at 6 cents	960	00
July 1.—To 1,721 pounds of rice, at 40 cents	688	40
9.—To 72 gallons vinegar, at $1	72	00
To 185 pounds candles, at 50 cents	92	50
To 1,187 pounds sugar, at 40 cents	478	80
To 32 gallons molasses, at $2	64	00

Aug. 7.—To 1,279 pounds beans, at 11 cents.............	$140	69
Sept. 7.—To 11,961 pounds beef, at 10 cents.............	1,196	10
To 17,000 pounds flour, at 6 cents.............	1,020	00
Oct. 26.—To 1,391 pounds sugar, at 40 cents.............	556	40
	6,200	59

GREAT SALT LAKE CITY, *November* 30, 1866.

I certify that the above account is correct; that the above supplies were purchased of Charles Byran, and issued to the Utah Territory militia while employed in the suppression of Indian hostilities in said Territory, and that they were necessary for that purpose.

ALBERT P. ROCKWOOD,
Commissary General Nauvoo Legion.

Received, Great Salt Lake City, November 30, 1866, of Albert P. Rockwood, commissary general Nauvoo Legion, six thousand two hundred dollars and fifty-nine cents, in full of the above account.

C. H. BRYAN.

UTAH TERRITORY, *Payson,* 1866.

The United States to John B. Fairbanks,	DR.	
May 1.—To 489 pounds coffee, at 40 cents................	$195	60
To 110 pounds soap, at 50 cents..................	55	00
To 396 pounds rice, at 40 cents..................	158	40
To 10 bushels potatoes, at $1....................	10	00
To 125 pounds salt, at 5 cents..................	6	25
To 25 gallons vinegar, at $1.....................	25	00
To 591 pounds sugar, at 40 cents................	236	40
To 3,000 pounds flour, at 6 cents................	180	00
To 1,460 pounds of beef, at 10 cents.............	146	00
20.—To 215 pounds salt, at 5 cents...................	10	75
To 26 bushels potatoes, at $1...................	26	00
To 211 pounds soap, at 50 cents.................	105	50
To 655 pounds sugar, at 40 cents................	262	00
To 4,890 pounds beef, at 10 cents...............	489	00
To 6,000 pounds flour, at 6 cents...............	360	00
June 1.—To 210 pounds soap, at 50 cents..............	105	00
To 36 gallons vinegar, at $1....................	36	00
To 25 bushels potatoes, at $1...................	25	00
To 200 pounds salt, at 5 cents..................	10	00
July 15.—To 5,780 pounds beef, at 10 cents.............	578	00
To 6,000 pounds flour, at 6 cents...............	360	00
To 860 pounds beans, at 11 cents................	94	60
To 595 pounds coffee, at 40 cents...............	238	00
To 40 pounds candles, at 50 cents...............	20	00
To 25 gallons molasses, at $1...................	25	00
Aug. 2.—To 240 pounds soap, at 50 cents..............	120	00
To 23 bushels potatoes, at $1...................	23	00
To 125 pounds candles, at 50 cents..............	62	50
To 36 gallons vinegar, at $1....................	36	00
To 595 pounds sugar, at 40 cents................	238	00

Aug. 2.—	To 521 pounds beans, at 11 cents	$57	31
	To 375 pounds rice, at 40 cents	150	00
	To 200 pounds coffee, at 40 cents	80	00
	To 7,000 pounds flour, at 6 cents	420	00
	To 5,886 pounds beef, at 10 cents	588	60
Sept. 15.—	To 196 pounds soap, at 50 cents	98	00
	To 10 bushels potatoes, at $1	10	00
	To 200 pounds salt, at 5 cents	10	00
	To 100 pounds candles, at 50 cents	50	00
	To 195 pounds sugar, at 40 cents	78	00
	To 25 gallons vinegar, at $1	25	00
	To 3,100 pounds flour, at 6 cents	186	00
	To 2,680 pounds beef, at 10 cents	268	00
Oct. 20.—	To 1,400 pounds beef, at 10 cents	140	00
		6,397	91

GREAT SALT LAKE CITY, *November* 30, 1866.

I certify that the above account is correct; that the above supplies were purchased of John B. Fairbanks, and issued to the Utah Territory militia while employed in the suppression of Indian hostilities in said Territory, in the year 1866, and that they were necessary for that purpose.

ALBERT P. ROCKWOOD,
Commissary General Nauvoo Legion.

Received, Great Salt Lake City, November 30, 1866, of Albert P. Rockwood, commissary general Nauvoo Legion, six thousand three hundred and ninety-seven dollars and ninety-one cents, in full payment of the above account.

JOHN B. FAIRBANKS.

UTAH TERRITORY, *American Fork*, 1866.

The United States to Leonard E. Harrington,   DR.

May 25.—	To 480 pounds rice, at 40 cents	$192	00
	To 490 pounds coffee, at 40 cents	196	00
	To 615 pounds beans, at 11 cents	67	65
	To 596 pounds sugar, at 40 cents	238	40
	To 3,160 pounds beef, at 10 cents	316	00
June 1.—	To 8,000 pounds flour, at 6 cents	480	00
	To 5,896 pounds beef, at 10 cents	589	60
	To 25 bushels potatoes, at $1	25	00
	To 100 pounds candles, at 50 cents	50	00
15.—	To 72 gallons vinegar, at $1	72	00
	To 589 pounds rice, at 40 cents	235	60
	To 2,240 pounds beef, at 10 cents	244	00
	To 36 gallons molasses, at $2	72	00
25.—	To 26 bushels potatoes, at $1	26	00
	To 125 pounds salt, at 5 cents	6	25
	To 108 pounds soap, at 50 cents	54	00
	To 8,000 pounds flour, at 6 cents	480	00
	To 6,921 pounds beef, at 10 cents	692	10

June 25.—To 390 pounds rice, at 40 cents	$156	00
To 590 pounds coffee, at 40 cents	236	00
To 669 pounds beans, at 11 cents	73	59
To 36 gallons vinegar, at $1	36	00
To 62 pounds candles, at 50 cents	31	00
To 650 pounds sugar, at 40 cents	260	00
To 3,516 pounds beef, at 10 cents	351	60
July 3.—To 36 gallons vinegar, at $1	36	00
20.—To 589 pounds beans, at 11 cents	73	59
To 481 pounds rice, at 40 cents	192	41
To 496 pounds coffee, at 40 cents	198	40
To 680 pounds sugar, at 40 cents	272	00
29.—To 96 pounds salt, at 5 cents	4	80
To 21 bushels potatoes, at $1	21	00
To 70 pounds soap, at 50 cents	35	00
To 9,500 pounds flour, at 6 cents	570	00
To 2,370 pounds beef, at 10 cents	237	00
To 36 pounds candles, at 50 cents	18	00
To 36 gallons vinegar, at $1	36	00
To 496 pounds sugar, at 40 cents	198	40
To 529 pounds beans, at 11 cents	58	19
To 450 pounds coffee, at 40 cents	180	00
To 298 pounds rice, at 40 cents	119	20
Aug. 2.—To 159 pounds salt, at 5 cents	7	95
26.—To 371 pounds coffee, at 40 cents	148	40
Sept. 2.—To 1,200 pounds flour, at 6 cents	72	00
To 1,200 pounds beef, at 10 cents	120	00
10.—To 100 pounds coffee, at 40 cents	40	00
Oct. 8.—To 2,391 pounds beef, at 10 cents	239	10
To 2,500 pounds flour, at 6 cents	150	00
To 150 pounds soap, at 50 cents	75	00
To 15 bushels potatoes, at $1	15	00
To 50 pounds salt, at 5 cents	2	50
To 175 pounds beans, at 11 cents	19	25
	8,319	98

GREAT SALT LAKE CITY, *November* 30, 1866.

I certify that the above account is correct; that the above supplies were purchased of Leonard E. Harrington and issued to the Utah Territory militia while employed in the suppression of Indian hostilities in said Territory, in the year 1866, and that they were necessary for that purpose.

ALBERT P. ROCKWOOD,
Commissary General Nauvoo Legion.

Received, Great Salt Lake City, November 30, 1866, of Albert P. Rockwood, commissary general Nauvoo Legion, eight thousand three hundred and nineteen dollars and ninety-eight cents, in full payment of the above account.

LEONARD E. HARRINGTON.

UTAH TERRITORY, *Great Salt Lake City*, 1866.

The United States to Edward Hunter,   DR.

May 1.—To 1,875 pounds coffee, at 40 cents..............	$750 00
June 12.—To 1,741 pounds beans, at 11 cents..............	191 50
To 321 pounds candles, at 50 cents..............	160 50
To 1,165 pounds coffee, at 40 cents..............	466 00
To 2,390 pounds sugar, at 40 cents..............	956 00
To 721 pounds salt, at 5 cents..............	36 05
23.—To 597 pounds rice, at 40 cents..............	238 80
To 155 bushels potatoes, at $1..............	155 00
27.—To 149 pounds sugar, at 40 cents..............	598 80
To 891 pounds coffee, at 40 cents..............	356 40
To 175 pounds candles, at 50 cents..............	87 50
July 4.—To 25,000 pounds flour, at 6 cents..............	1,500 00
To 21,000 pounds beef, at 10 cents..............	2,100 00
To 568 pounds soap, at 50 cents..............	284 00
Aug. 16.—To 15,781 pounds beef, at 10 cents..............	1,578 10
To 2,119 pounds coffee, at 40 cents..............	847 60
To 295 pounds candles, at 50 cents..............	147 50
Sept. 22.—To 27,191 pounds beef, at 10 cents..............	2,719 10
To 156 gallons vinegar, at $1..............	156 00
To 690 pounds coffee, at 40 cents..............	276 00
28.—To 1,857 pounds beans, at 11 cents..............	204 27
Oct. 3.—To 1,757 pounds rice, at 40 cents..............	712 80
11.—To 2,275 pounds sugar, at 40 cents..............	910 00
To 796 pounds coffee, at 40 cents..............	308 40

15,740 32

GREAT SALT LAKE CITY, *November* 30, 1866.

I certify that the above account is correct; that the above supplies were purchased of Edward Hunter and issued to the Utah Territory militia while employed in the suppression of Indian hostilities in said Territory in the year 1866, and that they were necessary for that purpose.
ALBERT P. ROCKWOOD,
Commissary General Nauvoo Legion.

Received, Great Salt Lake City, November 30, 1866, of Albert P. Rockwood, commissary general Nauvoo Legion, fifteen thousand seven hundred and forty dollars and thirty-two cents, in full of the above account.

EDWARD HUNTER.

UTAH TERRITORY, *Springville*, 1866.

The United States to Aaron Johnson,   DR.

May 9.—To 4,000 pounds flour, at 6 cents per pound......	$240 00
To 1,690 pounds beef, at 10 cents per pound......	169 00
To 150 pounds soap, at 50 cents per pound.......	75 00
To 139 pounds salt, at 5 cents per pound........	6 95
To 25 bushels potatoes, at $1 per bushel........	25 00
To 36 gallons vinegar, at $1 per gallon..........	36 00

May 9.—To 49 pounds candles, at 50 cents per pound.....	$24 50	
To 580 pounds beans, at 11 cents per pound.....	63 80	
To 461 pounds rice, at 40 cents per pound.......	184 40	
To 300 pounds coffee, at 40 cents per pound......	120 00	
June 15.—To 105 pounds salt, at 5 cents per pound........	5 25	
To 30 bushels potatoes, at $1..................	30 00	
To 895 pounds sugar, at 40 cents per pound.....	358 00	
To 36 gallons vinegar, at $1 per gallon..........	36 00	
To 59 pounds candles, at 50 cents per pound.....	29 50	
To 96 pounds soap, at 50 cents per pound........	48 00	
To 6,000 pounds flour, at 6 cents per pound......	360 00	
July 3.—To 250 pounds salt, at 5 cents per pound........	12 50	
To 15 bushels potatoes, at $1 per bushel..........	15 00	
To 590 pounds sugar, at 40 cents per pound......	236 40	
To 100 pounds candles, at 50 cents per pound....	50 00	
To 760 pounds beans, at 11 cents per pound......	83 60	
To 410 pounds rice, at 40 cents per pound........	164 00	
To 300 pounds coffee, at 40 cents per pound......	120 00	
To 195 pounds soap, at 50 cents per pound........	97 50	
To 4,000 pounds flour, at 6 cents per pound......	240 00	
To 6,900 pounds beef, at 10 cents per pound......	690 00	
Aug. 16.—To 429 pounds rice, at 40 cents per pound........	171 60	
To 369 pounds coffee, at 40 cents per pound......	147 60	
To 380 pounds beans, at 11 cents per pound......	41 80	
To 400 pounds sugar, at 40 cents per pound......	160 00	
To 4,921 pounds beef, at 10 cents per pound......	492 10	
To 4,500 pounds flour, at 6 cents per pound......	270 00	
Sept. 7.—To 268 pounds beans, at 11 cents per pound.....	31 46	
	4,834 96	

GREAT SALT LAKE CITY, *November* 30, 1866.

I certify that the above account is correct; that the above supplies were purchased of Aaron Johnson, and issued to the Utah Territory militia while employed in the suppression of Indian hostilities in said Territory, in the year 1866, and that they were necessary for that purpose.

ALBERT P. ROCKWOOD,
Commissary General Nauvoo Legion.

Received, Great Salt Lake City, November 30, 1866, of Albert P. Rockwood, four thousand eight hundred and thirty-four dollars and ninety-six cents, in full payment of the above account.

A. JOHNSON.

UTAH TERRITORY, *Fountain Green*, 1866.

The United States to Robert L. Johnson,   DR.

May 29.—To 761 pounds beans, at 11 cents per pound......	$83 71	
To 556 pounds soap, at 50 cents per pound.......	278 00	
To 793 pounds coffee, at 40 cents per pound......	317 20	
June 10.—To 7,800 pounds beef, at 10 cents per pound......	780 00	
To 19,000 pounds flour, at 6 cents per pound.....	1,140 00	
To 96 bushels potatoes, at $1 per bushel.........	96 00	

July 20.—To 1,017 pounds rice, at 40 cents per pound...... $406 80
          To 2,180 pounds sugar, at 40 cents per pound....   872 00
Sept. 16.—To 11,000 pounds flour, at 6 cents per pound.....   660 00
          To 87 gallons vinegar, at $1 per gallon..........   87 00
          To 36 gallons molasses, at $2 per gallon.........   72 00

                                                               4,792 71

GREAT SALT LAKE CITY, *November 30, 1866.*

I certify that the above account is correct; that the above supplies were purchased of Robert L. Johnson, and issued to the Utah Territory militia while employed in the suppression of Indian hostilities in said Territory, in the year 1866, and that they were necessary for that purpose.

                                ALBERT P. ROCKWOOD,
                                Commissary General Nauvoo Legion.

Received, Great Salt Lake City, November 30, 1866, of Albert P. Rockwood, commissary general Nauvoo Legion, four thousand seven hundred and ninety-two dollars and seventy-one cents, in full of the above account.

                                R. L. JOHNSON.

———

UTAH TERRITORY, *Fort Gunnison, 1866.*

The United States to H. H. Kearnes,   DR.

May   1.—To 3,971 pounds beef, at 10 cents per pound...... $397 10
          To 10,000 pounds flour, at 6 cents per pound.....   600 00
       5.—To 1,197 pounds beans, at 11 cents per pound....   131 67
       6.—To 1,590 pounds sugar, at 40 cents per pound....   636 00
          To 100 gallons vinegar, at $1 per gallon.........   100 00
June   3.—To 480 pounds soap, at 50 cents per pound.......   240 00
          To 35 gallons molasses, at $2 per gallon.........   70 00
July 30.—To 1,482 pounds beans, at 11 cents per pound....   163 02
Aug.   7.—To 1,385 pounds coffee, at 40 cents per pound....   554 00
       9.—To 119 pounds candles, at 50 cents per pound....   59 50
      19.—To 396 pounds soap, at 50 cents per pound......   198 00
      23.—To 1,792 pounds rice, at 40 cents per pound......   716 80
Sept. 1.—To 230 pounds soap, at 50 cents per pound.......   115 00
          To 101 pounds candles, at 50 cents per pound....   50 50
Oct.   1.—To 15,955 pounds beef, at 10 cents per pound....   1,595 50
          To 9,000 pounds flour, at 6 cents per pound......   540 00

                                                               6,167 09

GREAT SALT LAKE CITY, *November 30, 1866.*

I certify that the above account is correct; that the above bill of articles were purchased of H. H. Kearnes, and issued to the Utah Territory militia while employed in the suppression of Indian hostilities in said Territory, in the year 1866.

                                ALBERT P. ROCKWOOD,
                                Commissary General Nauvoo Legion.

Received, Great Salt Lake City, November 30, 1866, of Albert P. Rockwood, commissary general Nauvoo Legion, six thousand one hundred and sixty-seven dollars and nine cents, in full of the above account.

HAMILTON H. KEARMES.

UTAH TERRITORY, *Great Salt Lake City*, 1866.

The United States to Joseph Kingsbury,   DR.

May 14.—To 1,754 pounds coffee, at 40 cents per pound....		8701 60
16.—To 987 pounds of rice, at 40 cents per pound.....		394 80
June 27.—To 1,089 pounds beans, at 11 cents per pound....		121 79
July 15.—To 21,000 pounds flour, at 6 cents per pound.....		1,260 00
20.—To 7,990 pounds beef, at 10 cents per pound.....		799 00
Aug. 29.—To 1,821 pounds beans, at 11 cents per pound....		210 31
To 61 bushels potatoes, at $1 per bushel.........		61 00
To 1,971 pounds sugar, at 40 cents per pound....		788 40
Sept. 28.—To 100 gallons vinegar, at $1 per gallon.........		100 00
To 181 pounds candles, at 50 cents per pound....		90 50
To 1,690 pounds sugar, at 40 cents per pound....		676 00
To 1,940 pounds coffee, at 40 cents per pound....		776 00
To 621 pounds salt, at 5 cents per pound........		31 05
To 51 bushels potatoes, at $1 per bushel.........		51 00
To 31 gallons molasses, at $2 per gallon........		62 00
To 485 pounds soap, at 50 cents per pound......		242 50
Oct. 15.—To 12,200 pounds beef, at 10 cents per pound....		1,220 00
To 1,436 pounds beans, at 11 cents per pound....		157 96
To 521 pounds salt, at 5 cents per pound........		26 05
		7,769 96

GREAT SALT LAKE CITY, *November* 30, 1866.

I certify that the above account is correct; that the above supplies were purchased of Joseph Kingsbury, and issued to the Utah Territory militia while employed in the suppression of Indian hostilities in said Territory, in the year 1866, and that they were necessary for that purpose.

ALBERT P. ROCKWOOD,
Commissary General Nauvoo Legion.

Received, Great Salt Lake City, November 30, 1866, of Albert P. Rockwood, commissary general Nauvoo Legion, seven thousand seven hundred and sixty-nine dollars and ninety-six cents, in full of the above account.

J. C. KINGSBURY.

UTAH TERRITORY, *Springtown*, 1866.

The United States to C. G. Larsen,   DR.

May 15.—To 95 gallons vinegar, at $1		$95 00
To 250 pounds candles, at 50 cts.................		125 00
To 11,000 pounds flour, at 6 cts.................		660 00
To 7,916 pounds beef, at 10 cts		791 60
22.—To 35 gallons molasses, at $2		70 00

June	7.—To 1,576 pounds rice, at 40 cts................		$630 40
	To 1,686 pounds sugar, at 40 cts................		674 40
	To 389 pounds salt, at 5 cts...................		19 45
July	13.—To 1,527 pounds beans, at 11 cts............		167 97
	To 983 pounds rice, at 40 cts..................		393 20
	To 1,090 pounds soap, at 50 cts................		545 00
	To 1,497 pounds coffee, at 40 cts.............		598 80
Aug.	11.—To 17,000 pounds flour, at 6 cts.............		1,020 00
	To 2,470 pounds sugar, at 40 cts..............		988 00
	To 180 gallons vinegar, at $1.................		180 00
Sept.	6.—To 33 gallons molasses, at $2..............		72 00

7,030 82

GREAT SALT LAKE CITY, *November* 30, 1866.

I certify that the above account is correct; that the above supplies were purchased of —— Larsen and issued to the Utah Territory militia while employed in the suppression of Indian hostilities in said Territory in the year 1866, and that they were necessary for that purpose.

ALBERT P. ROCKWOOD,
Commissary General Nauvoo Legion.

Received, Great Salt Lake City, November 30, 1866, of Albert P. Rockwood, commissary general Nauvoo Legion, seven thousand and thirty dollars and eighty-two cents, in full of the above account.

C. G. LARSEN.

UTAH TERRITORY, *Wasatch County*, 1866.

The United States to Joseph Murdock,   DR.

May	1.—To 1,350 pounds beef, at 10 cts...............		$135 00
	To 2,300 pounds flour, at 6 cts................		138 00
	To 270 pounds sugar, at 40 cts................		168 00
	To 270 pounds rice, at 40 cts................		168 00
	To 60 pounds soap, at 50 cts..................		30 00
	To 150 pounds coffee, at 40 cts..............		60 00
June	5.—To 1,500 pounds beef, at 10 cts..............		150 00
	To 2,500 pounds flour, at 6 cts...............		150 00
	To 200 pounds sugar, at 40 cts...............		80 00
	To 200 pounds rice, at 40 cts................		80 00
	To 50 pounds candles, at 50 cts..............		25 00
July	2.—To 2,500 pounds beef, at 10 cts..............		250 00
	To 4,500 pounds flour, at 6 cts		270 00
	To 500 pounds sugar, at 40 cts...............		200 00
	To 50 bushels potatoes, at $1		50 00
	To 400 pounds coffee, at 40 cts..............		160 00
	To 500 pounds rice, at 40 cts................		200 00
	To 200 pounds soap, at 50 cts................		100 00
Aug.	6.—To 3,000 pounds beef, at 10 cts..............		300 00
	To 5,000 pounds flour, at 6 cts...............		300 00
	To 590 pounds sugar, at 40 cts		236 00
	To 570 pounds rice, at 40 cts		228 00
	To 100 pounds soap, at 50 cts................		50 00
	To 100 pounds candles, at 50 cts.............		50 00
	To 200 pounds coffee, at 40 cts..............		80 00

Sept.	10.—To 2,896 pounds beef, at 10 cts................	$289 60
	To 5,000 pounds flour, at 6 cts	300 00
	To 587 pounds sugar, at 40 cts.................	234 80
	To 390 pounds coffee, at 40 cts.................	156 00
	To 595 pounds rice, at 40 cts.................	238 00
	To 145 pounds soap, at 50 cts.................	72 50
	To 50 bushel potatoes, at $1.................	50 00
	To 50 gallons molasses, at $2.................	100 00
	To 500 pounds beans, at 11 cts................	55 00
		5,163 90

GREAT SALT LAKE CITY, *December* 31, 1866.

I certify that the above account is correct; that the above supplies were purchased of Joseph Murdock and issued to the Wasatch County militia while employed in the suppression of Indian hostilities in said and adjoining counties, in the year 1868.

ALBERT P. ROCKWOOD,
Commissary General Nauvoo Legion.

Received, Great Salt Lake City, December 31, 1866, of Albert P. Rockwood, commissary general Nauvoo Legion, five thousand one hundred and sixty-three dollars and ninety cents, in full payment of the above account.

JOSEPH L. MURDOCK.

UTAH TERRITORY, *Provo*, 1866.

The United States to William Miller,		DR.
May	4.—To 987 pounds beef, at 10 cts.................	98 70
	7.—To 1,690 pounds beef, at 10 cts.................	169 00
	13.—To 1,561 pounds beef, at 10 cts.................	156 10
	20.—To 6,000 pounds flour, at 6 cts	360 00
	To 665 pounds beans, at 11 cts	73 15
	To 36 gallons vinegar, at $1	36 00
	To 100 pounds candles, at 50 cts...............	50 00
June	4.—To 789 pounds sugar, at 40 cts.................	315 60
	To 590 pounds rice, at 40 cts.................	236 00
	To 396 pounds coffee, at 40 cts...............	158 40
	To 749 pounds beans, at 11 cts................	82 39
July	13.—To 20 bushels potatoes, at $1.................	20 00
	To 89 pounds salt, at 5 cts	4 45
	To 90 pounds soap, at 50 cts.................	45 00
Aug.	26.—To 498 pounds sugar, at 40 cts.................	199 20
	To 96 pounds candles, at 50 cts...............	48 00
	To 36 gallons vinegar, at $1.................	36 00
	To 200 pounds salt, at 5 cts.................	10 00
	To 35 bushels potatoes, at $1.................	35 00
	To 451 pounds beans, at 11 cts................	49 51
	To 200 pounds rice, at 40 cts.................	80 00
	To 2,780 pounds beef, at 10 cts.................	278 00
	To 5,000 pounds flour, at 6 cts.................	300 00
	To 160 pounds soap, at 50 cts.................	80 00
		2,920 50

GREAT SALT LAKE CITY, *November* 30, 1866

I certify that the above account is correct; that the above supplies were purchased of William Miller and issued to the Utah Territory militia while employed in the suppression of Indian hostilities in said Territory, in the year 1866, and that they were necessary for that purpose.

ALBERT P. ROCKWOOD,
Commissary General Nauvoo Legion.

Received, Great Salt Lake City, November 30, 1866, of Albert P. Rockwood, commissary general Nauvoo Legion, two thousand nine hundred and twenty dollars and fifty cents, in full payment of the above account.
WM. MILLER.

UTAH TERRITORY, *Manti*, 1866.

The United States to Andrew Moffitt,   DR.

May 1.—To 580 pounds salt, at 5 cents per pound.........	$29 00
To 1,186 pounds sugar, at 40 cents per pound....	474 40
To 36 gallons vinegar, at $1 per gallon...........	36 00
To 125 pounds candles, at 50 cents per pound....	62 50
To 36 gallons molasses, at $2 per gallon..........	72 00
To 651 pounds beans, at 11 cents per pound......	71 61
4.—To 11,421 pounds beef, at 10 cents per pound.....	1,142 10
To 15,000 pounds flour, at 6 cents per pound......	900 00
16.—To 1,727 pounds rice, at 40 cents per pound......	700 80
June 28.—To 3,000 pounds flour, at 6 cents per pound......	180 00
To 360 pounds soap, at 50 cents per pound.......	180 00
To 569 pounds salt, at 5 cents per pound.........	28 45
July 21.—To 1,765 pounds beans, at 11 cents per pound....	194 15
25.—To 1,534 pounds beef, at 10 cents per pound......	153 40
Aug. 1.—To 23,000 pounds flour, at 6 cents per pound.....	1,380 00
11.—To 1,583 pounds rice, at 40 cents per pound......	633 20
Sept. 19.—To 1,876 pounds sugar, at 40 cents per pound....	750 40
To 1,981 pounds beans, at 11 cents per pound....	217 91
To 165 pounds candles, at 50 cents per pound....	82 50
To 675 pounds soap, at 50 cents per pound.......	337 50
Oct. 5.—To 15,000 pounds flour, at 6 cents per pound......	900 00
To 407 pounds salt, at 5 cents per pound........	20 35
	8,546 27

GREAT SALT LAKE CITY, *November* 30, 1866.

I certify that the above account is correct; that the above supplies were purchased of Andrew Moffitt, and issued to the Utah Territory militia while employed in the suppression of Indian hostilities in said Territory, in the year 1866, and that they were necessary for that purpose.
ALBERT P. ROCKWOOD,
Commissary General Nauvoo Legion.

Received, Great Salt Lake City, November 30, 1866, of Albert P. Rockwood, commissary general Nauvoo Legion, eight thousand five hundred and forty-six dollars and twenty-seven cents, in full of the above account.

ANDREW MOFFITT.

UTAH TERRITORY, *Fort Ephraim*, 1866.

The United States to Canute Peterson,   DR.

May 11.—To 9,000 pounds flour, at 6 cents per pound......	$540 00
To 9,781 pounds beef, at 10 cents per pound......	978 10
To 390 pounds soap, at 50 cents per pound.......	195 00
To 96 bushels potatoes, at $1 per bushel.........	96 00
To 960 pounds salt, at 5 cents per pound.........	48 00
To 2,080 pounds sugar, at 40 cents per pound....	832 00
21.—To 1,757 pounds beans, at 11 cents per pound...	195 27
June 10.—To 981 pounds coffee, at 40 cents per pound......	392 40
To 691 pounds soap, at 50 cents per pound.......	345 50
July 15.—To 180 gallons vinegar, at $1 per gallon.........	180 00
To 35 gallons molasses, at $2 per gallon..........	70 00
To 830 pounds salt, at 5 cents per pound.........	41 50
To 110 bushels potatoes, at $1 per bushel........	110 00
31.—To 11,471 pounds beef, at 10 cents per pound.....	1,147 10
Aug. 13.—To 1,893 pounds beans, at 11 cents per pound....	208 23
19.—To 22,000 pounds flour, at 6 cents per pound......	1,320 00
To 742 pounds salt, at 5 cents per pound........	37 10
Sept. 9.—To 56 gallons vinegar, at $1 per gallon..........	56 00
To 211 pounds candles, at 50 cents per pound....	105 50
To 87 bushels potatoes, at $1 per bushel.........	87 00
To 2,565 pounds sugar, at 40 cents per pound....	1,026 00
To 1,369 pounds coffee, at 40 cents per pound....	547 60
Oct. 8.—To 31 gallons molasses, at $2 per gallon..........	62 00
To 179 pounds candles, at 50 cents per pound....	89 50
To 580 pounds coffee, at 40 cents per pound......	232 00
	8,941 80

GREAT SALT LAKE CITY, *November* 30, 1866.

I certify that the above account is correct; that the above supplies were purchased of Canute Peterson, and issued to the Utah Territory militia while employed in the suppression of Indian hostilities in said Territory, in the year 1866, and that they were necessary for that purpose.

     ALBERT P. ROCKWOOD,
     Commissary General Nauvoo Legion.

Received, Great Salt Lake City, November 30, 1866, of Albert P. Rockwood, commissary general Nauvoo Legion, eight thousand nine hundred and forty-one dollars and eighty cents, in full of the above account.

     CANUTE PETERSON.

UTAH TERRITORY, *Great Salt Lake City*, 1866.

The United States to Briant Stringham,   DR.

May 4.—To 1,978 pounds rice, at 40 cents per pound......	$791 20
9.—To 96 pounds candles, at 50 cents per pound......	48 00
To 71 gallons molasses, at $2 per gallon..........	142 00
To 396 pounds salt, at 5 cents per pound.........	19 80
June 19.—To 19,597 pounds beef, at 10 cents per pound.....	1,959 70
To 416 pounds soap, at 50 cents per pound.......	208 00
To 190 gallons vinegar, at $1 per gallon..........	190 00

July 4.—To 1,921 pounds beans, at 11 cents per pound....	$211	31
To 798 pounds sugar, at 40 cents per pound......	319	20
To 1,567 pounds coffee, at 40 cents per pound....	632	80
To 116 pounds candles, at 50 cents per pound ...	58	00
To 461 pounds salt, at 5 cents per pound.........	23	05
To 95 bushels potatoes, at $1 per bushel.........	95	00
Aug. 22.—To 1,585 pounds beans, at 11 cents per pound....	174	35
To 76 bushels potatoes, at $1 per bushel..........	76	00
To 160 gallons vinegar, at $1 per gallon..........	160	00
To 175 pounds candles, at 50 cents per pound....	87	50
To 1,185 pounds sugar, at 40 cents per pound....	474	00
26.—To 25,321 pounds beef, at 10 cents per pound.'....	2,532	10
Sept. 3.—To 1,145 pounds rice, at 40 cents per pound......	458	00
To 721 pounds coffee, at 40 cents per pound......	288	40
To 598 pounds soap, at 50 cents per pound.......	299	00
Oct. 20.—To 989 pounds sugar, at 40 cents per pound....	395	60
To 675 pounds coffee, at 40 cents per pound......	270	00
To 797 pounds beans, at 11 cents per pound......	87	67
To 96 gallons vinegar, at $1 per gallon...........	96	00
To 228 pounds candles, at 50 cents per pound.....	114	00
To 20 gallons molasses, at $2 per gallon..........	40	00
To 361 pounds soap, at 50 cents per pound.......	190	50
	10,531	18

GREAT SALT LAKE CITY, *November* 30, 1866.

I certify that the above account is correct; that the above supplies were purchased of Briant Stringham, and issued to the Utah Territory militia while employed in the suppression of Indian hostilities in said Territory, in the year 1866, and that they were necessary for that purpose.

ALBERT P. ROCKWOOD,
Commissary General Nauvoo Legion.

Received, Great Salt Lake City, November 30, 1866, of Albert P. Rockwood, commissary general Nauvoo legion, ten thousand five hundred and thirty-one dollars and eighteen cents, in full of the above account.

BRIANT STRINGHAM.

UTAH TERRITORY, *Mt. Pleasant*, 1866.

The United States to William Seely,   DR.

May 20.—To 321 pounds soap, at 50 cents	$160	50
To 160 gallons of vinegar, at $1	160	00
To 35 gallons molasses, at $2................	70	00
To 59 bushels potatoes, at $1....................	59	00
To 1,989 pounds sugar, at 40 cents............	795	60
To 13,221 pounds beef, at 10 cents	1,322	10
June 2.—To 2,391 pounds beans, at 11 cents.............	263	01
To 17,000 pounds flour, at 6 cents.............	1,020	00
To 1,191 pounds rice, at 40 cents	476	40
July 25.—To 17,000 pounds flour, at 6 cents.............	1,020	00
To 220 gallons vinegar, at $1...................	220	00
To 260 pounds candles, at 50 cents	130	00

July 25.—To 1,636 pounds coffee, at 40 cents.............. $654 40
         To 2,578 pounds sugar, at 40 cents.............. 1,031 20
         To 309 pounds soap, at 50 cents 154 50
Aug. 5.—To 18,400 pounds beef, at 10 cents 1,840 00
Sept. 9.—To 2,140 pounds beans, at 11 cents.............. 235 40
      25.—To 14,000 pounds flour, at 6 cents.............. 840 00
         To 1,926 pounds rice, at 40 cents.............. 770 40
Oct. 11.—To 490 pounds soap, at 50 cents 245 00
         To 110 bushels potatoes, at $1................. 110 00

                                                        11,577 51

GREAT SALT LAKE CITY, *November* 30, 1866.

I certify that the above account is correct; that the above supplies were purchased of William Seely, and issued to the Utah Territory militia while employed in the suppression of Indian hostilities in said Territory, in the year 1866, and that they were necessary for that purpose.

ALBERT P. ROCKWOOD,
Commissary General Nauvoo Legion.

Received, Great Salt Lake City, November 30, 1866, of Albert P. Rockwood, commissary general Nauvoo Legion, eleven thousand five hundred and seventy dollars and fifty-one cents, in full of the above account.

WM. SEELY.

UTAH TERRITORY, *Fairview*, 1866.

The United States to Amasa Tucker,   DR.

May 24.—To 17,550 pounds beef, at 10 cents per pound $1,755 00
June 1.—To 7,000 pounds flour, at 6 cents per pound...... 420 00
     20.—To 1,583 pounds beans, at 11 cents per pound.... 174 13
         To 31 gallons molasses, at $2 per gallon........ 62 00
July 28.—To 1,921 pounds rice, at 40 cents per pound...... 768 40
         To 56 bushels potatoes, at $1 per bushel......... 56 00
         To 31 gallons molasses, at $2 per gallon......... 62 00
         To 180 pounds candles, at 50 cents per pound.... 90 00
Aug. 25.—To 740 pounds soap, at 50 cents per pound 370 00
         To 981 pounds coffee, at 40 cents per pound...... 392 40
         To 39 gallons molasses, at $2 per gallon......... 78 00
         To 475 pounds salt, at 5 cents per pound 23 75
Sept. 4.—To 6,700 pounds beef, at 10 cents per pound...... 670 00
Oct. 10.—To 1,321 pounds beans, at 11 cents per pound.... 145 31

                                                        5,066 99

GREAT SALT LAKE CITY, *November* 30, 1866.

I certify that the above account is correct; that the above supplies were purchased of Amasa Tucker, and issued to the Utah Territory militia while employed in the suppression of Indian hostilities in said Territory, in the year 1866, and that they were necessary for that purpose.

ALBERT P. ROCKWOOD,
Commissary General Nauvoo Legion.

Received, Great Salt Lake City, November 30, 1866, of Albert P. Rockwood, commissary general Nauvoo Legion, five thousand and sixty-six dollars and ninety-nine cents, in full of the above account.

AMASA TUCKER.

VOUCHERS FOR QUARTERMASTER SUPPLIES FOR 1866.

UTAH TERRITORY, Moroni, 1866.

The United States to George W. Bradley,	DR.
May 11.—To 5,890 pounds hay, at 1 cent per pound........	$58 90
To 3,691 pounds hay, at 1 cent per pound........	36 91
15.—To 478 bushels oats, at $1 per bushel........	478 00
June 4.—To 5,921 pounds hay, at 1 cent per pound........	59 21
16.—To 3,521 pounds hay, at 1 cent per pound........	35 21
25.—To 3,920 pounds hay, at 1 cent per pound........	39 20
Aug. 13.—To 410 bushels oats, at $1 per bushel........	410 00
25.—To 363 bushels oats, at $1 per bushel........	363 00
Sept. 14.—To 587 bushels oats, at $1 per bushel........	587 00
To 5,975 pounds hay, at 1 cent per pound........	59 75
29.—To 5,891 pounds hay, at 1 cent per pound........	58 91
Oct. 13.—To 6,871 pounds hay, at 1 cent per pound........	68 71
26.—To 410 bushels oats, at $1 per bushel........	410 00
	2,664 80

GREAT SALT LAKE CITY, December 25, 1866.

I certify that the above account is correct; that the above supplies were purchased of George W. Bradley, and issued to the Utah Territory militia while employed in the suppression of Indian hostilities in said Territory in the year 1866, and that they were necessary for that purpose.

LEWIS ROBISON,
Quartermaster General Nauvoo Legion.

Received, Great Salt Lake City, December 25, 1866, of Lewis Robison quartermaster general Nauvoo Legion, two thousand six hundred and sixty-six dollars and eighty cents, in full of the above account.

GEORGE W. BRADLEY.

UTAH TERRITORY, Salt Creek, 1866.

The United States to Charles Bryan,	DR.
May 23.—To 460 bushels oats, at $1 per bushel........	$460 00
Sept. 1.—To 221 bushels oats, at $1 per bushel........	221 00
To 3,516 pounds hay, at 1 cent per pound........	35 16
	716 16

GREAT SALT LAKE CITY, *December 25, 1866.*

I certify that the above account is correct; that the above supplies were purchased of Charles Bryan, and issued to the Utah Territory militia while employed in the suppression of Indian hostilities in said Territory in the year 1866, and that they were necessary for that purpose.

LEWIS ROBISON,
Quartermaster General, Nauvoo Legion.

Received, Great Salt Lake City, December 25, 1866, of Lewis Robison, quartermaster general Nauvoo Legion, seven hundred and sixteen dollars and sixteen cents, in full payment of the above account.

CH. BRYAN.

UTAH TERRITORY, *Great Salt Lake City*, 1866.

The United States to Edward Hunter,	DR.
May 1.—To 180 bushels oats, at $1 per bushel.............	$180 00
To 5,100 pounds hay, at 1 cent per pound........	51 00
June 4.—To 516 bushels oats, at $1 per bushel.............	516 00
28.—To 468 bushels oats, at $1 per bushel.............	468 00
July 21.—To 592 bushels oats, at $1 per bushel.............	592 00
Aug. 5.—To 380 bushels oats, at $1 per bushel.............	380 00
Sept. 5.—To 159 bushels oats, at $1 per bushel.............	159 00
	2,346 00

GREAT SALT LAKE CITY, *December 25, 1866.*

I certify that the above account is correct; that they were purchased of Edward Hunter, and issued to the Utah Territory militia while employed in the suppression of Indian hostilities in said Territory in the year 1866, and that they were necessary for that purpose.

LEWIS ROBISON,
Quartermaster General Nauvoo Legion.

Received, Great Salt Lake City, December 25, 1866, of Lewis Robison, quartermaster general Nauvoo Legion, two thousand three hundred and forty-six dollars, in full payment for the above account.

EDW. HUNTER.

UTAH TERRITORY, *Fountain Green*, 1866.

The United States to Charles Johnson,	DR.
June 2.—To 311 bushels oats, at $1 per bushel.............	$311 00
28.—To 4,875 pounds hay, at 1 cent per pound........	48 75
July 7.—To 367 bushels oats, at $1 per bushel.............	367 00
To 3,740 pounds hay, at 1 cent per pound........	37 40
21.—To 5,840 pounds hay, at 1 cent per pound........	58 40
Aug. 8.—To 4,490 pounds hay, at 1 cent per pound........	49 90
10.—To 2,651 pounds hay, at 1 cent per pound........	26 51
13.—To 4,621 pounds hay, at 1 cent per pound........	46 21

Aug. 23.—To 3,816 pounds hay, at 1 cent per pound........ $38 16
Sept. 5.—To 2,391 pounds hay, at 1 cent per pound........ 23 91
    25.—To 4,621 pounds hay, at 1 cent per pound........ 46 21

                                                         _____
                                                         1,053 45
                                                         ========

GREAT SALT LAKE CITY, *December* 24, 1866.

I certify that the above account is correct; that the above supplies were purchased of Charles Johnson, and issued to the militia of Utah Territory while employed in the suppression of Indian hostilities in said Territory in the year 1866, and that they were necessary for that purpose.

_____ _____,
Quartermaster General Nauvoo Legion.

Received, Great Salt Lake City, December 24, 1866, of Lewis Robison, quartermaster general, Nauvoo Legion, one thousand and fifty-three dollars and forty-five cents, in full payment of the above account.
                                         R. L. JOHNSON.

_____

UTAH TERITORY, *Fort Gunnison*, 1866.

The United States to H. H. Kearmes,   DR.

May 9.—To 691 bushels oats, at $1 per bushel............ $691 00
June 7.—To 464 bushels oats, at $1 per bushel............ 464 00
    23.—To 576 bushels oats, at $1 per bushel............ 576 00
July 4.—To 4,891 pounds hay, at 1 cent per pound........ 48 91
    16.—To 6,990 pounds hay, at 1 cent per pound........ 69 90
July 25.—To 4,969 pounds hay, at 1 cent per pound........ 49 69
Aug.10.—To 295 bushels oats, at $1 per bushel............ 295 00
    27.—To 441 bushels oats, at $1 per bushel............ 441 00
Oct. 5.—To 491 bushels oats, at $1 per bushel............ 491 00
    10.—To 391 bushels oats, at $1 per bushel............ 391 00
        To 3,840 pounds hay, at 1 cent per pound........ 38 40
    16.—To 7,590 pounds hay, at 1 cent per pound........ 75 90

                                                         _____
                                                         3,651 80
                                                         ========

GREAT SALT LAKE CITY, *December* 25, 1866.

I certify that the above account is correct; that the above supplies were purchased of H. H. Kearmes, and issued to the Utah Territory militia while employed in the suppression of Indian hostilities in said Territory in the year 1866, and that they were necessary for that purpose.
                                         LEWIS ROBISON,
                              Quartermaster General Nauvoo Legion.

Received, Great Salt Lake City, December 25, 1866, of Lewis Robison, quartermaster general Nauvoo Legion, three thousand six hundred and fifty-one dollars and eighty cents, in full of the above account.
                                         HAMILTON H. KEARMES.

UTAH TERRITORY, *Springtown*, 1866.

The United States to C. G. Larsen, DR.

May 31.—To 115 bushels oats, at $1 per bushel............... $115 00
June 10.—To 5,940 pounds hay, at 1 cent per pound.......... 59 40
    23.—To 5,860 pounds hay, at 1 cent per pound.......... 58 60
July 12.—To 4,575 pounds hay, at 1 cent per pound.......... 45 75
    28.—To 5,731 pounds hay, at 1 cent per pound.......... 57 31
Aug. 5.—To 3,875 pounds hay, at 1 cent per pound.......... 38 75
Sept. 7.—To 228 bushels oats, at $1 per bushel............... 228 00
Oct. 5.—To 4,861 pounds hay, at 1 cent per pound 48 61
    '7.—To 5,942 pounds hay, at 1 cent per pound.......... 59 42
    23.—To 5,975 pounds hay, at 1 cent per pound........... 59 75

                                          770 59

GREAT SALT LAKE CITY, *December 25*, 1866.

I certify that the above account is correct; that the above supplies were purchased of C. G. Larsen and issued to the Utah Territory militia while employed in the suppression of Indian hostilities in said Territory in the year 1866, and that they were necessary for that purpose.

                 LEWIS ROBISON,
       Quartermaster General Nauvoo Legion.

Received, Great Salt Lake City, December 25, 1866, of Lewis Robison, quartermaster general Nauvoo Legion, seven hundred and seventy dollars and fifty-nine cents, in full payment of the above account.

                 C. G. LARSEN.

UTAH TERRITORY, *Wasatch County*, 1866.

The United States to Joseph Murdock, DR.

May 3.—To 150 bushels oats, at $1 per bushel............. $150 00
    To 4,000 pounds hay, at 1 cent per pound....... 40 00
June —To 150 bushels oats, at $1 per bushel............. 150 00
    To 3,500 pounds hay, at 1 cent per pound......... 35 00
Aug. 5.—To 300 bushels oats, at $1 per bushel 300 00
    To 5,000 pounds hay, at 1 cent per pound....... 50 00
    20.—To 325 bushels oats, at $1 per bushel............. 325 00
Sept. 6.—To 450 bushels oats, at $1 per bushel............. 250 00
    15.—To 275 bushels oats, at $1 per bushel............. 275 00
    25.—To 90 bushels oats, at $1 per bushel............. 90 00
Oct. 5.—To 500 bushels oats, at $1 per bushel............. 500 00
    20.—To 89 bushels oats, at $1 per bushel............. 89 00
    To 5,000 pounds hay, at 1 cent per pound....... 50 00

                                     2,254 00

GREAT SALT LAKE CITY, *December 24*, 1866.

I certify that the above account is correct; that the above supplies were purchased of Joseph Murdock, and issued to the Utah Territory militia while employed in the suppression of Indian hostilities in said Territory in the year 1866, and that they were necessary for that purpose.

LEWIS ROBISON,
Quartermaster General Nauvoo Legion.

Received, Great Salt Lake City, December 24, 1866, of Lewis Robison two thousand two hundred and fifty-four dollars, in full payment of the above account.

JOSEPH L. MURDOCK.

UTAH TERRITORY, *Manti*, 1866.

The United States to Andrew Moffitt,   DR.

May	5.—To 525 bushels oats, at $1 per bushel............	$525 00
	To 7,320 pounds hay, at 1 cent per pound........	73 20
May	19.—To 581 bushels oats, at $1 per bushel............	581 00
June	14.—To 609 bushels oats, at $1 per bushel............	609 00
	To 6,890 pounds hay, at 1 cent per pound......	68 90
	25.—To 303 bushels oats, at $1 per bushel..........	303 00
July	9.—To 386 bushels oats, at $1 per bushel............	386 00
	28.—To 583 bushels oats, at $1 per bushel...........	583 00
	30.—To 5,990 pounds hay, at 1 cent per pound......	59 90
Aug.	3.—To 2,790 pounds hay, at 1 cent per pound	27 90
	To 175 bushels oats, at $1 per bushel..........	175 00
	17.—To 540 bushels oats, at $1 per bushel............	540 00
Sept.	19.—To 681 bushels oats, at $1 per bushel............	681 00
	29.—To 465 bushels oats, at $1 per bushel............	465 00
Oct.	2.—To 6,195 pounds hay, at 1 cent per pound	61 95
	7.—To 536 bushels oats, at $1 per bushel...........	536 00
	26.—To 5,390 pounds hay, at 1 cent per pound	53 90

5,729 75

GREAT SALT LAKE CITY, *December 25, 1866.*

I certify that the above account is correct; that the above supplies were purchased of Andrew Moffitt, and issued to the Utah Territory militia while employed in the suppression of Indian hostilities in said Territory in the year 1866, and that they were necessary for that purpose.

LEWIS ROBISON,
Quartermaster General Nauvoo Legion.

Received, Great Salt Lake City, December 25, 1866, of Lewis Robison, quartermaster general Nauvoo Legion, five thousand seven hundred and twenty-nine dollars and seventy-five cents, in full of the above account.
ANDREW MOFFITT.

UTAH TERRITORY, *Fort Ephraim*, 1866.

The United States to Kanute Peterson,   DR.

May	2.—To 320 bushels oats, at $1 per bushel..............	$320 00
	11.—To 318 bushels oats, at $1 per bushel..............	318 00
	27.—To 632 bushels oats, at $1 per bushel..............	632 00

May 27.—To 9,327 pounds hay, at 1 cent per pound..........	893	27
June 2.—To 3,986 pounds hay, at 1 cent per pound..........	39	86
19.—To 4,953 pounds hay, at 1 cent per pound..........	49	53
To 453 bushels oats, at $1 per bushel..........	453	00
July 16.—To 646 bushels oats, at $1 per bushel............	646	00
30.—To 515 bushels oats, at $1 per bushel..............	515	00
Aug. 17.—To 5,980 pounds hay, at 1 cent per pound..........	59	80
27.—To 4,550 pounds hay, at 1 cent per pound..........	45	50
Sept. 3.—To 396 bushels oats, at $1 per bushel............	396	00
10.—To 390 bushels oats, at $1 per bushel............	390	00
25.—To 397 bushels oats, at $1 per bushel............	397	00
Oct. 13.—To 683 bushels oats, at $1 per bushel............	683	00
23.—To 581 bushels oats, at $1 per bushel............	581	00
	5,618	96

GREAT SALT LAKE CITY, *December* 25, 1866.

I certify that the above account is correct; that the above supplies were purchased of Kanute Peterson, and issued to the Utah Territory militia while employed in the suppression of Indian hostilities in said Territory in the year 1866, and that they were necessary for that purpose.

LEWIS ROBISON,
Quartermaster General Nauvoo Legion.

Received, Great Salt Lake City, December 25, 1866, of Lewis Robison, quartermaster general Nauvoo Legion, five thousand six hundred and eighteen dollars and ninety-six cents, in full of the above account.

CANUTE PETERSON.

UTAH TERRITORY, *Mount Pleasant*, 1866.

The United States to William Seeley,	DR.	
May 2.—To 6,200 pounds hay, at 1 cent per pound........	862	00
To 8,400 pounds hay, at 1 cent per pound........	84	00
23.—To 11,680 pounds hay, at 1 cent per pound	116	80
June 10.—To 531 bushels oats, at $1 per bushel............	531	00
16.—To 308 bushels oats, at $1 per bushel............	308	00
July 4.—To 479 bushels oats, at $1 per bushel............	479	00
25.—To 495 bushels oats, at $1 per bushel............	495	00
Aug. 8.—To 460 bushels oats, at $1 per bushel............	460	00
23.—To 371 bushels oats, at $1 per bushel............	371	00
29.—To 352 bushels oats, at $1 per bushel............	352	00
Sept. 3.—To 3,840 pounds hay, at 1 cent per pound........	38	40
7.—To 3,561 pounds hay, at 1 cent per pound........	35	61
19.—To 6,936 pounds hay, at 1 cent per pound........	69	36
Oct. 2.—To 582 bushels oats, at $1 per bushel............	582	00
16.—To 740 bushels oats, at $1 per bushel............	740	00
	4,724	17

GREAT SALT LAKE CITY, *December* 25, 1866.

I certify that the above account is correct; that the above supplies were purchased of William Seeley, and issued to the Utah Territory militia while employed in the suppression of Indian hostilities in said Territory in the year 1866, and that they were necessary for that purpose.

LEWIS ROBISON,
Quartermaster General Nauvoo Legion.

Received, Great Salt Lake City, December 25, 1866, of Lewis Robison, quartermaster general Nauvoo Legion, four thousand seven hundred and twenty-four dollars and seventeen cents, in full of the above account.

WM. SEELEY.

UTAH TERRITORY, *Fauvien*, 1866.

The United States to Amasa Tucker,	DR.	
May 15.—To 10,480 pounds hay, at 1 cent per pound	$104	80
7.—To 4,790 pounds hay, at 1 cent per pound	47	90
July 9.—To 3,920 pounds hay, at 1 cent per pound	39	20
12.—To 457 bushels oats, at $1 per bushel	457	00
Aug. 20.—To 494 bushels oats, at $1 per bushel	494	00
To 4,869 pounds hay, at 1 cent per pound	48	69
25.—To 3,760 pounds hay, at 1 cent per pound	37	60
Sept. 1.—To 3,516 pounds hay, at 1 cent per pound	35	16
10.—To 3,840 pounds hay, at 1 cent per pound	38	40
	1,302	75

GREAT SALT LAKE CITY, *December 25, 1866.*

I certify that the above account is correct; that the above supplies were purchased of Amasa Tucker, and issued to the Utah Territory militia while employed in the suppression of Indian hostilities in said Territory in the year 1866, and that they were necessary for that purpose.

LEWIS ROBISON,
Quartermaster General Nauvoo Legion.

Received, Great Salt Lake City, December 25, 1866, of Lewis Robison, quartermaster general Nauvoo Legion, one thousand three hundred and two dollars and seventy-five cents, in full payment of the above account.

AMASA TUCKER.

UTAH TERRITORY, *Mount Pleasant,* 1866.

The United States to William Seeley,	DR.	

For the use of horses, mules, and wagons, hauling baggage, provisions, and forage, Captain George Tucker's company of cavalry, while employed in the suppression of Indian hostilities in Sanpete and Sevier counties, in the year 1866.

May 1 to Nov. 1.—To 5 four-mule teams 184 days, at $5 per day each	$4,600	00
To 6 pack animals 184 days, at 40 cents per day each	441	60
	5,041	60

GREAT SALT LAKE CITY, *December* 31, 1866.

I certify that the above animals and wagons were engaged in and for the service and time specified above.

LEWIS ROBISON,
Quartermaster General Nauvoo Legion.

Received, Great Salt Lake City, December 31, 1866, of Lewis Robison, quartermaster general, Nauvoo Legion, five thousand forty-one dollars and sixty cents, in full payment of the above account.

WM. SEELY.

———

UTAH TERRITORY, *Great Salt Lake City*, 1866.

The United States to Bryant Stringham, DR.

For the use of horses, mules, and wagons, hauling baggage and provisions, with Major William W. Caspers's company of Infantry, while employed in the suppression of Indian hostilities in Sanpete and Sevier counties, Utah Territory, in the year 1866.

June 1 to Sept. 30.—To 5 four-mule teams 121 days, at $5 per
day each............................... $3,025

GREAT SALT LAKE CITY, *December* 31, 1866.

I certify that the above animals and wagons were engaged in and for the service and time specified.

LEWIS ROBISON,
Quartermaster General Nauvoo Legion.

Received, Great Salt Lake City, December 31, 1866, of Lewis Robison, quartermaster general Nauvoo Legion, three thousand and twenty-five dollars, in full payment of the above account.

BRIANT STRINGAM.

———

UTAH TERRITORY, *Great Salt Lake City*, 1866.

The United States to Bryant Stringham, DR.

May 1 to Aug. 30.—To 4 four-mule teams 122 days, at $5 per
day each............................... $2,440
To 10 pack animals 122 days, at 40 cents per
day each........................... 448
_____
2,928
=======

GREAT SALT LAKE CITY, *December* 31, 1866.

I certify that the above animals and wagons were engaged in and for the service and time specified.

LEWIS ROBISON,
Quartermaster General Nauvoo Legion.

Received, Great Salt Lake City, December 31, 1866, of Lewis Robison, quartermaster general Nauvoo Legion, two thousand nine hundred and twenty-eight dollars, in full payment of the above account.

BRIANT STRINGAM.

UTAH TERRITORY, *Great Salt Lake City*, 1866.

The United States to Bryant Stringham,   DR.

For the use of horses, mules, and wagons, hauling baggage and provisions, with Major Andrew Burt's company of Infantry, while employed
in the suppression of Indian hostilities in Sanpete and Sevier counties,
Utah Territory, in the year 1866.

July 25 to Nov. 3.—To 6 four-mule teams 102 days, at $5 per
          day each........................... $3,060

GREAT SALT LAKE CITY, *December* 31, 1866.

I certify that the above animals and wagons were engaged in and for
the service and time specified.

LEWIS ROBISON,
Quartermaster General Nauvoo Legion.

Received, Great Salt Lake City, December 31, 1866, of Lewis Robison,
quartermaster general Nauvoo Legion, three thousand and sixty dollars,
in full payment of the above account.

BRIANT STRINGAM.

UTAH TERRITORY, *Mante*, 1866.

The United States to Andrew Moffitt,   DR.

For the use of horses, mules, and wagons, hauling baggage, provisions,
and forage, with Captain George Sidwells's company of cavalry while
employed in the suppression of Indian hostilities in Sanpete and Sevier counties, Utah Territory, in the year 1866.

May 1 to Nov. 1.—To 5 four-mule teams, 184 days, at $5 per day
          each.................................. $4,600
          To 5 pack animals 184 days, at 40 cents per day
          each..................................   368

                                                4,968

GREAT SALT LAKE CITY, *December* 31, 1866.

I certify that the above animals and wagons were engaged in and for
the service and time specified above.

LEWIS ROBISON,
Quartermaster General Nauvoo Legion.

Received, Great Salt Lake City, December 31, 1866, of Lewis Robison,
quartermaster general Nauvoo Legion, four thousand nine hundred and
sixty-eight dollars, in full payment of the above account.

ANDREW MOFFITT.

UTAH TERRITORY, *Provo*, 1866.

The United States to William Miller,   DR.

For the use of horses, mules, and wagons, hauling baggage, provisions,
and forage, with Captain Caleb Haws's company of cavalry, while em-

ployed in the suppression of Indian hostilities in Sanpete and Sevier counties, Utah Territory, in the year 1866.

August 16 to October 24.—To 5 four-mule teams 70 days, at $5
      per day each...................... $1,750
      To 7 pack animals 70 days, at 40 cents
      per day each 196

                              1,946

GREAT SALT LAKE CITY, *December* 31, 1866.

I certify that the above animals and wagons were engaged in and for the service and time specified.

                     LEWIS ROBISON,
              Quartermaster General Nauvoo Legion.

Received, Great Salt Lake City, December 31, 1866, of Lewis Robison, quartermaster general Nauvoo Legion, one thousand nine hundred and forty-six dollars, in full payment of the above account.

                         WM. MILLER.

UTAH TERRITORY, *Provo*, 1866.

   The United States to William Miller,   DR.

For the use of horses, mules, and wagons, hauling baggage, provisions, and forage, with Major Joseph Cluff's company cavalry, while employed in the suppression of Indian hostilities in Sanpete and Sevier counties, Utah Territory, in the year 1866.

June 10 to July 25.—To 2 four-mule teams 45 days, at $5 per
      day each........................ $450

GREAT SALT LAKE CITY, *December* 31, 1866.

I certify that the above animals and wagons were engaged in and for the service and time specified.

                     LEWIS ROBISON,
              Quartermaster General Nauvoo Legion.

Received, Great Salt Lake City, December 31, 1866, of Lewis Robison, quartermaster general Nauvoo Legion, four hundred and fifty dollars, in full of the above account.

                         WM. MILLER.

UTAH TERRITORY, *Wasatch County*, 1866.

   The United States to Joseph Murdock,   DR.

For the use of horses, mules, wagons, hauling baggage, provisions, and forage, with the Wasatch County militia, cavalry, and infantry, while employed in the suppression of Indian hostilities in Wasatch, Summit, and adjoining counties, in the year 1866.

May 1 to July 30.—To 1 four-mule team 90 days, at $5 per
      day each........................... $450
      To 2 four-mule teams 60 days, at $5 per
      day each....................... 600

June 1 to July 30.—To 4 four-mule teams 60 days, at $5 per
     day each............................ $1,200
July 1 to Aug. 30.—To 3 four-mule teams 60 days, at $5 per
     day each............................   900
Aug. 1 to Sept. 30.—To 2 four-mule teams 60 days, at $5 per
     day each............................   600
Aug. 1 to Oct. 30.—To 4 four-mule teams 90 days, at $5 per
     day each............................   1,800
     To 6 pack animals 90 days, at 40 cents
     per day each.........................   216
                                               5,766

GREAT SALT LAKE CITY, *December* 31, 1866.

I certify that the above animals and wagons were engaged in and for
the service and time specified above.

LEWIS ROBISON,
Quartermaster General Nauvoo Legion.

Received, Great Salt Lake City, December 31, 1866, of Lewis Robison,
quartermaster general Nauvoo Legion, five thousand seven hundred and
sixty-six dollars, in full payment of the above account.

JOSEPH L. MURDOCK.

UTAH TERRITORY, *Springville*, 1866.

The United States to Aaron Johnson,   DR.

For the use of horses, mules, and wagons, hauling baggage and provisions, with Captain Franklin P. Whitmore's company infantry, while
employed in the suppression of Indian hostilities in Sanpete and Sevier
counties, Utah Territory, in the year 1866.

June 16 to July 26.—To 2 four-mule teams 42 days, at $5 per
     day each.......................... $420

GREAT SALT LAKE CITY, *December* 31, 1866.

I certify that the above animals and wagons were engaged in and for
the service and time specified.

LEWIS ROBISON,
Quartermaster General Nauvoo Legion.

Received, Great Salt Lake City, December 31, 1866, of Lewis Robison,
quartermaster general Nauvoo Legion, four hundred and twenty dollars,
in full payment of the above account.

A. JOHNSON.

UTAH TERRITORY, *Springville*, 1866.

The United States to Aaron Johnson,   DR.

For the use of horses, mules, and wagons, hauling baggage, provisions,
and forage, with Captain A. J. Conner's company cavalry, while

employed in the suppression of Indian hostilities in Sanpete and Sevier counties, Utah Territory, in the year 1866.

May 1 to July 18.—To 4 four-mule teams 80 days, at $5 per
day each........................... $1,600
To 10 pack animals 80 days, at 40 cents
per day each..................... 320

—————
1,920
=====

GREAT SALT LAKE CITY, *December* 31, 1866.

I certify that the above animals and wagons were engaged in and for the service and time specified.

LEWIS ROBISON,
Quartermaster General Nauvoo Legion.

Received, Great Salt Lake City, December 31, 1866, of Lewis Robison, quartermaster general Nauvoo Legion, one thousand nine hundred and twenty dollars, in full payment of the above account.

A. JOHNSON.

———

UTAH TERRITORY, *Great Salt Lake City,* 1866.

The United States to Arsa N. Hinkley,   DR.

For the use of horses, mules, and wagons, hauling baggage, provisions and forage, with Lieutenant Colonel John R. Winder's company cavalry, while employed in the suppression of Indian hostilities in Sanpete and Sevier counties, Utah Territory, in the year 1866.

June 1 to Sept. 30.—To 2 four-mule teams 122 days, at $5 per
day each........................... $1,220 00
To 1 two-mule team 122 days, at $4 per
day each........................... 488 00
To 4 pack animals 122 days, at 40 cents
per day each..................... 195 20

—————
1,903 20
=====

GREAT SALT LAKE CITY, *December* 31, 1866.

I certify that the above animals and wagons were engaged in and for the service and time specified.

LEWIS ROBISON,
Quartermaster General Nauvoo Legion.

Received, Great Salt Lake City, December 31, 1866, of Lewis Robison, quartermaster general Nauvoo Legion, one thousand nine hundred and three dollars and twenty cents, in full payment of the above account.

A. N. HINKLEY.

———

UTAH TERRITORY, *Farmington,* 1866.

The United States to John W. Hess,   DR.

For the use of horses, mules, and wagons, hauling baggage, provisions, and forage, with Captain Andrew J. Bigler's company cavalry, while employed in the suppression of Indian hostilities in Sanpete and Sevier counties, Utah Territory, in the year 1866.

July 1 to Oct. 30.—To 4 four-mule teams 122 days, at $5 per
    day each...................................... $2,440 00
    To 6 pack animals 122 days, at 40 cents
    per day each........................... 292 80
                                     2,732 80

GREAT SALT LAKE CITY, *December* 31, 1866.

I certify that the above animals and wagons were engaged in and for the service and time specified.

LEWIS ROBISON,
Quartermaster General Nauvoo Legion.

Received, Great Salt Lake City, December 31, 1866, of Lewis Robison, quartermaster general Nauvoo Legion, two thousand seven hundred and thirty-two dollars and eighty cents, in full payment of the above account.

JOHN W. HESS.

UTAH TERRITORY, *American Fork*, 1866.

The United States to Leonard E. Harrington,   DR.

For the use of horses, mules, and wagons, hauling baggage, provisions, and forage, with Captain Alva Green's company cavalry, while employed in the suppression of Indian hostilities in Sanpete and Sevier counties, Utah Territory, in the year 1866.

Aug. 7 to Oct. 7.—To 2 four-mule teams 60 days, at $5 per
    day each........................... $600 00
    To 3 pack animals 60 days, at 40 cents per
    day each............................... 72 00
                                     672 00

GREAT SALT LAKE CITY, *December* 31, 1866.

I certify that the above animals and wagons were engaged in and for the service and time specified.

LEWIS ROBISON,
Quartermaster General Nauvoo Legion.

Received, Great Salt Lake City, December 31, 1866, of Lewis Robison, quartermaster general Nauvoo Legion, six hundred and seventy-two dollars, in full payment of the above account.

LEONARD E. HARRINGTON.

UTAH TERRITORY, *Payson*, 1866.

The United States to John B. Fairbanks,   DR.

For the use of horses, mules, and wagons, hauling baggage, provisions, and forage, with Captain Jonathan Pages's company cavalry, while employed in the suppression of Indian hostilities in Sanpete and Sevier counties, Utah Territory, in the year 1866.

July 3 to Aug. 24.—To 4 four-mule teams 52 days, at $5 per
day each.......................... $1,040 00
To 8 pack animals 52 days, at 40 cents
per day each...... .... 166 40

1,206 40

GREAT SALT LAKE CITY, *December* 31, 1866.

I certify that the above animals and wagons were engaged in and for the service and time specified.

LEWIS ROBISON,
Quartermaster General Nauvoo Legion.

Received, Great Salt Lake City, December 31, 1866, of Lewis Robison, quartermaster general Nauvoo Legion, one thousand two hundred and six dollars and forty cents, in full payment of the above account.

JOHN B. FAIRBANKS.

———

UTAH TERRITORY, *Payson*, 1866.

The United States to John B. Fairbanks, DR.

For the use of horses, mules, and wagons, hauling baggage, provisions, and forage, with Captain Jonathan Page's company cavalry, while employed in the suppression of Indian hostilities in Sanpete and Sevier counties, Utah Territory, in the year 1864.

May 11 to July 2.—To 3 four-mule teams 52 days, at $5 per
day each...... .... $780 00
To 10 pack animals 52 days, at 40 cents
per day each 208 00

988 00

GREAT SALT LAKE CITY, *December* 31, 1866.

I certify that the above animals and wagons were engaged in and for the service and time specified.

LEWIS ROBISON,
Quartermaster General Nauvoo Legion.

Received, Great Salt Lake City, December 31, 1866, of Lewis Robison, quartermaster general Nauvoo Legion, nine hundred and eighty-eight dollars, in full payment of the above account.

JOHN B. FAIRBANKS.

———

UTAH TERRITORY, *Lehi*, 1866.

The United States to David Evans, DR.

For the use of horses, mules, and wagons, hauling baggage, provisions, and forage, with Captain William Wimm's company cavalry, while employed in the suppression of Indian hostilities in Sanpete and Sevier counties, Utah Territory, in the year 1866.

June 13 to Aug. 13.—To 2 four-mule teams 60 days, at $5 per
day each $600 00

GREAT SALT LAKE CITY, *December* 31, 1866.

I certify that the above animals and wagons were engaged in and for the service and time specified.

LEWIS ROBISON,
Quartermaster General Nauvoo Legion.

Received, Great Salt Lake City, December 31, 1866, of Lewis Robison, quartermaster general Nauvoo Legion, six hundred dollars, in full payment of the above account.

DAVID EVANS.

UTAH TERRITORY, *Fillmore*, 1866.

The United States to Thomas Callister,   DR.

For the use of horses, mules, and wagons, hauling baggage, provisions, and forage, with Captain James C. Owen's company cavalry, while employed in the suppression of Indian hostilities in Sanpete and Sevier counties, Utah Territory, in the year 1866.

June 10 to June 20.—To 4 four-mule teams 10 days, at $5 per
    day each $200 00
        To 6 pack animals 10 days, at 40 cents
        per day each 24 00
                                          _____
                                          224 00

GREAT SALT LAKE CITY, *December* 31, 1866.

I certify that the above animals and wagons were engaged in and for the service and time specified.

LEWIS ROBISON,
Quartermaster General Nauvoo Legion.

Received, Great Salt Lake City, December 31, 1866, of Lewis Robison, quartermaster general Nauvoo Legion, two hundred and twenty-four dollars, in full payment of the above account.

THOMAS CALLISTER.

UTAH TERRITORY, *Kaysville*, 1866.

The United States to Christopher Layton,   DR.

For the use of horses, mules, and wagons, hauling baggage, provisions, and forage, with Captain Robert Burton's company cavalry, while employed in the suppression of Indian hostilities in Sanpete and Sevier counties, Utah Territory, in the year 1866.

Sept. 1 to Nov. 30.—To 4 four-mule teams 90 days, at $5 per
    day each $1,800 00
        To 7 pack animals 90 days, at 40 cents
        per day each.....................   144 00
                                          _____
                                          1,944 00

GREAT SALT LAKE CITY, *December* 31, 1866.

I certify that the above animals and wagons were engaged in and for the service and time specified.

LEWIS ROBISON,
Quartermaster General Nauvoo Legion.

Received, Great Salt Lake City, December 31, 1866, of Lewis Robison, quartermaster general Nauvoo Legion, one thousand nine hundred and forty-four dollars, in full payment of the above account.

CHRISTOPHER ^{his} + LAYTON.
^{mark.}

Witness:
T. ABELBUH.

Recapitulation of expenses incurred by the Territory of Utah in the suppression of Indian hostilities in said Territory during the year 1866.

Names of commanding officers of companies.	Service rendered.	Commissary supplies.	Quartermaster supplies.	For transportation.	Total.
George Tucker	$17,146 36				
George Sidwell	17,744 86				
John Tidwell	11,935 86				
John D. Chase	13,265 86				
Lars Soneusen	11,473 86				
H. P. Kimball	9,615 92				
John W. Irous	11,473 92				
Amasa Tucker	11 819 50				
John R. Winder	6,603 28				
Joseph S. Day	11,819 50				
Isaac M. Behuunun	11,588 50				
William H. Winn	2,358 98				
James Guyman	12,150 51				
Joseph Cluff	1,555 47				
Frederick Nielson	11,945 47				
Alva A. Green	2,301 98				
James M. Allred	11,357 50				
Daniel Henrie	10,067 50				
A. J. Conover	6,579 95				
John Tuttle	11,242 95				
Jonathan Page	3,074 95				
Neels C. Christiansen	10,664 51				
Caleb W. Haws	6,189 01				
William Bench, sr	13,496 01				
Franklin P. Whitmore	1,173 20				
Peter Isaacson	11,126 51				
Morten Mortensen	11,935 50				
Field and staff, Utah county	25,130 50				
Jonathan Page	3,965 55				
George Gardner	11,588 50				
William C. Wightman	5,841 50				
Charles C. Burr	2,242 80				
Andrew J. Bigler	7,687 44				
John D. Holladay	4,800 60				
Daniel Stark	5,040 60				
William Wall	6,193 95				
John M. Murdock	2,320 95				
Ira N. Jacobs	3,031 95				
Thomas E. Daniels	4,384 80				
Field and staff, Sanpete	36,598 98				
Thomas Todd	2,634 98				
Andrew Burt	8,222 98				
John Galagher	1,891 98				
Peter Sutton	4,761 30				
Joseph McCarrol	1,869 48				
Field and staff, Wasatch	3,712 48				
William W. Casper	10,556 48				
Robert W. Burton	4,896 96				
Edward Dalton	6,024 45				
Joseph Betterson	575 48				
James Andrews	5,012 96				
James C. Owens	658 78				
Total	431,285 54	*430,545 86	†430,832 43	‡39,795 00	632,458 83

*As per Commissary General's vouchers. †As per Quartermaster General's vouchers.
‡As per Quartermaster General's vouchers.

I certify that the above account is correct.

H. B. CLAWSON,
Adjutant General Militia Utah Territory.

Pay-roll of Captain George Tucker's company —— cavalry, Utah Territory militia, employed in the suppression of Indian hostilities in Sanpete and Sevier counties, Utah Territory, from April 1 to November 1, 1866.

We, the undersigned, acknowledge to have received from James W. Cummings, paymaster Utah Territory militia, the sums set opposite to our names, in full payment for our services for the time specified.

Number.	Names.	Rank.	Period of service. Commencement.	Period of service. Expiration.	Months.	Pay per month.	Monthly allowance for clothing.	Total monthly pay and allowance.	40 cts. per day for use and risk of horse and horse equipment.	Total pay and allowance.	Signatures.	Witnesses.
1	George Tucker	Captain	April 1, 1866	Nov. 1, 1866	7			$159 50	$24 00	$290 50	George Tucker	Wm. Morrison.
2	Orange Seely	1st lieut.	April 1, 1866	Nov. 1, 1866	7			112 83	84 00	873 81	Orange Seely	Do.
3	Sidney Allred	2d lieut.	April 1, 1866	Nov. 1, 1866	7			112 83	84 00	873 81	Sidney Allred	Do.
4	Rodolphe Bennett	do.	April 1, 1866	Nov. 1, 1866	7			112 83	84 03	873 91	Rodolphe Bennet	Do.
5	John F. Sanders	do.	April 1, 1866	Nov. 1, 1866	7			112 83	84 00	873 81	John F. Sanders	Do.
6	Thomas B. Allred	do.	April 1, 1866	Nov. 1, 1866	7			112 83	84 00	873 81	Thomas B. Allred	John Kirkman.
7	Lars Christensen	do.	April 1, 1866	Nov. 1, 1866	7			112 83	84 00	873 81	Lars Christensen	Do.
8	Jeremiah D. Page	Sergeant	April 1, 1866	Nov. 1, 1866	7	$17 00	$3 50	20 50	84 00	227 50	Jeremiah D. Page	Wm. Morrison.
9	John Carter	do.	April 1, 1866	Nov. 1, 1866	7	17 00	3 50	20 50	84 00	227 50	John Carter	Do.
10	Jordan Brady	do.	April 1, 1866	Nov. 1, 1866	7	17 00	3 50	20 50	84 00	227 50	Jordan Brady	Do.
11	Stephen Allred	do.	April 1, 1866	Nov. 1, 1866	7	17 00	3 50	20 50	84 00	227 50	Stephen H. Allred	John Kirkman.
12	Peter Christiansen	do.	April 1, 1866	Nov. 1, 1866	7	17 00	3 50	20 50	84 00	227 50	Peter Christensen	Do.
13	Martin Aldrich	Private	April 1, 1866	Nov. 1, 1866	7	13 00	3 50	16 50	84 00	199 50	Martin Aldrich	Wm. Morrison.
14	Alma Staker	do.	April 1, 1866	Nov. 1, 1866	7	13 00	3 50	16 50	84 00	199 50	Alma Staker	Do.
15	George Fransen	do.	April 1, 1866	Nov. 1, 1866	7	13 00	3 50	16 50	84 00	199 50	George Fransen	H. P. Miller.
16	Niels Madsen	do.	April 1, 1866	Nov. 1, 1866	7	13 00	3 50	16 50	84 00	199 50	Niels Madsen	Do.
17	Eskild C. Peterson	do.	April 1, 1866	Nov. 1, 1866	7	13 00	3 50	16 50	84 00	199 50	Eskild C. Peterson	Wm. Morrison.
18	Peter Frederickson	do.	April 1, 1866	Nov. 1, 1866	7	13 00	3 50	16 50	84 00	199 50		Do.
19	Andres Larsen	do.	April 1, 1866	Nov. 1, 1866	7	13 00	3 50	16 50	84 00	199 50	Andrew Larsen	Wm. Morrison.
20	Peter Miller	do.	April 1, 1866	Nov. 1, 1866	7	13 00	3 50	16 50	84 00	199 50	Peter Miller	Do.
	James Burns	do.	April 1, 1866	Nov. 1, 1866	7	13 00	3 50	16 50	84 00	199 50	James Burns	Do.
	John Young	do.	April 1, 1866	Nov. 1, 1866	7	13 00	3 50	16 50	84 00	199 50	John Young	Do.
	Rasmus Fransden	do.	April 1, 1866	Nov. 1, 1866	7	13 00	3 50	16 50	84 00	199 51	Rasmus Fransden	Do.
	George Coates	do.	April 1, 1866	Nov. 1, 1866	7	13 00	3 50	16 50	84 00	199 50	George Coates	Do.
	Christian Jensen	do.	April 1, 1866	Nov. 1, 1866	7	13 00	3 50	16 50	84 00	199 50	Christian Jensen	Do.
	Wilford W. Brandon	do.	April 1, 1866	Nov. 1, 1866	7	13 00	3 50	16 50	84 00	199 50	Wilford W. Brandon	Do.
	Christian Nebeville	do.	April 1, 1866	Nov. 1, 1866	7	13 00	3 50	16 50	84 00	199 50		
	Christian Petersen	do.	April 1, 1866	Nov. 1, 1866	7	13 00	3 50	16 50	84 00	199 50	Christian Petersen	H. P. Miller.
	Lyman Peters	do.	April 1, 1866	Nov. 1, 1866	7	13 00	3 50	16 50	84 00	199 50	Lyman Peters	Wm. Morrison.
	Martin Rasmussen	do.	April 1, 1866	Nov. 1, 1866	7	13 00	3 50	16 50	84 00	199 50	Martin Rasmussen	Do.
	Levi B. Reynolds	do.	April 1, 1866	Nov. 1, 1866	7	13 00	3 50	16 50	84 00	199 51	Levi B. Reynolds	Do.
	Samuel Allen	do.	April 1, 1866	Nov. 1, 1866	7	13 00	3 50	16 50	84 00	199 50	Samuel Allen	Geo. Brough.

No.	Name		Mustered in	Mustered out							Name	By whom enlisted
21	Elias Cox	do.	April 1, 1866	Nov. 1, 1866	7	13 00	3 50	16 50	84 00	199 50	Elias Cox	Wm. Morrison.
22	Noah Guymon	do.	April 1, 1866	Nov. 1, 1866	7	13 00	3 50	16 50	84 00	199 50	Noah Guymon	Geo. Brough.
23	Mormon Miner	do.	April 1, 1866	Nov. 1, 1866	7	13 00	3 50	16 50	84 00	199 50	Mormon Miner	Wm. Morrison.
24	Hyrum Wilson	do.	April 1, 1866	Nov. 1, 1866	7	13 00	3 50	16 50	84 00	199 50	Hyrum Wilson	Jno.
25	John Remuera	do.	April 1, 1866	Nov. 1, 1866	7	13 00	3 50	16 50	84 00	199 50	John Remuera, (his + mark)	Do.
26	David Sanders	do.	April 1, 1866	Nov. 1, 1866	7	13 00	3 50	16 50	84 00	199 50	David Sanders	Do.
27	James Anderson	do.	April 1, 1866	Nov. 1, 1866	7	13 00	3 50	16 50	84 00	199 50	James Anderson	Do.
28	John Cox	do.	April 1, 1866	Nov. 1, 1866	7	13 00	3 50	16 50	84 00	199 50	John Cox	Do.
29	Orson M. Terry	do.	April 1, 1866	Nov. 1, 1866	7	13 00	3 50	16 50	84 00	199 50	Orson M. Terry	Do.
30	Jacob Jones	do.	April 1, 1866	Nov. 1, 1866	7	13 00	3 50	16 50	84 00	199 50	Jacob Jones, (his + mark)	Geo. Brough.
31	Sandford Allred	do.	April 1, 1866	Nov. 1, 1866	7	13 00	3 50	16 50	84 00	199 50	Sandford Allred	Do.
32	William Scott	do.	April 1, 1866	Nov. 1, 1866	7	13 00	3 50	16 50	84 00	199 50	William Scott	Do.
33	John Frantzen	do.	April 1, 1866	Nov. 1, 1866	7	13 00	3 50	16 50	84 00	199 50	John Frantzen	Do.
34	Sidney R. Allred	do.	April 1, 1866	Nov. 1, 1866	7	13 00	3 50	16 50	84 00	199 50	Sidney R. Allred	Do.
35	Peter L. Taud	do.	April 1, 1866	Nov. 1, 1866	7	13 00	3 50	16 50	84 00	199 50	Peter L. Taud	Do.
36	James Munsen	do.	April 1, 1866	Nov. 1, 1866	7	13 00	3 50	16 50	84 00	199 50	James Munsen	Do.
37	Henry Iversen	do.	April 1, 1866	Nov. 1, 1866	7	13 00	3 50	16 50	84 00	199 50	Henry Eckertsen	Do.
38	Andrew J. Allred	do.	April 1, 1866	Nov. 1, 1866	7	13 00	3 50	16 50	84 00	199 50	Andrew J. Allred	Do.
39	Nephi Allred	do.	April 1, 1866	Nov. 1, 1866	7	13 00	3 50	16 50	84 00	199 50	Nephi Allred	Do.
40	William Osborn	do.	April 1, 1866	Nov. 1, 1866	7	13 00	3 50	16 50	84 00	199 50	William Osborn	John Kirkman.
41	John Edelsen	do.	April 1, 1866	Nov. 1, 1866	7	13 00	3 50	16 50	84 00	199 50	John Elearsen	Do.
42	James Vorgensen	do.	April 1, 1866	Nov. 2, 1866	7	13 00	3 50	16 50	84 00	199 50	Jens Vorgensen	Do.
43	Nephi Reese	do.	April 1, 1866	Nov. 1, 1866	7	13 00	3 50	16 50	84 00	199 50	Nephi Rees	Do.
44	James Jensen, jr	do.	April 1, 1866	Nov. 1, 1866	7	13 00	3 50	16 50	84 00	199 50	Joseph Jolley, jr	Do.
45	Joseph Jolley	do.	April 1, 1866	Nov. 1, 1866	7	13 00	3 50	16 50	84 00	199 50	Joseph Jolley	Do.
46	Andrew Leslie	do.	April 1, 1866	Nov. 1, 1866	7	13 00	3 50	16 50	84 00	199 50	Andrew Leeslie	Do.
47	Peter Allen	do.	April 1, 1866	Nov. 1, 1866	7	13 00	3 50	16 50	84 00	199 50	Peter Allen	Do.
48	John Mott	do.	April 1, 1866	Nov. 1, 1866	7	13 00	3 50	16 50	84 00	199 50	John Mott	Do.
49	Charles West	do.	April 1, 1866	Nov. 1, 1866	7	13 00	3 50	16 50	84 00	199 50	Charles West	Do.
50	Samuel C. West	do.	April 1, 1866	Nov. 1, 1866	7	13 00	3 50	16 50	84 00	299 50	Samuel C. West	Wm. Morrison.
51	Thomas Fuller	do.	April 1, 1866	Nov. 1, 1866	7	13 00	3 50	16 50	84 00	199 50	Thomas Fuller	Do.

This company was mustered into service at Mount Pleasant, Sanpete county, April 1, 1866, by Brigadier General Warren S. Snow, and by him assigned to duty in the north and eastern mountains. They were on several expeditions to Fish Lake, Castle Valley, Green River, and up the Sevier River to Circleville. They were constantly scouting through the mountains, and on active service every day until mustered out, November 1, 1866.

I certify that the above account is correct.

H. B. CLAWSON,
Adjutant General Nauvoo Legion.

Pay-roll of Captain George Sidwell's company —— cavalry, Utah Territory militia, employed in the suppression of Indian hostilities in Sanpete and Serier counties, from April 1 to November 1, 1866.

We, the undersigned, acknowledge to have received from James W. Cummings, paymaster Utah Territory militia, the sums set opposite to our names, in full payment for our services, and for the time specified.

Number	Names	Rank	Commencement	Expiration	Months	Pay per month	Monthly allowance for clothing	Total monthly pay and allowance	40 cts. per day for horse and horse use and risk of equipment	Total pay and allowance	Signatures	Witnesses
1	George Sidwell	Captain	April 1, 1866	Nov. 1, 1866	7			109 50	84 00	290 50	George Sidwell	W. T. Reid
1	William Branch, jr	1st lieut	April 1, 1866	Nov. 1, 1866	7			112 83	84 00	273 71	William Branch, jr	Do.
1	Lucy Stillson	2d lieut	April 1, 1866	Nov. 1, 1866	7			112 83	84 00	273 71	Lucy Stillson	Do.
2	Andrew Jensen	do	April 1, 1866	Nov. 1, 1866	7			112 83	84 00	273 71	Andrew Jensen	W. B. Parr.
3	Lewis Larsen	do	April 1, 1866	Nov. 1, 1866	7			112 83	84 00	273 71	Lewis Larsen	Do.
4	Henry Beal	do	April 1, 1866	Nov. 1, 1866	7			112 83	84 00	273 71	Henry Beal	W. T. Reid.
5	Joseph Bartholomew	do	April 1, 1866	Nov. 1, 1866	7			257 50	84 00	287 50	Joseph Bartholomew	Do.
1	John Dobie	Sergeant	April 1, 1866	Nov. 1, 1866	7	17 00	3 50	20 50	84 00	257 50	John Dobie	Do.
2	Peter Hangard	do	April 1, 1866	Nov. 1, 1866	7	17 00	3 50	20 50	84 00	257 50	Peter Hoogaard	W. B. Parr.
3	John Williams	do	April 1, 1866	Nov. 1, 1866	7	17 00	3 50	20 50	84 00	257 50	J. Williams	Do.
4	Charles Whitlock	do	April 1, 1866	Nov. 1, 1866	7	17 00	3 50	20 50	84 00	257 50	Charles Whitlock	Do.
1	John Bartholomew	do	April 1, 1866	Nov. 1, 1866	7	17 00	3 50	20 50	84 00	227 50	John Bartholomew	Do.
2	Antone Christian	Private	April 1, 1866	Nov. 1, 1866	7	13 00	3 50	16 50	84 00	199 50	Anton Christowsmen	Do.
3	Alfred Bailey	do	April 1, 1866	Nov. 1, 1866	7	13 00	3 50	16 50	84 00	199 50	Alfred Bailey	W. T. Reid.
4	Archibald Buchannah	do	April 1, 1866	Nov. 1, 1866	7	13 00	3 50	16 50	84 00	199 53	A. W. Buchanan	Do.
5	Sanford Fairinsh	do	April 1, 1866	Nov. 1, 1866	7	13 00	3 50	16 50	84 00	199 50	Sanford Fairln-sh	Do.
6	Christian Christopherson	do	April 1, 1866	Nov. 1, 1866	7	13 00	3 50	16 50	84 00	199 50	Christian C. Christoffersen	Do.
7	Heber K. Petty	do	April 1, 1866	Nov. 1, 1866	7	13 00	3 50	16 50	84 00	199 50	Heber K. Petty	Do.
8	William Richey	do	April 1, 1866	Nov. 1, 1866	7	13 00	3 50	16 50	84 00	199 50	William Richey	Do.
9	David Lewis	do	April 1, 1866	Nov. 1, 1866	7	13 00	3 50	16 50	84 00	199 50	David Lewis	Do.
10	John Wilkinson	do	April 1, 1866	Nov. 1, 1866	7	13 00	3 50	16 50	84 00	199 50	John Wilkinson	W. B. Parr.
11	Wm. H. Peacock	do	April 1, 1866	Nov. 1, 1866	7	13 00	3 50	16 50	84 00	199 50	Wm. H. Peacock	W. T. Reid.
12	Peter Marker	do	April 1, 1866	Nov. 1, 1866	7	13 00	3 50	16 50	84 00	199 50	Peter Marker	Do.
13	Harrison Edwards	do	April 1, 1866	Nov. 1, 1866	7	13 00	3 50	16 50	84 00	199 50	Harrison Edwards	Do.
14	Frnst Nielson	do	April 1, 1866	Nov. 1, 1866	7	13 00	3 50	16 50	84 00	199 50	Frnst Nielson	Do.
15	Johnson Black	do	April 1, 1866	Nov. 1, 1866	7	13 00	3 50	16 50	84 00	199 50	Johnson Black	Do.
16	Peter Claws	do	April 1, 1866	Nov. 1, 1866	7	13 00	3 50	16 50	84 00	199 50	Peter Claws	Do.
17	William Funk	do	April 1, 1866	Nov. 1, 1866	7	13 00	3 50	16 50	84 00	199 50	William Funk	Do.
18	Andrew Vanburen	do	April 1, 1866	Nov. 1, 1866	7	13 00	3 50	16 50	84 00	199 50	A. C. Van Buren	Do.
19	John H. Clark	do	April 1, 1866	Nov. 1, 1866	7	13 00	3 50	16 50	84 00	199 50	John H. Clark	Do.
20	Ezra Shoemaker	do	April 1, 1866	Nov. 1, 1866	7	13 00	3 50	16 50	84 00	199 50	Ezra Shoemaker	Do.
	Amasa E. Merriam	do	April 1, 1866	Nov. 1, 1866	7	13 00	3 50	16 50	84 00	199 50	Amasa E. Merriam	Do.

No.	Name		Enlisted	Discharged								Name	Remarks
21	Adam Beal	do.	April 1, 1866	Nov. 1, 1866	7	13 00	3 50	16 50	84 00	199 50	Adam Beal	Do.
22	George Allred	do.	April 1, 1866	Nov. 1, 1866	7	13 00	3 50	16 50	84 00	199 50	Georg Allred	W. B. Parr.
23	James Larsen	do.	April 1, 1866	Nov. 1, 1866	7	13 00	3 50	16 50	84 00	199 50	James Larsen	Do.
24	Lewis Olsen	do.	April 1, 1866	Nov. 1, 1866	7	13 00	3 50	16 50	84 00	199 50	Lewis Olsen	Do.
25	Neils Thompson	do.	April 1, 1866	Nov. 1, 1866	7	13 00	3 50	16 50	84 00	199 50	Neils Thompson	Do.
26	Peter Taylor	do.	April 1, 1866	Nov. 1, 1866	7	13 00	3 50	16 50	84 00	199 50	Peter Taylor	Do.
27	Rasmus Clawson	do.	April 1, 1866	Nov. 1, 1866	7	13 00	3 50	16 50	84 00	199 50	Rasmus Clawson	Do.
28	Paul Polson	do.	April 1, 1866	Nov. 1, 1866	7	13 00	3 50	16 50	84 00	199 50	Paul Poulsen	Do.
29	Lars P. Peterson	do.	April 1, 1866	Nov. 1, 1866	7	13 00	3 50	16 50	84 00	199 50	Lars P. Petersen	Do.
30	George Taylor	do.	April 1, 1866	Nov. 1, 1866	7	13 00	3 50	16 50	84 00	199 50	Georg Taylor	Do.
31	Henry Jensen	do.	April 1, 1866	Nov. 1, 1866	7	13 00	3 50	16 50	84 00	199 50	Henri Jensen	Do.
32	Martin Thomason	do.	April 1, 1866	Nov. 1, 1866	7	13 00	3 50	16 50	84 00	199 50	Martines Thomason	Do.
33	Peter Larsen	do.	April 1, 1866	Nov. 1, 1866	7	13 00	3 50	16 50	84 00	199 50	Peter Larsen	Do.
34	Son A. Sorensen	do.	April 1, 1866	Nov. 1, 1866	7	13 00	3 50	16 50	84 00	199 50	Soren A. Sorensen	Do.
35	Henry Green	do.	April 1, 1866	Nov. 1, 1866	7	12 00	3 50	16 50	84 00	199 50	Henry Green	Do.
36	Christian Larsen	do.	April 1, 1866	Nov. 1, 1866	7	13 00	3 50	16 50	84 00	199 50	Christen Larsen	Do.
37	Jens G. Jensen	do.	April 1, 1866	Nov. 1, 1866	7	13 00	3 30	16 50	84 00	199 50	Jens G. Jensaller	Do.
38	Ole Olson	do.	April 1, 1866	Nov. 1, 1866	7	13 00	3 50	16 50	84 00	199 50	Ole Olson	Do.
39	Andrew C. Nelson	do.	April 1, 1866	Nov. 1, 1866	7	13 00	3 50	16 50	84 00	199 50	Andrew C. Nielsen	W. T. Reid.
40	Michael Yansen	do.	April 1, 1866	Nov. 1, 1866	7	13 00	3 50	16 50	84 00	199 50	Michael Yarnsen	W. B. Parr.
41	Peter Johnston	do.	April 1, 1866	Nov. 1, 1866	7	13 00	3 50	16 50	84 00	199 50	Peter Johnsen	Do.
42	James Mcdrolf	do.	April 1, 1866	Nov. 1, 1866	7	13 00	3 30	16 30	84 00	199 50	James Mcdrolf	Do.
43	James Mallow	do.	April 1, 1866	Nov. 1, 1866	7	13 00	3 50	16 30	84 00	199 53	James Mallow	Do.
44	John Z. Medcalf	do.	April 1, 1866	Nov. 1, 1866	7	13 00	3 50	16 30	84 00	199 50	Jhon Y. Medcalf	Do.
45	Philip Dark	do.	April 1, 1866	Nov. 1, 1866	7	13 00	3 50	16 50	84 00	199 50	Phillip Dark	Do.
46	Joseph Graham	do.	April 1, 1866	Nov. 1, 1866	7	13 00	3 50	16 50	84 00	199 50	Joseph Graham	Do.
47	H. Kearns	do.	April 1, 1866	Nov. 1, 1866	7	13 00	3 00	16 50	84 00	199 50	H. Kearns	Do.
48	C. A. Madsen	do.	April 1, 1866	Nov. 1, 1866	7	13 00	3 50	16 50	84 00	199 50	C. A. Madsen	Do.
49	Lars C. Madsen	do.	April 1, 1866	Nov. 1, 1866	7	13 00	3 50	16 50	84 00	199 50	Lars G. Madsen	Do.
50	Ruben Stephens	do.	April 1, 1866	Nov. 1, 1866	7	13 00	3 50	16 50	84 00	199 50	Reuthen Strevens	Do.
51	Simon Hanson	do.	April 1, 1866	Nov. 1, 1866	7	13 00	3 50	16 50	84 00	199 50	Simon Hanson	Do.
52	Ezra Funk	do.	April 1, 1866	Nov. 1, 1866	7	13 00	3 50	16 50	84 00	199 50	E. K. Funk	W. T. Reid.

This company was mustered into service at Manti City, Sanpete County, April 1, 1866, by Brigadier General Warren S. Snow, and by him assigned to duty in the Sevier Valley. They were on several expeditions to Fish Lake, Castle Valley, Green River, and Thistle Valley. They were constantly in active service, by night and day, through the mountains for two hundred miles; had several skirmishes with the enemy, and was on duty for the full time specified above, and was mustered out November 1, 1866.

I certify that the above account is correct.

H. B. CLAWSON,
Adjutant General Nauvoo Legion

Pay-roll of Captain Tidwell's company —— infantry, Utah Territory militia, employed in the suppression of Indian hostilities in Sanpete County, from April 1 to November 1, 1866.

We, the undersigned, acknowledge to have received from James W. Cummings, paymaster Utah Territory militia, the sums set opposite to our names, in full payment for our services for the time specified.

Number	Names	Rank	Period of service. Commencement.	Period of service. Expiration.	Months.	Pay per month.	Monthly allowance for clothing.	Total monthly pay and allowance.	Total pay and allowance.	Signatures.	Witnesses.
1	John Tidwell, sen	Captain	Apr. 1, 1866	Nov. 1, 1866	7	$17 00		118 50	$835 50	John Tidwell	H. P. Miller.
1	Carstiat C. Rowe	1st lieutenant	Apr. 1, 1866	Nov. 1, 1866	7	17 00		112 50	739 50	C. C. Rowe	Do.
1	Christian Hansen	2d lieutenant	Apr. 1, 1866	Nov. 1, 1866	7			103 50	724 50	C. Hansen	Do.
2	Mads Jensen	do	Apr. 1, 1866	Nov. 1, 1866	7			103 50	724 50	Mas Jensen	Do.
3	John Barton	do	Apr. 1, 1866	Nov. 1, 1866	7			103 50	724 50	John Barton	Do.
4	Ebbe Yessen	do	Apr. 1, 1866	Nov. 1, 1866	7			103 50	724 50	Ebbe Yessen	Do.
5	Christopher Johnson	do	Apr. 1, 1866	Nov. 1, 1866	7			103 50	724 50	C. Johnson	Do.
1	Peter Anderson	Sergeant	Apr. 1, 1866	Nov. 1, 1866	7	$17 00	$3 50	20 50	143 50	P. Anderson	Do.
2	Mikael Rasmussen	do	Apr. 1, 1866	Nov. 1, 1866	7	17 00	3 50	20 50	143 50	Michel Rasmussen	Do.
3	Auasay Scoville	do	Apr. 1, 1866	Nov. 1, 1866	7	17 00	3 50	20 50	143 50	Amasa Scovil	Do.
4	Joe Yessen	do	Apr. 1, 1866	Nov. 1, 1866	7	17 00	3 50	20 50	143 50	Jes Yessen	Do.
5	Rasmus Meiklesen	do	Apr. 1, 1866	Nov. 1, 1866	7	20 50	3 50	20 50	143 50	R. Michelsen	Do.
1	William N. Rowe	Private	Apr. 1, 1866	Nov. 1, 1866	7	13 00	3 50	16 50	115 50	William N. Rowe	Do.
2	James H. Tidwell	do	Apr. 1, 1866	Nov. 1, 1866	7	13 00	3 50	16 50	115 50	James H. Tidwell	Do.
3	Peter Jensen	do	Apr. 1, 1866	Nov. 1, 1866	7	13 00	3 50	16 50	115 50	Peter Yessen	Do.
4	Nathan Staker	do	Apr. 1, 1866	Nov. 1, 1866	7	13 00	3 50	16 50	115 50	Nathan Staker	Do.
5	William Lake	do	Apr. 1, 1866	Nov. 1, 1866	7	13 00	3 50	16 50	115 50	William Lake	Do.
6	Henning P. Peil	do	Apr. 1, 1866	Nov. 1, 1866	7	13 00	3 50	16 50	115 50	H. P. Peil, his + mark	Do.
7	George Miller	do	Apr. 1, 1866	Nov. 1, 1866	7	13 00	3 50	16 50	115 50	Geo. Miller, his + mark	Do.
8	James Anderson	do	Apr. 1, 1866	Nov. 1, 1866	7	13 00	3 50	16 50	115 50	James Anderson	Do.
9	Mikael Christiansen	do	Apr. 1, 1866	Nov. 1, 1866	7	13 00	3 50	16 50	115 50	Mikael Christiansen	Do.
10	Peter Borg	do	Apr. 1, 1866	Nov. 1, 1866	7	13 00	3 50	16 50	115 50	Peter Borg	Do.
11	Jens C. Nielsen	do	Apr. 1, 1866	Nov. 1, 1866	7	13 00	3 51	16 50	115 50	Jens C. Nielsen	Do.
12	Anders Petersen, 2d	do	Apr. 1, 1866	Nov. 1, 1866	7	13 00	3 50	16 50	115 50	Andres Petersen, 2d	Do.
13	Christian Broderson	do	Apr. 1, 1866	Nov. 1, 1866	7	13 00	3 50	16 50	115 50	Cristian Broderson	Do.
14	Christian N. Christiansen	do	Apr. 1, 1866	Nov. 1, 1866	7	13 00	3 50	16 50	115 50	C. N. Christiansen	Do.
15	Thomas C. Jensen	do	Apr. 1, 1866	Nov. 1, 1866	7	13 00	3 50	16 50	115 50	Thomas C. Jensen	Do.
16	James R. McLenahan	do	Apr. 1, 1866	Nov. 1, 1866	7	13 00	3 50	16 50	115 50	James R. McClenahan	Do.
17	Anders Limberg	do	Apr. 1, 1866	Nov. 1, 1866	7	13 00	3 50	16 50	115 50	Andrew Limberg	Do.
18	Giomler Erickson	do	Apr. 1, 1866	Nov. 1, 1866	7	13 00	3 50	16 50	115 50	Gund, Erickson	Do.
19	Christian Jensen	do	Apr. 1, 1866	Nov. 1, 1866	7	13 00	3 50	16 50	115 50	Christian Jensen	Do.
20	Peter Niels Oman	do	Apr. 1, 1866	Nov. 1, 1866	7	13 00	3 50	16 50	115 50	Peter N. Oman	Do.
21	Christian Larsen	do	Apr. 1, 1866	Nov. 1, 1866	7	13 00	3 59	16 50	115 50	Christian Larsen	Do.

	Name									Name	
53	John Tidwell, jun	do	Apr. 1, 1866	Nov. 1, 1866	7	13 00	3 50	16 50	115 50	John Tidwell, jun	Do.
54	Job E. Green	do	Apr. 1, 1866	Nov. 1, 1866	7	13 00	3 50	16 50	115 50	John E. Green	Do.
55	James B. Porter	do	Apr. 1, 1866	Nov. 1, 1866	7	13 00	3 50	16 50	115 50	James B. Porter	Do.
56	James Meyrick	do	Apr. 1, 1866	Nov. 1, 1866	7	13 00	3 50	16 50	115 50	James Meyrick	Do.
57	John Trescot	do	Apr. 1, 1866	Nov. 1, 1866	7	13 00	3 50	16 50	115 50	John Trescot	Do.
58	William Cresswell	do	Apr. 1, 1866	Nov. 1, 1866	7	13 00	3 50	16 50	115 50	William Cresswell	Do.
59	Justice W. Seely	do	Apr. 1, 1866	Nov. 1, 1866	7	13 00	3 50	16 50	115 50	Justus W. Seely	Do.
29	Anders Peterson	do	Apr. 1, 1866	Nov. 1, 1866	7	13 00	3 50	16 50	115 50	Andrew Peterson	Do.
30	Daniel Page	do	Apr. 1, 1866	Nov. 1, 1866	7	13 00	3 50	16 50	115 50	Daniel Page	Do.
30	Hans C. Davidson	do	Apr. 1, 1866	Nov. 1, 1866	7	13 00	3 50	16 50	115 50	Hans C. Davidson	Do.
31	Peter Larsen	do	Apr. 1, 1866	Nov. 1, 1866	7	13 00	3 50	16 50	115 50	Peter Larsen	Do.
32	Astmus Wildermassen	do	Apr. 1, 1866	Nov. 1, 1866	7	13 00	3 50	16 50	115 50	Astmus Wildemassen	Do.
34	Elisha Wilcocks	do	Apr. 1, 1866	Nov. 1, 1866	7	13 00	3 50	16 50	115 50	Elisha Wilcocks	Do.
35	Joseph Anderson	do	Apr. 1, 1866	Nov. 1, 1866	7	13 00	3 50	16 50	115 50	Josep Anderson	Do.
36	Hans Christopherson	do	Apr. 1, 1866	Nov. 1, 1866	7	13 00	3 50	16 50	115 50	Hans Christopherren	Do.
37	Niels Wittergren	do	Apr. 1, 1866	Nov. 1, 1866	7	13 00	3 50	16 30	115 30	Nils Witcgrin	Do.
38	Cyrus H. Wheelock	do	Apr. 1, 1866	Nov. 1, 1866	7	13 00	3 50	16 50	115 50	Cyrus H. Wheelock	Do.
39	Adreas Braudsted	do	Apr. 1, 1866	Nov. 1, 1866	7	13 00	3 50	16 50	115 50	A. Braudstad	Do.
40	Olof Lovegreen	do	Apr. 1, 1866	Nov. 1, 1866	7	13 00	3 50	16 50	115 50	Olof Ledgren	Do.
41	Ole C. Jensen	do	Apr. 1, 1866	Nov. 1, 1866	7	13 00	3 50	16 50	115 50	Ole C. Jensen	Do.
42	Ole Yessen	do	Apr. 1, 1866	Nov. 1, 1866	7	13 00	3 50	16 50	115 50	Ole Yessen	Do.
43	Adolph Fredrickson	do	Apr. 1, 1866	Nov. 1, 1866	7	13 00	3 50	16 50	115 50	Adolph Fredricksen	Do.
44	Washington P. McArthur	do	Apr. 1, 1866	Nov. 1, 1866	7	13 00	3 50	16 50	115 50	W. P. McArthur	Do.
45	Lars Jorgensen	do	Apr. 1, 1866	Nov. 1, 1866	7	13 00	3 50	16 50	115 50	Lars Jorgensen	Do.
46	John Coates	do	Apr. 1, 1866	Nov. 1, 1866	7	13 00	3 50	16 50	115 50	John Coates	Do.
47	Maurly Peterson	do	Apr. 1, 1866	Nov. 1, 1866	7	13 00	3 50	16 50	115 50	Morits Peterson	Do.
48	Lars Johnson	do	Apr. 1, 1866	Nov. 1, 1866	7	13 00	3 50	16 50	115 50	Lars Johnsen	Do.
49	James Riste	do	Apr. 1, 1866	Nov. 1, 1866	7	13 00	3 50	16 50	115 50	James Riste	Do.
50	Niels C. Carlson	do	Apr. 1, 1866	Nov. 1, 1866	7	13 00	3 50	16 50	115 50	Neis C. Carlson	Do.
51	Petter Peterson	do	Apr. 1, 1866	Nov. 1, 1866	7	13 00	3 50	16 50	115 50	Petter Peterson	Do.
52	Lucas K. Scovillo	do	Apr. 1, 1866	Nov. 1, 1866	7	13 00	3 50	16 50	115 50	Lucas K. Scovil	Do.

This company was mustered into service at Mount Pleasant, Sanpete County, April 1, 1866, by Brigadier General Warren S. Snow, and by him assigned to duty in the vicinity of said settlement for the protection of life and property. They were in active service every day until mustered out, November 1, 1866.

I certify that the above account is correct.

H. B. CLAWSON,
Adjutant General Nauvoo Legion.

Pay-roll of Captain John D. Chase's company —— infantry, Utah Territory militia, employed in the suppression of Indian hostilities in Sanpete County, Utah Territory, from April 1 to November 1, 1866.

We, the undersigned, acknowledge to have received from James W. Cummings, paymaster Utah Territory militia, the sums set opposite to our names, in full payment for our services for the time specified.

Number	Names	Rank	Commencement	Expiration	Months	Pay per month	Monthly allowance for clothing	Total monthly pay and allowance	Total pay and allowance	Signatures	Witnesses
	John D. Chase	Captain	April 1, 1866	Nov. 1, 1866	7			108 50	$229 50	John D. Chase	John Kirkman.
	Lars Eliason	1st lieut	April 1, 1866	Nov. 1, 1866	7			108 53	759 50	John Lars Eliason	Do.
	Joseph Shepherd	2d lieut	April 1, 1866	Nov. 1, 1866	7			103 50	724 50	Joseph Shepherd	Do.
	Soren Yorgensen	do	April 1, 1866	Nov. 1, 1866	7			103 50	724 50	Soren Jorginson	Do.
	John Bailey	do	April 1, 1866	Nov. 1, 1866	7			103 50	724 50	John Bailey	Do.
	Lars Alx. Josisen	do	April 1, 1866	Nov. 1, 1866	7			103 50	724 50	Lars Alx. Judisen, his + mark	John R. Winder.
	James C. Anderson	do	April 1, 1866	Nov. 1, 1866	7			103 50	724 50	James C. Anderson	Do.
	Paul E. Koffed	do	April 1, 1866	Nov. 1, 1866	7			20 50	143 50	P. E. Koffed	John Kirkman.
	William Prestwich	Sergeant	April 1, 1866	Nov. 1, 1866	7	$17	$3 50	20 50	143 50	William Prestwich	Do.
	Soren Christiansen	do	April 1, 1866	Nov. 1, 1866	7	17	3 50	20 50	143 50	Soren Christiansen	Do.
	Jens C. Petersen	do	April 1, 1866	Nov. 1, 1866	7	17	3 50	20 51	143 50	Jens C. Pettersen	John R. Winder.
	James Anderson Allred	do	April 1, 1866	Nov. 1, 1866	7	17	3 50	20 50	143 50	James A. Allred	Do.
	John Robinson	do	April 1, 1866	Nov. 1, 1866	7	17	3 50	20 51	143 50	John Robinson	Do.
	Raesmn Jensen	do	April 1, 1866	Nov. 1, 1866	7	13	3 50	16 50	115 50	Rasmus Jensen	
	John Irons, jr	Private	April 1, 1866	Nov. 1, 1866	7	13	3 50	16 50	115 50		
	George Monroe	do	April 1, 1866	Nov. 1, 1866	7	13	3 50	16 53	115 53	Eppe Christesen	John Kirkman.
	Eppa Christiansen	do	April 1, 1866	Nov. 1, 1866	7	13	3 50	16 50	115 50	Knud Nelson	Do.
	Knud Nelson	do	April 1, 1866	Nov. 1, 1866	7	13	3 50	16 50	115 50	Edward Mallison	Do.
	Edward Mallison	do	April 1, 1866	Nov. 1, 1866	7	13	3 50	16 50	115 20	Charles P. Thomas	Do.
	Charles P. Thomas	do	April 1, 1866	Nov. 1, 1866	7	13	3 50	16 50	115 50	Ole P. Anderson	Do.
	O. C. Anderson	do	April 1, 1866	Nov. 1, 1866	7	13	3 50	16 50	115 50	William Newton	Do.
	William Newton	do	April 1, 1866	Nov. 1, 1866	7	13	3 50	16 50	115 50	Peder Jensen	Do.
	Peter Yensen	do	April 1, 1866	Nov. 1, 1866	7	13	3 50	16 50	115 50	David Hutchison	Do.
	David Hutchinson	do	April 1, 1866	Nov. 1, 1866	7	13	3 50	16 50	115 50	Banget Munson	Do.
	Bennett Monson	do	April 1, 1866	Nov. 1, 1866	7	13	3 50	16 50	115 50	Joseph Allen	Do.
	Joseph Allen	do	April 1, 1866	Nov. 1, 1866	7	13	3 50	16 50	115 50	Petter Thomsen	Do.
	Peter Thompson	do	April 1, 1866	Nov. 1, 1866	7	13	3 50	16 50	115 57	Lars Hansen	Do.
	Lars Hansen	do	April 1, 1866	Nov. 1, 1866	7	13	3 50	16 50	115 50	Johan Stenstrom	Do.
	John Stendstrom	do	April 1, 1866	Nov. 1, 1866	7	13	3 53	16 50	115 50	Rasmus Rasumssen	Do.
	Rasmus Rasumssen	do	April 1, 1866	Nov. 1, 1866	7	13	3 50	16 50	115 50	Swend Olson	Do.
	Swend Olsen	do	April 1, 1866	Nov. 1, 1866	7	13	3 50	16 50	115 50	Benjamin Jackson	Do.
	Benjamin Jackson	do	April 1, 1866	Nov. 1, 1866	7	13	3 50	16 50	115 50	George Jackson	Do.
	George Jackson	do	April 1, 1866	Nov. 1, 1866	7	13	3 50	16 50	115 50	Petter Petterson	Do.
	Peter Peterson	do	April 1, 1866	Nov. 1, 1866	7	13	3 50	16 50	115 50		

No.	Name		Mustered in	Mustered out	7	13				Received by	Remarks
21	Peter Butler	do	April 1, 1866	Nov. 1, 1866	7	13	3 50	16 50	115 50	Peter Butler	Do.
22	James Butler	do	April 1, 1866	Nov. 1, 1866	7	13	3 50	16 50	115 50		Do.
23	Jens Jensen	do	April 1, 1866	Nov. 1, 1866	7	13	3 50	16 50	115 50	Jens Yensen	Do.
24	John Price	do	April 1, 1866	Nov. 1, 1866	7	13	3 50	16 50	115 50	John Price	Do.
25	Rice Williams	do	April 1, 1866	Nov. 1, 1866	7	13	3 50	16 50	115 50	Rice Williams	Do.
26	David Nicklaus	do	April 1, 1866	Nov. 1, 1866	7	13	3 50	16 50	115 50	David Nicholas	Do.
27	Thomas Reese	do	April 1, 1866	Nov. 1, 1866	7	13	3 50	16 50	115 50	Thomas Reese	Do.
28	Daniel Lewis	do	April 1, 1866	Nov. 1, 1866	7	13	3 50	16 50	115 50	Daniel Lewis	Do.
29	William Draper	do	April 1, 1866	Nov. 1, 1866	7	13	3 50	16 50	115 50	William Draper	Do.
30	Nathan Nickerson	do	April 1, 1866	Nov. 1, 1866	7	13	3 50	16 50	115 50		Do.
31	William Williams	do	April 1, 1866	Nov. 1, 1866	7	13	3 50	16 50	115 50		Stephen Allred.
32	George Crisp	do	April 1, 1866	Nov. 1, 1866	7	13	3 50	16 50	115 50	George Crisp	Do.
33	James Allred, sr	do	April 1, 1866	Nov. 1, 1866	7	13	3 50	16 50	115 50	James Allred, sr	Do.
34	William Stoddard	do	April 1, 1866	Nov. 1, 1866	7	13	3 50	16 50	115 50	Wm. Stodard	Do.
35	Louis Zabriska	do	April 1, 1866	Nov. 1, 1866	7	13	3 50	16 50	115 50	Lewis G. Zabrisiko	Do.
36	Joseph Broadhead	do	April 1, 1866	Nov. 1, 1866	7	13	3 50	16 50	115 50	Joseph Broad Heat	Do.
37	Yorgen Hansen	do	April 1, 1866	Nov. 1, 1866	7	13	3 50	16 50	115 51	Hans Jorgen Hansen	Do.
38	Peter Munson	do	April 1, 1866	Nov. 1, 1866	7	13	3 50	16 50	115 50	Peter Munsen	Do.
39	Isaac Allred, sr	do	April 1, 1866	Nov. 1, 1866	7	13	3 50	16 50	115 50	Isaac Allred, sr	Do.
40	Lars Franson	do	April 1, 1866	Nov. 1, 1866	7	13	3 50	16 50	115 50	Lars Fransden	Do.
41	William Seofield	do	April 1, 1866	Nov. 1, 1866	7	13	3 50	16 50	115 50	William Schofner	Do.
42	James Merks	do	April 1, 1866	Nov. 1, 1866	7	13	3 50	16 50	115 50	James Merks	Do.
43	Luke Nield	do	April 1, 1866	Nov. 1, 1866	7	13	3 50	16 50	115 50	Luke Neild	Do.
44	Peter Mickleson	do	April 1, 1866	Nov. 1, 1866	7	13	3 50	16 50	115 50	Peter Mikkelson	Do.
45	James P. Riterson	do	April 1, 1866	Nov. 1, 1866	7	13	3 50	16 50	115 50	J. P. Peterson, his + mark	Do.
46	Eleazer King	do	April 1, 1866	Nov. 1, 1866	7	13	3 50	16 50	115 50	Fleazur King	Do.
47	Louis Barney	do	April 1, 1866	Nov. 1, 1866	7	13	3 50	16 50	115 50	Lewis Barny	Do.
48	Paul D. S. Lund	do	April 1, 1866	Nov. 1, 1866	7	13	3 50	16 50	115 50	P. D. S. Lund	Do.
49	James Commander	do	April 1, 1866	Nov. 1, 1866	7	13	3 50	16 50	115 50	James Cammamiro	Do.
50	Samuel Akins	do	April 1, 1866	Nov. 1, 1866	7	13	3 50	16 50	115 50	Samuel Akins	Do.
51	Peter Gereron	do	April 1, 1866	Nov. 1, 1866	7	13	3 50	16 50	115 50	Peter Sorenson	Do.
52	Andrew Anderson	do	April 1, 1866	Nov. 1, 1866	7	13	3 50	16 50	115 50	Andrew Anderson	Do.
53	Lars Helverson	do	April 1, 1866	Nov. 1, 1866	7	13	3 50	16 50	115 50	Lars Halvesen, his + mark	Do.
54	Venus Jensen	do	April 1, 1866	Nov. 1, 1866	7	13	3 50	16 50	115 50	Jens Jensen	Do.
55	William Hudson	do	April 1, 1866	Nov. 1, 1866	7	13	3 50	16 50	115 50	William Hudson	Do.
56	Corn Peterson	do	April 1, 1866	Nov. 1, 1866	7	13	3 50	16 50	115 50	Soren Pedersen	Do.
57	Lars Larsen	do	April 1, 1866	Nov. 1, 1866	7	13	3 50	16 50	115 50	Lars Larsen	Do.
58	Samuel Fretwell	do	April 1, 1866	Nov. 1, 1866	7	13	3 50	16 50	115 50	Samuel Fretwell	Do.
59	James Bluck	do	April 1, 1866	Nov. 1, 1866	7	13	3 50	16 50	115 50	Jew M. Bluck	Do.
60	Louis Larsen	do	April 1, 1866	Nov. 1, 1866	7	13	3 50	16 50	115 50	Louis Lausen	Do.
61	Joseph Blaine	do	April 1, 1866	Nov. 1, 1866	7	13	3 50	16 50	115 50		John Kirkman.
62	Orson Alred	do	April 1, 1866	Nov. 1, 1866	7	13	3 50	16 50	115 50		

This company was mustered into service at Moroni City, Sanpete county, April 1, 1866, by Brigadier General Warren S. Snow, and by him assigned to duty in the vicinity of said settlement for the protection of life and property. They were in active service every day for the time specified above, and were mustered out November 1, 1866.

I certify that the above account is correct.

H. B. CLAWSON,
Adjutant General Nauvoo Legion.

Pay-roll of Captain Lars Swensen's company —— infantry, Utah Territory militia, employed in the suppression of Indian hostilities in Sanpete county, Utah Territory, from April 1 to November 30, 1866.

We, the undersigned, acknowledge to have received from James W. Cummings, paymaster Utah Territory militia, the sums set opposite to our names, in full payment for our services for the time specified.

Number	Names	Rank	Commencement	Expiration	Months	Pay per month	Monthly allowance for clothing	Total monthly pay and allowance	Total pay and allowance	Signatures	Witnesses
1	Lars Swensen	Captain	April 1, 1866	Nov. 30, 1866	7			$118 50	$829 50	Lars Swensen	Jabez Faux.
1	Jens C. Nielsen	1st lieutenant	April 1, 1866	Nov. 30, 1866	7			104 50	730 50	J. C. Nellsen	Do.
1	Carl Rosburg	2d lieutenant	April 1, 1866	Nov. 30, 1866	7			103 50	724 50	Carl Rosburg	Do.
2	Christian P. Nielsen	do	April 1, 1866	Nov. 30, 1866	7			103 50	724 50	Christian P. Nielson	Do.
2	Peter A. Nielson	do	April 1, 1866	Nov. 30, 1866	7			103 50	724 50	P. A. Nilson	Do.
3	Christian A. Christiansen	do	April 1, 1866	Nov. 30, 1866	7			103 50	724 50	C. A. Christensen	Do.
4	John Reese	do	April 1, 1866	Nov. 30, 1866	7			103 50	724 50	John Reese	Do.
5	Jens C. Olsen	Sergeant	April 1, 1866	Nov. 30, 1866	7	$17 00	$3 50	20 50	143 50	Jens C. Olsen	Do.
1	Rasmus Anderson	do	April 1, 1866	Nov. 30, 1866	7	17 00	3 50	20 50	143 50	Rasmus Anderson	Do.
2	Michael Johnson	do	April 1, 1866	Nov. 30, 1866	7	17 00	3 50	20 50	143 50	Michael Johnson	Do.
3	Toren N. Peterson	do	April 1, 1866	Nov. 30, 1866	7	17 00	3 50	20 50	143 50	Toren N. Peterson	Do.
4	Thomas Davis	do	April 1, 1866	Nov. 30, 1866	7	17 40	3 50	20 50	143 50	Thomas Davies	Do.
1	Hans Hansen	Private	April 1, 1866	Nov. 30, 1866	7	13 00	3 50	16 50	115 50	Hans Hansen	Do.
2	Joel H. Child	do	April 1, 1866	Nov. 30, 1866	7	13 00	3 50	16 50	115 50	Joel H. Child	Do.
3	Niels Jacobson	do	April 1, 1866	Nov. 30, 1866	7	13 00	3 50	16 50	115 50	Niels Jacobsen	Do.
4	Niels Olsen	do	April 1, 1866	Nov. 30, 1866	7	13 00	3 50	16 50	115 50	Nils Olsen	Do.
5	Peter Holm	do	April 1, 1866	Nov. 30, 1866	7	13 00	3 50	16 50	115 50	Peter Holm, his x mark	Do.
6	Nels P. Olsen	do	April 1, 1866	Nov. 30, 1866	7	13 00	3 50	16 50	115 50	Nils P. Olsen, his x mark	Do.
7	Andrew Jensen, jr.	do	April 1, 1866	Nov. 30, 1866	7	13 00	3 50	16 50	115 50	Andrew Jensen, jr	Do.
8	Lives Peterson	do	April 1, 1866	Nov. 30, 1866	7	13 00	3 50	16 50	115 50	Lois Petersen	Do.
9	Sim Nielson	do	April 1, 1866	Nov. 30, 1866	7	13 00	3 50	16 50	115 50	Sim Nielson	Do.
10	Carl Byelker	do	April 1, 1866	Nov. 30, 1866	7	13 00	3 50	16 50	115 50	Carl Bialki	Do.
11	Jacob Cloward	do	April 1, 1866	Nov. 30, 1866	7	13 00	3 50	16 50	115 50	Jacob Cloward	Do.
12	Phillip Marks	do	April 1, 1866	Nov. 30, 1866	7	13 00	3 50	16 50	115 50	Phillip Marx	Do.
13	Peter Rasmussen	do	April 1, 1866	Nov. 30, 1866	7	13 00	3 50	16 50	115 50	Petter Rasmussen	Do.
14	Marcus Jacobson	do	April 1, 1866	Nov. 30, 1866	7	13 00	3 50	16 50	115 50	Marcus Jacobsen	Do.
15	Peter R. Christiansen	do	April 1, 1866	Nov. 30, 1866	7	13 00	3 50	16 50	115 50	Petter R. Christensen	Do.
16	Peter Meekelsen	do	April 1, 1866	Nov. 30, 1866	7	13 00	3 50	16 50	115 50	Peter Meekelsen	Do.
17	Christian A. Peterson	do	April 1, 1866	Nov. 30, 1866	7	13 00	3 50	16 50	115 50	A. Petterson	Do.
18	James Garrard	do	April 1, 1866	Nov. 30, 1866	7	13 00	3 50	16 50	115 50	James Gammel	Do.
19	Erastus Curtis	do	April 1, 1866	Nov. 30, 1866	7	13 00	3 50	16 50	115 50	Erastus Curtis	Do.
20	Lauritz Larsen	do	April 1, 1866	Nov. 30, 1866	7	13 00	3 50	16 50	115 50	Lauritz Lauritzsen	Do.
21	Michael Sorensen	do	April 1, 1866	Nov. 30, 1866	7	13 00	3 50	16 50	115 50	Mikel Sorensen	Do.

No.	Name		Mustered in	Mustered out						Name	
22	John Lewellen	do	April 1, 1866	Nov. 30, 1866	7	13 00	3 50	16 50	115 50	John Lewellyn	Do.
23	Andrew Anderson	do	April 1, 1866	Nov. 30, 1866	7	13 00	3 50	16 50	115 50	Andrew Anderson	Do.
24	Jens Johnson	do	April 1, 1866	Nov. 30, 1866	7	13 00	3 50	16 50	115 50	Jens Jonsen	Do.
25	Christ Christiansen	do	April 1, 1866	Nov. 30, 1866	7	13 00	3 50	16 50	115 50	Charest Christesen	Do.
26	Lars C. Anderson	do	April 1, 1866	Nov. 30, 1866	7	13 00	3 50	20 50	115 50	Lars C. And'rsen	Do.
27	Andrew Anderson	do	April 1, 1866	Nov. 30, 1866	7	13 00	3 50	16 50	115 50	Andrew Anderson	Do.
28	O. C. Swensen	do	April 1, 1866	Nov. 30, 1866	7	13 00	3 50	16 50	115 50	O. C. Svensen	Do.
29	Peter Yorgensen	do	April 1, 1866	Nov. 30, 1866	7	13 00	3 50	16 50	115 50	Peter Yorgenson	Do.
30	Swen Anderson	do	April 1, 1866	Nov. 30, 1866	7	13 00	3 50	16 50	115 50	Sven Anderson	Do.
31	Lars Yorgensen	do	April 1, 1866	Nov. 30, 1866	7	13 00	3 50	16 50	115 50	Lars Jorgensen	Do.
32	Niels Rasmussen	do	April 1, 1866	Nov. 30, 1866	7	13 00	3 50	16 50	115 50	Neels Resmusen	Do.
33	John Bailey	do	April 1, 1866	Nov. 30, 1866	7	13 00	3 50	16 50	115 50	John Bailey	Do.
34	Henry N. Latter	do	April 1, 1866	Nov. 30, 1866	7	13 00	3 50	16 50	115 50	Henry N. Latter	Do.
35	Isaac Morley	do	April 1, 1866	Nov. 30, 1866	7	13 00	3 50	16 50	115 50	Isaac Morley	Do.
36	Andrew Jensen, jr.	do	April 1, 1866	Nov. 30, 1866	7	13 00	3 50	16 50	115 50	Andorn Jensen, 2d	Do.
37	Peter Christiansen, 2d.	do	April 1, 1866	Nov. 30, 1866	7	13 00	3 50	16 50	115 50	Petter Christesen	Do.
38	O. C. Olsen	do	April 1, 1866	Nov. 31, 1866	7	13 00	3 50	16 50	115 50		Do.
39	Peter Anderson, jr	do	April 1, 1866	Nov. 30, 1866	7	13 00	3 50	16 50	115 50	Peter Anderson	Do.
40	George P. Simpson	do	April 1, 1866	Nov. 30, 1866	7	13 00	3 50	16 50	115 50	George P. Simpson	Do.
41	Francis Simpson	do	April 1, 1866	Nov. 30, 1866	7	13 00	3 50	16 50	115 50	Francis Simpson	Do.
42	John N. Larsen	do	April 1, 1866	Nov. 30, 1866	7	13 00	3 50	16 50	115 50	John N. Larson	Do.
43	Andrew Borgeson	do	April 1, 1866	Nov. 30, 1866	7	13 00	3 50	16 50	115 50	Andrew Borgesen	Do.
44	Henry Rees	do	April 1, 1866	Nov. 30, 1866	7	13 00	3 50	16 50	115 50	Henry Rees	Do.
45	Richard Price	do	April 1, 1866	Nov. 30, 1866	7	13 00	3 50	16 50	115 50	Richard Price	Do.
46	Nathan Edmunds	do	April 1, 1866	Nov. 30, 1866	7	13 00	3 50	16 5	115 50	Nathan Edmunds	Do.
47	Edward Lewellen	do	April 1, 1866	Nov. 30, 1866	7	13 00	3 50	16 50	115 50	Edward Lewellyn	Do.
48	Peter Olsen	do	April 1, 1866	Nov. 30, 1866	7	13 00	3 50	16 50	115 50	Peter Olsen	Do.
49	Nephi Rees	do	April 1, 1866	Nov. 30, 1866	7	13 00	3 50	16 50	115 50	Nephi Rees	Do.

This company was mustered into service at Moroni City, Sanpete county, April 1, 1866, by Brigadier General Warren S. Snow, and by him assigned to duty in the mountains and passes north of said city. They performed regular service every day until mustered out.

I certify that the above account is correct.

NOVEMBER 1, 1866

H. B. CLAWSON,
Adjutant General Nauvoo Legion.

Pay-roll of Colonel H. P. Kimball's company, —— cavalry, Utah Territory militia, employed in the suppression of Indian hostilities in Sanpete and Sevier counties, Utah Territory, from May 1, 1866, to August 30, 1866.

We, the undersigned, acknowledge to have received from James W. Cummings, paymaster Utah Territory militia, the sums set opposite to our names, in full payment for our services for the time specified.

Number.	Names.	Rank.	Period of service. Commencement.	Period of service. Expiration.	Months.	Pay per month.	Monthly allowance for clothing.	Total monthly pay and allowance.	40 cts. per day for use and risk of horse and horse equipments.	Total pay and allowance.	Signatures.	Witnesses.
1	Hebrt P. Kimball	Colonel	May 1, 1866	August 30, 1866	4	$17 00		$211 00	$48 00	$892 00	H. P. Kimball	L. S. Hills
2	John Clark	Major	May 1, 1866	August 30, 1866	4			163 00	48 00	700 00	John Clark	Do.
3	Albert Dewey	1st lieutenant	May 1, 1866	August 30, 1866	4	13 00	$3 50	112 83	48 00	499 32	Albert Dewey	Do.
4	Howard O. Spencer	2d lieutenant	May 1, 1866	August 30, 1866	4	13 00	3 50	112 83	48 00	499 32	Howard O. Spencer	Do.
5	Malin Weiler	do.	May 1, 1866	August 30, 1866	4	13 00	3 50	112 83	48 00	499 32	Malin Weiler	Do.
6	A. R. Jackman	do.	May 1, 1866	August 30, 1866	4	13 00	3 50	112 83	48 00	499 32	A. R. Jackman	Do.
7	Seymour B. Young	do.	May 1, 1866	August 30, 1866	4	13 00	3 50	112 83	48 00	499 32	Seymour B. Young	Do.
8	William Howard	Sergeant	May 1, 1866	August 30, 1866	4	13 00	3 50	29 50	48 00	130 00	William Howard	Do.
9	E. D. Woolley, jr.	do.	May 1, 1866	August 30, 1866	4	13 00	3 50	29 50	48 00	130 00	E. D. Woolley, jr	Do.
10	William Rigby	Private	May 1, 1866	August 30, 1866	4	13 00	3 50	16 50	48 00	114 00	William Rigby	Do.
11	Thomas Jeremy	do.	May 1, 1866	August 30, 1866	4	13 00	3 50	16 50	48 00	114 00	Thomas Jeremy	Do.
12	William Dougal	Bugler	May 1, 1866	August 30, 1866	4	13 00	3 50	16 50	48 00	114 00	William Dougal	Do.
13	Homer Roberts	Private	May 1, 1866	August 30, 1866	4	13 00	3 50	16 50	48 00	114 00	Homer Roberts	Do.
1	E. L. Butterfield	do.	May 1, 1866	August 30, 1866	4	13 00	3 50	16 50	48 00	114 00	E. L. Butterfield	Do.
2	John Ashby	do.	May 1, 1866	August 30, 1866	4	13 00	3 50	16 50	48 00	114 00	John Ashby	Do.
3	Milton Davis	do.	May 1, 1866	August 30, 1866	4	13 00	3 50	16 50	48 00	114 00	Milton Davis	Do.
4	Orson Littlefield	do.	May 1, 1866	August 30, 1866	4	13 00	3 50	16 50	48 00	114 00	Orson Littlefield	Do.
5	Alma Pratt	do.	May 1, 1866	August 30, 1866	4	13 00	3 50	16 50	48 00	114 00	Alma Pratt	Do.
6	Albert Davis	do.	May 1, 1866	August 30, 1866	4	13 00	3 50	16 50	48 00	114 00	Albert W. Davis	Do.
7	Joseph Richards	do.	May 1, 1866	August 30, 1866	4	13 00	3 50	16 50	48 00	114 00	Joseph Richards	Do.
8	David Hillhouse	do.	May 1, 1866	August 30, 1866	4	13 00	3 50	16 50	48 00	114 00	David Hillhouse	Do.
9	Orson P. Arnold	do.	May 1, 1866	August 30, 1866	4	13 00	3 50	16 50	48 00	114 00	Orson P. Arnold	Do.
10	Joseph Arnold	do.	May 1, 1866	August 30, 1866	4	13 00	3 50	16 50	48 00	114 00	Joseph Arnold	Do.
11	Henry Snell	do.	May 1, 1866	August 30, 1866	4	13 00	3 50	16 50	48 00	114 00	H. Y. Snell	Do.
12	Conrad Wilkenson	do.	May 1, 1866	August 30, 1866	4	13 00	3 50	16 50	48 00	114 00	Conrad Wilkinson	Do.
13	James Hague, jr	do.	May 1, 1866	August 30, 1866	4	13 00	3 50	16 50	48 00	114 00	James Hague, jr	Do.
14	Robert Mycroft	do.	May 1, 1866	August 30, 1866	4	13 00	3 50	16 50	48 00	114 00	Robert Mycroft	Do.
15	Solomon F. Kimball	do.	May 1, 1866	August 30, 1866	4	13 00	3 50	16 50	48 00	114 00	Solomon F. Kimball	Do.
16	Jasper Conrad	do.	May 1, 1866	August 30, 1866	4	13 00	3 50	16 50	48 00	114 00	Jasper Conrad	Do.
17	William Goforth	do.	May 1, 1866	August 30, 1866	4	13 00	3 50	16 50	48 00	114 00	William Goforth	Do.
18	George Tribe	do.	May 1, 1866	August 30, 1866	4	13 00	3 50	16 50	48 00	114 00	George Tribe	Do.
19	William H. Piggott	do.	May 1, 1866	August 30, 1866	4	13 00	3 50	16 50	48 00	114 00	William H. Piggott	Do.
20	Joseph Goddard	do.	May 1, 1866	August 30, 1866	4	13 00	3 50	16 50	48 00	114 00	Joseph Goddard	Do.

	Name										Name	Remarks
53	Edward Fletcher	do.	May 1, 1866	August 30, 1866	4	13 00	3 50	16 50	48 00	114 00	Edwin Fletcher	Do.
54	Eldridge Tufts	do.	May 1, 1866	August 30, 1866	4	13 00	3 50	16 50	48 00	114 00	Eldridge Tufts	Do.
55	E. R. Young, jr	do.	May 1, 1866	August 30, 1866	4	13 00	3 50	16 50	48 00	114 00	E. R. Young, jr	Do.
56	R. B. Neff	do.	May 1, 1866	August 30, 1866	4	13 00	3 50	16 50	48 00	114 00	R. B. Neff	Do.
57	Peter Hanson	do.	May 1, 1866	August 30, 1866	4	13 00	3 50	16 50	48 00	114 00	Peter Hanson	Do.
58	Daniel Wostenholm	do.	May 1, 1866	August 30, 1866	4	13 00	3 50	16 50	48 00	114 00	Daniel Wolstenholm	Do.
29	George Chatlin	do.	May 1, 1866	August 30, 1866	4	13 00	3 50	16 50	48 00	114 00	George Chatlin	Do.
30	William Groesbeek	do.	May 1, 1866	August 30, 1866	4	13 00	3 50	16 50	48 00	114 00	William Groesbeck	Do.
31	H. B. Rich	do.	May 1, 1866	August 30, 1866	4	13 00	3 50	16 50	48 00	114 00	H. B. Rich	Do.
32	Richard V. Morris	do.	May 1, 1866	August 30, 1866	4	13 00	3 50	16 50	48 00	114 00	R. V. Morris	Do.
33	William H. Hill	do.	May 1, 1866	August 30, 1866	4	13 10	3 50	16 50	48 00	114 00	William H. Hill	Do.
34	Hyrum Murphy	do.	May 1, 1866	August 30, 1866	4	13 00	3 50	16 50	48 00	114 00	Hyrum Murphy	Do.
35	Ephraim Scott	do.	May 1, 1866	August 30, 1866	4	13 00	3 50	16 50	48 00	114 00	Ephraim Scott	Do.
36	William Boden	do.	May 1, 1866	August 30, 1866	4	13 00	3 50	16 50	48 00	114 00	William Bowden	Do.
37	John Arrowsmith	do.	May 1, 1866	August 30, 1866	4	13 00	3 50	16 50	48 00	114 00	Jown Arrowsmith	Do.
38	James Wolff	do.	May 1, 1866	August 30, 1866	4	13 00	3 50	16 50	48 00	114 00	James Wolff	Do.
39	William Carney	do.	May 1, 1866	August 30, 1866	4	13 00	3 50	16 50	48 00	114 00	William Carnie	Do.
40	*Charles Brown	do.	May 1, 1866	August 30, 1866	4	13 00	3 50	16 50	48 00	114 00		
41	John Hamilton	do.	May 1, 1866	August 30, 1866	4	13 00	3 50	16 50	48 00	114 00	John Hamilton	Do.
42	James H. Wells	do.	May 1, 1866	August 30, 1866	4	13 00	3 50	16 50	48 00	114 00	James H. Wells	Do.

*Killed in battle at Thistle Valley.

This company was mustered into service at Salt Lake City, May 1, 1866, by order of Lieutenant General Daniel H. Wells, and on that day started for Sanpete County; arrived at Manto May 5, 1866, and was assigned to duty by Brigadier General Warren S. Snow, at Circleville, Sevier County. They were in active service at this place fifteen days; then moved to Thistle Valley. Here they had a battle with the Indians: one man killed and several wounded; some Indians killed and wounded. The company was again sent to the Sevier Valley, and made two expeditions to Fish Lake, Castle Valley, and Green River. They were continually traveling, every day, until relieved, when they returned to Salt Lake City and were mustered out August 30, 1866.

I certify that the above account is correct.

H. B. CLAWSON,
Adjutant General Utah Territory Militia.

Pay-roll of Captain John W. Irons's company —— infantry, Utah Territory militia, employed in the suppression of Indian hostilities in Sanpete County, Utah Territory, from April 1, 1866, to November 1, 1866.

We, the undersigned, acknowledge to have received from James W. Cummings, paymaster Utah Territory militia, the sums set opposite to our names, in full payment for our services for the time specified.

Number	Names	Rank	Commencement	Expiration	Months	Pay per month	Monthly allowance for clothing	Total monthly pay and allowance	Total pay and allowance	Signatures	Witnesses
1	John W. Irons	Captain	April 1, 1866	Nov. 1, 1866	7		$3 50	$108 50	$759 50	John W. Irons	John Kirkman
2	James Harvey	1st lieutenant	April 1, 1866	Nov. 1, 1866	7		3 50	103 50	724 50	James Harvey	Do.
3	Niels Christensen	2d lieutenant	April 1, 1866	Nov. 1, 1866	7		3 50	103 50	724 50	Niels Christensen	Do.
4	Lars Larson	Sergeant	April 1, 1866	Nov. 1, 1866	7	$17 00	3 50	20 50	143 50	Lars N. Larson	Do.
5	Charles Longson	do	April 1, 1866	Nov. 1, 1866	7	17 00	3 50	20 50	143 50	Charles Longson	Do.
6	Lewis Hatch	do	April 1, 1866	Nov. 1, 1866	7	17 00	3 50	20 50	143 50	Lewis Hatch	Do.
7	John Tilby	do	April 1, 1866	Nov. 1, 1866	7	17 00	3 50	20 50	143 50	John Tilby	Do.
8	Nathan Fanx	do	April 1, 1866	Nov. 1, 1866	7	17 00	3 50	20 50	143 50	Nathan Fanx	Do.
9	James Cloward	Private	April 1, 1866	Nov. 1, 1866	7	13 00	3 50	16 50	115 50	James Cloward	Do.
10	Herbert Longson	do	April 1, 1866	Nov. 1, 1866	7	13 00	3 50	16 50	115 50	H. Longson	Do.
11	Aaron Hardy	do	April 1, 1866	Nov. 1, 1866	7	13 00	3 50	16 50	115 50	Aaron Hardy	Do.
12	John Kinder	do	April 1, 1866	Nov. 1, 1866	7	13 00	3 50	16 50	115 50	John Kinder	Do.
13	Peter Anderson	do	April 1, 1866	Nov. 1, 1866	7	13 00	3 50	16 50	115 50	Peter Anderson	Do.
14	Moroni Bradley	do	April 1, 1866	Nov. 1, 1866	7	13 00	3 50	16 50	115 50	Moroni Bradley	Do.
15	George Simpson, jr	do	April 1, 1866	Nov. 1, 1866	7	13 00	3 50	16 50	115 50	George Simpson, jr	Do.
16	Joseph Bagnel	do	April 1, 1866	Nov. 1, 1866	7	13 00	3 50	16 50	115 50	Joseph Bagnull	Do.
17	Peter Anderson, jr	do	April 1, 1866	Nov. 1, 1866	7	13 00	3 50	16 50	115 50	Peter Anderson	Do.
18	Hans P. Olsen	do	April 1, 1866	Nov. 1, 1866	7	13 00	3 50	16 50	115 50	Hans P. Olsen	Do.
19	George Mills	do	April 1, 1866	Nov. 1, 1866	7	13 00	3 50	16 50	115 50	George Mills	Do.
20	Morris Monson	do	April 1, 1866	Nov. 1, 1866	7	13 00	3 50	16 50	115 50	Morris Monson	Do.
21	Samuel Martin	do	April 1, 1866	Nov. 1, 1866	7	13 00	3 50	16 50	115 50	Samuel Martin	Do.
22	Charles Kemp	do	April 1, 1866	Nov. 1, 1866	7	13 00	3 50	16 50	115 50	Charles Kemp	Do.
23	Anders Jensen	do	April 1, 1866	Nov. 1, 1866	7	13 00	3 50	16 50	115 50	Andrew Jensen	Do.
24	Eli Ashcroft	do	April 1, 1866	Nov. 1, 1866	7	13 00	3 50	16 50	115 50	Bill Ashcraft	Do.
25	Martin Olsen	do	April 1, 1866	Nov. 1, 1866	7	13 00	3 50	16 50	115 50	Martin Olsen	Do.
26	George H. Bradley	do	April 1, 1866	Nov. 1, 1866	7	13 00	3 50	16 50	115 50	G. H. Bradley	Do.
27	Edward Scott	do	April 1, 1866	Nov. 1, 1866	7	13 00	3 50	16 50	115 50	Edward Scott	Do.
28	Amra Jensen	do	April 1, 1866	Nov. 1, 1866	7	13 00	3 50	16 50	115 50	Amra Jensen	Do.
29	Henry Draper	do	April 1, 1866	Nov. 1, 1866	7	13 00	3 50	16 50	115 50	Henry Draper	Do.
30	Moses Draper	do	April 1, 1866	Nov. 1, 1866	7	13 00	3 50	16 50	115 50	Moses Draper	Do.
31	Marion Jolly	do	April 1, 1866	Nov. 1, 1866	7	13 00	3 50	16 50	115 50	Marion Jolly	Do.
32	Charles Higgins	do	April 1, 1866	Nov. 1, 1866	7	13 00	3 50	16 50	115 50	Charles Higgins	Do.

No.	Name	Mustered in	Mustered out	Days					Remarks	Name
51	Amos A. Bradley	April 1, 1866	do.		13 00	3 50	16 50	115 50	Do.	Amos Bradley
52	James Larsen	April 1, 1866	do.		13 00	3 50	16 50	115 50	Do.	James Larsen
53	Robert Mallinson	April 1, 1866	do.		13 00	3 50	16 50	115 50	Do.	Robert Mallinson
54	James Done	April 1, 1866	do.		13 00	3 50	16 50	115 50	Do.	James Done
55	George Windows	April 1, 1866	do.		13 00	3 50	16 50	115 50	Do.	George Windows
56	William Hatch	April 1, 1866	do.		13 00	3 50	16 50	115 50	Do.	William Hatch
57	Reuben Ames	April 1, 1866	do.		13 00	3 50	16 50	115 50	Do.	Reuben Ames
58	Samuel Blackham	April 1, 1866	do.		13 00	3 50	16 50	115 50	Do.	Samuel Blackham
59	John Killett	April 1, 1866	do.		13 00	3 50	16 50	115 50	Do.	John Kellett
60	James Killett	April 1, 1866	do.		13 00	3 50	16 50	115 50	Do.	James Kellett
31	William Blackham	April 1, 1866	do.		13 00	3 50	16 50	115 50	Do.	John Mallinson
32	John Mallinson	April 1, 1866	do.		13 00	3 50	16 50	115 50	Do.	John Harris
33	John Harris	April 1, 1866	do.		13 00	3 50	16 50	115 50	Do.	James Christenson
34	James Christiansen	April 1, 1866	do.		13 00	3 50	16 50	115 50	Do.	John Done
35	John Done	April 1, 1866	do.		13 00	3 50	16 50	115 50	Do.	Anders Jensen
36	Andrew Jensen	April 1, 1866	do.		13 00	3 50	16 50	115 50	Do.	Jens Jensen
37	Jens Jensen	April 1, 1866	do.		13 00	3 50	16 50	115 50	Do.	George T. Jackson
38	George T. Jackson	April 1, 1866	do.		13 00	3 50	16 50	115 50	Do.	Thomas Brandon
39	Thomas Brandon	April 1, 1866	do.		13 00	3 50	16 60	115 50	Do.	Christen Jensen
40	Christian Jensen	April 1, 1866	do.		13 00	3 50	16 50	115 50	Do.	James Blackham
41	James Blackham	April 1, 1866	do.		13 00	3 50	14 50	115 50	Do.	Alexander Adamson
42	Alexander Adamson	April 1, 1866	do.		13 00	3 50	16 50	115 50	Do.	John Fowler
43	John Fowler	April 1, 1866	do.		13 00	3 50	16 50	115 50	Do.	Jens P. Christensen
44	Jens P. Christiansen	April 1, 1866	do.		13 00	3 50	16 50	115 50	Do.	David Scott
45	David Scott	April 1, 1866	do.		13 00	3 50	16 50	115 50	Do.	Peter Anderson
46	Peter Anderson, jr.	April 1, 1866	do.		13 00	3 50	16 50	115 50	Do.	John Blackham
47	John Blackham	April 1, 1866	do.		13 00	3 50	16 50	115 50	Do.	David Nicholas
48	David Nicholson	April 1, 1866	do.		13 00	3 50	16 50	115 50	Do.	John Davidson
49	John Davidson	April 1, 1866	do.		13 00	3 50	16 50	115 50	Do.	

This company was mustered into service at Moroni City, Sanpete County, April 1, 1866, by Brigadier General Warren S. Snow, and by him assigned to duty in the vicinity of said city, for the protection of life and property. They were in active service every day until mustered out, November 1, 1866.

I certify that the above account is correct.

H. B. CLAWSON,
Adjutant General Nauvoo Legion.

Pay-roll of Captain Amasa Tucker's company —— infantry, Utah Territory militia, employed in the suppression of Indian hostilities in Sanpete County, Utah Territory, from April 1 to November 1, 1866.

We, the undersigned, acknowledge to have received from James W. Cummings, paymaster Utah Territory militia, the sums sets opposite to our names, in full payment for our service for the time specified.

Number	Names	Rank	Commencement	Expiration	Months	Pay per month	Monthly allowance for clothing	Total monthly pay and allowance	Total pay and allowance	Signatures	Witnesses
1	Amasa Tucker	Captain	April 1, 1866	Nov. 1, 1866	7			$118 50	$829 50	Amasa Tucker	David Candland.
1	Jacob Christian	1st lieutenant	April 1, 1866	Nov. 1, 1866	7			108 50	759 50	Jacob Christenson	Do.
2	Andrew Madsen	2d lieutenant	April 1, 1866	Nov. 1, 1866	7			103 50	724 50	Andrew Madsen	Do.
3	Christian Sorensen	do	April 1, 1866	Nov. 1, 1866	7			103 50	724 50	Christen Sorensen, his + mark.	Do.
4	Peter M. Peil	do	April 1, 1866	Nov. 1, 1866	7			103 50	724 50	P. M. Peil	Do.
5	Harold Beanman	do	April 1, 1866	Nov. 1, 1866	7			103 50	724 50	H. Beanman	Do.
1	Jens Jorgensen	Sergeant	April 1, 1866	Nov. 1, 1866	7	17 00	3 50	20 50	143 50	Jens Jorgensen	Do.
2	Edward Cliff	do	April 1, 1866	Nov. 1, 1866	7	17 00	3 50	20 50	143 50	Edward Cliff	Do.
3	Hans Paulsen	do	April 1, 1866	Nov. 1, 1866	7	17 00	3 50	20 50	143 50	Hans Paulsen	Do.
4	Hans P. Miller	do	April 1, 1866	Nov. 1, 1866	7	17 00	3 50	20 50	143 50	H. P. Miller	Do.
5	Lars Rasmussen	do	April 1, 1866	Nov. 1, 1866	7	17 00	3 50	20 50	143 50	L. Rasmussen	Do.
1	Lauritz Larsen	Private	April 1, 1866	Nov. 1, 1866	7	13 00	3 50	16 50	115 50	Lauritz Larsen	Do.
2	Silvester Bartow	do	April 1, 1866	Nov. 1, 1866	7	13 00	3 50	16 50	115 50	Selvester Bartow	Do.
3	Jens C. Jensen	do	April 1, 1866	Nov. 1, 1866	7	13 00	3 50	16 50	115 50	Jens C. Jensen	Do.
4	Aaron P. Amen	do	April 1, 1866	Nov. 1, 1866	7	13 00	3 50	16 50	115 51	A. P. Oman	Do.
5	Rasmus Hansen	do	April 1, 1866	Nov. 1, 1866	7	13 00	3 50	16 50	115 50	Erik Gunderson	Do.
6	Niels P. Hansen	do	April 1, 1866	Nov. 1, 1866	7	13 00	3 50	16 50	115 50	Rasmus Hansen	Do.
7	Made Madsen	do	April 1, 1866	Nov. 1, 1866	7	13 00	3 50	16 50	115 30	Niele P. Hansen	Do.
8	Peter Larsen	do	April 1, 1866	Nov. 1, 1866	7	13 00	3 50	16 50	115 50	Made Madsen	Do.
9	Christian Madsen	do	April 1, 1866	Nov. 1, 1866	7	13 00	3 50	16 50	115 50	Peter Larsen	Do.
10	Calvin W. Moore	do	April 1, 1866	Nov. 1, 1866	7	13 00	3 50	16 50	115 50	Christian Madsen	Do.
11	Peter Christiansen	do	April 1, 1866	Nov. 1, 1866	7	13 00	3 50	16 50	115 50	C. W. Mors	Do.
12	George Farnsworth	do	April 1, 1866	Nov. 1, 1866	7	13 00	3 50	16 50	115 50	Peter Christenson	Do.
13	Niels Rosenlouf	do	April 1, 1866	Nov. 1, 1866	7	13 40	3 50	16 50	115 50	Geo. Farnsworth	Do.
14	James Walker	do	April 1, 1866	Nov. 1, 1866	7	13 00	3 50	16 50	115 50	N. Rosenlouf	Do.
15	Augustus Newberry	do	April 1, 1866	Nov. 1, 1866	7	13 00	3 50	16 50	115 50	James Walker	Do.
16	Peter Peterson	do	April 1, 1866	Nov. 1, 1866	7	13 00	3 50	16 50	115 50	Angus Newberg	Do.
17	Morten S. Mortensen	do	April 1, 1866	Nov. 1, 1866	7	13 00	3 50	16 50	115 50	Peter Petersen	Do.
18	Niels Nielsen	do	April 1, 1866	Nov. 1, 1866	7	13 00	3 50	16 50	115 50	S. Mortensen	Do.
19	Hyrum Winters	do	April 1, 1866	Nov. 1, 1866	7	13 00	3 50	16 50	115 50	Niele Nilson	Do.
20	John Lee	do	April 1, 1866	Nov. 1, 1866	7	13 00	3 50	16 50	115 50	Hyrum Winters	Do.
										John Lee	Do.

No.	Name		Mustered in	Mustered out						Signature	
21	Christian P. Jensen, jr.	do.	April 1, 1866	Nov. 1, 1866	7	13 00	3 50	16 50	115 50	Joseph Lee	David Candlund
22	Joseph Lee	do.	April 1, 1866	Nov. 1, 1866	7	13 00	3 50	16 50	115 50	William F. Reynolds	Do.
23	William F. Reynolds	do.	April 1, 1866	Nov. 1, 1866	7	13 00	3 50	16 50	115 50	Wm. Smith	Do.
24	William Smith	do.	April 1, 1866	Nov. 1, 1866	7	13 00	3 50	16 50	115 50	Hyram Seely	Do.
25	Hyram Seeley	do.	April 1, 1866	Nov. 1, 1866	7	13 00	3 50	16 50	115 50	Jens Hemriksen	Do.
26	Jens Henderksen	do.	April 1, 1866	Nov. 1, 1866	7	13 00	3 50	16 50	115 50	N. P. Nielsen	Do.
27	Niels P. Nielsen	do.	April 1, 1866	Nov. 1, 1866	7	13 00	3 50	16 50	115 50	Peter Frolersen	Do.
28	Peter Frederickson, 2d	do.	April 1, 1866	Nov. 1, 1866	7	13 00	3 50	16 50	115 50	John Gladhill	Do.
29	John Gladhill	do.	April 1, 1866	Nov. 1, 1866	7	13 00	3 50	16 50	115 50	John Wald-marson	Do.
30	John Waldmansen	do.	April 1, 1866	Nov. 1, 1866	7	13 00	3 50	16 50	115 50	Giannel Erickson	Do.
31	Giannel Erickson	do.	April 1, 1866	Nov. 1, 1866	7	13 00	3 50	16 50	115 50	B. Green	Do.
32	Benoni Green	do.	April 1, 1866	Nov. 1, 1866	7	13 00	3 50	16 50	115 50	Niels Johansen	Do.
33	Niels Johansen	do.	April 1, 1866	Nov. 1, 1866	7	13 00	3 50	16 50	115 50	Lauritz Hansen	Do.
34	Lars Hansen	do.	April 1, 1866	Nov. 1, 1866	7	13 00	3 50	16 50	115 50	Martin Johnson	Do.
35	Martin Johnson	do.	April 1, 1866	Nov. 1, 1866	7	13 00	3 50	16 50	115 50	Hans Martenzen, his + mark	Do.
36	Hans Martinsen	do.	April 1, 1866	Nov. 1, 1866	7	13 00	3 50	16 50	115 50	James Johnsen	Do.
37	James Johnson	do.	April 1, 1866	Nov. 1, 1866	7	13 00	3 50	16 50	115 50	A. G. Omann	Do.
38	August G. Oemann	do.	April 1, 1866	Nov. 1, 1866	7	13 00	3 50	16 50	115 50	William Evins	Do.
39	William Evins	do.	April 1, 1866	Nov. 1, 1866	7	13 00	3 50	16 50	115 50	J. G. Wheeler	Do.
40	John G. Wheeler	do.	April 1, 1866	Nov. 1, 1866	7	13 00	3 50	16 50	115 50	S. Green	Do.
41	Samuel Green	do.	April 1, 1866	Nov. 1, 1866	7	13 00	3 50	16 50	115 50	Hyram Coats	Do.
42	Hyram Coates	do.	April 1, 1866	Nov. 1, 1866	7	13 00	3 50	16 50	115 50	Niels Johansen	Do.
43	Niels Johansen	do.	April 1, 1866	Nov. 1, 1866	7	13 00	3 50	16 50	115 50	Martin Miller	Do.
44	Martin Miller	do.	April 1, 1866	Nov. 1, 1866	7	13 00	3 50	16 50	115 50	Soren Rasmusen	Do.
45	Soren Rasmussen	do.	April 1, 1866	Nov. 1, 1866	7	13 00	3 50	16 50	115 50	Niels Jacobsen	Do.
46	Niels Jacobson	do.	April 1, 1866	Nov. 1, 1866	7	13 00	3 50	16 50	115 50	H. J. Brown	Do.
47	Hans Jorgen Brown	do.	April 1, 1866	Nov. 1, 1866	7	13 00	3 50	16 50	115 50	Ole Arfdsen	Do.
48	Ole Arfdsen	do.	April 1, 1866	Nov. 1, 1866	7	13 00	3 50	16 50	115 50	Hans C. H. Beck	Do.
49	Hans C. H. Beck	do.	April 1, 1866	Nov. 1, 1866	7	13 00	3 50	16 50	115 50	P. Nielsen	Do.
50	Peter Nielsen	do.	April 1, 1866	Nov. 1, 1866	7	13 00	3 50	16 50	115 50	Henri Arnkruksen	Do.
51	Henry Erickson	do.	April 1, 1866	Nov. 1, 1866	7	13 00	3 50	16 50	115 50	Swen O. Nielsen	Do.
52	Swen Ole Nielsen	do.	April 1, 1866	Nov. 1, 1866	7	13 00	3 50	16 50	115 50		Do.

This company was mustered into service at Mount Pleasant, Sanpete County, April 1, 1866, by Brigadier General Warren S. Snow, and by him assigned to duty in the vicinity of said city to defend it against the Indians. They were in active service every day until mustered out, November 1, 1866.

I certify that the above account is correct.

H. B. CLAWSON,
Adjutant General Nauvoo Legion.

Pay-roll of Lieutenant Colonel John R. Winder's company —— cavalry, employed in the suppression of Indian hostilities in Sanpete and Sevier counties, Utah Territory, from June 1, 1866, to September 30, 1866.

We, the undersigned, acknowledge to have received from James W. Cummings, paymaster Utah Territory militia, the sums set opposite to our names, in full payment for our services for the time specified.

Number.	Names.	Rank.	Commencement.	Expiration.	Months.	Pay per month.	Monthly allowance for clothing.	Total monthly pay and allowance.	40 cents per day for use and risk of horse and horse equipments.	Total pay and allowance.	Signatures.	Witnesses.
1	John R. Winder	Lt. col.	June 1, 1866	Sept. 30, 1866	4	...	...	...	$48 00	$796 00	A. N. Hinkley	
1	A. N. Hinkle	1st lieut.	June 1, 1866	Sept. 30, 1866	4	...	...	112 83	48 00	499 32	William Harris	
1	William Harris	2d lieut.	June 1, 1866	Sept. 30, 1866	4	...	...	112 83	48 00	499 32	James Crane	
2	James Crane	do.	June 1, 1866	Sept. 30, 1866	4	...	...	112 83	48 00	499 32	C. A. North	
3	C. A. North	do.	June 1, 1866	Sept. 30, 1866	4	...	...	112 83	48 00	499 32	Samuel Riter	
4	Samuel Riter	Sergeant.	June 1, 1866	Sept. 30, 1866	4	$17 00	$2 50	20 50	48 00	120 00	Willard Snow	
1	Willard Snow	do.	June 1, 1866	Sept. 30, 1866	4	17 00	3 50	20 50	48 00	130 00	D. C. Thompson	
3	D. C. Thompson	do.	June 1, 1866	Sept. 30, 1866	4	17 00	3 50	20 50	48 00	130 00	Samuel Russell	
1	Samuel Russell	Private.	June 1, 1866	Sept. 30, 1866	4	13 00	3 50	16 50	48 00	114 00	George Naylor	
2	George Naylor	do.	June 1, 1866	Sept. 30, 1866	4	13 00	3 50	16 50	48 00	114 00	Josiah Lees	
3	Josiah Lees	do.	June 1, 1866	Sept. 30, 1866	4	13 00	3 50	16 50	48 00	114 00	Helaman Pratt	
4	Helaman Pratt	do.	June 1, 1866	Sept. 30, 1866	4	13 00	3 50	16 50	48 00	114 00	Josiah Lees	
5	S. B. Rose	do.	June 1, 1866	Sept. 30, 1866	4	13 00	3 50	16 50	48 00	114 00	Helaman Pratt	
6	William B. Clark	do.	June 1, 1866	Sept. 30, 1866	4	13 00	3 50	16 50	48 00	114 00	S. B. Rose	
7	C. J. Lambert	do.	June 1, 1866	Sept. 30, 1866	4	13 00	3 50	16 50	48 00	114 00	William B. Clark	
8	George Peart	do.	June 1, 1866	Sept. 30, 1866	4	13 00	3 50	16 50	48 00	114 00	C. J. Lambert	
9	James Briggs	do.	June 1, 1866	Sept. 30, 1866	4	13 00	3 50	16 50	48 00	114 00	George A. Peart	
10	Oliver Free	do.	June 1, 1866	Sept. 30, 1866	4	13 00	3 50	16 50	48 00	114 00	James Briggs	
11	William Moir	do.	June 1, 1866	Sept. 30, 1866	4	13 00	3 50	16 50	48 00	114 00	Oliver Free	
12	Ernstus Hall	do.	June 1, 1866	Sept. 30, 1866	4	13 00	3 50	16 50	48 00	114 00	William Moir	
13	Hanmer Wells	do.	June 1, 1866	Sept. 30, 1866	4	13 00	3 50	16 50	48 00	114 00	Ernstus Hall	
14	John Gabbott	do.	June 1, 1866	Sept. 30, 1866	4	13 00	3 50	16 50	48 00	114 00	Hanmer Wells	
15	John M. Cook	do.	June 1, 1866	Sept. 30, 1866	4	13 00	3 50	16 50	48 00	114 00	John Gabbot	
16	William H. Rhodes	do.	June 1, 1866	Sept. 30, 1866	4	13 00	3 50	16 50	48 00	114 00	John M. Cook	
17	Joseph Helm	do.	June 1, 1866	Sept. 30, 1866	4	13 00	3 50	16 50	48 00	114 00	William H. Rhodes	
18	William Clark	do.	June 1, 1866	Sept. 30, 1866	4	13 00	3 50	16 50	48 00	114 00	Joseph Helm	
19	Richard Howe	do.	June 1, 1866	Sept. 30, 1866	4	13 00	3 50	16 50	48 00	114 00	William Clark	
20	John R. Allen	do.	June 1, 1866	Sept. 30, 1866	4	13 00	3 50	16 50	48 00	114 00	Richard Howe	
21	William C. Allen	do.	June 1, 1866	Sept. 30, 1866	4	13 00	3 50	16 50	48 00	114 00	John R. Allen	
22	George Cottrall	do.	June 1, 1866	Sept. 30, 1866	4	13 00	3 50	16 50	48 00	114 00	William C. Allen	
23	D. M. Palmer	do.	June 1, 1866	Sept. 30, 1866	4	13 00	3 50	16 50	48 00	114 00	George Cottrall	
24	Zekeriah Derrick	do.	June 1, 1866	Sept. 30, 1866	4	13 00	3 50	16 50	48 00	114 00	Z. T. Derrick	

25	Absolom Smith	do....	June 1, 1866	Sept. 30, 1866	4	13 00	3 50	16 50	48 00	114 00	Absolom Smith
26	B. F. Stewart	do....	June 1, 1866	Sept. 30, 1866	4	13 00	3 50	16 50	48 00	114 00	B. F. Stewart
27	Robert Sharkey	do....	June 1, 1866	Sept. 30, 1866	4	13 00	3 50	16 50	48 00	114 00	Robert Sharkie
28	Robert Smithies	do....	June 1, 1866	Sept. 30, 1866	4	13 00	3 50	16 50	48 00	114 00	Robert Smithies
29	John Hardie	do....	June 1, 1866	Sept. 30, 1866	4	13 00	3 50	16 50	48 00	114 00	John Hardie
30	E. M. Murphy	do....	June 1, 1866	Sept. 30, 1866	4	13 00	3 50	16 50	48 00	114 00	E. M. Murphy

This company was mustered into service at Salt Lake City, June 1, 1866, by order of Lieutenant General Daniel H. Wells, and on that day started, in company with the lieutenant general, as an escort, to Sanpete County. They marched two hundred miles, and arrived at Selina June 5, 1866. They were then assigned to duty in Sevier County, patrolling and scouting in the mountains and passes for two hundred miles in extent; took part in the expeditions to Fish Lake, Castle Valley, and Green River. They were in active service every day until permitted to return to Salt Lake City, and were mustered out September 30, 1866.

I certify that the above account is correct.

H. B. CLAWSON,
Adjutant General Utah Territory Militia.

Pay-roll of Captain Joseph S. Day's company —— infantry, Utah Territory militia, employed in the suppression of Indian hostilities in Sanpete County, Utah Territory, from April 1 to November 1, 1866.

We, the undersigned, acknowledge to have received from James W. Cummings, paymaster Utah Territory militia, the sums set opposite to our names, in full payment for our services for the time specified.

Number.	Names.	Rank.	Period of service. Commencement.	Expiration.	Months.	Pay per month.	Monthly allowance for clothing.	Total monthly pay and allow.	Total pay and al. allowance.	Signatures.	Witnesses.
1	Joseph S. Day	Captain	April 1, 1866	Nov. 1, 1866	7	$17		$118 50	$829 50	Joseph S. Day	William Morrison.
1	Niels Waldermussen	1st lieut.	April 1, 1866	Nov. 1, 1866	7			106 50	759 50	Neils Waldernasson	Do.
2	John Myrick	2d lieut.	April 1, 1866	Nov. 1, 1866	7			103 50	724 50	John Meyrick	Do.
3	James Gunnison	do	April 1, 1866	Nov. 1, 1866	7			103 50	724 50	Jens Gundersen	Do.
3	Thomas C. Christiansen	do	April 1, 1866	Nov. 1, 1866	7			103 50	724 50	Thomas C. Christiansen	Do.
4	Paul Dehlin	do	April 1, 1866	Nov. 1, 1866	7			103 50	724 50	Paul Dehlin	Do.
5	Neils Jensen	do	April 1, 1866	Nov. 1, 1866	7			103 50	724 50	Nils Yensson	Do.
1	Peter Godfersen	Sergeant	April 1, 1866	Nov. 1, 1866	7		$3 50	20 50	143 50	Peter Godfersen	Do.
2	Hans Nielson	do	April 1, 1866	Nov. 1, 1866	7		3 50	20 50	143 50	Hans Neilson	Do.
3	James Sthal	do	April 1, 1866	Nov. 1, 1866	7		3 50	20 50	143 50	Jens Stahl	Do.
4	Andrew Saudergard	do	April 1, 1866	Nov. 1, 1866	7		3 50	20 50	143 50	Anders Syndergaard	Do.
5	Charles Hampshire	do	April 1, 1866	Nov. 1, 1866	7		3 50	20 50	143 50	Charles Hampshire	Do.
1	F. O. Witterling	Private	April 1, 1866	Nov. 1, 1866	7	13	3 50	16 50	115 50	F. O. Wetterling	Do.
2	Joseph Caldwell	do	April 1, 1866	Nov. 1, 1866	7	13	3 50	16 50	115 50	Yoseph Caldwell	Do.
3	Henry Wilcox	do	April 1, 1866	Nov. 1, 1866	7	13	3 50	16 50	115 50	Henry Wilcox	Do.
4	Bennett Rolfson	do	April 1, 1866	Nov. 1, 1866	7	13	3 50	16 50	115 50	Bendt Rolfsen	Do.
5	Martin Bonnie	do	April 1, 1866	Nov. 1, 1866	7	13	3 50	16 50	115 50	Martin Bonnee	Do.
6	John Johnson	do	April 1, 1866	Nov. 1, 1866	7	13	3 50	16 50	115 50	John Johnson	Do.
7	Counterret Rowe, jr	do	April 1, 1866	Nov. 1, 1866	7	13	3 50	16 50	115 50	Conderret Rowe	Do.
8	John Peterson	do	April 1, 1866	Nov. 1, 1866	7	13	3 50	16 50	115 50	John Petersen	Do.
9	John Nickleson	do	April 1, 1866	Nov. 1, 1866	7	13	3 50	16 50	115 50	John Nickolsen	Do.
10	Henry Olsen	do	April 1, 1866	Nov. 1, 1866	7	13	3 50	16 50	115 50	Henry Olsen	Do.
11	James Myrick, jr	do	April 1, 1866	Nov. 1, 1866	7	13	3 50	16 50	115 50	James Meyrick, jr	Do.
12	Claudius Wheeler	do	April 1, 1866	Nov. 1, 1866	7	13	3 50	16 50	115 50	Claudius Wheeler	Do.
13	Henry Bonnie	do	April 1, 1866	Nov. 1, 1866	7	13	3 50	16 50	115 50	Henry Bonnie	Do.
14	Jens Olsen	do	April 1, 1866	Nov. 1, 1866	7	13	3 50	16 50	115 50	Jens Olsen	Do.
15	Christian Jensen	do	April 1, 1866	Nov. 1, 1866	7	13	3 50	16 50	115 50	Christen Yensen	Do.
16	Adam Swensen	do	April 1, 1866	Nov. 1, 1866	7	13	3 50	16 50	115 50	Adam Swensen	Do.
17	Edward Dalley	do	April 1, 1866	Nov. 1, 1866	7	13	3 50	16 50	115 50	Edward Dally	Do.
18	Joseph Wilcox	do	April 1, 1866	Nov. 1, 1866	7	13	3 50	16 50	115 50	Joseph Wilcox	Do.
19	Thomas J. Hausekeeper	do	April 1, 1866	Nov. 1, 1866	7	13	3 50	16 50	115 50	Thomas J. Houskeeper	Do.
20	Theodore Hausekeeper	do	April 1, 1866	Nov. 1, 1866	7	13	3 50	16 50	115 50	Theodore Houskeeper	Do.

	Name		Date	Date						Name	
21	Niels R. Nielson	do	April 1, 1866	Nov. 1, 1866	7	13	3 50	16 50	115 50	Niels R. Nielson	Do.
22	Dolof Olsen	do	April 1, 1866	Nov. 1, 1866	7	13	3 50	16 50	115 50	Dolof Olsen	Do.
23	Rasmus Rasmussen	do	April 1, 1866	Nov. 1, 1866	7	13	3 50	16 50	115 50	Rasmus Rasmussen	Do.
24	Mads Anderson	do	April 1, 1866	Nov. 1, 1866	7	13	3 50	16 50	115 50	Mads Anderson	Do.
25	Franz Christiansen	do	April 1, 1866	Nov. 1, 1866	7	13	3 50	16 50	115 50	Franz Christonsin	Do.
26	Rasmus Brown	do	April 1, 1866	Nov. 1, 1866	7	13	3 50	16 50	115 50	Rasmus Brown	Do.
27	John Williams	do	April 1, 1866	Nov. 1, 1866	7	13	3 50	16 50	115 50	Johan Williams	Do.
28	Erick Erickson	do	April 1, 1866	Nov. 1, 1866	7	13	3 50	16 50	115 50	Erick Erickson	Do.
29	Hans Y. Hansen	do	April 1, 1866	Nov. 1, 1866	7	13	3 50	16 50	115 50	Hans Y. Hansen	Do.
30	Jens M. Christiansen	do	April 1, 1866	Nov. 1, 1866	7	13	3 50	16 50	115 50	Jens M. Christensen	Do.
31	Olof Rosenlouf	do	April 1, 1866	Nov. 1, 1866	7	13	3 50	16 50	115 50	Oloff Rosenlouf	Do.
32	Henry Mills	do	April 1, 1866	Nov. 1, 1866	7	13	3 50	16 50	115 50	Henry Mills	Do.
33	Christian Widergreen	do	April 4, 1866	Nov. 1, 1866	7	13	3 50	16 50	115 50	Christian Widergreen	Do.
34	Joseph Peterson	do	April 1, 1866	Nov. 1, 1866	7	13	3 50	16 50	115 50	Joseph Peterson	Do.
35	Ephraim Green	do	April 1, 1866	Nov. 1, 1866	7	13	3 50	16 50	115 50	Ephraim Green	Do.
36	Hazard Wilcox	do	April 1, 1866	Nov. 1, 1866	7	13	3 50	16 50	115 50	Hazard Wilcox	Do.
37	John Green	do	April 1, 1866	Nov. 1, 1866	7	13	3 50	16 50	115 50	John Green	Do.
38	Olof Sorensen	do	April 1, 1866	Nov. 1, 1866	7	13	3 50	16 50	115 50	Olof Sorenson	Do.
39	Alonzo Wheelock	do	April 1, 1866	Nov. 1, 1866	7	13	3 50	16 50	115 50	H. A. Wheelock	Do.
40	George Porter	do	April 1, 1866	Nov. 1, 1866	7	13	3 50	16 50	115 50	George Porter	Do.
41	Lars Borg	do	April 1, 1866	Nov. 1, 1866	7	13	3 50	16 50	115 50	Lars Borg	Do.
42	Hans Brodersen	do	April 1, 1866	Nov. 1, 1866	7	13	3 50	16 50	115 50	Hans Brodersen	Do.
43	George Toft	do	April 1, 1866	Nov. 1, 1866	7	13	3 50	16 50	115 50	George Toft	Do.
44	Frederick Peterson	do	April 1, 1866	Nov. 1, 1866	7	13	3 50	16 50	115 50	Frederick Petersen	Do.
45	Carloss Seely	do	April 1, 1866	Nov. 1, 1866	7	13	3 50	16 50	115 50	Carloss Seely	Do.
46	Ezra Day	do	April 1, 1866	Nov. 1, 1866	7	13	3 50	16 50	115 50	Ezra Day	Do.
47	Abraham Day, Jr	do	April 1, 1866	Nov. 1, 1866	7	13	3 50	16 50	115 50	Abraham Day	Do.
48	James Jason	do	April 1, 1866	Nov. 1, 1866	7	13	3 50	16 50	115 50	James Yeson	Do.
49	Thomas Allen	do	April 1, 1866	Nov. 1, 1866	7	13	3 50	16 50	115 50	Thomas Allen	Do.
50	Samuel C. Mills	do	April 1, 1866	Nov. 1, 1866	7	13	3 50	16 50	115 50	Samuel C. Mills	Do.
51	Ira Day	do	April 1, 1866	Nov. 1, 1866	7	13	3 50	16 50	115 50	Ira Day	Do.

This company was mustered into service at Mount Pleasant, Sanpete County, Utah Territory, April 1, 1866, by Brigadier General Warren S. Snow, and by him assigned to duty in the vicinity of said city for the protection of life and property. They were in active service every day until mustered out, November 1, 1866.

I certify that the above account is correct.

H. B. CLAWSON,
Adjutant General Nauvoo Legion.

Pay-roll of Captain Isaac M. Behunin's company —— infantry, Utah Territory militia, employed in the suppression of Indian hostilities in Sanpete County, Utah Territory, from April 1 to November 1, 1866.

We, the undersigned, acknowledge to have received from James W. Cummings, paymaster Utah Territory militia, the sums set opposite to our names, in full payment for our services for the time specified.

Number	Names	Rank	Period of service. Commencement.	Expiration.	Months.	Pay per month.	Monthly allowance for clothing.	Total monthly pay and allowance.	Total pay and allowance.	Signatures.	Witnesses.
1	Isaac M. Behunin	Captain	April 1, 1866	Nov. 1, 1866	7	$17 00		$118 50	$829 50	Isaac M. Behunin	William Blain.
1	James T. S. Allred	1st lieutenant	April 1, 1866	Nov. 1, 1866	7			108 50	750 50	J. T. S. Allred	Do.
2	Niels Clansen	2d lieutenant	April 1, 1866	Nov. 1, 1866	7			103 50	724 50	Niels Clawson	Do.
3	John Niehl	do	April 1, 1866	Nov. 1, 1866	7			103 50	724 50	John Neild	Do.
3	William S. Barney	do	April 1, 1866	Nov. 1, 1866	7			103 50	724 50	Wm. S. Barney	Do.
4	Samuel G. Bunnell	do	April 1, 1866	Nov. 1, 1866	7			103 50	724 50	Samuel G. Bunnell	Do.
5	Christian J. Larsen	do	April 1, 1866	Nov. 1, 1866	7			103 50	724 50	Christain J. Larsen	Do.
2	Peter Rasmussen	Sergeant	April 1, 1866	Nov. 1, 1866	7	$17 00	$3 50	20 50	143 50	Peter Rasmusen	Do.
3	William W. Major	do	April 1, 1866	Nov. 1, 1866	7	17 00	3 50	20 50	143 50	W. W. Mazor	Do.
4	Robert Blain	do	April 1, 1866	Nov. 1, 1866	7	17 00	3 50	20 50	143 50	Robert Blain, his + mark	Do.
5	William Blain	do	April 1, 1866	Nov. 1, 1866	7	17 00	3 50	20 50	143 50	William Blain	Do.
5	Abraham Acord	Private	April 1, 1866	Nov. 1, 1866	7	17 00	3 50	20 50	143 50	Abraham Acord	Do.
6	L. P. Anderson	do	April 1, 1866	Nov. 1, 1866	7	13 00	3 50	16 50	115 50	L. P. Anderson	Do.
2	John Zabriskie	do	April 1, 1866	Nov. 1, 1866	7	13 00	3 50	16 50	115 50	John Zabrisky	Do.
3	Soren P. Sorensen	do	April 1, 1866	Nov. 1, 1866	7	13 00	3 50	16 50	115 50	Soren P. Sorensen, his + mark	Do.
5	Nichole C. Land	do	April 1, 1866	Nov. 1, 1866	7	13 00	3 50	16 50	115 50	N. C. Land	Do.
6	Heming Olson	do	April 1, 1866	Nov. 1, 1866	7	13 00	3 50	16 50	115 50	Heming Olson	Do.
7	Peter Justisen	do	April 1, 1866	Nov. 1, 1866	7	13 00	3 50	16 50	115 50	Harry Ellertsen	Do.
8	Isaac N. Allred	do	April 1, 1866	Nov. 1, 1866	7	13 00	3 50	16 50	115 50	Peter Justusen	Do.
9	Joseph N. Major	do	April 1, 1866	Nov. 1, 1866	7	13 00	3 50	16 50	115 50	I. N. Allred	Do.
10	Niels Nielson	do	April 1, 1866	Nov. 1, 1866	7	13 00	3 50	16 50	115 50	J. S. Mazor	Do.
11	Mads Nielson	do	April 1, 1866	Nov. 1, 1866	7	13 00	3 50	16 50	115 50	Neils Nielsen	Do.
12	William Hudson	do	April 1, 1866	Nov. 1, 1866	7	13 00	3 50	16 50	115 55	Mads Nielsen	Do.
13	Jens Peterson	do	April 1, 1866	Nov. 1, 1866	7	13 00	3 50	16 50	115 50	William Hudson	Do.
14	John Broadbent	do	April 1, 1866	Nov. 1, 1866	7	13 00	3 50	16 50	115 50	Jens Pedersen	Do.
15	Frederick Wall	do	April 1, 1866	Nov. 1, 1866	7	13 00	3 50	16 50	115 50	John Broadbent	Do.
16	James L. Allred	do	April 1, 1866	Nov. 1, 1866	7	13 00	3 50	16 50	115 50	Frederick Wall	Do.
17	Peter Peterson	do	April 1, 1866	Nov. 1, 1866	7	13 00	3 50	16 50	115 50	James R. Allred	Do.
18	Axel Fulgreen	do	April 1, 1866	Nov. 1, 1866	7	13 00	3 50	16 50	115 50	Peter Peterson	Do.
19	Lewis Barney	do	April 1, 1866	Nov. 1, 1866	7	13 00	3 50	16 50	115 50	Axel Fulgreen	Do.
20	Jens Jensen	do	April 1, 1866	Nov. 1, 1866	7	13 00	3 50	16 50	115 50	Lewis Barney	Do.
										Jens Jensen	Do.

21	Peter Hanson	do.	April 1, 1866	7	Nov. 1, 1866	13 00	3 50	16 50	115 50	Peter Hanson	Do.
22	Green W. Allred	do.	April 1, 1866	7	Nov. 1, 1866	13 00	3 50	16 50	115 50	Green W. Allred	Do.
23	Caleb Stodard	do.	April 1, 1866	7	Nov. 1, 1866	13 00	3 50	16 50	115 50	Caleb Stodard	Do.
24	George Blain	do.	April 1, 1866	7	Nov. 1, 1866	13 00	3 50	16 50	115 50	George Blain	Do.
25	David H. Allred	do.	April 1, 1866	7	Nov. 1, 1866	13 00	3 50	16 50	115 50	David H. Allred	Do.
26	Yens Yensen	do.	April 1, 1866	7	Nov. 1, 1866	13 00	3 50	16 50	115 50	Jens Jensen	Do.
27	Niels H. Borsen	do.	April 1, 1866	7	Nov. 1, 1866	13 00	3 50	16 50	115 50	Niels H. Borresen	Do.
28	Lars Borsen	do.	April 1, 1866	7	Nov. 1, 1866	13 00	3 50	16 50	115 50	Lars Borresen	Do.
29	Andrew Johnson	do.	April 1, 1866	7	Nov. 1, 1866	13 00	3 50	16 50	115 50	Andrew Jonsen	Do.
30	Samuel B. Frost, jr	do.	April 1, 1866	7	Nov. 1, 1866	13 00	3 50	16 50	115 50	S. B. Frost, jr	Do.
31	John Larsen	do.	April 1, 1866	7	Nov. 1, 1866	13 00	3 50	16 50	115 50	John Larsen	Do.
32	Jonh Bertsen	do.	April 1, 1866	7	Nov. 1, 1866	13 00	3 50	16 50	115 50	John Elbertsen	Do.
33	John Lambert	do.	April 1, 1866	7	Nov. 1, 1866	13 00	3 50	16 50	115 50	John Lambert	Do.
34	Samuel Allred	do.	April 1, 1866	7	Nov. 1, 1866	13 00	3 50	16 50	115 50	Samuel Allred	Do.
35	Redick R. Allred	do.	April 1, 1866	7	Nov. 1, 1866	13 00	3 50	16 50	115 50	R. R. Allred	Do.
36	Andrew P. Miller	do.	April 1, 1866	7	Nov. 1, 1866	13 00	3 50	16 50	115 50	Andre P. Miller	Do.
37	James Christiansen	do.	April 1, 1866	7	Nov. 1, 1866	13 00	3 50	16 50	115 50	James Christiansen	Do.
38	John Robinson	do.	April 1, 1866	7	Nov. 1, 1866	13 00	3 50	16 50	115 50	John Robinson	Do.
39	Joseph A. Allred	do.	April 1, 1866	7	Nov. 1, 1866	13 00	3 50	16 50	115 50	Joseph A. Allred	Do.
40	Christian G. Larsen	do.	April 1, 1866	7	Nov. 1, 1866	13 00	3 50	16 50	115 50	Christian G. Larsen	Do.
41	Lauritz Larsen	do.	April 1, 1866	7	Nov. 1, 1866	13 00	3 50	16 50	115 50	Lauritz Larsen	Do.
42	Niels B. Eletter	do.	April 1, 1866	7	Nov. 1, 1866	13 00	3 50	16 50	115 50	Neils B. Eletter	Do.
43	Niels P. Stole	do.	April 1, 1866	7	Nov. 1, 1866	13 00	3 50	16 50	115 50	Niels P. Stole	Do.
44	Thomas B. Schroder	do.	April 1, 1866	7	Nov. 1, 1866	13 00	3 50	16 50	115 50	Thomas B. Schroder	Do.
45	Joseph P. Allred	do.	April 1, 1866	7	Nov. 1, 1866	13 00	3 50	16 50	115 50	Josep P. Allred	Do.
46	Nathan S. Barney	do.	April 1, 1866	7	Nov. 1, 1866	13 00	3 50	16 50	115 50	Nathan S. Barney	Do.
47	Wesley Simons	do.	April 1, 1866	7	Nov. 1, 1866	13 00	3 50	16 50	115 50		
48	John Benton	do.	April 1, 1866	7	Nov. 1, 1866	13 00	3 50	16 50	115 50	John Benton	Do.
49	William Williams	do.	April 1, 1866	7	Nov. 1, 1866	13 00	3 50	16 50	115 50	William Williams	Do.
50	John J. Spencer	do.	April 1, 1866	7	Nov. 1, 1866	13 00	3 50	16 50	115 50	John J. Spencer	Do.
51	Nathan Hardee	do.	April 1, 1866	7	Nov. 1, 1866	13 00	3 50	16 50	115 50		

This company was mustered into service at Springtown, Sanpete County, April 1, 1866, by Brigadier General Warren S. Snow, and by him assigned to duty in the vicinity of said city for the protection of life and property. They were in active service every day until mustered out, November 1, 1866.

I certify that the above account is correct.

H. B. CLAWSON,
Adjutant General Nauvoo Legion.

Pay-roll of Captain William H. Winn's company — cavalry, Utah Territory militia, employed in the suppression of Indian hostilities in Sanpete and Sevier counties, in the months of June, July, and August, 1866.

We, the undersigned, acknowledge to have received from James W. Cummings, paymaster Utah Territory militia, the sums set opposite to our names, in full payment for our services for the time specified.

Number	Names	Rank	Commencement	Expiration	Months	Pay per month	Monthly allowance for clothing	Total monthly pay and allowance	40 cts. per day for use and risk of horse and equipment	Total pay and allowance	Signatures	Witnesses
1	William H. Winn	Captain	June 13, 1866	August 13, 1866	2	$17 00		$129 50	$24 00	$253 00	Wm. H. Winn	J. Evans.
1	Robert E. King	1st lieut.	June 13, 1866	August 13, 1866	2			112 83	24 00	249 66	Robert E. King	Wm. Greenwood.
1	John Zimmerman	2d lieut.	June 13, 1866	August 13, 1866	2			112 83	24 10	249 66	John Zimmerman	J. Evans.
2	Richard Carlisle	do	June 13, 1866	August 13, 1866	2			112 83	24 00	249 66	Richard Carlisle	Wm. Greenwood.
1	Jasper Rolfe	Sergeant	June 13, 1866	August 13, 1866	2	$17 00	$3 50	20 50	24 00	65 00	Jasper Rolfe	J. Evans.
2	Frederick Thorne	do	June 13, 1866	August 13, 1866	2	17 00	3 50	20 50	24 00	65 00	Frederick Thorne	Wm. Greenwood.
1	Loren Olmsted	Private	June 13, 1866	August 13, 1866	2	13 00	3 50	16 50	24 00	57 00	Loren Olmsted	J. Evans.
2	John Bushman	do	June 13, 1866	August 13, 1866	2	13 00	3 50	16 50	24 00	57 00	John Bushman	Do.
3	Henry Millett	do	June 13, 1866	August 13, 1866	2	13 00	3 50	16 50	24 00	57 00	Henry Millett	Do.
4	Edwin A. Goodwin	do	June 13, 1866	August 13, 1866	2	13 00	3 50	16 50	24 00	57 00	Edwin A. Goodwin	Do.
5	Samuel Taylor	do	June 13, 1866	August 13, 1866	2	13 00	3 50	16 50	24 00	57 00	Samuel Taylor	Do.
6	Alfred Turner	do	June 13, 1866	August 13, 1866	2	13 00	3 50	16 50	24 00	57 00	Alfred Turner	Do.
7	William Bone	do	June 13, 1866	August 13, 1866	2	13 00	3 50	16 50	24 00	57 00	William Bone	Do.
8	Joseph Adams	do	June 13, 1866	August 13, 1866	2	13 00	3 50	16 50	24 00	57 00	Joseph Adams	Do.
9	Benjamin Greenwood	do	June 13, 1866	August 13, 1866	2	13 00	3 50	16 50	21 00	57 00	Benjamin Greenwood	Wm. Greenwood.
10	Alva North	do	June 13, 1866	August 13, 1866	2	13 00	3 50	16 50	24 00	57 00	Alva North	Do.
11	Frank Bears	do	June 13, 1866	August 13, 1866	2	13 00	3 50	16 50	24 00	57 00	Frank Bears	Do.
12	James McDaniels	do	June 13, 1866	August 13, 1866	2	13 00	3 50	16 50	24 00	57 00	James McDaniles	Do.
13	George Bennett	do	June 13, 1866	August 13, 1866	2	13 00	3 50	16 50	24 00	57 00	George Bennett	Do.
14	James Bush	do	June 13, 1866	August 13, 1866	2	13 00	3 50	16 50	24 10	57 00	James Bush	Do.
15	J. W. Chappin	do	June 13, 1866	August 13, 1866	2	13 00	3 50	16 50	24 00	57 00	J. W. Chappin	Do.
16	John Kettle	do	June 13, 1866	August 13, 1866	2	13 00	3 50	16 50	24 00	57 00	John Kettle	Do.
17	Henry Buckwater	do	June 13, 1866	August 13, 1866	2	13 00	3 50	16 50	24 00	57 00	Henry Buckwater	Do.
18	George Firkin	do	June 13, 1866	August 13, 1866	2	13 00	3 50	16 50	24 00	57 00	Geo. Firkin	Do.
19	David Wagstaff	do	June 13, 1866	August 13, 1866	2	13 00	3 50	16 50	24 00	57 00	David Wagstaff	Do.
20	Thomas Steel	do	June 13, 1866	August 13, 1866	2	13 00	3 50	16 50	24 10	57 00	Thomas Steel	Do.
21	Heber Robinson	do	June 13, 1866	August 13, 1866	2	13 00	3 50	16 50	24 00	57 00	Heber Robinson	Do.

This company was mustered into service at American Fork, Utah County, June 13, 1866, by order of Major General Aaron Johnson, and assigned to duty in Sanpete and Sevier counties. They started on the 13th of June, and arrived at

Pay-roll of Captain James Guyman's company —— infantry, Utah Territory militia, employed in the suppression of Indian hostilities in Sanpete County, Utah Territory, from April 1 to November 1, 1866.

We, the undersigned, acknowledge to have received from James W. Cummings, paymaster Utah Territory militia, the sums set opposite to our names, in full payment for our services for the time specified.

Number.	Names.	Rank.	Commencement.	Expiration.	Months.	Pay per month.	Monthly allowance for clothing.	Total monthly pay and allowance.	Total pay and allowance.	Signatures.	Witnesses.
1	James Guyman	Captain	April 1, 1866	Nov. 1, 1866	7	$17 00	---	$118 50	$829 50	James Guyman	Samuel Jewkes.
1	Samuel Jukes	1st lieutenant	April 1, 1866	Nov. 1, 1866	7	17 00	---	108 50	759 50	Samuel Jewkes	Rees. R. Lewellyn.
1	William Jolley	2d lieutenant	April 1, 1866	Nov. 1, 1866	7	14 00	---	103 50	724 50	Wm. Tolley	Samuel Jewkes.
2	Edward Collard	do	April 1, 1866	Nov. 1, 1866	7	14 00	---	103 50	724 50	Edward Collard	Do.
3	Cornelius Collard	do	April 1, 1866	Nov. 1, 1866	7	14 00	---	103 50	724 50	Cornelius Collard	Do.
4	Roger Openshaw	do	April 1, 1866	Nov. 1, 1866	7	14 00	---	103 50	724 50	Roger Openshaw	Do.
5	William Huggins	do	April 1, 1866	Nov. 1, 1866	7	14 00	---	103 50	724 50	Wm. Huggins	Do.
1	Nephi Robertson	Sergeant	April 1, 1866	Nov. 1, 1866	7	17 00	$3 50	20 50	143 50	Nephi Robertson	Rees. R. Lewellyn.
2	Thomas Crowther	do	April 1, 1866	Nov. 1, 1866	7	17 00	3 50	20 50	143 50	Thomas Crowther	Do.
3	Soren Christiansen	do	April 1, 1866	Nov. 1, 1866	7	17 00	3 50	20 50	143 50	Soren Christensen	Do.
4	Andrew Bertelsen	do	April 1, 1866	Nov. 1, 1866	7	17 00	3 50	20 50	143 50	Andreas Bertelsen	Do.
5	George Coombs	do	April 1, 1866	Nov. 1, 1866	7	17 00	3 50	20 50	143 50	George Coombs	Do.
1	Christian Christiansen	Private	April 1, 1866	Nov. 1, 1866	7	13 00	3 50	16 50	115 50	Christian Christensen	Samuel Jewkes.
2	William Cordingly	do	April 1, 1866	Nov. 1, 1866	7	13 00	3 50	16 50	115 50	William Cordingley	Do.
3	Richard H. Johnson	do	April 1, 1866	Nov. 1, 1866	7	13 00	3 50	16 50	115 50	Richard H. Johnson	Do.
4	Christian Ottison	do	April 1, 1866	Nov. 1, 1866	7	13 00	3 50	16 50	115 50	Christen Ottesen	Do.
5	Albert Collard	do	April 1, 1866	Nov. 1, 1866	7	13 00	3 50	16 50	115 50	Albert Collard	Do.
6	Edwin Robertson	do	April 1, 1866	Nov. 1, 1866	7	13 00	3 50	16 50	115 50	Edwin Robertson	Do.
7	William H. Adams	do	April 1, 1866	Nov. 1, 1866	7	13 00	3 50	16 50	115 50	William H. Adams	Do.
8	Lewis Lund	do	April 1, 1866	Nov. 1, 1866	7	13 00	3 50	16 50	115 50	Lewis Lund	Do.
9	William F. Cook	do	April 1, 1866	Nov. 1, 1866	7	13 00	3 50	16 50	115 50	Wm. F. Cook	Rees. R. Lewellen.
10	Lars Nielson	do	April 1, 1866	Nov. 1, 1866	7	13 00	3 50	16 50	115 50	Lars Nielson	Do.
11	Henry Sagers	do	April 1, 1866	Nov. 1, 1866	7	13 00	3 50	16 50	115 50	Henry Sagers	Do.
12	George Smith	do	April 1, 1866	Nov. 1, 1866	7	13 00	3 50	16 50	115 50	George Smith	Do.
13	James Woodward	do	April 1, 1866	Nov. 1, 1866	7	13 00	3 50	16 50	115 50	James Woodward	Do.
14	James Jukes	do	April 1, 1866	Nov. 1, 1866	7	13 00	3 50	16 50	115 50	James Jukes	Samuel Jewkes.
15	Richard Crowther	do	April 1, 1866	Nov. 1, 1866	7	13 00	3 50	16 50	115 50	Richard Crowther	Do.
16	William H. Johnson	do	April 1, 1866	Nov. 1, 1866	7	13 00	3 50	16 50	115 50	William H. Johnson	Do.
17	Erastus S. Wakefield	do	April 1, 1866	Nov. 1, 1866	7	13 00	3 50	16 50	115 50	Erastus S. Wakefield	Do.
18	John Green	do	April 1, 1866	Nov. 1, 1866	7	13 00	3 50	16 50	115 50	John Green	Do.
19	James Collard	do	April 1, 1866	Nov. 1, 1866	7	13 00	3 50	16 50	115 50	James Collard	Do.
20	Andrew Ougard	do	April 1, 1866	Nov. 1, 1866	7	13 00	3 50	16 50	115 50	Andrew Ougard	Rees. R. Lewellyn.
21	James A. Guyman	do	April 1, 1866	Nov. 1, 1866	7	13 00	3 50	16 50	115 50	James A. Guyman	Do.

No.	Name											By whom mustered
22	George Combs, jr	do.	115	50	16	50	3	50	13	00	7	Nov. 1, 1866	April 1, 1866	Do.
23	Ole Sorrenson	do.	115 50	16 50	3 50	13 00	7	Nov. 1, 1866	April 1, 1866	Do.
24	Reuben Carter	do.	115 50	16 50	3 50	13 00	7	Nov. 1, 1866	April 1, 1866	Samuel Jewkes.
25	Ole Jensen	do.	115 50	16 50	3 50	13 00	7	Nov. 1, 1866	April 1, 1866	Do.
26	John Shawcroft	do.	115 50	16 50	3 50	13 00	7	Nov. 1, 1866	April 1, 1866	Do.
27	Thomas Caldwell	do.	115 50	16 50	3 50	13 00	7	Nov. 1, 1866	April 1, 1866	Do.
28	William Combs	do.	115 50	16 50	3 50	13 00	7	Nov. 1, 1866	April 1, 1866	Do.
29	Thomas Wakefield	do.	115 50	16 50	3 50	13 00	7	Nov. 1, 1866	April 1, 1866	Rees. R. Lewellyn.
30	Samuel Jolley	do.	115 50	16 50	3 50	13 00	7	Nov. 1, 1866	April 1, 1866	Do.
31	Ephraim Combs	do.	115 50	16 50	3 50	13 00	7	Nov. 1, 1866	April 1, 1866	Do.
32	George Carter	do.	115 50	16 50	3 50	13 00	7	Nov. 1, 1866	April 1, 1866	Do.
33	Charles Johnson	do.	115 50	16 50	3 50	13 00	7	Nov. 1, 1866	April 1, 1866	Do.
34	James Nielson	do.	115 50	16 50	3 50	13 00	7	Nov. 1, 1866	April 1, 1866	Do.
35	Thomas Morgan	do.	115 50	16 50	3 50	13 00	7	Nov. 1, 1866	April 1, 1866	Samuel Jewkes
36	George Waylate	do.	115 50	16 50	3 50	13 00	7	Nov. 1, 1866	April 1, 1866	Do.
37	Soren Sorrensen	do.	115 50	16 50	3 50	13 00	7	Nov. 1, 1866	April 1, 1866	Do.
38	Bernard Snow	do.	115 50	16 50	3 50	13 00	7	Nov. 1, 1866	April 1, 1866	Do.
39	Rasmir Nielson	do.	115 50	16 50	3 50	13 00	7	Nov. 1, 1866	April 1, 1866	Do.
40	Andrew Larsen	do.	115 50	16 50	3 50	13 00	7	Nov. 1, 1866	April 1, 1866	Do.
41	Reese R. Lewellen	do.	115 50	16 50	3 50	13 00	7	Nov. 1, 1866	April 1, 1866	Rees. R. Lewellyn.
42	Thomas Robertson	do.	115 50	16 50	3 50	13 00	7	Nov. 1, 1866	April 1, 1866	Do.
43	Christian Christiansen	do.	115 50	16 50	3 50	13 00	7	Nov. 1, 1866	April 1, 1866	Do.
44	William Green	do.	115 50	16 50	3 50	13 00	7	Nov. 1, 1866	April 1, 1866	Do.
45	Jens Osgard	do.	115 50	16 50	3 50	13 00	7	Nov. 1, 1866	April 1, 1866	Do.
46	Robert L. Johnson	do.	115 50	16 50	3 50	13 00	7	Nov. 1, 1866	April 1, 1866	Do.
47	Jens Nielson, 3d	do.	115 50	16 50	3 50	13 00	7	Nov. 1, 1866	April 1, 1866	Samuel Jewkes.
48	Niels Jensen	do.	115 50	16 50	3 50	13 00	7	Nov. 1, 1866	April 1, 1866	Do.
49	Paul C. Peterson	do.	115 50	16 50	3 50	13 00	7	Nov. 1, 1866	April 1, 1866	Do.
50	William H. Sagers	do.	115 50	16 50	3 50	13 00	7	Nov. 1, 1866	April 1, 1866	Do.
51	Soren Hansen	do.	115 50	16 50	3 50	13 00	7	Nov. 1, 1866	April 1, 1866	Do.
52	Joshua Combs	do.	115 50	16 50	3 50	13 00	7	Nov. 1, 1866	April 1, 1866	Do.
53	George Huggins	do.	115 50	16 50	3 50	13 00	7	Nov. 1, 1866	April 1, 1866	Do.

This company was mustered into service at Fountain Green, Sanpete County, April 1, 1866, by Brigadier General Warren S. Snow, and by him assigned to duty in the hills and mountain passes north of said city. They were in active service every day until mustered out, November 1, 1866.

I certify that the above account is correct.

H. B. CLAWSON,
Adjutant General Utah Territory Militia.

Pay-roll of Captain Joseph Cluff's company ——— cavalry, Utah Territory militia, employed in the suppression of Indian hostilities in Sanpete County, Utah Territory, in the months of June and July, 1866.

We, the undersigned, acknowledge to have received from James W. Cummings, paymaster Utah Territory militia, the sums set opposite to our names, in full payment for our services for the time specified.

Number	Names	Rank	Commencement	Expiration	Months	Days	Pay per month	Monthly allowance for clothing	Total monthly pay and allowance	40 cts. per day for horse use and risk of horse and equipment	Total pay and allowance	Signatures	Witnesses
1	Joseph Cluff	Captain	June 10, 1866	July 25, 1866	1	15			$129 50	$18 00	$212 25	Joseph Cluff	James E. Daniels.
1	George W. Haws	1st lieut.	June 10, 1866	July 25, 1866	1	15			112 83	18 00	187 24	G. W. Haws	Do.
1	Elisha G. Goff	2d lieut.	June 10, 1866	July 25, 1866	1	15			112 83	18 00	187 24	E. G. Goff	Do.
2	Ezra H. Curtis	do	June 10, 1866	July 25, 1866	1	15			112 83	18 00	187 24	E. H. Curtis	Do.
1	Oscar Wilkins	Sergeant	June 10, 1866	July 25, 1866	1	15	$17 00	$3 50	20 50	18 00	48 75	Oscar Wilkins	Do.
2	Hyram Pratt	do	June 10, 1866	July 25, 1866	1	15	17 00	3 50	20 50	18 00	48 75	Hyram Pratt	Do.
1	Lewis Lewis	Private	June 10, 1866	July 25, 1866	1	15	13 00	3 50	16 50	18 00	42 75	Lewis Lewis	Do.
2	Abraham Penrod	do	June 10, 1866	July 25, 1866	1	15	13 00	3 50	16 50	18 00	42 75	Abram Penrod	Do.
3	Thomas Vincent	do	June 10, 1866	July 25, 1866	1	15	13 00	3 50	16 50	18 00	42 75	Thos. Vincent	Do.
4	William Brown	do	June 10, 1866	July 25, 1866	1	15	13 00	3 50	16 50	18 00	42 75	Wm. Brown	Do.
5	George Thatcher	do	June 10, 1866	July 25, 1866	1	15	13 00	3 50	16 50	18 00	42 75	Geo. Thatcher	Do.
6	Henry Cluff	do	June 10, 1866	July 25, 1866	1	15	13 00	3 50	16 50	18 00	42 75	Henry Cluff	Do.
7	James W. King	do	June 10, 1866	July 25, 1866	1	15	13 00	3 50	16 50	18 00	42 75	James W. King	Do.
8	Robert Boardman	do	June 10, 1866	July 25, 1866	1	15	13 00	3 50	16 50	18 00	42 75	Robt. Boardman	Do.
9	James Jones	do	June 10, 1866	July 25, 1866	1	15	13 00	3 50	16 50	18 00	42 75	James Jones	Do.
10	George Evans	do	June 10, 1866	July 25, 1866	1	15	13 00	3 50	16 50	18 00	42 75	George Evens	Do.
11	Andrew J. Johnson	do	June 10, 1866	July 25, 1866	1	15	13 00	3 50	16 50	18 00	42 75	J. A. Johnson	Do.
12	Enock Riehins	do	June 10, 1866	July 25, 1866	1	15	13 00	3 50	16 50	18 00	42 75	Enock Riehins	Do.
13	George Elliott	do	June 10, 1866	July 25, 1866	1	15	13 00	3 50	16 50	18 00	42 75	George Elliott	Do.
14	William Nelson	do	June 10, 1866	July 25, 1866	1	15	13 00	3 50	16 50	18 00	42 75	Wm. Nelson	Do.
15	John Baum	do	June 10, 1866	July 25, 1866	1	15	13 00	3 50	16 50	18 00	42 75	John Baum	Do.
16	Elisha Hubbard	do	June 10, 1866	July 25, 1866	1	15	13 00	3 50	16 50	18 00	42 75	Elisha Hubbard	Do.

This company was mustered into service at Provo City, June 10, 1866, by order of Major General Aaron Johnson, and on that day started for Sanpete County; arrived at Fort Gunnison June 14th, and was assigned to duty at Circleville, in

Pay-roll of Captain Frederick Nelson's company —— infantry, Utah Territory militia, employed in the suppression of Indian hostilities in Sanpete County, Utah Territory, from April 1 to November 1, 1866.

We, the undersigned, acknowledge to have received from James W. Cummings, paymaster Utah Territory militia, the sums set opposite to our names, in full payment for our services for the time specified.

Number.	Names.	Rank.	Period of service. Commencement.	Expiration.	Months.	Pay per month.	Monthly allowance for clothing.	Total monthly pay and allowance.	Total pay and allowance.	Signatures.	Witnesses.
1	Frederick Nelson	Captain	April 1, 1866	Nov. 1, 1866	7			$118 50	$829 50	Frederick Neilson	William Morrison.
1	Joseph Page	1st lieutenant	April 1, 1866	Nov. 1, 1866	7			108 50	739 50	Joseph Page	Do.
1	Jens Nielson	2d lieutenant	April 1, 1866	Nov. 1, 1866	7			103 50	724 50	Jens Nilsen	Do.
2	Andrew Flexirom	do	April 1, 1866	Nov. 1, 1866	7			103 50	724 50	Andrew Beehstrom	Do.
2	Jens Jensen	do	April 1, 1866	Nov. 1, 1866	7			103 50	724 50	Jens Jensen	Do.
3	James Hansen	do	April 1, 1866	Nov. 1, 1866	7			103 50	724 50	Jens Hansen	Do.
4	Antone H. Lund	do	April 1, 1866	Nov. 1, 1866	7			103 50	724 50	Anthon H. Lund	Do.
5	August Wall	Sergeant	April 1, 1866	Nov. 1, 1866	7	$17 00	$3 50	20 50	143 50	August Wall	Do.
1	Daniel Baxtrom	do	April 1, 1866	Nov. 1, 1866	7	17 00	3 50	20 50	143 50	Daniel Bicstrom	Do.
2	Andrew Nirlson	do	April 1, 1866	Nov. 1, 1866	7	17 00	3 50	20 50	143 50	Andrew Neilson	Do.
3	Christian Jensen	do	April 1, 1866	Nov. 1, 1866	7	17 00	3 50	20 50	143 50	Christian Jensen	Do.
4	Peter Madsen	do	April 1, 1866	Nov. 1, 1866	7	17 00	3 50	20 50	143 50	Peter Madsen	Do.
5	John Bone	Private	April 1, 1866	Nov. 1, 1866	7	13 00	3 50	16 50	115 50	John Bohn	Do.
1	Oscar Josephson	do	April 1, 1866	Nov. 1, 1866	7	13 00	3 50	16 50	115 50	Oscar Josephson	Do.
2	Olof S. Anderson	do	April 1, 1866	Nov. 1, 1866	7	13 00	3 50	16 50	115 50	Ole S. Andersen	Do.
3	Jens Jensen	do	April 1, 1866	Nov. 1, 1866	7	13 00	3 50	16 50	115 50	Jens Jensen	Do.
4	Johannes Krutsen	do	April 1, 1866	Nov. 1, 1866	7	13 00	3 50	16 50	115 50	Johannes Krutsen	Do.
5	Jens H. Frontwain	do	April 1, 1866	Nov. 1, 1866	7	13 00	3 50	16 50	115 50	Jens H. Transwein	Do.
6	Alina Gabriskie	do	April 1, 1866	Nov. 1, 1866	7	13 00	3 50	16 50	115 50	Alina Gabriskie	Do.
7	Peter Joiansen	do	April 1, 1866	Nov. 1, 1866	7	13 00	3 50	16 50	115 50	Peter Johansen	Do.
8	Rasmus Anderson	do	April 1, 1866	Nov. 1, 1866	7	13 00	3 50	16 50	115 50	Rasmus Anderson	Do.
9	Peter Rasmussen	do	April 1, 1866	Nov. 1, 1866	7	13 00	3 50	16 50	115 50	Peter Rasmussen	Do.
10	Jacob Anderson	do	April 1, 1866	Nov. 1, 1866	7	13 00	3 50	16 50	115 50	Jacob Anderson	Do.
11	Nephi Seeley	do	April 1, 1866	Nov. 1, 1866	7	13 00	3 50	16 50	115 50	Nephi Seely	Do.
12	Hogan Anderson	do	April 1, 1866	Nov. 1, 1866	7	13 00	3 50	16 50	115 50	Hogan Andoson	Do.
13	Andrew Peterson	do	April 1, 1866	Nov. 1, 1866	7	13 00	3 50	16 50	115 50	Andrew Peterson	Do.
14	Jens C. Meiling	do	April 1, 1866	Nov. 1, 1866	7	13 00	3 50	16 50	115 50	Jens C. Milleing	Do.
15	Jens Christiansen, 2d	do	April 1, 1866	Nov. 1, 1866	7	13 00	3 50	16 50	115 50	Jens Christiansen, 2d	Do.
16	Frederick Fieler	do	April 1, 1866	Nov. 1, 1866	7	13 00	3 50	16 50	115 50	Frederick Fieler	Do.
17	Ogen Olsen	do	April 1, 1866	Nov. 1, 1866	7	13 00	3 50	16 50	115 50	Ogen Olsen	Do.
18	Peter Mogensen	do	April 1, 1866	Nov. 1, 1866	7	13 00	3 50	16 50	115 50	Peter Morgenson	Do.
19	Niels Rasmussen	do	April 1, 1866	Nov. 1, 1866	7	13 00	3 50	16 50	115 50	Niels Rasen	Do.
20	Duncan McArthur	do	April 1, 1866	Nov. 1, 1866	7	13 00	3 50	16 50	115 50	Duncan McArthur	Do.
21											

No.	Name		Mustered in	Mustered out						Name	Remarks
23	Bendt Swensen	do.	April 1, 1866	Nov. 1, 1866	7	13 00	3 50	16 50	115 50	Bent Swensen	Do.
24	Melvin McArther	do.	April 1, 1866	Nov. 1, 1866	7	13 00	3 50	16 50	115 50	Melvin McArthur	Do.
25	William Barton	do.	April 1, 1866	Nov. 1, 1866	7	13 00	3 50	16 50	115 50	William G. Barton	Do.
26	Ole Nielsen	do.	April 1, 1866	Nov. 1, 1866	7	13 00	3 50	16 50	115 50	Ole Nielsen	Do.
27	Morony Seely	do.	April 1, 1866	Nov. 1, 1866	7	13 00	3 50	16 50	115 50	Morony Seely	Do.
28	Christian Christiansen	do.	April 1, 1866	Nov. 1, 1866	7	13 00	3 50	16 50	115 50	Christian Christiansen	Do.
29	Carl Johansen	do.	April 1, 1866	Nov. 1, 1866	7	13 00	3 50	16 50	115 50	Carl Jansen	Do.
30	Gustavo Nielsen	do.	April 2, 1866	Nov. 1, 1866	7	13 00	3 50	16 50	115 50	Gustave Nielsen	Do.
31	Rasmus Borggnist	do.	April 1, 1866	Nov. 1, 1866	7	13 00	3 50	16 50	115 50	Rasmus Borgquist	Do.
32	Sylvester Barton	do.	April 1, 1866	Nov. 1, 1866	7	13 00	3 50	16 50	115 50	Sylvester Barton	Do.
33	George Reynolds	do.	April 1, 1866	Nov. 1, 1866	7	13 00	3 50	16 50	115 50	George Reynolds	Do.
34	Benilt Hansen	do.	April 1, 1866	Nov. 1, 1866	7	13 00	3 50	16 50	115 50	Benitt Hansen	Do.
35	Peter Sondergard	do.	April 1, 1866	Nov. 1, 1866	7	13 00	3 50	16 50	115 50	Peder Syndergaard	Do.
36	Hans C. Simpson	do.	April 1, 1866	Nov. 1, 1866	7	13 00	3 50	16 50	115 50	Hans C. Simpson	Do.
37	Jens C. Jensen	do.	April 1, 1866	Nov. 1, 1866	7	13 00	3 50	16 50	115 50	Jens C. Jensen	Do.
38	Niels Hansen	do.	April 1, 1866	Nov. 1, 1866	7	13 00	3 50	16 50	115 50	Niels Hansen	Do.
39	Andrew Jensen	do.	April 1, 1866	Nov. 1, 1866	7	13 00	3 50	16 50	115 50	Andrew Jenson	Do.
40	Soren Jacobsen	do.	April 1, 1866	Nov. 1, 1866	7	13 00	3 50	16 50	115 50	Soren Jacobsen	Do.
41	Frederick Nielsen	do.	April 1, 1866	Nov. 1, 1866	7	13 00	3 50	16 50	115 50	Fredrvick Nielson	Do.
42	Wellington Seeley, jr.	do.	April 1, 1866	Nov. 1, 1866	7	13 00	3 50	16 50	115 50	Wellington Seely, jr.	Do.
43	William Seeley, 2d	do.	April 1, 1866	Nov. 1, 1866	7	13 00	3 50	16 50	115 50	William Seely, 2d	Do.
44	Soren Christiansen	do.	April 1, 1866	Nov. 1, 1866	7	13 00	3 50	16 50	115 50	Soren C. Christiansen	Do.
45	Christian Petersen	do.	April 1, 1866	Nov. 1, 1866	7	13 00	3 50	16 50	115 50	Christian Pedersen	Do.
46	James C. Harbro	do.	April 1, 1866	Nov. 1, 1866	7	13 00	3 50	16 50	115 50	James C. Harbro	Do.
47	Oscar Barton	do.	April 1, 1866	Nov. 1, 1866	7	13 00	3 50	16 50	115 50	Oscar Barton	Do.
48	William Morrison	do.	April 1, 1866	Nov. 1, 1866	7	13 00	3 50	16 50	115 50	William Morrison	Do.
49	Hans P. Hansen	do.	April 1, 1866	Nov. 1, 1866	7	13 00	3 50	16 50	115 50	Hans P. Hansen	Do.
50	John Seely	do.	April 1, 1866	Nov. 1, 1866	7	13 00	3 50	16 50	115 50	John Seely	Do.
51	Bonte Brodersen	do.	April 1, 1866	Nov. 1, 1866	7	13 00	3 50	16 50	115 50	Bonte Brod-rson	Do.
52	Martin Brodersen	do.	April 1, 1866	Nov. 1, 1866	7	13 00	3 50	16 50	115 50	Martin Brodersen	Do.
	Moroni Wheeler	do.	April 1, 1866	Nov. 1, 1866	7	13 00	3 50	16 50	115 50	Moroni Wheeler	Do.

This company was mustered into service at Mount Pleasant, Sanpete County, April 1, 1866, by Brigadier General Warren S. Snow, and assigned to duty by him in the mountains east of said city; they performed regular and daily service for the time specified above, and were mustered out November 1, 1866.

I certify that the above account is correct.

H. B. CLAWSON,
Adjutant General Utah Territory Militia.

Pay-roll of Captain Alva A. Green's company ——— cavalry, Utah Territory militia, employed in the suppression of Indian hostilities in Sanpete and Sevier counties, Utah Territory, in the months of June and July, 1866.

We, the undersigned, acknowledge to have received from James W. Cummings, paymaster of Utah Territory militia, the sums set opposite to our names, in full payment for our services for the time specified.

Number.	Names.	Rank.	Commencement.	Expiration.	Months.	Pay per month.	Monthly allowance for clothing.	Total monthly pay and allowance.	40 cts. per day for use and risk of horse and horse equipment.	Total pay and allowance.	Signatures.	Witnesses.
1	Alva A. Green	Captain	Aug. 7, 1866	Oct. 7, 1866	2			$129 50	$24 00	$353 00	Alva Green	William Greenwood.
1	Laburn L. Fuller	1st lieut.	Aug. 7, 1866	Oct. 7, 1866	2			112 83	24 00	249 66	L. L. Fuller	W. B. Parr.
2	George T. Peay	2d lieut.	Aug. 7, 1866	Oct. 7, 1866	2			112 83	24 00	249 66	Geo. T. Peay	Do.
2	Austin Maybew	do.	Aug. 7, 1866	Oct. 7, 1866	2			112 83	24 00	249 66	Austin Maybew	William Greenwood.
2	Jesse Knight	Sergeant	Aug. 7, 1866	Oct. 7, 1866	2	$17 00		20 50	24 00	65 00	Jesse Knight	W. B. Parr.
1	Stephen Ross	do.	Aug. 7, 1866	Oct. 7, 1866	2	17 00	$2 50	20 50	24 00	63 00	Stephen Ross	Do.
1	Henry Turner	Private	Aug. 7, 1866	Oct. 7, 1866	2	13 00	3 50	16 50	24 00	57 00	Henry Turner	Do.
2	Hyrum Chaff	do.	Aug. 7, 1866	Oct. 7, 1866	2	13 00	3 50	16 50	24 00	57 00	Hyrum Chaff	Do.
3	William Beasley	do.	Aug. 7, 1866	Oct. 7, 1866	2	13 00	3 50	16 50	24 00	57 00	William Beasley	Do.
4	Joseph Clark, jr	do.	Aug. 7, 1866	Oct. 7, 1866	2	13 00	3 50	16 50	24 00	57 00	Joseph Clark, Jr	Do.
5	Asa Avery	do.	Aug. 7, 1866	Oct. 7, 1866	2	13 00	3 50	16 50	24 00	57 00	Asea Avery	Do.
6	Orrace Newell	do.	Aug. 7, 1866	Oct. 7, 1866	2	13 00	3 50	16 50	24 00	57 00	Orrace Newel	Do.
7	Alex. Thornton	do.	Aug. 7, 1866	Oct. 7, 1866	2	13 00	3 50	16 50	24 00	57 00	Alex. Thornton	William Greenwood.
8	Nathaniel Williams	do.	Aug. 7, 1866	Oct. 7, 1866	2	13 00	3 50	16 50	24 00	57 00	Nathaniel Williams	W. B. Parr.
9	B. K. Bullock, jr	do.	Aug. 7, 1866	Oct. 7, 1866	2	13 00	3 50	16 50	24 00	57 00	B. K. Bullock	Do.
10	James Dunn	do.	Aug. 7, 1866	Oct. 7, 1866	2	13 00	3 50	16 50	24 00	57 00	James Dunn	Wm. Greenwood.
11	Robert Debeck	do.	Aug. 7, 1866	Oct. 7, 1866	2	13 00	3 50	16 50	24 00	57 00	Robert Debeck	
12	Stephen Farnsworth	do.	Aug. 7, 1866	Oct. 7, 1866	2	13 00	3 50	16 50	24 00	57 00	Stephen Farnsworth	Do.
13	John Wing	do.	Aug. 7, 1866	Oct. 7, 1866	2	13 00	3 50	16 50	24 00	57 00	John Wing	
14	John Peters	do.	Aug. 7, 1866	Oct. 7, 1866	2	13 00	3 50	16 50	24 00	57 00	John Peters	
15	John Roberts	do.	Aug. 7, 1866	Oct. 7, 1866	2	13 00	3 50	16 50	24 00	57 00	John Roberts	
16	Jacob Cox	do.	Aug. 7, 1866	Oct. 7, 1866	2	13 00	3 50	16 50	24 00	57 00	Jacob Cox	Do.
17	Joseph Shelley	do.	Aug. 7, 1866	Oct. 7, 1866	2	13 00	3 50	16 50	24 00	57 00	Joseph Shelley	
18	David Pearce	do.	Aug. 7, 1866	Oct. 7, 1866	2	13 00	3 50	16 50	24 00	57 00	David Pearce	Do.
19	John Mitchell	do.	Aug. 7, 1866	Oct. 7, 1866	2	13 00	3 50	16 50	24 00	57 00	John Mitchel	Do.
20	George T. Baker	do.	Aug. 7, 1866	Oct. 7, 1866	2	13 00	3 50	16 50	24 00	57 00	George T. Baker	Do.

This company was mustered into service at American Fork, Utah County, August 7, 1866, by order of Lieutenant General Daniel H. Wells, and on that day started on the march for Sanpete County; arrived at Fort Gunnison August 10,

Pay-roll of Captain James Allred's company —— infantry, Utah Territory militia, employed in the suppression of Indian hostilities in Sanpete County, Utah Territory, from April 1 to November 1, 1866.

We, the undersigned, acknowledge to have received from James W. Cunnings, paymaster Utah Territory militia, the sums set opposite to our names, in full payment for our services for the time specified.

Number.	Names.	Rank.	Period of service. Commencement.	Expiration.	Months.	Pay per month.	Monthly allowance for clothing.	Total monthly pay and allowance.	Total pay and allowance.	Signatures.	Witnesses.
1	James M. Allred	Captain	April 1, 1866	Nov. 1, 1866	7	$17 00		$118 56	$829 56	James M. Allred	A. Anderson.
1	Philip Hurst	1st lieutenant	April 1, 1866	Nov. 1, 1866	7	17 00		108 50	759 50	Philip Hurst	Do.
1	Arick Anderson	2d lieutenant	April 1, 1866	Nov. 1, 1866	7	17 00		103 50	724 50	Arick Anderson	W. B. Parr.
2	John A. Vance	do	April 1, 1866	Nov. 1, 1866	7	17 00		103 50	724 50	John A. Vance	A. Anderson.
3	Andrew Nielsen	do	April 1, 1866	Nov. 1, 1866	7	17 00		103 51	724 50	Andrew Nielson	Do.
4	Jens Jenson	do	April 1, 1866	Nov. 1, 1866	7	17 00		103 50	724 50	Jens Jenson	Do.
5	Elias W. Howell	do	April 1, 1866	Nov. 1, 1866	7	17 00		103 50	724 50	Elias W. Howell	Do.
1	John Anderson	Sergeant	April 1, 1866	Nov. 1, 1866	7	17 00	$3 50	20 50	143 50	John Anderson	Do.
2	Louis Jordie	do	April 1, 1866	Nov. 1, 1866	7	17 00	3 50	20 50	143 50	Lewis Jordie	Do.
3	George Denton	do	April 1, 1866	Nov. 1, 1866	7	17 00	3 50	20 51	143 50	George Denton	Do.
4	Andrew Isaamussen	do	April 1, 1866	Nov. 1, 1866	7	17 00	3 50	20 50	143 50	Andrew Isaamusen	Do.
5	William Taylor	do	April 1, 1866	Nov. 1, 1866	7	17 00	3 50	20 50	143 50	William Taylor	Do.
2	James Stewart	Private	April 1, 1866	Nov. 1, 1866	7	13 00	3 50	16 50	115 50	Samuel Gudmanson	Do.
3	John Saline	do	April 1, 1866	Nov. 1, 1866	7	13 00	3 50	16 50	115 50	James Stewart	Do.
4	Isaac N. Wilson	do	April 1, 1866	Nov. 1, 1866	7	13 00	3 50	16 50	115 50	Isae N. Willson	Do.
5	John A. Mower	do	April 1, 1866	Nov. 1, 1866	7	13 00	3 50	16 50	115 50	John Saline	Do.
6	George Graham	do	April 1, 1866	Nov. 1, 1866	7	13 00	3 50	16 20	115 50	George Grahm	Do.
7	Francis Wilson	do	April 1, 1866	Nov. 1, 1866	7	13 00	3 50	16 50	115 50	William Avry	Do.
8	Justice Jordan	do	April 1, 1866	Nov. 1, 1866	7	13 00	3 50	16 50	115 50	Frances Wilson	Do.
9	Warren Brady	do	April 1, 1866	Nov. 1, 1866	7	13 00	3 50	16 50	115 50	Justice Jordan	Do.
10	Hans A. Anderson	do	April 1, 1866	Nov. 1, 1866	7	13 00	3 50	16 50	115 50	Warren B. Brady	Do.
11	Alonzo Vanvalkenburgh	do	April 1, 1866	Nov. 1, 1866	7	13 00	3 50	16 50	115 50	Lars Johanson	Do.
12	William Oliver	do	April 1, 1866	Nov. 1, 1866	7	13 00	3 50	16 50	115 50	Alonzo Vanvalkenburgh	Do.
13	William Zabrookie	do	April 1, 1866	Nov. 1, 1866	7	13 00	3 50	16 50	115 50	William Oliver	William Oliver.
14	Samuel N. B. Pritchett	do	April 1, 1866	Nov. 1, 1866	7	13 00	3 50	16 50	115 50	S. N. B. Pritchott	
15	James Vance	do	April 1, 1866	Nov. 1, 1866	7	13 00	3 50	16 50	115 50	James Vance	S. N. B.
16	George Vance	do	April 1, 1866	Nov. 1, 1866	7	13 00	3 50	16 50	115 50	George H. Vance, his X mark	A. Anderson.
17	Orson Kelsey	do	April 1, 1866	Nov. 1, 1866	7	13 00	3 50	16 50	115 50	Orison Kelsey, his X mark	Do.
18	Lindsay A. Brady	do	April 1, 1866	Nov. 1, 1866	7	13 00	3 50	16 50	115 50	Lindsey A. Brady	Do.
19	Ole Arisen	do	April 1, 1866	Nov. 1, 1866	7	13 00	3 50	16 50	115 50	Ole Arisen	Do.

52	Ole Ogleson	do.	April 1, 1866	Nov. 1, 1866	7	13 00	3 50	16 50	115 50	Lara Larson, his X mark	Do.	
53	Lars Larsen	do.	April 1, 1866	Nov. 1, 1866	7	13 00	3 50	16 50	115 50	Henry Carlson	Do.	
55	Henry Carlson	do.	April 1, 1866	Nov. 1, 1866	7	13 00	3 50	16 50	115 50	Elias Hutchins, his X mark	Do.	
55	Elias Hutchins	do.	April 1, 1866	Nov. 1, 1866	7	13 00	3 50	16 50	115 50	Charles Cruser	Do.	
56	Charles Cruser	do.	April 1, 1866	Nov. 1, 1866	7	13 00	3 50	16 50	115 50	Martin Guyman	Do.	
57	Martin Guyman	do.	April 1, 1866	Nov. 1, 1866	7	13 00	3 50	16 50	115 50	Albert Guyman	Do.	
58	Albert Guyman	do.	April 1, 1866	Nov. 1, 1866	7	13 00	3 50	16 50	115 50	James Jones	Do.	
59	James Jones	do.	April 1, 1866	Nov. 1, 1866	7	13 00	3 50	16 50	115 50	Andrew Petersen	Do.	
30	Andrew Peterson	do.	April 1, 1866	Nov. 1, 1866	7	13 00	3 50	16 50	115 50		Do.	
31	John Carlson	do.	April 1, 1866	Nov. 1, 1866	7	13 00	3 50	16 50	115 50	Benjamin Vance	Do.	
32	Benjamin Vance	do.	April 1, 1866	Nov. 1, 1866	7	13 00	3 50	16 50	115 50	Hans Gulbrandsen	Do.	
33	Hans Gulbrandsen	do.	April 1, 1866	Nov. 1, 1866	7	13 00	3 50	16 50	115 50	Peder Ostensen	Do.	
34	Peter Ostensen	do.	April 1, 1866	Nov. 1, 1866	7	13 00	3 50	16 50	115 50	James Munro	Do.	
35	James Monro	do.	April 1, 1866	Nov. 1, 1866	7	13 00	3 50	16 50	115 50	Orville Cox	Do.	
36	Orville Cox	do.	April 1, 1866	Nov. 1, 1866	7	13 00	3 50	16 50	115 50	Wesley Billes	Do.	
37	Wesley Billes	do.	April 1, 1866	Nov. 1, 1866	7	13 00	3 50	16 50	115 50	Charles Green	Do.	
38	Charles Green	do.	April 1, 1866	Nov. 1, 1866	7	13 00	3 50	16 50	115 50	Nile Andersen, his X mark	Do.	
39	Niels Anderson	do.	April 1, 1866	Nov. 1, 1866	7	13 00	3 50	16 50	115 50	John Thomson	Do.	
40	John Johnson	do.	April 1, 1866	Nov. 1, 1866	7	13 00	3 50	16 50	115 50	William Johnson	Do.	
41	William Johnson	do.	April 1, 1866	Nov. 1, 1866	7	13 00	3 50	16 50	115 50	Noah T. Guyman	Do.	
42	Noah T. Guyman	do.	April 1, 1866	Nov. 1, 1866	7	13 00	3 50	16 50	115 50	Peder N. Hen-on	Do.	
43	Peter N. Hansen	do.	April 1, 1866	Nov. 1, 1866	7	13 00	3 50	16 50	115 50	Andre Christensen	Do.	
44	Andrew Christensen	do.	April 1, 1866	Nov. 1, 1866	7	13 00	3 50	16 50	115 50	Nicla Larsen	Do.	
45	Niels Larsen	do.	April 1, 1866	Nov. 1, 1866	7	13 00	3 50	16 50	115 50	Niels Nielsen	Do.	
46	Niels Nielsen	do.	April 1, 1866	Nov. 1, 1866	7	13 00	3 50	16 50	115 50	Andrew Oelsen, his X mark	John R. Winder,	
47	Andrew Olsen	do.	April 1, 1866	Nov. 1, 1866	7	13 00	3 50	16 50	115 50	Bengamin Lovern	A. Anderson,	
48	Benjamin Lovern	do.	April 1, 1866	Nov. 1, 1866	7	13 00	3 50	16 50	115 50	Louis A. Pine	Do.	
49	Louis A. Pine	do.	April 1, 1866	Nov. 1, 1866	7	13 00	3 50	16 50	115 50	Samuel Bills	Do.	
50	Samuel Bills	do.	April 1, 1866	Nov. 1, 1866	7	13 00	3 50	16 50	115 50			
51	Jacob Bills	do.	April 1, 1866	Nov. 1, 1866	7	13 00	3 50	16 50	115 50			
52	Richard Grahain	do.	April 1, 1866	Nov. 1, 1866	7	13 00	3 50	16 50	115 50	Richard Grahain	Do.	

This company was mustered into service at Fairview, Sanpete County, April 1, 1866, by Brigadier General Warren S. Snow, and by him assigned to duty in the vicinity of Thistle Valley, in the mountains and passes leading into Sanpete Valley. They were in active service every day until mustered out, November 1, 1866.

I certify that the above account is correct.

H. B. CLAWSON,
Adjutant General Nauvoo Legion.

Pay-roll of Captain Daniel Henrie's company ——— infantry, Utah Territory militia, employed in the suppression of Indian hostilities in Sanpete County, Utah Territory, from April 1, 1866, to November 1, 1866.

We, the undersigned, acknowledge to have received from James W. Cummings, paymaster Utah Territory militia, the sums set opposite to our names, in full payment for our services for the time specified.

Number	Names	Rank	Commencement	Expiration	Months	Pay per month	Monthly allowance for clothing	Total monthly pay and allowance	Total pay and allowance	Signatures	Witnesses
1	Daniel Henrie	Captain	April 1, 1866	Nov. 1, 1866	7			$118 50	$829 50	Daniel Henrie	W. T. Reid.
2	John P. Squires	1st lieutenant	April 1, 1866	Nov. 1, 1866	7			118 50	750 50	John P. Squires	Do.
3	John Patten	2d lieutenant	April 1, 1866	Nov. 1, 1866	7			103 50	724 50	John Patten	Do.
4	Alfonzo Wingate	do.	April 1, 1866	Nov. 1, 1866	7			103 50	724 50	Alfonzo Winget	Do.
5	Albert Beach	do.	April 1, 1866	Nov. 1, 1866	7			103 50	724 50	Albert Beach	Do.
6	James C. Brown	do.	April 1, 1866	Nov. 1, 1866	7			103 50	724 50	James C. Brown	Do.
7	John Hall	do.	April 1, 1866	Nov. 1, 1866	7			103 51	724 50	John Hall	Do.
8	James F. Edwards	Sergeant	April 1, 1866	Nov. 1, 1866	7	$17 00	$3 50	20 50	143 50	James F. Edwards	Do.
9	Angus Stocks	do.	April 1, 1866	Nov. 1, 1866	7	17 00	3 50	20 50	143 50	Angus Stocks	Do.
10	Jens Larsen	do.	April 1, 1866	Nov. 1, 1866	7	17 00	3 50	20 50	143 50	Jens Larsen	Do.
11	Soren Nielson	do.	April 1, 1866	Nov. 1, 1866	7	17 00	3 50	20 50	143 50	Soren Nielson	Do.
12	John Lewis	do.	April 1, 1866	Nov. 1, 1866	7	17 00	3 50	20 50	143 50	John Lewis	Do.
13	John Morwick	Private	April 1, 1866	Nov. 1, 1866	7	13 00	3 50	16 50	115 50	John Morwick	Do.
14	Alma Beal	do.	April 1, 1866	Nov. 1, 1866	7	13 00	3 50	16 50	115 50	Alma Beal	Do.
15	John Buchanan	do.	April 1, 1866	Nov. 1, 1866	7	13 00	3 50	16 50	115 50	John Buchanan	Do.
16	Thomas Boyington	do.	April 1, 1866	Nov. 1, 1866	7	13 00	3 50	16 50	115 50	Thomas Boyington	Do.
17	Zenas Winget	do.	April 1, 1866	Nov. 1, 1866	7	13 00	3 50	16 50	115 50	Zenas Winget	Do.
18	George Braithwaite	do.	April 1, 1866	Nov. 1, 1866	7	13 00	3 50	16 50	115 50	George Braithwaite	Do.
19	John Mackay	do.	April 1, 1866	Nov. 1, 1866	7	13 00	3 50	16 50	115 50		Do.
20	Independence Mikesell	do.	April 1, 1866	Nov. 1, 1866	7	13 00	3 50	16 50	115 50	Independence Mikesell	Do.
21	William Rudd	do.	April 1, 1866	Nov. 1, 1866	7	13 00	3 50	16 50	115 50	William Rudd	Do.
22	George E. Beach	do.	April 1, 1866	Nov. 1, 1866	7	13 00	3 50	16 50	115 50	George E. Beach	Do.
23	Isaac Voorhees	do.	April 1, 1866	Nov. 1, 1866	7	13 00	3 50	16 50	115 50	Isaac Voorhees	Do.
24	Anthon Jensen	do.	April 1, 1866	Nov. 1, 1866	7	13 00	3 50	16 50	115 50		Do.
25	William Whiting	do.	April 1, 1866	Nov. 1, 1866	7	13 00	3 50	16 50	115 50	William Whiting	Do.
26	Jeptha Shoemaker	do.	April 1, 1866	Nov. 1, 1866	7	13 00	3 50	16 50	115 50	Jeptha Shoemaker	Do.
27	Samuel Devenport	do.	April 1, 1866	Nov. 1, 1866	7	13 00	3 50	16 50	115 50	Samuel Devenport	Do.
28	Lars C. Kear, jr	do.	April 1, 1866	Nov. 1, 1866	7	13 00	3 50	16 50	115 50	Lars C. Kear, jr	Do.
29	William F. Maylett	do.	April 1, 1866	Nov. 1, 1866	7	13 00	3 50	16 50	115 50	Wm. F. Maylett	Do.
30	Elias Crane	do.	April 1, 1866	Nov. 1, 1866	7	13 00	3 50	16 50	115 50	Elias Crane	Do.
31	Cyrus Winget	do.	April 1, 1866	Nov. 1, 1866	7	13 00	3 50	16 50	115 50	Cyrus Winget	Do.
32	Peter Poulsen	do.	April 1, 1866	Nov. 1, 1866	7	13 00	3 50	16 50	115 50	Peter Poulsen	Do.

No.	Name		Mustered in	Mustered out						Remarks	
21	Joseph Tuttle	do.	April 1, 1866	Nov. 1, 1866	7	13 00	3 50	16 50	115 50	Joseph Tuttle	In.
22	Joseph Snow	do.	April 1, 1866	Nov. 1, 1866	7	13 00	3 50	16 50	115 50	Joseph Snow	In.
23	Sanford Forbush, jr	do.	April 1, 1866	Nov. 1, 1866	7	13 00	3 50	16 50	115 50	Sanford Forbush	In.
24	Hyrum Forbush	do.	April 1, 1866	Nov. 1, 1866	7	13 00	3 50	16 50	115 50	Hyrum Forbush	In.
25	Franklin Spencer	do.	April 1, 1866	Nov. 1, 1866	7	13 00	3 50	16 50	115 50	Franklin Spencer	In.
26	Daniel B. Funk	do.	April 1, 1866	Nov. 1, 1866	7	13 00	3 50	16 50	115 50		
27	Daniel B. Funk, jr	do.	April 1, 1866	Nov. 1, 1866	7	13 00	3 50	16 50	115 50	Samuel Mackay	Do.
28	Samuel Mackay, jr	do.	April 1, 1866	Nov. 1, 1866	7	13 00	3 50	16 50	115 50	Henry Parsons	Do.
29	Henry Parsons	do.	April 1, 1866	Nov. 1, 1866	7	13 00	3 50	16 50	115 50		
30	James Marker	do.	April 1, 1866	Nov. 1, 1866	7	13 00	3 50	16 50	115 50		
31	Joseph Clingman	do.	April 1, 1866	Nov. 1, 1866	7	13 00	3 50	16 50	115 50	Elias Denill	Do.
32	Elias Denill	do.	April 1, 1866	Nov. 1, 1866	7	13 00	3 50	16 50	115 50		
33	Frederick W. Cox, jr	do.	April 1, 1866	Nov. 1, 1866	7	13 00	3 50	16 50	115 50		
34	Michael Jensen	do.	April 1, 1866	Nov. 1, 1866	7	13 00	3 50	16 50	115 50		
35	Nathan Lewis	do.	April 1, 1866	Nov. 1, 1866	7	13 00	3 50	16 50	115 50	Gardner Snow, 2d	Do.
36	Gardner Snow, 2d	do.	April 1, 1866	Nov. 1, 1866	7	13 00	3 50	16 50	115 50	Edwin Cox	Do.
37	Edwin Cox	do.	April 1, 1866	Nov. 1, 1866	7	13 00	3 50	16 50	115 50	Jeremiah Stringham	In.
38	Jeremiah Stringham	do.	April 1, 1866	Nov. 1, 1866	7	13 00	3 50	16 50	115 50	John L. Beach	In.
39	John L. Beach	do.	April 1, 1866	Nov. 1, 1866	7	13 00	3 50	16 50	115 50	Marcus Froelson	Do.
40	Marcus Trawlsen	do.	April 1, 1866	Nov. 1, 1866	7	13 00	3 50	16 50	115 50		
41	John Hannah	do.	April 1, 1866	Nov. 1, 1866	7	13 00	3 50	16 50	115 50		
42	Byron Cox	do.	April 1, 1866	Nov. 1, 1866	7	13 40	3 50	16 50	115 50	Byron Cox	Do.
43	Christen Anderson	do.	April 1, 1866	Nov. 1, 1866	7	13 00	3 50	16 50	115 50		
44	John Stalala	do.	April 1, 1866	Nov. 1, 1866	7	13 40	3 50	16 50	115 50	John Stalala	Do.
45	Dwight Atwool	do.	April 1, 1866	Nov. 1, 1866	7	13 00	3 50	16 50	115 50		
46	John Williams	do.	April 1, 1866	Nov. 1, 1866	7	13 00	3 50	16 50	115 50		
47	John Lowry, Jr	do.	April 1, 1866	Nov. 1, 1866	7	13 00	3 50	16 50	115 50	John Lowry, jr	Do.
48	Richard Hall, jr	do.	April 1, 1866	Nov. 1, 1866	7	13 00	3 50	16 50	115 50		
49	Laskey Shoemaker	do.	April 1, 1866	Nov. 1, 1866	7	13 00	3 50	16 50	115 50	Lahn Homaker	Do.
50	Peter Andersen	do.	April 1, 1866	Nov. 1, 1866	7	13 40	3 50	16 50	115 50	Peter Andersen	Do.
51	Emmanuel Petersen	do.	April 1, 1866	Nov. 1, 1866	7	13 40	3 50	16 50	115 50		
52	Christian Nielson	do.	April 1, 1866	Nov. 1, 1866	7	13 00	3 50	16 50	115 50		

This company was mustered into service at Manto City, Sanpete County, April 1, 1866, by Brigadier General Warren S. Snow, and by him assigned to duty in the mountains and passes east of said city. They were in active service every day until mustered out, November 1, 1866.

I certify that the above account is correct.

H. B. CLAWSON,
Adjutant General Nauvoo Legion.

Pay-roll of Captain Abraham G. Conover's company —— cavalry, Utah Territory militia, employed in the suppression of Indian hostilities in Sanpete and Sevier counties, Utah Territory, in the months of May, June, and July, 1866.

We, the undersigned, acknowledge to have received from James W. Cummings, paymaster Utah Territory militia, the sums set opposite to our names, in full payment for our services for the time specified.

Number	Names	Rank	Commencement	Expiration	Months	Days	Pay per month	Monthly allowance for clothing	Total monthly pay and allowance	40 cts. per day for use and risk of horse and horse equipment	Total pay and allowance	Signatures	Witnesses
1	Abraham G. Conover	Captain	May 1, 1866	July 18, 1866	2	19			$119 50	$31 60	$372 22	A. G. Conover	A. F. Macdonald.
1	John Leetham	1st lieutenant	May 1, 1866	July 18, 1866	2	19			112 83	31 60	325 38	John Leetham	Do.
1	Henry Rodgers	2d lieutenant	May 1, 1866	July 18, 1866	2	19			112 83	31 60	325 38	Henry Rodgers	Do.
2	Alonzo Farnsworth	do.	May 1, 1866	July 18, 1866	2	19			112 83	31 60	325 38	Alonzo Farnsworth	William Greenwood.
3	John H. Noakes	do.	May 1, 1866	July 18, 1866	2	19			112 83	31 60	325 38	John H. Noakes	A. F. Macdonald.
4	Samuel M. Hicks	do.	May 1, 1866	July 18, 1866	2	19			112 83	31 60	325 38	S. M. Hicks	Do.
5	Horatio Calkin	do.	May 1, 1866	July 18, 1866	2	19			112 83	31 60	325 38	Horatio Calking	William Heaton.
1	William H. Gray	Sergeant	May 1, 1866	July 18, 1866	2	19	$17 00	$3 50	20 50	31 60	85 58	Wm. H. Gray	A. F. Macdonald.
2	Moroni Pratt	do.	May 1, 1866	July 18, 1866	2	19	17 00	3 50	20 50	31 60	85 58	Moroni Pratt	J. Evans.
3	Theodore M. Medina	do.	May 1, 1866	July 18, 1866	2	19	17 00	3 50	20 50	31 60	85 58	J. M. Medina	A. F. Macdonald.
4	James Lamb	do.	May 1, 1866	July 18, 1866	2	19	17 00	3 50	20 50	31 60	85 58	James Lamb	J. Evans.
5	Joseph H. Wright	Bugler	May 1, 1866	July 18, 1866	2	19	13 00	3 50	16 50	31 60	75 05	Joseph H. Wright	A. F. Macdonald.
1	Charles Stephenson	Private	May 1, 1866	July 18, 1866	2	19	13 00	3 50	16 50	31 60	75 05	Charles Stevenson	Do.
2	Daniel Vincent	do.	May 1, 1866	July 18, 1866	2	19	13 00	3 50	16 50	31 60	75 05	Dan'l Vincent, his + mark	Do.
3	Lorin S. Glazier	do.	May 1, 1866	July 18, 1866	2	19	13 00	3 50	16 50	31 60	75 05	Loren S. Glazier	Do.
4	John Twelves	do.	May 1, 1866	July 18, 1866	2	19	13 00	3 50	16 50	31 60	75 05	John Twelves	Do.
5	Joseph Rogers	do.	May 1, 1866	July 18, 1866	2	19	13 00	3 50	16 50	31 60	75 05	Joseph Rogers	Do.
6	William Gannon	do.	May 1, 1866	July 18, 1866	2	19	13 00	3 50	16 50	31 60	75 05	William Gannon	Do.
7	William Strong	do.	May 1, 1866	July 18, 1866	2	19	13 00	3 50	16 50	31 60	75 05	Wm. Strong	Do.
8	Albert Haws	do.	May 1, 1866	July 18, 1866	2	19	13 00	3 50	16 50	31 60	75 05	Albert Haws	Do.
9	Joel A. Bascom	do.	May 1, 1866	July 18, 1866	2	19	13 00	3 50	16 50	31 60	75 05	J. A. Bascom	Do.
10	Samuel Cluff	do.	May 1, 1866	July 18, 1866	2	19	13 00	3 50	16 50	31 60	75 05	Samuel Cluff	Do.
11	William J. Taylor	do.	May 1, 1866	July 18, 1866	2	19	13 00	3 50	16 50	31 60	75 05	W. J. Taylor	J. Evans.
12	Robert Cobley	do.	May 1, 1866	July 18, 1866	2	19	13 00	3 50	16 50	31 60	75 05	Robert Cobley	Do.
13	Thomas Fowler	do.	May 1, 1866	July 18, 1866	2	19	13 00	3 50	16 50	31 60	75 05	Thomas Fowler	Do.
14	Matias Peterson	do.	May 1, 1866	July 18, 1866	2	19	13 00	3 50	16 50	31 60	75 05	Matias Peterson	Do.
15	Evander White	do.	May 1, 1866	July 18, 1866	2	19	13 00	3 50	16 50	31 60	75 05	Evander White	Do.
16	Robert Fox	do.	May 1, 1866	July 18, 1866	2	19	13 00	3 50	16 50	31 60	75 05	Robert Fox	Do.
17	John Kraus	do.	May 1, 1866	July 18, 1866	2	19	13 00	3 50	16 50	31 60	75 05	John Kraus	Do.
18	Albert Marsh	do.	May 1, 1866	July 18, 1866	2	19	13 00	3 50	16 50	31 60	75 05	Albert Marsh	Do.
19	Henry Moyle	do.	May 1, 1866	July 18, 1866	2	19	13 00	3 50	16 50	31 60	75 05	Henry Moyle	Do.
20	Robert Loder	do.	May 1, 1866	July 18, 1866	2	19	13 00	3 50	16 50	31 60	75 05	Robert Loder	William Greenwood.
21	George Williams	do.	May 1, 1866	July 18, 1866	2	19	13 00	3 50	16 50	31 60	75 05	George Williams	A. F. Macdonald.

No.	Names		When enrolled	When mustered into service							Names	By whom mustered
21	Henry Curtis	do.	May 1, 1866	July 18, 1866	19	13 00	3 50	16 50	31 60	75 05	Henry Curtis	Do.
22	William Tumbridge	do.	May 1, 1866	July 18, 1866	19	13 00	3 50	16 50	31 60	75 05	William Tumbridge	Do.
23	*Henry Jennings	do.	May 1, 1866	July 18, 1866	19	13 00	3 50	16 50	31 60	75 05	Henry Jennings	Do.
24	Ewall Stewart	do.	May 1, 1866	July 18, 1866	19	13 00	3 50	16 50	31 60	75 05	Ewell Stewart	Do.
25	William Hull	do.	May 1, 1866	July 18, 1866	19	13 00	3 50	16 50	31 60	75 05	William Hull	Do.
26	Eliel Curtis	do.	May 1, 1866	July 18, 1866	19	13 00	3 50	16 50	31 60	75 05	Eliel Curtis	Do.
27	William Johnson	do.	May 1, 1866	July 18, 1866	19	13 00	3 50	16 50	31 60	75 05	William Johnson	J. Evans.
28	Henry Miller	do.	May 1, 1866	July 18, 1866	19	13 00	3 50	16 50	31 60	75 05	Henry Miller	William Greenwood.
29	Niel Christensen	do.	May 1, 1866	July 18, 1866	19	13 00	3 50	16 50	31 60	75 05	Niel Christsen	Do.
30	Brigham Ney	do.	May 1, 1866	July 18, 1866	19	13 00	3 50	16 50	31 60	75 05	Brigham Ney	A. F. Macdonald.
31	Edward P. Thomas	do.	May 1, 1866	July 18, 1866	19	13 00	3 50	16 50	31 60	75 05	Edward P. Thomas	Do.
32	John Jones	do.	May 1, 1866	July 18, 1866	19	13 00	3 50	16 50	31 60	75 05	John Jones	Do.
33	John Hoton	do.	May 1, 1866	July 18, 1866	19	13 00	3 50	16 50	31 60	75 05	John Hoton	Do.
34	Alfred R. Beck	do.	May 1, 1866	July 18, 1866	19	13 00	3 50	16 50	31 60	75 05	Alfred R. Beck	Do.
35	John Rockhill	do.	May 1, 1866	July 18, 1866	19	13 00	3 50	16 50	31 60	75 05	John Rockhill	J. Evans.
36	Hensen Walker	do.	May 1, 1866	July 18, 1866	19	13 00	3 50	16 50	31 60	75 05	Hensen Walker	William Heaton.
37	Mathew Daley	do.	May 1, 1866	July 18, 1866	19	13 40	3 50	16 50	31 60	75 05	Mathew Daley	Do.
38	William Loveless	do.	May 1, 1866	July 18, 1866	19	13 00	3 50	16 50	31 60	75 05	William Loveless	Do.
39	John H. Moore, Jr.	do.	May 1, 1866	July 18, 1866	19	13 00	3 50	16 50	31 60	75 05	John H. Moore, Jr.	Do.
40	James L. Scarled	do.	May 1, 1866	July 18, 1866	19	13 00	3 50	16 50	31 60	75 05	James L. Scarles	Do.
41	Elijah Hancock	do.	May 1, 1866	July 18, 1866	19	13 00	3 50	16 50	31 60	75 05	Elijah Hancock	Do.
42	Alma Bagley	do.	May 1, 1866	July 18, 1866	19	13 00	3 50	16 50	31 60	75 05	Alma Bagley	Do.
43	John Reed	do.	May 1, 1866	July 18, 1866	19	13 00	3 50	16 50	31 60	75 05	John Reel	Do.
44	Peter Winward	do.	May 1, 1866	July 18, 1866	19	13 00	3 50	16 50	31 60	75 05	Peter Winward	Do.
45	John Kay	do.	May 1, 1866	July 18, 1866	19	13 00	3 50	16 50	31 60	75 03	John Kay	Do.
46	Henry Elmere	do.	May 1, 1866	July 18, 1866	19	13 00	3 50	16 50	31 60	75 05	Henry Elmero	Do.
47	John Tuner	do.	May 1, 1866	July 18, 1866	19	13 00	3 50	16 50	31 60	75 05	John Tuner	Do.
48	Moroni Manwill	do.	May 1, 1866	July 18, 1866	19	13 00	3 50	16 50	31 60	75 05	Moroni Manwill	Do.
49	Amasa Potter	do.	May 1, 1866	July 18, 1866	19	13 00	3 50	16 20	31 60	75 05	Amasa Potter	Do.
50	Amos Warren	do.	May 1, 1866	July 18, 1866	19	13 00	3 50	16 50	31 60	75 05	Amos Warren	A. F. Macdonald.

*Wounded in battle at Gravelly Ford.

This company was mustered into service at Provo City, May 1, 1866, by order of Lieutenant General D. H. Wells, and on that day started for Sanpete County; arrived at Manti May 4, 1866, and was assigned to duty at Selina, in the Sevier Valley; was in active service ten days, and then sent to Circleville, Sevier County; remained here thirty days, and returned to Fort Gunnison, and was assigned to duty again at Selina and vicinity; and on the tenth day of June fought a severe battle for four hours with the Indians at Gravelly Ford; continued in active service until the expiration of the time above stated; returned and was mustered out at Provo City, July 18, 1866.

I certify that the above account is correct.

H. B. CLAWSON,
Adjutant General Utah Territory Militia.

Pay-roll of Captain John Tuttle's company —— infantry, Utah Territory militia, employed in the suppression of Indian hostilities in Sanpete County, Utah Territory, from April 1, 1866, to November 1, 1866.

We, the undersigned, acknowledge to have received from James W. Cummings, paymaster Utah Territory militia, the sums set opposite to our names, in full payment for our services for the time specified.

Number.	Names.	Rank.	Commencement.	Expiration.	Months.	Pay per month.	Monthly allowance for clothing.	Total monthly pay and allowance.	Total pay and allowance.	Signatures.	Witnesses.
1	John Tuttle	Captain	April 1, 1866	Nov. 1, 1866	7			$118 50	$829 50	John H. Tuttle	Luther Tuttle,
1	Erick Ludrickson	1st lieutenant	April 1, 1866	Nov. 1, 1866	7			108 50	759 50	Erick Ludrigson	Do.
1	James Crawford	2d lieutenant	April 1, 1866	Nov. 1, 1866	7			103 50	724 50	James Crawford	Do.
2	Yeace Hansen	do	April 1, 1866	Nov. 1, 1866	7			103 50	724 50	Yence Hansen	Do.
3	Peter Marker	do	April 1, 1866	Nov. 1, 1866	7			103 50	724 50	Peter Marker	Do.
4	Niels C. Enburgh	do	April 1, 1866	Nov. 1, 1866	7			103 50	724 50	Niels C. Enburgh	Do.
5	Peter Mickelson	do	April 1, 1866	Nov. 1, 1866	7			103 50	724 50	Peter Mickelson	Do.
1	Christian Yensen	Sergeant	April 1, 1866	Nov. 1, 1866	7	$17 00	3 50	20 50	143 50	Christian Jensen	Do.
2	Jeace Christiansen	do	April 1, 1866	Nov. 1, 1866	7	17 00	3 50	20 50	143 50	Jeace Christiansen	Do.
3	Hanson Dennison	do	April 1, 1866	Nov. 1, 1866	7	17 00	3 50	20 50	143 50	Hans Dienesen	Do.
4	Christianson Peterson	do	April 1, 1866	Nov. 1, 1866	7	17 00	3 50	20 50	143 50	Christen Peterson	Do.
5	Christian Barnson	do	April 1, 1866	Nov. 1, 1866	7	17 00	3 50	20 50	143 50	Christian Berensen	Do.
1	David Shand	Private	April 1, 1866	Nov. 1, 1866	7	13 00	3 50	16 50	115 50	David Shand	Do.
2	Robert Johnson	do	April 1, 1866	Nov. 1, 1866	7	13 00	3 50	16 50	115 50	John N. Wilson	Do.
3	John Wilson	do	April 1, 1866	Nov. 1, 1866	7	13 00	3 50	16 50	115 50	Jens Dienesen	Do.
4	Yence Dennison	do	April 1, 1866	Nov. 1, 1866	7	13 00	3 50	16 50	115 50	William Beams	Do.
5	William Beams	do	April 1, 1866	Nov. 1, 1866	7	13 00	3 50	16 50	115 50	Samuel Ware	Do.
6	Samuel Ware	do	April 1, 1866	Nov. 1, 1866	7	13 00	3 50	16 50	115 50	Delen Cox	Do.
7	Delon Cox	do	April 1, 1866	Nov. 1, 1866	7	13 00	3 50	16 50	115 50	Brig. Casto	Do.
8	Brigham Casto	do	April 1, 1866	Nov. 1, 1866	7	13 00	3 50	16 50	115 50	James Hannah	Do.
9	James Hannah	do	April 1, 1866	Nov. 1, 1866	7	13 00	3 50	16 50	115 50	Lars Madsen	Do.
10	Lewis Mason	do	April 1, 1866	Nov. 1, 1866	7	13 00	3 50	16 50	115 50	George Casto	Do.
11	George Casto	do	April 1, 1866	Nov. 1, 1866	7	13 00	3 50	16 50	115 50	Jens Nielsen	Do.
12	Yvace Nielson	do	April 1, 1866	Nov. 1, 1866	7	13 00	3 50	16 50	115 50		Do.
13	Hans Dennison	do	April 1, 1866	Nov. 4, 1866	7	13 00	3 50	16 50	115 50		Do.
14	Fredrick E. Miller	do	April 1, 1866	Nov. 1, 1866	7	13 00	3 50	16 50	115 50	Friedrich Miller	Do.
15	Ola Larson	do	April 1, 1866	Nov. 1, 1866	7	13 00	3 50	16 50	115 50	Ola Larson	Do.
16	Peter C. Larson	do	April 1, 1866	Nov. 1, 1866	7	13 00	3 50	16 50	115 50	Peter C. Larson	Do.
17	Ola Nielson	do	April 1, 1866	Nov. 1, 1866	7	13 00	3 50	16 50	115 50	Ole Nielsen	Do.
18	Jacob Nielson	do	April 1, 1866	Nov. 1, 1866	7	13 00	3 50	16 50	115 50		
19	Peter Monk	do	April 1, 1866	Nov. 1, 1866	7	13 00	3 50	16 50	115 50	Peter Monk	Do

No.	Name		Enlisted	Discharged						Name	Remarks
20	Frederick C. Hansen	do.	April 1, 1866	Nov. 1, 1866	7	13 00	3 50	16 50	115 50	Frederick C. Hansen	Do.
21	Peter Mickelson	do.	April 1, 1866	Nov. 1, 1866	7	13 00	3 50	16 50	115 50	Robert Braithwaite	Do.
22	Robert Braithwaite	do.	April 1, 1866	Nov. 1, 1866	7	13 00	3 50	16 50	115 50	George Johnson	Do.
23	George Johnson	do.	April 1, 1866	Nov. 1, 1866	7	13 00	3 50	16 50	115 50	Hans Ottosen	Do.
24	Hance Otsen	do.	April 1, 1866	Nov. 1, 1866	7	13 00	3 50	16 50	115 50		
25	Joseph Smith	do.	April 1, 1866	Nov. 1, 1866	7	13 00	3 50	16 50	115 50	Fredric Gess	Do.
26	Fredrick Gess	do.	April 1, 1866	Nov. 1, 1866	7	13 00	3 50	16 50	115 50	Samuel Marlol	Do.
27	Samuel Marlol	do.	April 1, 1866	Nov. 1, 1866	7	13 00	3 50	16 50	115 50	David Johnson	Do.
28	David Johnson	do.	April 1, 1866	Nov. 1, 1866	7	13 00	3 50	16 50	115 50	John Alder	Do.
29	John Alder	do.	April 1, 1866	Nov. 1, 1866	7	13 00	3 50	16 50	115 50	Hance Hansen	Do.
30	Hance Hansen	do.	April 1, 1866	Nov. 1, 1866	7	13 00	3 50	16 50	115 50	Joseph Braithwaite	Do.
31	Joseph Braithwaite	do.	April 1, 1866	Nov. 1, 1866	7	13 00	3 50	16 50	115 50	Jorgen Madsen	Do.
32	Yorgen Museum	do.	April 1, 1866	Nov. 1, 1866	7	13 00	3 50	16 50	115 50		
33	Robert Christianson	do.	April 1, 1866	Nov. 1, 1866	7	13 00	3 50	16 50	115 50	Robert Johnston	Do.
34	Robert Johnson, jr	do.	April 1, 1866	Nov. 1, 1866	7	13 00	3 50	16 50	115 50	Peter Smith	Do.
35	Yence Mullen	do.	April 1, 1866	Nov. 1, 1866	7	13 00	3 50	16 50	115 50	Mats Matsen	Do.
36	Peter Smith	do.	April 1, 1866	Nov. 1, 1866	7	13 00	3 50	16 50	115 50	Hans Madsen	Do.
37	Mads Madsen	do.	April 1, 1866	Nov. 1, 1866	7	13 00	3 50	16 50	115 50	Hyrem Chapman	Do.
38	Hans Museum, 1st	do.	April 1, 1866	Nov. 1, 1866	7	13 00	3 50	16 50	115 50	Levi Chapman	Do.
39	Hyram Chapman	do.	April 1, 1866	Nov. 1, 1866	7	13 00	3 50	16 50	115 50	Nathan Lewis, jr	Do.
40	Levi Chapman	do.	April 1, 1866	Nov. 1, 1866	7	13 00	3 50	16 50	115 50	Lyman Beach	Do.
41	Nathan Lewis, jr	do.	April 1, 1866	Nov. 1, 1866	7	13 00	3 50	16 50	115 50	Charles O. Larko	Do.
42	Lyman Beach	do.	April 1, 1866	Nov. 1, 1866	7	13 00	3 50	16 50	115 50	Ole Peterson	Do.
43	Charles O. Larko	do.	April 1, 1866	Nov. 1, 1866	7	13 00	3 50	16 50	115 50		
44	Ola Peterson	do.	April 1, 1866	Nov. 1, 1866	7	13 00	3 50	16 50	115 50		
45	Hans Hansen, 2d	do.	April 1, 1866	Nov. 1, 1866	7	13 00	3 50	16 50	115 50	Jens Hansen	Do.
46	Yence Hansen, 2d	do.	April 1, 1866	Nov. 1, 1866	7	13 00	3 50	16 50	115 50	Jorgen Christensen	Do.
47	Yorgen Christiansen	do.	April 1, 1866	Nov. 1, 1866	7	13 00	3 50	16 50	115 50	Reuben Dewitt	Do.
48	Reuben Dewitt	do.	April 1, 1866	Nov. 1, 1866	7	13 00	3 50	16 50	115 50		
49	Ethelbert Barton	do.	April 1, 1866	Nov. 1, 1866	7	13 00	3 50	16 50	115 50	Henry Cook, X	Do.
50	Henry Cook	do.	April 1, 1866	Nov. 1, 1866	7	13 00	3 50	16 50	115 50	Geo. Peacock, X	Do.
51	George Peacock, jr	do.	April 1, 1866	Nov. 1, 1866	7	13 00	3 50	16 50	115 50	Joseph Wilson	Do.
52	Joseph Wilson	do.	April 1, 1866	Nov. 1, 1866	7	13 00	3 50	16 50	115 50	Wm. Larke	Do.
53	William Lurke	do.	April 1, 1866	Nov. 1, 1866	7	13 00	3 50	16 50	115 50	Neels Hansen	Do.
54	Neils Hansen	do.	April 1, 1866	Nov. 1, 1866	7	13 00	3 50	16 50	115 50	Selah Atwood	Do.
55	Seiah Atwood	do.	April 1, 1866	Nov. 1, 1866	7	13 00	3 50	16 50	115 50		

This company was mustered into service at Manti City, Sanpete County, April 1, 1866, by Brigadier General Warren S. Snow, and by him assigned to duty in the mountains and passes, for the protection of the city and its inhabitants. They performed regular service every day for the time specified above, and were mustered out November 1, 1866.

I certify that the above account is correct.

H. B. CLAWSON,
Adjutant General Utah Territory Militia.

Pay-roll of Captain Jonathan S. Page's company —— cavalry, Utah Territory militia, employed in the suppression of Indian hostilities in Payson, Pondtown, and Santaquin, Utah County, in the months of May, June, and July, 1866.

We, the undersigned, acknowledge to have received from James W. Cummings, paymaster Utah Territory militia, the sums set opposite to our names, in full payment for our services for the time specified.

Number	Names	Rank	Commencement	Expiration	Months	Days	Pay per month	Monthly allowance for clothing	Total monthly pay and allowance	40 cts. per day for use and risk of horse and horse equipment	Total pay and allowance	Signatures	Witnesses
1	Jonathan S. Page	Captain	May 11, 1866	July 2, 1866	1	21	$17 00		$129 50	$29 40	$240 55	Jonathan S. Page	William Heaton
1	Russell Kelley	1st lieutenant	May 11, 1866	July 2, 1866	1	21	17 00		112 83	20 40	212 21	Russel Kelley	Do.
1	James Manwell	2d lieutenant	May 11, 1866	July 2, 1866	1	21	17 00		112 83	20 40	212 21	James Manwell	Do.
2	Samuel Peery	do	May 11, 1866	July 2, 1866	1	21	17 00		112 83	20 40	212 21	Samuel Peery	Do.
3	Horatio Calkin	do	May 11, 1866	July 2, 1866	1	21	17 00		112 83	20 40	212 21	Horatio Calkin	Do.
4	Joseph Daniels	do	May 11, 1866	July 2, 1866	1	21	17 00		112 83	20 40	212 21	Joseph Daniels	Do.
5	John C. Searle	Sergeant	May 11, 1866	July 2, 1866	1	21	17 00		112 83	20 40	212 21	John C. Searle	Do.
1	George S. Rust	do	May 11, 1866	July 2, 1866	1	21	13 00	$3 50	20 50	20 40	55 95	Geo. S. Rust	Do.
2	Joseph H. Wright	do	May 11, 1866	July 2, 1866	1	21	13 00	3 50	20 50	20 40	55 95	Joseph H. Wright	Do.
3	Charles B. Oliver	do	May 11, 1866	July 2, 1866	1	21	13 00	3 50	20 50	20 40	55 25	Charles B. Oliver	Do.
1	Warren S. Pace	Private	May 11, 1866	July 2, 1866	1	21	13 00	3 50	16 50	20 40	55 25	Warren S. Pace	Do.
2	George S. Todd	do	May 11, 1866	July 2, 1866	1	21	13 00	3 50	16 50	20 40	48 45	George Todd	Do.
3	Thomas Wimmer	do	May 11, 1866	July 2, 1866	1	21	13 00	3 50	16 50	20 40	48 45	Thomas Wimmer	Do.
4	Benjamin F. Stewart	do	May 11, 1866	July 2, 1866	1	21	13 00	3 50	16 50	20 40	48 45	B. F. Stewart	Do.
5	Ammon Nebeker	do	May 11, 1866	July 2, 1866	1	21	13 00	3 50	16 50	20 40	48 45	Ammon Nebeker	Do.
6	Smith Tanner	do	May 11, 1866	July 2, 1866	1	21	13 00	3 50	16 50	20 40	48 45	W. S. Tanner	Do.
7	Henry Fairbanks	do	May 11, 1866	July 2, 1866	1	21	13 00	3 50	16 50	20 40	48 45	Henry Fairbanks	Do.
8	Daniel Manwell	do	May 11, 1866	July 2, 1866	1	21	13 00	3 50	16 50	20 40	48 45		Do.
9	Matthew Daley	do	May 11, 1866	July 2, 1866	1	21	13 00	3 50	16 50	20 40	48 45	Mathew Daley	Do.
10	John H. Moore, Jr	do	May 21, 1866	July 2, 1866	1	21	13 00	3 50	16 50	20 40	48 45	John H. Moore, jr	Do.
11	Henry Elmore	do	May 11, 1866	July 2, 1866	1	21	13 00	3 50	16 50	20 40	48 45	Henry Elmore	Do.
12	William Loveless	do	May 11, 1866	July 2, 1866	1	21	13 00	3 50	16 50	20 40	48 45	William Loveless	Do.
13	Elijah Hancock	do	May 11, 1866	July 2, 1866	1	21	13 00	3 50	16 50	20 40	48 43	Elijah Hancock	Do.
14	Lafayette Searle	do	May 11, 1866	July 2, 1866	1	21	13 00	3 50	16 50	20 40	48 45	Laffayette Searle	Do.
15	John Kreel	do	May 11, 1866	July 2, 1866	1	21	13 00	3 50	16 50	20 40	48 45	John Kreel	Do.
16	John Kay	do	May 11, 1866	July 2, 1866	1	21	13 00	3 50	16 50	20 40	48 45	John Kay	Do.
17	Alma Bagley	do	May 11, 1866	July 2, 1866	1	21	13 00	3 50	16 50	20 40	48 45	Alma Bayley	Do.
18	John Douglas	do	May 11, 1866	July 2, 1866	1	21	13 00	3 50	16 50	20 40	48 45	Wm. John Douglass	Do.
20	John Burr	do	May 11, 1866	July 2, 1866	1	21	13 00	3 50	16 50	20 40	48 45	John Burr	Do.
21	John Wimmer	do	May 11, 1866	July 2, 1866	1	21	13 00	3 50	16 50	20 40	48 45	John Wimmer	Do.
22	Charles Hancock	do	May 11, 1866	July 2, 1866	1	21	13 00	3 50	16 50	20 40	48 45	Charles Hancock	Do.

			Mustered in	Mustered out								
23	O. M. Manwell	do	May 11, 1866	July 2, 1866	1 21	13 00	3 50	16 50	20 40	48 45	O. M. Manwell	Do.
24	Israel Calkins	do	May 11, 1866	July 2, 1866	1 21	13 00	3 50	16 50	20 40	48 45	Israel Calkins	Do.
25	Bradley Wilson	do	May 11, 1866	July 2, 1866	1 21	13 00	3 50	16 50	20 40	48 45	Bradley Wilson	Do.
26	Heber Reed	do	May 11, 1866	July 2, 1866	1 21	13 00	3 50	16 50	20 40	48 45	Heber Reed	Do.
27	Solomon Hancock	do	May 11, 1866	July 2, 1866	1 21	13 00	3 50	16 50	20 40	48 45	Solomon Hancock	Do.
28	Joseph Tanner	do	May 11, 1866	July 2, 1866	1 21	13 00	3 50	16 50	20 40	48 45	Joseph Tanner	Do.
29	Joseph Whighthead	do	May 11, 1866	July 2, 1866	1 21	13 00	3 50	16 50	20 40	48 45	Joseph Whit-head	Do.
30	Daniel Tanner	do	May 11, 1866	July 2, 1866	1 21	13 00	3 50	16 50	20 40	48 45	Daniel Tanner	Do.
31	Delmot Webb	do	May 11, 1866	July 2, 1866	1 21	13 00	3 50	16 50	20 40	48 45	Delmot Webb	Do.
32	Lewis White	do	May 11, 1866	July 2, 1866	1 21	13 00	3 50	16 50	20 40	48 45	Lewis White	Do.
33	William Wimmer	do	May 11, 1866	July 2, 1866	1 21	13 00	3 50	16 50	20 40	48 45	W. D. Wimmer	Do.
34	John Tanner	do	May 11, 1866	July 2, 1866	1 21	13 00	3 50	16 50	20 40	48 45	John Tanner	Do.

This company was mustered into service at Payson, Utah County, May 11, 1866, by order of Major General Aaron Johnson, and assigned to duty by him in the eastern mountains and passes, for the protection of the southern settlements in Utah County, viz., Pondtown, Payson, and Santaquin; they were in active service every day, until mustered out at Payson, July 2, 1866.

I certify that the above account is correct.

H. B. CLAWSON,
Adjutant General Utah Territory Militia.

Pay-roll of Captain Niels C. Christiansen's company —— infantry, Utah Territory militia, employed in the suppression of Indian hostilities in Sanpete County, Utah Territory, from April 1, 1866, to November 1, 1866.

We, the undersigned, acknowledge to have received from James W. Cummings, paymaster Utah Territory militia, the sums set opposite to our names, in full payment for our services for the time specified.

Number.	Names.	Rank.	Commencement.	Expiration.	Months.	Pay per month.	Monthly allowance for clothing.	Total monthly pay and allowance.	Total pay and allowance.	Signatures.	Witnesses.
1	Niels C. Christiansen	Captain	April 1, 1866	Nov. 1, 1866	7	----	$3 50	$118 50	$829 50	Niels Chs. Christianson	H. F. Peterson.
1	Robert Olsen	1st lieutenant	April 1, 1866	Nov. 1, 1866	7	----	3 50	108 50	759 50	Rasmus Ol-on	Do.
1	Jens M. Lyon	2d lieutenant	April 1, 1866	Nov. 1, 1866	7	----	3 50	103 50	724 50	Jem M. Lyon	Do.
2	Jens T. Bell	do	April 1, 1866	Nov. 1, 1866	7	----	3 50	103 50	724 50	Jens Thomsen Balle	Do.
3	Stephen Williams	do	April 1, 1866	Nov. 1, 1866	7	----	3 50	103 50	724 50	Stephen Williams	Do.
4	Christian A. Thorum	do	April 1, 1866	Nov. 1, 1866	7	----	3 50	103 50	724 50	Christen A. Thorm	Do.
5	Andrew L. Jensen	do	April 1, 1866	Nov. 1, 1866	7	----	3 50	103 50	724 50	Ander Jensan Langavo	Do.
6	Soren H. Larsen	Sergeant	April 1, 1866	Nov. 1, 1866	7	$17 00	3 50	20 50	143 50	Soren H. Larsen	Do.
3	Jens A. Oveson	do	April 1, 1866	Nov. 1, 1866	7	17 00	3 50	20 50	143 50	J. A. Oveson	Do.
4	Hans Hansen	do	April 1, 1866	Nov. 1, 1866	7	17 00	3 50	20 50	143 50	Hans Hausen	Do.
5	Hans A. Hansen	do	April 1, 1866	Nov. 1, 1866	7	17 00	3 50	20 50	143 50	Hans A. Hansen	Do.
6	Peter Petersen	do	April 1, 1866	Nov. 1, 1866	7	17 00	3 50	20 50	143 50	Peter Peterson	Do.
7	John Larsen	Private	April 1, 1866	Nov. 1, 1866	7	13 00	3 50	16 50	115 50		Do.
8	Bent Malingreen	do	April 1, 1866	Nov. 1, 1866	7	13 00	3 50	16 50	115 50		Do.
9	Abraham Hansen	do	April 1, 1866	Nov. 1, 1866	7	13 00	3 50	16 50	115 50	Abrahm Hansen	Do.
4	Johan A. Jensen	do	April 1, 1866	Nov. 1, 1866	7	13 00	3 50	16 50	115 50	John A. Jensen	Do.
5	Jesse Rosengreen	do	April 1, 1866	Nov. 1, 1866	7	13 00	3 50	16 50	115 50	Jesse Rosengreen	Do.
6	Bartel Brihl	do	April 1, 1866	Nov. 1, 1866	7	13 00	3 50	16 50	115 50		Do.
7	Andrew B. Hansen	do	April 1, 1866	Nov. 1, 1866	7	13 00	3 50	16 50	115 50	Andrew B. Hansen	Do.
8	Erick Johnson	do	April 1, 1866	Nov. 1, 1866	7	13 00	3 50	16 50	115 50		Do.
9	Andrew A. Hansen	do	April 1, 1866	Nov. 1, 1866	7	13 00	3 50	16 50	115 50	Andru Hansen	Do.
10	Peter Hansen	do	April 1, 1866	Nov. 1, 1866	7	13 00	3 50	16 50	115 50	Peter Hansen	Do.
11	Niels Johnson	do	April 1, 1866	Nov. 1, 1866	7	13 00	3 50	16 50	115 50	Niels Johnson, his X mark	Do.
12	Peter P. Thompson	do	April 1, 1866	Nov. 1, 1866	7	13 00	3 50	16 50	115 50	P. P. Thomsen	Do.
13	Jesse Ottestrom	do	April 1, 1866	Nov. 1, 1866	7	13 00	3 50	16 50	115 50	James Ott-strom	Do.
14	Jens C. Gorgensen	do	April 1, 1866	Nov. 1, 1866	7	13 00	3 50	16 50	115 50	Jens C. Gorgensen, X	Do.
15	Andrew Lovensen	do	April 1, 1866	Nov. 1, 1866	7	13 00	3 50	16 50	115 50	Anders Sorensen	Do.
16	Lars Poulsen	do	April 1, 1866	Nov. 1, 1866	7	13 00	3 50	16 50	115 50	Lars Pousisen	Do.
17	Chris Willardson	do	April 1, 1866	Nov. 1, 1866	7	13 00	3 50	16 50	115 50	Cr-sten Willerdson	Do.
18	Rasmus Larsen	do	April 1, 1866	Nov. 1, 1866	7	13 00	3 50	16 50	115 50	Rosmue Larsen	Do.
19	Niels Sorensen	do	April 1, 1866	Nov. 1, 1866	7	13 00	3 50	16 50	115 50	Niels Sorensen	Do.
20	Hans A. Pedersen	do	April 1, 1866	Nov. 1, 1866	7	13 00	3 50	16 50	115 50	Hans A. Peterson	Do.
21	Peter Madsen	do	April 1, 1866	Nov. 1, 1866	7	13 00	3 50	16 50	115 50	Peter Madsen	Do

	Name		From	To						Name	
21	Niels Clemmensen	do.	April 1, 1866	Nov. 1, 1866	7	13.00	3.50	16.50	115.50	Niels Clemmensen	Do.
52	Peter C. Anderson	do.	April 1, 1866	Nov. 1, 1866	7	13.00	3.50	16.50	115.50	P. C. Anderson	Do.
53	Rasmus Johnson	do.	April 1, 1866	Nov. 1, 1866	7	13.00	3.50	16.50	115.50	Rasmus Johnson	Do.
55	Soren S. Mohler	do.	April 1, 1866	Nov. 1, 1866	7	13.00	3.50	16.50	115.50		
57	Andrew S. Frost	do.	April 1, 1866	Nov. 1, 1866	7	13.00	3.50	16.50	115.50	Niels T. Peterson, ×	Do.
58	Niels P. Peterson	do.	April 1, 1866	Nov. 1, 1866	7	13.00	3.50	16.50	115.50	Hans Lawson	Do.
59	Hans R. Larsen	do.	April 1, 1866	Nov. 1, 1866	7	13.00	3.50	16.50	115.50		
30	Hans C. Jensen	do.	April 1, 1866	Nov. 1, 1866	7	13.00	3.50	16.50	115.50	Peter Wulff	Do.
31	Peter Wulff	do.	April 1, 1866	Nov. 1, 1866	7	13.00	3.50	16.50	115.50	Ole Peter Larsen, ×	Do.
32	Ole Peter Larsen	do.	April 1, 1866	Nov. 1, 1866	7	13.00	3.50	16.50	115.50		
33	Niels N. Haugen	do.	April 1, 1866	Nov. 1, 1866	7	13.00	3.50	16.50	115.50	John Beal	Do.
33	John Beal	do.	April 1, 1866	Nov. 1, 1866	7	13.00	3.50	16.50	115.50	Lars Anderson	Do.
31	Lars Anderson	do.	April 1, 1866	Nov. 1, 1866	7	13.00	3.50	16.50	115.50	Niels Pederson	Do.
35	Niels Peterson	do.	April 1, 1866	Nov. 1, 1866	7	13.00	3.50	16.50	115.50	N. P. Anderson	Do.
36	Niels P. Anderson	do.	April 1, 1866	Nov. 1, 1866	7	13.00	3.50	16.50	115.50	Peter H. Sorenson	Do.
37	Peter H. Sorensen	do.	April 1, 1866	Nov. 1, 1866	7	13.00	3.53	16.50	115.50	Jens Chrestian Madsen	Do.
38	Jens C. Madsen	do.	April 1, 1866	Nov. 1, 1866	7	13.99	3.50	16.50	115.50		
39	Andrew N. Biorgard	do.	April 1, 1866	Nov. 1, 1866	7	13.00	3.50	16.50	115.50		Rasmus Olson.
40	Jens T. Peterson	do.	April 1, 1866	Nov. 1, 1866	7	13.00	3.50	16.50	115.50	Soren Rasmusson, ×	H. F. Peterson.
41	Soren Rasmussen	do.	April 1, 1866	Nov. 1, 1866	7	13.00	3.50	16.50	115.50	Christian Nevison	Do.
42	Christian Nielson	do.	April 1, 1866	Nov. 1, 1866	7	13.00	3.50	16.50	115.50	Thos. C. Hadden	Do.
43	Thomas C. Hadden	do.	April 1, 1866	Nov. 1, 1866	7	13.04	3.50	16.50	115.50		Do.
44	Ole Huge	do.	April 1, 1866	Nov. 1, 1866	7	13.00	3.50	16.50	115.50	Andw. P. Jonson	Do.
45	Andrew P. Jonsen	do.	April 1, 1866	Nov. 1, 1866	7	13.00	3.50	16.51	115.51	Andrew P. Nilson, ×	Do.
46	Andrew P. Nielson	do.	April 1, 1866	Nov. 1, 1866	7	13.00	3.50	16.50	115.50	Frederik C. Schwalbe	Do.
47	Frederick C. Schwalbe	do.	April 1, 1866	Nov. 1, 1866	7	13.00	3.50	16.50	115.50	Ardrew Overlade	Do.
48	Andrew Overlade	do.	April 1, 1866	Nov. 1, 1866	7	13.00	3.50	16.50	115.50	Christoffar Olson, ×	Do.
49	Christopher Olsen	do.	April 1, 1866	Nov. 1, 1866	7	13.00	3.50	16.51	115.51	William Quinn	Do.
49	William Quinn	do.	April 1, 1856	Nov. 1, 1866	7	13.00	3.50	16.50	115.50	Andrew Rosquist, ×	Do.
51	Andrew Rosquist	do.	April 1, 1866	Nov. 1, 1866	7	13.00	3.50	16.50	115.50	Iver Peterson	Do.
52	Iver Peterson	do.	April 1, 1866	Nov. 1, 1866	7	13.00	3.50	16.50	115.50		Do.
53	Frederick Christiansen	do.	April 1, 1866	Nov. 1, 1866	7	13.00	3.50	16.50	115.50		
54	Johans Larsen	do.	April 1, 1866	Nov. 1, 1866	7	13.00	3.50	16.50	115.50		

This company was mustered into service at Fort Ephraim, Sanpete County, April 1, 1866, by Brigadier General Warren S. Snow, and by him assigned to duty in the mountains east of said city; they were in active service every day for the time specified above, and mustered out November 1, 1866.

I certify that the above account is correct.

H. B. CLAWSON,
Adjutant General Nauvoo Legion.

Pay-roll of Captain Caleb W. Haws's company —— cavalry, Utah Territory militia, employed in the suppression of Indian hostilities in Sanpete and Sevier counties, Utah Territory, in the months of August, September, and October, 1866.

We, the undersigned, acknowledge to have received from James W. Cummings, paymaster Utah Territory militia, the sums set opposite to our names, in full payment for our services for the time specified.

Number	Names	Rank	Commencement	Expiration	Months	Days	Pay per month	Monthly allowance for clothing	Total monthly pay and allowance	40 cents per day for use and risk of horse and horse equipment	Total pay and allowance	Signatures	Witnesses
1	Caleb W. Haws	Captain	Aug. 16, 1866	Oct. 24, 1866	2	8			$129 50	$37 20	$239 93	C. W. Haws	S. S. Jones.
2	John K. Ferre	1st lieutenant	Aug. 16, 1866	Oct. 24, 1866	2	8			112 83	27 20	282 94	Jno. K. Ferre	Do.
3	William Harrison	2d lieutenant	Aug. 16, 1866	Oct. 24, 1866	2	8			112 83	27 20	282 94	William Harrison	Do.
4	Richard Westwood	do	Aug. 16, 1866	Oct. 24, 1866	2	8			112 83	27 20	222 94	Richard Westwood	Do.
5	Kenion T. Butler	do	Aug. 16, 1866	Oct. 24, 1866	2	8			112 83	27 20	222 94	K. T. Butler	William Heaton.
6	David Sergeant	do	Aug. 16, 1866	Oct. 24, 1866	2	8			112 83	27 20	222 94	D. E. Sargent	S. S. Jones.
7	John Cook	do	Aug. 16, 1866	Oct. 24, 1866	2	8			112 83	27 20	222 94	John Cook	Do.
8	Joseph McEwan	Sergeant	Aug. 16, 1866	Oct. 24, 1866	2	8	$17 00	$3 50	20 50	27 20	73 66	Joseph McEwan	Do.
9	James Lisonbee	do	Aug. 16, 1866	Oct. 24, 1866	2	8	17 00	3 50	20 50	27 20	73 66	James Lisonbee	Do.
10	Ephraim Cuffall	do	Aug. 16, 1866	Oct. 24, 1866	2	8	17 00	3 50	20 50	27 20	73 66	Ephraim Cuffall	Do.
11	George W. Thomas	do	Aug. 16, 1866	Oct. 24, 1866	2	8	17 00	3 50	20 50	27 20	73 66	Jos. G. W. Thomas	Do.
12	Frederick W. Bee	Private	Aug. 16, 1866	Oct. 24, 1866	2	8	13 00	3 50	16 50	27 20	64 60	Fred. Bee	Do.
13	Albert Bishop	do	Aug. 16, 1866	Oct. 24, 1866	2	8	13 00	3 50	16 50	27 20	64 60		Do.
14	Amasa Mecham	do	Aug. 16, 1866	Oct. 24, 1866	2	8	13 00	3 50	16 50	27 20	64 60	Amasa Mecham	Do.
15	Andrew Hoover	do	Aug. 16, 1866	Oct. 24, 1866	2	8	13 00	3 50	16 50	27 20	64 60	Andrew Hoover	Do.
16	Martin Davis	do	Aug. 16, 1866	Oct. 24, 1866	2	8	13 00	3 50	16 50	27 20	64 60	Martin Davis	Do.
17	Samuel Mecham	do	Aug. 16, 1866	Oct. 24, 1866	2	8	13 00	3 50	16 50	27 20	64 60	Sam'l Mecham	Do.
18	Thomas Harding	do	Aug. 16, 1866	Oct. 24, 1866	2	8	13 00	3 50	16 50	27 20	64 60	Thomas Harding	Do.
19	George Richardson	do	Aug. 16, 1866	Oct. 24, 1866	2	8	13 00	3 50	16 55	27 20	64 60	George Richardson	Do.
20	Allen Lambson	do	Aug. 16, 1866	Oct. 24, 1866	2	8	13 00	3 50	16 50	27 20	64 60	Allen Lambson	Do.
21	N. P. Beebe	do	Aug. 16, 1866	Oct. 24, 1866	2	8	13 00	3 50	16 50	27 20	64 60	N. P. Beebe	Do.
22	Daniel Allman	do	Aug. 16, 1866	Oct. 24, 1866	2	8	13 00	3 50	16 50	27 20	64 60	Daniel Allman	Do.
23	Francis C. Beyer	do	Aug. 16, 1866	Oct. 24, 1866	2	8	13 00	3 50	16 50	27 20	64 60	Francis C. Boyer	Do.
24	Moroni Fuller	do	Aug. 16, 1866	Oct. 24, 1866	2	8	13 00	3 50	16 50	27 20	64 60	Moroni Fuller	Do.
25	William D. Johnson	do	Aug. 16, 1866	Oct. 24, 1866	2	8	13 00	3 50	16 50	27 20	64 60	Wm. D. Johnson	Do.
26	Walter Wheeler	do	Aug. 16, 1866	Oct. 24, 1866	2	8	13 00	3 50	16 50	27 20	64 60	Walter Wheeler	Do.
27	Samuel Guley	do	Aug. 16, 1866	Oct. 24, 1866	2	8	13 00	3 50	16 50	27 20	64 60	Samuel Guley	Do.
28	Don C. Huntington	do	Aug. 16, 1866	Oct. 24, 1866	2	8	13 00	3 50	16 50	27 20	64 60	Don C. Huntington	Do.
29	Nephi Jennings	do	Aug. 16, 1866	Oct. 24, 1866	2	8	13 00	3 50	16 50	27 20	64 60	Nephi Jennings	Do.
30	Thomas Brown	do	Aug. 16, 1866	Oct. 24, 1866	2	8	13 00	2 50	16 50	27 20	64 60	Thomas Brown	Do.
31	Samuel Tew	do	Aug. 16, 1866	Oct. 24, 1866	2	8	13 00	3 50	16 50	27 20	64 60	Samuel Tew	Do.
32	Raswell Ferre	do	Aug. 16, 1866	Oct. 24, 1866	2	8	13 00	3 50	16 50	27 20	64 63	Roswell Ferre	Do.

No.	Names	Enrolled	Mustered in	Mustered out			13 00	3 50	16 50	27 20	64 60	Names	Remarks
22	Robert Boyack	do.	Aug. 16, 1866	Oct. 24, 1866	2	10	13 00	3 50	16 50	27 20	64 60	Robert Boyack	Do.
23	Robert McHill	do.	Aug. 16, 1866	Oct. 24, 1866	2	10	13 00	3 50	16 50	27 20	64 60	Robert McKell	Do.
24	Albert Balcock	do.	Aug. 16, 1866	Oct. 24, 1866	2	10	13 00	3 50	16 50	27 20	64 60	Albert Babcock	Do.
25	Charles Hales	do.	Aug. 16, 1866	Oct. 24, 1866	2	10	13 00	3 50	16 50	27 20	64 60	Charles Hales	Do.
26	M. Brigham Gay	do.	Aug. 16, 1866	Oct. 24, 1866	2	10	13 00	3 50	16 50	27 20	64 60	Moses Brigham Gay	Do.
27	Hyrum Sterling	do.	Aug. 16, 1866	Oct. 24, 1866	2	10	13 00	3 50	16 50	27 20	64 60	Hyrum Sterlin	Do.
28	Joseph Chambers	do.	Aug. 16, 1866	Oct. 24, 1866	2	10	13 00	3 50	16 50	27 20	64 60	Joseph Chambers	Do.
29	Matthew Simmonds	do.	Aug. 16, 1866	Oct. 24, 1866	2	10	13 00	3 50	16 50	27 20	64 60	Matthew Simmonds	Do.
30	Joshua Brockbank	do.	Aug. 16, 1866	Oct. 24, 1866	2	10	13 00	3 50	16 50	27 20	64 60	Joshua Brockbank	Do.
31	Joseph Tibbetts	do.	Aug. 16, 1866	Oct. 24, 1866	2	10	13 00	3 50	16 50	27 20	64 61	Joseph Tibbetts	Israel Evans,
32	William Thomas	do.	Aug. 16, 1866	Oct. 24, 1866	2	10	13 00	3 50	16 50	27 20	64 60	William Thomas	William Heaton.
33	Solomon Hancock	do.	Aug. 16, 1866	Oct. 24, 1866	2	10	13 00	3 50	16 50	27 20	64 61	Solomon Hancock	Do.
34	Hyrum Spencer	do.	Aug. 16, 1866	Oct. 24, 1866	2	10	13 00	3 50	16 51	27 20	64 61	Hyrum Spencer	Do.
35	David Holliday	do.	Aug. 16, 1866	Oct. 24, 1866	2	10	13 00	3 50	16 50	27 20	64 60	David Holliday	L. Evans.
36	George Barker	do.	Aug. 16, 1866	Oct. 24, 1866	2	10	13 00	3 50	16 50	27 20	64 60	George Barker	William Heaton.
37	Israel Calkin	do.	Aug. 16, 1866	Oct. 24, 1866	2	10	13 00	3 50	16 50	27 20	64 61	Israel Calkins	Do.
38	Delmont Webb	do.	Aug. 16, 1866	Oct. 24, 1866	2	10	13 00	3 50	16 50	27 20	64 60	Delmot Webb	Do.
39	Joseph Whitehead	do.	Aug. 16, 1866	Oct. 24, 1866	2	10	13 03	3 50	16 50	27 20	64 61	Joseph Whitehead	Do.
40	Heber Reed	do.	Aug. 16, 1866	Oct. 24, 1866	2	10	13 00	3 50	16 50	27 20	64 63	Heber Reed	Do.
41	Sidney Teeples	do.	Aug. 16, 1866	Oct. 24, 1866	2	10	13 00	3 50	16 50	27 30	64 60	Sidney Teeples	Do.
42	Thomas Holliday	do.	Aug. 16, 1866	Oct. 24, 1866	2	10	13 00	3 50	16 50	27 30	64 60	Thomas Holladay	Do.
43	Thomas Clayson	do.	Aug. 16, 1866	Oct. 24, 1866	2	10	13 00	3 30	16 50	27 30	64 60	Thomas Clayson	Do.
44	Joseph Tanner	do.	Aug. 16, 1866	Oct. 24, 1866	2	10	13 00	3 50	16 50	27 30	64 60	Joseph Tanner	Israel Evans.
45	George W. Hancock	do.	Aug. 16, 1866	Oct. 24, 1866	2	10	13 01	3 50	16 50	27 30	64 61	George W. Hancock	Do.
46	William Clyde	do.	Aug. 16, 1866	Oct. 24, 1866	2	10	13 00	3 50	16 50	27 30	64 67	William Clyde	Do.
47	Jacob McKinney	do.	Aug. 16, 1866	Oct. 24, 1866	2	10	13 00	3 50	16 50	27 30	64 60	Jacob McKinney	Do.
48	Jacob Cunnington	do.	Aug. 16, 1866	Oct. 24, 1866	2	10	13 00	3 50	16 50	27 30	64 61	Jacob Cunnington	Do.
49	David Lafelt	do.	Aug. 16, 1866	Oct. 24, 1866	2	10	13 00	3 51	16 51	27 30	64 61	David Lafelt	Do.
50	John E. Booth	do.	Aug. 16, 1866	Oct. 24, 1866	2	10	13 00	3 50	16 50	27 30	64 61	John E. Booth	Do.
51	Bradley Wilson	do.	Aug. 16, 1866	Oct. 24, 1866	2	10	13 00	3 50	16 51	27 30	64 61	Bradley Wilson	Wm. Greenwood.
52	Martin Taylor	do.	Aug. 16, 1866	Oct. 24, 1866	2	10	13 00	3 50	16 50	27 30	64 60	Martin Taylor	Do.
53	Samuel Brown	do.	Aug. 16, 1866	Oct. 24, 1866	2	10	13 00	3 50	16 50	27 30	64 60	Samuel Brown	Do.
54	James Pullin	do.	Aug. 16, 1866	Oct. 24, 1866	2	10	13 00	2 30	16 50	27 30	64 60	James Pullin	Do.
55	George Longmore	do.	Aug. 16, 1866	Oct. 24, 1866	2	10	13 00	3 50	16 50	27 30	64 60	George Longmore	Israel Evans.
56	James Shaw	do.	Aug. 16, 1866	Oct. 24, 1866	2	10	13 00	3 50	16 50	27 30	64 60	James Shaw	Do.
57	George McOrmic	do.	Aug. 16, 1866	Oct. 24, 1866	2	10	13 00	3 50	16 51	27 30	64 60	George McComie	Do.
58	George Bennett	do.	Aug. 16, 1866	Oct. 24, 1866	2	10	13 00	3 50	16 50	27 30	64 60	George Bennett	Do.
59	Henry Jackson	do.	Aug. 16, 1866	Oct. 24, 1866	2	10	13 00	3 50	16 50	27 30	64 61	Henry Jackson	Do.
60	William Beardshaw	do.	Aug. 16, 1866	Oct. 24, 1866	2	10	13 00	3 50	16 50	27 30	64 61	William Beardshaw	Do.
61	Charles Crawforth	do.	Aug. 16, 1866	Oct. 24, 1866	2	10	13 00	3 50	16 50	27 30	64 30	Chas. Crawforth	S. S. Jones.

This company was mustered into service in Provo City, Utah County, by order of Lieutenant General Daniel H. Wells, August 16, 1866, and on that day started for Sanpete County. Arrived at Manti August 19, and was assigned to duty in Severe and Pinte counties. They were in active service every day until they returned to Provo City and were mustered out, the 24th day of October, 1866.

I certify that the above account is correct.

H. B. CLAWSON, *Adjutant General Utah Territory Militia.*

Pay-roll of Captain William Beuch's Company —— infantry, Utah Territory militia, employed in the suppression of Indian hostilities in Sanpete County, Utah Territory, from April 1, 1866, to November 1, 1866.

We, the undersigned, acknowledge to have received from James W. Cummings, paymaster Utah Territory militia, the sums set opposite to our names, in full payment for our services for the time specified.

Number	Names	Rank	Commencement	Expiration	Months	Pay per month	Monthly allowance for clothing	Total monthly pay and allowance	Total pay and allowance	Signatures	Witnesses
1	William Beuch, sr	Captain	April 1, 1866	Nov. 1, 1866	7			$118 50	$829 50	William Beuch, sr	W. T. Reid.
1	William Anderson	1st lieut.	April 1, 1866	Nov. 1, 1866	7			108 50	739 50	William Anderson	Do.
2	John Lowry	2d lieut.	April 1, 1866	Nov. 1, 1866	7			103 50	724 50	Jno. Lowry, sr	Do.
3	Azariah Tuttle, sr	do	April 1, 1866	Nov. 1, 1866	7			103 50	724 50	Azariah Tuttle, sr	Do.
3	Gardner Snow	do	April 1, 1866	Nov. 1, 1866	7			103 50	724 50	Gardner Snow	Do.
4	Hause Larsen	do	April 1, 1866	Nov. 1, 1866	7			103 50	721 50	Hause Larsen	Do.
5	Peter Graves	do	April 1, 1866	Nov. 1, 1866	7			103 50	721 50	Peter Graves	Do.
6	Andrew Hendrickson	do	April 1, 1866	Nov. 1, 1866	7			103 50	721 50	A. Hendriksen	Do.
1	Elisha Edwards	Sergeant	April 1, 1866	Nov. 1, 1866	7	$17 00	$3 50	20 50	143 50	Elisha Edwards	Do.
2	James Tooth	do	April 1, 1866	Nov. 1, 1866	7	17 00	3 50	20 50	143 50	James Tooth	Do.
3	Richard Hall	do	April 1, 1866	Nov. 1, 1866	7	17 00	3 50	20 50	143 50	R. Hall	Do.
4	Andrew Poulson	do	April 1, 1866	Nov. 1, 1866	7	17 00	3 50	20 50	143 50	Andrew Poulson	Do.
5	Thomas Woolsey	do	April 1, 1866	Nov. 1, 1866	7	17 00	3 50	20 50	143 50	Tunnis Woolsey	Do.
6	George Jensen	do	April 1, 1866	Nov. 1, 1866	7	17 00	3 50	20 50	143 50	George Jensen	Do.
1	Hance C. Hansen	Private	April 1, 1866	Nov. 1, 1866	7	13 00	3 50	16 50	115 50	Hance C. Hansen	Do.
2	William Beal	do	April 1, 1866	Nov. 1, 1866	7	13 00	3 50	16 50	115 50	William Beall	Do.
3	Robert Logan	do	April 1, 1866	Nov. 1, 1866	7	13 00	3 50	16 50	115 50	Robert Logan	Do.
4	Claws Rasmussen	do	April 1, 1866	Nov. 1, 1866	7	13 00	3 50	16 50	115 50	Claws Rasmussen, X	Do.
5	Peder Larsen	do	April 1, 1866	Nov. 1, 1866	7	13 00	3 50	16 50	115 50	Peter Larsen	Do.
6	Jense Jensen	do	April 1, 1866	Nov. 1, 1866	7	13 00	3 50	16 50	115 50	Jense Jensen	Do.
7	Jesse P. Marker	do	April 1, 1866	Nov. 1, 1866	7	13 00	3 50	16 50	115 50	Jesse Peter Marker	Do.
8	Peter Jensen	do	April 1, 1866	Nov. 1, 1866	7	13 00	3 50	16 50	115 50	Peder Jensen	Do.
9	Christian Monk	do	April 1, 1866	Nov. 1, 1866	7	13 00	3 50	16 50	115 50	Christian Monk	Do.
10	Christian Stark	do	April 1, 1866	Nov. 1, 1866	7	13 00	3 51	16 50	115 50	Cristian Stack	Do.
11	Samuel Mackay, sr	do	April 1, 1866	Nov. 1, 1866	7	13 00	3 50	16 50	115 50	Samuel Mackey	Do.
12	Abraham Washburn	do	April 1, 1866	Nov. 1, 1866	7	13 00	3 50	16 53	115 50	Abrahum Worshburn	Do.
13	Peter C. Nielson	do	April 1, 1866	Nov. 1, 1866	7	13 00	3 50	16 50	115 50	N. C. Nielson	Do.
14	Niels P. Doungard	do	April 1, 1866	Nov. 1, 1866	7	13 00	3 50	16 50	115 50	Niels P. Doungard	Do.
15	Jezreel Shonaker	do	April 1, 1866	Nov. 1, 1866	7	13 00	3 50	16 50	115 50	Jezreel Shonaker	Do.
16	Albert Smith	do	April 1, 1866	Nov. 1, 1866	7	13 00	3 50	16 50	115 50	Albert Smith	Do.
17	Azariah Smith	do	April 1, 1866	Nov. 1, 1866	7	13 00	3 50	16 50	115 50	Azariah Smith	Do.
18	Kern Peterson	do	April 1, 1866	Nov. 1, 1866	7	13 00	3 50	16 50	115 50	Sonen Pederson	Do.
19	Niels Madsen	do	April 1, 1866	Nov. 1, 1866	7	13 00	3 50	16 50	115 50	Niels Madsen	Do.
20	Jens Marker	do	April 1, 1866	Nov. 1, 1866	7	13 00	3 50	16 50	115 50	J. J. Marker	Do.

No.	Name	Mustered in	Mustered out	Days					Name	Remarks
21	Nathan Lewis, sr.	April 1, 1866	Nov. 1, 1866	7	13 00	3 50	16 50	115 50	Nathan Lewis, sr	Do.
22	Freeborn Demill	April 1, 1866	Nov. 1, 1866	7	13 00	3 50	16 50	115 50	Freeborn Demill	Do.
23	Sern Christopherson	April 1, 1866	Nov. 1, 1866	7	13 00	3 50	16 50	115 50	Seneca Christoffersen	Do.
24	Mathias Anderson	April 1, 1866	Nov. 1, 1866	7	13 00	3 50	16 50	115 50	Mattzias Anderson	Do.
25	Ole Pederson	April 1, 1866	Nov. 1, 1866	7	13 00	3 50	16 50	115 50	Ole Pederson	Do.
26	John Pederson	April 1, 1866	Nov. 1, 1866	7	13 00	3 50	16 50	115 50	John Pederson	Do.
27	Ludwick Norril	April 1, 1866	Nov. 1, 1866	7	13 00	3 50	16 50	115 50	Ludwick Norril	Do.
28	Andrew Nielsen	April 1, 1866	Nov. 1, 1866	7	13 00	3 50	16 50	115 50	Anders Nick, sr.	Do.
29	Rasmus Hogard	April 1, 1866	Nov. 1, 1866	7	13 00	3 50	16 50	115 50	Rasmus Haugord	Do.
30	Allen Wilkinson	April 1, 1866	Nov. 1, 1866	7	13 00	3 50	16 50	115 50	Allen Wilkinson, his X mark	Do.
31	Hans Madson	April 1, 1866	Nov. 1, 1866	7	13 00	3 50	16 50	115 50	Hans Madsen	Do.
32	Lars C. Kjar, sr.	April 1, 1866	Nov. 1, 1866	7	13 00	3 50	16 50	115 50	L. C. Kjar, sr.	Do.
33	Hans Jenson	April 1, 1866	Nov. 1, 1866	7	13 00	3 50	16 50	115 50	Hans Jensen	Do.
34	Alexander Scowlio	April 1, 1866	Nov. 1, 1866	7	13 00	3 50	16 50	115 50	Ict, Skowhye	Do.
35	Christian Nielson	April 1, 1866	Nov. 1, 1866	7	13 00	3 50	16 50	115 50	Christian Nelson	Do.
36	John Sheers	April 1, 1866	Nov. 1, 1866	7	13 00	3 50	16 50	115 50	Yohonans Sheers	Do.
37	Jens Nyman	April 1, 1866	Nov. 1, 1866	7	13 00	3 50	16 50	115 50	Jens Nymand	Do.
38	Ole Madson	April 1, 1866	Nov. 1, 1866	7	13 00	3 50	16 50	115 50	Ole Madern	Do.
39	James Cook	April 1, 1866	Nov. 1, 1866	7	13 00	3 50	16 50	115 50	James Cook	Do.
40	James Works	April 1, 1866	Nov. 1, 1866	7	13 00	3 50	16 50	115 50	James Works	Do.
41	Frederick W. Cox, sr	April 1, 1866	Nov. 1, 1866	7	13 00	3 50	16 50	115 50	F. W. Cox, sr.	Peter Greaves.
42	Sylvester Hewlet	April 1, 1866	Nov. 1, 1866	7	13 00	3 50	16 50	115 50	Sylvester Hublit	Do.
43	Hans Nielson	April 1, 1866	Nov. 1, 1866	7	13 00	3 50	16 50	115 50	Hans Nellsen	Do.
44	Andrew Nichleson	April 1, 1866	Nov. 1, 1866	7	13 00	3 50	16 50	115 50	Andrew Nicolsen	Do.
45	Andrew Whitlock	April 1, 1866	Nov. 1, 1866	7	13 00	3 50	16 50	115 50	Andro Whitlock	Do.
46	Rasmus Rasmussen	April 1, 1866	Nov. 1, 1866	7	13 00	3 50	16 50	115 50	Rasms Rasmusen	Do.
47	Lowe C. Larsen	April 1, 1866	Nov. 1, 1866	7	13 00	3 50	16 50	115 50	L. C. Larsen	Do.
48	Andrew R. Anderson	April 1, 1866	Nov. 1, 1866	7	13 00	3 50	16 50	115 50	A. R. Andersen	Do.
49	Thomas Torpe	April 1, 1866	Nov. 1, 1866	7	13 00	3 50	16 50	115 50	Thomas Thorp	Do.
50	Christian Nielson	April 1, 1866	Nov. 1, 1866	7	13 00	3 50	16 50	115 50		Do.
51	Peter Anderson	April 1, 1866	Nov. 1, 1866	7	13 00	3 50	16 50	115 50	Peter Anderson	Do.
52	John C. Frost	April 1, 1866	Nov. 1, 1866	7	13 00	3 50	16 50	115 50	John C. Frost	Do.
53	Joseph Stephens	April 1, 1866	Nov. 1, 1866	7	13 00	3 50	16 50	115 50	Joseph Stevens	Do.
54	Andrew O. Anderson	April 1, 1866	Nov. 1, 1866	7	13 00	3 50	16 50	115 50		Do.
55	Thomas Thompson	April 1, 1866	Nov. 1, 1866	7	13 00	3 50	16 50	115 50	Thomas Thomsen	Do.
56	William Beal	April 1, 1866	Nov. 1, 1866	7	13 00	3 50	16 50	115 50	William Beal	Do.
57	James Olsen	April 1, 1866	Nov. 1, 1866	7	13 00	3 50	16 50	115 50	James Olsen	Do.
58	Andrew Thompson	April 1, 1866	Nov. 1, 1866	7	13 00	3 50	16 30	115 30	Andrew Thomsen	Do.
59	Jens Anderson	April 1, 1866	Nov. 1, 1866	7	13 00	3 50	16 50	115 50	Jens Andersen	Do.
60	Lewis Thompson	April 1, 1866	Nov. 1, 1866	7	13 00	3 50	16 50	115 50		
61	Christian C. Christiansen	April 1, 1866	Nov. 1, 1866	7	13 00	3 50	16 50	115 50	Christian C. Christen	Do.
62	Caleb Edwards	April 1, 1866	Nov. 1, 1866	7	13 00	3 50	16 50	115 30		

This company was mustered into service at Manti City, Sanpete County, April 1, 1866, by Brigadier General Warren S. Snow, and by him assigned to duty in the mountains and passes east of said city. They were in active service every day until mustered out, November 1, 1866.

I certify that the above account is correct.

H. B. CLAWSON, *Adjutant General Nauvoo Legion.*

Pay-roll of Captain Franklin P. Whitmore's company —— infantry, Utah Territory militia, employed in the suppression of Indian hostilities in Sanpete and Sevier counties, Utah Territory, in the months of June and July, 1866.

We, the undersigned, acknowledge to have received from James W. Cummings, paymaster Utah Territory militia, the sums set opposite to our names, in full payment for our services for the time specified.

Number.	Names.	Rank.	Commencement.	Expiration.	Months.	Days.	Pay per month.	Monthly allowance for clothing.	Total monthly pay and allowance.	Total pay and allowance.	Signatures.	Witnesses.
1	Franklin P. Whitmore	Captain	June 14, 1866	July 26, 1866	1	12			$118.50	$165.90	Franklin P. Whitmore	
2	Benjamin Isaacs	1st lieut.	June 14, 1866	July 26, 1866	1	12			108.50	151.90	Benjamin Isaac	
3	William W. Davis	2d lieut.	June 14, 1866	July 26, 1866	1	12			103.50	144.90	William W. Davis	
	Ephraim Dimick	do	June 14, 1866	July 26, 1866	1	12			103.50	144.90	Ephraim Dimick	
	George Harrison	Sergeant	June 14, 1866	July 26, 1866	1	12	$17	$3.50	20.50	29.70	George Harrison	
	William Stoker	do	June 14, 1866	July 26, 1866	1	12	17	3.50	20.50	29.50	William Stoker	
	Joseph Humphries	Private	June 14, 1866	July 26, 1866	1	12	13	3.50	16.50	23.10	Joseph Humphrys	
	William Kerswell	do	June 14, 1866	July 26, 1866	1	12	13	3.50	16.50	23.10	William Kerswell	
	Crandell Ellison	do	June 14, 1866	July 26, 1866	1	12	13	3.50	16.50	23.10	Crandle Ellison	
	Francis Beardhall	do	June 14, 1866	July 26, 1866	1	12	13	3.50	16.50	23.10	Francis Beardhall	
	Moses D. Childs	do	June 14, 1866	July 26, 1866	1	12	13	3.50	16.50	23.10	Moses D. Child	
	Daniel Thomas	do	June 14, 1866	July 26, 1866	1	12	13	3.50	16.50	23.10	Daniel Z. Thomas	
	John Staley	do	June 14, 1866	July 26, 1866	1	12	13	3.50	16.50	23.10	John Staly	
	George Jabitus	do	June 14, 1866	July 26, 1866	1	12	13	3.50	16.50	23.10	George Jabitus	
	Edwin Lee	do	June 14, 1866	July 26, 1866	1	12	13	3.50	16.50	23.10	Edwin Lee	
	Richard Loynd	do	June 14, 1866	July 26, 1866	1	12	13	3.50	16.50	23.10	Rich'd Loynd	
	John Mason	do	June 14, 1866	July 26, 1866	1	12	13	3.50	16.50	23.10	John Mason	
	Samuel Grange	do	June 14, 1866	July 26, 1866	1	12	13	3.50	16.50	23.10	Samuel Grange	
	Gillett Hales	do	June 14, 1866	July 26, 1866	1	12	13	3.50	16.50	23.10	Gillet Hales	
	William Lewis	do	June 14, 1866	July 26, 1866	1	12	13	3.50	16.50	23.10	William Lewis	
	Eli Ferguson	do	June 14, 1866	July 26, 1866	1	12	13	3.50	16.50	23.10	Eli Fergus-on	
	Augst Swenson	do	June 14, 1866	July 26, 1866	1	12	13	3.50	16.50	23.10	A. Swenson	
	Charles Brown	do	June 14, 1866	July 26, 1866	1	12	13	3.50	16.50	23.10	Charles Brown	
18	David Boyack	do	June 14, 1866	July 26, 1866	1	12	13	3.50	16.50	23.10	David Boyack	
19	Joseph Chambers	do	June 14, 1866	July 26, 1866	1	12	13	3.50	16.50	23.10	Joseph Chambers	
20	Henry Gay	do	June 14, 1866	July 26, 1866	1	12	13	3.50	16.50	23.10	Henry Gay	
21	Orson Creer	do	June 4, 1866	July 26, 1866	1	12	13	3.50	16.50	23.10	Orson Creer	
22	Even Gardner	do	June 14, 1866	July 26, 1866	1	12	13	3.50	16.50	23.10	Even Gardner	

This company was mustered into service at Springville, Utah County, June 14, 1866, by Major General Aaron John-

Pay-roll of Captain Peter Isaacson's company ——— infantry, Utah Territory militia, employed in the suppression of Indian hostilities in Sanpete and Sevier counties, Utah Territory, from April 1, 1866, to November 1, 1866.

We, the undersigned, acknowledge to have received from James W. Cummings, paymaster Utah Territory militia, the sums set opposite to our names, in full payment for our services for the time specified.

Number.	Names.	Rank.	Commencement.	Expiration.	Months.	Pay per month.	Monthly allowance for clothing.	Total monthly pay and allowance.	Total pay and allowance.	Signatures.	Witnesses.
1	Peter Isaacson	Captain	April 1, 1866	Nov. 1, 1866	7			$118.50	$829.50	Peder Isaacson	Peter Greaves.
1	John F. Doremus	1st lieut	April 1, 1866	Nov. 1, 1866	7			108.50	759.50	John F. Dorius	Do.
1	Henry H. Brown	2d lieut	April 1, 1866	Nov. 1, 1866	7			103.50	724.50	H. H. Brown	Do.
2	Larse Anderson	do	April 1, 1866	Nov. 1, 1866	7			103.50	724.50	Lars S. Anderson	Do.
3	Christian L. Thorpe	do	April 1, 1866	Nov. 1, 1866	7			103.50	724.50	Christen L. Thorpe	Do.
4	Even Forgeson	do	April 1, 1866	Nov. 1, 1866	7			103.50	724.50	Even Forgeson	Do.
5	Niels L. Christiansen	do	April 1, 1866	Nov. 1, 1866	7			103.50	724.50	Niels L. Christiansen	Do.
6	Frederick Jensen	Sergeant	April 1, 1866	Nov. 1, 1866	7	$17	$3.50	20.50	143.50	Frederick Jensen	Do.
2	Michael P. Nielson	do	April 1, 1866	Nov. 1, 1866	7	17	3.50	20.50	143.50	M. P. Nielsen	Do.
3	J. Peter Hanson	do	April 1, 1866	Nov. 1, 1866	7	17	3.50	20.50	143.50	J. Peter Hanson	Do.
4	Ole C. Olsen	do	April 1, 1866	Nov. 1, 1866	7	17	3.50	20.50	143.50	Ole C. Olson	Do.
5	Niels Anderson	do	April 1, 1866	Nov. 1, 1866	7	17	3.50	20.50	143.50	N. Anderson	Do.
1	Christian Anderson	Private	April 1, 1866	Nov. 1, 1866	7	13	3.50	16.50	115.50	Christian Andersen	Do.
2	Jens Otterstrom	do	April 1, 1866	Nov. 1, 1866	7	13	3.50	16.50	115.50	Jens Otterstrom	Do.
3	John C. Jensen	do	April 1, 1866	Nov. 1, 1866	7	13	3.50	16.50	115.50	John C. Jensen	Do.
4	Soren Tigrsen	do	April 1, 1866	Nov. 1, 1866	7	13	3.50	16.50	115.50	Soren O. Tillgrsen	Do.
5	Christian Jensen	do	April 1, 1866	Nov. 1, 1866	7	13	3.50	16.50	115.50		
6	Aaron Lerburg	do	April 1, 1866	Nov. 1, 1866	7	13	3.50	16.50	115.50		
7	Peter Peterson	do	April 1, 1866	Nov. 1, 1866	7	13	3.50	16.50	115.50	Peter Petersen	Do.
8	Jorgen Christiansen	do	April 1, 1866	Nov. 1, 1866	7	13	3.50	16.50	115.50		
9	Peter Nielson	do	April 1, 1866	Nov. 1, 1866	7	13	3.50	16.50	115.50	Peter Nielson	Do.
10	Christian S. Jensen	do	April 1, 1866	Nov. 1, 1866	7	13	3.50	16.50	115.50	Christian S. Jensen	Do.
11	William Dickson	do	April 1, 1866	Nov. 1, 1866	7	13	3.50	16.50	115.50	Willim Dixon	Do.
12	Peter C. Jensen	do	April 1, 1866	Nov. 1, 1866	7	13	3.50	16.50	115.50	P. C. Jensen	Do.
13	Niels P. Bartholomew	do	April 1, 1866	Nov. 1, 1866	7	13	3.50	16.50	115.50	Niels P. Bartholm	Do.
14	Marcus Hansen	do	April 1, 1866	Nov. 1, 1866	7	13	3.50	16.50	115.50	Marine Hansen	Do.
15	Larse Hansen	do	April 1, 1866	Nov. 1, 1866	7	13	3.50	16.50	115.50	Lars Hansen	Do.
16	Niels Mortensen	do	April 1, 1866	Nov. 1, 1866	7	13	3.50	16.50	115.50	Nicls Mortensen	Do.
17	Andrew C. Hansen	do	April 1, 1866	Nov. 1, 1866	7	13	3.50	16.50	115.50		Do.
18	Paul Hammer	do	April 1, 1866	Nov. 1, 1866	7	13	3.50	16.50	115.50	Poul Hammer	Do.
19	Christian Olsen	do	April 1, 1866	Nov. 1, 1866	7	13	3.50	16.50	115.50	Christian Oleson	Do.
20	James V. Stephenson	do	April 1, 1866	Nov. 1, 1866	7	13	3.50	16.50	115.50	James V. Stevenson	Do.
21	Andrew Anderson	do	April 1, 1866	Nov. 1, 1866	7	13	3.50	16.50	113.50	Andrew Anderson	Do.

No.	Name		Enrolled	Mustered out							
52	Christian Anderson	do	April 1, 1866	Nov. 1, 1866	7	13	3 50	16 50	115 50	Niels C. Anderson	Do.
53	Niels C. Anderson	do	April 1, 1866	Nov. 1, 1866	7	13	3 50	16 50	115 50	Frederik Julius	Do.
54	Frederick Julius	do	April 1, 1866	Nov. 1, 1866	7	13	3 50	16 50	115 50	Rasmus Anderson	Do.
55	Rasmus Anderson	do	April 1, 1866	Nov. 1, 1866	7	13	3 50	16 50	115 50	Peter Ahlstrou	Do.
56	Peter Allstrom	do	April 1, 1866	Nov. 1, 1866	7	13	3 50	16 50	115 50	John Johnson	Do.
57	John Johnston	do	April 1, 1866	Nov. 1, 1866	7	13	3 50	16 50	115 50		Do.
58	Jens C. Nickson	do	April 1, 1866	Nov. 1, 1866	7	13	3 50	16 50	115 50	Ras Jensen	Do.
59	Rasmus Jenson	do	April 1, 1866	Nov. 1, 1866	7	13	3 50	16 50	115 50	James Hugg	Do.
30	James Hugg	do	April 1, 1866	Nov. 1, 1866	7	13	3 50	16 50	115 50	Freitz Molier	Do.
31	Fritz Mawler	do	April 1, 1866	Nov. 1, 1866	7	13	3 50	16 53	115 50	Even Forgeson	Do.
32	Even Forgeson	do	April 1, 1866	Nov. 1, 1866	7	13	3 50	16 50	115 50	Andrew Vestergard	Do.
33	Andrew Vestergard	do	April 1, 1866	Nov. 1, 1866	7	13	3 50	16 50	115 50	Hans Boson	Do.
34	Hans Boson	do	April 1, 1866	Nov. 1, 1866	7	13	3 50	16 50	115 50	Andrew Peterson	Po.
35	Andrews Peterson	do	April 1, 1866	Nov. 1, 1866	7	13	3 50	16 50	115 50	Jens Nielsen Engager	Do.
36	Jens Nielson Engager	do	April 1, 1866	Nov. 1, 1866	7	13	3 50	16 50	115 50	Made Larson	Do.
37	Made Larson	do	April 1, 1866	Nov. 1, 1866	7	13	3 50	16 50	115 50	Christian Christianson	Do.
38	Christian Christiansen	do	April 1, 1866	Nov. 1, 1866	7	13	3 50	16 50	115 51	Augnst Johansen	Do.
39	Augnst Johnson	do	April 1, 1866	Nov. 1, 1866	7	13	3 50	16 50	115 50	Nicls P. Nielson	Do.
40	Nicla P. Nielson	do	April 1, 1866	Nov. 1, 1866	7	13	3 50	16 50	115 59	Tohmas Byergard	Do.
41	Thomas Biergard	do	April 1, 1866	Nov. 1, 1866	7	13	3 50	16 50	115 50	Lars Niels n	Do.
42	Lars Nielson	do	April 1, 1866	Nov. 1, 1866	7	13	3 50	16 50	115 50	Tohmas Christoffar	Do.
43	Rasmus Christofersen	do	April 1, 1866	Nov. 1, 1866	7	13	3 50	16 50	115 50	Samuel Beal	Do.
44	Samuel Beal	do	April 1, 1866	Nov. 1, 1866	7	13	3 59	16 50	115 50	N. L. Petrsen	Do.
45	Niels L. Peterson	do	April 1, 1866	Nov. 1, 1866	7	13	3 50	16 50	115 50	Christian Jenson	Do.
46	Christian Jenson	do	April 1, 1866	Nov. 1, 1866	7	13	3 50	16 50	115 50	M. Nilson	Do.
47	Margens Nielson	do	April 1, 1866	Nov. 1, 1866	7	13	3 50	16 50	115 50	Johan Anderson	Do.
48	John Anderson	do	April 1, 1866	Nov. 1, 1866	7	13	3 50	16 50	115 50	Tory Thurston	Do.
49	Toro Thurston	do	April 1, 1867	Nov. 1, 1866	7	13	3 50	16 50	115 50	Peter Tommander	Do.
50	Peter Tommander	do	April 1, 1866	Nov. 1, 1866	7	13	3 50	16 50	115 50	Hans W. Nessen	Do.
51	Hans M. Nesson	do	April 1, 1866	Nov. 1, 1866	7	13	3 50	16 50	115 50		Do.

This company was mustered into service at Fort Ephraim, in Sanpete County, by Brigadier General Warren S. Snow, and by him assigned to duty in the mountains east of Fort Ephraim. They performed daily service in the defense of said city for the whole time specified above, and was mustered out November 1, 1866.

I certify that the above account is correct.

H. B. CLAWSON,
Adjutant General Utah Territory Militia.

Pay-roll of Captain Morten Mortenson's company —— infantry, employed in the suppression of Indian hostilities in Sanpete County, Utah Territory, from April 1, 1866, to November 1, 1866.

We, the undersigned, acknowledge to have received from James W. Cummings, paymaster Utah Territory militia, the sums set opposite to our names, in full payment for our services for the time specified.

Number.	Names.	Rank.	Period of service — Commencement.	Period of service — Expiration.	Months.	Pay per month.	Monthly allowance for clothing.	Total monthly pay and allowance.	Total pay and allowance.	Signatures.	Witnesses.
1	Morten Mortenson	Captain	April 1, 1866	Nov. 1, 1866	7			$118 50	$825 50	Morten Mortensen	William K. Barton.
1	Sethe Childs	1st lieut.	April 1, 1866	Nov. 1, 1866	7			108 50	759 50	Seth Childs	Do.
1	Jonathan Lancaster	2d lieut.	April 1, 1866	Nov. 1, 1866	7			103 50	724 50	Jonathan Lancaster	Do.
2	Johannes Sorensen	do	April 1, 1866	Nov. 1, 1866	7			103 50	724 50	Johannes Sorensen	Do.
3	Thomas Wasden	do	April 1, 1866	Nov. 1, 1866	7			103 50	724 50	Thomas Wasden	Do.
4	John Picket	do	April 1, 1866	Nov. 1, 1866	7			103 50	724 50	John Pickett	Do.
5	Hamloton Garrick	do	April 1, 1866	Nov. 1, 1866	7			103 50	724 50	IL Garrick	Do.
1	Austin Kearnes	Sergeant	April 1, 1866	Nov. 1, 1866	7	$17	$3 50	20 50	143 50	Austin Karen	Do.
2	Lars P. Fyeldsted	do	April 1, 1866	Nov. 1, 1866	7	17	3 50	20 50	143 50	Lars P. Fyeldsted	Do.
3	Lorenzo Babcock	do	April 1, 1866	Nov. 1, 1866	7	17	3 50	20 50	143 50	Lorenzo Babcock	Do.
4	George F-rsn	do	April 1, 1866	Nov. 1, 1866	7	17	3 50	20 50	143 50	George Fenn	Do.
5	Allen C. Bigelow	do	April 1, 1866	Nov. 1, 1866	7	17	3 50	20 50	143 50	Alen C. Biglow	Do.
2	Peter Brown	Private	April 1, 1866	Nov. 1, 1866	7	13	3 50	16 50	115 50	Peter Brown	Do.
3	Hans Jorgenson	do	April 1, 1866	Nov. 1, 1866	7	13	3 50	16 50	115 50	Hans Jorgensen	Do.
4	Andrew Nielson, Jr	do	April 1, 1866	Nov. 1, 1866	7	13	3 50	16 50	115 50	Andru Nielson, Jr	Do.
5	William Nay	do	April 1, 1866	Nov. 1, 1866	7	13	3 50	16 50	115 50	William Nay	Do.
6	Theodore Christiansen	do	April 1, 1866	Nov. 1, 1866	7	13	3 50	16 50	115 50	Theodor Christensen	Do.
7	Carl Bengland	do	April 1, 1866	Nov. 1, 1866	7	13	3 50	16 50	115 50	Carl Berglund	Do.
8	Heber Mawkin	do	April 1, 1866	Nov. 1, 1866	7	13	3 50	16 50	115 50	Heber Maxhum	Do.
9	John Fresin	do	April 1, 1866	Nov. 1, 1866	7	13	3 50	16 50	115 50	John Tresin	Do.
10	Peter F. Rasmussen	do	April 1, 1866	Nov. 1, 1866	7	13	3 50	16 50	115 50	Peter F. Rasmuson	Do.
11	Alexander Jimerson	do	April 1, 1866	Nov. 1, 1866	7	13	3 50	16 50	115 50	Alexander Jinarsen	Do.
12	Julius Christiansen	do	April 1, 1866	Nov. 1, 1866	7	13	3 50	16 50	115 50	Julius Christensen	Do.
13	Frederick Wasden	do	April 1, 1866	Nov. 1, 1866	7	13	3 50	16 50	115 50	Fredrick Wasden	Do.
14	Marl C. Anderson	do	April 1, 1866	Nov. 1, 1866	7	13	3 50	16 50	115 50	Mads C. Andersen	Do.
15	Heyman Lublin	do	April 1, 1866	Nov. 1, 1866	7	13	3 50	16 50	115 50	Herman Lublin	Do.
16	John E. Metcalf, Jr	do	April 1, 1866	Nov. 1, 1866	7	13	3 50	16 50	115 50	J. E. Metcalf, Jr	Do.
17	Jens M. Nielson	do	April 1, 1866	Nov. 1, 1866	7	13	3 50	16 50	115 50	Jens M. Nielsen	Do.
18	Niels Johansen	do	April 1, 1866	Nov. 1, 1866	7	13	3 50	16 50	115 50	John Christianson	Do.
19	Ole Okerlund	do	April 1, 1866	Nov. 1, 1866	7	13	3 50	16 50	115 50	Neuben Johansen	Do.
20	Christian P. Sorensen	do	April 1, 1866	Nov. 1, 1866	7	13	3 50	16 50	115 50	Ole Akerlund	Do.
21	Charles Gladell	do	April 1, 1866	Nov. 1, 1866	7	13	3 50	16 50	115 50	C. P. Sorensen	Do.
										Charles Gladell	Do.

No.	Name		Mustered in	Mustered out						Name	
22	Erick Lindburgh	do....	April 1, 1866	Nov. 1, 1866	7	13	3 50	16 50	115 50	Erick Lindburgh	Do.
23	James Hansen	do....	April 1, 1866	Nov. 1, 1866	7	13	3 50	16 50	115 50	James Hansen	Do.
24	George Beunut	do....	April 1, 1866	Nov. 1, 1866	7	13	3 50	16 50	115 50	George Beunus	Do.
25	William Babcock	do....	April 1, 1866	Nov. 1, 1866	7	13	3 50	16 50	115 50	William Babcock	Do.
26	Peter Marker	do....	April 1, 1866	Nov. 1, 1866	7	13	3 50	16 50	115 50	Peter Marker	Do.
27	Hans H. Peterson	do....	April 1, 1866	Nov. 1, 1866	7	13	3 50	16 50	115 50	Hans H. Peterson	Do.
28	Parlen McFarlin	do....	April 1, 1866	Nov. 1, 1866	7	13	3 50	16 50	115 50	Parlen McFarlin	Do.
29	Hans C. Hansen	do....	April 1, 1866	Nov. 1, 1866	7	13	3 50	16 50	115 50	Hans C. Hansen	Do.
30	John Boshard	do....	April 1, 1866	Nov. 1, 1866	7	13	3 50	16 50	115 50	John Boshard	Do.
31	Chris Christiansen	do....	April 1, 1866	Nov. 1, 1866	7	13	3 50	16 50	115 50	Chris Christiansen	Do.
32	James Sorensen	do....	April 1, 1866	Nov. 1, 1866	7	13	3 50	16 50	115 50	James Sorensen	Do.
33	Rasmus Jensen	do....	April 1, 1866	Nov. 1, 1866	7	13	3 50	16 50	115 50	Rasmus Jensen	Do.
34	Thomas Schofield	do....	April 1, 1866	Nov. 1, 1866	7	13	3 50	16 50	115 50	Thomas Schofield	Do.
35	Edward Ashworth	do....	April 1, 1866	Nov. 1, 1866	7	13	3 50	16 50	115 50	Edward Ashworth	Do.
36	John Overnburgh	do....	April 1, 1866	Nov. 1, 1866	7	13	3 50	16 50	115 50	John Gramberg	Do.
37	Ludwig Overnburgh	do....	April 1, 1866	Nov. 1, 1866	7	13	3 50	16 50	115 50	Ludwig Gramberg	Do.
38	Joseph Bardsley	do....	April 1, 1866	Nov. 1, 1866	7	13	3 50	16 50	115 50	Joseph Bardsley	Do.
39	William Andrews	do....	April 1, 1866	Nov. 1, 1866	7	13	3 50	16 50	115 50	William Andrew	Do.
40	Peter Poulson	do....	April 1, 1866	Nov. 1, 1866	7	13	3 50	16 50	115 50	Peter Poulson	Do.
41	Justruff Senier	do....	April 1, 1866	Nov. 1, 1866	7	13	3 50	16 50	115 50	Justruff Sinier	Do.
42	Ludwig Dustrip	do....	April 1, 1866	Nov. 1, 1866	7	13	3 50	16 50	115 50	Ludwig Dustrup	Do.
43	Jens Larsen	do....	April 1, 1866	Nov. 1, 1866	7	13	3 50	11 50	Jens Larsen		Do.
44	John Babcock	do....	April 1, 1866	Nov. 1, 1866	7	13	3 50	16 50	115 50	John Babcock	Do.
45	William McFadgen	do....	April 1, 1866	Nov. 1, 1866	7	13	3 50	16 50	115 50	William McFadgen	Do.
46	Henrie McKinney	do....	April 1, 1866	Nov. 1, 1866	7	13	3 50	16 50	115 50	Henrie McKinney	Do.
47	Sylvester Gribble	do....	April 1, 1866	Nov. 1, 1866	7	13	3 50	16 50	115 50	Sylvester Gribble	Do.
48	Ole Jensen	do....	April 1, 1866	Nov. 1, 1866	7	13	3 50	16 50	115 50	Ole Jensen	Do.
49	Jens C. Hansen	do....	April 1, 1866	Nov. 1, 1866	7	13	3 50	16 50	115 50	Jens C. Hansen	Do.
50	William Childs	do....	April 1, 1866	Nov. 1, 1866	7	13	3 50	16 50	115 50	William Childs	Do.
51	Hans P. Hansen	do....	April 1, 1866	Nov. 1, 1866	7	13	3 50	16 50	115 50	Hans P. Hansen	Do.
52	Joseph Bartholomew	do....	April 1, 1866	Nov. 1, 1866	7	13	3 50	16 50	115 50	Joseph Bartholomew	Do.

This company was mustered into service at Fort Gunnison, Sanpete County, April 1, 1866, by Brigadier General Warren S. Snow, and by him assigned to duty in the vicinity of Fort Gunnison, for the defense and protection of said city and its inhabitants. They performed regular service every day until mustered out, November 1, 1866.

I certify that the above account is correct.

H. B. CLAWSON,
Adjutant General Utah Militia.

Pay-roll of field and staff officers commanding the Utah Territory militia, employed in the suppression of Indian hostilities in Utah County, Utah Territory, in the months of June, July, August, and September, 1866.

We, the undersigned, acknowledge to have received from James W. Cummings, paymaster Utah Territory militia, the sums set opposite to our names, in full payment for our services for the time specified.

Names.	Staff; appointment office.	Rank.	Commencement.	Expiration.	Months.	Total monthly pay and allowance.	40 cts. per day for use and risk of horse and horse equipment.	Total pay and allowance.	Signatures.	Witnesses.
SECOND DIVISION.										
Aaron Johnson	Division adjutant	Major general	June 1, 1866	September 30, 1866	4	$345 00	$48 00	$1,898 00	Aaron Johnson	S. S. Jones
Lyman S. Woods	Division quartermaster	Colonel	June 1, 1866	September 30, 1866	4	211 00	48 00	892 00	Lyman S. Wood	Do.
William Miller	Division quartermaster	...do	June 1, 1866	September 30, 1866	4	211 00	48 00	892 00	William Miller	Do.
Derr P. Curtis	Division aide-de-c'p	...do	June 1, 1866	September 30, 1866	4	211 00	48 00	892 00	D. P. Curtis	Do.
William T. Lane	Division surgeon	Lieutenant colonel	June 1, 1866	September 30, 1866	4	187 00	48 00	700 00		Do.
Andrew R. Wild	Division aide-de-c'p	Major	June 1, 1866	September 30, 1866	4	163 00	48 00	700 00	Andrew B. Wild	Do.
Richard Bird	...do	...do	June 1, 1866	September 30, 1866	4	163 00	48 00	700 00	Rich'd Bird	Do.
FIRST BRIGADE.										
William B. Pace	Brigade adjutant	Brigadier general	June 1, 1866	September 30, 1866	4	299 00	48 00	1,244 00	Wm. B. Pace	S. S. Jones
Alexander F. McDonald	Brigade quartermaster	Lieutenant colonel	June 1, 1866	September 30, 1866	4	187 00	48 00	796 00	A. F. Macdonald	Do.
George W. Bean	Brigade aide-de-c'p	...do	June 1, 1866	September 30, 1906	4	187 00	48 00	796 00	Geo. W. Bean	Do.
John Leetham	Brigade aide-de-c'p	...do	June 1, 1866	September 30, 1866	4	187 00	48 00	796 00	John Leetham	Do.
John Riggs	Brigade surgeon	Major	June 1, 1866	September 30, 1866	4	163 00	48 00	700 00	John Riggs	Do.
Thadeus E. Fleming	Brigade aide-de-c'p	Captain	June 1, 1866	September 30, 1866	4	129 50	48 00	566 00	Thadeus E. Fleming	Do.
FIRST REGIMENT.										
Leonard J. Nuttall		Colonel	June 1, 1866	September 30, 1866	4	211 00	48 00	892 00	L. John Nuttall	S. S. Jones
James E. Daniels		Lieutenant colonel	June 1, 1866	September 30, 18-6	4	187 00	48 00	796 00	James E. Daniels	Do.
Samuel S. Jones	Regimental adjutant	Major	June 1, 1866	September 30, 1866	4	163 00	48 00	700 00	Samuel S. Jones	W. B. Pace.
Peter Stubbs	Reg. quartermaster	Captain	June 1, 1866	September 30, 1866	4	129 50	48 00	566 00	Peter Stubbs	S. S. Jones.
William W. Haws		Major	June 1, 1846	September 30, 1866	4	163 00	48 10	700 00	Wm. W. Haws	Do.
John P. R. Jones	Battalion adjutant	Captain	June 1, 1866	September 30, 1866	4	129 50	45 10			
William W. Alken	...do	...do	June 1, 1866	September 30, 1866	4	129 50	48 00			
SECOND REGIMENT.										
William E. McClellan		Colonel	June 1, 1866	September 30, 1866	4	211 00	48 00	892 00	Wm. C. McClellan	S. S. Jones.
Joseph W. Bates		Lieutenant colonel	June 1, 1866	September 30, 1866	4	187 01	48 00	766 00	Joseph W. Bates	Do.

Name		Rank	From	To					Name	Remarks
William Heaton	Regimental adjutant	Major	June 1, 1866	September 30, 1866	4	163 00	48 00	700 00	William Heaton	
J B Fairbanks	Reg. surgeon	Captain	June 1, 1866	September 30, 1866	4	129 50	48 00	566 00	William Dughau	Do.
William Douglas	Reg. quarterm'r	do	June 1, 1866	September 30, 1866	4	163 00	48 00	700 00	H. G. Boyle	Do.
Henry G. Boyle		Major	June 1, 1866	September 30, 1866	4	163 00	48 00	700 00	Geo. W. Haucock	Do.
George W. Haucock		do	June 1, 1866	September 30, 1866	4	163 00	48 00	700 00	William McBride	Do.
William McBride		do								
THIRD REGIMENT.										
William M. Bromley		Colonel	June 1, 1866	September 30, 1866	4	211 00	48 00	892 00	Wm. M. Bromley	S. S. Jones.
George D. Snell		Lieutenant colonel	June 1, 1866	September 30, 1866	4	187 00	48 00	796 00	George B. Snell	Do.
Joseph W. Bissell	Regimental adjutant	Major	June 1, 1866	September 30, 1866	4	163 00	48 00	700 00	J. W. Biswell	Do.
Charles D Evans	Reg. surgeon	Captain	June 1, 1866	September 30, 1866	4	129 50	48 00	565 00	Charles D. Evans	Do.
William D. Johnson		Major	June 1, 1866	September 30, 1866	4	163 00	48 00	700 00	Wm. D. Johnson	Do.
Gideon D. Wood		do	June 1, 1866	September 30, 1866	4	163 00	48 00	700 00	G. D. Wood	Do.
William Creer		do	June 1, 1866	September 30, 1866	4	163 00	48 00			
Samuel Thompson		do	June 1, 1866	September 30, 1866	4	163 00	48 00			
Henry E. Hudson		do	June 1, 1866	September 30, 1866	4	161 00	48 00	700 00	Henry E. Hudson	Do.
William Vest	Battalion adjutant	Captain	June 1, 1866	September 30, 1866	4	129 50	48 00	566 00	William Vest	Do.

The above field and staff officers of Utah County, Utah Territory, were mustered into service by order of Lieutenant General Daniel H. Wells. They were assigned to duty where their services were the most needed, in Utah, Juab, Sanpete, and Sevier counties. They were in active service every day for the time specified above, and mustered out on the 30th day of September, 1866.

I certify that the above account is correct.

H. B. CLAWSON,
Adjutant General Nauvoo Legion.

Pay-roll of Captain Jonathan S. Page's company ——— cavalry, Utah Territory militia, employed in the suppression of Indian hostilities in Sanpete and Sevier counties, in the months of July and August, 1866.

We, the undersigned, acknowledge to have received from James W. Cummings, paymaster Utah Territory militia, the sums set opposite to our names, in full payment for our services for the time specified.

No.	Names	Rank	Commencement	Expiration	Months	Days	Pay per month	Monthly allowance for clothing	Total monthly pay and allowance	40 cts. per day for use and risk of horse and horse equipment	Total pay and allowance	Signatures	Witnesses
1	Jonathan S. Page	Captain	July 3, 1866	Aug. 25, 1866	1	21		$3 50	$139 50	$20 40	$240 55	Jonathan S. Page	J. M. Coombs
1	Russell Kelley	1st lieutenant	July 3, 1866	Aug. 25, 1866	1	21		3 50	112 83	30 40	212 55	Russell Kelley	Do.
1	James Maxwell	2d lieutenant	July 3, 1866	Aug. 25, 1866	1	21		3 50	112 83	30 40	212 55	James Maxwell	Do.
2	R. S. Mendenhall	do.	July 3, 1866	Aug. 25, 1866	1	21		3 50	112 83	30 40	212 55	R. S. Mendenhall	A. F. Macdonald.
3	Roger Farrer	do.	July 3, 1866	Aug. 25, 1866	1	21		3 50	112 83	30 40	212 55	Roger Farrer	Do.
4	Joseph Foutz	do.	July 3, 1866	Aug. 25, 1866	1	21		3 50	112 83	30 40	212 55	Joseph Foutz	J. M. Coombs.
5	Charles Robinson	do.	July 3, 1866	Aug. 25, 1866	1	21		3 50	112 83	30 40	212 55	Charles Robinson	Do.
1	John C. Searle	Sergeant	July 3, 1866	Aug. 25, 1866	1	21	$17 00	3 50	20 50	30 40	55 55	John C. Searle	Do.
2	Henry Holden	do.	July 3, 1866	Aug. 25, 1866	1	21	17 00	3 50	20 50	30 40	55 55	H. J. Moore	A. F. Macdonald.
3	Francis Holden	do.	July 3, 1866	Aug. 25, 1866	1	21	17 00	3 50	20 50	30 40	55 55	Henry Holden	J. Evans.
4	F. D. Shaffer	do.	July 3, 1866	Aug. 25, 1866	1	21	17 00	3 50	20 50	30 40	55 55	Francs Molen	
1	Warren S. Pace	Private	July 3, 1866	Aug. 25, 1866	1	21	13 00	3 50	16 50	30 40	44 45	W. S. Pace	J. M. Coombs.
2	Thomas Wimmer	do.	July 3, 1866	Aug. 25, 1866	1	21	13 00	3 50	16 50	30 40	44 45	Thomas Wimmer	Do.
3	George Todd	do.	July 3, 1866	Aug. 25, 1866	1	21	13 00	3 50	16 50	30 40	44 45	George Todd	Do.
4	Benjamin F. Stewart	do.	July 3, 1866	Aug. 25, 1866	1	21	13 00	3 50	16 50	30 40	44 45	B. F. Stewart	Do.
5	Henry Fairbanks	do.	July 3, 1866	Aug. 25, 1866	1	21	13 00	3 50	16 50	30 40	44 45	Henry Fairbanks	Do.
6	Ammon Nebeker	do.	July 3, 1866	Aug. 25, 1866	1	21	13 00	3 50	16 50	30 40	44 45	Ammon Nebeker	Do.
7	Samuel Perry	do.	July 3, 1866	Aug. 25, 1866	1	21	13 00	3 50	16 50	30 40	44 45	Samuel Peerry	Do.
8	Daniel Maxwell	do.	July 3, 1866	Aug. 25, 1866	1	21	13 00	3 50	16 50	30 40	44 45	Daniel Maxwell	Do.
9	George Rust	do.	July 3, 1866	Aug. 25, 1866	1	21	13 00	3 50	16 50	30 40	44 45	George S. Rust	Do.
10	Warren Hancock	do.	July 3, 1866	Aug. 25, 1866	1	21	13 00	3 50	16 50	30 40	44 45	Warren Hancock	Do.
11	R. S. Mendenhall	do.	July 3, 1866	Aug. 25, 1866	1	21	13 00	3 50	16 50	30 40	44 45		Do.
12	H. J. Moore	do.	July 3, 1866	Aug. 25, 1866	1	21	13 00	3 50	16 50	30 40	44 45		Do.
13	John Davis	do.	July 3, 1866	Aug. 25, 1866	1	21	13 00	3 50	16 50	30 40	44 45	John Davis	A. F. Macdonald.
14	Albert Harmer	do.	July 3, 1866	Aug. 25, 1866	1	21	13 00	3 50	16 50	30 40	44 45	Albert Harmer	Do.
15	William Chisholm	do.	July 3, 1866	Aug. 25, 1866	1	21	13 00	3 50	16 50	30 40	44 45	William Chisom	Do.
16	Martin Farr	do.	July 3, 1866	Aug. 25, 1866	1	21	13 00	3 50	16 50	30 40	44 45	Martin Parr	Do.
17	Bartlett Neilson	do.	July 3, 1866	Aug. 25, 1866	1	21	13 00	3 50	16 50	30 40	44 45	Bartlett Neilson	Do.
18	Henry Babcock	do.	July 3, 1866	Aug. 25, 1866	1	21	13 00	3 50	16 50	30 40	44 45	Henry Babcock	Do.
19	Benjamin Buchanan	do.	July 3, 1866	Aug. 25, 1866	1	21	13 00	3 50	16 50	30 40	44 45	Benjamin Buchanan	Do.
20	George Ainge	do.	July 3, 1866	Aug. 25, 1866	1	21	13 00	3 50	16 50	30 40	44 45	George Ainge	Do.
21	Alma C. Davis	do.	July 3, 1866	Aug. 25, 1866	1	21	13 00	3 50	16 50	30 40	44 45	Alma C. Davis	Do.

No.	Name		Mustered in	Mustered out							Name	Remarks
22	Samuel Buckley	do.	July 3, 1866	Aug. 25, 1866	21	13 00	3 50	16 50	20 40	48 45	Samuel Buckley	Do.
23	Roger Farrer	do.	July 3, 1866	Aug. 25, 1866	21	13 00	3 50	16 50	20 40	48 45	Roger Farrer	J. M. Coombs.
24	Henry Holden	do.	July 3, 1866	Aug. 25, 1866	21	13 00	3 50	16 50	20 40	48 45	T. J. Patton	A. F. Macdonald.
25	T. J. Patton	do.	July 3, 1866	Aug. 25, 1866	21	13 00	3 50	16 50	20 40	48 45	A. Jones	Do.
26	Albert Jones	do.	July 3, 1866	Aug. 25, 1866	21	13 00	3 50	16 50	20 40	48 45	Watson Bell	Do.
27	Watson Bell	do.	July 3, 1866	Aug. 25, 1866	21	13 00	3 50	16 50	20 40	48 45	John Johnson	Do.
28	John Johnson	do.	July 3, 1866	Aug. 25, 1866	21	13 00	3 50	16 50	20 40	48 45	George Bann	Do.
29	George Bann	do.	July 3, 1866	Aug. 25, 1866	21	13 00	3 50	16 50	20 40	48 45	Lewellen Lewis	Do.
30	Lewellen Lewis	do.	July 3, 1866	Aug. 25, 1866	21	13 00	3 50	16 50	20 40	48 45	James Herbert	Do.
31	James Herbert	do.	July 3, 1866	Aug. 25, 1866	21	13 00	3 50	16 50	20 40	48 45	Alpheus Conover	Do.
32	Alpheus Conover	do.	July 3, 1866	Aug. 25, 1866	21	13 00	3 50	16 50	20 40	48 45	John T. Morgan	Do.
33	John T. Morgan	do.	July 3, 1866	Aug. 25, 1866	21	13 00	3 50	16 50	20 41	48 45	A. D. Shepherd	J. Evans.
34	A. D. Shepherd	do.	July 3, 1866	Aug. 25, 1866	21	13 00	3 50	16 50	20 40	48 45	Orlando Herron	Do.
35	Orlando Herron	do.	July 3, 1866	Aug. 25, 1866	21	13 00	3 50	16 50	20 40	48 45	George McConnell	Do.
36	George McConnell	do.	July 3, 1866	Aug. 25, 1866	21	13 00	3 50	16 50	20 40	48 45	Daniel Thomas	Do.
37	Daniel Thomas	do.	July 3, 1866	Aug. 25, 1866	21	13 00	3 50	16 50	20 40	48 45	Newell Brown	Do.
38	Newell Brown	do.	July 3, 1866	Aug. 25, 1866	21	13 00	3 50	16 50	20 40	48 45	Joseph Ashton	Do.
39	Joseph Ashton	do.	July 3, 1866	Aug. 25, 1866	21	13 00	3 50	16 50	20 40	48 45	William Matthews	Do.
40	William Matthews	do.	July 3, 1866	Aug. 25, 1866	21	13 00	3 50	16 50	20 40	48 45	John E. Ross	Do.
41	John E. Ross	do.	July 3, 1866	Aug. 25, 1866	21	13 00	3 50	16 50	20 40	48 45	Joseph Errard	Do.
42	Joseph Errard	do.	July 3, 1866	Aug. 25, 1866	21	13 00	3 50	16 50	20 40	48 45	Robert Kirkman	A. F. Macdonald.
43	Robert Kirkman	do.	July 3, 1866	Aug. 25, 1866	21	13 00	3 50	16 50	20 40	48 45	Theodore Harrington	William Greenwood.
44	Theodore Harrington	do.	July 3, 1866	Aug. 25, 1866	21	13 00	3 50	16 50	20 40	48 45	George Huggard	Do.
45	George Huggard	do.	July 3, 1866	Aug. 25, 1866	21	13 00	3 50	16 50	20 40	48 45	John Roberts	Do.
46	John Roberts	do.	July 3, 1866	Aug. 25, 1866	21	13 00	3 50	16 50	20 40	48 45	James Hickerson	Do.
47	James Hickerson	do.	July 3, 1866	Aug. 25, 1866	21	13 00	3 50	16 50	20 40	48 45	Thomas Crookstan	Do.
48	Thomas Crookstan	do.	July 3, 1866	Aug. 25, 1866	21	13 00	3 50	16 50	20 40	48 45	Thomas Karren	Do.
49	Thomas Karren	do.	July 3, 1866	Aug. 25, 1866	21	13 00	3 50	16 50	20 40	48 45		J. Evans.

This company was mustered into service at Payson, Utah County, by order of Major General Aaron Johnson, July 3, 1866, and on that day started for Sanpete County; arrived at Fort Gunnison, in said county, July 6, 1866, and was assigned to duty by Lieutenant General D. H. Wells, in the eastern mountains and passes on the Severe River, in Severe and Piute counties. They were in active service every day until they returned to Payson, and mustered out on the 25th day of August, 1866.

I certify that the above account is correct.

H. B. CLAWSON,
Adjutant General Utah Territory Militia.

Pay-roll of Captain George Gardner's company ——— infantry, Utah Territory militia, employed in the suppression of Indian hostilities in Sanpete and Sevier counties, from April 1, 1866, to November 1, 1866.

We, the undersigned, acknowledge to have received from James W. Cummings, paymaster Utah Territory militia, the sums set opposite to our names, in full payment for our services for the time specified.

Number.	Names.	Rank.	Commencement.	Expiration.	Months.	Pay per month.	Monthly allowance for clothing.	Total monthly pay and allowance.	Total pay and allowance.	Signatures.	Witnesses.
1	George Gardner	Captain	April 1, 1866	Nov. 1, 1866	7			$118 50	$829 50	George Gardener	William K. Barton.
1	Hans Tonasen	1st lieut.	April 1, 1866	Nov. 1, 1866	7			108 50	759 50	Hans Thuneson	Do.
1	Jonathan Heaton	2d lieut.	April 1, 1866	Nov. 1, 1866	7			103 50	724 50	Johnathan Eaton	Do.
2	Peter Field	do	April 1, 1866	Nov. 1, 1866	7			103 50	724 50	Peter Freave	Do.
3	Niels Tueson	do	April 1, 1866	Nov. 1, 1866	7			103 50	724 50	Niels Tueleln	Do.
4	Andrew Jorgensen	do	April 1, 1866	Nov. 1, 1866	7			103 50	724 50	Andrew Jorgensen	Do.
5	Hans Toft	do	April 1, 1866	Nov. 1, 1866	7			103 50	724 50	Hans Toft	Do.
1	Henry K. Maxham	Sergeant	April 1, 1866	Nov. 1, 1866	7	$17	$3 50	20 50	143 50	Henry K. Maxham	Do.
2	Jens Jepsen	do	April 1, 1866	Nov. 1, 1866	7	17	3 50	20 50	143 50	Jens Jepsen	Do.
3	Lars Peterson	do	April 1, 1866	Nov. 1, 1866	7	17	3 50	20 50	141 50	Lars Pettersen	Do.
4	Morten Brown	do	April 1, 1866	Nov. 1, 1866	7	17	3 50	20 50	143 50	Morten Brunn	Do.
5	Hans Larsen	do	April 1, 1866	Nov. 1, 1866	7	17	3 50	20 50	143 50	Hans Larsen	Do.
1	Jacob Inlander	Private	April 1, 1866	Nov. 1, 1866	7	13	3 50	16 50	115 50	Jacob Inlander	Do.
2	William Bartholomew	do	April 1, 1866	Nov. 1, 1866	7	13	3 50	16 50	115 50	Will Bartholomew	Do.
3	Anthony Metcalf	do	April 1, 1866	Nov. 1, 1866	7	13	3 50	16 50	115 50	Anthony Metcalf	Do.
4	William Muther	do	April 1, 1866	Nov. 1, 1866	7	13	3 50	16 50	115 50	William Mallor	Do.
5	Frederick Ludrigsen	do	April 1, 1866	Nov. 1, 1866	7	13	3 50	16 50	115 50	Frederick Ludvigsen	Do.
6	Anthony Wing	do	April 1, 1866	Nov. 1, 1866	7	13	3 50	16 50	115 50	Anthony Wing	Do.
7	Mads P. Sorensen	do	April 1, 1866	Nov. 1, 1866	7	13	3 50	16 50	115 50	Mads P. Sor-nsen	Do.
8	Henry Rodgers	do	April 1, 1866	Nov. 1, 1866	7	13	3 50	16 50	115 50	Henry Roper	Do.
9	Thomas Jones	do	April 1, 1866	Nov. 1, 1866	7	13	3 50	16 50	115 50	Thomas Jones, his + mark	Do.
10	Ole Olsen	do	April 1, 1866	Nov. 1, 1866	7	13	3 50	16 50	115 50	Ole Olsen	Do.
11	Jens F. Mortensen	do	April 1, 1866	Nov. 1, 1866	7	13	3 50	16 50	115 50	Jens F. Mortensen	Do.
12	Fredman Gregory	do	April 1, 1866	Nov. 1, 1866	7	13	3 50	16 50	115 50	William Inkender	Do.
13	Lewis Jensen	do	April 1, 1866	Nov. 1, 1866	7	13	3 50	16 50	115 50	Rand Jensen	Do.
14	William Bradley	do	April 1, 1866	Nov. 1, 1866	7	13	3 50	16 50	115 50	William Bradsky	Do.
15	George Hansen	do	April 1, 1866	Nov. 1, 1866	7	13	3 50	16 50	115 50		Do.
16	William Brown	do	April 1, 1866	Nov. 1, 1866	7	13	3 50	16 50	115 50	William Brown	Do.
17	James Kearnes	do	April 1, 1866	Nov. 1, 1866	7	13	3 50	16 50	115 50	James Kennes	Do.
18	Brigham Ney	do	April 1, 1866	Nov. 1, 1866	7	13	3 50	16 50	115 50	Brigham Ney	Do.
19	Joshua Silvester	do	April 1, 1866	Nov. 1, 1866	7	13	3 50	16 50	115 50		Do.
20	Ledrick Christiansen	do	April 1, 1866	Nov. 1, 1866	7	13	3 50	16 50	115 50	Ledrick Christensen	Do.

No.	Name		Enlisted	Discharged						Name	
22	John Sorensen, jr	do	April 1, 1866	Nov. 1, 1866	7	13	3 50	16 50	115 50	John Sorensen	Do.
23	Soren Sorensen	do	April 1, 1866	Nov. 1, 1866	7	13	3 50	16 50	115 50	Soren Sorensen	Do.
24	Liberty Millett	do	April 1, 1866	Nov. 1, 1866	7	13	3 50	16 50	115 50	Hans Toft, sen'r.	Do.
25	Hans Toft, jr.	do	April 1, 1866	Nov. 1, 1866	7	13	3 50	16 50	115 50	Amos Stevens	Do.
26	Amos Stephens	do	April 1, 1866	Nov. 1, 1866	7	13	3 50	16 50	115 50	John Warsden	Do.
27	John Wasdom	do	April 1, 1866	Nov. 1, 1866	7	13	3 50	16 50	115 51	George Sorensen	Do.
28	George Sorenson	do	April 1, 1866	Nov. 1, 1866	7	13	3 50	16 50	115 50	Ole G. Olson	Do.
29	Ole G. Olson	do	April 1, 1866	Nov. 1, 1866	7	13	3 50	16 50	115 50	Soren Jenson	Do.
30	Soren Jensen	do	April 1, 1866	Nov. 1, 1866	7	13	3 50	16 50	115 50	J. P. Frileard	Do.
31	John Peter Frileard	do	April 1, 1866	Nov. 1, 1866	7	13	3 50	16 50	115 50	Toumas Peterson	Do.
32	Thomas Peterson	do	April 1, 1866	Nov. 1, 1866	7	13	3 50	16 50	115 50	Henry Keaues	Do.
33	Henry Keaues	do	April 1, 1866	Nov. 1, 1866	7	13	3 50	16 50	115 50	Brigham Inlander	Do.
34	Brigham Vilander	do	April 1, 1866	Nov. 1, 1866	7	13	3 30	16 50	115 50	Christen Hansen	Do.
35	Christen Hansen	do	April 1, 1866	Nov. 1, 1866	7	13	3 50	16 50	115 50	Samuel Lublin	Do.
36	Samuel Lutbland	do	April 1, 1866	Nov. 1, 1866	7	13	3 50	16 50	115 50	Ole Andersen	Do.
37	Ole Anderson	do	April 1, 1866	Nov. 1, 1866	7	13	3 50	16 50	115 50	N. Landstrum	Do.
38	Niels Lundstrum	do	April 1, 1866	Nov. 1, 1866	7	13	3 50	14 50	115 50	Samuel Bardsley	Do.
39	Samuel Braadsley	do	April 1, 1866	Nov. 1, 1866	7	13	3 30	16 50	115 30	William Christinsen	Do.
40	William Christensen	do	April 1, 1866	Nov. 1, 1866	7	13	3 50	16 50	115 50	Lars Madson	Do.
41	Lars Madson	do	April 1, 1866	Nov. 1, 1866	7	13	3 50	10 50	115 50	Lars Eskhind	Do.
42	Lars Eskland	do	April 1, 1866	Nov. 1, 1866	7	13	3 50	16 50	115 50	George Hawley	Do.
43	George Hawlep	do	April 1, 1866	Nov. 1, 1866	7	13	3 50	16 50	115 50	Harman Christensen	Do.
44	Harman Christenson	do	April 1, 1866	Nov. 1, 1866	7	13	3 50	16 50	115 50	James Silvester	Do.
45	James Sylvestor	do	April 1, 1866	Nov. 1, 1866	7	13	3 50	16 50	115 50	Rund Jensen	Do.
46	Rund Jeusen	do	April 1, 1866	Nov. 1, 1866	7	13	3 30	16 50	115 50	Daniel Brown	Do.
47	Daniel Brown	do	April 1, 1866	Nov. 1, 1866	7	13	3 50	16 50	115 50	Mads Jonson	Do.
48	Muts Jensen	do	April 1, 1866	Nov. 1, 1866	7	13	3 50	16 50	115 50	John Swenson	Do.
49	John Swensen	do	April 1, 1866	Nov. 1, 1866	7	13	3 50	16 50	115 50	Soren P. Peterson	Do.
50	Soren P. Peterson	do	April 1, 1866	Nov. 1, 1866	7	13	3 50	10 50	115 50	Ivor Hendriksen, X	Do.
51	Ivoy Hendry, sr.	do	April 1, 1866	Nov. 1, 1866	7	13	3 50	16 50	115 50	James Steel	Do.
52	James Steel	do	April 1, 1866	Nov. 1, 1866	7	13	3 50	10 50	115 50	Morten Brown	Do.
53	Morten Brown	do	April 1, 1866	Nov. 1, 1866	7	13	3 50	10 50	115 50		Do.

This company was mustered into service at Fort Gunnison, Sanpete County, April 1, 1866, by Brigadier General Warren S. Snow, and by him assigned to duty in the vicinity of said city. They were in active service every day for the time specified above, and were mustered out November 1, 1866.

I certify that the above account is correct.

H. B. CLAWSON,
Adjutant General Nauvoo Legion.

Pay-roll of Captain *William C. Whightman's* company —— infantry, Utah Territory militia, employed in the suppression of Indian hostilities in Payson, Pondtown, Santiquin, and Goshen, Utah County, Utah Territory, *from May 11, 1866, to August 29, 1866.*

We, the undersigned, acknowledge to have received from James W. Cummings, paymaster Utah Territory militia, the sums set opposite to our names, in full payment for our services for the time specified.

Number	Names	Rank	Commence-ment	Expiration	Months	Days	Pay per month	Monthly allow-ance for cloth-ing	Total monthly pay and allow-ance	Total pay and allowance	Signatures	Witnesses
1	William C. Whightman	Captain	May 11, 1866	Aug. 29, 1866	3	18			$118 50	$436 60	Wm. C. Wightman	William Heaton.
1	Ephraim Ellsworth	1st lieut.	May 11, 1866	Aug. 29, 1866	3	18			108 50	390 60	Ephraim Ellsworth	Do.
1	Parley P. Loveless	2d lieut.	May 11, 1866	Aug. 29, 1866	3	18			103 50	372 60	Parley P. Loveless	Do.
2	Charles Brewerton	do	May 11, 1866	Aug. 29, 1866	3	18			103 50	372 60	Chas. Brewerton	Do.
3	David E. Seargent	do	May 11, 1866	Aug. 29, 1866	3	18			103 50	372 60	David E. Sargent	Do.
4	Samuel Curtis	do	May 11, 1866	Aug. 29, 1866	3	18			103 50	372 60	Samuel T. Curtis	Do.
5	John Zundal	do	May 11, 1866	Aug. 29, 1866	3	18			103 50	372 60		Do.
6	Henry E. Gardner	Sergeant	May 11, 1866	Aug. 29, 1866	3	18	$17 00	$3 50	20 50	73 40	Henry E. Gardiner	Do.
1	Joseph Jones	do	May 11, 1866	Aug. 29, 1866	3	18	17 00	3 50	20 50	73 40	Joseph Jones	Do.
2	Joseph Hewish	do	May 11, 1866	Aug. 29, 1866	3	18	17 00	3 50	20 50	73 40	Joseph Huish	Do.
3	Jesse Taylor	do	May 11, 1866	Aug. 29, 1866	3	18	17 00	3 50	20 50	73 40	Jesse S. Taylor	Do.
4	Everett Richmond	do	May 11, 1866	Aug. 29, 1866	3	18	17 00	3 50	20 50	73 40	Everett Richmond	Do.
5	F. M. Ewell	Private	May 11, 1866	Aug. 29, 1866	3	18	13 00	3 50	16 50	59 40	F. M. Ewell	Do.
1	William P. Stewart	do	May 11, 1866	Aug. 29, 1866	3	18	13 00	3 50	16 50	59 40	Wm. P. Stewart	Do.
2	William Depew	do	May 11, 1866	Aug. 29, 1866	3	18	13 00	3 50	16 50	59 40	William Depew	Do.
3	Charles Long	do	May 11, 1866	Aug. 29, 1866	3	18	13 00	3 50	16 50	59 40	Charles Long	Do.
4	William Powell	do	May 11, 1866	Aug. 29, 1866	3	18	13 00	3 50	16 50	59 40	Wm. Powell	Do.
5	Norman Filmore	do	May 11, 1866	Aug. 29, 1866	3	18	13 00	3 50	16 50	59 40	Norman Filmore	Do.
6	Joseph Whightman	do	May 11, 1866	Aug. 29, 1866	3	18	13 00	3 50	16 50	59 40	Joseph Wightman	Do.
7	Thomas P. Cloward	do	May 11, 1866	Aug. 29, 1866	3	18	13 00	3 50	16 50	59 40	T. P. Cloward	Do.
8	Cornelius Melinger	do	May 11, 1866	Aug. 29, 1866	3	18	13 00	3 50	16 50	59 40	Cornelius Mellinger	Do.
9	O. Knowlton	do	May 11, 1866	Aug. 29, 1866	3	18	13 00	3 50	16 50	59 40	Far	Do.
10	James E. Jones	do	May 11, 1866	Aug. 29, 1866	3	18	13 00	3 50	16 50	59 40	James E. Jones	Do.
11	Albert Kempton	do	May 11, 1866	Aug. 29, 1866	3	18	13 00	3 50	16 50	59 40	Alvin Krempton	Do.
12	Hyram Spencer	do	May 11, 1866	Aug. 29, 1866	3	18	13 00	3 50	16 50	59 40	Hyrum Spencer	Do.
13	Thomas Clayson	do	May 11, 1866	Aug. 29, 1866	3	18	13 00	3 50	16 50	59 40	Thomas Clayson	Do.
14	Nephi A. Loveless	do	May 11, 1866	Aug. 29, 1866	3	18	13 00	3 50	16 50	59 40	N. A. Lovel-ss	Do.
15	Francis Keel	do	May 11, 1866	Aug. 29, 1866	3	18	13 00	3 50	16 50	59 40	Francis M. Reel	Do.
16	Henry Terbit	do	May 11, 1866	Aug. 29, 1866	3	18	13 00	3 50	16 50	59 40		Do.
17	Jonathan G. Davis	do	May 11, 1866	Aug. 29, 1866	3	18	13 00	3 51	16 50	59 40	Jonathan Davis	Do.
18	Alexander G. Davis	do	May 11, 1866	Aug. 29, 1866	3	18	13 00	3 50	16 50	59 40	A. G. Davis	Do.

No.	Name		Enrolled							Mustered	Name	
19	Edward K. Roberts	do.	May 11, 1866	3	18	13 00	3 50	16 50	59 40	Aug. 29, 1866	E. K. Roberts	Do.
20	Peter Winward	do.	May 11, 1866	3	18	13 00	3 50	16 50	59 40	Aug. 29, 1866	Peter Winward	Do.
21	James Knight	do.	May 11, 1866	3	18	13 00	3 50	16 50	59 40	Aug. 29, 1866	James Knights	Do.
22	William Keel	do.	May 11, 1866	3	18	13 00	3 50	16 50	59 40	Aug. 29, 1866	William Keel	Do.
23	Dabery Keel	do.	May 11, 1866	3	18	13 00	3 50	16 50	59 40	Aug. 29, 1866	Dabery Keel	Do.
24	John Spencer	do.	May 11, 1866	3	18	13 00	3 50	16 50	59 40	Aug. 29, 1866	John Spencer	Do.
25	George Williams	do.	May 11, 1866	3	18	13 00	3 50	16 50	59 40	Aug. 29, 1866	George Williams	Do.
26	David Sabin	do.	May 11, 1866	3	18	13 00	3 50	16 50	59 40	Aug. 29, 1866	David Sabin	Do.
27	Richard Betts	do.	May 11, 1866	3	18	13 00	3 50	16 50	59 40	Aug. 29, 1866	Richard Betts	Do.
28	Benjamin Hancock	do.	May 11, 1866	3	18	13 00	3 50	16 50	59 40	Aug. 29, 1866	Benj'n Hancock	Do.
29	Durant Searle	do.	May 11, 1866	3	18	13 00	3 50	16 50	59 40	Aug. 29, 1866	Delmot Searle	Do.
30	Andrew Box	do.	May 11, 1866	3	18	13 00	3 50	16 50	59 40	Aug. 29, 1866	Andrew Box	Do.
31	Parley Sabin	do.	May 11, 1866	3	18	13 00	3 50	16 50	59 40	Aug. 29, 1866	Parley Sabin	Do.
32	James Ellsworth	do.	May 11, 1866	3	18	13 00	3 50	16 50	59 40	Aug. 29, 1866	James Elkworth	Do.
33	James Huish	do.	May 11, 1866	3	18	13 00	3 50	16 50	59 40	Aug. 29, 1866	James W. Huish	Do.
34	William Cloward	do.	May 11, 1866	3	18	13 00	3 50	16 50	59 40	Aug. 29, 1866	William Cloward	Do.
35	Jo'n Maxwell	do.	May 11, 1866	3	18	13 00	3 50	16 50	59 40	Aug. 29, 1866	John Maxwel	Do.
36	Ransome Filmore	do.	May 11, 1866	3	18	13 00	3 50	16 50	59 40	Aug. 29, 1866	Ransom Fillmore	Do.
37	Thomas Zundal	do.	May 11, 1866	3	18	13 00	3 50	16 50	59 40	Aug. 29, 1866	Thomas Zundle	Do.
38	Harry Clark	do.	May 11, 1866	3	18	13 00	3 50	16 50	59 40	Aug. 29, 1866	Harvey Clark	Do.
39	Ruben Jolly	do.	May 11, 1866	3	18	13 00	3 50	16 50	59 40	Aug. 29, 1866	Reuben Jolley	Do.
40	James Memmot	do.	May 11, 1866	3	18	13 00	3 50	16 50	59 40	Aug. 29, 1866	James Memmat	Do.
41	John Juckson	do.	May 11, 1866	3	18	13 00	3 50	16 50	59 40	Aug. 29, 1866	John Juckson	Do.
42	David Wilson	do.	May 11, 1866	3	18	13 00	3 50	16 50	59 40	Aug. 29, 1866	David Wilson	Do.
43	Henry Kay	do.	May 11, 1866	3	18	13 00	3 50	16 50	59 40	Aug. 29, 1866	Henery Key	Do.
44	Thomas G. Wilson	do.	May 11, 1866	3	18	13 00	3 50	16 50	59 40	Aug. 29, 1866	T. G. Wilson	Do.
45	John Mikesell	do.	May 11, 1866	3	18	13 00	3 50	16 50	59 40	Aug. 29, 1866	John Mikesell, jr.	Do.
46	George Nebeker	do.	May 11, 1866	3	18	13 00	3 50	16 50	59 40	Aug. 29, 1866	George Nebeker	Do.
47	William P. Bell	do.	May 11, 1866	3	18	13 00	3 50	16 50	59 40	Aug. 29, 1866		J. M. Combs.
48	Jerman Johnson	do.	May 11, 1866	3	18	13 00	3 50	16 50	59 40	Aug. 29, 1866	German Johnson	Do.
49	Joseph Wignall	do.	May 11, 1866	3	18	13 00	3 50	16 50	59 40	Aug. 29, 1866	Joseph Wignall	Do.
50	Hyrum Loveless	do.	May 11, 1866	3	18	13 00	3 50	16 50	59 40	Aug. 29, 1866	Hyrum Loveless	Do.

This company was mustered into service at Payson, Utah County, May 11, 1866, by order of Major General Aaron Johnson, and assigned to duty by him in the vicinity of Goshen and surrounding country; they were in active service until mustered out, August 29, 1866.

I certify that the above account is correct.

H. B. CLAWSON,
Adjutant General Utah Territory Militia.

Pay-roll of Captain Charles C. Burr's company —— infantry, Utah Territory militia, employed in the suppression of Indian hostilities in Payson, Pondtown, Santaquin, and Goshen, Utah County, Utah Territory, from May 11, 1866, to August 29, 1866.

We, the undersigned, acknowledge to have received from James W. Cummings, paymaster Utah Territory militia, the sums set opposite to our names, in full payment for our services for the time specified.

Number	Names	Rank	Commencement	Expiration	Months	Days	Pay per month	Monthly allowance for clothing	Total monthly pay and allowance	Total pay and allowance	Signatures	Witnesses
1	Charles C. Burr	Captain	May 11, 1866	Aug. 29, 1866	3	18			$118 50	$486 60	C. C. Burr	W. B. Pace.
2	John Butler	1st lieut	May 11, 1866	Aug. 29, 1866	3	18			108 50	390 63	John Butler	Do.
3	James Hall	Private	May 11, 1866	Aug. 29, 1866	3	18	$13 00	$3 50	16 50	59 40	James Hall	Do.
4	Charles B. Whightman	do	May 11, 1866	Aug. 29, 1866	3	18	13 00	3 50	16 50	59 40	C. B. Wightman	Do.
5	Hyrum Elmore	do	May 11, 1866	Aug. 29, 1866	3	18	13 00	3 50	16 50	59 40	Hiram Elmer	Do.
6	George Killian	do	May 11, 1866	Aug. 29, 1866	3	18	13 00	3 50	16 50	59 40	George Killian	Do.
7	Curtis E. Botton	do	May 11, 1866	Aug. 29, 1866	3	18	13 00	3 50	16 50	59 40	Curtis E. Botton	Do.
8	John H. Moore, sen	do	May 11, 1866	Aug. 29, 1866	3	18	13 00	3 50	16 50	59 40	John H. Moore, sen	Do.
9	William W. Rust	do	May 11, 1866	Aug. 29, 1866	3	18	13 00	3 50	16 50	59 40	Wm. W. Rust	Do.
10	Joseph Curtis	do	May 11, 1866	Aug. 29, 1866	3	18	13 00	3 50	16 50	59 40	Joseph Curtis	Do.
11	David S. Colvin	do	May 11, 1866	Aug. 29, 1866	3	18	13 00	3 50	16 50	59 40	David S. Colvin	Do.
12	Barton H. Phelps	do	May 11, 1866	Aug. 29, 1866	3	18	13 00	3 50	16 50	59 40	Barton H. Phelps	Do.
13	Christopher Dixon	do	May 11, 1866	Aug. 29, 1866	3	18	13 00	3 50	16 50	59 40	Christopher Dixon	Do.
14	William Calkins	do	May 11, 1866	Aug. 29, 1866	3	18	13 00	3 50	16 50	59 40	William Kalkins	Do.
15	Philo Johnson	do	May 11, 1866	Aug. 29, 1866	3	18	13 00	3 50	16 50	59 40	Philo Johnson	Do.
16	Anson Sheffield	do	May 11, 1866	Aug. 29, 1866	3	18	13 00	3 50	16 50	59 40	Anson Sheffield	Do.
17	David Lamb	do	May 11, 1866	Aug. 29, 1866	3	18	13 00	3 50	16 50	59 40	David Lant	Do.
18	Charles B. Hancock	do	May 11, 1866	Aug. 19, 1866	3	18	13 00	3 50	16 50	59 40	C. B. Hancock	Do.
19	James Butler	do	May 11, 1866	Aug. 29, 1866	3	18	13 00	3 50	16 50	59 40	James Butler	Do.
20	Jeremiah Bingham	do	May 11, 1866	Aug. 29, 1866	3	18	13 00	3 50	16 50	59 40	Jeremiah Bingham	Do.
21	Richard Brown	do	May 11, 1866	Aug. 29, 1866	3	18	13 00	3 50	16 50	59 40	Richard Brown	Do.
22	Henry Savage	do	May 11, 1866	Aug. 29, 1866	3	18	13 00	3 50	16 50	59 40	Henry Savage	Do.
23	Phillip Ballard	do	May 11, 1866	Aug. 29, 1866	3	18	13 00	3 50	16 50	59 40	Phillip Ballard	Do.
24	Cyprian Marsh	do	May 11, 1866	Aug. 29, 1866	3	18	13 00	3 50	16 50	59 40	Cyprian Marsh	Do.
25	James McClellan	do	May 11, 1866	Aug. 29, 1866	3	18	13 00	3 50	16 50	59 40	James McClelan	Do.
26	Daniel Filmore	do	May 11, 1866	Aug. 29, 1866	3	18	13 00	3 50	16 50	59 40	Daniel Fillmore	Do.

This company was mustered into service at Payson, Utah County, May 11, 1866, by order of Major General Johnson,

H. B. CLAWSON,
Adjutant General Utah Territory Militia.

Pay-roll of Captain Andrew Bigler's company ——— cavalry, Utah Territory militia, employed in the suppression of Indian hostilities in Sanpete and Sevier counties, Utah Territory, from July 1, 1866, to September 30, 1866.

We, the undersigned, acknowledge to have received from James W. Cunnings, paymaster Utah Territory militia, the sums set opposite to our names, in full payment for our services for the time specified.

Number	Names	Rank	Period of service. Commencement.	Period of service. Expiration.	Months.	Pay per month.	Monthly allowance for clothing.	Total monthly pay and allowance.	40 cents per day for horse and risk of use and horse equipment.	Total pay and allowance.	Signatures.	Witnesses.
1	Andrew Bigler	Captain.	July 1, 1866	Sept. 30, 1866	3			$128 50	$36 00	$321 56	Andrew Bigler	Job Wellings.
1	Thomas Abbott	1st lieut	July 1, 1866	Sept. 30, 1866	3			112 83	36 00	371 49	Thomas Abat	Do.
1	Elias Vanfleet	2d lieut	July 1, 1866	Sept. 30, 1866	3			112 83	36 00	374 49	Elias Vanfleet	Do.
2	William Foxley	do.	July 1, 1866	Sept. 30, 1866	3			112 83	36 00	374 49	William Foxley	Do.
3	Joseph Holbrook	do.	July 1, 1866	Sept. 30, 1866	3			112 83	36 00	374 49	Joseph Holbrok	Do.
3	Isaac Atkinson	do.	July 1, 1866	Sept. 30, 1866	3			112 83	36 00	374 49	Isaac Atkinson	Do.
4	Henry Yates	Sergeant.	July 1, 1866	Sept. 30, 1866	3	$17 00	$3 50	20 50	36 00	97 50	Henry Yates	Do.
5	Timothy B. Clark	do.	July 1, 1866	Sept. 30, 1866	3	17 00	3 50	20 50	36 00	97 50	Timothy B. Clark	Do.
3	John Bloxam	do.	July 1, 1866	Sept. 30, 1866	3	17 00	3 50	20 50	36 00	97 50	Joh Bloxom	Do.
3	John Duncan	do.	July 1, 1866	Sept. 30, 1866	3	17 00	3 50	20 50	36 00	97 50	John Duncan	Do.
4	Ephraim Hatch	do.	July 1, 1866	Sept. 30, 1866	3	17 00	3 50	20 50	36 00	97 50	Ephraim Hatch	Do.
5	Charles Layton	do.	July 1, 1866	Sept. 31, 1866	3	13 00	3 50	16 50	36 00	85 50	Charlrs Layton	Do.
1	Hubert Bark	Private.	July 1, 1866	Sept. 30, 1866	3	13 00	3 50	16 50	36 00	85 50	Hubert Bark	Do.
2	Ameenas Miller	do.	July 1, 1866	Sept. 30, 1866	3	13 00	3 50	16 50	36 00	85 50	Ameenas Miller	Do.
3	William Glover	do.	July 1, 1866	Sept. 30, 1866	3	13 00	3 50	16 50	36 00	85 50	William Glover	Do.
4	William Haight	do.	July 1, 1866	Sept. 30, 1866	3	13 00	3 50	16 50	36 00	85 50	William Haight	Do.
5	Hyrum Rice	do.	July 1, 1866	Sept. 30, 1866	3	13 00	3 50	16 50	36 00	85 50	Hyrum Rice	Do.
6	Alma Hayn	do.	July 1, 1866	Sept. 30, 1866	3	13 00	3 50	16 50	36 00	85 50	Alma Hayle	Do.
7	William Rice	do.	July 1, 1866	Sept. 30, 1866	3	13 00	3 50	16 50	36 00	85 50	William Rice	Do.
8	Joel Grover	do.	July 1, 1866	Sept. 30, 1866	3	13 00	3 50	16 50	36 00	85 50	Joel Grover	Do.
9	David Clawson	do.	July 1, 1866	Sept. 30, 1866	3	13 00	3 50	16 50	36 00	85 50	David Clonse	Do.
10	Joseph Miller	do.	July 1, 1866	Sept. 30, 1866	3	13 00	3 50	16 50	36 00	85 50	Joseph Miller	Do.
11	William Galbreath	do.	July 1, 1866	Sept. 30, 1866	3	13 00	3 50	16 50	36 00	85 50	Willium Galbraith	Do.
12	George Stoddard	do.	July 1, 1866	Sept. 30, 1866	3	13 00	3 50	16 50	36 00	85 50	George Stoddard	Do.
13	Peter Billings	do.	July 1, 1866	Sept. 30, 1866	3	13 00	3 50	16 50	36 00	85 50	Peter Billings	Do.
14	John Flint	do.	July 1, 1866	Sept. 30, 1866	3	13 00	3 50	16 50	36 00	85 50	John Flint	Do.
15	Robert Bodley	do.	July 1, 1866	Sept. 30, 1866	3	13 00	3 50	16 50	36 00	85 50	Robert Bodly	Do.
16	Hyrum King	do.	July 1, 1866	Sept. 30, 1866	3	13 00	3 50	16 50	36 00	85 50	Hyrum King	Do.
17	Enoch Harris	de.	July 1, 1866	Sept. 30, 1866	3	13 00	3 50	16 50	36 00	85 50	Enoch Harris	Do.
18	John Manning	do.	July 1, 1866	Sept. 30, 1866	3	13 00	3 50	16 50	36 00	85 50	John Manning	Do.
19	Thomas Barton	do.	July 1, 1866	Sept. 30, 1866	3	13 00	3 50	16 50	36 00	85 50	Thomas Barton	Do.
20	Joseph Woolley	do.	July 1, 1866	Sept. 30, 1866	3	13 00	3 50	16 50	36 00	85 50	Joseph Woolley	Do.

No.	Name		From	To						Name	
21	John Fisher	do.	July 1, 1866	Sept. 30, 1866	3	13 00	3 50	16 50	36 00	85 50	John Fisher	Do.
22	Wallace Willey	do.	July 1, 1866	Sept. 30, 1866	3	13 00	3 50	16 50	36 00	85 50	Wallace Willey	Do.
23	Luther Barlow	do.	July 1, 1866	Sept. 30, 1866	3	13 00	3 50	16 50	36 00	85 50	Luthins Barlow	Do.
24	William Corbrigo	do.	July 1, 1866	Sept. 30, 1866	3	13 00	3 50	16 50	36 00	85 50	William Corbrige	Do.
25	George Davis	do.	July 1, 1866	Sept. 30, 1866	3	13 00	3 50	16 50	36 00	85 50	George Davis	Do.
26	William Jackson	do.	July 1, 1866	Sept. 30, 1866	3	13 00	3 50	16 50	36 00	85 50	William Jackson	Do.
27	David Stoker	do.	July 1, 1866	Sept. 30, 1866	3	13 00	3 50	16 50	36 00	85 50	David Stoker	Do.
28	David Thompson	do.	July 1, 1866	Sept. 30, 1866	3	13 00	3 50	16 50	36 00	85 50	David Thompson	Do.
29	Chester Call	do.	July 1, 1866	Sept. 30, 1866	3	13 00	3 50	16 50	36 00	85 50	Chester Call	Do.
30	Orvil Thompson	do.	July 1, 1866	Sept. 30, 1866	3	13 00	3 50	16 50	36 00	85 50	Orvil Thompson	Do.
31	Daniel Moss	do.	July 1, 1866	Sept. 30, 1866	3	13 00	3 50	16 50	36 00	85 50	Daniel Moss	Do.
32	John Perkins	do.	July 1, 1866	Sept. 30, 1866	3	13 00	3 50	16 50	36 00	85 50	John H. Perkins	Do.
33	Thomas Atkinson	do.	July 1, 1866	Sept. 30, 1866	3	13 00	3 50	16 50	36 00	85 50	Thomas Atkinson	Do.
34	George Pace	do.	July 1, 1866	Sept. 30, 1866	3	13 00	3 50	16 50	36 00	85 50	George Pace	Do.
35	William Gillespie	do.	July 1, 1866	Sept. 30, 1866	3	13 00	3 50	16 50	36 00	85 50	William Gillespie	Do.
36	Joseph Argyle	do.	July 1, 1866	Sept. 30, 1866	3	13 00	3 50	16 50	36 00	85 50	Joseph Aragle	Do.
37	Natanel Cherry	do.	July 1, 1866	Sept. 30, 1866	3	13 00	3 50	16 50	36 00	85 50	Nanal Cheny	Do.
38	Benjamin Cherry	do.	July 1, 1866	Sept. 30, 1866	3	13 00	3 50	16 50	36 00	85 50	Benjamin Cherry	Do.
39	Charles Irwin	do.	July 1, 1866	Sept. 30, 1866	3	13 00	3 50	16 50	36 00	85 50	Charles Irwin	Do.
40	Charles Crawford	do.	July 1, 1866	Sept. 30, 1866	3	13 00	3 50	16 50	36 00	85 50	William Barns	Do.
41	William Barns	do.	July 1, 1866	Sept. 30, 1866	3	13 00	3 50	16 50	36 00	85 50	Levi Webster	Do.
42	Levi Webster	do.	July 1, 1866	Sept. 30, 1866	3	13 00	3 50	16 50	36 00	85 50	John Phillips	Do.
43	John Phillips	do.	July 1, 1866	Sept. 30, 1866	3	13 00	3 50	16 50	36 00	85 50		
44	Thomas Evans	do.	July 1, 1866	Sept. 30, 1866	3	13 00	3 50	16 50	36 00	85 50	Thomas Evans	Do.
45	William Duffin	do.	July 1, 1866	Sept. 30, 1866	3	13 00	3 50	16 50	36 00	85 50	William Duffin	Do.
46	Joseph Robbins	do.	July 1, 1866	Sept. 30, 1866	3	13 00	3 50	16 50	36 00	85 50	Joseph Robbins	Do.
47	George Gailey	do.	July 1, 1866	Sept. 30, 1866	3	13 00	3 50	16 50	36 00	85 50	George Gailey	Do.
48	Edward Phillips	do.	July 1, 1866	Sept. 30, 1866	3	13 00	3 50	16 50	36 00	85 50		
49	James Rogers	do.	July 1, 1866	Sept. 30, 1866	3	13 00	3 50	16 50	36 00	85 50	James Rogers	Do.
50	Frank Lincoln	do.	July 1, 1866	Sept. 30, 1866	3	13 00	3 50	16 50	36 00	85 50	Frank Lincon	Do.
51	Jasper Perkins	do.	July 1, 1866	Sept. 30, 1866	3	13 00	3 50	16 50	36 00	85 50	Jasper Perkins	Do.
52	Christian Crawford	do.	July 1, 1866	Sept. 30, 1866	3	13 00	3 50	16 50	36 00	85 50	Christian Crawford	Do.
53	John Smith	do.	July 1, 1866	Sept. 30, 1866	3	13 00	3 50	16 50	36 00	85 50	John Smith	Do.
54	James A. Baird	do.	July 1, 1866	Sept. 30, 1866	3	13 00	3 50	16 50	36 00	85 50	James A. Baird	Do.
55	Richard Pilling	do.	July 1, 1866	Sept. 30, 1866	3	13 00	3 50	16 50	36 00	85 50	Richard Pilling	Do.

This company was mustered into service July 1, 1866, at Farmington, Davis County, by Brigadier General Lott Smith, and on that day started for Sanpete, marched two hundred miles to the vicinity of Fort Ephraim, and were there assigned to duty by Lieutenant General D. H. Wells, who was then in the field. The company was in active service in Sanpete and Sevier counties for three months, returned to Farmington, and was mustered out on 30th day of September, 1866.

I certify that the above account is correct.

H. B. CLAWSON,

Adjutant General Utah Territory Militia.

Pay-roll of Captain John D. Holliday's company —— infantry, Utah Territory militia, employed in the suppression of Indian hostilities in Payson, Pondtown, Santaquin, and Goshen, from May 11, 1866, to August 29, 1866.

We, the undersigned, acknowledge to have received from James W. Cummings, paymaster Utah Territory militia, the sums, set opposite to our names, in full payment for our services for the time specified.

Number.	Names.	Rank.	Commencement.	Expiration.	Months.	Days.	Pay per month.	Monthly allow. for clothing.	Total, monthly pay and allowance.	Total pay and allowance.	Signatures.	Witnesses.
1	John D. Holliday	Captain	May 11, 1866	Aug. 29, 1866	3	18			$118 50	$426 60	John D. Holliday	W. B. Parr.
1	Thomas R. Heelis	1st lieutenant	May 11, 1866	Aug. 29, 1866	3	18			108 50	390 60	Thomas R. Heelis	Do.
1	David H. Holliday	2d lieutenant	May 11, 1866	Aug. 29, 1866	3	18			103 50	372 60	David H. Holliday	Do.
2	William W. Barnett	do.	May 11, 1866	Aug. 29, 1866	3	18			103 50	372 60	W. W. Barnett	Do.
3	Albert Stickney	do.	May 11, 1866	Aug. 29, 1866	3	18			103 50	372 60	Albert Stickney	Do.
4	Niels Nielson	Sergeant	May 11, 1866	Aug. 29, 1866	3	18	$17 00	$3 50	20 50	73 80	Neels Nelson	Do.
1	Samuel Openshaw	do.	May 11, 1866	Aug. 29, 1866	3	18	17 00	3 50	20 50	73 80	Samuel Openshaw	Do.
2	George Crompton	do.	May 11, 1866	Aug. 29, 1866	3	18	17 00	3 50	20 50	73 80	George Crompton	Do.
3	John Greenalch	do.	May 11, 1866	Aug. 29, 1866	3	18	17 00	3 50	20 50	73 80	John Greenalch	Do.
4	Lars Anstrom	do.	May 11, 1866	Aug. 29, 1866	3	18	17 00	3 50	20 50	73 80	Lars Anstnn	Do.
1	William F. Carter	Private	May 11, 1866	Aug. 29, 1866	3	18	13 00	3 50	16 50	59 40	William P. Carter	Do.
2	James A. McBride	do.	May 11, 1866	Aug. 29, 1866	3	18	13 00	3 50	16 50	59 40	James A. McBride	Do.
3	Thomas Holliday	do.	May 11, 1866	Aug. 29, 1866	3	18	13 00	3 50	16 50	59 40	Thomas Holliday	Do.
4	Martin Taylor	do.	May 11, 1866	Aug. 29, 1866	3	18	13 00	3 50	16 50	59 40	Martin Taylor	Do.
5	Norman Taylor	do.	May 11, 1866	Aug. 29, 1866	3	18	13 00	3 50	16 50	59 40	Norman Taylor	Do.
6	Lester Taylor	do.	May 11, 1866	Aug. 29, 1866	3	18	13 00	3 50	16 50	59 40	Lester Taylor	Do.
7	Frank Johnson	do.	May 11, 1866	Aug. 29, 1866	3	18	13 00	3 50	16 50	59 40	Franklin Johnson	Do.
8	Eli Openshaw	do.	May 11, 1866	Aug. 29, 1866	3	18	13 00	3 50	16 50	59 40	Eli Openshaw	Do.
9	Robert Kinneson	do.	May 11, 1866	Aug. 29, 1866	3	18	13 00	3 50	16 50	59 40	Robert Kinlson	Do.
10	Wm. Robert Smith	do.	May 11, 1866	Aug. 29, 1866	3	18	13 00	3 50	16 50	59 40	Wm. R. Smith	Do.
11	Chester Montague	do.	May 11, 1866	Aug. 29, 1866	3	18	13 00	3 50	16 50	59 40	Charles Montague	Do.
12	James Green	do.	May 11, 1866	Aug. 29, 1866	3	18	13 00	3 50	16 50	59 40	James Green	Do.
13	Eugene Degraw	do.	May 11, 1866	Aug. 29, 1866	3	18	13 00	3 50	16 50	59 40	Eugene Degraw	Do.
14	Morssil Degraw	do.	May 11, 1866	Aug. 29, 1866	3	18	13 00	3 50	16 50	59 40	Marvin Degraw	Do.
15	Chester Nizouger	do.	May 11, 1866	Aug. 29, 1866	3	18	13 00	3 50	16 50	59 40	Chester Nizenger	Do.
16	Howa Cushing	do.	May 11, 1866	Aug. 29, 1866	3	18	13 00	3 50	16 50	59 40	Howa Cushing	Do.
17	Ezekiel Greenalch	do.	May 11, 1866	Aug. 29, 1866	3	18	13 00	3 50	16 50	59 40	Ezekle Grunnlch	Do.
18	James Stoure	do.	May 11, 1866	Aug. 29, 1866	3	18	13 00	3 50	16 50	59 40	James Stoure	Do.
19	Levi Openshaw	do.	May 11, 1866	Aug. 29, 1866	3	18	13 00	3 50	16 50	59 40	Levi Openshaw	Do.
20	J. G. Vannmedal	do.	May 11, 1866	Aug. 29, 1866	3	18	13 00	3 50	16 50	59 40	J. G. Vannmedal	Do.
21	David Jernin	do.	May 11, 1866	Aug. 29, 1866	3	18	13 00	3 50	16 50	59 40	David Jermin	Do.
22	Thomas Jarvis	do.	May 11, 1866	Aug. 29, 1866	3	18	13 00	3 50	16 50	59 40	Thomas Jarvis	Do.
23	Henry McGee	do.	May 11, 1866	Aug. 29, 1866	3	18	13 00	3 50	16 50	59 40	Henry McGee	Do.

24	Pleasant Minchey	do	59 40	16 50	3 50	13 00	18	3	May 11, 1866	Aug. 29, 1866	Pleasant Minchey	Do.
25	Ernest Tietichen	do	59 40	16 50	3 50	13 00	18	3	May 11, 1866	Aug. 29, 1866	Ernest Feitjen	Do.
26	Morris Larsen	do	59 40	16 50	3 50	13 00	18	3	May 11, 1866	Aug. 29, 1866	Morris Larsen	Do.
27	Andrew Olsen	do	59 40	16 50	3 50	13 00	18	3	May 11, 1866	Aug. 29, 1866	Andrew Olsen, his + mark	Do.
28	Samuel Malinburgh	do	59 40	16 50	3 50	13 00	18	3	May 11, 1866	Aug. 29, 1866	Samuel Malinberg, his + mark	Do.
29	Andrew Burgison	do	59 40	16 50	3 50	13 00	18	3	May 11, 1866	Aug. 29, 1866	Andrus Borjson	Do.
30	Charles Saunuelson	do	59 40	16 50	3 50	13 00	18	3	May 11, 1866	Aug. 29, 1866	Charles Saunnelson	Do.
31	Charles Tietihan	do	59 40	16 50	3 50	13 00	18	3	May 11, 1866	Aug. 29, 1866	Charles Feitjen, his + mark	Do.
32	Sivvus Johnson	do	59 40	16 50	3 50	13 00	18	3	May 11, 1866	Aug. 29, 1866	Sven Jonson	Do.
33	William Sundbury	do	59 40	16 50	3 50	13 00	18	3	May 11, 1866	Aug. 29, 1866	Wm. Sandbery	Do.
34	James Hickersley	do	59 40	16 50	3 50	13 00	18	3	May 11, 1866	Aug. 29, 1866	James Heckersley	Do.
35	David Thorpe	do	59 40	16 50	3 50	13 00	18	3	May 11, 1866	Aug. 29, 1866	David Sharp	Do.
36	Peter Ocklebury	do	59 40	16 50	3 50	13 00	18	3	May 11, 1866	Aug. 29, 1866	Peter Ocklebury	Do.
37	Jacob Degraw	do	59 40	16 50	3 50	13 00	18	3	May 11, 1866	Aug. 29, 1866	Jacob Degraw	Do.

This company was mustered into service at Santaquin, Utah County, May 11, 1866, by order of Major General Aaron Johnson, and assigned to duty by him in the mountains east of Santaquin, and were in active service until mustered out, August 29, 1866.

I certify that the above account is correct.

H. B. CLAWSON,
Adjutant General Utah Territory Militia.

Pay-roll of Captain Daniel Stark's company —— infantry, Utah Territory militia, employed in the suppression of Indian hostilities in Payson, Pondtown, Santaquin, and Goshen, Utah County, Utah Territory, from May 11, 1866, to August 29, 1866.

We, the undersigned, acknowledge to have received from James W. Cummings, paymaster Utah Territory militia, the sums set opposite to our names in full payment for our services for the time specified.

Number	Names	Rank	Commencement	Expiration	Months	Days	Pay per month	Monthly allowance for clothing	Total monthly pay and allowance	Total pay and allowance	Signatures	Witnesses
1	Daniel Stark	Captain	May 11, 1866	Aug. 29, 1866	3	18	$17 00		$118 50	$426 60	Daniel Stark	William Heaton.
1	Isaiah M. Coombs	1st lieutenant	May 11, 1866	Aug. 29, 1866	3	18	17 00		108 50	390 60	Isaiah M. Coombs	Do.
1	Amasa Potter	2d lieutenant	May 11, 1866	Aug. 29, 1866	3	18			103 50	372 60	Amasa Potter	Do.
2	William Wighthead	do	May 11, 1866	Aug. 29, 1866	3	18			103 50	372 60	William Whitehed	Do.
3	James Reese	do	May 11, 1866	Aug. 29, 1866	3	18			103 50	372 60	James Reece	Do.
4	John Shields	do	May 11, 1866	Aug. 29, 1866	3	18			103 50	372 60	John Shields	Do.
5	Robert Davis	do	May 11, 1866	Aug. 29, 1866	3	18			103 50	372 60	Robert Davis	Do.
1	Charles W. Wright	Sergeant	May 11, 1866	Aug. 29, 1866	3	18	17 00	$3 50	20 50	73 80	Charles W. Wright	Do.
2	Ira Tiffany	do	May 11, 1866	Aug. 29, 1866	3	18	17 00	3 50	20 50	73 80	Ira Tiffany	Do.
3	Wilford Crocket	do	May 11, 1866	Aug. 29, 1866	3	18	17 00	3 50	20 50	73 80	Wilford Crocket	Do.
1	Isaac Hancock	Private	May 11, 1866	Aug. 29, 1866	3	18	13 00	3 50	16 50	59 40	Isaac Hancock	Do.
2	Robert E. Collet	do	May 11, 1866	Aug. 29, 1866	3	18	13 00	3 50	16 50	59 40	Robert E. Collet	Do.
3	William H. Seabury	do	May 11, 1866	Aug. 29, 1866	3	18	13 00	3 50	16 50	59 40	W. H. Seabury	Do.
4	Thomas Jack-on	do	May 11, 1866	Aug. 29, 1866	3	18	13 00	3 50	16 50	59 40	Thomas Jack-on	Do.
5	John B. Fairbanks	do	May 11, 1866	Aug. 29, 1866	3	18	13 00	3 50	16 50	59 40	John B. Fairbanks	Do.
6	Thomas H. Wilson	do	May 11, 1866	Aug. 29, 1866	3	18	13 00	3 50	16 50	59 40	Thomas H. Wilson	Do.
7	Pardon Webb	do	May 11, 1866	Aug. 29, 1866	3	18	13 00	3 50	16 50	59 40	Pardon Webb	Do.
8	Newell Potter	do	May 11, 1866	Aug. 29, 1866	3	18	13 00	3 50	16 50	59 40	Newel Potter	Do.
9	Shadrack Richardson	do	May 11, 1866	Aug. 29, 1866	3	18	13 00	3 50	16 50	59 40	Shedriuk Racherson	Do.
10	George Pickering	do	May 11, 1866	Aug. 29, 1866	3	18	13 00	3 50	16 50	59 40	George Pickering	Do.
11	Joseph Crook, sen	do	May 11, 1866	Aug. 29, 1866	3	18	13 00	3 50	16 50	59 40	Joseph Crook, sen	Do.
12	Henry Neloker	do	May 11, 1866	Aug. 29, 1866	3	18	13 00	3 50	16 50	59 40	Henry Neloker	Do.
13	Walter H. Hewish	do	May 11, 1866	Aug. 29, 1866	3	18	13 00	3 50	16 50	59 40	Walter H. Ilaiah	Do.
14	Joseph Keer	do	May 11, 1866	Aug. 29, 1866	3	18	13 00	3 50	16 50	59 40		
15	William Wignall	do	May 11, 1866	Aug. 29, 1866	3	18	13 00	3 50	16 50	59 40		
16	James Finlason	do	May 11, 1866	Aug. 29, 1866	3	18	13 00	3 50	16 50	59 40	James Finlayson	Do.
17	James Reese	do	May 11, 1866	Aug. 29, 1866	3	18	13 00	3 50	16 50	59 40	James Reece	Do.
18	Joseph Race	do	May 11, 1866	Aug. 29, 1866	3	18	13 00	3 50	16 50	59 40	Joseph Race	Do.
19	Hugh Wilson	do	May 11, 1866	Aug. 29, 1866	3	18	13 00	3 50	16 50	59 40	Hugh Wilson	Do.
20	John Marry	do	May 11, 1866	Aug. 29, 1866	3	18	13 00	3 50	16 50	59 40	John Murray	Do.
21	John Vist	do	May 11, 1866	Aug. 29, 1866	3	18	13 00	3 50	16 50	59 40	John Vest	Do.
22	Levi A. O. Colvin	do	May 11, 1866	Aug. 29, 1866	3	18	13 00	3 50	16 50	59 40	L. O. A. Colvin	Do.
23	Alma Durphy	do	May 11, 1866	Aug. 29, 1866	3	18	13 00	3 50	16 50	49 50		

24	Jason Harris	do	May 11, 1866	Aug. 29, 1866	3 18	13 00	3 50	16 50	59 40	Jason Haws	Do.
25	Monroe Curtis	do	May 11, 1866	Aug. 29, 1866	3 18	13 00	3 50	16 50	59 40	Monroe M. Curtis	Do.
26	Joseph Jones	do	May 11, 1866	Aug. 29, 1866	3 18	13 00	3 50	16 50	59 40		
27	F. A. Curtis	do	May 11, 1866	Aug. 29, 1866	3 18	13 00	3 50	16 50	59 40	F. A. Curtis	Do.
28	William W. Haws	do	May 11, 1866	Aug. 29, 1866	3 18	13 00	3 50	16 50	59 40	William W. Haws	Do.
29	A. G. Moore	do	May 11, 1866	Aug. 29, 1866	3 18	13 00	3 50	16 50	59 40		
30	Aquilla Hopper	do	May 11, 1866	Aug. 29, 1866	3 18	13 00	3 50	16 50	59 40	Alfilla Hopper	Do.
31	Elijah Haws	do	May 11, 1866	Aug. 29, 1866	3 18	13 00	3 50	16 50	59 40	Elijah Haws	Do.
32	George Hanks	do	May 11, 1866	Aug. 29, 1866	3 18	13 00	3 50	16 50	59 40	George Hanks	Do.
33	Joseph Tryon	do	May 11, 1866	Aug. 29, 1866	3 18	13 00	3 50	16 50	59 40	Joseph Tryon	Do.
34	P. M. Elliott	do	May 11, 1866	Aug. 29, 1866	3 18	13 00	3 50	16 50	59 40	P. M. Elliott	Do.
35	William Davis, jun	do	May 11, 1866	Aug. 29, 1866	3 18	13 00	3 50	16 50	59 40	William Davis	Do.
36	William Davis, sen	do	May 11, 1866	Aug. 29, 1866	3 18	13 00	3 50	16 50	59 40	William Davis	Do.
37	Lyman Curtis	do	May 11, 1866	Aug. 29, 1866	3 18	13 00	3 50	16 50	59 40	Lyman Curtis	Do.
38	Samuel Farris	do	May 11, 1866	Aug. 29, 1866	3 18	13 00	3 50	16 50	59 40	Samuel J. Ferris	Do.
39	Joseph Curtis	do	May 11, 1866	Aug. 29, 1866	3 18	13 00	3 50	16 50	59 40	Joseph Curtis	Do.
40	Moses Curtis	do	May 11, 1866	Aug. 29, 1866	3 18	13 00	3 50	16 50	59 40	Moses Curtis	Do.
41	Samuel Curtis	do	May 11, 1866	Aug. 29, 1866	3 18	13 00	3 50	16 50	59 40	Samuel B. Curtis	Do.

This company was mustered into service at Payson, Utah County, May 11, 1866, by order of Major General Aaron Johnson, and assigned to duty by him in the mountains in the vicinity of Pondtown, Payson, and Spanish Fork, Utah County; they were in active service every day until mustered out at Payson, August 29, 1866.

I certify that the above account is correct.

H. B. CLAWSON,

Adjutant General Utah Territory Militia.

Pay-roll of Captain William Wall's company —— cavalry, Utah Territory militia, employed in the suppression of Indian hostilities in Wasatch County, Utah Territory, from August 1, 1866, to October 31, 1866.

We, the undersigned, acknowledge to have received from James W. Cummings, paymaster Utah Territory militia, the sums set opposite to our names, in full payment for our services for the time specified.

Number.	Names.	Rank.	Commencement.	Expiration.	Months.	Pay per month.	Monthly allowance for clothing.	Total monthly pay and allowance.	40 cts. per day for use and risk of horse and horse equipment.	Total pay and allowance.	Signatures.	Witnesses.
1	William Wall	Captain	Aug. 1, 1866	Oct. 31, 1866	3			$129 50	$36 00	$424 50	William Wall	William McDonald.
1	William McDonald	1st lieutenant	Aug. 1, 1866	Oct. 31, 1866	3			112 83	36 00	374 79	William McDonald	George Clyde.
2	Joseph McDonald	2d lieutenant	Aug. 1, 1866	Oct. 31, 1866	3			112 83	36 00	374 79	Joseph McDonald	Calvin Henry.
2	Patrick Carroll	...do	Aug. 1, 1866	Oct. 31, 1866	3			112 83	36 00	374 79	Patrick Carroll	Do.
3	Andrew Ross	...do	Aug. 1, 1866	Oct. 31, 1866	3			112 83	36 00	374 79	Andrew Ross	William McDonald.
4	Benjamin Norris	Sergeant	Aug. 1, 1866	Oct. 31, 1866	3	$17 00		20 50	36 00	97 50	Benjamin Norris	Andrew Ross.
2	John McDonald	...do	Aug. 1, 1866	Oct. 31, 1866	3	17 00		20 50	36 00	97 50	John McDonald	Josephus Murdock.
3	Philip Smith	...do	Aug. 1, 1866	Oct. 31, 1866	3	17 00	$3 50	21 50	36 00	97 50	Philip Smith	William McDonald.
3	Richard Jones	...do	Aug. 1, 1866	Oct. 31, 1866	3	17 00	3 50	20 50	36 00	97 50	Richard Jones	Joseph McDonald.
1	William Forman	...do	Aug. 1, 1866	Oct. 31, 1866	3	17 00	3 50	20 50	36 00	97 50	William Forman	William McDonald.
2	George Clyde	Bugler	Aug. 1, 1866	Oct. 31, 1866	3	13 00	3 50	16 50	36 00	85 50	George Clyde	Do.
3	Jacob Harris	Private	Aug. 1, 1866	Oct. 31, 1866	3	13 00	3 50	16 50	36 00	85 50	Jacob Harris	William G. Giles.
2	Ephraim Smith	...do	Aug. 1, 1866	Oct. 31, 1866	3	13 00	3 50	16 50	36 00	85 50	Ephraim Smith	Andrew Ross.
3	John Acomb	...do	Aug. 1, 1866	Oct. 31, 1866	3	13 00	3 50	16 50	36 00	85 50	John Acomb	Joseph Thomas.
4	John Cummings	...do	Aug. 1, 1866	Oct. 31, 1866	3	13 00	3 50	16 50	36 00	85 50	John Cummings	Sidney Carter.
5	George Froughton	...do	Aug. 1, 1866	Oct. 31, 1866	3	13 00	3 50	16 50	36 00	85 50	George Froughton	Patrick Carroll.
6	Wm. Gallagher	...do	Aug. 1, 1866	Oct. 31, 1866	3	13 00	3 50	16 50	36 00	85 50	Wm. Gallagher	William McDonald.
7	Joseph Thomas	...do	Aug. 1, 1866	Oct. 31, 1866	2	13 00	3 50	16 50	36 00	85 50	Joseph Thomas	William G. Giles.
8	Stanley Davis	...do	Aug. 1, 1866	Oct. 31, 1866	3	13 00	3 50	16 50	36 00	85 50	Stanley Davis	William McDonald.
9	Robert Broadhead	...do	Aug. 1, 1866	Oct. 31, 1866	3	13 00	3 50	16 50	36 00	85 50	Robert Broadhead	S. M. Rooker.
10	Nymphus Murdock	...do	Aug. 1, 1866	Oct. 31, 1866	3	13 00	3 50	16 50	36 00	85 50	Nymphus Murdock	Murray Harvey.
11	George Giles	...do	Aug. 1, 1866	Oct. 31, 1866	3	13 00	3 50	16 50	36 00	85 50	George Giles	John Gallagher.
12	William Nuttall	...do	Aug. 1, 1866	Oct. 31, 1866	3	13 00	3 50	16 50	36 00	85 50	William Nuttall	William McDonald.
13	William Giles	...do	Aug. 1, 1866	Oct. 31, 1866	3	13 00	3 50	16 50	36 00	85 50	William Giles	Patrick Carroll.
14	Hyrum Oaks	...do	Aug. 1, 1866	Oct. 31, 1866	3	13 00	3 50	16 50	36 00	85 50	Hyrum Oaks	Richard Jones.
15	David A. Sessions	...do	Aug. 1, 1866	Oct. 31, 1866	3	13 00	3 50	16 50	36 00	85 50	David A. Sessions	John Gallagher.
16	George Carlyle	...do	Aug. 1, 1866	Oct. 31, 1866	3	13 00	3 50	16 50	36 00	85 50	George Carlyle	William Giles.
17	William G. Giles	...do	Aug. 1, 1866	Oct. 31, 1866	3	13 00	3 50	16 50	36 00	85 50	William G. Giles	William McDonald.
18	Calvin Henry	...do	Aug. 1, 1866	Oct. 31, 1866	3	13 00	3 50	16 50	36 00	85 50	Calvin Henry	Patrick Carroll.
19	George Giles, jr.	...do	Aug. 1, 1866	Oct. 31, 1866	3	13 00	3 50	16 50	36 00	85 50	George Giles, jr.	John Cronk.
20	William Cummings	...do	Aug. 1, 1866	Oct. 31, 1866	3	13 00	3 50	16 50	36 00	85 50	William Cummings	John Harvey.
21	William Averett	...do	Aug. 1, 1866	Oct. 31, 1866	3	13 00	3 50	16 50	36 00	85 50	William Averett	William McDonald.

No.	Name								Name
22	Albert McMullen	do.	Aug. 1, 1866	Oct. 31, 1866	3	13 00	3 50	16 50	36 00	85 50	Albert McMullen	Joseph Thomas
23	John Harvey, Jr.	do.	Aug. 1, 1866	Oct. 31, 1866	3	13 00	3 50	16 50	36 00	85 50	John Harvey, Jr.	Joseph Parker
24	John Harvey	do.	Aug. 1, 1866	Oct. 31, 1866	3	13 00	3 50	16 50	36 00	85 50	John Harvey	Sidney Carter
25	Isaac Cummings	do.	Aug. 1, 1866	Oct. 31, 1866	3	13 00	3 50	16 50	36 00	85 50	Isaac Cummings	John M. Harvey
26	Sidney Carter	do.	Aug. 1, 1866	Oct. 31, 1866	3	13 00	3 50	16 50	36 00	85 50	Sidney Carter	William G. Giles
27	Joseph Parker	do.	Aug. 1, 1866	Oct. 31, 1866	3	13 00	3 50	16 50	36 00	85 50	Joseph Parker	William McDonald
28	George Bunnell	do.	Aug. 1, 1866	Oct. 31, 1866	3	13 00	3 50	16 50	36 00	85 50	George Bunnell	Hyrum Oaks
29	Henry Olewhiler	do.	Aug. 1, 1866	Oct. 31, 1866	3	13 00	3 50	16 50	36 00	85 50	Henry Olewhiler	Sidney Carter
30	Isaac Bunn	do.	Aug. 1, 1866	Oct. 31, 1866	3	13 00	3 50	16 50	36 00	85 50	Isaac Bunn	Richard Jones
31	Richard Sessions	do.	Aug. 1, 1866	Oct. 31, 1866	3	13 00	3 50	16 50	36 00	85 50	Richard Sessions	George Clyde
32	Darvin Walton	do.	Aug. 1, 1866	Oct. 31, 1866	3	13 00	3 50	16 50	36 00	85 50	Darwin Walton	John Gallagher
33	Thomas Nichols	do.	Aug. 1, 1866	Oct. 31, 1866	3	13 00	3 50	16 50	36 00	85 50	Thomas Nichols	John M. Harvey
34	Lybeous T. Coon, jr.	do.	Aug. 1, 1866	Oct. 31, 1866	3	13 00	3 50	16 50	36 00	85 50	Lybeous T. Coon, jr.	George Perry
35	Murry Harvey	do.	Aug. 1, 1866	Oct. 31, 1866	3	13 00	3 50	16 50	36 00	85 50	Murray Harvey	John M. Harvey
36	Soul Sessions	do.	Aug. 1, 1866	Oct. 31, 1866	3	13 00	3 50	16 50	36 00	85 50	Soul Sessions	John Gallagher
37	Elijah Thomas	do.	Aug. 1, 1866	Oct. 31, 1866	3	13 00	3 50	16 50	36 00	85 50	Elijah Thomas	William McDonald
38	Alfred Shelton	do.	Aug. 1, 1866	Oct. 31, 1866	3	13 00	3 50	16 50	36 00	85 50	Alfred Shelton	John Gallagher
39	William Cole	do.	Aug. 1, 1866	Oct. 31, 1866	3	13 00	3 50	16 50	36 00	85 50	William Cole	Elishe Thomas
40	James Carlyle	do.	Aug. 1, 1866	Oct. 31, 1866	3	13 00	3 50	16 50	36 00	85 50	James Carlyle, his x mark	Robert Jones

This company was mustered into service at Heber City, August 1, 1866, by order of Lieutenant General Daniel H. Wells. They were assigned to duty and had charge of all the country lying between Wasatch County range and the Uinta reservation. They had several skirmishes with Indians; at one time killed two and wounded several. They performed active service every day for three months, and were mustered out October 31, 1866.

I certify that the above account is correct.

H. B. CLAWSON,
Adjutant General Utah Territory Militia.

Pay-roll of Captain John M. Murdock's company —— infantry, Utah Territory militia, employed in the suppression of Indian hostilities in Wasatch County, Utah Territory, from May 1, 1866, to June 30, 1866.

We, the undersigned, acknowledge to have received from James W. Cummings, paymaster Utah Territory militia, the sums set opposite to our names, in full payment for our services for the time specified.

Number	Names	Rank	Period of service. Commencement.	Period of service. Expiration.	Months.	Pay per month.	Monthly allowance for clothing.	Total monthly pay and allowance.	Total pay and allowance.	Signatures.	Witnesses.
1	John M. Murdock	Captain	May 1, 1866	June 30, 1866	2		$3 50	$118 50	$237 00	John M. Murdock	John Crook.
1	John Muir	1st lieutenant	May 1, 1866	June 30, 1866	2		3 50	108 50	217 00	John Muir	J. M. Murdock.
1	John Jordan	2d lieutenant	May 1, 1866	June 30, 1866	2		3 50	103 50	207 00	John Jordan	Do.
2	William Davidson	do	May 1, 1866	June 30, 1866	2		3 50	103 50	207 00	William Davidson	John Muir.
3	Archibald Serougie	do	May 1, 1866	June 30, 1866	2	$17 00	3 50	103 50	207 00	Archibald Serougie	John Murdock.
3	James McNaughton	Sergeant	May 1, 1866	June 30, 1866	2	17 00	3 50	20 50	41 00	James McVaughton	John Muir.
3	Robert Cunningham	do	May 1, 1866	June 30, 1866	2	17 00	3 50	20 50	41 00	Robert Cunningham	John Murdock.
3	Ruben Allred	do	May 1, 1866	June 30, 1866	2	13 00	3 50	20 50	41 00	Ruben Allred	Do.
4	Joseph Moulton	Private	May 1, 1866	June 30, 1866	2	13 00	3 50	16 50	33 00	Joseph Moulton	John Muir.
5	Joseph Taylor	do	May 1, 1866	June 30, 1866	2	13 00	3 50	16 50	33 00	Joseph Taylor	Do.
6	William Clegg	do	May 1, 1866	June 30, 1866	2	13 00	3 50	16 50	33 00	William Clegg	William Aird.
4	Freeman Manning	do	May 1, 1866	June 30, 1866	2	13 00	3 50	16 50	33 00	Fremon Manning	John Muir.
5	Thomas Hudson	do	May 1, 1866	June 30, 1866	2	13 00	3 50	16 50	33 00	Thomas Hudson	Do.
6	William Aird	do	May 1, 1866	June 30, 1866	2	13 00	3 50	16 50	33 00	William Aird	John Jordan.
7	Stephen Bond	do	May 1, 1866	June 30, 1866	2	13 00	3 50	16 50	33 00	Stephen Bond	Do.
8	Robert Baird	do	May 1, 1866	June 30, 1866	2	13 00	3 50	16 50	33 00	Robert Baird	John Muir.
9	James Given	do	May 1, 1866	June 30, 1866	2	13 00	3 50	16 50	33 00	James Given	John Murdock.
10	William Thompson	do	May 1, 1866	June 30, 1866	2	13 00	3 50	16 50	33 00	William Thompson	Do.
11	William Clegg	do	May 1, 1866	June 30, 1866	2	13 00	3 50	16 50	33 00	William Clegg, sr	William Aird.
12	John Grant	do	May 1, 1866	June 30, 1866	2	13 00	3 50	16 50	33 00	John Grant	John Murdock.
13	David Adams	do	May 1, 1866	June 30, 1866	2	13 00	3 50	16 50	33 00	David Adams	Do.
14	Mark Jeffs	do	May 1, 1866	June 30, 1866	2	13 00	3 50	16 50	33 00	Mark Jeffs	John Jordan.
15	William McMillen	do	May 1, 1866	June 30, 1866	2	13 00	3 50	16 50	33 00	William McMillen	Do.
16	James Adams	do	May 1, 1866	June 30, 1866	2	13 00	3 50	16 50	33 00	James Adams	Do.
17	George Muir	do	May 1, 1866	June 30, 1866	2	13 00	3 50	16 50	33 00	George Muir	Do.
18	John Turner	do	May 1, 1866	June 30, 1866	2	13 00	3 50	16 50	33 00	John Turner	John Muir.
19	Joseph Batson	do	May 1, 1866	June 30, 1866	2	13 00	3 50	16 50	33 00	Joseph Betson	Do.
20	William Lindsay	do	May 1, 1866	June 30, 1866	2	13 00	3 50	16 50	33 00	William Lindsay	Do.
21	Peter Cunningham	do	May 1, 1866	June 30, 1866	2	13 00	3 50	16 50	33 00	Peter Cunningham	Do.
22	William Oakes	do	May 1, 1866	June 30, 1866	2	13 00	3 50	16 50	33 00	William Oakes	Do.
23	John Jordan	do	May 1, 1866	June 30, 1866	2	13 00	3 50	16 50	33 00	John P. Jordan	William Aird.
24	Lewis Meckham	do	May 1, 1866	June 30, 1866	2	13 00	3 50	16 50	33 00	Lewis Meckham	John Muir.
25	Edward Garr	do	May 1, 1866	June 30, 1866	2	13 00	3 50	16 50	33 00	Edward Garr	Do.

No.	Name		Mustered in	Mustered out						Name	Remarks
26	William Johnson	do	May 1, 1866	June 30, 1866	2	13 00	3 50	16 50	33 00	Isaac Wall	Do.
27	Isaac Wall	do	May 1, 1866	June 30, 1866	2	13 00	3 50	16 50	33 00	William Johnson	Do.
28	Francis Kirby	do	May 1, 1866	June 30, 1866	2	13 00	3 50	16 50	33 00	Francis Kirby	John Jordan.
29	John Mecklum	do	May 1, 1866	June 30, 1866	2	13 00	3 50	16 50	33 00	John Mecklum	Do.
30	John Griffith	do	May 1, 1866	June 30, 1866	2	13 00	3 50	16 50	33 00	John Griffith	John Muir.
31	William Adams	do	May 1, 1866	June 30, 1866	2	13 00	3 50	16 50	33 00	William Adams	Do.
32	Arthur Kirk	do	May 1, 1866	June 3, 1866	2	13 00	3 50	16 50	33 00	Arthur Kirk	Do.
33	James Allred	do	May 1, 1866	June 30, 1866	2	13 00	3 50	16 50	33 00	James Alred	Do.
34	William Ryan, Jr.	do	May 1, 1866	June 30, 1866	2	13 00	3 50	16 50	31 00	William Ryan, Jr	Do.
35	Peter Gurr	do	May 1, 1866	June 30, 1866	2	13 00	3 50	16 50	33 00	Peter Gurr	Do.

This company was mustered into service at Heber City, May 1, 1866, by order of Daniel H. Wells, and assigned to duty in the Northern Mountain range, where they performed active service for two months, and was mustered out on the 30th day of June, 1866.

I certify that the above account is correct,

H. B. CLAWSON,
Adjutant General Utah Territory Militia.

Pay-roll of Captain Ira N. Jacobs's company —— infantry, Utah Territory militia, employed in the suppression of Indian hostilities in Wasatch County, Utah Territory, from June 1, 1866, to July 30, 1866.

We, the undersigned, acknowledge to have received from James W. Cummings, paymaster Utah Territory militia, the sums set opposite to our names, in full payment for our services for the time specified.

Number.	Names.	Rank.	Commencement.	Expiration.	Months.	Pay per month.	Monthly allowance for clothing.	Total monthly allowance.	Total pay and allowance.	Signatures.	Witnesses.
1	Ira N. Jacobs	Captain	June 1, 1866	July 30, 1866	2			$118 50	$237	I. N. Jacob	David Van Wagonen.
1	William W. Wilson	1st lieut	June 1, 1866	July 30, 1866	2			104 50	217	Wm. W. Wilson	Do.
2	Robert Cunningham	2d lieut	June 1, 1866	July 30, 1866	2			103 50	207	Robert Cunningham	Joseph McCarrel.
3	George Dablin	do	June 1, 1866	July 30, 1866	2			103 50	207	George Dabling	Do.
3	William McGhee a	do	June 1, 1866	July 30, 1866	2			103 50	207		
4	Peter Apt-nalp	do	June 1, 1866	July 30, 1866	2			103 50	207	Peter Aplexortp	David Van Wagonen.
5	James Low	do	June 1, 1866	July 30, 1866	2			103 50	207	James Low	Joseph McCarrel.
6	Samuel Thompson	do	June 1, 1866	July 30, 1866	2			103 50	207	Samuel Thompson	Do.
2	John O'Ni-il b	Sergeant	June 1, 1866	July 30, 1866	2	$17	$3 50	20 50	41		
3	John G. Gerber c	do	June 1, 1866	July 30, 1866	2	17	3 50	20 50	41		
3	George Wilson	do	June 1, 1866	July 30, 1866	2	17	3 50	20 50	41	George Wilson	Do.
4	John Huber d	do	June 1, 1866	July 30, 1866	2	17	3 50	20 50	41	John Huber	John Fonsett.
5	John Sutherland	do	June 1, 1866	July 30, 1866	2		3 50	20 50	41		
6	John Fawcett	Private	June 1, 1866	July 30, 1866	2		3 50	20 50	41	John Fonsett	John Huber.
1	John Robertson	do	June 1, 1866	July 30, 1866	2	13	3 50	16 50	33	John Robertson	Joseph McCarrel.
2	Thomas Fisher	do	June 1, 1866	July 30, 1866	2	13	3 50	16 50	33	Thomas Fisher	David Van Wagonen.
3	Morone Blood	do	June 1, 1866	July 30, 1866	2	13	3 50	16 50	33	Moroni Blood, his + mark	Joseph McCarrel.
4	James O'Niel b	do	June 1, 1866	July 30, 1866	2	13	3 50	16 50	33		
5	Allen Morton	do	June 1, 1866	July 30, 1866	2	13	3 50	16 50	33	Allan Morton	Do.
6	Joseph Jacobs	do	June 1, 1866	July 30, 1866	2	13	3 50	16 50	33		
7	George W. Clift	do	June 1, 1866	July 30, 1866	2	13	3 50	16 50	33	George S. Clift	I. N. Jacob.
8	Samuel S. Hickenbottom	do	June 1, 1866	July 30, 1866	2	13	3 50	16 50	33	Simon S. Hickenbotham	David Van Wagonen.
9	Thompson Ritter	do	June 1, 1866	July 30, 1866	2	13	3 50	16 50	33	Thompson Ritter, his + mark	Do.
10	James Gurr	do	June 1, 1866	July 30, 1866	2	13	3 50	16 50	33	James Guerre	
11	William Buhler	do	June 1, 1866	July 30, 1866	2	13	3 50	16 50	33	Wm. R. Beclar	Do.
12	Marino McOlney	do	June 1, 1866	July 30, 1866	2	13	3 50	16 50	33		
13	Adam Thompson	do	June 1, 1866	July 30, 1866	2	13	3 50	16 50	33	Adam Thompson	Joseph McCarrel.
14	John Rosef	do	June 1, 1866	July 30, 1866	2	13	3 50	16 50	33		
15	Lewis Gerber	do	June 1, 1866	July 30, 1866	2	13	3 50	16 50	33	Louis Gerber, his + mark	David Van Wagonen.
16	David F. Hamilton	do	June 1, 1866	July 30, 1866	2	13	3 50	16 50	33	David F. Hamilton	Nathan C. Springer.
17	Thomas Thornton e	do	June 1, 1866	July 30, 1866	2	13	3 50	16 50	33		
18	Jacob Duel	do	June 1, 1866	July 30, 1866	2	13	3 50	16 50	33	Jacob Duel	David Van Wagonen.
19	Attuwall Wooten	do	June 1, 1866	July 30, 1866	2	13	3 50	16 50	33	Attewell Wooton	Do.
20	Edward Condar g	do	June 1, 1866	July 30, 1866	2	13	3 50	16 50	33		

No.	Name		In	Out						Signature	Witness
21	Lucien H. Jacob b h	do	June 1, 1866	July 30, 1866	2	13	3 50	16 50	33	William Coleman	Wm. W. Wilson.
22	William Coleman	do	June 1, 1866	July 30, 1866	2	13	3 50	16 50	33	Joshua Ward, his + mark	David Van Wagonen.
23	Joshua Weed	do	June 1, 1866	July 30, 1866	2	13	3 50	16 50	33	George Bonner	Do.
24	George Bonner i	do	June 1, 1866	July 30, 1866	2	13	3 50	16 50	33	Harry Meeks	Do.
25	Harvey Meeks	do	June 1, 1866	July 30, 1866	2	13	3 50	16 50	33	John Davis	Do.
26	John Davis	do	June 1, 1866	July 30, 1866	2	13	3 50	16 50	33	Enock Davis	Do.
27	Enock Davis	do	June 1, 1866	July 30, 1866	2	13	3 50	16 50	33		
28	John Robertson j	do	June 1, 1866	July 30, 1866	2	13	3 50	16 50	33	Kourad Aboeglin	Do.
29	Henry Love k	do	June 1, 1866	July 30, 1866	2	13	3 50	16 50	33	Jakob Butler	Do.
30	Conrad Aboeglin	do	June 1, 1866	July 30, 1866	2	13	3 50	16 50	33	Jakob Bargener	Do.
31	Jacob Butler	do	June 1, 1866	July 30, 1866	2	13	3 50	16 50	33	Casper Suljer	Do.
32	Jacob Bergener	do	June 1, 1866	July 30, 1866	2	13	3 50	16 50	33	John Suljer his + mark	Do.
33	Casper Suljer	do	June 1, 1866	July 30, 1866	2	13	3 50	16 50	33	Martin Nargeil + mark	John Huler.
34	John Suljer	do	June 1, 1866	July 24, 1866	2	13	3 50	16 50	33	Hyrum Shelton, his + mark	David Van Wagonen.
35	Martin Nagle	do	June 1, 1866	July 30, 1866	2	13	3 50	16 50	33		
36	Hyrum Shelton	do	June 1, 1866	July 30, 1866	2	13	3 50	16 50	33		
37	Herbet Homer l	do	June 1, 1866	July 30, 1866	2	13	3 50	16 50	33		
38	Joseph Allen l	do	June 1, 1866	July 30, 1866	2	13	3 50	16 50	33		
39	Charles Allen l	do	June 1, 1866	July 30, 1866	2	13	3 50	16 50	33	Edwin Wardle	I. N. Jacob.
40	Edwin Wardle	do	June 1, 1866	July 30, 1866	2	13	3 50	16 50	33	James W. Provost	David F. Hamilton.
41	James Provost	do	June 1, 1866	July 30, 1866	2	13	3 50	16 50	33	Mark Smith	David Van Wagonen.
42	Mark Smith	do	June 1, 1866	July 30, 1866	2	13	3 50	16 50	33	David Provost, his + mark	Do.
43	David Provost	do	June 1, 1866	July 30, 1866	2	13	3 50	16 50	33	John Hold n, his + mark	Do.
44	John Holden	do	June 1, 1866	July 30, 1866	2	13	3 50	16 50	33	James W. Fisher	Do.
45	James W. Fisher	do	June 1, 1866	July 30, 1866	2	13	3 50	16 50	33	Jas. Mayer	Do.
46	John Mayer	do	June 1, 1866	July 30, 1866	2	13	3 50	16 50	33	George Wardle	I. N. Jacob.
47	George Wardle	do	June 1, 1866	July 30, 1866	2	13	3 50	16 50	33	David Wood	David Van Wagonen.
48	David Wood	do	June 1, 1866	July 30, 1866	2	13	3 50	16 50	33	Andrew M. Hamilton	George Dabling.
49	Andrew Hamilton	do	June 1, 1866	July 30, 1866	2	13	3 50	16 50	33	Jeremiah Roby	David Van Wagonen.
50	Jeremiah Roby	do	June 1, 1866	July 30, 1866	2	13	3 50	16 50	33	Jacob Ertzinger	Do.
51	Jacob Ertzinger	do	June 1, 1866	July 30, 1866	2	13	3 50	16 50	33	John H. Van Wagonen	Do.
52	John Van Wagoner	do	June 1, 1866	July 30, 1866	2	13	3 50	16 50	33	James Davis	Do.
53	James Davis	do	June 1, 1866	July 30, 1866	2	13	3 50	16 50	33	Christian Orbueglun	Do.
54	Christian Aboeglin	do	June 1, 1866	July 30, 1866	2	13	3 50	16 50	33	Ulrich Orbueglun	Do.
55	Ulrich Aboeglin m	do	June 1, 1866	July 30, 1866	2	13	3 50	16 50	33		

a Big Cottonwood. b Green River. c Wanship, Summit County. d Cottonwood. e American Fork. f Moved to Summit Creek, Utah County. g Moved to American Fork. k Moved to Ruby Valley. i Wounded through the leg near Uinta reservation, June 16, 1866. j Moved to American Fork, Utah County. k Moved to Ruby Valley, Nevada. l Moved to Springville. m Name accidentally omitted.

This company was mustered into service by order of Lieutenant General D. H. Wells at Heber City, June 1, 1866, and assigned to duty in the eastern mountains and passes. They were in active service for two months, and were mustered out at Heber City July 30, 1866.

I certify that the above account is correct.

H. B. CLAWSON,
Adjutant General Utah Territory Militia.

Pay-roll of Captain Thomas E. Daniels's company —— infantry, Utah Territory militia, employed in the suppression of Indian hostilities in Payson, Pondtown, Santaquin, and Goshen, Utah County, from May 11, 1866, to August 29, 1866.

We, the undersigned, acknowledge to have received from James W. Cummings, paymaster Utah Territory militia, the sums set opposite to our names, in full payment for our services for the time specified.

Number.	Names.	Rank.	Commencement.	Expiration.	Months.	Days.	Pay per month.	Monthly allowance for clothing.	Total monthly pay and allow.	Total pay and allowance.	Signatures.	Witnesses.
1	Thomas E. Daniels	Captain	May 11, 1866	Aug. 29, 1866	3	18		$3 50	$118 50	$436 60	Thomas E. Daniels	J. M. Coombs.
1	Edward Ried	1st lieut.	May 11, 1866	Aug. 29, 1866	3	18		3 30	108 50	390 60	Edward Reid	Do.
1	Warren Hancock	2d lieut.	May 11, 1866	Aug. 29, 1866	3	18		3 50	103 50	372 60	Warren Hancock	Do.
2	David Mitchell	do	May 11, 1866	Aug. 29, 1866	3	18		3 50	103 50	372 60	D. Mitchell	Do.
3	Henry W. Barnett	do	May 11, 1866	Aug. 29, 1866	3	18		3 50	103 50	372 60	H. W. Barnett	Do.
4	David Russell	do	May 11, 1866	Aug. 29, 1866	3	18		3 50	104 50	372 60	David Russell	Do.
1	Henry Butler	Sergeant	May 11, 1866	Aug. 29, 1866	3	18	$17 00	3 50	20 50	73 80	Henry Butler	Do.
2	Joseph Robinson	do	May 11, 1866	Aug. 29, 1866	3	12	17 00	3 30	20 50	73 80	Joseph Robinson	Do.
3	John Reddington	do	May 11, 1866	Aug. 29, 1866	3	18	17 00	3 50	20 50	73 80	John Redington	Do.
4	John Holden	do	May 11, 1866	Aug. 29, 1866	3	12	17 00	3 50	20 51	73 20	John Holden, his X mark	Do.
1	William Clayson	Private	May 11, 1866	Aug. 29, 1866	3	18	13 00	3 50	16 50	59 40	William Clayson	Do.
2	Thomas Gange	do	May 11, 1866	Aug. 29, 1866	3	18	13 00	3 50	16 50	59 40	Thomas Gange	Do.
3	Jacob Dean	do	May 11, 1866	Aug. 29, 1866	3	12	13 00	3 50	16 50	59 40	Jacob Dien	Do.
4	Robert Ford	do	May 11, 1866	Aug. 29, 1866	3	18	13 00	3 50	16 50	59 40	Robert Forde	Do.
5	David Butler	do	May 11, 1866	Aug. 29, 1866	3	18	13 00	3 50	16 50	59 40	David Butler	Do.
6	John Reid	do	May 11, 1866	Aug. 29, 1866	3	12	13 00	3 50	16 50	59 40	John Reid	Do.
7	Samuel Worsencroft	do	May 11, 1866	Aug. 29, 1866	3	18	13 00	3 50	16 50	59 40	Samuel Worsencroft	Do.
8	Charles Davis	do	May 11, 1866	Aug. 29, 1866	3	18	13 00	3 50	16 50	59 40	Chas. Davis	Do.
9	John W. Jackson	do	May 11, 1866	Aug. 29, 1866	3	18	13 00	3 51	16 50	59 40	John W. Jackson	Do.
10	William Salmon	do	May 11, 1866	Aug. 29, 1866	3	18	13 00	3 50	16 50	59 40	William Salmon	Do.
11	Joseph Crompton	do	May 11, 1866	Aug. 29, 1866	3	18	13 00	3 50	16 50	59 40	Joseph Crompton	Do.
12	J. R. Ross	do	May 11, 1866	Aug. 29, 1866	3	12	13 00	3 50	16 50	59 40	J. R. Ross	Do.
13	John F. Bellows	do	May 11, 1866	Aug. 29, 1866	3	18	13 00	3 50	16 50	59 40	John F. Bellows	Do.
14	John K. Reid	do	May 11, 1866	Aug. 29, 1866	3	18	13 00	3 50	16 50	59 40	John K. Reid	Do.
15	Thomas E. Gange	do	May 11, 1866	Aug. 29, 1866	3	18	13 00	3 50	16 50	59 40	Thomas E. Gange	Do.
16	James Boyle	do	May 11, 1866	Aug. 29, 1866	3	12	13 00	3 50	16 50	59 40	James Boyle	Do.
17	Russell Chandler	do	May 11, 1866	Aug. 29, 1866	3	18	13 00	3 50	16 50	59 40	Russell Chandler	Do.
18	Robert Shin	do	May 11, 1866	Aug. 29, 1866	3	18	13 00	3 50	16 50	59 40	Robert Shin	Do.
19	Alven Hershay	do	May 11, 1866	Aug. 29, 1866	3	18	13 00	3 50	16 50	59 40	Alven Hershy	Do.
20	Richard Smyth	do	May 11, 1866	Aug. 29, 1866	3	14	13 00	3 50	16 50	59 40	Richard Smyth	Do.
21	Ferdinand Overruned	do	May 11, 1866	Aug. 29, 1866	3	18	13 00	3 50	16 50	59 40	Ferdinand Oberhänsly	Do.
22	Thomas Miller	do	May 11, 1866	Aug. 29, 1866	3	18	13 00	3 30	16 50	59 40	Thomas Miller	Do.

23	John Armet	do	May 11, 1866	Aug. 29, 1866	3 18	13 00	3 50	16 50	59 40	H. M. Russell	Do.
24	Henry Russell	do	May 11, 1866	Aug. 29, 1866	3 18	13 00	3 50	16 50	59 40	Jackson Russell	Do.
25	Jackson Russell	do	May 11, 1866	Aug. 29, 1866	3 18	13 00	3 50	16 50	59 40	Alexander Gowan	Do.
26	Alexander Gowan	do	May 11, 1866	Aug. 29, 1866	3 18	13 00	3 50	16 50	59 40	George Hatch	Do.
27	George Hatch	do	May 11, 1866	Aug. 29, 1866	3 18	13 00	3 50	16 50	59 40	Shadrick Richerson	Do.
28	Shadrack Richardson	do	May 11, 1866	Aug. 29, 1866	3 18	13 00	3 50	16 50	59 40	William L. Court	Do.
29	William L. Court	do	May 11, 1866	Aug. 29, 1866	3 18	13 00	3 50	16 50	59 40	Henry Worthington	Do.
30	Henry Worthington	do	May 11, 1866	Aug. 29, 1866	3 18	13 00	3 50	16 50	59 43	Daniel Mott	Do.
31	Daniel Mott	do	May 11, 1866	Aug. 29, 1866	3 18	13 00	3 50	16 50	59 40		Do.

This company was mustered into service at Payson, Utah County, May 11, 1866, by order of Major General Aaron Johnson, and assigned to duty in the mountains east of Pondtown, Payson, and Santaquin. They were in active service in this vicinity every day until mustered out, August 29, 1866.

I certify that the above account is correct.

H. B. CLAWSON,
Adjutant General Utah Territory Militia.

Pay-roll of field and staff officers commanding the Utah militia employed in the suppression of Indian hostilities in Sanpete, Sevier, and Piute counties, Utah Territory, from May 1, 1866, to November 1, 1866.

We, the undersigned, acknowledge to have received from James W. Cummings, paymaster Utah Territory militia, the sums set opposite to our names in full payment for our services for the time specified.

Number.	Names.	Staff appointment; office.	Rank.	Period of service. Commencement.	Period of service. Expiration.	Months.	Pay per month.	Monthly allowance for clothing.	Total monthly pay and allowance.	40 cents per day for use and risk of horse and horse equipment.	Total pay and allowance.	Signatures.	Witnesses.
	Warren S. Snow	Brigade adj't	Brig. general	May 1, 1866	Nov. 1, 1866	6			299 50	72 00	1,869 00	W. S. Snow	C. F. Twede.
	George Peacock	Brigade adj't	Lt. colonel	May 1, 1866	Nov. 1, 1866	6			187 00	72 00	1,194 00	George Peacock	Do.
	Frederick Robinson	Brigade Q. M	do	May 1, 1866	Nov. 1, 1866	6			187 00	72 00	1,194 00	Frederick Robinson	Do.
	Luther Tuttle	Aide-de-camp	do	May 1, 1866	Nov. 1, 1866	6			187 00	72 00	1,194 00	Luther Tuttle	Do.
	Madison D. Hambleton	do	Captain	May 1, 1866	Nov. 1, 1866	6			129 50	72 00	849 00	M. D. Hambleton	Do.
	Rural M. Rogers	Surgeon	do	May 1, 1866	Nov. 1, 1866	6			129 50	72 00	849 00	R. M. Rogers	Do.
	George Snow	Chief of music	1st lieuten't	May 1, 1866	Nov. 1, 1866	6			112 83	72 00	748 98	George Snow	Do.
	Redick N. Allred	Colonel	Colonel	May 1, 1866	Nov. 1, 1866	6			211 00	72 00	1,338 00	Redick N. Allred	Do.
	John L. Ivie		Lt. colonel	May 1, 1866	Nov. 1, 1866	6			187 00	72 00	1,191 00	John L. Ivie	Do.
	Joseph T. Ellis	Regim'l adj't	Major	May 1, 1866	Nov. 1, 1866	6			163 00	72 00	1,050 00	Jos. T. Ellis	Do.
	Joseph S. Wing	Surgeon	Captain	May 1, 1866	Nov. 1, 1866	6			129 50	72 00	849 00	Jos. S. Wing	John R. Winder.
	David Candland	Post adj't	do	May 1, 1866	Nov. 1, 1866	6			129 50	72 00	849 00	David Candland	Do.
	Ruben W. Allred		Major	May 1, 1866	Nov. 1, 1866	6			163 00	72 00	1,050 00	Reuben W. Allred	C. F. Twede.
	Samuel R. Frost	Battalion adj't	Captain	May 1, 1866	Nov. 1, 1866	6			129 50	72 00	849 00	Samuel R. Frost	Do.
	George W. Bradley		Major	May 1, 1866	Nov. 1, 1866	6			129 50	72 00	1,050 00	George W. Bradley	Do.
	Abner Lowry	Battalion adj't	Captain	May 1, 1866	Nov. 1, 1866	6			129 50	72 00	849 00	Abner Lowry	Do.
	William S. Seeley		Major	May 1, 1866	Nov. 1, 1866	6			129 50	72 00	1,050 00	Wm. S. Seeley	Do.
	William N. Tidwell	Battalion & lt.	Captain	May 1, 1866	Nov. 1, 1866	6			129 50	72 00	849 00	Wm. N. Tidwell	Do.
	John Hitchcock		Major	May 1, 1866	Nov. 1, 1866	6			129 50	72 00	1,050 00	John Hitchcock	Do.
	Rasmus Justesen	Battalion adj't	Captain	May 1, 1866	Nov. 1, 1866	6			129 50	72 00	849 00	Rasmus Justesen	Do.
	Henry W. Sanderson		Major	May 1, 1866	Nov. 1, 1866	6			163 00	72 00	1,050 00	Henry W. Sanderson	Do.
	Lyurgus Wilson	Battalion adj't	Captain	May 1, 1866	Nov. 1, 1866	6			129 50	72 00	849 00	Lyurgus Wilson	Do.
	Nathaniel S. Beach		Colonel	May 1, 1866	Nov. 1, 1866	6			211 00	72 40	1,338 00	N. S. Beach	Do.
	Foster R. Kerner	Regim'l adj't	Lt. colonel	May 1, 1866	Nov. 1, 1866	6			167 00	72 00	1,144 00	F. R. Kerner	Do.
	Edward W. Fox	Surgeon	Major	May 1, 1866	Nov. 1, 1866	6			163 00	72 00	1,050 00	Edward W. Fox	Do.
	Oliver C. Ormsby		Captain	May 1, 1866	Nov. 1, 1866	6			129 50	72 00	849 00	Oliver C. Ormsby	Do.
	George P. Billings	Battalion adj't	Major	May 1, 1866	Nov. 1, 1866	6			163 03	72 03	1,050 00	Geo. P. Billings	Do.
	Hans Massen		Captain	May 1, 1866	Nov. 1, 1866	6			163 00	72 00	849 00	Hans Madsen	Do.
	William K. Burton	Battalion adj't	Major	May 1, 1866	Nov. 1, 1866	6			163 00	72 00	1,050 00	William K. Burton	Do.
	Thomas Greer		Captain	May 1, 1866	Nov. 1, 1866	6			129 50	72 00	849 00	Thomas Green	Do.

Caleb G. Edwards	Major	May 1, 1866	Nov. 1, 1866	6		163 00	72 00	1,050 00	Caleb G. Edwards	Do.
Hans F. Peterson	Battalion adj't	May 1, 1866	Nov. 1, 1866	6		129 50	72 00	949 00	H. F. Peterson	Do.
C. C. N. Dorius	Major	May 1, 1866	Nov. 1, 1866	6		163 00	72 00	1,050 00	C. C. N. Dorius	Do.
J. P. Christiansen	Battalion adj't	May 1, 1866	Nov. 1, 1866	6		129 50	72 00	949 00	J. P. Christiansen	Do.
Robert G. Frazier	Major	May 1, 1866	Nov. 1, 1866	6		163 00	72 00	1,050 00	Robert G. Frazier	Do.
Christian A. Madsen	Battalion adj't	May 1, 1866	Nov. 1, 1866	6		129 00	72 00	949 00	Christian A. Madsen	Do.
Silas S. Smith	Major	Mar. 21, 1866	June 21, 1866	3		163 00	36 00	525 00	Silas S. Smith	W. B. Parr.
James Whittaker, jr	Battalion adj't	Mar. 21, 1866	June 21, 1866	3		129 50	36 00	496 50	James Whittaker, jr	Do.

The above field and staff officers, of Sanpete, Sevier, Piute, and Iron counties, were mustered into service by order of Lieutenant General Daniel H. Wells, and assigned to duty by him in the above-named counties. They were in active service every day for the time above specified until they were mustered out November 1, 1866.

I certify that the above account is correct.

H. B. CLAWSON,
Adjutant General Nauvoo Legion.

Pay-roll of Captain Thomas Todd's company —— infantry, Utah Territory militia, employed in the suppression of Indian hostilities in Wasatch County, Utah Territory, from July 1, 1866, to August 30, 1866.

We, the undersigned, acknowledge to have received from James W. Cummings, paymaster Utah Territory militia, the sums set opposite to our names, in full payment for our services for the time specified.

Number	Names	Rank	Commencement	Expiration	Months	Pay per month	Monthly allowance for clothing	Total monthly pay and allow.	Total pay and allowance	Signatures	Witnesses
1	Thomas Todd	Captain	July 1, 1866	August 30, 1866	2	$17 00		$118 50	$237 00	Thomas Todd	John Crook.
1	Charles N. Carroll	1st lieut	July 1, 1866	August 30, 1866	2	17 00		108 50	217 00	Charles N. Carroll	Thomas Todd.
1	Frederick Giles	2d lieut	July 1, 1866	August 30, 1866	2	17 00		103 50	207 00	Frederick Giles	Charles N. Carroll.
2	Henry McMullin	do	July 1, 1866	August 31, 1866	2	17 00		103 50	207 00	Henry McMullin	Henry McMullin.
3	Richard Greer	do	July 1, 1866	August 30, 1866	2	17 00		103 50	207 00	Richard Greer	Frederick Giles.
3	Henry Hamilton	do	July 1, 1866	August 30, 1866	2	17 00		103 50	207 00	Henery Hamilton	Do.
2	William Monlton	Sergeant	July 1, 1866	August 30, 1866	2	17 00	$3 50	20 50	41 00	William Monlton	Thomas Todd.
3	William McGee	do	July 1, 1866	August 30, 1866	2	17 00	3 50	20 50	41 00	William McGee	Charles N. Carroll.
3	William Hows	do	July 1, 1866	August 30, 1866	2	17 00	3 50	20 50	41 00	William Hows	Thomas Todd.
4	George A. Wilson	do	July 1, 1866	August 30, 1866	2	17 00	3 50	20 50	41 00	George A. Wilson	Charles N. Carroll.
2	Jonathan Clegg	Private	July 1, 1866	August 30, 1866	2	13 00	3 50	16 50	33 00	Jonathan Clegg	Thomas Todd.
3	James Shanks†	do	July 1, 1866	August 30, 1866	2	13 00	3 50	16 50	33 00	James Shanks	Frederick Giles.
4	James Duke*	do	July 1, 1866	August 35, 1866	2	13 00	3 50	16 50	33 00	James Duke	Jonathan Clegg.
5	Jonathan M. Duke	do	July 1, 1866	August 30, 1866	2	13 00	3 50	16 50	33 00	Jonethan M. Duke	Frederick Giles.
6	Jesse Bond	do	July 1, 1866	August 30, 1866	2	13 00	3 50	16 50	33 00	Jesse Bond	Thomas Todd.
7	Thomas Handley	do	July 1, 1866	August 30, 1866	2	13 00	3 50	16 50	33 00	Thomas Handly	Do.
7	Willard Carroll	do	July 1, 1866	August 30, 1866	2	13 00	3 50	16 50	33 00	Willard Carroll	Charles N. Carroll.
8	Jacob Bann	do	July 1, 1866	August 30, 1866	2	13 00	3 50	16 50	33 00	Jachob Bann	Frederick Giles.
9	William Chatwin	do	July 1, 1866	August 30, 1866	2	13 00	3 50	16 50	33 00	William Chatwin	Do.
10	Edward Payne	do	July 1, 1866	August 30, 1866	2	13 00	3 50	16 50	33 00	Edward Payne	Thomas Todd.
11	Alfred Ward	do	July 1, 1866	August 30, 1866	2	13 00	3 50	16 50	33 00	Alfred Ward	Frederick Giles.
12	Thomas Rasband	do	July 1, 1866	August 30, 1866	2	13 00	3 50	16 50	33 00	Thomas Rasband	Jonathan Clegg.
13	James Cole	do	July 1, 1866	August 30, 1866	2	13 00	3 50	16 50	33 00	James Coal	Charles N. Carroll.
14	Thomas Hicken	do	July 1, 1866	August 30, 1866	2	13 00	3 50	16 50	33 00	Thomas Hicken	Jesse Baud.
15	David Stephenson	do	July 1, 1866	August 30, 1866	2	13 00	3 50	16 50	33 00	David Stephenson	Charles N. Carroll.
16	William Richardson	do	July 1, 1866	August 30, 1866	2	13 00	3 50	16 50	33 00	William Richardson	Do.
17	John Kirbie	do	July 1, 1866	August 30, 1866	2	13 00	3 50	16 50	33 00	John Kirbie	John Crook.
18	William Watson	do	July 1, 1866	August 30, 1866	2	13 00	3 50	16 50	33 00	William Watson	Do.
19	Samuel McFee	do	July 1, 1866	August 30, 1866	2	13 00	3 50	16 50	33 00	Samuel McFee	Do.
20	Henry Nelson	do	July 1, 1866	August 30, 1866	2	13 00	3 50	16 50	33 00	Henry Nelson	Do.
21	Noah Mayab	do	July 1, 1866	August 30, 1866	2	13 00	3 50	16 50	33 00	Noah Mayab	Do.
22	Jasper Booren	do	July 1, 1866	August 30, 1866	2	13 00	3 50	16 50	33 00	Jacper Boren	Do.
23	Edward Stocks	do	July 1, 1866	August 30, 1866	2	13 00	3 50	16 50	33 00	Edward Stock	Do.

21	James Garr	do	July 1, 1866	August 30, 1866	2?	13 00	3 50	16 50	33 00	James Garr	Do.
25	Hiram Biglow	do	July 1, 1866	August 30, 1866	2?	13 00	3 50	16 50	33 00	Hiram Biglow	Do.
26	Alva Hanks	do	July 1, 1866	August 30, 1866	2?	13 00	3 50	16 50	33 00	Alva Hanks	Do.
27	Francis Kirby	do	July 1, 1866	August 30, 1866	2?	13 00	3 50	16 50	33 00	Francis Kirley	Do.
28	George Brown	do	July 1, 1866	August 30, 1866	2?	21 00	3 50	16 50	33 00	George Brown	Do.
29	Moroni Meckham	do	July 1, 1866	August 30, 1866	2?	13 00	3 50	16 50	33 00	Moroni Meckham	Thomas Todd.
30	Reuben Garr	do	July 1, 1866	August 30, 1866	2?	13 00	3 50	16 50	33 0?	Ruben Garr	Do.
31	John Andrews	do	July 1, 1866	August 30, 1866	2?	13 00	3 50	16 50	33 00	John Andrew	Do.
32	J. R. Miller	do	July 1, 1866	August 30, 1866	2?	13 00	3 50	16 50	33 00	James R. Miller	Do.
33	Lewis Poiree	do	July 1, 1866	August 30, 1866	2?	13 00	3 50	16 50	33 00	Lewis Poiree	Do.
35	John Davis	do	July 1, 1866	August 30, 1866	2?	13 00	3 50	16 50	33 00	John Davis	Do.
36	Frank Wilson	do	July 1, 1866	August 30, 1866	2?	13 00	3 50	16 50	33 00	Frank Wilson	Do.

* A mistake; he is drum-major.   † A mistake; he is fife-major.   ‡ Drum-major's adjutant.

This company was mustered into service in Wasatch County, for the protection of the inhabitants in Rhode's Valley and surrounding country. They were actively engaged during the two months, and were mustered out August 30, 1866. I certify that the above account is correct.

H. B. CLAWSON,
Adjutant General Utah Territory Militia.

Pay-roll of Major Andrew Burt's company —— infantry, Utah Territory militia, employed in the suppression of Indian hostilities in Sanpete and Sevier counties, from July 25, 1866, to November 3, 1866.

We, the undersigned, acknowledge to have received from James W. Cummings, paymaster Utah Territory militia, the sums set opposite to our names, in full payment for our services for the time specified.

Number	Names	Rank	Commencement	Expiration	Months	Days	Pay per month	Monthly allowance for clothing	Total monthly pay and allowance	Total pay and allowance	Signatures	Witnesses
1	Andrew Burt	Major	July 25, 1866	Nov. 3, 1866	3	22	$17 00	3 50	$163 00	$554 90	Andrew Burt	John Reading.
2	Wm. L. N. Allen, batt. adjutant	Captain	July 25, 1866	Nov. 3, 1866	3	22	17 00	3 50	118 50	402 90	William L. N. Allen	Do.
3	James C. Livingston	do.	July 25, 1866	Nov. 3, 1866	3	22	17 00	3 50	118 50	402 90	James C. Livingston	Do.
1	Charles Crow	1st lieutenant	July 25, 1866	Nov. 3, 1866	3	22	17 00	3 50	118 50	402 90	Charles H. Crow	Do.
2	Charles Livingston	2d lieutenant	July 25, 1866	Nov. 3, 1866	3	22	17 00	3 50	108 50	368 90	Charles Livingston	Do.
3	Milford B. Shipp	do.	July 25, 1866	Nov. 3, 1866	3	22	17 00	3 50	108 50	368 90	Milford B. Shipp	Do.
4	James Banting	do.	July 25, 1866	Nov. 3, 1866	3	22	17 00	3 50	103 50	351 90	James Banting	Do.
5	Charles Ringwood	do.	July 25, 1866	Nov. 3, 1866	3	22	17 00	3 50	103 50	351 90	Charles Ringwood	Do.
6	John Reading	do.	July 25, 1866	Nov. 3, 1866	3	22	17 00	3 50	103 50	351 90	John Reading	Do.
7	Joseph Bean	do.	July 25, 1866	Nov. 3, 1866	3	22	17 00	3 50	103 50	351 90	Joseph Bean	Do.
8	Henry Coulan	do.	July 25, 1866	Nov. 3, 1866	3	22	17 00	3 50	103 50	351 90	Henry Coulan	Do.
9	William F. Allbran	do.	July 25, 1866	Nov. 3, 1866	3	22	17 00	3 50	103 50	351 90	William F. Allbran	Do.
1	Robert Sneddon	Sergeant	July 25, 1866	Nov. 3, 1866	3	22	17 00	3 50	20 50	68 70	Robert Sneddon	Do.
2	Thomas Goodman	do.	July 25, 1866	Nov. 3, 1866	3	22	17 00	3 50	20 50	68 70	Thos. Goodman	Do.
3	William Phillips	do.	July 25, 1866	Nov. 3, 1866	3	22	17 00	3 50	20 50	68 70	William Phillips	Do.
4	John W. Sharp	do.	July 25, 1866	Nov. 3, 1866	3	22	17 00	3 50	20 50	68 70	John W. Sharp	Do.
5	Nathan Meade	do.	July 25, 1866	Nov. 3, 1866	3	22	17 00	3 50	20 50	68 70	Nathan Meade	Do.
1	Erastus F. Carter	do.	July 25, 1866	Nov. 3, 1866	3	22	13 00	3 50	16 50	56 10	Erastus F. Carter	Do.
2	Isaac Asa	Private	July 25, 1866	Nov. 3, 1866	3	22	13 00	3 50	16 50	56 10	Isaac Asa	Do.
3	Richard Camp	do.	July 25, 1866	Nov. 3, 1866	3	22	13 00	3 50	16 50	56 10	Richard Camp	Do.
4	Samuel Corbett	do.	July 25, 1866	Nov. 3, 1866	3	22	13 00	3 50	16 50	56 10	Samuel Corbett	Do.
5	William Crabb	do.	July 25, 1866	Nov. 3, 1866	3	22	13 00	3 50	16 50	56 10	William Crabb	Do.
6	George W. Davis	do.	July 25, 1866	Nov. 3, 1866	3	22	13 00	3 50	16 50	56 10	Geo. W. Davis	Do.
7	Archibald Erskine	do.	July 25, 1866	Nov. 3, 1866	3	22	13 00	3 50	16 50	56 10	Archibald Erskine	Do.
8	William Goodman	do.	July 25, 1866	Nov. 3, 1866	3	22	13 00	3 50	16 50	56 10	William Goodman	Do.
9	Peter Gray	do.	July 25, 1866	Nov. 3, 1866	3	22	13 00	3 50	16 50	56 10	Peter Gray	Do.
10	Nathan Gray	do.	July 25, 1866	Nov. 3, 1866	3	22	13 00	3 50	16 50	56 10	Nathan Gray	Do.
11	Alexander Gibson	do.	July 25, 1866	Nov. 3, 1866	3	22	13 00	3 50	16 50	56 10	Alexander Gibson	Do.
12	Thomas Higham	do.	July 25, 1866	Nov. 3, 1866	3	22	13 00	3 50	16 50	56 10	Thomas Higham	Do.
13	Mark Lindsay	do.	July 25, 1866	Nov. 3, 1866	3	22	13 00	3 50	16 50	56 10	Mark Lindsay	Do.
14	Henry Lewis	do.	July 25, 1866	Nov. 3, 1866	3	22	13 00	3 50	16 50	56 10	Henry Lewis	Do.
15	Thomas Lewis	do.	July 25, 1866	Nov. 3, 1866	3	22	13 00	3 50	16 50	56 10	Thomas Lewis	Do.
16	John A. Lewis	do.	July 25, 1866	Nov. 3, 1866	3	22	13 00	3 50	16 50	56 10	John A. Lewis	Do.
17	John Mazzell	do.	July 25, 1866	Nov. 3, 1866	3	12	13 00	3 50	16 50	56 10	John Mazzell	Do.

No.	Name											Name	
17	William Major		56 10	16 50	3 50	13 00	12 12	3	Nov. 3, 1866	July 25, 1866	do.	William Major	Do.
18	John McCulloch		56 10	16 50	3 50	13 00	12 12	3	Nov. 3, 1866	July 25, 1866	do.	John McCulloch	Do.
19	John Midgley		56 10	16 50	3 50	13 00	12 12	3	Nov. 3, 1866	July 25, 1866	do.	John Midgley	Do.
20	Samuel P. Neve		56 10	16 50	3 50	13 00	12 12	3	Nov. 3, 1866	July 25, 1866	do.	Samuel P. Neve	Do.
21	George W. Rogers		56 10	16 50	3 50	13 00	12 12	3	Nov. 3, 1866	July 25, 1866	do.	George W. Rogers	Do.
22	James Rogers		56 10	16 50	3 50	13 00	12 12	3	Nov. 3, 1866	July 25, 1866	do.	James Rogers	Do.
23	Henry Robbins		56 10	16 50	3 50	13 00	12 12	3	Nov. 3, 1866	July 25, 1866	do.	Henry Robbins	Do.
24	John Squires		56 10	16 50	3 50	13 00	12 12	3	Nov. 3, 1866	July 25, 1866	do.	John Squires	Do.
25	Ralph Snowball		56 10	16 50	3 50	13 00	12 12	3	Nov. 3, 1866	July 25, 1866	do.	Ralph Snowball	Do.
26	Thomas F. Thomas		56 10	16 50	3 50	13 00	12 12	3	Nov. 3, 1866	July 25, 1866	do.	Thomas F. Thomas	Do.
27	William Turner		56 10	16 50	3 50	13 00	12 12	3	Nov. 3, 1866	July 25, 1866	do.	William Turner	Do.
28	James White		56 10	16 50	3 50	13 00	12 12	3	Nov. 3, 1866	July 25, 1866	do.	James White	Do.
29	James Wickens		56 10	16 50	3 50	13 00	12 12	3	Nov. 3, 1866	July 25, 1866	do.	James Wickens	Do.
30	William Ajax		56 10	16 50	3 50	13 00	12 12	3	Nov. 3, 1866	July 25, 1866	do.	Wm. Ajax	Do.
31	Edmund Bird		56 10	16 50	3 50	13 00	12 12	3	Nov. 3, 1866	July 25, 1866	do.	Edmund Bird	Do.
32	Charles H. Banks		56 10	16 50	3 50	13 00	12 12	3	Nov. 3, 1866	July 25, 1866	do.	Charles H. Banks	Do.
33	William Colton		56 10	16 50	3 50	13 00	12 12	3	Nov. 3, 1866	July 25, 1866	do.	William Colton	Do.
34	William Cornwall		56 10	16 50	3 50	13 00	12 12	3	Nov. 3, 1866	July 25, 1866	do.	William Cornwall	Do.
35	Charles Cottrell		56 10	16 50	3 50	13 00	12 12	3	Nov. 3, 1866	July 25, 1866	do.	Charles Cottrell	Do.
36	Henry Dixon		56 10	16 50	3 50	13 00	12 12	3	Nov. 3, 1866	July 25, 1866	do.	Henry A. Dixon	Do.
37	Anders Frantzen		56 10	16 50	3 50	13 00	12 12	3	Nov. 3, 1866	July 25, 1866	do.	Anders Frantzen	Do.
38	Thomas Hewlett		56 10	16 50	3 50	13 00	12 12	3	Nov. 3, 1866	July 25, 1866	do.	Thomas Hewlett	Do.
39	Harold Hunniholl		56 10	16 50	3 50	13 00	12 12	3	Nov. 3, 1866	July 25, 1866	do.	Harold Hunniholl	Do.
40	John Holmberg		56 10	16 50	3 50	13 00	12 12	3	Nov. 3, 1866	July 25, 1866	do.	John Holmberg	Do.
41	Charles R. Jones		56 10	16 50	3 50	13 00	12 12	3	Nov. 3, 1866	July 25, 1866	do.	Charles R. Jones	Do.
42	John Kingdom		56 10	16 50	3 50	13 00	12 12	3	Nov. 3, 1866	July 25, 1866	do.	John Kingdom	Do.
43	John Miller		56 10	16 50	3 50	13 00	12 12	3	Nov. 3, 1866	July 25, 1866	do.	John Miller	Do.
44	Thomas Manning		56 10	16 50	3 50	13 00	12 12	3	Nov. 3, 1866	July 25, 1866	do.	Thomas Manning	Do.
45	Frederick Myers		56 10	16 50	3 50	13 00	12 12	3	Nov. 3, 1866	July 25, 1866	do.	Fredrick Myer	Do.
46	William Mathews		56 10	16 50	3 50	13 00	12 12	3	Nov. 3, 1866	July 25, 1866	do.	William Mathews	Do.
47	Robert Mawson		56 10	16 50	3 50	13 00	12 12	3	Nov. 3, 1866	July 25, 1866	do.	Robert Mawson	Do.
48	William C. Neal		56 10	16 50	3 50	13 00	12 12	3	Nov. 3, 1866	July 25, 1866	do.	William C. Neal	Do.
49	Horace Nelson		56 10	16 50	3 50	13 00	12 12	3	Nov. 3, 1866	July 25, 1866	do.	Horace Nelson	Do.
50	William H. Pitt		56 10	16 50	3 50	13 00	12 12	3	Nov. 3, 1866	July 25, 1866	do.	William H. Pitt	Do.
51	Walter Pike		56 10	16 50	3 50	13 00	12 12	3	Nov. 3, 1866	July 25, 1866	do.	Walter Pike	Do.
52	Lorenzo Pettit		56 10	16 50	3 50	13 00	12 12	3	Nov. 3, 1866	July 25, 1866	do.	Lorenzo Pettit	Do.
53	Peter Rasmusson		56 10	16 50	3 50	13 00	12 12	3	Nov. 3, 1866	July 25, 1866	do.	Peter Rasmusson	Do.
54	William F. Raybold		56 10	16 50	3 50	13 00	12 12	3	Nov. 3, 1866	July 25, 1866	do.	William F. Raybold	Do.
55	Ira Reed		56 10	16 50	3 50	13 00	12 12	3	Nov. 3, 1866	July 25, 1866	do.	Ira Reed	Do.
56	Frank Sprowle		56 10	16 50	3 50	13 00	12 12	3	Nov. 3, 1866	July 25, 1866	do.	Frank Sprowle	Do.
	Jabez Taylor		56 10	16 50	3 50	13 00	12 12	3	Nov. 3, 1866	July 25, 1866	do.	Jabez Taylor	Do.

This company was mustered into service at Great Salt Lake City, July 25, 1866, by Major General Robert T. Burton, and on that day started for Sanpete, marched one hundred and fifty miles to Moroni, and was assigned to duty in the mountains by Lieutenant General D. H. Wells. Was in active service every day until relieved. Returned to Salt Lake City, and was mustered out by Major General R. T. Burton on the 3d day of November, 1866.

I certify that the above account is correct.

H. B. CLAWSON,
Adjutant General Utah Territory Militia.

Pay-roll of Captain John Gallagher's company —— infantry, Utah Territory militia, employed in the suppression of Indian hostilities in Wasatch County, Utah Territory, from August 1, 1866, to September 30, 1866.

We, the undersigned, acknowledge to have received from James W. Cummings, paymaster Utah Territory militia, the sums set opposite to our names, in full payment for our services for the time specified.

Number	Names	Rank	Commencement	Expiration	Months	Pay per month	Monthly allowance for clothing	Total monthly pay and allowance	Total pay and allowance	Signatures	Witnesses
1	John Gallagher	Captain	Aug. 1, 1866	Sept. 30, 1866	2	$115 00	$3 50	$118 50	$237 00	John Gallagher	Wm. P. Reynolds
2	William Reynolds	1st lieutenant	Aug. 1, 1866	Sept. 30, 1866	2	105 00	3 50	108 50	217 00	William Reynolds	John Gallagher
3	John Lee	2d lieutenant	Aug. 1, 1866	Sept. 30, 1866	2	100 00	3 50	103 50	207 00	John Lee	John Lee
4	Henry Chatwin	do	Aug. 1, 1866	Sept. 30, 1866	2	100 00	3 50	103 50	207 00	Henry Chatwin	Do.
5	Samuel Thompson	do	Aug. 1, 1866	Sept. 30, 1866	2	100 00	3 50	103 50	207 00	George Thompson, his + mark	Daniel McMillan
6	Samuel Rooker	Sergeant	Aug. 1, 1866	Sept. 30, 1866	2	17 00	3 50	20 50	41 00	Samuel Rooker	John Gallagher
7	Robert McKnight	Private	Aug. 1, 1866	Sept. 30, 1866	2	13 00	3 50	16 50	33 00	Robert McKnight	Do.
8	Cornelius White	do	Aug. 1, 1866	Sept. 30, 1866	2	13 00	3 50	16 50	33 00	Cornelius White	Henry Chatwin
9	James Watson	do	Aug. 1, 1866	Sept. 30, 1866	2	13 00	3 50	16 50	33 00	James Watson	John Gallagher
10	David Barney	do	Aug. 1, 1866	Sept. 30, 1866	2	13 00	3 50	16 50	33 00	David Barney	Do.
11	William Giles	do	Aug. 1, 1866	Sept. 30, 1866	2	13 00	3 50	16 50	33 00	William Giles, his + mark	John Crook
12	Thomas Moulton	do	Aug. 1, 1866	Sept. 30, 1866	2	13 00	3 50	16 50	33 00	Thomas Moulton	John Gallagher
13	John Cummings	do	Aug. 1, 1866	Sept. 30, 1866	2	13 00	3 50	16 50	33 00	John Cummings, his + mark	Do.
14	William Thompson	do	Aug. 1, 1866	Sept. 30, 1866	2	13 00	3 50	16 50	33 00	William Thompson	W. P. Reynolds
15	Richard Smith	do	Aug. 1, 1866	Sept. 30, 1866	2	13 00	3 50	16 50	33 00	Richard Smith	John Gallagher
16	George Noaks	do	Aug. 1, 1866	Sept. 30, 1866	2	13 00	3 50	16 50	33 00	Georg Noaks	Do.
17	Elijah Jones	do	Aug. 1, 1866	Sept. 30, 1866	2	13 00	3 50	16 50	33 00	Elijah Jones	W. P. Reynolds
18	Anthony Brown	do	Aug. 1, 1866	Sept. 30, 1866	2	13 00	3 50	16 50	33 00	Anthony Brown	John Gallagher
19	Daniel McMillan	do	Aug. 1, 1866	Sept. 30, 1866	2	13 00	3 50	16 50	33 00	Daniel McMillan	Do.
20	Frances Kirby	do	Aug. 1, 1866	Sept. 30, 1866	2	13 00	3 50	16 50	33 00	Frances Kirby	John Lee
21	Freeman Manning	do	Aug. 1, 1866	Sept. 30, 1866	2	13 00	3 50	16 50	33 00	Freeman Manning	John Gallagher
22	James Reed	do	Aug. 1, 1866	Sept. 30, 1866	2	13 00	3 50	16 50	33 00	James Reed	John Crook
23	James Taylor	do	Aug. 1, 1866	Sept. 30, 1866	2	13 00	3 50	16 50	33 00	James Taylor, his + mark	John Gallagher
24	Thomas B. Sessions	do	Aug. 1, 1866	Sept. 30, 1866	2	13 00	3 50	16 50	33 00	Thomas B. Sessions	John Lee
25	Peter Backstrom	do	Aug. 1, 1866	Sept. 30, 1866	2	13 00	3 50	16 50	33 00	Peter Backstrom	Thomas Smith
26	Thomas Giles	do	Aug. 1, 1866	Sept. 30, 1866	2	13 00	3 50	16 50	33 00	Thos. Giles	Do.
27	William Ryan	do	Aug. 1, 1866	Sept. 30, 1866	2	13 00	3 50	16 50	33 00	William Ryan	Do.
28	John Dabell	do	Aug. 1, 1866	Sept. 30, 1866	2	13 00	3 50	16 50	33 00	John Dabell	John Gallagher
29	John Christman	do	Aug. 1, 1866	Sept. 30, 1866	2	13 00	3 50	16 50	33 00	John Chrisman	John Gallagher

* Mistake in given name.   "George" instead of "Samuel."

Pay-roll of Major Peter Sutton's company —— cavalry, Utah Territory militia, employed in the suppression of Indian hostilities in the Sanpete and Juab counties, from April 8, 1866, to June 8, 1866.

We, the undersigned, acknowledge to have received from James W. Cummings, paymaster Utah Territory militia, the sums set opposite to our names, in full payment for the time specified.

Number.	Names.	Rank.	Commencement.	Expiration.	Months.	Pay per month.	Monthly allowance for clothing.	Total monthly pay and allowance.	40 cts. per day for use and risk of horse and horse equipment.	Total pay and allowance.	Signatures.	Witnesses.
1	Peter Sutton	Major	April 8, 1866	June 8, 1866	2	---	---	$163 50	$24 00	$350 00	Peter Sutton	Charles Foote.
1	Charles Foot, (adjutant)	Captain	April 8, 1866	June 8, 1866	2	---	---	129 50	24 00	283 00	Charles Foote	Peter Sutton.
2	Samuel Cazier	do	April 8, 1866	June 8, 1866	2	---	---	129 50	24 00	283 00	Samuel Cazier	Thomas Webster.
1	Eli Randall	1st lieut.	April 8, 1866	June 8, 1866	2	---	---	112 83	24 00	249 66	Eli Randall	Charles Foote.
2	Charles Sperry	2d lieut.	April 8, 1866	June 8, 1866	2	---	---	112 83	24 00	249 66	Charles Sperry	William L. Sperry.
3	Gideon Wilson	do	April 8, 1866	June 8, 1866	2	---	---	112 83	24 00	249 66	Gideon Wilson	Richard Jenkins.
4	William Sperry	do	April 8, 1866	June 8, 1866	2	---	---	112 83	26 00	249 66	William Sperry	William Bryan.
	William Bryan	do	April 8, 1866	June 8, 1866	2	---	---	112 83	24 00	249 66	William Bryan	David Udall.
1	David Udall	Sergeant	April 8, 1866	June 8, 1866	2	$17 00	$3 50	20 50	24 00	65 00	David Udall	David Vickers.
2	David Cazier	do	April 8, 1866	June 8, 1866	2	17 00	3 50	20 50	24 00	65 00	David Cazier	Thomas Carter.
3	Edwin Booth	do	April 8, 1866	June 8, 1866	2	17 00	3 50	20 50	24 00	65 00	Edwin Booth	Robert Rollins.
4	Samuel Tulley	do	April 8, 1866	June 8, 1866	2	17 00	3 50	20 50	24 00	65 00	Samuel Tulley	Henry J. Jenkins.
1	Abraham Baswell	Private	April 8, 1866	June 8, 1866	2	13 00	3 50	16 50	24 00	57 00	Abraham Boswell	Richard Jenkins.
2	Edward Williams	do	April 8, 1866	June 8, 1866	2	13 00	3 50	16 50	24 00	57 00	E. H. Williams	William Warner.
3	William Turner	do	April 8, 1866	June 8, 1866	2	13 00	3 50	16 50	24 00	57 00	William Turner	Charles Oekey.
4	William Warner	do	April 8, 1866	June 8, 1866	2	13 00	3 50	16 50	24 00	57 00	William Warner	Samuel Tulley.
5	Henry Sutton	do	April 8, 1866	June 8, 1866	2	13 00	3 50	16 50	21 00	57 00	Henry J. Sutton	John Ellion.
6	Samuel Jackson	do	April 8, 1866	June 8, 1866	2	13 00	3 50	16 50	25 00	57 00	Samuel Jackson	Gideon Wilson.
7	Thomas Wright	do	April 8, 1866	June 8, 1866	2	13 00	3 50	16 50	24 00	57 00	Thomas Wright	William Cole.
8	Cyrus Foot	do	April 8, 1866	June 8, 1866	2	13 00	3 50	16 50	24 00	57 00	Cyrus Foot	Amos Rollins.
9	Robert Rollins	do	April 8, 1866	June 8, 1866	2	13 00	3 50	16 50	24 00	57 00	Robert Rollins	Edwin Booth.
10	Thomas Carter	do	April 8, 1866	June 8, 1866	2	13 00	3 50	16 50	24 00	57 00	Thomas Carter	Charles Andrews.
11	Henry Goldsbrough	do	April 8, 1866	June 8, 1866	2	13 00	3 50	16 50	24 00	57 00	Henry Goldsbrough	E. H. Williams.
12	John Cazier	do	April 8, 1866	June 8, 1866	2	13 00	3 50	16 50	24 00	57 00	John Cazier	Martin Rollins.
13	Charles Oekey	do	April 8, 1866	June 8, 1866	2	13 00	3 50	16 50	24 00	57 00	Charles Oekey	Eli Randall.
14	John Ellison	do	April 8, 1866	June 8, 1866	2	13 00	3 50	16 50	24 00	57 00	Richard Jenkins	David Udall.
15	Richard Jenkins	do	April 8, 1866	June 8, 1866	2	13 00	3 50	16 50	24 00	57 00	John Ellison	E. H. Williams.
16	John Hague	do	April 8, 1866	June 8, 1866	2	13 00	3 50	16 50	24 00	57 00	John Hague	William Warner.
17	John Vickers	do	April 8, 1866	June 8, 1866	2	13 00	3 50	16 50	24 00	57 00	John Vickers	John Sidwell.
18	William Cole	do	April 8, 1866	June 8, 1866	2	13 00	3 50	16 50	24 00	57 00	William Vickers	John Beasley.
19	Charles Andrews	do	April 8, 1866	June 8, 1866	2	13 00	3 50	16 51	24 00	57 00	Charles Andrews	Amos Rollins.
20	Nephi Jackson	do	April 8, 1866	June 8, 1866	2	13 00	3 50	16 50	24 00	57 00	Nephi Jackson	

21	John Beagley	do.	April 8, 1866	June 8, 1866	2	13 00	3 50	16 50	24 00	57 00	John Worwood.
22	Thomas Gustin	do.	April 8, 1866	June 8, 1866	2	13 00	3 50	16 50	24 00	57 00	Eli Randall.
23	Amos Rollins	do.	April 8, 1866	June 8, 1866	2	13 00	3 50	16 50	24 00	57 00	Abraham Boswell.
24	John Worwood	do.	April 8, 1866	June 8, 1866	2	13 00	3 50	16 50	24 00	57 00	Peter Sutton.
25	John W. Cazier	do.	April 8, 1866	June 8, 1866	2	13 00	3 50	16 50	24 00	57 00	Nephi Jackson.
26	Charles Searles	do.	April 8, 1866	June 8, 1866	2	13 00	3 50	16 50	24 00	57 00	John Worwood.
27	William Tulley	do.	April 8, 1866	June 8, 1866	2	13 00	3 50	16 50	24 00	57 00	David Bigler.
28	Clinton Brown	do.	April 8, 1866	June 8, 1866	2	13 00	3 50	16 50	24 00	57 00	A. C. Sapp.
29	A. C. Sapp	do.	April 8, 1866	June 8, 1866	2	13 00	3 50	16 50	24 00	57 00	Clinton Brown.
30	John Sidwell	do.	April 8, 1866	June 8, 1866	2	13 00	3 50	16 50	24 00	57 00	Abraham Boswell.
31	Henry Ockey	do.	April 8, 1866	June 8, 1866	2	13 00	3 50	16 50	24 00	57 00	George Ostler.
32	Samuel Linton	do.	April 8, 1866	June 8, 1866	2	13 00	3 50	16 50	24 00	57 00	Cyrus Mangun.
33	Martin Rollins	do.	April 8, 1866	June 8, 1866	2	13 00	3 50	16 50	24 00	57 00	Peter Sutton.
34	Thomas Vickers	do.	April 8, 1866	June 8, 1866	2	13 00	3 50	16 50	24 00	57 00	William Tulley.
35	Jacob Bowers	do.	April 8, 1866	June 8, 1866	2	13 00	3 50	16 50	24 00	57 00	C. H. Williams.
36	David Bigler	do.	April 8, 1866	June 8, 1866	2	13 00	3 50	16 50	24 00	57 00	William Sidwell.
37	Cyrus Mangun	do.	April 8, 1866	June 8, 1866	2	13 00	3 50	16 50	24 00	57 00	Samuel Linton.
38	George Ostler	do.	April 8, 1866	June 8, 1866	2	13 00	3 50	16 50	24 00	57 00	Charles Searles.
39	Henry Carter	do.	April 8, 1866	June 8, 1866	2	13 00	3 50	16 50	24 00	57 00	Thomas Vickers.
40	James Belliston	do.	April 8, 1866	June 8, 1866	2	13 00	3 50	16 50	24 00	57 00	Chas. Foot.
41	William Sidwell	do.	April 8, 1866	June 8, 1866	2	13 00	3 50	16 50	24 00	57 00	Edwin Booth.

This company was mustered into service April 8, 1866, at Nephi, Juab County, and was assigned to duty in said county by Lieutenant General D. H. Wells. They were in active service, scouting and guarding the mountain passes, for two months, and June 8, 1866, were mustered out by order of Lieutenant General D. H. Wells.

I certify that the above account is correct.

H. B. CLAWSON,
Adjutant General Utah Territory Militia.

Pay-roll of Captain Joseph McCarroll's company —— cavalry, Utah Territory militia, employed in the suppression of Indian hostilities in Wasatch County, Utah Territory, from May 1, 1866, to July 30, 1866.

We, the undersigned, acknowledge to have received from James W. Cummings, paymaster Utah Territory militia, the sums set opposite to our names, in full payment for our services for the time specified.

Number	Names	Rank	Commencement	Expiration	Months	Pay per month	Monthly allowance for clothing	Total monthly pay and allowance	40 cts. per day for use and risk of horse and horse equipment	Total pay and allowance	Signatures	Witnesses
1	Joseph McCarroll	Captain	May 1, 1866	July 30, 1866	3			$129 50	$36 00	$421 59	Joseph McCarrol	John Huber.
1	Edwin Bronson*	1st lieut.	May 1, 1866	July 30, 1866	3			112 83	36 00	374 49	Edwin Bronson	David Van Wagonen.
1	Jesse McCarroll	2d lieut.	May 1, 1866	July 30, 1866	3			112 83	36 00	374 49	Jesse McCarrol	Do.
1	Ephraim Van Wagoner	Sergeant	May 1, 1866	July 30, 1866	3	$17	$3 50	20 53	36 00	97 50	Ephraim Van Wagonens	Do.
2	James B. Hamilton	Private	May 1, 1866	July 30, 1866	3	13	3 50	16 50	36 00	85 50	James B. Hamilton, his + mark	Do.
3	William Bagley	do	May 1, 1866	July 30, 1866	3	13	3 50	16 50	36 00	85 50	Wm. Boogley	Do.
3	Jeremiah Robey, Jr	do	May 1, 1866	July 30, 1866	3	13	3 50	16 50	36 00	85 51	Jeremiah A. Robey, Jun	Do.
4	Henry Coleman‡	do	May 1, 1866	July 30, 1866	3	13	3 50	16 50	36 00	85 50		
5	Rich'd Shurlock‡	do	May 1, 1866	July 30, 1866	3	13	3 50	16 50	36 00	85 50		
6	James Jackson	do	May 1, 1866	July 30, 1866	3	13	3 50	16 50	36 00	85 50	James Jackson	Do.
7	William Gibson§	do	May 1, 1866	July 30, 1866	3	13	3 50	16 50	36 00	85 50		
8	Charles Gurney	do	May 1, 1866	July 30, 1866	3	13	3 50	16 50	36 00	85 50	Charles Gurney	Do.
9	Emanuel Richman	do	May 1, 1866	July 30, 1866	3	13	3 50	16 50	36 00	85 50	Emanuel Richman	Do.
10	Ezekiel Bates	do	May 1, 1866	July 30, 1866	3	13	3 50	16 50	36 00	85 50	Ezekiel Bates	Do.

* Battalion adjutant. † Deceased. ‡ Moved to South Pass City, Dacotah. § Moved to American Fork.

This company was mustered into service May 1, 1866, at Heber City, Wasatch County, by Major John Witt, by order of Lieutenant General D. H. Wells. They were in active service, scouting in the mountains, thereby protecting the inhabitants from further ravages of the enemy, and were mustered out at Heber City July 30, 1866, by Major John Witt.

I certify that the above account is correct.

H. B. CLAWSON,
Adjutant General Utah Territory Militia.

Pay-roll of field and staff officers commanding the Wasatch County, Utah Territory, militia, employed in the suppression of Indian hostilities in Wasatch County, Utah Territory, from May 1, 1866, to October 30, 1866.

We, the undersigned, acknowledge to have received from James W. Cummings, paymaster Utah Territory militia, the sums set opposite to our names, in full payment for our services for the time specified.

Number.	Names.	Staff appointment; office.	Rank.	Period of service. Commencement.	Expiration.	Months.	Total monthly pay and allowance.	40cts. per day for use and risk of horse and horse equipment.	Total pay and allowance.	Signatures.	Witnesses.
1	John W. Witt		Major	May 1, 1866	Oct. 30, 1866	6	$162 00	$72 00	$1,050 00	John W. Witt	C. H. Wilcken.
2	John Hamilton		do	May 1, 1866	July 30, 1866	3	151 00	36 00	489 00	John Hamilton	John Crook.
3	Sidney Epperson		do	Aug. 1, 1866	Oct. 30, 1866	3	151 00	36 00	489 00	Sidney Epperson	John W. Witt.
1	Charles Wilcken	Battalion adj't	Captain	May 1, 1866	Oct. 30, 1866	6	129 50	72 00	849 00	C. H. Wilcken	Do.
2	John Crook	do	do	May 1, 1866	July 30, 1866	3	118 50	72 00	427 50	John Crook	John Hamilton.
3	David Van Wagoner	do	do	Aug. 1, 1866	Oct. 30, 1866	3	118 50	72 00	427 50	David Van Wagoner	Sidney Epperson.

The above field and staff officers of Wasatch County were mustered into service by order of Lieutenant General Daniel H. Wells, and by him assigned to duty in said county. They were in active service every day for the time specified above, and mustered out as above stated.

I certify that the above account is correct.

H. B. CLAWSON,
Adjutant General Utah Territory Militia.

Pay-roll of Major William W. Casper's company —— infantry, Utah Territory militia, employed in the suppression of Indian hostilities in Sanpete and Sevier counties, Utah Territory, from June 1, 1866, to September 30, 1866.

We, the undersigned, acknowledge to have received from James W. Cummings, paymaster Utah Territory militia, the sums set opposite to our names, in full payment for our services for the time specified.

Number	Names	Rank	Commencement	Expiration	Months	Pay per month	Monthly allowance for clothing	Total monthly pay and allowance	Total pay and allowance	Signatures	Witnesses
1	William W. Casper	Major	June 1, 1866	September 30, 1866	4			$151 00	$604 00	William W. Casper	G. W. Groo.
2	Peter Sinclair, (battalion adjutant)	Captain	June 1, 1866	September 30, 1866	4			118 50	474 00	Peter Sinclair	Do.
3	Henry Skidmore	do.	June 1, 1866	September 30, 1866	4			118 50	474 00	Henry Skidmore	Do.
4	Jesse West	1st lieutenant	June 1, 1866	September 30, 1866	4			118 50	474 00	Jesse West	Do.
5	William Douglas	2d lieutenant	June 1, 1866	September 30, 1866	4			108 50	434 00	William Douglas	Do.
6	George S. Smith	do.	June 1, 1866	September 30, 1866	4			108 50	434 00	George S. Smith	Do.
7	Alexander Bart	do.	June 1, 1866	September 30, 1866	4			103 50	414 00	Alex. Bart	Do.
8	John Jereny	do.	June 1, 1866	September 30, 1866	4			103 50	414 00	John Jereny	Do.
9	Joseph Reese	do.	June 1, 1866	September 30, 1866	4			103 50	414 00	Joseph Reese	Do.
10	Aaron Nelson	do.	June 1, 1866	September 30, 1866	4			103 50	414 00	Aaron Nelson	Do.
11	John Mycroft	do.	June 1, 1866	September 30, 1866	4			103 50	414 00	John Mycroft	Do.
12	Byron Groo	Sergeant	June 1, 1866	September 30, 1866	4	$17 00	$3 50	20 50	82 00	Byron Groo	Do.
13	John W. Andrews	do.	June 1, 1866	September 30, 1866	4	17 00	3 50	20 50	82 00	John W. Andrews	Do.
14	Thomas J. Williams	do.	June 1, 1866	September 30, 1866	4	17 00	3 50	20 50	82 00	Thomas J. Williams	Do.
15	William Newell	do.	June 1, 1866	September 30, 1866	4	17 00	3 50	20 50	82 00	William Newell	Do.
16	James Hansen	do.	June 1, 1866	September 30, 1866	4	17 00	3 50	20 50	82 00	Yens Hansen	Do.
17	Andrew Forsyth	Private	June 1, 1866	September 30, 1866	4	13 00	3 50	16 50	66 00	Andrew Forsyth	Do.
18	George Ellis	do.	June 1, 1866	September 30, 1866	4	13 00	3 50	16 50	66 00	George Ellis	Do.
19	William A. Garrett	do.	June 1, 1866	September 30, 1866	4	13 00	3 50	16 50	66 00	William Garret	Do.
20	Clark Walker	do.	June 1, 1866	September 30, 1866	4	13 00	3 50	16 50	66 00	Charles Walker	Do.
21	William McGregor	do.	June 1, 1866	September 30, 1866	4	13 00	3 50	16 50	66 00	William McGregor	Do.
22	Thomas Tinnon	do.	June 1, 1866	September 30, 1866	4	13 00	3 50	16 50	66 00	Thomas Tinnon	Do.
23	Alexander Glen	do.	June 1, 1866	September 30, 1866	4	13 00	3 50	16 50	66 00	Alexander Glen	Do.
24	Niels Rosengren	do.	June 1, 1866	September 30, 1866	4	13 00	3 50	16 50	66 00	Nels Rosengren	Do.
25	Paul Poulson	do.	June 1, 1866	September 30, 1866	4	13 00	3 50	16 50	66 00	Baul Bonsen	Do.
26	James P. Towson	do.	June 1, 1866	September 30, 1866	4	13 00	3 50	16 50	66 00	Jems P. Twelson	Do.
27	George T. Taylor	do.	June 1, 1866	September 30, 1866	4	13 00	3 50	16 50	66 00	George G. Taylor	Do.
28	Archibald Wallen	do.	June 1, 1866	September 30, 1866	4	13 00	3 50	16 50	66 00		Do.
29	Richard Carr	do.	June 1, 1866	September 30, 1866	4	13 00	3 50	16 50	66 00	Richard Carr	Do.
30	Jacob Bowman	do.	June 1, 1866	September 30, 1866	4	13 00	3 50	16 50	66 00	Jakob Bauman	Do.
31	J. R. Peirce	do.	June 1, 1866	September 30, 1866	4	13 00	3 50	16 50	66 00	J. R. Pierce	Do.
32	G. C. Lang	do.	June 1, 1866	September 30, 1866	4	13 00	3 50	16 50	66 00	G. C. Lang	Do.
33	Hyram Strong	do.	June 1, 1866	September 30, 1866	4	13 00	3 50	16 50	66 00	H. Strong	Do.

No.	Name								Date	Date		Do.
16	John Golightly		66 00	16 50	3 50	13 00	4		September 30, 1866	June 1, 1866	do.	Do.
17	Samuel Shenaerdine		66 00	16 50	3 50	13 00	4		September 30, 1866	June 1, 1866	do.	Do.
18	George W. Kennedy		66 00	16 50	3 50	13 00	4		September 30, 1866	June 1, 1866	do.	Do.
19	Vaughan Jacobsen		66 00	16 50	3 50	13 00	4		September 30, 1866	June 1, 1866	do.	Do.
20	Martin Hunner		66 00	16 50	3 50	13 00	4		September 30, 1866	June 1, 1866	do.	Do.
21	John Chamberlain		66 03	16 50	3 50	13 00	4		September 30, 1866	June 1, 1866	do.	Do.
22	Chris Larsen		66 00	16 50	3 50	13 00	4		September 30, 1866	June 1, 1866	do.	Do.
23	Edward Newby		66 00	16 50	3 50	13 00	4		September 30, 1866	June 1, 1866	do.	Do.
24	John Ainsworth		66 03	16 50	3 50	13 00	4		September 21, 1866	June 1, 1866	do.	Do.
25	James Thompson		66 03	16 50	3 50	13 00	4		September 30, 1866	June 1, 1866	do.	Do.
26	Henry Rook		66 00	16 50	3 50	13 00	4		September 30, 1866	June 1, 1866	do.	Do.
27	A. P. Trane		66 00	16 50	3 50	13 00	4		September 30, 1866	June 1, 1866	do.	Do.
28	Andrew Holvorsen		66 00	16 50	3 50	13 00	4		September 30, 1866	June 1, 1866	do.	Do.
29	Jens Larsen		66 03	16 50	3 50	13 00	4		September 30, 1866	June 1, 1866	do.	Do.
30	Andrew Franklin		66 00	16 50	3 50	13 00	4		September 30, 1866	June 1, 1866	do.	Do.
31	John Woodbury		66 00	16 50	3 50	13 00	4		September 30, 1866	June 1, 1866	do.	Do.
32	G. C. Lambert		66 00	16 50	3 50	13 00	4		September 30, 1866	June 1, 1866	do.	Do.
33	Alexander Leetham		66 00	16 50	3 50	13 00	4		September 30, 1866	June 1, 1866	do.	Do.
34	Edward Rushton		66 00	16 50	3 50	13 00	4		September 30, 1866	June 1, 1866	do.	Do.
35	James Hunter		66 00	16 50	3 50	13 00	4		September 30, 1866	June 1, 1866	do.	Do.
36	A. P. Fordham		66 00	16 50	3 50	13 00	4		September 30, 1866	June 1, 1866	do.	Do.
37	Lorenzo Price		61 00	16 50	3 50	13 00	4		September 30, 1866	June 1, 1866	do.	Do.
38	James Allen		66 00	16 50	3 50	13 00	4		September 30, 1866	June 1, 1866	do.	Do.
39	Gibson Condie		66 00	16 50	3 50	13 00	4		September 30, 1866	June 1, 1866	do.	Do.
40	Thomas Suarr		66 00	16 50	3 50	13 00	4		September 30, 1866	June 1, 1866	do.	Do.
41	William Evans		66 00	16 50	3 50	13 00	4		September 31, 1866	June 1, 1866	do.	Do.
42	Lucien Phippen		66 00	16 50	3 50	13 00	4		September 30, 1866	June 1, 1866	do.	Do.
43	John Smith		66 00	16 50	3 50	13 01	4		September 30, 1866	June 1, 1866	do.	Do.
44	Charles Cooper		66 00	16 50	3 50	13 00	4		September 30, 1866	June 1, 1866	do.	Do.
45	Andrew Peterson		66 00	16 50	3 50	13 00	4		September 30, 1866	June 1, 1866	do.	Do.
46	John R. Jones		66 00	16 50	3 50	13 00	4		September 30, 1866	June 1, 1866	do.	Do.
47	John Smith		66 00	16 50	3 50	13 00	4		September 31, 1866	June 1, 1866	do.	Do.
48	John G. Boker		66 00	16 50	3 50	13 00	4		September 30, 1866	June 1, 1866	do.	Do.
49	William D. Johnson, jr.		66 00	16 50	3 50	13 00	4		September 30, 1866	June 1, 1866	do.	Do.
50	David R. Parry		66 00	16 50	3 50	13 00	4		September 30, 1866	June 1, 1866	do.	Do.
51	Robert Granger		66 00	16 50	3 50	13 00	4		September 30, 1866	June 1, 1866	do.	Do.
52	William H. Bess		66 01	16 50	3 50	13 00	4		September 30, 1866	June 1, 1866	do.	Do.
53	Richard I. Keep		66 00	16 50	3 50	13 00	4		September 30, 1866	June 1, 1866	do.	Do.
54	John J. Wixey		66 00	16 50	3 53	13 00	4		September 30, 1866	June 1, 1866	do.	Do.
55	Ole Olson		66 00	16 51	3 50	13 00	4		September 30, 1866	June 1, 1866	do.	Do.
56	James Ure		66 07	16 50	3 50	13 00	4		September 30, 1866	June 1, 1866	do.	Do.
57	Hans Christiansen		66 00	16 50	3 50	13 00	4		September 30, 1866	June 1, 1866	do.	Do.
58	Dalro Onenson		66 00	16 50	3 50	13 00	4		September 30, 1866	June 1, 1866	do.	Do.
59	Henry Harker		66 00	16 50	3 50	13 00	4		September 30, 1866	June 1, 1866	do.	Do.
60	Ephraim Bennett		66 00	16 50	3 50	13 00	4		September 31, 1866	June 1, 1866	do.	Do.
61	James Tempest		66 00	16 50	3 50	13 00	4		September 30, 1866	June 1, 1866	do.	Do.
62	John Spencer		66 00	16 50	3 50	13 00	4		September 30, 1866	June 1, 1866	do.	Dr.
63	William Wayne		66 00	16 50	3 50	13 00	4		September 30, 1866	June 1, 1866	do.	Do.
64	George Wardle		66 00	16 50	3 50	13 00	4		September 30, 1866	June 1, 1866	do.	Do.
65	William Dowling		66 00	16 50	3 50	13 00	4		September 30, 1866	June 1, 1866	do.	Do.
66	Richard Gilbert		66 00	16 50	3 50	13 00	4		September 30, 1866	June 1, 1866	do.	Do.
67	William Wardle		66 00	16 50	3 50	13 00	4		September 30, 1866	June 1, 1866	do.	Do.

Pay-roll of Major William W. Casper's company —— infantry, Utah Territory militia, &c.—Continued.

Number.	Names.	Rank.	Period of Service.		Months.	Pay per month.	Monthly allowance for clothing.	Total monthly pay and allowance.	Total pay and allowance.	Signatures.	Witnesses.
			Commencement.	Expiration.							
68	James J. Sharp	Private	June 1, 1866	September 30, 1866	4	$13 00	$3 50	$16 50	$66 00	James J. Sharp	G. W. Gros.
69	Loren E. Forbush	do	June 1, 1866	September 30, 1866	4	13 00	3 50	16 50	66 00	Loren E. Forbush	Do.
70	David Jones	do	June 1, 1866	September 30, 1866	4	13 00	3 50	16 50	66 00	David Jones	Do.
71	William L. Turpin	do	June 1, 1866	September 30, 1866	4	13 00	3 50	16 50	66 00	William Turpin	Do.
72	Aaron Nielson	do	June 1, 1866	September 30, 1866	4	13 00	3 50	16 50	66 00	Aaron Nelson	John R. Winder.

This company was mustered into service at Salt Lake City, June 1, 1866, and on that day started for Sanpete County, and in four days marched one hundred and twenty-five miles, to Moroni City, and was assigned to duty in the hills and mountain passes north of Moroni, Fountain Green, and North Bend. They were in active service every day for four months. They returned to Salt Lake City and were mustered out the 30th day of September, 1866.

I certify that the above account is correct.

H. B. CLAWSON,
Adjutant General Utah Territory Militia.

Pay-roll of Captain Robert W. Burton's company ——— cavalry, Utah Territory militia, employed in the suppression of Indian hostilities in Sanpete and Sevier counties, from October 1, 1866, to November 30, 1866.

We, the undersigned, acknowledge to have received from James W. Cummings, paymaster Utah Territory militia, the sums set opposite to our names, in full payment for our services for the time specified.

Number	Names	Rank	Period of service. Commencement.	Expiration.	Months.	Pay per month.	Monthly allowance for clothing.	Total monthly pay and allowance.	40 cents per day for use and risk of horse and equipment.	Total pay and allowance.	Signatures.	Witnesses.
1	Robert W. Burton	Captain	Oct. 1, 1866	Nov. 30, 1866	2			$128 50	$24 00	$291 00	Robert W. Burton	Job Wellings.
1	Robert W. Egbert	1st lieut	Oct. 1, 1866	Nov. 31, 1866	2			112 83	24 00	249 66	Robert N. Egbert	Do.
1	William Carbine	2d lieut	Oct. 1, 1866	Nov. 30, 1866	2			112 83	24 00	249 66	William Carbine	Do.
2	James Green	do	Oct. 1, 1866	Nov. 30, 1866	2			112 83	24 00	249 66	James Green	Do.
3	Philip Germs	do	Oct. 1, 1866	Nov. 30, 1866	2			112 83	24 00	249 66	Philip Germ	Do.
4	Carlos Sessions	do	Oct. 1, 1866	Nov. 30, 1866	2			112 83	24 00	249 66	Carlos Sessions	Do.
5	Allen Frost	do	Oct. 1, 1866	Nov. 30, 1866	2			112 83	24 00	249 66	Allen Frost	Do.
6	Joseph Morris	Sergeant	Oct. 1, 1866	Nov. 30, 1866	2	$17 00	$3 50	20 50	24 00	65 00	Joseph Morris	Do.
7	Joseph Allerd	do	Oct. 1, 1866	Nov. 30, 1866	2	17 00	3 50	20 50	24 00	65 00	Joseph Alford	Do.
8	Henry Hort	do	Oct. 1, 1866	Nov. 30, 1866	2	17 00	3 50	20 50	24 00	65 00	Henry Hoit	Do.
9	Stephen Ellis	do	Oct. 1, 1866	Nov. 30, 1866	2	17 00	3 50	20 50	24 00	65 00	Stephen H. Ellis	Do.
1	Edward Simmons	do	Oct. 1, 1866	Nov. 30, 1866	2	17 00	3 50	20 50	24 00	65 00	Edward Simon	Do.
2	Alvirus Gleason	Private	Oct. 1, 1866	Nov. 30, 1866	2	13 00	3 50	16 50	24 00	57 00	Alvirus Gleason	Do.
3	James Skelton	do	Oct. 1, 1866	Nov. 30, 1866	2	13 00	3 50	16 50	24 00	57 00	James Skelton	Do.
4	Moroni Secrist	do	Oct. 1, 1866	Nov. 30, 1866	2	13 00	3 50	16 50	24 00	57 00	Moroni Secrist	Do.
5	Melvin Potter	do	Oct. 1, 1866	Nov. 30, 1866	2	13 00	3 50	16 50	24 00	57 00	Melvin Potter	Do.
6	Calvin Wilson	do	Oct. 1, 1866	Nov. 30, 1866	2	13 00	3 50	16 50	24 00	57 00	Calvin Wilson	Do.
7	Joseph Wise	do	Oct. 1, 1866	Nov. 30, 1866	2	13 00	3 50	16 50	24 00	57 00	Joseph Wise	Do.
8	Daniel Tubbs	do	Oct. 1, 1866	Nov. 30, 1866	2	13 00	3 50	16 50	24 00	57 00	Daniel Tubbs	Do.
9	John James	do	Oct. 1, 1866	Nov. 30, 1866	2	13 00	3 50	16 50	24 00	57 00	John James	Do.
10	Jacob Giffin	do	Oct. 1, 1866	Nov. 30, 1866	2	13 00	3 50	16 50	24 00	57 00	Jacob Griffen	Do.
11	William Jones	do	Oct. 1, 1866	Nov. 30, 1866	2	13 00	3 50	16 50	24 00	57 03	William Jones	Do.
12	John Hendricks	do	Oct. 1, 1866	Nov. 30, 1866	2	13 00	3 50	16 50	24 00	57 00	John Hendrix	Do.
13	George Stevens	do	Oct. 1, 1866	Nov. 30, 1866	2	13 00	3 50	16 50	24 00	57 00	George Stevens	Do.
14	Thomas Harris	do	Oct. 1, 1866	Nov. 30, 1866	2	13 00	3 50	16 50	24 00	57 00	Thomas Harris	Do.
15	John Green	do	Oct. 1, 1866	Nov. 30, 1866	2	13 00	3 50	16 50	24 00	57 00	John Green	Do.
16	Jabez Brandon	do	Oct. 1, 1866	Nov. 30, 1866	2	13 00	3 50	16 50	24 00	57 00	Jabez Brandon	Do.
17	Joshua Harris	do	Oct. 1, 1866	Nov. 30, 1866	2	13 00	3 50	16 50	24 00	57 00	Joshua Harris	Do.
18	John Egbert	do	Oct. 1, 1866	Nov. 30, 1866	2	13 00	3 50	16 50	24 00	57 00	John Egbert	Do.
19	George Adams	do	Oct. 1, 1866	Nov. 30, 1866	2	13 00	3 50	16 50	24 00	57 00	George Adams	Do.
19	John Hudson	do	Oct. 1, 1866	Nov. 30, 1866	2	13 00	3 50	16 50	24 00	57 00	John Hudson	Do.

No.	Name		Mustered in	Mustered out							Name	
20	John Collins	do	Oct. 1, 1866	Nov. 30, 1866	2	13 00	3 50	16 50	21 00	57 00	John Colings	Do.
21	Josiah Hoskins	do	Oct. 1, 1866	Nov. 30, 1866	2	13 00	3 50	16 50	21 00	57 00	Joseph Hoskins	Do.
22	Isaac Barton	do	Oct. 1, 1866	Nov. 30, 1866	2	13 00	3 50	16 50	21 00	57 00	Isac Barton	Do.
23	Isaac Bloxom	do	Oct. 1, 1866	Nov. 30, 1866	2	13 00	3 50	16 50	21 00	57 00	Isac Bloxom	Do.
24	James Martin	do	Oct. 1, 1866	Nov. 30, 1866	2	13 00	3 50	16 50	21 00	57 00	James Martin	Do.
25	Abner McPherson	do	Oct. 1, 1866	Nov. 30, 1866	2	13 00	3 50	16 50	21 00	57 00	Abner McPherson	Do.
26	George Webster	do	Oct. 1, 1866	Nov. 30, 1866	2	13 00	3 50	16 50	21 00	57 00	George Webster	Do.
27	William Young	do	Oct. 1, 1866	Nov. 30, 1866	2	13 00	3 50	16 50	21 00	57 00	William Young	Do.
28	James Watson	do	Oct. 1, 1866	Nov. 30, 1866	2	13 00	3 50	16 50	21 00	57 00	James Watson	Do.
29	Samuel Rigby	do	Oct. 1, 1866	Nov. 30, 1866	2	13 00	3 50	16 50	21 00	57 00	Samuel Rigby	Do.
30	James Walke	do	Oct. 1, 1866	Nov. 30, 1866	2	13 00	3 50	16 50	21 00	57 00	James Walke	Do.
31	Alfred Spencer	do	Oct. 1, 1866	Nov. 30, 1866	2	13 00	3 50	16 50	24 00	57 00	Alfred Spencer	Do.
32	Jeremiah Willey	do	Oct. 1, 1866	Nov. 30, 1866	2	13 00	3 50	16 50	24 00	57 00	Jemiah Willey	Do.
33	John Lewis	do	Oct. 1, 1866	Nov. 30, 1866	2	13 00	3 50	16 50	24 00	57 00	John Lewis	Do.
34	Edwin Fackwell	do	Oct. 1, 1866	Nov. 30, 1866	2	13 00	3 50	16 50	24 00	57 00	Edwin Fackwell	Do.
35	William Mann	do	Oct. 1, 1866	Nov. 30, 1866	2	13 00	3 50	16 50	24 00	57 00	William Mann	Do.
36	Richard Jones	do	Oct. 1, 1866	Nov. 30, 1866	2	13 00	3 50	16 50	24 00	57 00	Richard Jones	Do.
37	John Parkin	do	Oct. 1, 1866	Nov. 30, 1866	2	13 00	3 50	16 50	21 00	57 00	John Parkin	Do.
38	Malcom McDuff	do	Oct. 1, 1866	Nov. 30, 1866	2	13 00	3 50	16 50	21 00	57 00	Malcon McDuff	Do.
39	Joseph Boyce	do	Oct. 1, 1866	Nov. 30, 1866	2	13 00	3 50	16 50	21 00	57 00	Joseph Boyce	Do.
40	William Wisbey	do	Oct. 1, 1866	Nov. 30, 1866	2	13 00	3 50	16 50	21 00	57 00	Albert Maby	Do.
41	Albert Mayby	do	Oct. 1, 1866	Nov. 30, 18 6	2	13 00	3 50	16 50	21 00	57 00	Israel Barlow	Do.
42	Israel Barlow	do	Oct. 1, 1866	Nov. 30, 1866	2	13 00	3 50	16 50	21 00	57 00	John Kynaston	Do.
43	John Kynaston	do	Oct. 1, 1866	Nov. 31, 1866	2	13 00	3 50	16 50	24 00	57 00	William Jones	Do.
44	William Jones	do	Oct. 1, 1866	Nov. 30, 1866	2	13 00	3 50	16 50	24 00	57 00	Benjamin Ashby	Do.
45	Benjamin Ashby	do	Oct. 1, 1866	Nov. 30, 1866	2	13 00	3 50	16 50	21 00	57 00	Thomas Carliss	Do.
46	Thomas Carliss	do	Oct. 1, 1866	Nov. 30, 1866	2	13 00	3 50	16 50	21 00	57 00	William Bruce	Do.
47	William Bruce	do	Oct. 1, 1866	Nov. 30, 1866	2	13 00	3 50	16 50	24 00	57 00	Neaphii Hayes	Do.
48	Nephi Hayes	do	Oct. 1, 1866	Nov. 30, 1866	2	13 00	3 50	16 50	24 00	57 00	Ephraim Mantle	Do.
49	Ephraim Mantle	do	Oct. 1, 1866	Nov. 30, 1866	2	13 00	3 50	16 50	24 00	57 00	Elijah Pilling	Do.
50	Elijah Pilling	do	Oct. 1, 1866	Nov. 30, 1866	2	13 00	3 50	16 50	24 00	57 00		Do.

This company was mustered into service by Brigadier General Lott Smith, October 1, 1866, at Kaysville, Davis County, and on that day started to Sanpete, marched two hundred miles, and were assigned to duty in the Severe Valley and vicinity, where they remained in active service for two months; returned to Kaysville, and were mustered out by Brigadier General Lott Smith on the 30th day of November, 1866.

I certify that the above account is correct.

H. B. CLAWSON,
Adjutant General Utah Territory Militia.

Pay-roll of Captain Edward Dalton's company —— cavalry, Utah Territory militia, employed in the suppression of Indian hostilities in Iron, Piute, and Sevier counties, Utah Territory, from March 21, 1865, to June 21, 1866.

We, the undersigned, acknowledge to have received from James W. Cummings, paymaster Utah Territory militia, the sums set opposite to our names, in full payment for our services for the time specified.

Number	Names	Rank	Commencement	Expiration	Months	Days	Pay per month	Monthly allowance for clothing	Total monthly pay and allowance	40cts. per day for use and risk of horse and horse equipment	Total pay and allowance	Signatures	Witnesses
1	Edward Dalton	Captain	Mar. 21, 1866	June 21, 1866	3				$129 50	$36 00	$424 50	Edward Dalton	David Ward
2	James Whitaker, jr	1st lieut.	Mar. 21, 1866	June 21, 1866	3				112 83	36 00	374 49	James Whittaker, jr	Benj. Arthur
3	Collins R. Hakes	2d lieut.	Mar. 21, 1866	June 21, 1866	3				112 83	36 00	374 49	Collins R. Hakes	John R. Winder
4	Sidney R. Burton	do	Mar. 21, 1866	June 21, 1866	3				112 83	36 00	374 49	Sidney R. Burton	Charles Adams
5	Isaac Turley	do	Mar. 21, 1866	June 21, 1866	3				112 83	36 00	374 49		James Whittaker
6	James Anderson	do	Mar. 21, 1866	June 21, 1866	3				112 83	36 00	374 49	James Anderson	Isaac Turley
7	Stephen S. Barton	Sergeant	Mar. 21, 1866	June 21, 1866	3		$17 00	$3 50	20 50	36 00	97 50	Stephen S. Barton	Stephen Thornton
8	John Topham	do	Mar. 21, 1866	June 21, 1866	3		17 00	3 50	20 50	36 00	97 50	John Topham	John Morrill
9	William Ashworth	do	Mar. 21, 1866	June 21, 1866	3		17 00	3 50	20 50	36 00	97 50	William Ashworth	Maximilian Parker
10	William Richards	do	Mar. 21, 1866	June 21, 1866	3		17 00	3 50	20 50	36 00	97 50	William Richards	William Ashworth
11	William Adams	Private	Mar. 21, 1866	June 21, 1866	3		13 00	3 50	16 50	36 00	85 50	William Adams	Charles Adams
12	George W. Crouch	do	Mar. 21, 1866	June 21, 1866	3		13 00	3 50	16 50	36 00	85 50	George W. Crouch	Benj. A. Arthur
13	Hyrum S. Combs	do	Mar. 21, 1866	June 21, 1866	3		13 00	3 50	16 50	36 00	85 50	Hyrum S. Coombs	John R. Winder
14	William Carter	do	Mar. 21, 1866	June 21, 1866	3		13 00	3 50	16 50	36 00	85 50	William Carter	Edward Dalton
15	John Davenport	do	Mar. 21, 1866	June 21, 1866	3		13 00	3 50	16 50	36 00	85 50	John Davenport	Charles Adams
16	Franklin Fish	do	Mar. 21, 1866	June 21, 1866	3		13 00	3 50	16 50	16 03	85 50	Franklin Fish	Do
17	Ebenezer Hanks	do	Mar. 21, 1866	April 6, 1866		15	13 00	3 50	16 50	6 00	14 25	Ebenezer Hanks	E. Dalton
18	Robert E. Miller	do	Mar. 21, 1866	April 6, 1866		15	13 00	3 50	16 50	6 00	14 25	Robert E. Miller	Do
19	John Willden	do	Mar. 21, 1866	April 6, 1866		15	13 00	3 50	16 50	6 00	14 25	John Willder	William Ashworth
20	John G. Pindar	do	Mar. 21, 1866	June 21, 1866	3		13 00	3 50	16 50	36 00	85 50	John G. Pindar, his + mark	Benj. A. Arthur
21	Samuel Orton	do	Mar. 21, 1866	June 21, 1866	3		13 00	3 50	16 50	36 00	85 50	Samuel Orton	John Morrill
22	Jonathan Prothero	do	Mar. 21, 1866	June 21, 1866	3		13 00	3 50	16 50	36 00	85 50	Jonathan Prothero	R. A. Robinson
23	Christian Rasmussen	do	Mar. 21, 1866	June 21, 1866	3		13 00	3 50	16 50	36 00	85 50	Christen Rasmussen	Edward Dalton
24	Alma Steele	do	Mar. 21, 1866	June 21, 1866	3		13 00	3 50	16 50	36 00	85 50	Alma Steele	John R. Winder
25	Stephen Thornton	do	Mar. 21, 1866	June 21, 1866	3		13 00	3 50	16 50	36 00	85 50	Stephen Thornton	Charles Adams
26	William M. West	do	Mar. 21, 1866	June 21, 1866	3		13 00	3 50	16 50	36 00	85 50	John A. West	Wm. C. Mitchell
27	John A. West	do	Mar. 21, 1866	June 21, 1866	3		13 00	3 50	16 50	36 00	85 50	William M. West	D. P. Clark
28	Peter Winmer	do	Mar. 21, 1866	June 21, 1866	3		13 00	3 50	16 50	36 00	85 50	Peter Winmer	John Morrill
29	David Ward	do	Mar. 21, 1866	June 21, 1866	3		13 00	3 50	16 50	36 00	85 50	David Ward	Charles Adams
30	Daniel P. Clark	do	Mar. 21, 1866	June 21, 1866	3		13 00	3 50	16 50	36 00	85 50	D. P. Clark	J. A. West
31	John Blackburn, jr	do	Mar. 21, 1866	June 21, 1866	3		13 00	3 50	16 50	36 00	85 50	John Blackburn, jr, his + mark	Benj. A. Arthur
32	Elias Blackburn	do	Mar. 21, 1866	June 21, 1866	3		13 00	3 50	16 50	36 00	85 50	Elias Blackburn, his + mark	Do
33	Joseph Brunyer	do	Mar. 21, 1866	June 21, 1866	3		13 00	3 50	16 50	36 00	85 50	Joseph Brunyer, his + mark	Do

24	Philip Baker	do	Mar. 21, 1866	June 21, 1866	3		13 00	3 50	16 50	36 00	85 50	Philip Baker	Matthew McEwen.
25	Philo T. Farnsworth	do	Mar. 21, 1866	June 21, 1866	3		13 00	3 50	16 50	36 00	85 50	Philo Farnsworth	George Willahire.
26	Duckworth Grimshaw	do	Mar. 21, 1866	June 21, 1866	3		13 00	3 50	16 50	36 00	85 50	Duckworth Grimshaw	Philo Farnsworth.
27	George Horton	do	Mar. 21, 1866	June 21, 1866	3		13 00	3 50	16 50	36 00	85 50	George Horton	Benj. A. Arthur.
28	Christian Johnson	do	Mar. 21, 1866	June 21, 1866	3		13 00	3 50	16 50	36 00	85 50	Christien Johnson	Hezekiah Simpkins.
29	Joseph Levin	do	Mar. 21, 1866	June 21, 1866	3		13 00	3 50	16 50	36 00	85 50	Joseph Levir, his + mark	Joseph Turley.
30	William Moren	do	Mar. 21, 1866	June 21, 1866	3		13 00	3 50	16 50	36 00	85 50	William Moyre	William Ashworth.
31	Matthew McEwan	do	Mar. 21, 1866	June 21, 1866	3		13 00	3 50	16 50	36 40	85 50	Matthew McEwen his + mark	Jas. Whittaker, jr.
32	Rupard Lee	do	Mar. 21, 1866	June 21, 1866	3		13 00	3 50	16 50	36 00	85 50	Rupard Lee, his + mark	Benj. A. Arthur.
33	Joseph Turley	do	Mar. 21, 1866	June 21, 1866	3		13 00	3 50	16 50	36 00	85 50	Joseph Turley	Feargus O. Willden.
34	James Thompson	do	Mar. 21, 1866	June 21, 1866	3		13 00	3 50	16 50	36 40	85 50	James Thompson	James Gide.
35	James Wiley	do	Mar. 21, 1866	June 21, 1866	3		13 00	3 50	16 50	36 00	85 50	James Wiley	George Willahire.
36	Fergus Wilden	do	Mar. 21, 1866	June 21, 1866	3		13 00	3 50	16 50	36 00	85 50	Feargus O. Willden	Benj. A. Arthur.
37	Thomas Willis	do	Mar. 21, 1866	June 21, 1866	3		13 00	3 50	16 50	36 00	85 50	Thomas Willis	Do.
38	George Wilbahire	do	Mar. 21, 1866	June 21, 1866	3		13 00	3 50	16 50	36 00	85 50	George Wilbahire	Jas. Whittaker, jr.
39	Maximillian Parker	do	Mar. 21, 1866	June 21, 1866	3		13 00	3 50	16 50	36 00	85 50	Maximillian Parker	Jas. Whittaker.

This company was mustered into service at Parowan City, Iron County, March 21, 1866, by order of Brigadier General George A. Smith, and assigned to duty by him in Piute County. They built Fort Sanford under the command and direction of Major Silas Smith. They were in active service every day as scouts and patrols in the mountains and passes, and had several skirmishes with the enemy. They were mustered out June 21, 1866.

I certify that the above account is correct.

H. B. CLAWSON,
Adjutant General Nauvoo Legion.

Pay-roll of Captain Joseph Betterson's company —— cavalry, Utah Territory militia, employed in the suppression of Indian hostilities in Iron, Piute, and Sevier Counties, Utah Territory, from June 6, 1866, to June 21, 1866.

We, the undersigned, acknowledge to have received from James W. Cummings, paymaster Utah Territory militia, the sums set opposite to our names, in full payment for our services for the time specified.

Number	Names	Rank	Period of service.			Pay per month.	Monthly allowance for clothing.	Total monthly pay and allowance.	40 cts. per day for horse use and risk of horse and equipment.	Total pay and allowance.	Signatures.
			Commencement.	Expiration.	Days.						
1	Joseph Betterson	Captain	June 6, 1866	June 21, 1866	15	------	------	$129 50	$6 00	$70 75	Joseph Betterson.
2	Hezekiah Simpkins	1st lieutenant	June 6, 1866	June 21, 1866	15	------	------	112 83	6 00	62 41	Hezekiah Simkins.
3	James Lowe	2d lieutenant	June 6, 1866	June 21, 1866	15	------	------	112 83	6 00	62 41	James Lowe.
4	Cunningham Aurther	Sergeant	June 6, 1866	June 21, 1866	15	$17 00	$3 50	20 50	6 00	16 25	Cunningham Mathews.
5	Benjamin Arither	do	June 6, 1866	June 21, 1866	15	17 00	3 50	20 50	6 00	16 25	Benjamin Arthur.
6	James Farrer	Private	June 6, 1866	June 21, 1866	15	13 00	3 50	16 50	6 00	14 25	James Farrer.
7	Robert Patterson	do	June 6, 1866	June 21, 1866	15	13 00	3 50	16 50	6 00	14 25	Robert Patterson.
8	David Law	do	June 6, 1866	June 21, 1866	15	13 00	3 50	16 50	6 00	14 25	David Law.
9	Jetson Button	do	June 6, 1866	June 21, 1866	15	13 00	3 50	16 50	6 00	14 25	Jetson Button.
10	Joseph Lillywhite	do	June 6, 1866	June 21, 1866	15	13 00	3 50	16 50	6 00	14 25	Joseph Lillywhite.
11	Benjamin Lillywhite	do	June 6, 1866	June 21, 1866	15	13 00	3 50	16 50	6 00	14 25	Benjamin Lillywhite.
12	Isaac Riddle	do	June 6, 1866	June 21, 1866	15	13 00	3 50	16 50	6 00	14 25	Isaac Riddle.
13	Albert Goodwin	do	June 6, 1866	June 21, 1866	15	13 00	3 50	16 50	6 01	14 25	Albert Goodwin.
14	Horace Skinner	do	June 6, 1866	June 21, 1866	15	13 00	3 50	16 50	6 00	14 25	William J. Cox.
15	William J. Cox	do	June 6, 1866	June 21, 1866	15	13 00	3 50	16 50	6 00	14 25	Horace Skinner.
16	Gideon Murdock	do	June 6, 1866	June 21, 1866	15	13 00	3 50	16 50	6 00	14 25	Gideon Murdock.
17	Edward W. Thompson	do	June 6, 1866	June 21, 1866	15	13 00	3 50	46 50	6 00	14 25	Edward W. Thompson.
18	William Thompson, jr	do	June 6, 1866	June 21, 1866	15	13 00	3 50	16 50	6 00	14 25	William Thompson, jr.
19	Ethan Stewart	do	June 6, 1866	June 21, 1866	15	13 00	3 50	16 50	6 00	14 25	Ethan Stewart.
20	Charles Tyler	do	June 6, 1866	June 21, 1866	15	13 00	3 50	16 50	6 00	14 25	Charles Tyler.
21	Lafayette Shephard	do	June 6, 1866	June 21, 1866	15	13 00	3 50	16 50	6 00	14 25	Lafayette Shepherd.
22	Joseph Huntington	do	June 6, 1866	June 21, 1866	15	13 00	3 50	16 50	6 00	14 25	Joseph Huntington.
23	Joseph McGuffie	do	June 6, 1866	June 21, 1866	15	13 00	3 50	16 50	6 00	14 23	Joseph McGuffie.
24	Zachariah B. Decker	do	June 6, 1866	June 21, 1866	15	13 00	3 50	16 50	6 00	14 00	Z. B. Decker.
25	Calvin C. Pendleton	do	June 6, 1866	June 21, 1866	15	13 00	3 50	16 50	6 00	14 25	C. C. Pendleton.
26	Joseph Fish	do	June 6, 1866	June 21, 1866	15	13 00	3 50	16 50	6 00	14 25	Joseph Fish.

This company was mustered into service at Beaver City, Beaver County, June 6, 1866, by order of Brigadier General

Pay-roll of Captain James Andrus's company — cavalry, Utah Territory militia, employed in the suppression of Indian hostilities in Washington and Kane counties, Utah Territory; from August 16, 1866, to October 6, 1866.

We, the undersigned, acknowledge to have received from James W. Cummings, paymaster Utah Territory militia, the sums set opposite to our names, in full payment for our services for the time specified.

Number.	Names.	Rank.	Period of service. Commencement.	Expiration.	Months.	Pay per month.	Monthly allowance for clothing.	Total monthly pay and allowance.	40 cts. per day for use and risk of horse and horse equipment.	Total pay and allowance.	Signatures.	Witnesses.
1	James Andrus	Captain	Aug. 16, 1866	Oct. 16, 1866	2			$129 50	$24 00	$283 00	James Andrus	M. P. Romney.
	Franklin B. Woolley	1st lieutenant	Aug. 16, 1866	Oct. 16, 1866	2			112 83	24 00	249 66	Franklin B. Woolley	Do.
	Willis Copland	2d lieutenant	Aug. 16, 1866	Oct. 16, 1866	2			112 83	24 00	249 66	Willis Copland	Wm. H. Carpenter.
2	Woodruff John Freeman	do.	Aug. 16, 1866	Oct. 16, 1866	2			112 83	24 00	249 66	Woodruff John Freeman	R. C. Lund.
3	Thomas Dennett	do.	Aug. 16, 1866	Oct. 16, 1866	2			112 83	24 00	249 66	Thomas Dennett	Daniel Bagley.
4	Albert Minerly	do.	Aug. 16, 1866	Oct. 16, 1866	2			112 83	24 00	249 66	Albert Minerly	George H. Crosby.
5	Joseph Fish	do.	Aug. 16, 1866	Oct. 16, 1866	2			112 83	24 00	249 66	Joseph Fish	Richard Bentley.
	George W. Gould	Sergeant	Aug. 16, 1866	Oct. 16, 1866	2	$17 00	$3 50	20 50	24 00	65 00	George W. Gould	James G. Bleak.
2	Thales H. Haskell	do.	Aug. 16, 1866	Oct. 16, 1866	2	17 00	3 50	20 50	24 00	65 04	Thales H. Haskell	F. R. Woolley.
3	George Petty	do.	Aug. 16, 1866	Oct. 16, 1866	2	17 00	3 50	20 50	24 00	65 00	George Petty	Do.
4	Elijah H. Maxfield	do.	Aug. 16, 1866	Oct. 16, 1866	2	17 00	3 50	20 50	24 00	65 00	Elijah H. Maxfield	William B. Lang.
5	William C. McGregor	do.	Aug. 16, 1866	Oct. 16, 1866	2	17 00	3 50	20 50	24 00	65 00	Wm. C. McGregor	Joseph Fish.
1	Charles John Thomas	Bugler	Aug. 16, 1866	Oct. 16, 1866	2	13 00	3 50	16 50	24 00	57 00	Charles John Thomas	F. B. Woolley.
	Jesse W. Crosby, jr	Private	Aug. 16, 1866	Oct. 16, 1866	2	13 00	3 50	16 50	24 00	57 00	Jesse W. Crosby, jr	M. P. Romney.
2	James Cragan	do.	Aug. 16, 1866	Oct. 16, 1866	2	13 00	3 50	16 50	24 00	57 00	James Cragan	F. B. Woolley.
3	John Houston	do.	Aug. 16, 1866	Oct. 16, 1866	2	13 00	3 50	16 50	24 00	57 00	John Houston	M. P. Romney.
4	David Cameron	do.	Aug. 16, 1866	Oct. 16, 1866	2	13 00	3 50	16 50	24 00	57 00	David Cameron	Do.
5	Mahonri Snow	do.	Aug. 16, 1866	Oct. 16, 1866	2	13 00	3 50	16 50	24 00	57 00	Mahonri Snow	Do.
6	William Meeks	do.	Aug. 16, 1866	Oct. 16, 1866	2	13 00	3 50	16 50	24 00	57 00	William Meeks	Robert C. Lund.
7	William E. Cowley	do.	Aug. 16, 1866	Oct. 16, 1866	2	13 00	3 50	16 50	24 00	57 00	William E. Cowley	M. P. Romney.
8	Henry McFate	do.	Aug. 16, 1866	Oct. 16, 1866	2	13 00	3 50	16 30	24 00	57 00	Henry McFate	F. B. Woolley.
9	Archibald Sullivan	do.	Aug. 16, 1866	Oct. 16, 1866	2	13 00	3 50	16 50	24 00	57 00	Archibald Sullivan	Do.
	John Lay	do.	Aug. 16, 1866	Oct. 16, 1866	2	13 00	3 50	16 50	24 00	57 00	John Lay	R. C. Lund.
11	Alfred Ford	do.	Aug. 16, 1866	Oct. 16, 1866	2	13 00	3 50	16 50	24 00	57 00	Alfred Ford	Erastus Snow.
12	Hiram Pollock	do.	Aug. 16, 1866	Oct. 16, 1866	2	13 00	3 50	16 50	24 00	57 00	Hiram Pollock	Do.
13	Thomas J. Clark	do.	Aug. 16, 1866	Oct. 16, 1866	2	13 00	3 50	16 50	21 00	57 00	Thomas J. Clark	Do.
14	Samuel N. Adair	do.	Aug. 16, 1866	Oct. 16, 1866	2	13 00	3 50	16 50	21 00	57 00	Samuel N. Adair	R. C. Lund.
15	Frederick D. Ruggs	do.	Aug. 16, 1866	Oct. 16, 1866	2	13 00	3 50	16 50	21 03	57 00	Frederick D. Ruggs	Do.
16	Lehi Smithson	do.	Aug. 16, 1866	Oct. 16, 1866	2	13 00	3 50	16 50	24 00	57 00	Lehi Smithson	F. B. Woolley.
17	William Gardner	do.	Aug. 16, 1866	Oct. 16, 1866	2	13 00	3 50	16 50	24 00	57 00	William Gardner	Do.
18	William Slade	do.	Aug. 16, 1866	Oct. 16, 1866	2	13 00	3 50	16 50	24 00	57 00	William Slade	Do.
19	Bennet Brucken	do.	Aug. 16, 1866	Oct. 16, 1866	2	13 00	3 50	16 50	24 00	57 00	Bennett Brucken	Do.
20	Benjamin Knell	do.	Aug. 16, 1866	Oct. 16, 1866	2	13 00	3 50	16 50	24 00	57 00	Benjamin Knell	Do.

No.	Name		Mustered in	Mustered out								Name	Remarks
21	William A. Bringhurst	do	Aug. 16, 1866	Oct. 16, 1866	2	13 00	3 50	16 50	24 00	57 00		William A. Bringhurst	William R. Lang.
22	John S. Adams	do	Aug. 16, 1866	Oct. 16, 1866	2	13 00	3 50	16 50	24 00	57 00		John S. Adams	F. B. Woolley.
23	Joseph S. McClevo	do	Aug. 16, 1866	Oct. 16, 1866	2	13 00	3 50	16 50	24 00	57 00		Joseph S. McClevo	Do.
24	John Batty	do	Aug. 16, 1866	Oct. 16, 1866	2	13 00	3 50	16 50	24 00	57 00		John Batty	Do.
25	George A. Wardsworth	do	Aug. 16, 1866	Oct. 16, 1866	2	13 00	3 50	16 50	24 00	57 00		George A. Wardsworth	Do.
26	Lemuel H. Redd	do	Aug. 16, 1866	Oct. 16, 1866	2	13 00	3 50	16 50	24 00	57 00		Lemuel H. Redd	Do.
27	Francis Prince	do	Aug. 16, 1866	Oct. 16, 1866	2	13 00	3 50	16 50	24 00	57 00		Francis Prince	Do.
28	Robert Richardson	do	Aug. 16, 1866	Oct. 16, 1866	2	13 00	3 50	16 50	24 00	57 00		Robert Richardson	Do.
29	Eli N. Pace	do	Aug. 16, 1866	Oct. 16, 1866	2	13 00	3 50	16 50	24 00	57 00		Eli N. Pace	Lorenzo W. Ronnch.
30	James P. Thompson	do	Aug. 16, 1866	Oct. 16, 1866	2	13 00	3 50	16 50	24 00	57 00		James P. Thompson	Richard Beatley.
31	Enock Wardle	do	Aug. 16, 1866	Oct. 16, 1866	2	13 00	3 50	16 50	24 00	57 00		Enoch Wardell	Do.
32	George Richards	do	Aug. 16, 1866	Oct. 16, 1866	2	13 00	3 50	16 50	24 00	57 00		George Richards	Do.
33	Thomas Robb	do	Aug. 16, 1866	Oct. 16, 1866	2	13 00	3 50	16 50	24 00	57 00		Thomas Robb	Do.
34	John White	do	Aug. 16, 1866	Oct. 16, 1866	2	13 00	3 50	16 50	24 00	57 00		John White	Do.
35	Thomas Rowley	do	Aug. 16, 1866	Oct. 16, 1866	2	13 00	3 50	16 50	24 00	57 00		Thomas Rowley	Do.
36	Richard H. Benson	do	Aug. 16, 1866	Oct. 16, 1866	2	13 00	3 50	16 50	24 00	57 00		Richard H. Benson	Do.
37	Edward Parry	do	Aug. 16, 1866	Oct. 16, 1866	2	13 00	3 50	16 50	24 00	57 00		Edward Parry	Do.
38	Samuel Wood	do	Aug. 16, 1866	Oct. 16, 1866	2	13 00	3 50	16 50	24 00	57 00		Samuel Wood	Do.
39	Andrew Corry	do	Aug. 16, 1866	Oct. 16, 1866	2	13 00	3 50	16 50	24 00	57 00		Andrew Corry	Henry Lunt.
40	Horatio Morrill	do	Aug. 16, 1866	Oct. 16, 1866	2	13 00	3 50	16 30	24 00	57 00		Horatio Morrill	Erastus Snow.
41	George Williams	do	Aug. 16, 1866	Oct. 16, 1866	2	13 00	3 50	16 50	24 00	57 00		George Williams	Do.
42	Albert Beebee	do	Aug. 16, 1866	Oct. 16, 1866	2	13 00	3 50	16 50	24 00	57 00		Albert Beebee	Do.
43	George Isom	do	Aug. 16, 1866	Oct. 16, 1866	2	13 00	3 50	16 50	24 00	57 00		George Isom	Do.
44	Charles Finney	do	Aug. 16, 1866	Oct. 16, 1866	2	13 00	3 50	16 50	24 00	57 00		Charles Finney	Do.
45	James A. Stratton	do	Aug. 16, 1866	Oct. 16, 1866	2	13 00	3 50	16 50	24 00	57 00		James A. Stratton	Do.
46	Robert H. Boun	do	Aug. 16, 1866	Oct. 16, 1866	2	13 00	3 50	16 50	24 00	57 00		Robert H. Brown	Do.
47	Elijah Everett, jr*	do	Aug. 16, 1866	Oct. 16, 1866	2	13 00	3 50	16 50	24 00	57 00			
48	Gardner Potter	do	Aug. 16, 1866	Oct. 16, 1866	2	13 00	3 50	16 50	24 00	57 00		Gardner Potter	Do.
49	Walter Winsor	do	Aug. 16, 1866	Oct. 16, 1866	2	13 00	3 50	16 50	24 00	57 00		Walter Winsor	Do.
50	William Riggs	do	Aug. 16, 1866	Oct. 16, 1866	2	13 00	3 50	16 50	24 00	57 00		William Riggs	Do.

* Killed by Indians, on the expedition.

This company was mustered into service at St. George, Washington County, on the 15th day of August, by Brigadier General Erastus Snow, and by him assigned to duty in the valleys and mountains in Southern Utah. They were on several expeditions, and performed service every day until mustered out, October 16, 1866.

I certify that the above account is correct.

H. B. CLAWSON,
Adjutant General Nauvoo Legion.

Pay-roll of Captain James C. Orenu's company —— cavalry, Utah Territory militia, employed in the suppression of the Indian hostilities in Sanpete and Sevier counties, Utah Territory, in the month of June, 1866.

We, the undersigned, acknowledge to have received from James W. Cummings, paymaster Utah Territory militia, the sums set opposite to our names, in full payment for our services for the time specified.

Number.	Names.	Rank.	Period of service. Commencement.	Period of service. Expiration.	Days.	Pay per month.	Monthly allowance for clothing.	Total monthly pay and allowance.	40 cts. per day, for use and risk of horse and equipment.	Total pay and allowance.	Signatures.	Witnesses.
1	James C. Owens	Captain	June 10, 1866	June 20, 1866	10			$129 50	$4 00	$47 00	James C. Owens	M. J. Shelton.
2	William King	1st lieutenant	June 10, 1866	June 20, 1866	10			112 63	4 40	41 62	William King	F. A. Robison.
3	Peter Huntsman	Private	June 10, 1866	June 20, 1866	10	$13 00	$3 50	16 50	4 00	9 34	Peter Huntsmnr	Do.
4	Marcelous Webb	do	June 10, 1866	June 20, 1866	10	13 00	3 50	16 50	4 00	9 34	Marcelous Webb	Do.
5	Volney King	do	June 10, 1866	June 20, 1866	10	13 00	3 50	16 50	4 00	9 34	Volney King	Do.
6	Henry Crump	do	June 10, 1866	June 20, 1866	10	13 00	3 50	16 50	4 00	9 34	Henry Crump	Do.
7	Josiah F. Gibbs	do	June 10, 1866	June 20, 1866	10	13 00	3 50	16 50	4 00	9 34	Josiah F. Gibbs	Do.
8	Platt Lyman	do	June 10, 1866	June 20, 1866	10	13 00	3 50	16 50	4 00	9 34	Platt Lyman	Do.
9	Jesse Huntsman	do	June 10, 1866	June 20, 1866	10	13 00	3 50	16 50	4 00	9 34	Jesse Huntsmnr	S. S. Smith.
10	George Croft	do	June 10, 1866	June 20, 1866	10	13 00	3 50	16 50	4 00	9 34	George Croft	Do.
11	Amasa Lyman	do	June 10, 1866	June 20, 1866	10	13 00	3 50	16 50	4 00	9 34	Amasa Lyman	Do.
12	William Hatton	do	June 10, 1866	June 20, 1866	10	13 00	3 50	16 50	4 00	9 34	William Hatton	Do.
13	Joseph Holbrook	do	June 10, 1866	June 20, 1866	10	13 00	3 50	16 50	4 00	9 34	Joseph Holbrook	Do.
14	Edward Webb	do	June 10, 1866	June 20, 1866	10	13 00	3 50	16 50	4 00	9 34	Edward Webb	Do.
15	John King	do	June 10, 1866	June 20, 1866	10	13 00	3 50	16 50	4 00	9 34	John King	Do.
16	Sims L. Mathina	do	June 10, 1866	June 20, 1866	10	13 00	3 50	16 50	4 00	9 34	S. L. Matheny	Do.
17	William Ray	do	June 10, 1866	June 20, 1866	10	13 00	3 50	16 50	4 00	9 34	William Ray	Do.
18	John Felshaw	do	June 10, 1866	June 20, 1866	10	13 00	3 50	16 50	4 00	9 34	John Felshaw	Do.
19	James Brooks	do	June 10, 1866	June 20, 1866	10	13 00	3 50	16 50	4 00	9 34	James Brook	Do.
20	Almon Robinson	do	June 10, 1866	June 20, 1866	10	13 00	3 50	16 50	4 00	9 34	Almon Robinson	Do.
21	Henry McCullough	do	June 10, 1866	June 20, 1866	10	13 00	3 50	16 50	4 00	9 34	Henry McCullough	Do.
22	Davis B. Warner	do	June 10, 1866	June 20, 1866	10	13 00	3 50	16 50	4 00	9 34	Davis B. Warner	Do.
23	John N. McBride	do	June 10, 1866	June 20, 1866	10	13 00	3 50	16 50	4 00	9 34	J. N. McBride	Do.
24	Henry Hatton	do	June 10, 1866	June 20, 1866	10	13 00	3 50	16 50	4 00	9 34	Henry Hatton	Do.
25	William H. Bishop	do	June 10, 1866	June 20, 1866	10	13 00	3 50	16 50	4 00	9 34	Wm. H. Bishop	Do.
26	Robert Henry	do	June 10, 1866	June 20, 1866	10	13 00	3 50	16 50	4 00	9 34	Robert Henry	Do.
27	Orson Holbrook	do	June 10, 1866	June 20, 1866	10	13 00	3 50	16 50	4 00	9 34	Orson Holbrook	Do.
28	Joseph Pugmire	do	June 10, 1866	June 20, 1866	10	13 00	3 50	16 50	4 00	9 34	Joseph H. Pugmire	Do.
29	Albert Robinson	do	June 10, 1866	June 20, 1866	10	13 00	3 50	16 50	4 00	9 34	Albert Robinson	Do.
30	William W. Trescott	do	June 10, 1866	June 20, 1866	10	13 00	3 50	16 50	4 00	9 34	William W. Trescot	Do.
31	Joseph Payne	do	June 10, 1866	June 20, 1866	10	13 00	3 50	16 50	4 00	9 34	Joseph Payne	Do.
	Franklin Carlin	do	June 10, 1866	June 20, 1866	10	13 00	3 50	16 50	4 00	9 34	Franklin Carlin	Do.
	Edward Partridge	do	June 10, 1866	June 20, 1866	10	13 00	3 50	16 50	4 00	9 34	Edward Partridge	Do.

No.	Name		Mustered in	Mustered out							Name	
32	James Knights	do.	June 10, 1866	June 20, 1866	10	13 00	3 50	16 50	4 00	9 34	James Knight	Do.
33	Henry Teples	do.	June 10, 1866	June 20, 1866	10	13 00	3 50	16 50	4 00	9 34	H. Teples	Dn.
34	James Haven	do.	June 10, 1866	June 20, 1866	10	13 00	3 50	16 50	4 00	9 34	James Haven	In.
35	James Lambert	do.	June 10, 1866	June 20, 1866	10	13 00	3 50	16 50	4 00	9 34	James Lambert	In.
36	Horas Russell	do.	June 10, 1866	June 20, 1866	10	13 00	3 50	16 50	4 00	9 34	Horace Russell	In.
37	Culbert King	do.	June 10, 1866	June 20, 1866	10	13 00	3 50	16 50	4 00	9 34	Culbert King	Do.
38	Nesson Bartholomew	do.	June 10, 1866	June 20, 1866	10	13 00	3 50	16 50	4 00	9 34		
39	Christian P. Beauregard	do.	June 10, 1866	June 20, 1866	10	13 00	3 50	16 50	4 00	9 34	Christian P. Beauregard	Do.
40	Christian Hansen	do.	June 10, 1866	June 20, 1866	10	13 00	3 50	16 50	4 00	9 34	Christian Hansen	Do.
41	John Pilling	do.	June 10, 1866	June 20, 1866	10	13 00	3 50	16 50	4 00	9 34	John Pilling	Do.
42	John Dudson	do.	June 10, 1866	June 20, 1866	10	13 00	3 50	16 50	4 00	9 34	John Dudson	Do.
43	Wesley Dame	do.	June 10, 1866	June 20, 1866	10	13 00	3 50	16 50	4 00	9 34	Wesley Dame	Do.
44	William Press	do.	June 10, 1866	June 20, 1866	10	13 00	3 50	16 50	4 00	9 34	William Press	Do.
45	James Daugherty	do.	June 10, 1866	June 20, 1866	10	13 00	3 50	16 50	4 00	9 34	James Daugherty	Do.
46	Brigham F. Young	do.	June 10, 1866	June 20, 1866	10	13 00	3 50	16 50	4 00	9 34	H. F. Young	Do.
47	William Holt	do.	June 10, 1866	June 20, 1866	10	13 00	3 50	16 50	4 00	9 34	Wm. Holt	Do.
48	Ephraim Tompkins	do.	June 10, 1866	June 20, 1866	10	13 00	3 50	16 50	4 00	9 34	Efraim Tomkins	Do.
49	Lewis Brunson	do.	June 10, 1866	June 20, 1866	10	13 00	3 50	16 50	4 00	9 34	Lewis Brunson	In.
50	John Avery	do.	June 10, 1866	June 20, 1866	10	13 00	3 50	16 50	4 00	9 34	John Avery	Do.
51	Robert Barrow	do.	June 10, 1866	June 20, 1866	10	13 00	3 50	16 50	4 00	9 34	Robert Barrow, X	Dr.
52	Edward Skinner	do.	June 10, 1866	June 20, 1866	10	13 00	3 50	16 50	4 00	9 34	Edward Skinner	Do.
53	Allen Russell	do.	June 10, 1866	June 20, 1866	10	13 00	3 50	16 50	4 00	9 34	Allen Russell	Do.
54	Minor Prisbey	do.	June 10, 1866	June 20, 1866	10	13 00	3 50	16 50	4 00	9 34	Minor Prisbey	Do.
55	Abraham Carlin	do.	June 10, 1866	June 20, 1866	10	13 00	3 50	16 50	4 00	9 34	Abraham Carlin	Do.
56	Joseph Prisby	do.	June 10, 1866	June 20, 1866	10	13 00	3 50	16 50	4 00	9 34	Joseph Prisbey	Do.
57	Mortimer Warner	do.	June 10, 1866	June 20, 1866	10	13 00	3 50	16 50	4 00	9 34	Mortimer Warner	Do.
58	James Ivy	do.	June 10, 1866	June 20, 1866	10	13 00	3 50	16 50	4 00	9 34	James Ivy	Do.
59	Richard Ivy	do.	June 10, 1866	June 20, 1866	10	13 00	3 50	16 50	4 00	9 34	Richard Ivy	Do.
60	Henry McArthur	do.	June 10, 1866	June 20, 1866	10	13 00	3 50	16 50	4 00	9 34	Frank Ivy	In.
61	— Ferguson	do.	June 10, 1866	June 20, 1866	10	13 00	3 50	16 50	4 00	9 34	Henry McArthur	Do.
62	Shindy Ivy	do.	June 10, 1866	June 20, 1866	10	13 00	3 50	16 50	4 00	9 33		

This company was mustered into service at Filmore, Millard County, June 10, 1866, by Colonel Thomas Callister, and started in pursuit of the Indians that made the raid on Round Valley; they followed them into Sevier County, came up about three hours after the battle at Gravelly Ford; they were then attached to General Pace's command, and followed up Selina Cañon. They were in active service ten days, and mustered out June 20, 1866.

I certify that the above account is correct.

H. B. CLAWSON,
Adjutant General Nauvoo Legion.

Recapitulation of expenses incurred by the Territory of Utah in the suppression of Indian hostilities in said Territory in the year 1867.

Names of commanding officers of companies.	Service rendered.	Commissary supplies.	Quartermaster supplies.	Transportation.	Total.
I. M. Behannau	$9,339 00				
S. B. Frost	6,267 00				
Jacob Christiansen	10,230 00				
Orson P. Miles	9,463 13				
Joseph S. Day	10,131 00				
J. T. S. Allred	10,585 92				
Frederick C. Nielson	10,230 00				
Erastus Curtis	9,559 92				
John Tidwell	9,636 00				
C. A. Madson	8,875 92				
James M. Allred	8,595 00				
A. W. Bessy	13,923 00				
John W. Irons	10,230 00				
John F. Sanders	6,563 94				
John D. Chase	6,069 00				
T. J. Holbrook	7,618 44				
John H. Tuttle	8,547 00				
Louis Larsen	13,670 88				
Daniel Henrie	10,230 00				
Orange Seeley	14,867 88				
Peter Isaacson	6,060 00				
William Bench	9,933 00				
Wm. L. Binder	4,975 00				
N. C. Christiansen	10,974 00				
C. P. Anderson	6,564 00				
Thomas Robinson	11,667 00				
Field and staff	32,205 26				
Christian Madsen	8,397 00				
Christian Tattistrup	8,094 00				
	300,112 19	*102,198 42	123,037 30	‡22,644 40	448,592 31

* As per Commissary General's vouchers.   † As per Quartermaster General's vouchers.
‡ As per Quartermaster General's vouchers.

I certify that the above account is correct.

H. B. CLAWSON,
Adjutant General Militia Utah Territory.

VOUCHERS FOR TRANSPORTATION FOR 1867.

UTAH TERRITORY, *Great Salt Lake City*, 1867.

The United States to Briant Stringham, DR.

For the use of horses, mules, and wagons, hauling baggage, provisions, and forage with Captain Orson P. Miles's company cavalry while on expedition against the Indians in Sanpete and Sevier counties, Utah Territory, in the year 1867.

April 26 to Aug. 6.—To 5 four-mule teams 106 days, at $5 per
day each........................ $2,650 00

GREAT SALT LAKE CITY, *December* 15, 1867.

I certify that the above animals and wagons were engaged in and for the service and time specified above.

LEWIS ROBISON,
Quartermaster General Nauvoo Legion.

Received, Great Salt Lake City, December 15, 1867, of Lewis Robison, quartermaster general Nauvoo Legion, two thousand six hundred and fifty dollars, in full payment of the above account.

BRIANT STRINGAM.

———

UTAH TERRITORY, *March*, 1867.

The United States to Andrew Moffitt, DR.

For the use of horses, mules, and wagons, hauling baggage, provisions, and forage with Captain Anthony Bessy's company cavalry while employed in the suppression of Indian hostilities in Sanpete and Sevier counties, in the year 1867.

May 1 to Nov. 1.—To 3 four-mule teams 184 days, at $5 per
day each........................ $2,760 00
To 4 pack animals 184 days, at 40 cents
per day each........................ 288 00
                                            —————
                                            3,048 00
                                            =====

GREAT SALT LAKE CITY, *December* 15, 1867.

I certify that the above animals and wagons were engaged in and for the service and time specified above.

LEWIS ROBISON,
Quartermaster General Nauvoo Legion.

Received, Great Salt Lake City, December 15, 1867, of Lewis Robison, quartermaster general Nauvoo Legion, three thousand and forty-eight dollars, in full payment of the above account.

ANDREW MOFFITT.

UTAH TERRITORY, *Mount Pleasant*, 1867.

The United States to William Seely,   DR.

For the use of horses, mules, and wagons, hauling baggage, provisions and forage with Captain Orang Seely's company cavalry while employed in the suppression of Indian hostilities in Sanpete and Sevier counties, Utah Territory, in the year 1867.

May 1 to Nov. 1.—To 4 four-mule teams 184 days, at $5 per
day each............................ $3,680 00
To 5 pack animals 184 days, at 40 cents
per day each...................... 368 00

4,048 00

GREAT SALT LAKE CITY, *December* 15, 1867.
I certify that the above animals and wagons were engaged in and for the service and time specified above.
LEWIS ROBISON,
Quartermaster General Nauvoo Legion.

Received, Great Salt Lake City, December 15, 1867, of Lewis Robison, quartermaster general Nauvoo Legion, four thousand and forty-eight dollars, in full payment of the above account.
WM. SEELY.

UTAH TERRITORY, *Fort Ephraim*, 1867.

The United States to Canute Peterson,   DR.

For the use of horses, mules, and wagons, hauling baggage, provisions, and forage, with Captain Louis Larsen's company cavalry, while employed in the suppression of Indian hostilities in Sanpete and Sevier counties, Utah Territory, in the year 1867.

May 1 to Nov. 1.—To 4 four-mule teams 184 days, at $5 per
day each............................ $3,680 00
To 4 pack animals 184 days, at 40 cents
per day each...................... 294 40

3,974 40

GREAT SALT LAKE CITY, *December* 15, 1867.
I certify that the above animals and wagons were engaged in and for the service and time specified above.
LEWIS ROBISON,
Quartermaster General Nauvoo Legion.

Received, Great Salt Lake City, December 15, 1867, of Lewis Robison, quartermaster general Nauvoo Legion, three thousand nine hundred and seventy-four dollars and forty cents, in full payment of the above account.
CANUTE PETERSON.

UTAH TERRITORY, *Fairview*, 1867.

The United States to Amasa Tucker, DR.

For the use of horses, mules, and wagons, hauling baggage, provisions, and forage, with Captain John F. Sanders's company cavalry, while employed in the suppression of Indian hostilities in Sanpete and Sevier counties, Utah Territory, in the year 1867.

May 1 to Nov. 1—To 1 four-mule team 184 days, at $5 per day .. $920 00

GREAT SALT LAKE CITY, *December* 15, 1867.

I certify that the above animals and wagon were engaged in and for the service and time specified above.

LEWIS ROBISON,
Quartermaster General Nauvoo Legion.

Received, Great Salt Lake City, December 15, 1867, of Lewis Robison, quartermaster general Nauvoo Legion, nine hundred and twenty dollars, in full payment of the above account.

AMASA TUCKER.

UTAH TERRITORY, *Morone*, 1867.

The United States to George W. Bradley, DR.

For the use of horses, mules, and wagons, hauling baggage, provisions, and forage, with Captain Erastus Curtiss' company cavalry, while employed in the suppression of Indian hostilities in Sanpete and Sevier counties, Utah Territory, in the year 1867.

May 1 to Nov. 1—To 2 four-mule teams, 184 days, at $5 per
day each $1,840 00

GREAT SALT LAKE CITY, *December* 15, 1867.

I certify that the above animals and wagons were engaged in and for the service and time specified above.

LEWIS ROBISON,
Quartermaster General Nauvoo Legion.

Received, Great Salt Lake City, December 15, 1867, of Lewis Robison, quartermaster general Nauvoo Legion, one thousand eight hundred and forty dollars, in full payment of the above account.

G. W. BRADLEY.

UTAH TERRITORY, *Fountain Green*, 1867.

The United States to R. L. Johnson, DR.

For the use of horses, mules, and wagons, hauling baggage, provisions, and forage, with Captain T. J. Holbrook's company cavalry, while employed in the suppression of Indian hostilities in Sanpete and Sevier counties, Utah Territory, in the year 1867.

May 1 to Nov. 1—To 2 four-mule teams 184 days, at $5 per
day each $1,840 00

GREAT SALT LAKE CITY, *December* 15, 1867.

I certify that the above animals and wagons were engaged in and for the service and time specified above.

LEWIS ROBISON,
Quartermaster General Nauvoo Legion.

Received, Great Salt Lake City, December 15, 1867, of Lewis Robison, quartermaster general Nauvoo Legion, one thousand eight hundred and forty dollars, in full payment of the above account.

R. L. JOHNSON.

UTAH TERRITORY, *Fort Gunnison*, 1867.

The United States to H. H. Kearnes,   DR.

For the use of horses, mules, and wagons, hauling baggage, provisions, and forage, with Captain C. A. Madson's company cavalry, while employed in the suppression of Indian hostilities in Sanpete and Sevier counties, in the year 1867.

May 1 to Nov. 1—To 1 four-mule team 184 days, at $5 per day.	$920 00
To 1 two-mule team 184 days, at $3 50 per day	644 00
	1,564 00

GREAT SALT LAKE CITY, *December* 15, 1867.

I certify that the above animals and wagons were engaged in and for the service and time specified above.

LEWIS ROBISON,
Quartermaster General Nauvoo Legion.

Received, Great Salt Lake City, December 15, 1867, of Lewis Robison, quartermaster general Nauvoo Legion, one thousand five hundred and sixty-four dollars, in full payment of the above account.

HAMILTON H. KEARNES.

UTAH TERRITORY, *Springtown*, 1867.

The United States to Christian G. Larsen,   DR.

For the use of horses, mules, and wagons, hauling baggage, provisions, and forage, with Captain James T. S. Allred's company cavalry, while employed in the suppression of Indian hostilities in Sanpete and Sevier counties, Utah Territory, in the year 1867.

May 1 to Nov. 1—To 3 four-mule teams 184 days, at $5 per day each	$2,760 00

GREAT SALT LAKE CITY, *December* 15, 1867.

I certify that the above animals and wagons were engaged in and for the service and time specified above.

LEWIS ROBISON,
Quartermaster General Nauvoo Legion.

Received, Great Salt Lake City, December 15, 1867, of Lewis Robison, quartermaster general Nauvoo Legion, two thousand seven hundred and sixty dollars, in full payment of the above account.

C. G. LARSEN.

VOUCHERS FOR QUARTERMASTER'S SUPPLIES FOR 1867.

UTAH TERRITORY, *Manti*, 1867.

The United States to *Andrew Moffitt,*	DR.
May 4.—To 500 bushels oats, at $1 per bushel............	$500 00
June 3.—To 753 bushels oats, at $1 per bushel............	753 00
8.—To 291 bushels oats, at $1 per bushel............	291 00
To 5,060 pounds hay, at 1 cent per pound........	50 60
24.—To 480 bushels oats, at $1 per bushel............	480 00
July 2.—To 195 bushels oats, at $1 per bushel............	195 00
8.—To 391 bushels oats, at $1 per bushel............	391 00
21.—To 243 bushels oats, at $1 per bushel............	243 00
Aug. 3.—To 439 bushels oats, at $1 per bushel............	439 00
To 4,270 pounds hay, at 1 cent per pound	42 70
Sept. 6.—To 587 bushels oats, at $1 per bushel............	587 00
10.—To 642 bushels oats, at $1 per bushel............	642 00
Oct. 20.—To 284 bushels oats, at $1 per bushel............	284 00
To 3,500 pounds hay, at 1 cent per pound........	35 00
	4,933 30

GREAT SALT LAKE CITY, *December 24, 1867.*

I certify that the above account is correct; that the above supplies were purchased of Andrew Moffitt and issued to the Utah Territory militia while employed in the suppression of Indian hostilities in said Territory in the year 1867.

LEWIS ROBISON,
Quartermaster General Nauvoo Legion.

Received, Great Salt Lake City, December 24, 1867, of Lewis Robison, quartermaster general Nauvoo Legion, four thousand nine hundred and thirty-three dollars and thirty cents, in full payment of the above account.

ANDREW MOFFITT.

UTAH TERRITORY, *Mount Pleasant*, 1867.

The United States to *William Seeley,*	DR.
May 1.—To 250 bushels oats, at $1 per bushel............	$250 00
15.—To 798 bushels oats, at $1 per bushel............	798 00
15.—To 4,000 pounds hay, at 1 cent per pound........	40 00
30.—To 3,000 pounds hay, at 1 cent per pound........	30 00
30.—To 329 bushels oats, at $1 per bushel	329 00
June 14.—To 386 bushels oats, at $1 per bushel............	386 00
14.—To 5,000 pounds hay, at 1 cent per pound........	50 00
July 3.—To 210 bushels oats, at $1 per bushel............	210 00

July 25.—To 534 bushels oats, at $1 per bushel..............	$534	00
25.—To 4,500 pounds hay, at 1 cent per pound.........	45	00
Aug. 20.—To 582 bushels oats, at $1 per bushel..............	582	00
Sept. 4.—To 398 bushels oats, at $1 per bushel..............	398	00
4.—To 3,500 pounds hay, at 1 cent per pound.........	35	00
21.—To 471 bushels oats, at $1 per bushel..............	471	00
21.—To 5,500 pounds hay, at 1 cent per pound.........	55	00
Oct. 1.—To 325 bushels oats, at $1 per bushel..............	325	00
9.—To 536 bushels oats, at $1 per bushel..............	536	00
22.—To 329 bushels oats, at $1 per bushel..............	329	00
12.—To 4,500 pounds hay, at 1 cent per pound.........	45	00
	5,448	

GREAT SALT LAKE CITY, *December 24, 1867.*

I certify that the above account is correct; that the above supplies were purchased of William Seeley and issued to the Utah Territory militia while employed in the suppression of Indian hostilities in said Territory in the year 1867.

LEWIS ROBISON,
Quartermaster General Nauvoo Legion.

Received, Great Salt Lake City, December 24, 1867, of Lewis Robison, quartermaster general Nauvoo Legion, five thousand four hundred and forty-eight dollars, in full payment of the above account.

WILLIAM SEELEY.

UTAH TERRITORY, *Fort Ephraim,* 1867.

The United States to Canute Peterson,   DR.

May 8.—To 379 bushels oats, at $1 per bushel..............	$379	00
8.—To 5,000 pounds hay, at 1 cent per pound.........	50	00
11.—To 4,500 pounds hay, at 1 cent per pound.........	45	00
21.—To 3,500 pounds hay, at 1 cent per pound.........	35	00
June 10.—To 537 bushels oats, at $1 per bushel..............	537	00
July 5.—To 460 bushels oats, at $1 per bushel..............	460	00
18.—To 569 bushels oats, at $1 per bushel..............	569	00
Aug. 6.—To 4,500 pounds hay, at 1 cent per pound.........	45	00
10.—To 6,000 pounds hay, at 1 cent per pound.........	60	00
10.—To 487 bushels oats, at $1 per bushel..............	487	00
24.—To 375 bushels oats, at $1 per bushel..............	375	00
Oct. 4.—To 297 bushels oats, at $1 per bushel..............	297	00
18.—To 469 bushels oats, at $1 per bushel..............	469	00
28.—To 522 bushels oats, at $1 per bushel..............	522	00
	4,330	

GREAT SALT LAKE CITY, *December 24, 1867.*

I certify that the above account is correct; that the above supplies were purchased of Canute Peterson, and issued to the Utah Territory militia, while employed in the suppression of Indian hostilities in said Territory in the year 1867.

LEWIS ROBISON,
Quartermaster General Nauvoo Legion.

Received, Great Salt Lake City, December 24, 1867, of Lewis Robison, quartermaster general Nauvoo Legion, four thousand three hundred and thirty dollars, in full payment of the above account.

CANUTE PETERSON.

UTAH TERRITORY, *Monroe*, 1867.

The United States to George W. Bradley,   DR.

May	11.—To 486 bushels oats, at $1	$486 00
	25.—To 862 bushels oats, at $1	862 00
July	11.—To 295 bushels oats, at $1	295 00
Aug.	6.—To 596 bushels oats, at $1	596 00
Sept.	7.—To 298 bushels oats, at $1	298 00
Oct.	6.—To 381 bushels oats, at $1	381 00
	15.—To 370 bushels oats, at $1	370 00
	25.—To 490 bushels oats, at $1	490 00
		3,778 00

GREAT SALT LAKE CITY, *December 24, 1867.*

I certify that the above account is correct; that the above supplies were purchased of George W. Bradley, and issued to the Utah Territory militia while employed in the suppression of Indian hostilities in the said Territory in the year 1867.

LEWIS ROBISON,
Quartermaster General Nauvoo Legion.

Received, Great Salt Lake City, December 24, 1867, of Lewis Robison, quartermaster general Nauvoo Legion, three thousand seven hundred and seventy-eight dollars, in full payment of the above account.

GEORGE W. BRADLEY.

UTAH TERRITORY, *Gunnison*, 1867.

The United States to H. H. Kearnes,   DR.

June	3.—To 360 bushels oats, at $1	$360 00
July	14.—To 387 bushels oats, at $1	387 00
Aug.	30.—To 582 bushels oats, at $1	582 00
	To 5,500 pounds hay, at 1 cent	55 00
Sept.	15.—To 353 bushels oats, at $1	353 00
Oct.	20.—To 284 bushels oats, at $1	284 00
	To 5,600 pounds hay, at 1 cent	56 00
	28.—To 3,500 pounds hay, at 1 cent	35 00
		2,112 00

GREAT SALT LAKE CITY, *December 24, 1867.*

I certify that the above account is correct; that the above supplies were purchased of H. H. Kearnes and issued to the Utah Territory militia while employed in the suppression of Indian hostilities in said Territory in the year 1867.

LEWIS ROBISON,
Quartermaster General Nauvoo Legion.

Received, Great Salt Lake City, December 24, 1867, of Lewis Robison, quartermaster-general Nauvoo Legion, two thousand one hundred and twelve dollars, in full payment of the above account.

HAMILTON H. KEARNES.

UTAH TERRITORY, *Salt Creek, 1867.*

The United States to Charles Bryan,   DR.

May	21.—To 318 bushels oats, at $1	$318 00
June	17.—To 578 bushels oats, at $1	578 00
	29.—To 492 bushels oats, at $1	492 00
July	30.—To 465 bushels oats, at $1	465 00
Aug.	15.—To 625 bushels oats, at $1	625 00
Sept.	29.—To 298 bushels oats, at $1	298 00
Oct.	12.—To 240 bushels oats, at $1	240 00
		3,036 00

GREAT SALT LAKE CITY, *December 24, 1867.*

I certify that the above account is correct; that the above supplies were purchased of Charles Bryan and issued to the Utah Territory militia while employed in the suppression of Indian hostilities in said Territory in the year 1867.

LEWIS ROBISON,
Quartermaster General Nauvoo Legion.

Received, Great Salt Lake City, December 24, 1867, of Lewis Robison, quartermaster general Nauvoo Legion, three thousand and thirty-six dollars, in full payment of the above account.

CH. BRYAN.

VOUCHERS FOR COMMISSARY SUPPLIES FOR 1867.

UTAH TERRITORY, *Great Salt Lake City, 1867.*

The United States to Briant Stringam,   DR.

May	14.—To 21,400 pounds flour, at 6 cents	$1,284 00
	To 2,100 pounds beans, at 11 cents	231 00
	To 2,289 pounds sugar, at 40 cents	915 60
	To 72 gallons vinegar, at $1	72 00
	To 72 gallons molasses, at $2	144 00
June	15.—To 11,765 pounds beef, at 10 cents	1,176 50

June	15.—To 15,700 pounds flour, at 6 cents............	$942 00
	To 1,529 pounds rice, at 40 cents	611 60
	To 540 pounds salt, at 5 cents	27 00
July	18.—To 1,570 pounds sugar, at 40 cents	628 00
	To 200 pounds candles, at 50 cents	100 00
	To 19,700 pounds flour, at 6 cents...........	1,182 00
	To 1,275 pounds rice, at 40 cents	510 00
Aug.	4.—To 1,729 pounds coffee, at 40 cents	691 60
	To 72 gallons vinegar, at $1..............	72 00
	To 205 pounds candles, at 50 cents	102 50
	To 1,590 pounds beans, at 11 cents	174 90
	To 1,370 pounds rice, at 40 cents	548 00
	To 371 pounds salt, at 5 cents	18 55
	To 62 gallons molasses, at $2..............	124 00
	To 580 pounds soap, at 50 cents	290 00
	To 78 bushels potatoes, at $1..............	78 00
Sept.	12.—To 9,782 pounds beef, at 10 cents	987 20
	To 2,240 pounds beans, at 11 cents	246 40
	To 1,581 pounds rice, at 40 cents	632 40
	To 59 bushels potatoes, at $1....:.......	59 00
	To 162 gallons vinegar, at $1..............	162 00
	To 890 pounds coffee, at 40 cents	356 00
Oct.	5.—To 391 pounds salt, at 5 cents	19 55
	To 150 gallons vinegar, at $1..............	150 00
	To 320 pounds candles, at 50 cents	160 00
	To 1,581 pounds beans, at 11 cents	173 91
	To 796 pounds rice, at 40 cents	318 40
		13,179 11

GREAT SALT LAKE CITY, *December* 20, 1867.

I certify that the above account is correct, that the above supplies were purchased of Briant Stringam and issued to the Utah Territory militia while employed in the suppression of Indian hostilities in said Territory in the year 1867.

ALBERT P. ROCKWOOD,
Commissary General Nauvoo Legion.

Received, Great Salt Lake City, December 20, 1867, of Albert P. Rockwood, commissary general Nauvoo Legion, thirteen thousand one hundred and seventy-nine dollars and eleven cents, in full payment of the above account.

BRIANT STRINGAM.

UTAH TERRITORY, *Great Salt Lake Ctiy*, 1867.

The United States to Edward Hunter, DR.

May	1.—To 10,500 pounds flour, at 6 cents	$630 00
	To 4,500 pounds beef, at 10 cents	450 00
	To 580 pounds beans, at 11 cents	63 80
	To 1,595 pounds rice, at 40 cents	638 00

May 1	—To 36 gallons molasses, at $2	$72 00
	To 65 bushels potatoes, at $1	65 00
	To 375 pounds soap. at 50 cents	187 50
	To 400 pounds salt, at 5 cents	20 00
June 10.	—To 1,775 pounds coffee, at 40 cents	710 00
	To 2,575 pounds sugar, at 40 cents	1,031 60
	To 250 gallons vinegar, at $1	250 00
	To 436 pounds soap, at 50 cents	218 00
	To 56 bushels potatoes, at $1	56 00
	To 590 pounds salt, at 5 cents	29 50
	To 11,200 pounds flour, at 6 cents	672 00
	To 7,962 pounds beef, at 10 cents	796 20
July 1.	—To 25,800 pounds flour, at 6 cents	1,548 00
	To 109 bushels potatoes, at $1	109 00
	To 748 pounds soap, at 50 cents	347 00
	To 178 pounds candles, at 50 cents	89 00
	To 2,250 pounds beans, at 11 cents	247 50
	To 1,856 pounds rice, at 40 cents	742 40
Aug. 14.	—To 1,590 pounds coffee, at 40 cents	636 00
Aug. 14.	—To 1,776 pounds sugar, at 40 cents	710 40
	To 198 pounds candles, at 50 cents	99 00
	To 90 gallons vinegar, at $1	90 00
	To 16,201 pounds beef, at 10 cents	1,620 10
	To 1,725 pounds rice, at 40 cents	690 00
	To 621 pounds soap, at 50 cents	310 50
	To 649 pounds salt, at 5 cents	32 45
Sept. 6.	—To 17,000 pounds flour, at 6 cents	1,020 00
	To 7,521 pounds beef, at 10 cents	752 10
	To 81 bushels potatoes, at $1	81 00
	To 486 pounds salt, at 5 cents	24 30
	To 35 gallons molasses, at $2	70 00
Oct. 2.	—To 1,290 pounds coffee, at 40 cents	516 00
	To 2,275 pounds sugar, at 40 cents	910 00
	To 2,490 pounds flour, at 6 cents	149 40
	To 15,771 pounds beef, at 10 cents	1,577 10
	To 648 pounds soap, at 50 cents	324 00
	To 121 bushels potatoes, at $1	121 00
	To 36 gallons molasses, at $2	72 00

18,754 85

GREAT SALT LAKE CITY, *December* 20, 1867.

I certify that the above account is correct; that the above supplies were purchased of Edward Hunter, and issued to the Utah Territory militia while employed in the suppression of Indian hostilities in said Territory in the year 1867.

ALBERT P. ROCKWOOD,
Commissary General Nauvoo Legion.

Received, Great Salt Lake City, December 20, 1867, of Albert P. Rockwood, commissary general Nauvoo Legion, eighteen thousand seven hundred and fifty-four dollars and eighty-five cents, in full payment of the above account.

EDW. HUNTER.

UTAH TERRITORY, *Manti*, 1867.

The United States to Andrew Moffitt, DR.

May 5.—To 9,275 pounds of beef, at 10 cents	$927	50
To 680 pounds salt, at 5 cents	34	00
To 795 pounds coffee, at 40 cents	318	00
To 1,750 pounds sugar, at 40 cents	700	00
To 1,200 pounds beans, at 11 cents	132	00
To 1,781 pounds rice, at 40 cents	712	40
To 15,800 pounds flour, at 6 cents	948	00
June 6.—To 890 pounds coffee, at 40 cents	356	00
To 72 gallons molasses, at $2	144	00
To 9,400 pounds flour, at 6 cents	384	00
To 2,480 pounds beans, at 11 cents	272	80
To 1,680 pounds rice, at 40 cents	672	00
July 12.—To 17,681 pounds beef, at 10 cents	1,768	10
To 1,971 pounds coffee, at 40 cents	788	40
To 2,590 pounds sugar, at 40 cents	1,036	00
To 196 gallons vinegar, at $1	196	00
To 35 gallons molasses, at $2	70	00
To 680 pounds salt, at 5 cents	28	00
Aug. 8.—To 1,684 pounds sugar, at 40 cents	673	60
Sept. 9.—To 11,800 pounds flour, at 6 cents	708	00
To 521 pounds salt, at 5 cents	26	05
To 36 gallons molasses, at $2	72	00
To 681 pounds soap, at 50 cents	340	50
To 1,590 pounds sugar, at 40 cents	636	00
Oct. 15.—To 11,430 pounds beef, at 10 cents	1,143	00
To 1,140 pounds beans, at 11 cents	125	40
To 21,700 pounds flour, at 6 cents	1,302	00
	14,513	75

GREAT SALT LAKE CITY, *December* 30, 1867.

I certify that the above account is correct; that the above supplies
were purchased of Andrew Moffitt, and issued to the Utah Territory
militia while employed in the suppression of Indian hostilities in said
Territory in the year 1867.

ALBERT P. ROCKWOOD,
Commissary General Nauvoo Legion.

Received, Great Salt Lake City, December 20, 1867, of Albert P. Rockwood, commissary general Nauvoo Legion, fourteen thousand five hundred and thirteen dollars and seventy-five cents, in full payment of the
above account.

ANDREW MOFFITT.

UTAH TERRITORY, *Mount Pleasant,* 1867.

The United States to William Seely, DR.

May 1.—To 690 pounds sugar, at 40 cents	$276	00
To 1,590 pounds coffee, at 40 cents	636	00
To 110 pounds candles, at 50 cents	55	00

May 1.—	To 36 gallons vinegar, at $1	$36 00
June 2.—	To 691 pounds soap, at 50 cents	345 50
	To 95 bushels potatoes, at $1	95 00
	To 389 pounds salt, at 5 cents	19 45
	To 140 gallons vinegar, at $1	140 00
	To 350 pounds candles, at 50 cents	175 00
	To 1,980 pounds sugar, at 40 cents	792 00
July 12.—	To 17,681 pounds beef, at 10 cents	1,768 10
	To 1,850 pounds beans, at 11 cents	203 50
	To 1,180 pounds rice, at 40 cents	472 00
	To 491 pounds soap, at 50 cents	245 50
	To 185 pounds candles, at 50 cents	92 50
	To 145 gallons vinegar, at $1	145 00
	To 1,997 pounds coffee, at 40 cents	438 80
Aug. 1.—	To 19,700 pounds beef, at 10 cents	1,970 00
	To 17,000 pounds flour, at 6 cents	1,020 00
Sept. 3.—	To 141 gallons vinegar, at $1	141 00
	To 219 pounds candles, at 50 cents	109 50
	To 2,160 pounds coffee, at 40 cents	864 00
	To 2,180 pounds sugar, at 40 cents	872 00
	To 195 pounds soap, at 50 cents	97 50
	To 1,950 pounds beans, at 11 cents	214 50
	To 1,875 pounds rice, at 40 cents	750 00
		11,973 85

GREAT SALT LAKE CITY, *December* 20, 1867.

I certify that the above account is correct; that the above supplies were purchased of William Seely, and issued to the Utah Territory militia while employed in the suppression of Indian hostilities in said Territory, in the year 1867.

ALBERT P. ROCKWOOD,
Commissary General Nauvoo Legion.

Received, Great Salt Lake City, December 20, 1867, of Albert P. Rockwood, commissary general Nauvoo Legion, eleven thousand nine hundred and seventy-three dollars and eighty-five cents, in full payment of the above account.

WM. SEELY.

UTAH TERRITORY, *Fort Ephraim*, 1867.

The United States to Canute Peterson,   DR.

May 20.—	To 1,796 pounds beans, at 11 cents per pound	$197 50
	To 490 pounds salt, at 5 cents per pound	24 50
	To 780 pounds soap, at 50 cents per pound	390 00
	To 110 bushels potatoes, at $1 per bushel	110 00
	To 150 gallons vinegar, at $1 per gallon	150 00
	To 11,480 pounds beef, at 10 cents per pound	1,148 00
June 22.—	To 9,300 pounds flour, at 6 cents per pound	558 00
	To 1,987 pounds beans, at 11 cents per pound	218 57
	To 7,430 pounds beef, at 10 cents per pound	743 00
	To 490 pounds salt, at 5 cents per pound	24 50

June 22.—To 58 bushels potatoes, at $1 per bushel.........		$58 00
To 597 pounds soap, at 50 cents per pound......		298 50
To 1,892 pounds sugar, at 40 cents per pound.....		756 80
To 1,595 pounds coffee, at 40 cents per pound....		638 00
To 110 gallons vinegar, at $1 per gallon..........		110 00
To 195 pounds candles, at 50 cents per pound....		87 50
July 19.—To 54 bushels potatoes, at $1 per bushel.........		54 00
To 591 pounds salt, at 5 cents per pound.........		29 55
Aug. 10.—To 22,000 pounds flour, at 6 cents per pound......		1,320 00
To 75 gallons vinegar, at $1 per gallon...........		75 00
To 65 bushels potatoes, at $1 per bushel..........		65 00
To 1,716 pounds beans, at 11 cents per pound....		188 76
Sept. 19.—To 11,500 pounds flour, at 6 cents per pound......		690 00
To 11,369 pounds beef, at 10 cents per pound.....		1,136 90
To 36 gallons molasses, at $2 per gallon..........		72 00
To 690 pounds salt, at 5 cents per pound.........		34 50
To 225 pounds candles, at 50 cents per pound....		112 50
To 250 pounds soap, at 50 cents per pound.......		125 00
Oct. 11.—To 750 pounds coffee, at 40 cents per pound......		300 00
To 1,989 pounds sugar, at 40 cents per pound....		795 60
To 791 pounds soap, at 50 cents per pound.......		395 50
To 1,259 pounds rice, at 40 cents per pound......		503 60
		11,410 78

GREAT SALT LAKE CITY, *December* 20, 1867.

I certify that the above account is correct; that the above supplies were purchased of Canute Peterson, and issued to the Utah Territory militia while employed in the suppression of Indian hostilities in said Territory, in the year 1867.

ALBERT P. LOCKWOOD,
Commissary General Nauvoo Legion.

Received, Great Salt Lake City, December 20, 1867, of Albert P. Rockwood, commissary general Nauvoo Legion, eleven thousand four hundred and ten dollars and seventy-eight cents, in full payment of the above account.

CANUTE PETERSON.

UTAH TERRITORY, *Fairview*, 1867.

The United States to Amasa Tucker,   DR.

May 22.—To 18,621 pounds beef, at 10 cents per pound.....		$1,862 10
To 1,641 pounds sugar, at 40 cents per pound.....		656 40
To 191 pounds soap, at 50 cents per pound.......		95 50
June 18.—To 36 gallons molasses, at $2 per gallon..........		72 00
July 27.—To 12,300 pounds flour, at 6 cents per pound......		738 00
To 970 pounds beans, at 11 cents per pound......		106 70
To 2,060 pounds sugar, at 40 cents per pound....		824 00
Aug. 25.—To 9,700 pounds flour, at 6 cents per pound......		582 00
To 1,321 pounds beans, at 11 cents per pound....		145 31
To 1,188 pounds rice, at 40 cents per pound......		475 20
To 520 pounds soap, at 50 cents per pound.......		260 00
To 68 bushels potatoes, at $1 per bushel.........		68 00

Aug. 25.—To 1,075 pounds coffee, at 40 cents per pound..... $430 00
     To 130 gallons vinegar, at $1 per gallon.........   130 00

                                                6,445 21

GREAT SALT LAKE CITY, *December* 20, 1867.

I certify that the above account is correct; that the above supplies were purchased of Amasa Tucker, and issued to the Utah Territory militia while employed in the suppression of Indian hostilities in said Territory, in the year 1867.

ALBERT P. ROCKWOOD,
Commissary General Nauvoo Legion.

Received, Great Salt Lake City, December 20, 1867, of Albert P. Rockwood, commissary general Nauvoo Legion, six thousand four hundred and forty-five dollars and twenty-one cents, in full payment of the above account.

AMASA TUCKER.

UTAH TERRITORY, *Morone*, 1867.

    The United States to George W. Bradley,   DR.

May 10.—To 13,972 pounds beef, at 10 cents............... $1,397 20
     To 79 bushels potatoes, at $1...................   79 00
     To 445 pounds soap, at 50 cents.................   222 50
     To 1,790 pounds coffee, at 40 cents.............   716 00
June 3.—To 15,600 pounds beef, at 10 cents............... 1,560 00
July 24.—To 61 bushels potatoes, at $1....................   61 00
     To 1,790 pounds beans, at 11 cents.............   196 90
Aug. 22.—To 1,590 pounds sugar, at 40 cents..............   736 00
     To 96 pounds candles, at 50 cents...............   48 00
     To 24,891 pounds beef, at 10 cents.............. 2,489 10
Oct. .20.—To 1,295 pounds sugar, at 40 cents.............   718 00
     To 500 pounds coffee, at 40 cents...............   200 00
     To 6,200 pounds flour, at 6 cents............... 6,372 00

                                              8,795 70

GREAT SALT LAKE CITY, *December* 20, 1867.

I certify that the above account is correct; that the above supplies were purchased of George W. Bradley, and issued to the Utah Territory militia while employed in the suppression of Indian hostilities in said Territory, in the year 1867.

ALBERT P. ROCKWOOD,
Commissary General Nauvoo Legion.

Received, Great Salt Lake City, December 20, 1867, of Albert P. Rockwood, commissary general Nauvoo Legion, eight thousand seven hundred and ninety-five dollars and seventy cents, in full payment of the above account.

GEORGE W. BRADLEY.

UTAH TERRITORY, *Provo*, 1867.

The United States to William Miller,	DR.
May 1.—To 110 pounds candles, at 50 cents................	$55 00
16.—To 220 pounds candles, at 50 cents................	110 00
To 1,160 pounds rice, at 40 cents................	464 00
May 25.—To 990 pounds beans, at 11 cents................	108 90
July 21.—To 14,769 pounds beef, at 10 cents...............	1,476 90
Sept. 23.—To 8,000 pounds flour, at 6 cents................	480 00
To 1,790 pounds beans, at 11 cents.............	196 90
To 1,780 pounds sugar, at 40 cents.............	712 00
Oct. 18.—To 862 pounds rice, at 40 cents.................	348 80
	3,944 50

GREAT SALT LAKE CITY, *December* 20, 1867.

I certify that the above account is correct; that the above supplies were purchased of William Miller, and issued to the Utah Territory militia while employed in the suppression of Indian hostilities in said Territory, in the year 1867.

ALBERT P. ROCKWOOD,
Commissary General Nauvoo Legion.

Received, Great Salt Lake City, December 20, 1867, of Albert P. Rockwood, commissary general Nauvoo Legion, three thousand nine hundred and forty-four dollars and fifty cents, in full payment of the above account.

WM. MILLER.

UTAH TERRITORY, *American Fork*, 1867.

The United States to Leonard E. Harrington,	DR.
May 28.—To 7,900 pounds flour, at 6 cents,................	$474 00
To 560 pounds coffee, at 40 cents................	224 00
June 25.—To 980 pounds rice, at 40 cents................	392 00
To 14,979 pounds beef, at 10 cents...............	1,497 90
Sept. 25.—To 1,217 pounds coffee, at 40 cents.............	486 80
To 979 pounds rice, at 40 cents................	391 60
Oct. 20.—To 18,690 pounds beef, at 10 cents.............	1,869 00
To 536 pounds soap, at 50 cents................	268 00
To 75 bushels potatoes, at $1.................	75 00
	5,678 30

GREAT SALT LAKE CITY, *December* 20, 1867.

I certify that the above account is correct, that the above supplies were purchased of Leonard E. Harrington and issued to the Utah Territory militia while employed in the suppression of Indian hostilities in said Territory, in the year 1867.

ALBERT P. ROCKWOOD,
Commissary General Nauvoo Legion.

Received, Great Salt Lake City, December 20, 1867, of Albert P. Rockwood, commissary general Nauvoo Legion, five thousand six hundred and seventy-eight dollars and thirty cents, in full payment of the above account.

LEONARD E. HARRINGTON.

UTAH TERRITORY, *Springville*, 1867.

The United States to Aaron Johnson,	DR.	
May 23.—To 5,200 pounds flour, at 6 cents per pound.....	$312	00
To 729 pounds rice, at 40 cents per pound.......	291	60
June 14.—To 420 pounds salt, at 5 cents per pound........	21	00
To 750 pounds beans, at 11 cents per pound.....	82	50
To 42 gallons molasses, at $2 per gallon.........	84	00
Aug. 17.—To 560 pounds salt, at 5 cents per pound......•.	28	00
Sept. 16.—To 21,600 pounds flour, at 6 cents per pound.....	1,296	00
Oct. 15.—To 209 pounds candles, at 50 cents per pound....	104	50
To 2,136 pounds beans, at 11 cents per pound....	234	96
	2,454	56

GREAT SALT LAKE CITY, *December* 20, 1867.

I certify that the above account is correct, that the above supplies were purchased of Aaron Johnson, and issued to the Utah Territory militia while employed in the suppression of Indian hostilities in said Territory, in the year 1867.

ALBERT P. ROCKWOOD,
Commissary General Nauvoo Legion.

Received, Great Salt Lake City, December 20, 1867, of Albert P. Rockford, commissary general Nauvoo Legion, two thousand four hundred and fifty-four dollars and fifty-six cents, in full payment of the above account.

A. JOHNSON.

UTAH TERRITORY, *Gunnison*, 1867.

The United States to H. H. Kearnes,	DR.	
May 4.—To 125 gallons vinegar, at $1 per gallon..........	$125	00
June 28.—To 11,900 pounds flour, at 6 cents per pound......	714	00
To 911 pounds beans, at 11 cents per pound......	100	21
July 21.—To 21 gallons vinegar, at $1 per gallon........	21	00
To 510 pounds soap, at 50 cents per pound.	255	00
To 1,287 pounds coffee, at 40 cents per pound.....	514	80
Aug. 20.—To 36 gallons molasses, at $2 per gallon..........	72	00
To 1,430 pounds beans, at 11 cents per pound.....	157	30
Sept. 25.—To 19,740 pounds beef, at 10 cents per pound.....	1,940	00
To 491 pounds soap, at 50 cents per pound........	245	50
To 98 bushels potatoes, at $1 per bushel..	98	00
To 1,160 pounds sugar, at 40 cents per pound.....	464	00
To 178 pounds candles, at 50 cents per pound.....	89	00
To 98 gallons vinegar, at $1 per gallon....... ...	98	00

Oct. 15.—To 320 pounds salt, at 5 cents per pound........ $160 00
      To 52 gallons molasses, at $2 per gallon..........   104 00

                                         5,047 81

SALT LAKE CITY, *December 20, 1867.*

I certify that the above account is correct, that the above supplies were purchased of H. H. Kearnes, and issued to the Utah Territory militia while employed in the suppression of Indian hostilities in said Territory, in the year 1867.

ALBERT P. ROCKWOOD,
Commissary General Nauvoo Legion.

Received, Great Salt Lake City, December 20, 1867, of Albert P. Rockwood, commissary general Nauvoo Legion, five thousand and forty-seven dollars and eighty-one cents, in full payment of the above account.

HAMILTON H. KEARNES.

PAY-ROLL FOR 1867.

Pay-roll of Captain Isaac M. Behannan's company, infantry, Utah Territory militia, employed in the suppression of Indian hostilities in Sanpete County, Utah Territory, from May 1, 1867, to November 1, 1867.

We, the undersigned, acknowledge to have received from James W. Cummings, paymaster Utah Territory militia, the sums set opposite to our names, in full payment for our services for the time specified.

Number.	Names.	Rank.	Period of service. Commencement.	Period of service. Expiration.	Months.	Pay per month.	Monthly allowance for clothing.	Total monthly pay and allowance.	Total pay and allowance.	Signatures.	Witnesses.
1	Isaac M. Behannan	Captain	May 1, 1867	Nov. 1, 1867	6			$18 50	$711 00	Isaac M. Behanin	William Bluin.
1	William Blain	1st lieutenant	May 1, 1867	Nov. 1, 1867	6			108 50	651 00	William Blain	Geo. Brough.
1	Niels Clawson	2d lieutenant	May 1, 1867	Nov. 1, 1867	6			103 50	621 00	Niels Clawson	William Bluin.
2	William Warren Major	do	May 1, 1867	Nov. 1, 1867	6			103 50	621 00	W. W. Mazar	Do.
3	William Street Barney	do	May 1, 1867	Nov. 1, 1867	6			103 50	621 00	Wm. S. Barney	Do.
4	Christian Larsen	do	May 1, 1867	Nov. 1, 1867	6			103 50	621 00	Christine Larsen	Do.
5	Samuel G. Bunnell	do	May 1, 1867	Nov. 1, 1867	6			103 50	621 00	Samuel G. Bunnel	Do.
1	Peter Rasmme 3	Sergeant	May 1, 1867	Nov. 1, 1867	6	$17 00	$3 50	20 50	123 00	Peter Rasmmsen	Do.
2	John Gledhill	do	May 1, 1867	Nov. 1, 1867	6	17 00	3 50	20 50	123 00	John Gladhill	Do.
3	John Acton	do	May 1, 1867	Nov. 1, 1867	6	17 00	3 50	20 50	123 00	John Acton	Do.
4	Thomas Gude Schroder	do	May 1, 1867	Nov. 1, 1867	6	17 00	3 50	20 50	123 00	Thomas Gude Schrodr	Do.
5	Adolph Peter Miller	do	May 1, 1867	Nov. 1, 1867	6	17 00	3 50	20 50	123 00	A. P. Miller	Do.
1	Peter Andersen	Private	May 1, 1867	Nov. 1, 1867	6	13 00	3 50	16 50	99 00	Peter Andersen	Do.
2	John H. Zabriskie	do	May 1, 1867	Nov. 1, 1867	6	13 00	3 50	16 50	99 00	John H. Zabrisky	Do.
3	Soren Peter Sorensen	do	May 1, 1867	Nov. 1, 1867	6	13 00	3 50	16 50	99 00	Soren Peter Sorenson, his + mark	Do.
4	Joseph S. Major	do	May 1, 1867	Nov. 1, 1867	6	13 00	3 50	16 50	99 00	J. S. Mazar	Do.
5	Heming Worgunan Olsen	do	May 1, 1867	Nov. 1, 1867	6	13 00	3 50	16 50	99 00	H. V. Olsen	Do.
6	Andrew Anderson	do	May 1, 1867	Nov. 1, 1867	6	13 00	3 50	46 50	99 00	Andrew Anderson	Do.
7	Samuel Allred	do	May 1, 1867	Nov. 1, 1867	6	13 00	3 50	16 50	99 00	Samuel Allred	Do.
8	Hans Jensen	do	May 1, 1867	Nov. 1, 1867	6	13 00	3 50	16 50	99 00	Hans Jensen	Do.
9	Joseph Zabriskie	do	May 1, 1867	Nov. 1, 1867	6	13 00	3 50	16 50	99 00	Joseph Zabriskie	Do.
10	John Blain	do	May 1, 1867	Nov. 1, 1867	6	13 00	3 50	16 50	99 00	John Blain, his + mark	Do.
11	James Bloxy Allred	do	May 1, 1867	Nov. 1, 1867	6	13 00	3 50	16 50	99 00	James K. Allred	Do.
12	Jens Petersen	do	May 1, 1867	Nov. 1, 1867	6	13 00	3 50	16 50	99 00	Jens Pedersen	Do.
13	Frederick Wall	do	May 1, 1867	Nov. 1, 1867	6	13 00	3 50	16 50	99 00	Frederick Wall	Do.
14	Axel Tulgreen	do	May 1, 1867	Nov. 1, 1867	6	13 00	3 50	16 50	99 00	Axel Fuleegren	Do.
15	George Robinson	do	May 1, 1867	Nov. 1, 1867	6	13 00	3 50	16 50	99 00	Gorge Robsen	Do.
16	Peter George Hanson	do	May 1, 1867	Nov. 1, 1867	6	13 00	3 50	16 50	99 00	P. G. Hansen	Do.
17	Lewis Barney	do	May 1, 1867	Nov. 1, 1867	6	13 00	3 50	16 50	99 00	Lewis Barney	Do.
18	John Broadbent	do	May 1, 1867	Nov. 1, 1867	6	13 00	3 50	16 50	99 00	John Broadbent	Do.

No.	Name										Name	
19	Philip Borrison	do	May 1, 1867	Nov. 1, 1867	6	13 00	3 50	16 50	98 00		Philip Borrison	Do.
20	Ole Olsen	do	May 1, 1867	Nov. 1, 1867	6	13 00	3 50	16 50	98 00		Ole Olsen	Do.
21	Caleb Stoddard	do	May 1, 1867	Nov. 1, 1867	6	13 00	3 50	16 50	98 00		Caleb Stoddard	Do.
22	Andrew Johnson, 1st	do	May 1, 1867	Nov. 1, 1867	6	13 00	3 50	16 50	98 00		Andrew Johnson	Do.
23	Andrew Johnson, 2d	do	May 1, 1867	Nov. 1, 1867	6	13 00	3 50	16 50	98 00		Andrew Johnson	Do.
24	Henry Taylor	do	May 1, 1867	Nov. 1, 1867	6	13 00	3 50	16 50	98 00		Henry Taylor	Do.
25	Lewis Larsen	do	May 1, 1867	Nov. 1, 1867	6	13 00	3 50	16 50	98 00		Lewis Larsen	Do.
26	William Henry Allred	do	May 1, 1867	Nov. 1, 1867	6	13 00	3 50	16 50	98 00		Wm. H. Allred	Do.
27	Alfred Grimes	do	May 1, 1867	Nov. 1, 1867	6	13 00	3 50	16 50	98 00		Alfred Grimes	Do.
28	Frederick Grimes	do	May 1, 1867	Nov. 1, 1867	6	13 00	3 50	16 50	98 00		Alfred Grimes, his + mark	Do.
29	George Blain	do	May 1, 1867	Nov. 1, 1867	6	13 00	3 50	16 50	98 00		George Blain	Do.
30	Nels Peterson Soule	do	May 1, 1867	Nov. 1, 1867	6	13 00	3 50	16 50	98 00		Nicls Peterson Soule	Do.
31	John Larsen	do	May 1, 1867	Nov. 1, 1867	6	13 00	3 50	16 50	98 00		Jens Larsen	Do.
32	John Ferdinand Bohn	do	May 1, 1867	Nov. 1, 1867	6	13 00	3 50	16 50	98 00		John Fardnand Bohlen	Do.
33	Chauncey Paine	do	May 1, 1867	Nov. 1, 1867	6	13 00	3 50	16 50	98 00		Chancey Paine	Do.
34	Soren Larsen	do	May 1, 1867	Nov. 1, 1867	6	13 00	3 50	16 50	98 00		Soren Larsen	Do.
35	Martin Bonie	do	May 1, 1867	Nov. 1, 1867	6	13 00	3 50	16 50	98 00		Marten Barney	Do.
36	Haman Hansen	do	May 1, 1867	Nov. 1, 1867	6	13 00	3 50	16 50	98 00		Hemming Hansen	Do.
37	Christian Clausen	do	May 1, 1867	Nov. 1, 1867	6	13 00	3 50	16 50	98 00		Christian Clawsen	Do.
38	Peter Hallen	do	May 1, 1867	Nov. 1, 1867	6	13 00	3 50	16 50	98 00		Peter Hallen	Do.
39	John Robinson	do	May 1, 1867	Nov. 1, 1867	6	13 00	3 50	16 50	98 00		John Robinson	Do.
40	Jens Christiansen	do	May 1, 1867	Nov. 1, 1867	6	13 00	3 50	16 50	98 00		Jens Christiansen	Do.
41	Walter Barney	do	May 1, 1867	Nov. 1, 1867	6	13 00	3 50	16 50	98 00		Walter Barny	Do.
42	Franklin Hanmer	do	May 1, 1867	Nov. 1, 1867	6	13 00	3 50	16 50	98 00		Franklin Hanmer	Do.
43	Ashworth Jackson	do	May 1, 1867	Nov. 1, 1867	6	13 00	3 50	16 50	98 00		Ashworth Jackson	Do.

This company was mustered into service at Springtown, Sanpete County, May 1, 1867, by Brigadier General W. B. Pace, and by him assigned to duty in the eastern mountains and passes. They were in active service every day as guards and patrols, until mustered out November 1, 1867.

I certify that the above account is correct.

H. B. CLAWSON,
Adjutant General Utah Territory Militia.

Pay-roll of Captain Samuel B. Frost's company —— infantry, Utah Territory militia, employed in the suppression of Indian hostilities in Sanpete County, Utah Territory, from May 1, 1867, to November 1, 1867.

We, the undersigned, acknowledge to have received from James W. Cummings, paymaster Utah Territory militia, the sums set opposite to our names, in full payment for our services for the time specified.

Number.	Names.	Rank.	Commencement.	Expiration.	Months.	Pay per month.	Monthly allowance for clothing.	Total monthly pay and allowance.	Total pay and allowance.	Signatures.	Witnesses.
1	Samuel B. Frost	Captain	May 1, 1867	Nov. 1, 1867	6			118 50	$711 00	S. B. Frost	William Blair.
1	James Anderson Allred	1st lieutenant	May 1, 1867	Nov. 1, 1867	6			108 50	651 00	James A. Allred	Do.
2	Jens Jensen	2d lieutenant	May 1, 1867	Nov. 1, 1867	6			103 50	621 00	Jens Jensen	Do.
3	Jens Christian Anderson	do	May 1, 1867	Nov. 1, 1867	6			103 50	621 00	Jens Christan Andersen	Do.
3	Paul Ernest Kofford	do	May 1, 1867	Nov. 1, 1867	6			103 50	621 00	P. E. Kofford	Do.
1	Paul D. S. Land	Sergeant	May 1, 1867	Nov. 1, 1867	6	$17 00	$3 50	20 50	123 00	P. D. S. Land	Do.
2	John Robinson	do	May 1, 1867	Nov. 1, 1867	6	17 00	3 50	20 50	123 00	John Robinson	Do.
3	William Stoddart	do	May 1, 1867	Nov. 1, 1867	6	17 00	3 50	20 50	123 00	Wm. Stoddard	Do.
1	Hans C. Hansen	Private	May 1, 1867	Nov. 1, 1867	6	$13 00	3 50	16 50	99 00	Hans C. Hansen	Do.
2	Eleazer King	do	May 1, 1867	Nov. 1, 1867	6	13 00	3 50	16 50	99 00	Eleazar King	Do.
3	Jens Peter Peterson	do	May 1, 1867	Nov. 1, 1867	6	13 00	3 50	16 50	99 00	J. P. Peterson	Do.
4	Peter Mikkelsen	do	May 1, 1867	Nov. 1, 1867	6	13 00	3 50	16 50	99 00	Peter Mikkelsen	Do.
5	William Hudson	do	May 1, 1867	Nov. 1, 1867	6	13 00	3 50	16 50	99 00	William Hudson	Do.
6	Lars Frantzen	do	May 1, 1867	Nov. 1, 1867	6	13 00	3 50	16 50	99 00	Lars Frantzen	Do.
7	Peter Monsen	do	May 1, 1867	Nov. 1, 1867	6	13 00	3 50	16 50	99 00	Peter Monsen	Do.
8	Hans Jorgen Hansen	do	May 1, 1867	Nov. 1, 1867	6	13 00	3 50	16 50	99 00	Hans Jorgen Hansen	Do.
9	John Schofield	do	May 1, 1867	Nov. 1, 1867	6	13 00	3 50	16 50	99 00	John Schofield	Do.
10	Lewis Curtis Zabriskie	do	May 1, 1867	Nov. 1, 1867	6	13 00	3 50	16 50	99 00	Lewis Curtis Zabriskie.	Do.
11	John Broadbent	do	May 1, 1867	Nov. 1, 1867	6	13 00	3 50	16 50	99 00	John Broadbent	Do.
12	James Commander	do	May 1, 1867	Nov. 1, 1867	6	13 00	3 50	16 50	99 00	James Commander	Do.
13	Peter Sorensen	do	May 1, 1867	Nov. 1, 1867	6	13 00	3 50	16 50	99 00	Peter Sorensen	Do.
14	Andrew Anderson	do	May 1, 1867	Nov. 1, 1867	6	13 00	3 50	16 50	99 00	Andrew Anderson	Do.
15	Lars Alverson	do	May 1, 1867	Nov. 1, 1867	6	13 00	3 50	16 50	99 00	Lars Halversen	Do.
16	Soren Peterson	do	May 1, 1867	Nov. 1, 1867	6	13 00	3 50	16 50	99 00	Soren Peterson	Do.
17	George Crisp	do	May 1, 1867	Nov. 1, 1867	6	13 00	3 50	16 50	99 00	George Crisp	Do.
18	James M. Black	do	May 1, 1867	Nov. 1, 1867	6	13 00	3 50	16 50	99 00	Jans M. Black	Do.
19	James Allred	do	May 1, 1867	Nov. 1, 1867	6	13 00	3 50	16 50	99 00	James Allred	Do.
20	Isaac Allred	do	May 1, 1867	Nov. 1, 1867	6	13 00	3 50	16 50	-99 00	Isaac Allred	Do.
21	William Schofield	do	May 1, 1867	Nov. 1, 1867	6	13 00	3 50	16 50	99 00	William Schofield	Do.
22	James Meek	do	May 1, 1867	Nov. 1, 1867	6	13 00	3 50	16 50	99 00	James Meek	Do.
23	Luke Neibl	do	May 1, 1867	Nov. 1, 1867	6	13 00	3 50	16 50	99 00	Luke Neibl	Do.
24	Lars Johansen	do	May 1, 1867	Nov. 1, 1867	6	13 00	3 50	16 50	99 00	Lars Johansen	Do.

25	Samuel M. F. Fretwell	...do...	May 1, 1867	Nov. 1, 1867	6	13 00	3 50	16 50	99 00	Samuel Fretwell	Do.
26	Andrew Johnson	...do...	May 1, 1867	Nov. 1, 1867	6	13 00	3 50	16 50	99 00	Ander Johanson	Do.
27	Knud Mortensen	...do...	May 1, 1867	Nov. 1, 1867	6	13 00	3 50	16 50	99 00	Knud Mortensen	Do.

This company was mustered into service at Springtown, Sanpete County, May 1, 1867, by Brigadier General W. B. Pace, and by him assigned to duty in the mountains east of said city. They were in active service every day as guards and patrols in the mountains and passes, until mustered out, November 1, 1867.

I certify that the above account is correct.

H. B. CLAWSON,
Adjutant General Utah Territory Militia.

Pay-roll of Captain Jacob Christiansen's company —— infantry, Utah Territory militia, employed in the suppression of Indian hostilities in Sanpete County, Utah Territory, from May 1, 1867, to November 1, 1867.

We, the undersigned, acknowledge to have received from James W. Cummings, paymaster Utah Territory militia, the sums set opposite to our names, in full payment for our services for the time specified.

Number	Names	Rank	Commencement	Expiration	Months	Pay per month.	Monthly allowance for clothing.	Total monthly pay and allowance.	Total pay and allowance.	Signatures.	Witnesses.
1	Jacob Christiansen	Captain	May 1, 1867	November 1, 1867	6	$17 00		$318 50	$711 00	Jacob Christensen	David Candland.
1	Hans Peter Miller	1st lieutenant	May 1, 1867	November 1, 1867	6	17 00		168 50	651 00	H. P. Miller	Do.
1	Andrew Madsen	2d lieutenant	May 1, 1867	November 1, 1867	6	17 00		103 50	621 00	Andrew Madsen	Do.
2	Lars Hansen	do	May 1, 1867	November 1, 1867	6	17 00		103 50	621 00	Lauritz Hansen	Do.
3	Peter Mad-en Piel	do	May 1, 1867	November 1, 1867	6	17 00		103 50	621 00	Peter M. Piel	Do.
4	Harold Christian Bremen	do	May 1, 1867	November 1, 1867	6	17 00		103 50	621 00	H. C. Rnemann	Do.
5	Jens Jorgensen	do	May 1, 1867	November 1, 1867	6	17 00		103 50	621 00	Jens Jorgensen	Do.
1	Edward Cliff	Sergeant	May 1, 1867	November 1, 1867	6	17 00	$3 50	20 50	123 00	Edward Cliff	Do.
2	Angustus Newberg	do	May 1, 1867	November 1, 1867	6	17 00	3 50	20 50	123 00	August Neuberg	Do.
3	Erick Christiansen	do	May 1, 1867	November 1, 1867	6	17 00	3 50	20 50	123 00	E. Christensen	Do.
4	Niels Johansen	do	May 1, 1867	November 1, 1867	6	17 00	3 50	20 50	123 00	Niels Johansen	Do.
5	Lauritz Larsen	do	May 1, 1867	November 1, 1867	6	17 00	3 50	20 50	123 00	Lauritz Larsen	Do.
1	Joseph Lee	Private	May 1, 1867	November 1, 1867	6	13 00	3 50	16 50	99 00	Joseph Lee	Do.
2	John Smith Jorgensen	do	May 1, 1867	November 1, 1867	6	13 00	3 50	16 50	99 00	John S. Jorgensen	Do.
3	Andrew Peter Oemann	do	May 1, 1867	November 1, 1867	6	13 00	3 50	16 50	99 00	Rasmus Hansen	Do.
4	Rasmus Hansen	do	May 1, 1867	November 1, 1867	6	13 00	3 50	16 50	99 00	A. P. Omann	Do.
5	Niels Peter Hansen	do	May 1, 1867	November 1, 1867	6	13 00	3 50	16 50	99 00	Niels P. Hansen	Do.
6	Mads Madsen	do	May 1, 1867	November 1, 1867	6	13 00	3 50	16 50	99 00	Mads Madsen	Do.
7	Thomas Pritchett	do	May 1, 1867	November 1, 1867	6	13 00	3 50	16 50	99 00	Thoms Pritchett	Do.
8	Jacob Larsen, 1st	do	May 1, 1867	November 1, 1867	6	13 00	3 50	16 50	99 00	Jacob Larsen	Do.
9	Rasmus Andersen	do	May 1, 1867	November 1, 1867	6	13 00	3 50	16 50	99 00	Rasmus Andersen	Do.
10	Orson Lee	do	May 1, 1867	November 1, 1867	6	13 00	3 50	16 50	99 00	Orson Lee	Do.
11	Christopher Johnson	do	May 1, 1867	November 1, 1867	6	13 00	3 50	16 50	99 00	Christofer Jonsen	Do.
12	Henry Johnson	do	May 1, 1867	November 1, 1867	6	13 00	3 50	16 50	99 00	Henry Johnson	Do.
13	Niels Rosenlof	do	May 1, 1867	November 1, 1867	6	13 00	3 50	16 50	99 00	N. Rosenloff	Do.
14	John Lee	do	May 1, 1867	November 1, 1867	6	13 00	3 50	16 50	99 00	John Lee	Do.
15	Andrew Christiansen	do	May 1, 1867	November 1, 1867	6	13 00	3 50	16 50	99 00	Anders Christensen	Do.
16	Nells Neilson	do	May 1, 1867	November 1, 1867	6	13 00	3 50	16 50	99 00	Nels Nelsen	Do.
17	John E. Josephson	do	May 1, 1867	November 1, 1867	6	13 00	3 50	16 50	99 00	John E. Josephsen	Do.
18	Ulrick Winkler	do	May 1, 1867	November 1, 1867	6	13 00	3 50	16 50	99 00	Ulrik Winkler	Do.
19	Hans Haarby	do	May 1, 1867	November 1, 1867	6	13 00	3 50	16 50	99 00	Hans Haarby	Do.
20	Olof Rosenlof	do	May 1, 1867	November 1, 1867	6	13 00	3 50	16 50	99 00	O. Rosenloff	Do.

No.	Name		From	To						Name	
21	Vigo Smith	do.	May 1, 1867	November 1, 1867	6	13 00	3 50	16 50	99 00	Wigo Smidt	Do.
22	John C. Johansen	do.	May 1, 1867	November 1, 1867	6	13 00	3 50	16 50	99 00	John C. Johansen	Do.
23	William F. Reynolds	do.	May 1, 1867	November 1, 1867	6	13 00	3 50	16 50	99 00	William F. Reynolds	Do.
24	Jens Henrickson	do.	May 1, 1867	November 1, 1867	6	13 00	3 50	16 50	99 00	Jens Hendrikson	Do.
25	William Smith	do.	May 1, 1867	November 1, 1867	6	13 00	3 50	16 50	99 00	Wm. Smith	Do.
26	Alma Staker	do.	May 1, 1867	November 1, 1867	6	13 00	3 50	16 50	99 00	Alma Staker	Do.
27	Jens Christian Jensen	do.	May 1, 1867	November 1, 1867	6	13 00	3 50	16 50	99 00	Jens C. Jensen	Do.
28	Augustus Nelson	do.	May 1, 1867	November 1, 1867	6	13 00	3 50	16 50	99 00	August Nielsen	Do.
29	Peter S. Olsen	do.	May 1, 1867	November 1, 1867	6	13 00	3 50	16 50	99 00	Peter S. Olsen	Do.
30	Christian Frederick Pell	do.	May 1, 1867	November 1, 1867	6	13 00	3 50	16 50	99 00	Christen F. Pell	Do.
31	George Reynolds	do.	May 1, 1867	November 1, 1867	6	13 00	3 50	16 50	99 00	George Reynolds	Do.
32	Joseph Burton	do.	May 1, 1867	November 1, 1867	6	13 00	3 50	16 50	99 00	Joseph Burten	Do.
33	Lars Rasmussen	do.	May 1, 1867	November 1, 1867	6	13 00	3 50	16 50	99 00	L. Rasmussen	Do.
34	Martin Johnson	do.	May 1, 1867	November 1, 1867	6	13 00	3 50	16 50	99 00	Martin Johnson	Do.
35	James Johnson	do.	May 1, 1867	November 1, 1867	6	13 00	3 50	16 50	99 00	Hans Mortensen, his X mark	Do.
36	Hans Mortenson	do.	May 1, 1867	November 1, 1867	6	13 00	3 50	16 50	99 00	James Johnsen	Do.
37	Aaron G. Osmun	do.	May 1, 1867	November 1, 1867	6	13 00	3 50	16 50	99 00	A. G. Osmun	Do.
38	Jacob Fisher	do.	May 1, 1867	November 1, 1867	6	13 00	3 50	16 50	99 00	Jakkols Heven	Do.
39	Jacob Haven	do.	May 1, 1867	November 1, 1867	6	13 00	3 50	16 50	99 00	Jacob Fisler	Do.
40	John P. Peterson	do.	May 1, 1867	November 1, 1867	6	13 00	3 50	16 50	99 00	Jona P. Petersen	Do.
41	Anton Breunu	do.	May 1, 1867	November 1, 1867	6	13 00	3 50	16 50	99 00	A. Buennan	Do.
42	Jacob Larsen	do.	May 1, 1867	November 1, 1867	6	13 00	3 50	16 50	99 00	Jacob Larsen	Do.
43	Nels Johansen	do.	May 1, 1867	November 1, 1867	6	13 00	3 50	16 50	99 00	Niels Johansen, 2d	Do.
44	Soren Rasmussen	do.	May 1, 1867	November 1, 1867	6	13 00	3 50	16 50	99 00	Soren Rasmussen	Do.
45	Neils Jacobsen	do.	May 1, 1867	November 1, 1867	6	13 00	3 50	16 50	99 00	Niels Jacobsen	Do.
46	Hans Jorgen Brown	do.	May 1, 1867	November 1, 1867	6	13 00	3 50	16 50	99 00	H. J. Brown	Do.
47	Hans Nick Hansen	do.	May 1, 1867	November 1, 1867	6	13 00	3 50	16 50	99 00	H. N. Hansen	Do.
48	Jens C. A. Welby	do.	May 1, 1867	November 1, 1867	6	13 00	3 50	16 50	99 00	Jens C. A. Weeby	Do.
49	Brigham Y. Lee	do.	May 1, 1867	November 1, 1867	6	13 00	3 50	16 50	99 00	Brigham Y. Lee.	Do.
50	John George Wheeler	do.	May 1, 1867	November 1, 1867	6	13 00	3 50	16 50	99 00	J. G. Wheeler	Do.
51	Claudius S. Wheeler	do.	May 1, 1867	November 1, 1867	6	13 00	3 50	16 50	99 00	Claudina S. Wheeler	Do.
52	Joseph Staker	do.	May 1, 1867	November 1, 1867	6	13 00	3 50	16 50	99 00	Jos. Starker	Do.

This company was mustered into service at Mount Pleasant, Sanpete County, May 1, 1867, by Brigadier General William B. Pace, and assigned to duty by him in the mountains and valleys east of said city. They were in active service every day as guards and patrols, until mustered out, November 1, 1867.

I certify that the above account is correct.

H. B. CLAWSON,
Adjutant General Utah Territory Militia.

Pay-roll of Captain Orson Pratt Miles's company ——— cavalry, Utah Territory militia, employed in the suppression of Indian hostilities in Sanpete and Sevier counties, from May 1, 1867, to November 1, 1867.

We, the undersigned, acknowledge to have received from James W. Cummings, paymaster Utah Territory militia, the sums set opposite to our names, in full payment for our services for the time specified.

Number	Names	Rank	Commencement	Expiration	Months	Days	Pay per month	Monthly allowance for clothing	Total monthly pay and allowance	40 cts. per day for use and risk of horse and horse equipment	Total pay and allowance	Signatures
1	Orson Pratt Miles	Captain	Apr. 22, 1867	Aug. 6, 1867	3	15	$126 00	$3 50	$129 50	$42 00	$495 25	Orson P. Miles.
2	Milton H. Davis	1st lieut.	Apr. 22, 1867	Aug. 6, 1867	3	15	109 33	3 50	112 83	42 00	436 90	Milton H. Davis.
3	Breninen B. Bittner	2d lieut.	Apr. 22, 1867	Aug. 6, 1867	3	15	109 33	3 50	112 83	42 00	426 90	Breneman B. Bitner.
4	John Gay	do.	Apr. 22, 1867	Aug. 6, 1867	3	15	109 33	3 50	112 83	42 00	436 90	John F. Gay.
5	Adam M. Paul	do.	Apr. 22, 1867	May 22, 1867	1		109 33	3 50	112 83	24 00	136 83	Adam M. Paul.
6	Leander Lemmon	do.	Apr. 22, 1867	Aug. 6, 1867	3	15	109 33	3 50	112 83	42 00	436 90	Leander Lemmon.
7	Daniel W. Thomas	do.	Apr. 22, 1867	Aug. 6, 1867	3	15	109 33	3 50	112 83	42 00	436 90	Daniel W. Thomas.
8	William Smith Tanner	do.	Apr. 22, 1867	June 22, 1867	2		109 33	3 50	112 83	24 00	249 66	W. S. Tanner.
9	John L. Blythe	do.	Apr. 22, 1867	Aug. 6, 1867	3	15	109 33	3 50	112 83	42 00	436 90	John L. Blythe.
10	Rodney C. Badger	Sergeant	Apr. 22, 1867	Aug. 6, 1867	3	15	17 00	3 50	20 50	42 00	113 75	R. C. Badger.
11	David Huffaker	do.	Apr. 22, 1867	June 7, 1867	1	11	17 00	3 50	20 50	16 40	44 24	David Huffaker.
12	Solon Wells Robinson	do.	Apr. 22, 1867	Aug. 6, 1867	3	15	17 00	3 50	20 50	42 00	113 75	Solon Wells Robinson.
13	Richard L. Mendenhall	do.	Apr. 22, 1867	May 22, 1867	1		17 00	3 50	20 50	12 00	32 50	Richard L. Mendenhall.
14	Joseph Lindsay	Bugler	Apr. 22, 1867	Aug. 6, 1867	3	15	17 00	3 50	20 50	42 00	113 75	Joseph Lindsey.
15	Moroni L. Pratt	Private	Apr. 22, 1867	Aug. 6, 1867	3	15	13 00	3 50	16 50	42 00	99 75	Moroni L. Pratt.
16	Joseph Smith	do.	Apr. 22, 1867	Aug. 6, 1867	3	15	13 00	3 50	16 50	42 00	99 75	Joseph Smith.
17	Nathan Tanner	do.	Apr. 22, 1867	Aug. 6, 1867	3	15	13 00	3 50	16 50	42 00	99 75	Nathan Tanner.
18	William J. F. McAllister	do.	Apr. 22, 1867	Aug. 6, 1867	3	15	13 00	3 50	16 50	42 00	99 75	W. J. F. McAllister.
19	James Rigdy	do.	Apr. 22, 1867	Aug. 6, 1867	3	15	13 00	3 50	16 50	42 00	99 75	James Rigdy.
20	George M. Webster	do.	Apr. 22, 1867	Aug. 6, 1867	3	15	13 00	3 50	16 50	42 00	99 75	George M. Webster.
21	William L. Bateman	do.	Apr. 22, 1867	Aug. 6, 1867	3	15	13 00	3 50	16 50	42 00	99 75	W. L. Bateman.
22	Alma Becksted	do.	Apr. 22, 1867	Aug. 6, 1867	3	15	13 00	3 50	16 50	42 00	99 75	Alma Becksted.
23	Charles Wright	do.	Apr. 22, 1867	Aug. 6, 1867	3	15	13 00	3 50	16 50	42 00	99 75	Charles Wright.
24	James Tibbetts	do.	Apr. 22, 1867	Aug. 6, 1867	3	15	13 00	3 50	16 50	42 00	99 75	James Tibbets.
25	Joseph Eldredge	do.	Apr. 22, 1867	Aug. 6, 1867	3	15	13 00	3 50	16 50	42 00	99 75	Joseph Eldredge.
26	William G. Goforth	do.	Apr. 22, 1867	Aug. 6, 1867	3	15	13 00	3 50	16 50	42 00	99 75	William G. Goforth.
27	Lyman Shurtliff	do.	Apr. 22, 1867	Aug. 6, 1867	3	15	13 00	3 50	16 50	42 00	99 75	Lymon Shertleff.
28	Richard Hardey	do.	Apr. 22, 1867	Aug. 6, 1867	3	15	13 00	3 50	16 50	42 00	99 75	Richard Hardey.
29	Alma Lutz	do.	Apr. 22, 1867	Aug. 6, 1867	3	15	13 00	3 50	16 50	42 00	99 75	Alma Lutz, his + mark.
30	James Standing	do.	Apr. 22, 1867	Aug. 6, 1867	3	15	13 00	3 50	16 50	42 00	99 75	James Standing.
31	John Derrick	do.	Apr. 22, 1867	Aug. 6, 1867	3	15	13 00	3 50	16 50	42 00	99 75	John Derrick.
32	Charles Rockwood	do.	Apr. 22, 1867	Aug. 6, 1867	3	15	13 00	3 50	16 50	42 00	99 75	Chas. W. Rockwool.
33	Stephen Newman	do.	Apr. 22, 1867	Aug. 6, 1867	3	15	13 00	3 50	16 50	42 00	99 75	Stephen R. Newman.
34	Benjamin Hoten	do.	Apr. 22, 1867	Aug. 6, 1867	3	15	13 00	3 50	16 50	42 00	99 75	Benjamin Hoten.

No.	Name	Enrolled	Mustered out							
20	George Butterfield	Apr. 22, 1867	Aug. 6, 1867	3	15	13 00	3 50	16 50	42 00	99 75
21	Melvin Miller	Apr. 22, 1867	Aug. 6, 1867	3	15	13 00	3 50	16 50	42 00	99 75
22	Samuel Helm	Apr. 22, 1867	Aug. 6, 1867	3	15	13 00	3 50	16 50	42 00	99 75
23	Henry Boyce	Apr. 22, 1867	May 22, 1867	1	15	13 00	3 50	16 50	12 00	29 50
24	Joseph Fordham	Apr. 22, 1867	Aug. 6, 1867	3	15	13 00	3 50	16 50	42 00	99 75
25	Edwin Bolton	Apr. 22, 1867	Aug. 6, 1867	3	15	13 00	3 50	16 50	42 00	99 75
26	Philo A. Colvin	Apr. 22, 1867	Aug. 6, 1867	3	15	13 00	3 50	16 50	42 00	99 75
27	Wiltus Webb	Apr. 22, 1867	Aug. 6, 1867	3	15	13 00	3 50	16 50	42 00	99 75
28	Thomas Stokes	Apr. 22, 1867	Aug. 6, 1867	3	15	13 00	3 50	16 50	42 00	99 75
29	James Terry	Apr. 22, 1867	Aug. 6, 1867	3	15	13 00	3 50	16 50	42 00	99 75
30	Oliver Smith	Apr. 22, 1867	Aug. 6, 1867	3	15	13 00	3 50	16 50	42 00	99 75
31	Stephen W. Ross	Apr. 22, 1867	Aug. 6, 1867	3	15	13 00	3 50	16 50	42 00	99 75
32	John Bushman	Apr. 22, 1867	Aug. 6, 1867	3	15	13 00	3 50	16 50	42 00	99 75
33	William Bone	Apr. 22, 1867	Aug. 6, 1867	3	15	13 00	3 50	16 50	42 00	99 75
34	Robert Thorne	Apr. 22, 1867	May 22, 1867	1	15	13 00	3 50	16 50	12 00	28 50
35	George McConnell	Apr. 22, 1867	Aug. 6, 1867	3	15	13 00	3 50	16 50	42 00	99 75
36	Joseph Wrigley	Apr. 22, 1867	Aug. 6, 1867	3	15	13 00	3 50	16 50	42 00	99 75
37	Benjamin Greenwood	Apr. 22, 1867	Aug. 6, 1867	3	15	13 00	3 50	16 50	42 00	99 75
38	John Armstrong	Apr. 22, 1867	Aug. 6, 1867	3	15	13 00	3 50	16 50	42 00	99 75
39	Isaac Plunkett	Apr. 22, 1867	Aug. 6, 1867	3	15	13 00	3 50	16 50	42 00	99 75
40	Byron W. Brown	Apr. 22, 1867	Aug. 6, 1867	3	15	13 00	3 50	16 50	42 00	99 75
41	William C. Tunbridge	Apr. 22, 1867	Aug. 6, 1867	3	15	13 00	3 50	16 50	42 00	99 75
42	Joseph M. Westwood	Apr. 22, 1867	Aug. 6, 1867	3	15	13 00	3 50	16 50	42 00	99 75
43	Henry Curtis	Apr. 22, 1867	Aug. 6, 1867	3	15	13 00	3 50	16 50	42 00	99 75
44	Elial Curtis	Apr. 22, 1867	Aug. 6, 1867	3	15	13 00	3 50	16 50	42 00	99 75
45	Alpea Beck	Apr. 22, 1867	Aug. 6, 1867	3	15	13 00	3 50	16 50	42 00	99 75
46	John Moore	Apr. 22, 1867	Aug. 6, 1867	3	15	13 00	3 50	16 50	42 00	99 75
47	Elijah Hancock	Apr. 22, 1867	Aug. 6, 1867	3	15	13 00	3 50	16 50	42 00	99 75
48	Delmont Webb	Apr. 22, 1867	Aug. 6, 1867	3	15	13 00	3 50	16 50	42 00	99 75
49	Joseph Tibbetts	Apr. 22, 1867	Aug. 6, 1867	3	15	13 00	3 50	16 50	42 00	99 75
50	Andrew Dudley	Apr. 22, 1867	Aug. 6, 1867	3	15	13 00	3 50	16 50	42 00	99 75
51	Joseph Myers	Apr. 22, 1867	Aug. 6, 1867	3	15	13 00	3 50	16 50	42 00	99 75
52	George Watt	Apr. 22, 1867	Aug. 6, 1867	3	15	13 00	3 50	16 50	42 00	99 75
53	William F. Pace	Apr. 22, 1867	Aug. 6, 1867	3	15	13 00	3 50	16 50	42 00	99 75
54	William B. Rowley	Apr. 22, 1867	Aug. 6, 1867	3	15	13 00	3 50	16 50	42 00	99 75
55	Laconius Colvin	Apr. 22, 1867	June 6, 1867	1	15	13 00	3 50	16 50	18 00	42 25
56	Thomas Laburn	Apr. 22, 1867	June 6, 1867	1	15	13 00	3 50	16 50	18 00	42 25

* Wounded May 22, 1867.   † Killed by Indians.

This company was mustered into service at Salt Lake City April 22, 1867, by order of Lieutenant General Daniel H. Wells, and assigned to duty by him in Sanpete and Sevier counties. They started from Salt Lake City on the 22d, and marched 200 miles to Fort Gunnison, where they arrived on the 26th. Brigadier General W. B. Pace, then in command of the district, assigned them to duty in the Sevier valley, to protect and assist the inhabitants of Richfield, Glenwood, Alma, and Selina to move away themselves and stock, as said settlements had to be abandoned in consequence of the continued depredations of the Indians. This company was in active service every day until mustered out at Salt Lake City, August 6, 1867.

I certify that the above account is correct.

H. B. CLAWSON, *Adjutant General Utah Territory Militia.*

Pay-roll of Captain Joseph Smith Day's company —— infantry, Utah Territory militia, employed in the suppression of Indian hostilities in Sanpete County, Utah Territory, from May 1, 1867, to November 1, 1867.

We, the undersigned, acknowledge to have received from James W. Cummings, paymaster Utah Territory militia, the sums set opposite to our names, in full payment for our services for the time specified.

Number	Names	Rank	Commencement	Expiration	Months	Pay per month	Monthly allowance for clothing	Total monthly pay and allowance	Total pay and allowance	Signatures	Witnesses
1	Joseph Smith Day	Captain	May 1, 1867	Nov. 1, 1867	6	$17		$118 50	$711	Joseph S. Day	H. P. Miller.
1	Neils Wald-rmasson	1st lieut.	May 1, 1867	Nov. 1, 1867	6			108 50	651	Neils Waldenmarson	Do.
1	John Meyrick	2d lieut.	May 1, 1867	Nov. 1, 1867	6			103 50	621	John Meyrick	Do.
2	James Gundersen	do.	May 1, 1867	Nov. 1, 1867	6			103 50	621	Jens Gundersen	Do.
3	Thomas Christiansen	do.	May 1, 1867	Nov. 1, 1867	6			103 50	621	Thomas C. Christensen	Do.
4	Paul Deblin	do.	May 1, 1867	Nov. 1, 1867	6			103 50	621	Paul Deblin	Do.
5	Neils Jensen	do.	May 1, 1867	Nov. 1, 1867	6			103 50	621	Nils Jensen	Do.
1	Peter Gollfreason	Sergeant	May 1, 1867	Nov. 1, 1867	6	$17		20 50	123	Peter Gottfreason	Do.
2	Hans Neilson	do.	May 1, 1867	Nov. 1, 1867	6	17	$3 50	20 50	123	Hans Neilsen	Do.
3	James Stohl	do.	May 1, 1867	Nov. 1, 1867	6	17	3 50	20 50	123	Jens Stahl	Do.
4	Neils Barker Nelson	do.	May 1, 1867	Nov. 1, 1867	6	17	3 50	20 50	123	Niels B. Nielson	Do.
1	Charles Hauushire	Private	May 1, 1867	Nov. 1, 1867	6	13	3 50	16 50	99	Charles Hanushier	Do.
2	Ephraim Green	do.	May 1, 1867	Nov. 1, 1867	6	13	3 50	16 50	99	Ephrom Green	Do.
3	Joseph Caldwell	do.	May 1, 1867	Nov. 1, 1867	6	13	3 50	16 50	99	Joseph Caldwell	Do.
4	Henry Wilcox	do.	May 1, 1867	Nov. 1, 1867	6	13	3 50	16 50	99	Henry Willcox	Do.
5	B-udt Rolfsen	do.	May 1, 1867	Nov. 1, 1867	6	13	3 50	16 50	99	Berndt Rolfsen	Do.
6	Peter Jensen	do.	May 1, 1867	Nov. 1, 1867	6	13	3 50	16 50	99	Peter Jensen	Do.
7	John Jonasen	do.	May 1, 1867	Nov. 1, 1867	6	13	3 50	16 50	99	John Johsen	Do.
8	John Nicholsen	do.	May 1, 1867	Nov. 1, 1867	6	13	3 50	16 50	99	John Nickelson	Do.
9	Henry Olsen	do.	May 1, 1867	Nov. 1, 1867	6	13	3 50	16 50	99	Henry Olsen	Do.
10	Jeremiah Page	do.	May 1, 1867	Nov. 1, 1867	6	13	3 50	16 50	99	Jeremiah Page	Do.
11	Andrew Larsen	do.	May 1, 1867	Nov. 1, 1867	6	13	3 50	16 50	99	Andru Larsen	Do.
12	Abraham Day, jun'r	do.	May 1, 1867	Nov. 1, 1867	6	13	3 50	16 50	99	Abraham Day	Do.
13	John P. Carl-son, 2d	do.	May 1, 1867	Nov. 1, 1867	6	13	3 50	16 50	99	John P. Carl-on	Do.
14	Christian Jensen, 2d	do.	May 1, 1867	Nov. 1, 1867	6	13	3 50	16 50	99	Chrisren Jeunsen, 2	Do.
15	James Olsen	do.	May 1, 1867	Nov. 1, 1867	6	13	3 50	16 50	90	Jenes Olsen	Do.
16	Adam Swensen	do.	May 1, 1867	Nov. 1, 1867	6	13	3 50	16 50	90	Adam Swensen	Do.
17	Edward Dalley	do.	May 1, 1867	Nov. 1, 1867	6	13	3 50	16 50	90	Edward Dally	Do.
18	Henry Bowie	do.	May 1, 1867	Nov. 1, 1867	6	13	3 50	16 50	90	Henry Bonnie	Do.
19	Thomas J. Hansekeeper	do.	May 1, 1867	Nov. 1, 1867	6	13	3 50	16 50	90	Thomas J. Houskeeper	Do.
20	Theodor F. Hansekeeper	do.	May 1, 1867	Nov. 1, 1867	6	13	3 50	16 50	90	Theodor F. Honskeeper	Do.
21	Soren Jacobsen	do.	May 1, 1867	Nov. 1, 1867	6	13	3 50	16 50	99	Soren Jacolnsen	Do.
21	Hans Gottfredsen	do.	May 1, 1867	Nov. 1, 1867	6	13	3 50	16 50	99	Hans Gottfridson	Do

22	Benjamin Green	do.	May 1, 1867	Nov. 1, 1867	6	13	3 50	16 50	99	Benjamin Green	Do.
23	Rasmus Rasmussen	do.	May 1, 1867	Nov. 1, 1867	6	13	3 50	16 50	99	Rasmus Rasmussen	Do.
24	Mads Anderson	do.	May 1, 1867	Nov. 1, 1867	6	13	3 50	16 50	99	Mads Anderson	Do.
25	Frantz Christiansen	do.	May 1, 1867	Nov. 1, 1867	6	13	3 50	16 50	99	Frantz C. Christensen	Do.
26	John Williams	do.	May 1, 1867	Nov. 1, 1867	6	13	3 50	16 50	99	John Williams	Do.
27	Hans Yorgen Hansen	do.	May 1, 1867	Nov. 1, 1867	6	13	3 50	16 50	99	Hans Y. Hansen	Do.
28	Mons Rolf	do.	May 1, 1867	Nov. 1, 1867	6	13	3 50	16 50	99	Mons Rolf	Do.
29	John Stohl	do.	May 1, 1867	Nov. 1, 1867	6	13	3 30	16 50	99	John Stohl	Do.
30	Andrew Poulsen	do.	May 1, 1867	Nov. 1, 1867	6	13	3 50	16 50	99	Andrn Ponlsen	Do.
31	Erastus Stohl	do.	May 1, 1867	Nov. 1, 1867	6	13	3 50	16 50	99	Erastus Stohl	Do.
32	Samuel Green	do.	May 1, 1867	Nov. 1, 1867	6	13	3 50	16 50	99	Samuel Green	Do.
33	Henry Mills	do.	May 1, 1867	Nov. 1, 1867	6	13	3 50	16 50	99	Henry Mills.	Do.
34	Jesper Peterson	do.	May 1, 1867	Nov. 1, 1867	6	13	3 50	16 50	99	Jesper Petterson	Do.
35	Hazard Wilcox	do.	May 1, 1867	Nov. 1, 1867	6	13	3 50	16 50	99	Hazard Willcox	Do.
36	John Green	do.	May 1, 1867	Nov. 1, 1867	6	13	3 50	16 50	99	John Green	Do.
37	Olof Sorenson	do.	May 1, 1867	Nov. 1, 1867	6	13	3 50	16 50	99	Olof Sorenson	Do.
38	Swen Olsen	do.	May 1, 1867	Nov. 1, 1867	6	13	3 50	16 50	99	Sven Olsen	Do.
39	Andrew Svensen	do.	May 1, 1867	Nov. 1, 1867	6	13	3 50	16 50	99	Anders Svendsen	Do.
40	Joseph Coates	do.	May 1, 1867	Nov. 1, 1867	6	13	3 50	16 50	99	Joseph Coats	Do.
41	Wellington Seely	do.	May 1, 1867	Nov. 1, 1867	6	13	3 50	16 50	99	Wellington Seely	Do.
42	William Seely	do.	May 1, 1867	Nov. 1, 1867	6	13	3 50	16 50	99	William Seely	Do.
43	Hans Broderson	do.	May 1, 1867	Nov. 1, 1867	6	13	3 50	16 50	99	Hans Broderson	Do.
44	George Toft	do.	May 1, 1867	Nov. 1, 1867	6	13	3 50	16 50	99	George Tuft	Do.
45	Don Carlos Seely	do.	May 1, 1867	Nov. 1, 1867	6	13	3 50	16 50	99	Don Carlos Seely	Do.
46	Ezra Day	do.	May 1, 1867	Nov. 1, 1867	6	13	3 50	16 50	99	Ezra Day	Do.
47	Neils Lund	do.	May 1, 1867	Nov. 1, 1867	6	13	3 30	16 50	99	Neils Lund	Do.
48	Christian Peterson	do.	May 1, 1867	Nov. 1, 1867	6	13	3 50	16 50	99	Christian Peteren	Do.
49	Andrew Harbro	do.	May 1, 1867	Nov. 1, 1867	6	13	3 50	16 50	99	Andrew Harbro	Do.
50	Hans Peter Peterson	do.	May 1, 1867	Nov. 1, 1867	6	13	3 50	16 50	99	Hans Peter Petersen	Do.
51	Martin Broderson	do.	May 1, 1867	Nov. 1, 1867	6	13	3 50	16 50	99	Martin Brodersen	Do.

This company was mustered into service at Mount Pleasant, Sanpete County, May 1, 1867, by Brigadier General W. B. Pace, and by him assigned to duty in vicinity of said settlement. They were in active service every day as guards and patrols in the mountains, and wherever duty called them, until mustered out November 1, 1867.

I certify that the above account is correct.

H. B. CLAWSON,

Adjutant General Utah Territory Militia.

Pay-roll of Captain James T. S. Allred's company —— cavalry, Utah Territory militia, employed in the suppression of Indian hostilities in Sanpete County, Utah Territory, from May 1, 1867, to November 1, 1867.

We, the undersigned, acknowledge to have received from James W. Cummings, paymaster Utah Territory militia, the sums set opposite to our names, in full payment for our services for the time specified.

Number	Names	Rank	Commencement.	Expiration.	Months.	Pay per month.	Monthly allowance for clothing.	Total monthly pay and allowance.	40 cts. per day for use and risk of horse and horse equipment.	Total pay and allowance.	Signatures.	Witnesses.
1	James T. S. Allred	Captain	May 1, 1867	November 1, 1867	6			$129 50	$72 00	$849 00	James T. S. Allred	Geo. Brough.
1	William Scott	1st lieut.	May 1, 1867	November 1, 1867	6			112 83	72 00	748 98	William Scott	Do.
1	Thomas B. Allred	2d lieut.	May 1, 1867	November 1, 1867	6			112 83	72 00	748 98	Thomas B. Allred	Do.
1	Lars A. Justesen	do	May 1, 1867	November 1, 1867	6			112 83	72 00	748 98	Lars A. Justesen	Do.
2	Abraham Acord	do	May 1, 1867	November 1, 1867	6	$17 00	$3 50	20 50	72 00	195 00	Abiham Acord	Do.
2	Sandford Acord	Sergeant	May 1, 1867	November 1, 1867	6	17 00	3 50	20 50	72 00	195 00	Sandford Acord	Do.
2	Stephen Allred	do	May 1, 1867	November 1, 1867	6	17 00	3 50	20 50	72 00	195 00	Stephen Allred	Do.
3	Samuel Frost	do	May 1, 1867	November 1, 1867	6	13 00	3 50	16 50	72 00	171 00	Samuel Frost	Do.
1	James Slater	Bugler	May 1, 1867	November 1, 1867	6	13 00	3 50	16 50	72 00	171 00	James Slater	Do.
2	Lewis P. Land	Private	May 1, 1867	November 1, 1867	6	13 00	3 50	16 50	72 00	171 00	Louis P. Land	Do.
3	James W. Monson	do	May 1, 1867	November 1, 1867	6	13 00	3 50	16 50	72 00	171 00	James W. Munsen	Do.
4	Frederick Neilson	do	May 1, 1867	November 1, 1867	6	13 00	3 50	16 50	72 00	171 00	Frederick Neilson	Do.
5	Neils Benson	do	May 1, 1867	November 1, 1867	6	13 00	3 50	16 50	72 00	171 00	Neils Benson	Do.
6	Mennus Lund	do	May 1, 1867	November 1, 1867	6	13 00	3 50	16 50	72 00	171 00	Marenus Lund	Do.
7	Nephi Allred	do	May 1, 1867	November 1, 1867	6	13 00	3 50	16 50	72 00	171 00	Nephi Allred	Do.
8	Elijah C. Behmann	do	May 1, 1867	November 1, 1867	6	13 00	3 50	16 50	72 00	171 00	Elijah C. Behmann	Do.
9	Sidney H. Allred	do	May 1, 1867	November 1, 1867	6	13 00	3 50	16 50	72 00	171 00	Sidney H. Allred	Do.
10	Green W. Allred	do	May 1, 1867	November 1, 1867	6	13 00	3 50	16 50	72 00	171 00	Green W. Allred	Do.
11	Sidney R. Allred	do	May 1, 1867	November 1, 1867	6	13 00	3 50	16 50	72 00	171 00	Sidney R. Allred	Do.
12	Isaac M. Allred	do	May 1, 1867	November 1, 1867	6	13 00	3 50	16 50	72 00	171 00	Isaac M. Allred	Do.
13	Andrew J. Allred	do	May 1, 1867	November 1, 1867	6	13 00	3 50	16 50	72 00	171 00	Andrew J. Allred	Do.
14	Isaac N. Allred	do	May 1, 1867	November 1, 1867	6	13 00	3 50	16 50	72 00	171 00	Isaac N. Allred	Do.
15	Carles Rofford	do	May 1, 1867	November 1, 1867	6	13 00	3 50	16 50	72 00	171 00	Charles Kofford	Do.
16	John Ellertson	do	May 1, 1867	November 1, 1867	6	13 00	3 50	16 50	72 00	171 00	John Ellertsen	Do.
17	Robert Blain	do	May 1, 1867	November 1, 1867	6	13 00	3 50	16 50	72 00	171 00	Robt. Blain	Do.
18	Robert Yensen	do	May 1, 1867	November 1, 1867	6	13 00	3 50	16 50	72 00	171 00	Robt. Yensen	Do.
19	Reuben W. Allred, jr.	do	May 1, 1867	November 1, 1867	6	13 00	3 50	16 50	72 00	171 00	Reuben W. Allred, jr.	Do.
20	Walter Barney, jr	do	May 1, 1867	November 1, 1867	6	13 00	3 50	16 50	72 00	171 00	Walter Barney, jr	Do.
21	John Neild	do	May 1, 1867	November 1, 1867	6	13 00	3 50	16 50	72 00	171 00	John Neild	Do.
22	Peter Justesen	do	May 1, 1867	November 1, 1867	6	13 00	3 50	16 50	72 00	171 00	Peter Justesen	Do.
23	David H. Allred	do	May 1, 1867	November 1, 1867	6	13 00	3 50	16 50	72 00	171 00	David H. Allred	Do.
24	John Thomas Lambert	do	May 1, 1867	November 1, 1867	6	13 00	3 50	16 50	72 00	171 00	John T. Lambert	Do.

25	John Frantzen	do	May 1, 1867	November 1, 1867	6	13 00	3 50	16 50	72 00	171 00	John Frantzen	Do.
26	Neils H. Borrison	do	May 1, 1867	November 1, 1867	6	13 00	3 50	16 50	72 00	171 00	Niels H. Borresen	Do.
27	Joseph Parley Allred	do	May 1, 1867	November 1, 1867	6	13 00	3 50	16 50	72 00	171 00	J. P. Allred	Do.
28	Joseph Tickle Ellis	do	May 1, 1867	November 1, 1867	6	13 01	3 50	16 50	72 00	171 00	Joseph T. Ellis	Do.
29	Christian G. Larsen	do	May 1, 1867	November 1, 1867	6	13 00	3 50	16 50	72 00	171 00	Christian G. Larsen	Do.
30	Nicolar Lund	do	May 1, 1867	November 1, 1867	6	13 00	3 50	16 50	72 10	171 00	Nickly Lund	Do.
31	Redick Redlen Allred	do	May 1, 1867	November 1, 1867	6	13 00	3 50	16 50	72 00	171 00	Redick R. Allred	Do.
32	Rastunus Justisen	do	May 1, 1867	November 1, 1867	6	13 00	3 50	16 50	72 00	171 00	Rastums Justisen	Do.
33	John Hitchcock	do	May 1, 1867	November 1, 1867	6	13 00	3 50	16 50	72 00	171 00	John Hitchcock	Do.
34	Cyrus H. Wheelock	do	May 1, 1867	November 1, 1867	6	13 00	3 50	16 50	72 00	171 00	C. H. Wheelock	Do.
35	Frederick Olsen	do	May 1, 1867	November 1, 1867	6	13 00	3 50	16 50	72 00	171 00	F. Olsen	Do.

This company was mustered into service at Springtown, Sanpete County, May 1, 1867, by Brigadier General Wm. B. Pace. They were in active service every day as patrol and scouting parties. They were also engaged in the battle at Thistle Creek Kanyon, under command of Lieutenant Colonel John L. Ivie; and also in the battle at the time of the Springtown raid, under command of Colonel R. M. Allred. They were in active service for the full time specified above, and mustered ont November 1, 1867.

I certify that the above account is correct.

H. B. CLAWSON,

Adjutant General Utah Territory Militia.

Pay-roll of Captain Frederick Neilson's company —— infantry, Utah Territory militia, employed in the suppression of Indian hostilities in Sanpete County, Utah Territory, from May 1, 1867, to November 1, 1867.

We, the undersigned, acknowledge to have received from James W. Cummings, paymaster Utah Territory militia, the sums set opposite to our names, in full payment for our services for the time specified.

Number	Names	Rank	Commencement	Expiration	Months	Pay per month	Monthly allowance for clothing	Total monthly pay and allowance	Total pay and allowance	Signatures	Witnesses
1	Frederick Neilsen	Captain	May 1, 1867	Nov. 1, 1867	6	$118 50		$118 50	$711 00	Frederick Neilsen	H. P. Miller
1	John Waldermasen	1st lieut	May 1, 1867	Nov. 1, 1867	6	108 50		108 50	651 00	John Waldemarson	Do.
1	Jens Neilson	2d lieut	May 1, 1867	Nov. 1, 1867	6	103 50		103 50	621 00	Jens Nilsen	Do.
2	Andrew Bextrom	do	May 1, 1867	Nov. 1, 1867	6	103 50		103 50	621 00	Andrew Bechstrom	Do.
3	Daniel Bextrom	do	May 1, 1867	Nov. 1, 1867	6	103 50		103 50	621 00	Daniel Bechstrom	Do.
4	Peter Syndergaard	do	May 1, 1867	Nov. 1, 1867	6	103 50		103 50	621 00	Peder Synder Juard	Do.
5	Antoine H. Lund	do	May 1, 1867	Nov. 1, 1867	6	103 50		103 50	621 00	Anthon H. Lund	Do.
1	August Wall	Sergeant	May 1, 1867	Nov. 1, 1867	6	$17 00	$3 50	20 50	123 00	August Wall	Do.
2	Hogan Anderson	do	May 1, 1867	Nov. 1, 1867	6	17 00	3 50	20 50	123 00	Hogan Anderson	Do.
3	Hans Simonsen	do	May 1, 1867	Nov. 1, 1867	6	17 00	3 50	20 50	123 00	Hans Simpson	Do.
4	James Yeser	do	May 1, 1867	Nov. 1, 1867	6	17 00	3 50	20 50	123 00	James Yesen	Do.
5	Joseph Larsen	do	May 1, 1867	Nov. 1, 1867	6	17 00	3 50	20 50	123 00	Joseph Larsen	Do.
1	John M. Bohn	Private	May 1, 1867	Nov. 1, 1867	6	13 00	3 50	16 50	99 00	John M. Bohn	Do.
2	Oscar Barton	do	May 1, 1867	Nov. 1, 1867	6	13 00	3 50	16 50	99 00	Oscar Barton	Do.
3	Ole S. Anderson	do	May 1, 1867	Nov. 1, 1867	6	13 00	3 50	16 50	99 00	Ole S. Andersen	Do.
4	Alma Zabrskie	do	May 1, 1867	Nov. 1, 1867	6	13 00	3 50	16 50	99 00	Alma Zabriskie	Do.
5	Jacob Rolfson	do	May 1, 1867	Nov. 1, 1867	6	13 00	3 50	16 50	99 00	Jacob Rolfsen	Do.
6	Samuel Allen	do	May 1, 1867	Nov. 1, 1867	6	13 00	3 50	16 50	99 00	Samuel Allen	Do.
7	Peter Madsen	do	May 1, 1867	Nov. 1, 1867	6	13 00	3 50	16 50	99 00	Peter Madsen	Do.
8	Soren Chri-tiansen	do	May 1, 1867	Nov. 1, 1867	6	13 00	3 50	16 50	99 00	Soren Christensen	Do.
9	Neils Pehi-on	do	May 1, 1867	Nov. 1, 1867	6	13 00	3 50	16 50	99 00	Neils Pehison	Do.
10	Carl Gu-taf Bjelka	do	May 1, 1867	Nov. 1, 1867	6	13 00	3 50	16 50	99 00	Carl Bjelke	Do.
11	Carl Johnson	do	May 1, 1867	Nov. 1, 1867	6	13 00	3 50	16 50	99 00	Carl Jonsen	Do.
12	Jens H. Frantwe-en	do	May 1, 1867	Nov. 1, 1867	6	13 00	3 50	16 50	99 00	Jens H. Trauutreen	Do.
13	Jens Christians-n, 2d	do	May 1, 1867	Nov. 1, 1867	6	13 00	3 50	16 50	99 00	Jens Christainsen, 2d	Do.
14	Frederick Fireelier	do	May 1, 1867	Nov. 1, 1867	6	13 00	3 50	16 50	99 00	Frederick Peiselier	Do.
15	Neils Rasmussen	do	May 1, 1867	Nov. 1, 1867	6	13 00	3 50	16 50	99 00	Niels Rasmussen	Do.
16	Oscar Josephsen	do	May 1, 1867	Nov. 1, 1867	6	13 00	3 50	16 50	99 00	Oscar Josephsen	Do.
17	Claudeau Anderson	do	May 1, 1867	Nov. 1, 1867	6	13 00	3 50	16 50	99 00	Claus Andersen	Do.
18	Soren Jacobsen	do	May 1, 1867	Nov. 1, 1867	6	13 00	3 50	16 50	99 00	Soren Jacobsen	Do.
19	Jens Christian Jemsen	do	May 1, 1867	Nov. 1, 1867	6	13 00	3 50	16 50	99 00	Yena C. Yemsen	Do.
20	Sejor Jensen	do	May 1, 1867	Nov. 1, 1867	6	13 00	3 50	16 50	99 00	Seler Jensen	Do.

No.	Name		Mustered in	Mustered out		$13 00	$3 50	$16 50	$99 00	Name	
21	Frederick Neilson, 2d	do	May 1, 1867	Nov. 1, 1867	6	13 00	3 50	16 50	99 00	Frederick Nielson, 2	Do.
22	Jens Jensen	do	May 1, 1867	Nov. 1, 1867	6	13 00	3 50	16 50	99 00	Jens Jensen	Do.
23	Johannes Knutson	do	May 1, 1867	Nov. 1, 1867	6	13 00	3 50	16 50	99 00	Johannes Knutsen	Do.
24	Magnus Rosenberg	do	May 1, 1867	Nov. 1, 1867	6	13 00	3 50	16 50	99 00	Magnus Rosenberg	Do.
25	Andrew Neilson	do	May 1, 1867	Nov. 1, 1867	6	13 00	3 50	16 50	99 00	Andrew Neilsen	Do.
26	Christian Christiansen	do	May 1, 1867	Nov. 1, 1867	6	13 00	3 50	16 20	99 00	Christian Christiansen	Do.
27	Morani Seely	do	May 1, 1867	Nov. 1, 1867	6	13 00	3 50	16 50	99 00	Morony Seely	Do.
28	Ole Neilsen	do	May 1, 1867	Nov. 1, 1867	6	13 00	3 50	16 50	99 00	Ole Neilsen	Do.
29	Peter Larsen	do	May 1, 1867	Nov. 1, 1867	6	13 00	3 50	16 20	99 00	Peter Larsen	Do.
30	Yoren Larsen	do	May 1, 1867	Nov. 1, 1867	6	13 00	3 50	16 50	99 00	Yoren Larsen	Do.
31	Hans Christian Neilsen	do	May 1, 1867	Nov. 1, 1867	6	13 00	3 50	16 50	99 00	Hans Christian Neilsen	Do.
32	John Walce	do	May 1, 1867	Nov. 1, 1867	6	13 00	3 50	16 50	99 00	John Walce	Do.
33	George Sinniforth	do	May 1, 1867	Nov. 1, 1867	6	13 00	3 50	16 50	99 03	George Stennefort	Do.
34	Andrew Berg	do	May 1, 1867	Nov. 1, 1867	6	13 00	3 50	16 50	99 00	Andru Berg	Do.
35	Frederick Peter Neilson	do	May 1, 1867	Nov. 1, 1867	6	13 00	3 50	16 50	99 00	Frederek P. Nielsen	Do.
36	Hans Hansen	do	May 1, 1867	Nov. 1, 1867	6	13 00	3 50	16 50	99 00	Hans Hansen	Do.
37	Peter Rasmussen	do	May 1, 1867	Nov. 1, 1867	6	13 00	3 50	16 50	99 00	Peter Rasmussen	Do.
38	Olof Bohn	do	May 1, 1867	Nov. 1, 1867	6	13 00	3 50	16 50	99 00	Olof Bohn	Do.
39	Nephi Seely	do	May 1, 1867	Nov. 1, 1867	6	13 00	3 50	16 50	99 00	Nephi Seely	Do.
40	Hyrum Wilcox	do	May 1, 1867	Nov. 1, 1867	6	13 00	3 50	16 50	99 00	Hyrum Vilcox	Do.
41	Andrew Rolfe	do	May 1, 1867	Nov. 1, 1867	6	13 00	3 50	16 50	99 00	Andrew Rolf	Do.
42	Bennet Larsen	do	May 1, 1867	Nov. 1, 1867	6	13 00	3 50	16 50	99 00	Bennet Larsen	Do.
43	Samuel Constantine	do	May 1, 1867	Nov. 1, 1867	6	13 00	3 50	16 50	99 00	Samuel Constantine	Do.
44	Sophus Johnson	do	May 1, 1867	Nov. 1, 1867	6	13 00	3 50	16 50	99 00	Sophus Johnson	Do.
45	Edmund Johnson	do	May 1, 1867	Nov. 1, 1867	6	13 00	3 50	16 50	99 00	Edmon Johson	Do.
46	George Fransem	do	May 1, 1867	Nov. 1, 1867	6	13 00	3 50	16 50	99 00	George Fransem	Do.
47	John Carter	do	May 1, 1867	Nov. 1, 1867	6	13 00	3 50	16 50	99 00	John Carter	Do.
48	Neils Christiansen	do	May 1, 1867	Nov. 2, 1867	6	13 00	3 50	16 50	99 00	Niels Christianson	Do.
49	Thomas West	do	May 1, 1867	Nov. 1, 1867	6	13 00	3 50	16 50	99 00	Tomas West	Do.
50	Hyram Coats	do	May 1, 1867	Nov. 1, 1867	6	13 00	3 50	16 50	99 00	Hyram Coats	Do.
51	William Rowe	do	May 1, 1867	Nov. 1, 1867	6	13 00	3 50	16 50	99 00	William Howe	Do.
52	Duncan McArthur	do	May 1, 1867	Nov. 1, 1867	6	13 00	3 50	16 50	99 00	Duncan McArthur	Do.

This company was mustered into service at Mount Pleasant, Sanpete County, May 1, 1867, by Brigadier General Wm. B. Pace, and by him assigned to duty in vicinity of same settlement; they were in active service every day as guards and patrols on the mountains and passes, until mustered out, November 1, 1867.

I certify that the above account is correct.

H. B. CLAWSON,
Adjutant General Utah Territory Militia.

Pay-roll of Captain Erastus Curtis's company ——— cavalry, Utah Territory militia, employed in the suppression of Indian hostilities in Sanpete County, Utah Territory, from May 1, 1867, to November 1, 1867.

We, the undersigned, acknowledge to have received from James W. Cummings, paymaster Utah Territory militia, the sums set opposite to our names, in full payment for our services for the time specified.

Number	Names	Rank	Commencement	Expiration	Months	Pay per month	Monthly allowance for clothing	Total monthly pay and allowance	40 cts. per day for use and risk of horse and horse equipment	Total pay and allowance	Signatures	Witnesses
1	Erastus Curtis	Captain	May 1, 1867	November 1, 1867	6			$129 50	$72 00	$849 00	Erastus Curtis	Jabez Faux.
1	Jens C. Neilson	1st lieut	May 1, 1867	November 1, 1867	6			112 83	72 00	748 98	Jens C. Neilson	Do.
2	John Reese	2d lieut	May 1, 1867	November 1, 1867	6			112 83	72 00	748 98	John Reese, his X mark	Do.
3	Lars Svensen	do	May 1, 1867	November 1, 1867	6			112 83	72 00	748 98	Lars Svensen	Do.
3	Parley Draper	do	May 1, 1867	November 1, 1867	6			112 83	72 00	748 98	Parley Draper	Do.
3	Moroni Bradley	Sergeant	May 1, 1867	November 1, 1867	6	$17 00	$3 50	20 50	72 00	195 00	Moroni Bradley	Do.
3	John N. Larsen	do	May 1, 1867	November 1, 1867	6	17 00	3 50	20 50	72 00	195 00	John N. Larson	Do.
3	William Pridmore	do	May 1, 1867	November 1, 1867	6	17 00	3 50	20 50	72 00	195 00	William Pridmore	Do.
1	George Simpson	Bugler	May 1, 1867	November 1, 1867	6	13 00	3 50	16 50	72 00	171 00	George Simpson	Do.
2	James Jorgensen	Private	May 1, 1867	November 1, 1867	6	13 00	3 50	16 50	72 00	171 00	James Jorgesen	Do.
3	Peter Christiansen	do	May 1, 1867	November 1, 1867	6	13 00	3 50	16 50	72 00	171 00	Petter Christiansen	Do.
4	Peter Anderson	do	May 1, 1867	November 1, 1867	6	13 00	3 50	16 50	72 00	171 00	Peter Anderson	Do.
5	Soren Christiansen	do	May 1, 1867	November 1, 1867	6	13 00	3 50	16 50	72 00	171 00	Soren Christisen	Do.
6	Thomas Blackham	do	May 1, 1867	November 1, 1867	6	13 00	3 50	16 50	72 00	171 00	Thomas Blackham	Do.
7	John Olsen	do	May 1, 1867	November 1, 1867	6	13 00	3 50	16 50	72 00	171 00	John Olsen	Do.
8	George Parker	do	May 1, 1867	November 1, 1867	6	13 00	3 50	16 50	72 00	171 00	George Parker	Do.
9	Amos Bradley	do	May 1, 1867	November 1, 1867	6	13 00	3 50	16 50	72 00	171 00	Amos Bradley	Do.
10	Henry Jolley	do	May 1, 1867	November 1, 1867	6	13 00	3 50	16 50	72 00	171 00	Henry Jolley	Do.
11	Samuel Rhodes	do	May 1, 1867	November 1, 1867	6	13 00	3 50	16 50	72 00	171 00	Samuel Rhodes	Do.
12	Andrew Jensen	do	May 1, 1867	November 1, 1867	6	13 00	3 50	16 50	72 00	171 00	Andrew Jensen	Do.
13	Andreas Jensen	do	May 1, 1867	November 1, 1867	6	13 00	3 50	16 50	72 00	171 00	Andreas Jensen	Do.
14	Peter C. Anderson	do	May 1, 1867	November 1, 1867	6	13 00	3 50	16 50	72 00	171 00	P-ter C. Anderson	Do.
15	Samuel Martin	do	May 1, 1867	November 1, 1867	6	13 00	3 50	16 50	72 00	171 00	Samuel Martin	Do.
16	Lars Jorgensen	do	May 1, 1867	November 1, 1867	6	13 00	3 50	16 50	72 00	171 00	Lars Jorgensen	Do.
17	Andrew Anderson	do	May 1, 1867	November 1, 1867	6	13 00	3 50	16 50	72 00	171 00	Andrew Anderson	Do.
18	Andrew C. Nelson	do	May 1, 1867	November 1, 1867	6	13 00	3 50	16 50	72 00	171 00	Andr-w C. Nelsen	Do.
19	Mons Monsen	do	May 1, 1867	November 1, 1867	6	13 00	3 50	16 50	72 00	171 00	Mons Monsen	Do.
20	David Bailey	do	May 1, 1867	November 1, 1867	6	13 40	3 50	16 50	72 00	111 00	David Bailey	Do.
21	Andrew C. Groldersen	do	May 1, 1867	November 1, 1867	6	13 00	3 50	16 50	72 00	171 00	Andrew C. Groldersen	Do.
22	Niels Christiansen	do	May 1, 1867	November 1, 1867	6	13 00	3 50	16 50	72 01	171 00	Nells Christiansen	Do.
23	Jens Jonsen	do	May 1, 1867	November 1, 1867	6	13 00	3 50	16 50	72 00	171 00	Jens Jonsen	Do.
24	William Hatch	do	May 1, 1867	November 1, 1867	6	13 00	3 50	16 50	72 00	171 00	William Hatch	Do.
	Christian P. Neilson	do	May 1, 1867	November 1, 1867	6	13 00	3 50	16 50	72 00	171 00	Christian P. Nelson	Do.

25	Jens M. Jorgensen	do	May 1, 1867	November 1, 1867	6	13 00	3 50	16 50	72 00	171 00	Jens M. Jorgensen	Do.
26	William Davis	do	May 1, 1867	November 1, 1867	6	13 00	3 50	16 50	72 00	171 00	William Davis	Do.
27	Jacob Cloward	do	May 1, 1867	November 1, 1867	6	13 00	3 50	16 50	72 00	171 00	Jacob Cloward	Do.
28	Joseph Jolley	do	May 1, 1867	November 1, 1867	6	13 00	3 50	16 50	72 00	171 00	Joseph Jolley	Do.
29	Lewis Hatch	do	May 1, 1867	November 1, 1867	6	13 00	3 50	16 50	72 00	171 00	Lewis Hatch	Do.

This company was mustered into service at Moroni, Sanpete County, May 1, 1867, by Brigadier General Wm. B. Pace, and assigned to duty by him as scouts and patrols in the mountains and passes. They were engaged every day. They were also in the battle at the time of the raid on Fountain Green, and also at the battle in Springtown. They were in active service for the full time specified above, and were mustered out November 1, 1867.

I certify that the above account is correct.

H. B. CLAWSON,
Adjutant General Utah Territory Militia.

Pay-roll of Captain John Tidwell, sen'r, company —— infantry, Utah Territory militia, employed in the suppression of Indian hostilities in Sanpete County, Utah Territory, from May 1, 1867, to November 1, 1867.

We, the undersigned, acknowledge to have received from James W. Cummings, paymaster Utah Territory militia, the sums set opposite to our names, in full payment for our services for the time specified.

Number.	Names.	Rank.	Period of service. Commencement.	Expiration.	Months.	Pay per month.	Monthly allowance for clothing.	Total monthly pay and allowance.	Total pay and allowance.	Signatures.	Witness.
1	John Tidwell, sen'r	Captain	May 1, 1867	Nov. 1, 1867	6			$118 50	$711 00	John Tidwell	H. P. Miller.
2	Garafret C. Rowe	1st lieutenant	May 1, 1867	Nov. 1, 1867	6			106 50	651 00	C. C. Rowe	Do.
3	Christian Hansen	2d lieutenant	May 1, 1867	Nov. 1, 1867	6			103 50	621 00	Christen Hansen	Do.
4	Michael Rasmussen	do	May 1, 1867	Nov. 1, 1867	6			103 50	621 00	Michel Rasmusen	Do.
5	John Barton	do	May 1, 1867	Nov. 1, 1867	6			103 50	621 00	John Barton	Do.
6	Jes Jessen	do	May 1, 1867	Nov. 1, 1867	6			103 50	621 00	Jes Jessen	Do.
7	Christopher Johnson	do	May 1, 1867	Nov. 1, 1867	6			103 50	621 00	Christopher Johnsen	Do.
8	Peter Anderson	Sergeant	May 1, 1867	Nov. 1, 1867	6	$17 00	$3 50	20 50	123 00	Peter Andersen	Do.
9	Christian Broderson	do	May 1, 1867	Nov. 1, 1867	6	17 00	3 50	20 50	123 00	Christian Brodersen	Do.
10	Amasa Scovil	do	May 1, 1867	Nov. 1, 1867	6	17 00	3 50	20 50	123 00	Amasa Scovil	Do.
11	Hans C. Davidson	do	May 1, 1867	Nov. 1, 1867	6	17 00	3 50	20 50	123 00	Hans C. Davidsen	Do.
12	Rasmus Mikelson	do	May 1, 1867	Nov. 1, 1867	6	17 00	3 50	20 50	123 00	R. Mickelsen	Do.
13	William N. Rowe	do	May 1, 1867	Nov. 1, 1867	6	17 00	3 50	20 50	123 00	William N. Rowe	Do.
14	George Miller	Private	May 1, 1867	Nov. 1, 1867	6	13 00	3 50	16 50	99 00	James H. Tidwell	Do.
15	James H. Tidwell	do	May 1, 1867	Nov. 1, 1867	6	13 00	3 50	16 50	99 00	Geo. Miller, his + mark	Do.
16	James Anderson	do	May 1, 1867	Nov. 1, 1867	6	13 00	3 50	16 50	99 00	James Anderson	Do.
17	Peter Yensen	do	May 1, 1867	Nov. 1, 1867	6	13 00	3 50	16 50	99 00	Peter Jensen	Do.
18	William Lake	do	May 1, 1867	Nov. 1, 1867	6	13 00	3 50	16 50	99 00	William Lake	Do.
19	Jens C. Neilsen	do	May 1, 1867	Nov. 1, 1867	6	13 00	3 50	16 50	99 00	Jens C. Neilsen	Do.
20	Nathan Staker	do	May 1, 1867	Nov. 1, 1867	6	13 00	3 50	16 50	99 00	Nathan Staker	Do.
21	Henning P. Peil	do	May 1, 1867	Nov. 1, 1867	6	13 00	3 50	16 50	99 00	H. P. Peel, his + mark	Do.
22	Peter Borg	do	May 1, 1867	Nov. 1, 1867	6	13 00	3 50	16 50	99 00	Peter Borg	Do.
23	Michael Christiansen	do	May 1, 1867	Nov. 1, 1867	6	13 00	3 50	16 50	99 00	Mickel Christensen, his + mark	Do.
24	Anders Linberg	do	May 1, 1867	Nov. 1, 1867	6	13 00	3 50	16 50	99 00	Andri Linberg	Do.
25	Gunder Enksen	do	May 1, 1867	Nov. 1, 1867	6	13 00	3 50	16 50	99 00	Gunder Encksen	Do.
26	Peter N. Oman	do	May 1, 1867	Nov. 1, 1867	6	13 00	3 50	16 50	99 00	Peter N. Oman	Do.
27	Gergen Hansen	do	May 1, 1867	Nov. 1, 1867	6	13 00	3 50	16 50	99 00	Jorgen Hansen	Do.
28	Thomas C. Jensen	do	May 1, 1867	Nov. 1, 1867	6	13 00	3 50	16 50	99 00	Thomas C. Jensen	Do.
29	James K. McCleanhan	do	May 1, 1867	Nov. 1, 1867	6	13 00	3 50	16 50	99 00	Jas. K. Jensen	Do.
30	Christian Larsen	do	May 1, 1867	Nov. 1, 1867	6	13 00	3 50	16 50	99 00	Christer Larsen	Do.
31	Neils Christian Neilsen	do	May 1, 1867	Nov. 1, 1867	6	13 00	3 50	16 50	99 00	N. C. Nielsen.	Do.

20	James B. Porter	do.	May 1, 1867	Nov. 1, 1867	6	13 00	3 50	16 50	99 00	Jas. B. Porter	Do.
21	Job Ephriam Green	do.	May 1, 1867	Nov. 1, 1867	6	13 00	3 50	16 50	99 00	Job E. Green	Do.
22	Daniel Page	do.	May 1, 1867	Nov. 1, 1867	6	13 00	3 50	16 50	99 00	Daniel Page	Do.
23	James Meyrick	do.	May 1, 1867	Nov. 1, 1867	6	13 00	3 50	16 50	99 00	James Meyrick	Do.
24	John Trescot	do.	May 1, 1867	Nov. 1, 1867	6	13 00	3 51	16 50	99 00	John Trescot	Do.
25	Asmus Waldermarson	do.	May 1, 1867	Nov. 1, 1867	6	13 00	3 50	16 50	99 00	Asmus Wald-marsen	Do.
26	John Tidwell, Jr.	do.	May 1, 1867	Nov. 1, 1867	6	13 00	3 50	16 50	99 00	John Tidwell, jr.	Do.
27	Justin W. Seely	do.	May 1, 1867	Nov. 1, 1867	6	13 00	3 50	16 50	99 00	Justus W. Seely	Do.
28	Ole Jessen	do.	May 1, 1867	Nov. 1, 1867	6	13 00	3 50	16 50	99 00	Ole Jessen	Do.
29	Ebbe Jessen	do.	May 1, 1867	Nov. 1, 1867	6	13 00	3 50	16 50	99 00	Ebbe Jessen	Do.
30	Joseph Anderson	do.	May 1, 1867	Nov. 1, 1867	6	13 00	3 50	16 50	99 00	Joseph Anderson	Do.
31	Peter Larsen	do.	May 1, 1867	Nov. 1, 1867	6	13 00	3 50	16 50	99 00	Peter Larsen	Do.
32	Neils Wittegreen	do.	May 1, 1867	Nov. 1, 1867	6	13 00	3 51	16 50	99 00	Nicls Wildegreen, his + mark.	Do.
33	Andus Petersen	do.	May 1, 1867	Nov. 1, 1867	6	13 00	3 50	16 50	99 00	Andrew Petersen	Do.
34	Ole Christian Jensen	do.	May 1, 1867	Nov. 1, 1867	6	13 00	3 50	16 50	99 00	Ole C. Jensen	Do.
35	Anders Braunsted	do.	May 1, 1867	Nov. 1, 1867	6	13 00	3 50	16 50	99 00	Anders Braunstad	Do.
36	Olof Lofgren	Do.	May 1, 1867	Nov. 1, 1867	6	13 00	3 50	16 50	99 03	Olof Lofgren	Do.
37	Ad olph Fredericksen	do.	May 1, 1867	Nov. 1, 1867	6	13 03	3 50	16 50	99 00	Adolph Fredericksen	Do.
38	Washington P. McArthur	do.	May 1, 1867	Nov. 1, 1867	6	13 00	3 50	16 50	99 00	W. P. McArthur.	Do.
39	Lars Jorgensen	do.	May 1, 1867	Nov. 1, 1867	6	13 00	3 50	16 51	99 00	Lars Jorgensen	Do.
40	John Couts	do.	May 1, 1867	Nov. 1, 1867	6	13 00	3 50	16 50	99 00	John Couts	Do.
41	Peter Petterson	do.	May 1, 1867	Nov. 1, 1867	6	13 00	3 50	16 50	99 00	Petter Pettersen	Do.
42	Mauritz Peterson	do.	May 1, 1867	Nov. 1, 1867	6	13 00	3 50	16 50	99 00	Morets Petersen	Do.
43	James Riste	do.	May 1, 1867	Nov. 1, 1867	6	13 00	3 50	16 50	99 00	James Riste	Do.
44	Neils Christian Carlsen	do.	May 1, 1867	Nov. 1, 1867	6	13 00	3 50	16 50	99 00	Nels C. Carlsen	Do.
45	John Winkleman	do.	May 1, 1867	Nov. 1, 1867	6	13 00	3 50	16 50	99 00	John Winkleman	Do.
46	William Marsh Farnsworth	do.	May 1, 1867	Nov. 1, 1867	6	13 00	3 50	16 53	99 00	Wm. M. Farnsworth	Do.

This company was mustered into service at Mount Pleasant, Sanpete County, May 1, 1867, by Brigadier General W. B. Pace, and by him assigned to duty in the vicinity of said settlement. They were in active service every day as guards and patrols in the mountains and passes until mustered out, November 1, 1867.

I certify that the above account is correct.

H. B. CLAWSON,
Adjutant General Utah Territory Militia.

Pay-roll of Captain Christian A. Madsen's company —— cavalry, Utah Territory militia, employed in the suppression of Indian hostilities in Sanpete County, from May 1, 1867, to November 1, 1867.

We, the undersigned, acknowledge to have received from James W. Cummings, paymaster Utah Territory militia, the sums set opposite to our names, in full payment for our services for the time specified.

Number.	Names.	Rank.	Commencement.	Expiration.	Months.	Pay per month.	Monthly allowance for clothing.	Total monthly pay and allowance.	40 cts. per day for use and risk of horse and horse equipment.	Total pay and allowance.	Signatures.	Witnesses.
1	Christian A. Madsen	Captain	May 1, 1867	Nov. 1, 1867	6	$17 00	$3 50	$129 50	$72 00	$819 00	Christian A. Madsen	A. E. Merriam.
1	Axel Inarsen	1st lieut.	May 1, 1867	Nov. 1, 1867	6	17 00	3 50	112 83	72 00	748 98	Ax-l Inersen	Do.
2	Oscar Kearns	2d lieut.	May 1, 1867	Nov. 1, 1867	6		3 50	112 83	72 00	748 98	Oscar Kearns	Do.
2	Elias Pearson	do.	May 1, 1867	Nov. 1, 1867	6		3 50	112 83	72 00	748 98	Elias Pearson	Do.
3	Peter Telle	do.	May 1, 1867	Nov. 1, 1867	6		3 50	112 83	72 00	748 98	Peter Telle	Do.
3	Lorenzo Dastrop	Sergeant	May 1, 1867	Nov. 1, 1867	6	$17 00	3 50	20 50	72 00	195 00	Lorenzo Dastruf	Do.
3	Christian Sorensen	do.	May 1, 1867	Nov. 1, 1867	6	17 00	3 50	20 50	72 00	195 00	Christian Sorensen	Do.
1	Frederick Ludvicksen	do.	May 1, 1867	Nov. 1, 1867	6		3 50	20 50	72 00	195 00	Fredrick Ludvigson	Do.
1	George Madsen	Bugler	May 1, 1867	Nov. 1, 1867	6	13 00	3 50	16 50	72 00	171 00	George Madsen	Do.
2	Hans Lorenzen	Private	May 1, 1867	Nov. 1, 1867	6	13 00	3 50	16 50	72 00	171 00	Hans Lorentzen	Do.
3	Simon Hansen	do.	May 1, 1867	Nov. 1, 1867	6	13 00	3 50	16 50	72 00	171 00	Simon Hansen	Do.
3	Neils C. Christiansen	do.	May 1, 1867	Nov. 1, 1867	6	13 00	3 50	16 50	72 00	171 00	Niels C. Christenson	Do.
4	Ole Jensen	do.	May 1, 1867	Nov. 1, 1867	6	13 00	3 50	16 50	72 00	171 00	Louns Christiansen	Do.
5	Soren Christiansen	do.	May 1, 1867	Nov. 1, 1867	6	13 00	3 50	16 50	72 00	171 00	Sylvester Grigble	Do.
6	Sylvester Gribble	do.	May 1, 1867	Nov. 1, 1867	6	13 00	3 50	16 50	72 00	171 00	Antony Christensen	Do.
7	Antony Christiansen	do.	May 1, 1867	Nov. 1, 1867	6	13 00	3 50	16 50	72 00	171 00	Johan Peterson	Do.
8	Johan Peterson	do.	May 1, 1867	Nov. 1, 1867	6	13 00	3 50	16 50	72 00	171 00	Tom. s P. Peterson	Do.
9	Thomas P. Peterson	do.	May 1, 1867	Nov. 1, 1867	6	13 00	3 50	16 50	72 00	171 00	Jens Jewson	Do.
11	Dan Perkins	do.	May 1, 1867	Nov. 1, 1867	6	13 00	3 50	16 50	72 00	171 00	Dan Perkins	Do.
12	John Bra-hard	do.	May 1, 1867	Nov. 1, 1867	6	13 00	3 50	16 50	72 00	171 00	John Brushard	Do.
13	Peter F. Rasmussen	do.	May 1, 1867	Nov. 1, 1867	6	13 00	3 50	16 50	72 00	171 00	Peter F. Rasumasen	Do.
14	Andrew Winge	do.	May 1, 1867	Nov. 1, 1867	6	13 00	3 50	16 50	72 00	171 03	Andruw Vinge	Do.
15	George Brunn	do.	May 1, 1867	Nov. 1, 1867	6	13 00	3 50	16 50	72 00	171 00	George Benns	Do.
16	Hans Yergensen	do.	May 1, 1867	Nov. 1, 1867	6	13 00	3 50	16 50	72 00	171 00	Hans Yergesen	Do.
17	Joseph Graham	do.	May 1, 1867	Nov. 1, 1867	6	13 00	3 50	16 50	72 00	171 00	Joseph Graham	Do.
18	Thomas Skofield	do.	May 1, 1867	Nov. 1, 1867	6	13 00	3 50	16 50	72 00	171 00	Thomas Scofield	Do.
19	Lars Soren-en	do.	May 1, 1867	Nov. 1, 1867	6	13 00	3 50	16 50	72 00	171 00	Lars Sorensen	Do.
20	Hans C. Hansen	do.	May 1, 1867	Nov. 1, 1867	6	13 00	3 50	16 50	72 00	171 00	Haue C. Hansen	Do.
21	Lars Madsen	do.	May 1, 1867	Nov. 1, 1867	6	13 00	3 50	16 50	72 00	171 00	Lars Madsen	Do.
22	Ole Acreland	do.	May 1, 1867	Nov. 1, 1867	6	13 00	3 50	16 50	72 00	171 03	Ch. Akerlund	Do.
23	Hans Larsen	do.	May 1, 1867	Nov. 1, 1867	6	13 00	3 50	16 50	72 00	171 00	Haus Larsen	Do.

| 24 | Ruben Stevens | do | May 1, 1867 | Nov. 1, 1867 | 6 | 13 00 | 3 50 | 16 50 | 72 00 | 171 00 | Ruben Stevens | Do. |
| 25 | John Sorensen | do | May 1, 1867 | Nov. 1, 1867 | 6 | 13 00 | 3 50 | 16 50 | 72 00 | 171 00 | John Sorensen | Do. |

This company was mustered into service at Fort Gunnison, Sanpete County, May 1, 1867, by Brigadier General William B. Pace, and assigned to duty by him in the Sevier Valley. They were in active service as scouts and patrols in the mountains and passes, and were actively engaged every day for the time specified above, and mustered out November 1, 1867.

I certify that the above account is correct.

H. B. CLAWSON,
Adjutant General Utah Territory Militia.

Pay-roll of Captain James Martin Allred's company —— infantry, Utah Territory militia, employed in the suppression of Indian hostilities in Sanpete County, Utah Territory, from May 1, 1867, to November 1, 1867.

We, the undersigned, acknowledge to have received from James W. Cummings, paymaster Utah Territory militia, the sums set opposite to our names in full payment for our services for the time specified.

Number.	Names.	Rank.	Commencement.	Expiration.	Months.	Pay per month.	Monthly allowance for clothing.	Total monthly pay and allowance.	Total pay and allowance.	Signatures.	Witness.
1	James Martin Allred	Captain	May 1, 1867	Nov. 1, 1867	6	$17 00	$3 50	$118 50	$711 00	James M. Allread	Henry W. Sanderson.
2	Philip Hurst	1st lieutenant	May 1, 1867	Nov. 1, 1867	6	17 00	3 50	108 50	651 00	Philip Hurst	Do.
3	John Alma Vance	2d lieutenant	May 1, 1867	Nov. 1, 1867	6	17 00	3 50	103 50	621 00	John A. Vance	Do.
	Archibald Anderson	do	May 1, 1867	Nov. 1, 1867	6	17 00	3 50	103 50	621 00	Arch'd Anderson	Do.
	Andrew Nelson	do	May 1, 1867	Nov. 1, 1867	6	17 00	3 50	103 50	621 00	Andrew Nielson	Do.
4	Otis L. Terry	do	May 1, 1867	Nov. 1, 1867	6	17 00	3 50	103 50	621 00	Otis L. Terry	Do.
5	James Vance	Sergeant	May 1, 1867	Nov. 1, 1867	6	$17 00	3 50	20 50	123 00	James Vance	Do.
6	John Anderson	do	May 1, 1867	Nov. 1, 1867	6	17 00	3 50	20 50	123 00	John Anderson	Do.
7	Orvill Cox	do	May 1, 1867	Nov. 1, 1867	6	17 00	3 50	20 50	123 00	Orville Cox	Do.
	Lindsey A. Brady	do	May 1, 1867	Nov. 1, 1867	6	17 00	3 50	20 50	123 00	Lindsey A. Brady	Do.
	Samuel Gudmunsen	do	May 1, 1867	Nov. 1, 1867	6	17 00	3 50	20 50	123 00	Samuel Gudmunson	Do.
8	James Stewart	Private	May 1, 1867	Nov. 1, 1867	6	13 00	3 50	16 50	99 00	James Stewart	Do.
9	Willard Vance	do	May 1, 1867	Nov. 1, 1867	6	13 00	3 50	16 50	99 00	Willard Vance, his + mark	Do.
	William Vance	do	May 1, 1867	Nov. 1, 1867	6	13 00	3 50	16 50	98 00	William Vance, his + mark	Do.
	Neils Larsen	do	May 1, 1867	Nov. 1, 1867	6	13 00	3 50	16 50	99 00	Nick Larsen	Do.
10	Joseph Garlick	do	May 1, 1867	Nov. 1, 1867	6	13 00	3 50	16 50	99 00	Joseph Garlick his + mark	Do.
	Andrew Petersen	do	May 2, 1867	Nov. 1, 1867	6	13 00	3 50	16 50	99 00	Andrew Peterson	Do.
	Isaac Newton Wilson	do	May 1, 1867	Nov. 1, 1867	6	13 00	3 50	16 50	99 00	J. N. Wilson	Do.
11	William Christiansen	do	May 1, 1867	Nov. 1, 1867	6	13 00	3 50	16 50	99 00	William Christenson	Do.
12	Elias Willes Howell	do	May 1, 1867	Nov. 1, 1867	6	13 00	3 50	16 50	99 00	E. W. Howell	Do.
13	Richard Brown	do	May 1, 1867	Nov. 1, 1867	6	13 00	3 50	16 50	99 00	Richard Brown	Do.
14	Charles Green	do	May 1, 1867	Nov. 1, 1867	6	13 00	3 50	16 50	99 00	Charles Green	Do.
15	Ranson Stevens	do	May 1, 1867	Nov. 1, 1867	6	13 00	3 50	16 50	99 00	R. A. Stevens	Do.
	Franklin Wilson	do	May 1, 1867	Nov. 1, 1867	6	13 00	3 50	16 50	99 00	F. Wilson	Do.
16	George Graham	do	May 1, 1867	Nov. 1, 1867	6	13 00	3 50	16 50	99 00	George Graham	Do.
17	John Graham	do	May 1, 1867	Nov. 1, 1867	6	13 00	3 50	16 50	99 00	John Graham	Do.
18	James Pritchett	do	May 1, 1867	Nov. 1, 1867	6	13 00	3 50	16 50	99 00	James Pritchett	Do.
19	Wesley Mower	do	May 1, 1867	Nov. 1, 1867	6	13 00	3 50	16 50	99 10	Wesley Mower	Do.
20	Henry Fowler	do	May 1, 1867	Nov. 1, 1867	6	13 00	3 50	16 50	99 00	Henry Fowler	Do.
	John Pritchett	do	May 1, 1867	Nov. 1, 1867	6	13 00	3 50	16 50	99 00	John Pritchett, his + mark	Do.
21	Peter Neils Hauson	do	May 1, 1867	Nov. 1, 1867	6	13 00	3 50	16 50	99 00	Fedor N. Hanson	Do.
22	Lars Larsen	do	May 1, 1867	Nov. 1, 1867	6	13 00	3 50	16 50	99 00	Lars Larson, his + mark	Do.

No.	Name		Mustered in	Mustered out						Name	
23	Charles Cruzier	do	May 1, 1867	Nov. 1, 1867	6	13 00	3 50	16 50	99 00	C. Cruse	Do.
24	Warren Brady	do	May 1, 1867	Nov. 1, 1867	6	13 00	3 50	16 50	99 00	Warren P. Brady	Do.
25	Elias Cox	do	May 1, 1867	Nov. 1, 1867	6	13 00	3 50	16 50	99 00	Elias Cox	Do.
26	Charles Tucker	do	May 1, 1867	Nov. 1, 1867	6	13 00	3 50	16 50	99 00	Charles Tucker	Do.
27	Andrew Christenson	do	May 1, 1867	Nov. 1, 1867	6	13 00	3 50	16 50	99 00	Andrew Christensen	Do.
28	Justus Jordon	do	May 1, 1867	Nov. 1, 1867	6	13 00	3 50	16 50	99 00	Justus Jason	Do.
29	Albert Guymun	do	May 1, 1867	Nov. 1, 1867	6	13 00	3 50	16 50	99 00	Albert Guynon	Do.
30	John Cox, sr	do	May 1, 1867	Nov. 1, 1867	6	13 00	3 50	16 50	99 00	John Cox, sr	Do.
31	Isaac Young Vance	do	May 1, 1867	Nov. 1, 1867	6	13 00	3 50	16 50	99 00	J. Y. Vance	Do.
32	Richard Graham	do	May 1, 1867	Nov. 1, 1867	6	13 00	3 50	16 50	99 00	Richard Graham	Do.
33	Henry Mower	do	May 1, 1867	Nov. 1, 1867	6	13 00	3 50	16 50	99 00	Henry Mower, Jr	Do.
34	John Nordstrom	do	May 1, 1867	Nov. 1, 1867	6	13 00	3 50	16 50	99 00	Johan Nordstrom	Do.
35	Nathaniel Stewart	do	May 1, 1867	Nov. 1, 1867	6	13 00	3 50	16 50	99 00	Peeth Nanlforss	Do.
36	Peter Nordfoss	do	May 1, 1867	Nov. 1, 1867	6	13 00	3 50	16 50	99 00	Naten Stewart	Do.
37	Archibald Anderson, sr	do	May 1, 1867	Nov. 1, 1867	6	13 00	3 50	16 50	99 00	Archibald Anderson, sr	Do.
38	Lars Johanson	do	May 1, 1867	Nov. 1, 1867	6	13 00	3 50	16 50	99 00	Lars Johanson	Do.
39	Peter Halversen	do	May 1, 1867	Nov. 1, 1867	6	13 00	3 50	16 50	99 00	Peter Halvorsen, his + mark	Do.
40	James Pritchett, sr	do	May 1, 1867	Nov. 1, 1867	6	13 00	3 50	16 50	99 00	James Pritchett, sr	Do.
41	William Hunter	do	May 1, 1867	Nov. 1, 1867	6	13 00	3 50	16 50	99 00	William Hunter	Do.
42	Lars Anderson	do	May 1, 1867	Nov. 1, 1867	6	13 00	3 50	16 50	99 00	Lars Anderson	Do.
43	Amasa Tucker	do	May 1, 1867	Nov. 1, 1867	6	13 00	3 50	16 50	99 00	Amasa Tucker	Do.

This company was mustered into service at North Bend, Sanpete County, May 1, 1867, by Brigadier General W. B Pace, and assigned to duty by him in the vicinity of said settlement. They were in active service every day as guards and patrols in the mountains and passes until mustered out November 1, 1867.

I certify that the above account is correct.

H. B. CLAWSON,
Adjutant General Utah Territory Militia.

Pay-roll of Anthony W. Bessey's company —— cavalry, Utah Territory militia, employed in the suppression of Indian hostilities in Sanpete County, Utah Territory, from May 1, 1867, to November 1, 1867.

We, the undersigned, acknowledge to have received from James W. Cummings, paymaster Utah Territory militia, the sums set opposite to our names, in full payment for our services for the time specified.

Number.	Names.	Rank.	Period of service. Commencement.	Period of service. Expiration.	Months.	Pay per month.	Monthly allowance for clothing.	Total monthly pay and allowance.	40 c. per day for use and risk of horse and horse equipment.	Total pay and allowance.	Signatures.	Witness.
1	Anthony W. Bessey	Captain	May 1, 1867	Nov. 1, 1867	6		$3 50	$129 50	$72 00	$849 00	A. W. Bessey	Luther Tuttle.
1	William Beach, Jr	1st lieut	May 1, 1867	Nov. 1, 1867	6		3 50	112 83	72 00	748 98	William Beach, jr	Do.
1	Archibald W. Buchanan	2d lieut	May 1, 1867	Nov. 1, 1867	6		3 50	112 83	72 00	748 98	A. W. Buchanan	Do.
2	William A. Cox	do	May 1, 1867	Nov. 1, 1867	6		3 50	112 83	72 00	748 99	W. A. Cox	Do.
3	John Hall	do	May 1, 1867	Nov. 1, 1867	6		3 50	112 83	72 00	748 98	John Hall	Do.
4	Haselnem Clarke	do	May 1, 1867	Nov. 1, 1867	6		3 50	112 83	72 00	748 98	Haselnem Clark	Do.
1	Fretz Neilson	Sergeant	May 1, 1867	Nov. 1, 1867	6	$17 00	3 50	20 50	72 00	195 00	Fretz Nielsjon	Do.
2	Marian Jolly	do	May 1, 1867	Nov. 1, 1867	6	17 00	3 50	20 50	72 00	195 00	Marin Jolley	Do.
3	William F. Maylett	do	May 1, 1867	Nov. 1, 1867	6	17 00	3 50	20 50	72 00	195 00	Wm. F. Maylett	Do.
4	George Sidwell	do	May 1, 1867	Nov. 1, 1867	6	17 00	3 50	20 50	72 00	195 00	George Sidwell	Do.
1	Alma Beal	Bugler	May 1, 1867	Nov. 1, 1867	6	13 00	3 50	16 50	72 00	171 00	Alma Beal	Do.
1	Frederick W. Cox	Private	May 1, 1867	Nov. 1, 1867	6	13 00	3 50	16 50	72 00	171 00	F. W. Cox	Do.
2	John Dobie	do	May 1, 1867	Nov. 1, 1867	6	13 00	3 50	16 50	72 00	171 00	John Dobee	Do.
3	Andrew C. Van Buren	do	May 1, 1867	Nov. 1, 1867	6	13 00	3 50	16 50	72 00	171 00	A. C. Van Buren	Do.
4	Peter Munk	do	May 1, 1867	Nov. 1, 1867	6	13 00	3 50	16 50	72 00	171 00	Peter Munk	Do.
5	Almy Brown	do	May 1, 1867	Nov. 1, 1867	6	13 00	3 50	16 50	72 00	171 00	Alma Brown	Do.
6	Albert Beach	do	May 1, 1867	Nov. 1, 1867	6	13 00	3 50	16 50	72 00	171 00	Albert Beach	Do.
7	Alonzo Wingate	do	May 1, 1867	Nov. 1, 1867	6	13 00	3 50	16 50	72 00	171 00	Alonzo Wingot	Do.
8	Jonathan Lemaster	do	May 1, 1867	Nov. 1, 1867	6	13 00	3 50	16 50	72 00	171 00	Jonathan Lemaster	Do.
9	Yence Madsen	do	May 1, 1867	Nov. 1, 1867	6	13 00	3 50	16 50	72 00	171 00	Jens Madsen	Do.
10	Luther Tuttle	do	May 1, 1867	Nov. 1, 1867	6	13 00	3 50	16 50	72 00	171 00	Luther Tuttle, jr	Do.
11	Ezra Shoemaker	do	May 1, 1867	Nov. 1, 1867	6	13 00	3 50	16 50	72 00	171 00	Ezra Shomaker	Do.
12	Dwight Atwood	do	May 1, 1867	Nov. 1, 1867	6	13 00	3 50	16 50	72 00	171 00	Dwight Atwood	Do.
13	John Mackey	do	May 1, 1867	Nov. 1, 1867	6	13 00	3 50	16 50	72 00	171 00	John Mackey	Do.
14	Daniel R. Funk	do	May 1, 1867	Nov. 1, 1867	6	13 00	3 50	16 50	72 00	171 00	D. B. Funk	Do.
15	Zeques Wingate	do	May 1, 1867	Nov. 1, 1867	6	13 00	3 50	16 50	72 00	171 00		
16	Michael Yausen	do	May 1, 1867	Nov. 1, 1867	6	13 00	3 50	16 50	72 00	171 10	Michael Yansen	Do.
17	Joseph Tuttle	do	May 1, 1867	Nov. 1, 1867	6	13 00	3 50	16 50	72 00	171 00	Joseph Tuttle	Do.
18	Ezra Funk	do	May 1, 1867	Nov. 1, 1867	6	13 00	3 50	16 50	72 00	171 00	E. K. Funk	Do.
19	Peter Smith	do	May 1, 1867	Nov. 1, 1867	6	13 00	3 50	16 50	72 00	171 00	Peder Smith	Do.
20	Orson Taylor	do	May 1, 1867	Nov. 1, 1867	6	13 00	3 50	16 50	72 00	171 00	Orson Taylor	Do.

21	Andrew Yunsen	do	May 1, 1867	Nov. 1, 1867	6	13 00	3 50	16 50	72 00	171 00	Andrew Jensen	Do.
22	Christian Anderson	do	May 1, 1867	Nov. 1, 1867	6	13 00	3 50	16 50	72 00	171 00	Christian Andresen	Do.
23	Sanford Forbush	do	May 1, 1867	Nov. 1, 1867	6	13 00	3 50	16 50	72 00	171 00	Sanford Forbush	Do.
24	George C. Johnson	do	May 1, 1867	Nov. 1, 1867	6	13 00	3 50	16 50	72 00	171 00	George C. Johnson	Do.
25	Peter Hougaard	do	May 1, 1867	Nov. 1, 1867	6	13 00	3 50	16 50	72 10	171 00	Peter Hougaard	Do.
26	Richard Hall	do	May 1, 1867	Nov. 1, 1867	6	13 00	3 50	16 50	72 00	171 00	Richard Hall	Do.
27	Harrison Edwards	do	May 1, 1867	Nov. 1, 1867	6	13 00	3 50	16 50	72 10	171 00	Harrison Edwards	Do.
28	Gardner Snow	do	May 1, 1867	Nov. 1, 1867	6	13 00	3 50	16 50	72 10	171 00	Gardner Snow	Do.
29	James P. Edwards	do	May 1, 1867	Nov. 1, 1867	6	13 00	3 50	16 50	72 00	171 00	James P. Edwards	Do.
30	Moss Madsen	do	May 1, 1867	Nov. 1, 1867	6	13 00	3 50	16 50	72 00	171 00	Mads Madsen	Do.
31	Seth Warchum	do	May 1, 1867	Nov. 1, 1867	6	13 00	3 50	16 50	72 00	171 00	Seth Warchum	Do.
32	Jorgen Hanson	do	May 1, 1867	Nov. 1, 1867	6	13 00	3 50	16 50	72 00	171 00	Jorgen Hanson	Do.
33	Joseph Watt	do	May 1, 1867	Nov. 1, 1867	6	13 00	3 50	16 50	72 00	171 00	Joseph Wall	Do.
34	William McDonald	do	May 1, 1867	Nov. 1, 1867	6	13 00	3 50	16 50	72 00	171 00	Wm. McDonald	Do.
35	Joseph S. Snow	do	May 1, 1867	Nov. 1, 1867	6	13 00	3 50	16 50	72 00	171 00	Joseph S. Snow	Do.
36	John Lewis	do	May 1, 1867	Nov. 1, 1867	6	13 00	3 50	16 50	72 00	171 00	John Lewis	Do.
37	Anna E. Merriam	do	May 1, 1867	Nov. 1, 1867	6	13 00	3 50	16 50	72 00	171 00	Anana E. Merriam	Do.
38	John C. Tatton, Jr.	do	May 1, 1867	Nov. 1, 1867	6	13 00	3 50	16 50	72 00	171 00	John C. Patton	Do.
39	William Richey	do	May 1, 1867	Nov. 1, 1867	6	13 00	3 50	16 50	72 00	171 00	William Richey	Do.
40	William Lake	do	May 1, 1867	Nov. 1, 1867	6	13 00	3 50	16 50	72 00	171 00	Wm. Lake	Do.
41	Selah Atwool	do	May 1, 1867	Nov. 1, 1867	6	13 00	3 50	16 50	72 00	171 00	Selah Atwool	Do.
42	Antony Bessy	do	May 1, 1867	Nov. 1, 1867	6	13 00	3 50	16 50	72 00	171 00	Antony Bessy	Do.
43	Lars Marross	do	May 1, 1867	Nov. 1, 1867	6	13 00	3 50	16 50	72 00	171 00	Lars Marrop	Do.
44	J.C. Welbyo	do	May 1, 1867	Nov. 1, 1867	6	13 00	3 50	16 50	72 00	171 00	J. C. Welbyo	Do.
45	P. C. Christiansen	do	May 1, 1867	Nov. 1, 1867	6	13 00	3 50	16 50	72 00	171 00	P. C. Christiansen	Do.
46	William H. Peacock	do	May 1, 1867	Nov. 1, 1867	6	13 00	3 50	16 50	72 00	171 00	William H. Peacock	Do.
47	Yens Steck	do	May 1, 1867	Nov. 1, 1867	6	12 00	3 50	16 50	72 00	171 00	Yens Steck	Do.
48	H. C. Hanson	do	May 1, 1867	Nov. 1, 1867	6	13 00	3 50	16 50	72 00	171 00	H. C. Hansen	Do.
49	John Crawford	do	May 1, 1867	Nov. 1, 1867	6	13 00	3 50	16 50	72 00	171 00	John Crawford	Do.
50	George Snow	do	May 1, 1867	Nov. 1, 1867	6	13 00	3 50	16 50	72 00	171 00	George Snow	Do.

This company was mustered into service at Manti City, Sanpete County May, 1, 1867, by Brigadier General William B. Pace, and were actively engaged as scouts and patrols for the protection of the most exposed points in this and Sevier counties; on the 2d day of June were engaged in the battle at Twelve-mile Creek, and on the 13th of August at the Spring-town battle. They were actively engaged every day for the time specified above, and mustered out November 1, 1867.

I certify that the above account is correct.

H. B. CLAWSON,
Adjutant General Utah Territory Militia.

Pay-roll of Captain John W. Irons's company, —— infantry, Utah Territory militia, employed in the suppression of Indian hostilities in Sanpete County, Utah Territory, from May 1, 1867, to November 1, 1867.

We, the undersigned, acknowledge to have received from James W. Cummings, paymaster Utah Territory militia, the sums set opposite to our names in full payment for our services for the time specified.

Number.	Names.	Rank.	Commencement.	Expiration.	Months.	Pay per month.	Monthly allowance for clothing.	Total monthly pay and allowance.	Total pay and allowance.	Signatures.	Witness.
1	John W. Irons	Captain	May 1, 1867	Nov. 1, 1867	6	$17 00		$118 50	$711 00	John W. Irons	John Kirkman.
1	Mikel Johnson	1st lieutenant	May 1, 1867	Nov. 1, 1867	6			108 50	651 00	Michael Johnson	Do.
1	Nathan Faux	2d lieutenant	May 1, 1867	Nov. 1, 1867	6			103 50	621 00	Nathan Faux	Do.
2	Lars N. Larsen	do.	May 1, 1867	Nov. 1, 1867	6			103 50	621 00	Lars N. Larsen	Do.
3	Charles Longson	do.	May 1, 1867	Nov. 1, 1867	6			103 50	621 00	Charles Longson	Do.
4	Rasmus Anderson	do.	May 1, 1867	Nov. 1, 1867	6			103 50	621 00	Rasmus Anderson	Do.
5	James Blackham	Sergeant	May 1, 1867	Nov. 1, 1867	6			103 50	621 00	James Blackham	Do.
1	Aaron Hardy	do.	May 1, 1867	Nov. 1, 1867	6	$17 00	$3 50	20 50	123 00	Aaron Hardy	Do.
2	Neils Anderson	do.	May 1, 1867	Nov. 1, 1867	6	17 00	3 50	20 50	123 00	Neils Anderson, his + mark	Do.
3	Herbert Longson	do.	May 1, 1867	Nov. 1, 1867	6	17 00	3 50	20 50	123 00	H. Longson	Do.
4	Thore N. Peterson	do.	May 1, 1867	Nov. 1, 1867	6	17 00	3 50	20 50	123 00	Thore N. Peterson	Do.
5	Aleck Adamson	do.	May 1, 1867	Nov. 1, 1867	6	17 00	3 50	20 50	123 00	Alexander Adamson	Do.
1	Jens Jensen	Private	May 1, 1867	Nov. 1, 1867	6	13 00	3 50	16 50	99 00	Jens Jensen	Do.
2	William Bolter	do.	May 1, 1867	Nov. 1, 1867	6	13 00	3 50	16 50	99 00	William Bolter	Do.
3	Joseph Bagnall	do.	May 1, 1867	Nov. 1, 1867	6	13 00	3 50	16 50	99 00	Joseph Bagnall	Do.
4	William H. Hatch	do.	May 1, 1867	Nov. 1, 1867	6	13 00	3 50	16 50	99 00	William H. Hatch	Do.
5	James Cloward	do.	May 1, 1867	Nov. 1, 1867	6	13 00	3 50	16 50	99 00	James Cloward	Do.
6	Charles Kemp	do.	May 1, 1867	Nov. 1, 1867	6	13 00	3 50	16 50	99 00	Charles Kemp	Do.
7	John Blackham	do.	May 1, 1867	Nov. 1, 1867	6	13 00	3 50	16 50	99 00	John Blackham	Do.
8	Alma White	do.	May 1, 1867	Nov. 1, 1867	6	13 00	3 50	16 50	99 00	Alma White	Do.
9	Andrew Rasmus	do.	May 1, 1867	Nov. 1, 1867	6	13 00	3 50	16 50	99 00	Anders Rasmussen	Do.
10	Peter Anderson	do.	May 1, 1867	Nov. 1, 1867	6	13 00	3 50	16 50	99 00	Peter Anderson	Do.
11	Samuel Blackham	do.	May 1, 1867	Nov. 1, 1867	6	13 00	3 50	16 50	99 00	Samuel Blackham	Do.
12	James Harvey	do.	May 1, 1867	Nov. 1, 1867	6	13 00	3 50	16 50	99 00	James Harvey	Do.
13	James Done	do.	May 1, 1867	Nov. 1, 1867	6	13 00	3 50	16 50	99 00	James Done	Do.
14	Amos Jensen	do.	May 1, 1867	Nov. 1, 1867	6	13 00	3 50	16 50	99 00	Amos Yeusson	Do.
15	Morten Olsen	do.	May 1, 1867	Nov. 1, 1867	6	13 00	3 50	16 50	99 00	Marten Olsen	Do.
16	William Prestwich	do.	May 1, 1867	Nov. 1, 1867	6	13 00	3 50	16 50	99 00	William Presturch	Do.
17	Peter Larsen	do.	May 1, 1867	Nov. 1, 1867	6	13 00	3 50	16 50	99 00	Peter Larsen	Do.
18	Peter Holm	do.	May 1, 1867	Nov. 1, 1867	6	13 00	3 50	16 50	99 00	Peter Holm	Do.
19	Neils P. Olsen	do.	May 1, 1867	Nov. 1, 1867	6	13 00	3 50	16 50	99 00	Nils P. Olson, his + mark	Do.
20	Margus Jacobsen	do.	May 1, 1867	Nov. 1, 1867	6	13 00	3 50	16 50	99 00	Markus Jakobsen	Do.

No.	Name		Enlisted	Discharged	6					Name	
21	Peter B. Hanmer	do.	May 1, 1867	Nov. 1, 1867	6	13 00	3 50	16 50	99 00	Ridau B. Hanmen	Do.
22	Eli Askeroft	do.	May 1, 1867	Nov. 1, 1867	6	13 00	3 50	16 50	99 00	Eli Asheroft	Do.
23	Robert Malinson	do.	May 1, 1867	Nov. 1, 1867	6	13 00	3 50	16 50	99 00	Robert Malinson	Do.
24	James Laren	do.	May 1, 1867	Nov. 1, 1867	6	13 00	3 50	11 50	99 00	James Larson	Do.
25	John Kellett	do.	May 1, 1867	Nov. 1, 1867	6	13 00	3 50	16 50	99 00	John Kellett	Do.
26	Reuben Ames	do.	May 1, 1867	Nov. 1, 1867	6	13 00	3 50	16 50	99 00	Reuben Ames	Do.
27	James Christiansen	do.	May 1, 1867	Nov. 1, 1867	6	13 00	3 50	16 50	99 00	James Christenson	Do.
28	George Windows	do.	May 1, 1867	Nov. 1, 1867	6	13 00	3 50	16 50	99 00	George Windows	Do.
29	George T. Jackson	do.	May 1, 1867	Nov. 1, 1867	6	13 00	3 50	16 50	99 00	George T. Jackson	Do.
30	George Hardy	do.	May 1, 1867	Nov. 1, 1867	6	13 00	3 50	16 50	99 00	Georges Hurdy	Do.
31	Anarm Jensen	do.	May 1, 1867	Nov. 1, 1867	6	13 00	3 50	16 50	99 00	Andres Jensen	Do.
32	Philip Marks	do.	May 1, 1867	Nov. 1, 1867	6	13 00	3 50	16 50	99 00	Philipp Mory	Do.
33	Peter Christiansen, 2d	do.	May 1, 1867	Nov. 1, 1867	6	13 00	3 50	16 50	99 00	Petter Christensen, 2d	Do.
34	William L. Lunblad	do.	May 1, 1867	Nov. 1, 1867	6	13 00	3 50	16 50	99 00	William Lunblad	Do.
35	Anders Jensen	do.	May 1, 1867	Nov. 1, 1867	6	13 00	3 50	16 50	99 00	Andros Jonsson	Do.
36	Swend Anderson	do.	May 1, 1867	Nov. 1, 1867	6	13 00	3 50	16 50	99 00	Sven Anderson	Do.
37	Jens C. Olsen	do.	May 1, 1867	Nov. 1, 1867	6	13 00	3 50	16 50	99 00	Jens C. Olsen	Do.
38	Peter Olsen	do.	May 1, 1867	Nov. 1, 1867	6	13 00	3 50	16 50	99 00	Peter Olsen	Do.
39	Christian A. Peterson	do.	May 1, 1867	Nov. 1, 1867	6	13 00	3 50	16 50	99 00	A. Pellerson	Do.
40	Neils R. Lindahl	do.	May 1, 1867	Nov. 1, 1867	6	13 00	3 50	16 50	99 00	N. R. Lindahl	Do.
41	Neils Olsen	do.	May 1, 1867	Nov. 1, 1867	6	13 00	3 50	16 50	99 00	Nils Olsen	Do.
42	Jens Jensen	do.	May 1, 1867	Nov. 1, 1867	6	13 00	3 50	16 50	99 00	Jens Jenson	Do.
43	John Kinder	do.	May 1, 1867	Nov. 1, 1867	6	13 00	3 50	16 50	99 00	John Hinder	Do.
44	William Kinder	do.	May 1, 1867	Nov. 1, 1867	6	13 00	3 50	16 50	99 00	William Kinder	Do.
45	Andrew Leslie	do.	May 1, 1867	Nov. 1, 1867	6	13 00	3 50	16 50	99 00	Andrew Lessliey	Do.
46	John Harris	do.	May 1, 1867	Nov. 1, 1867	6	13 00	3 50	16 50	99 00	John Harris	Do.
47	Thomas Brandon	do.	May 1, 1867	Nov. 1, 1867	6	13 00	3 50	16 50	99 00	Thomas Brandon	Do.
48	James P. Christianse	do.	May 1, 1867	Nov. 1, 1867	6	13 00	3 50	16 50	99 00	Jams P. Christeinsen	Do.
49	Christian Jensen	do.	May 1, 1867	Nov. 1, 1867	6	13 00	3 50	16 50	99 00	Christen Jensen	Do.
50	Rasmus Lorensen	do.	May 1, 1867	Nov. 1, 1867	6	13 00	3 50	16 50	99 00	Rasmus Lorenson	Do.
51	James Gan t	do.	May 1, 1867	Nov. 1, 1867	6	13 00	3 50	16 50	99 00	James Gannt	Do.
52	George Brandon	do.	May 1, 1867	Nov. 1, 1867	6	13 00	3 50	16 50	99 00	George Brandon	Do.

This company was mustered into service at Moroni City, Sanpete County, May 1, 1867, by Brigadier General W. B. Pace, and assigned to duty in the vicinity of said city for the protection of life and property. They were in active service every day as guards and patrols in the mountains and valleys until mustered out, November 1, 1867.

I certify that the above account is correct.

H. B. CLAWSON,
Adjutant General Utah Territory Militia.

Pay-roll of Captain John F. Sanders's company —— cavalry, Utah Territory militia, employed in the suppression of Indian hostilities in Sanpete County, Utah Territory, from May 1, 1867, to November 1, 1867.

We, the undersigned, acknowledge to have received from James W. Cummings, paymaster Utah Territory militia, the sums set opposite to our names, in full payment for our services for the time specified.

Number	Names	Rank	Commencement	Expiration	Months	Pay per month	Monthly allowance for clothing	Total monthly pay and allowance	40 cts. per day for use and risk of horse and equipment	Total pay and allowance	Signature	Witness
1	John F. Sanders	Captain	May 1, 1867	Nov. 1, 1867	6			$129 50	$72 00	$849 00	John F. Sanders	Henry W. Sanderson
1	George Tucker	1st lieut	May 1, 1867	Nov. 1, 1867	6			112 83	72 00	748 98	George Tucker	Do.
1	Mormon Miner	2d lieut	May 1, 1867	Nov. 1, 1867	6			112 83	72 00	748 98	Mormon Miner	Do.
2	Jordon Brady	—do—	May 1, 1867	Nov. 1, 1867	6			112 83	72 00	748 98	Jordan Brady	Do.
2	Orson Mont Terry	Sergeant	May 1, 1867	Nov. 1, 1867	6	$17 00	$3 50	20 50	72 00	195 00	Orson M. Terry	Do.
1	Jehu Cox, jr	—do—	May 1, 1867	Nov. 1, 1867	6	17 00	3 50	20 50	72 00	195 00	Jehu Cox	Do.
1	Lars Neilson	Bugler	May 1, 1867	Nov. 1, 1867	6	13 00	3 50	16 50	72 00	171 00		Do.
2	James Sanderson	Private	May 1, 1867	Nov. 1, 1867	6	13 00	3 50	16 50	72 00	171 00	James Sanderson	Do.
3	William S. Taylor	—do—	May 1, 1867	Nov. 1, 1867	6	13 00	3 50	16 50	72 00	171 00	William S. Taylor	Do.
4	John Romero	—do—	May 1, 1867	Nov. 1, 1867	6	13 00	3 50	16 50	72 00	171 00	John Romero, + his mark	Do.
5	Lindsay A. Brady, jr	—do—	May 1, 1867	Nov. 1, 1867	6	13 00	3 50	16 50	72 00	171 00	Lindsey A. Brady, jr	Do.
6	James Anderson	—do—	May 1, 1867	Nov. 1, 1867	6	13 00	3 50	16 50	72 00	171 00	James Anderson	Do.
7	Hyrum Wilson	—do—	May 1, 1867	Nov. 1, 1867	6	13 00	3 50	16 50	72 00	171 00	Hyrum Wilson	Do.
8	James M. Turpin	—do—	May 1, 1867	Nov. 1, 1867	6	13 00	3 50	16 50	72 00	171 00	James M. Turpin	Do.
9	John A. Mower	—do—	May 1, 1867	Nov. 1, 1867	6	13 00	3 50	16 50	72 00	171 00	John A. Mower	Do.
10	Franklin Pritchett	—do—	May 1, 1867	Nov. 1, 1867	6	13 00	3 50	16 50	72 00	171 00	Franklin Pritchett	Do.
11	Samuel N. B. Pritchett	—do—	May 1, 1867	Nov. 1, 1867	6	13 00	3 50	16 50	72 00	171 00	S. N. B. Pritchett	Do.
12	Samuel Bills	—do—	May 1, 1867	Nov. 1, 1867	6	13 00	3 50	16 50	72 00	171 00	Samuel Bills	Do.
13	George Vance	—do—	May 1, 1867	Nov. 1, 1867	6	13 00	3 50	16 50	72 00	171 00	George H. Vance, + his mark	Do.
14	William Avery	—do—	May 1, 1867	Nov. 1, 1867	6	13 00	3 50	16 50	79 00	171 00	William Avry	Do.
14	Jacob Jones	—do—	May 1, 1867	Nov. 1, 1867	6	13 00	3 50	16 50	72 00	171 00	Jacob Jones, + his mark	Do.
15	David W. Sanders	—do—	May 1, 1867	Nov. 1, 1867	6	13 00	3 50	16 50	72 00	171 00	David W. Sanders	Do.
16	Alma Miner	—do—	May 1, 1867	Nov. 1, 1867	6	13 00	3 50	16 50	72 01	171 00	Alma Miner	Do.
17	James Jones	—do—	May 1, 1867	Nov. 1, 1867	6	13 00	3 50	16 50	72 00	171 00	James Jones	Do.
18	Henry Fowles	—do—	May 1, 1867	Nov. 1, 1867	6	13 00	3 50	16 50	72 00	171 00	Henry Fowles	Do.

This company was mustered into service at Fairview, Sanpete county, May 1, 1867, by Brigadier General William B. Pace. They were actively engaged every day as scouts and patrols in the mountains and passes and most exposed points

Pay-roll of Captain John D. Chase's company —— infantry, Utah Territory militia, employed in the suppression of Indian hostilities in Sanpete County, Utah Territory, from May 1, 1867, to November 1, 1867.

We, the undersigned, acknowledge to have received from James W. Cummings, paymaster Utah Territory militia, the sums set opposite to our names, in full payment for our services for the time specified.

Number.	Names.	Rank.	Commencement.	Expiration.	Months.	Pay per month.	Monthly allowance for clothing.	Total monthly pay and allowance.	Total pay and allowance.	Signatures.	Witness.
1	John D. Chase	Captain	May 1, 1867	Nov. 1, 1867	6			118 50	711 00	John D. Chase	Jabez Faux.
2	Lars Eleason	1st lieutenant	May 1, 1867	Nov. 1, 1867	6			108 50	651 00	Lars Eleason	Do.
3	Joseph Shepherd	2d lieutenant	May 1, 1867	Nov. 1, 1867	6			103 50	621 00	Joseph Shepherd	Do.
4	Soren Yorgensen	do	May 1, 1867	Nov. 1, 1867	6			103 50	621 00	Soren Yorgenson	Do.
5	Rasmus P. Christiansen	do	May 1, 1867	Nov. 1, 1867	6			103 50	621 00	Rasmus P. Christensen	Do.
6	Jeppa Christiansen	Sergeant	May 1, 1867	Nov. 1, 1867	6	$17 00	$3 50	20 50	123 00	Jeppe Christensen, his + mark	Do.
7	Neils Rasmussen	do	May 1, 1867	Nov. 1, 1867	6	17 00	3 50	20 50	123 00	Nicls Rasmussen	Do.
8	Mikel Sorensen	do	May 1, 1867	Nov. 1, 1867	6	13 00	3 50	16 50	99 00	Mikel Sorensen	Do.
9	Jeppa Anderson	Private	May 1, 1867	Nov. 1, 1867	6	13 00	3 50	16 50	99 00	Jeppe Anderson	Do.
10	Kund Neilson	do	May 1, 1867	Nov. 1, 1867	6	13 00	3 50	16 50	99 00	Knud Nielsen	Do.
11	David Hutchinson	do	May 1, 1867	Nov. 1, 1867	6	13 00	3 50	16 50	99 00	David Hutchinson	Do.
12	Edward Mallinson	do	May 1, 1867	Nov. 1, 1867	6	13 00	3 50	16 50	99 00	Edward Mallinson	Do.
13	Lars Peterson	do	May 1, 1867	Nov. 1, 1867	6	13 00	3 50	16 50	99 00	Lars Petersen	Do.
14	William Prestwich	do	May 1, 1867	Nov. 1, 1867	6	13 00	3 50	16 50	99 00	William Prestwich	Do.
15	Ole Anderson	do	May 1, 1867	Nov. 1, 1867	6	13 00	3 50	16 50	99 00	Ole Andersen	Do.
16	Peter Y.bsen	do	May 1, 1867	Nov. 1, 1867	6	13 00	3 50	16 50	99 00	Peter Jensen	Do.
17	Bendt Monson	do	May 1, 1867	Nov. 1, 1867	6	13 00	3 50	16 50	99 00	Banyt Munson	Do.
18	Soren Christiansen	do	May 1, 1867	Nov. 1, 1867	6	13 00	3 50	16 50	99 00	Soren Christensen	Do.
19	Peter Thompson	do	May 1, 1867	Nov. 1, 1867	6	13 00	3 50	16 50	99 00	Peter Thompson, his + mark	Do.
20	Swend Olsen	do	May 1, 1867	Nov. 1, 1867	6	13 00	3 50	16 50	99 00	Sven Onson	Do.
21	Rasmus Rasmussen	do	May 1, 1867	Nov. 1, 1867	6	13 00	3 50	16 50	99 00	Rasmus Rasmunsen	Do.
22	Lars Hanson	do	May 1, 1867	Nov. 1, 1867	6	13 00	3 50	16 50	99 00	Laus Hanson	Do.
23	George Jackson	do	May 1, 1867	Nov. 1, 1867	6	13 00	3 50	16 50	99 00	George Jackson	Do.
24	Benjamin Jackson	do	May 1, 1867	Nov. 1, 1867	6	13 00	3 50	16 50	99 00	Benjamin Jackson	Do.
25	John Slent lion	do	May 1, 1867	Nov. 1, 1867	6	13 00	3 50	16 50	99 00	Johan Stenstion	Do.
26	Charles P. Thomas	do	May 1, 1867	Nov. 1, 1867	6	13 00	3 50	16 50	99 00	Charles P. Thomas, his + mark	Do.
27	John Bailey	do	May 1, 1867	Nov. 1, 1867	6	13 00	3 50	16 50	99 00	John Bailey	Do.
28	Jens C. Peterson	do	May 1, 1867	Nov. 1, 1867	6	13 00	3 50	16 50	99 00	Jens C. Pettersen	Do.
29	John Price	do	May 1, 1867	Nov. 1, 1867	6	13 00	3 50	16 50	99 00	John Price	Do.
30	Lars Larsen	do	May 1, 1867	Nov. 1, 1867	6	13 00	3 50	16 50	99 00	Lars Larsen	Do.
31	Jens Jensen	do	May 1, 1867	Nov. 1, 1867	6	13 00	3 50	16 50	99 00	Jens Jensen	Do.

| 24 | William Draper | .... | ...do......... | May 1, 1867 | Nov. 1, 1867 | 6 | 13 00 | 3 50 | 16 50 | 99 00 | William Draper | Do. |
| 25 | Peter Petterson | .... | ...do......... | May 1, 1867 | Nov. 1, 1867 | 6 | 13 00 | 3 50 | 16 50 | 99 00 | Petter Petterson | Do. |

This company was mustered into service at Moroni, Sanpete County, May 1, 1867, by Brigadier General W. B. Pace, and by him assigned to duty in the vicinity of said city for the protection of life and property. They were in active service every day until mustered out at Moroni City, November 1, 1867.

I certify that the above account is correct.

H. B. CLAWSON,
Adjutant General Utah Territory Militia.

Pay-roll of Captain Thomas J. Holbrook's company —— cavalry, Utah Territory militia, employed in the suppression of Indian hostilities in Sanpete County, Utah Territory, from May 1, 1867, to November 1, 1867.

We, the undersigned, acknowledge to have received from James W. Cummings, paymaster Utah Territory militia, the sums set opposite to our names, in full payment for our services for the time specified.

Number	Names	Rank	Commencement	Expiration	Month.	Pay per month.	Monthly allowance for clothing.	Total monthly pay and allowance.	40 cts. per day for use and risk of horse and horse equipment.	Total pay and allowance.	Signatures.	Witnesses.
1	Thomas J. Holbrook	Captain	May 1, 1867	Nov. 1, 1867	6			$129 50	$72 00	$849 50	Thomas J. Holbrook	Samuel Jenkes,
1	William Cordingly	1st lieut	May 1, 1867	Nov. 1, 1867	6			112 83	72 00	748 98	William Cordigly	Rees R. Lewellyn.
2	Matthew Caldwell	2d lieut	May 1, 1867	Nov. 1, 1867	6			112 83	72 00	748 98	Matthew Caldwell	Do.
2	Peter Johnson	do.	May 1, 1867	Nov. 1, 1867	6			112 83	72 00	748 98	Peter Jonsen	Do.
1	Nephi Robertson	do.	May 1, 1867	Nov. 1, 1867	6	$17	$3 50	20 50	72 00	195 00	Nephi Robertson	Do.
1	George Carter	Sergeant	May 1, 1867	Nov. 1, 1867	6	17	3 50	20 50	72 00	195 00	George Carter	Do.
2	Jasper Robertson*	do.	May 1, 1867	Nov. 1, 1867	6	13	3 50	16 50	72 00	171 00	Jasper Robertson	Do.
3	Albert Collard	Bugler	May 1, 1867	Nov. 1, 1867	6	13	3 50	16 50	72 00	171 00	Albert Collard	Do.
4	Noah T. Guyman	Private	May 1, 1867	Nov. 1, 1867	6	13	3 50	16 50	72 00	171 00	Noah T. Guymon	Do.
5	John Green	do.	May 1, 1867	Nov. 1, 1867	6	13	3 50	16 50	72 00	171 00	John Green	Do.
6	William Cook	do.	May 1, 1867	Nov. 1, 1867	6	13	3 50	16 50	72 00	171 00	Wm. F. Cook	Do.
7	James Johnson	do.	May 1, 1867	Nov. 1, 1867	6	13	3 50	16 50	72 00	171 00	James Johnson	Do.
8	Isaac Herring	do.	May 1, 1867	Nov. 1, 1867	6	13	3 50	16 50	72 00	171 00	Isaac Herring	Do.
9	William Cropb	do.	May 1, 1867	Nov. 1, 1867	6	13	3 50	16 50	72 00	171 00	William Cropp	Do.
10	George Crowther	do.	May 1, 1867	Nov. 1, 1867	6	13	3 50	16 50	72 00	171 00	George Crauther	Do.
11	George Combs	do.	May 1, 1867	Nov. 1, 1867	6	13	3 50	16 50	72 00	171 00	George Coombs	Do.
12	Christian Poulson	do.	May 1, 1867	Nov. 1, 1867	6	13	3 50	16 50	72 00	171 00	Christian Poulson	Do.
13	Louis Lund†	do.	May 1, 1867	Nov. 1, 1867	6	13	3 50	16 50	12 00	28 50		Do.
14	Christian Ottesen	do.	May 1, 1867	Nov. 1, 1867	6	13	3 50	16 50	72 00	171 00	Christen Ottesen	Do.
15	Andrew Aagard	do.	May 1, 1867	Nov. 1, 1867	6	13	3 50	16 50	72 00	171 00	Andrew Aggard	Do.
16	Hans P. Olsen	do.	May 1, 1867	Nov. 1, 1867	6	13	3 50	16 50	72 00	171 00	Hans P. Holsen	Do.
17	William H. Adams	do.	May 1, 1867	Nov. 1, 1867	6	13	3 50	16 50	72 00	171 00	William H. Adams	Do.
18	Curtis W. Caldwell	do.	May 1, 1867	Nov. 1, 1867	6	13	3 50	16 50	72 00	171 00	Curtis W. Caldwell	Do.
19	Sanford Holman	do.	May 1, 1867	Nov. 1, 1867	6	13	3 50	16 50	72 00	171 00	Sanford Holman	Do.
20	James A. Guyman	do.	May 1, 1867	Nov. 1, 1867	6	13	3 50	16 50	72 00	171 00	James A. Guymon	Do.
21	Hans A. Thompson	do.	May 1, 1867	Nov. 1, 1867	6	13	3 50	16 50	72 00	171 00	Hans A. Thomsen	Do.
22	Joseph Robertson	do.	May 1, 1867	Nov. 1, 1867	6	13	3 50	16 50	72 00	171 00	Joseph Robertson	Do.
23	George Huggins	do.	May 1, 1867	Nov. 1, 1867	6	13	3 50	16 50	72 00	171 00	George Huggins	Do.
24	Thomas Wakefield	do.	May 1, 1867	Nov. 1, 1867	6	13	3 50	16 50	72 00	171 00	Thomas Wakefield	Do.
	Charles H. Johnson	do.	May 1, 1867	Nov. 1, 1867	6	13	3 50	16 50	72 00	171 00	Charles H. Johnson	Do.
	Erastus S. Wakefield	do.	May 1, 1867	Nov. 1, 1867	6	13	3 50	16 50	72 00	171 00	Erastus Wakefield	Do.

*Wounded, June 1, 1867.   †Killed in battle, June 1, 1867.

Pay-roll of Captain John Henry Tuttle's company —— infantry, Utah Territory militia, employed in the suppression of Indian hostilities in Sanpete County, Utah Territory, from May 1, 1867, to November 1, 1867.

We, the undersigned, acknowledge to have received from James W. Cummings, paymaster Utah Territory militia, the sums set opposite to our names, in full payment for our services for the time specified.

Number	Names	Rank	Commencement	Expiration	Months	Pay per month	Monthly allowance for clothing	Total monthly pay and allowance	Total Pay and allowance	Signatures	Witness
1	John Henry Tuttle	Captain	May 1, 1867	November 1, 1867	6			118 50	$711 00	John H. Tuttle	Luther Tuttle.
1	Erick Ludvicksen	1st lieut	May 1, 1867	November 1, 1867	6			108 50	651 00	Erik Ludvigsen	Do.
1	James Crawford	2d lieut	May 1, 1867	November 1, 1867	6			103 50	621 00	James Crawford	Do.
2	Yence Dennison	do	May 1, 1867	November 1, 1867	6			103 50	621 00	Jons Dinnesen	Do.
3	Haure Ottosen	do	May 1, 1867	November 1, 1867	6			103 50	621 00	Hans Ottosen	Do.
4	Vorgan Christiansen	do	May 1, 1867	November 1, 1867	6			103 50	621 00	Jorgen Christensen	Do.
5	Jacob Krasel	do	May 1, 1867	November 1, 1867	6			103 50	621 00	Jacob Kinsel	Do.
1	Christian Yrasen	Sergeant	May 1, 1867	November 1, 1867	6	$17 00	$3 50	20 50	123 00	Christian Jensen	Do.
2	Robert Braithwaite	do	May 1, 1867	November 1, 1867	6	17 00	3 50	20 50	123 00	Robert Braithwaite	Do.
3	John Alder	do	May 1, 1867	November 1, 1867	6	17 00	3 50	20 50	123 00	John Alder	Do.
4	Christian Banson	do	May 1, 1867	November 1, 1867	6	17 00	3 50	20 50	123 00	Chrustun Borousen	Do.
5	Yence P. Hanson	do	May 1, 1867	November 1, 1867	6	17 00	3 50	20 50	123 00	Yens P. Hansen	Do.
1	Joseph Wilson	Private	May 1, 1867	November 1, 1867	6	13 00	3 50	16 50	99 00	Joseph Wilson	Do.
2	Haure Yensen	do	May 1, 1867	November 1, 1867	6	13 00	3 50	16 50	99 00	Hance Yensen	Do.
3	John Wilson	do	May 1, 1867	November 1, 1867	6	13 00	3 50	16 50	99 00	John Wilson	Do.
4	Yence Dennison	do	May 1, 1867	November 1, 1867	6	13 00	3 50	16 50	99 00	Jens Dirnesen	Do.
5	Samuel Ware	do	May 1, 1867	November 1, 1867	6	13 00	3 50	16 50	99 00	Samuel Ware	Do.
6	David Bennett	do	May 1, 1867	November 1, 1867	6	13 00	3 50	16 50	99 00	David Bennett	Do.
7	Brigham Casto	do	May 1, 1867	November 1, 1867	6	13 00	3 50	16 50	99 00	Brigham Casto	Do.
8	James Hannah	do	May 1, 1867	November 1, 1867	6	13 00	3 50	16 50	99 00	James Hannah	Do.
9	Louis Madsen	do	May 1, 1867	November 1, 1867	6	13 00	3 50	16 50	99 00	Lars Madsen	Do.
10	George C. Casto	do	May 1, 1867	November 1, 1867	6	13 00	3 50	16 50	99 00	Georg C. Casto	Do.
11	Yence Nielson	do	May 1, 1867	November 1, 1867	6	13 00	3 50	16 50	99 00	Jens Nielsen	Do.
12	Joseph L. Wall	do	May 1, 1867	November 1, 1867	6	13 00	3 50	16 50	99 00	Joseph L. Wall	Do.
13	Jacob Keller	do	May 1, 1867	November 1, 1867	6	13 00	3 50	16 50	99 00	Jakoh Keller	Do.
14	Jence Hanson	do	May 1, 1867	November 1, 1867	6	13 00	3 50	16 50	99 00	Jens Hansen	Do.
15	Frederick Miller	do	May 1, 1867	November 1, 1867	6	13 00	3 50	16 50	99 00		Do.
16	Peter C. Larsen	do	May 1, 1867	November 1, 1867	6	13 00	3 50	16 50	99 00	Peter C. Larson	Do.
17	Ole Larson	do	May 1, 1867	November 1, 1867	6	13 00	3 50	16 50	99 00	Ole Larsen	Do.
18	Ole Nielson	do	May 1, 1867	November 1, 1867	6	13 00	3 50	16 50	99 00	Ole Nielsen	Do.
19	Frederick C. Christiansen	do	May 1, 1867	November 1, 1867	6	13 00	3 50	16 50	99 00	Frederik C. Christesen	Do.
20	Christian Christiansen	do	May 1, 1867	November 1, 1867	6	13 00	3 50	16 50	99 00	Christian Christiausen	Do.
21	Walter R. Burton	do	May 1, 1867	November 1, 1867	6	13 00	3 50	16 50	99 00		Do.

22	Yorgan Madson	do	May 1, 1867	November 1, 1867	6	13 00	3 50	16 50	99 00	Yorgan Madson	Do.
53	Charles Shrum	do	May 1, 1867	November 1, 1867	6	13 00	3 50	16 50	99 00	Charls Shrum	Do.
51	Peter Madsen	do	May 1, 1867	November 1, 1867	6	13 00	3 50	16 50	99 00	Peder Madsen	Do.
55	Lars Nielsen	do	May 1, 1867	November 1, 1867	6	13 00	3 50	16 50	99 00	Lars Nielsen	Do.
26	Charles O. Lake	do	May 1, 1867	November 1, 1867	6	13 00	3 50	16 50	99 00	Charles O. Lake	Do.
27	Ole Peterson	do	May 1, 1867	November 1, 1867	6	13 00	3 50	16 50	99 00	Ole Petersen	Do.
28	Niels Hanson	do	May 1, 1867	November 1, 1867	6	13 00	3 50	16 50	99 00	Niels Hansen	Do.
29	Niels Christiansen	do	May 1, 1867	November 1, 1867	6	13 00	3 50	16 50	99 00	Niels Christiansen	Do.
30	Christian Peterson	do	May 1, 1867	November 1, 1867	6	13 00	3 50	16 50	99 00	Christian Pettersen	Do.
31	Yence Stock	do	May 1, 1867	November 1, 1867	6	13 00	3 50	16 50	99 00	Yens Starkt.	Do.
32	Peter Peterson	do	May 1, 1867	November 1, 1867	6	13 00	3 50	16 50	99 00	Petterre Peterson	Do.
33	Harrison Fugate	do	May 1, 1867	November 1, 1867	6	13 00	3 50	16 50	99 00	Harrison Fugate	Do.
34	Louis Madsen	do	May 1, 1867	November 1, 1867	6	13 10	3 50	16 50	99 00	Joseph Howe	Do.
35	Joseph Howe	do	May 1, 1867	November 1, 1867	6	13 00	3 50	16 50	99 00	Joseph Howe	Do.
36	Peter Hanson	do	May 1, 1867	November 1, 1867	6	13 00	3 50	16 30	99 00	Peter Hanson	Do.
37	Rasmus Madson	do	May 1, 1867	November 1, 1867	6	13 00	3 50	16 50	99 00	Rasmus Madsen	Do.

This company was mustered into service at Manti City, May 1, 1867, by Brigadier General W. B. Pace, and assigned to duty by him in the vicinity of said city, for the protection of life and property. They were in active service every day until mustered out, at Manti, November 1, 1867.

I certify that the above account is correct.

H. B. CLAWSON,
Adjutant General Utah Territory Militia.

Pay-roll of Captain Lewis Larsen's company —— cavalry, Utah Territory militia, employed in the suppression of Indian hostilities in Sanpete County, from May 1, 1867, to November 1, 1867.

We, the undersigned, acknowledge to have received from James W. Cummings, paymaster Utah Territory militia, the sums set opposite to our names, in full payment for our services for the time specified.

Number.	Names.	Rank.	Commencement.	Expiration.	Months.	Pay per month.	Monthly allowance for clothing.	Total monthly pay and allowance.	40cts. per day for use and risk of horse and horse equipment.	Total pay and allowance.	Signatures.	Witnesses.
1	Lewis Larsen	Captain	May 1, 1867	Nov. 1, 1867	6			$129 50	$72 00	$849 00	Lewis Larsen	H. F. Peterson.
1	John Williams	1st lieutenant	May 1, 1867	Nov. 1, 1867	6			112 83	72 00	748 98	J. Williams	Do.
2	Christian Larsen Thorp	2d lieutenant	May 1, 1867	Nov. 1, 1867	6			112 83	72 00	748 98	C. L. Thorp	Do.
3	Henry Beal	do.	May 1, 1867	Nov. 1, 1867	6			112 83	72 00	748 98	Henry Beal	Do.
4	Peter Greaves	do.	May 1, 1867	Nov. 1, 1867	6			112 83	72 00	748 98	Peter Greaves	Do.
5	Thomas Woolsey	do.	May 1, 1867	Nov. 1, 1867	6			112 83	72 00	748 98	Thomas H. Woolsey	Do.
6	Peter Peterson	do.	May 1, 1867	Nov. 1, 1867	6			195 00	72 00	748 98	Peter Petersen	Do.
1	Lewis Olsen	Sergeant	May 1, 1867	Nov. 1, 1867	6	$17 00	$3 50	20 50	72 00	195 00	Lewis Olsen	Do.
2	Jeure Anderson	do.	May 1, 1867	Nov. 1, 1867	6	17 00	3 50	20 50	72 00	195 00	Jens Andersen	Do.
3	George Taylor	do.	May 1, 1867	Nov. 1, 1867	6	17 00	3 50	20 50	72 00	195 00	George Taylor	Do.
4	Andrew Thomson	do.	May 1, 1867	Nov. 1, 1867	6	17 00	3 50	20 50	72 00	195 00	Andrew Thomsen	Do.
5	Haure Neilsen	do.	May 1, 1867	Nov. 1, 1867	6	17 00	3 50	20 50	72 00	195 00	Haus Neilsen	Do.
1	Andrew Nickison	Bugler	May 1, 1867	Nov. 1, 1867	6	13 00	3 50	16 50	72 00	171 00	Andrew Nickison	Do.
2	Mads Neilson	Private	May 1, 1867	Nov. 1, 1867	6	13 00	3 50	16 50	72 00	171 00	Mads Neilson	Do.
3	Andrew Anderson	do.	May 1, 1867	Nov. 1, 1867	6	13 00	3 50	16 50	72 00	171 00	Anders Anders	Do.
4	Marinus Thomson	do.	May 1, 1867	Nov. 1, 1867	6	13 00	3 50	16 50	72 00	171 00	Marinus Thomson	Do.
5	Thomas A. Williams	do.	May 1, 1867	Nov. 1, 1867	6	13 00	3 50	16 50	72 00	171 00	Tomas Williams	Do.
6	Andrew Whitlock	do.	May 1, 1867	Nov. 1, 1867	6	13 00	3 50	16 50	72 00	171 00	Audro H. Whitlock	Do.
7	Niels Anderson	do.	May 1, 1867	Nov. 1, 1867	6	13 00	3 50	16 50	72 00	171 00	Neile Anderson	Do.
8	Christian G. Neilson	do.	May 1, 1867	Nov. 1, 1867	6	13 00	3 50	16 50	72 00	171 00	Christen G. Neilsen	Do.
9	Henry G. Jensen	do.	May 1, 1867	Nov. 1, 1867	6	13 00	3 50	16 50	72 00	171 00	H. C. Jensen	Do.
10	Christian C. Neilson	do.	May 1, 1867	Nov. 1, 1867	6	13 00	3 50	16 50	72 01	171 00	C. C. Nielsen	Do.
11	John Christiannsen	do.	May 1, 1867	Nov. 1, 1867	6	13 00	3 50	16 50	72 00	171 00	John Chrestensen	Do.
12	Antoine Christiansen	do.	May 1, 1867	Nov. 1, 1867	6	13 00	3 50	16 50	72 00	171 00	Anton Christensen	Do.
13	Charles Whitlock	do.	May 1, 1867	Nov. 1, 1867	6	13 00	3 50	16 50	72 00	171 00	Charles Whitlock	Do.
14	Sern A. Sorensen	do.	May 1, 1867	Nov. 1, 1867	6	13 00	3 50	16 50	72 00	171 00	S. A. Lorensen	Do.
15	Sern N. Sorensen	do.	May 1, 1867	Nov. 1, 1867	6	13 00	3 50	16 50	72 00	171 00	S. N. Lorensen	Do.
16	George Aldred	do.	May 1, 1867	Nov. 1, 1867	6	13 00	3 50	16 50	72 00	171 00	George Alrede	Do.
17	James Larson	do.	May 1, 1867	Nov. 1, 1867	6	13 00	3 50	16 50	72 00	171 00	James P. Larsen	Do.
18	Peter Larsen	do.	May 1, 1867	Nov. 1, 1867	6	13 00	3 50	16 50	72 00	171 00	Petter Larson	Do.
19	Henry Ovett	do.	May 1, 1867	Nov. 1, 1867	6	13 00	3 50	16 50	72 00	171 00	Henry Oviutt	Do.
20	Lars C. Larson	do.	May 1, 1867	Nov. 1, 1867	6	13 00	3 50	16 50	72 00	171 00	Lars C. Larson	Do.
20	Peter T. Peterson	do.	May 1, 1867	Nov. 1, 1867	6	13 00	3 50	16 50	72 00	171 00	Peder Taylor Pederson	Do.

No.	Name									Name	
21	Louis Thomson	do	May 1, 1867	Nov. 1, 1867	6	13 00	3 50	16 50	72 00	171 00	Louis Thomson	Do.
22	Ole Oleson	do	May 1, 1867	Nov. 1, 1867	6	13 00	3 50	16 50	72 00	171 00	Ole Olson	Do.
23	Christian S. Yensen	do	May 1, 1867	Nov. 1, 1867	6	13 00	3 50	16 50	72 00	171 00	Christian S. Yenson	Do.
24	Andrew R. Anderson	do	May 1, 1867	Nov. 1, 1867	6	13 00	3 50	16 50	72 00	171 00	A. K. Anderson	Do.
25	Jence C. Frost	do	May 1, 1867	Nov. 1, 1867	6	13 00	3 50	16 50	72 00	171 00	J. Chr. Frost	Do.
26	George Jensen	do	May 1, 1867	Nov. 1, 1867	6	13 00	3 50	16 50	72 00	171 00	Georg Jensen	Do.
27	Michael Hansen	do	May 1, 1867	Nov. 1, 1867	6	13 00	3 50	16 50	72 00	171 00	Michael Hanson	Do.
28	Thomas Thorp	do	May 1, 1867	Nov. 1, 1867	6	13 00	3 50	16 50	72 00	171 00	Thomas Thorpe	Do.
29	Christian Larsen, jr.	do	May 1, 1867	Nov. 1, 1867	6	13 00	3 50	16 50	72 00	171 00		Do.
30	Peter Christemsen Jensen	do	May 1, 1867	Nov. 1, 1867	6	13 00	3 50	16 50	72 00	171 00	P. C. Jensen	Do.
31	Peter Peterson	do	May 1, 1867	Nov. 1, 1867	6	13 00	3 50	16 50	72 00	171 00		Do.
32	Poul Poulson	do	May 1, 1867	Nov. 1, 1867	6	13 00	3 50	16 50	72 00	171 00	Paul Paulsen	Do.
33	Marten Benson	do	May 1, 1867	Nov. 1, 1867	6	13 00	3 50	16 50	72 00	171 00		Do.
34	George Larsen	do	May 1, 1867	Nov. 1, 1867	6	13 00	3 50	16 50	72 00	171 00	Ole Larson	Do.
35	Ole Larsen	do	May 1, 1867	Nov. 1, 1867	6	13 00	3 50	16 50	72 00	171 00	R. Rasmussen	Do.
36	Rasmus Rasmussen	do	May 1, 1867	Nov. 1, 1867	6	13 00	3 50	16 50	72 00	171 00	Peter Anderson	Do.
37	Peter Anderson	do	May 1, 1867	Nov. 1, 1867	6	13 00	3 50	16 50	72 00	171 00	James V. Stevenson	Do.
38	James V. Stephens	do	May 1, 1867	Nov. 1, 1867	6	13 00	3 50	16 50	72 00	171 00	James Hanson	Do.
39	James Hanson	do	May 1, 1867	Nov. 1, 1867	6	13 00	3 50	16 50	72 00	171 00	Thomas Thomsen	Do.
40	Thomas Thomson	do	May 1, 1867	Nov. 1, 1867	6	13 00	3 50	16 50	72 00	171 00	Andrew O. Anderson	Do.
41	Andrew O. Anderson	do	May 1, 1867	Nov. 1, 1867	6	13 00	3 50	16 50	72 00	171 00	William Dixen	Do.
42	William Dixon	do	May 1, 1867	Nov. 1, 1867	6	13 00	3 50	16 50	72 00	171 00	Ole Pet rson	Do.
43	Ole Peterson	do	May 1, 1867	Nov. 1, 1867	6	13 00	3 50	16 50	72 00	171 00		Do.
44	Caleb C. Edwards	do	May 1, 1867	Nov. 1, 1867	6	13 00	3 50	16 50	72 00	171 00		Do.
45	Rasmus Clanson	do	May 1, 1867	Nov. 1, 1867	6	13 00	3 50	16 50	72 00	171 00	Andrew C. Anderson	Do.
46	Andrew C. Anderson	do	May 1, 1867	Nov. 1, 1867	6	13 00	3 50	16 50	72 00	171 00	Nels Thompson	Do.
47	Niels Thompson	do	May 1, 1867	Nov. 1, 1867	6	13 00	3 50	16 50	72 00	171 00	Joseph Stevens	Do.
48	Joseph Stephens	do	May 1, 1867	Nov. 1, 1867	6	13 00	3 50	16 50	72 00	171 00		Do.

This company was mustered into service at Fort Ephraim, Sanpete County, May 1, 1867, by Brigadier General William B. Pace. They were actively engaged every day in the mountains and passes as scouts and patrols. They were also engaged at the battle at Springtown, August 13, 1867, and were mustered out November 1, 1867.

I certify that the above account is correct.

H. B. CLAWSON,
Adjutant General Utah Territory Militia.

Pay-roll of Captain Daniel Henrie's company —— infantry, Utah Territory militia, employed in the suppression of Indian hostilities in Sanpete county, Utah Territory, from May 1, 1867, to November 1, 1867.

We, the undersigned, acknowledge to have received from James W. Cummings, paymaster Utah Territory militia, the sums set opposite to our names, in full payment for our services for the time specified.

Number.	Names.	Rank.	Period of service. Commencement.	Period of service. Expiration.	Months.	Pay per month.	Monthly allowance for clothing.	Total monthly pay and allowance.	Total pay and allowance.	Signatures.	Witness.
1	Daniel Henrie	Captain	May 1, 1867	Nov. 1, 1867	6			$118 50	$711 00	Daniel Henrie	W. T. Reid.
1	John P. Squires	1st lieutenant	May 1, 1867	Nov. 1, 1867	6			108 50	651 00	John P. Squires	Do.
1	John Patten	2d lieutenant	May 1, 1867	Nov. 1, 1867	6			103 50	621 00	John Patten	Do.
2	Samuel Mackey	do	May 1, 1867	Nov. 1, 1867	6			103 50	621 00	Samuel Mackey	Do.
3	James C. Brown	do	May 1, 1867	Nov. 1, 1867	6			103 50	621 00	James C. Brown	Do.
4	William Sampson	do	May 1, 1867	Nov. 1, 1867	6			103 50	621 00	William Sampton	Do.
5	John Curtis	do	May 1, 1867	Nov. 1, 1867	6			103 50	621 00	John Curtis	Do.
1	Peter Anderson	Sergeant	May 1, 1867	Nov. 1, 1867	6	$17 00	$3 50	20 50	123 00	Peter Andersen	Do.
2	Jeptha Shoemaker	do	May 1, 1867	Nov. 1, 1867	6	17 00	3 50	20 50	123 00	Jephthah Shoemaker	Do.
3	John Greer	do	May 1, 1867	Nov. 1, 1867	6	17 00	3 50	20 50	123 00	John Grier	Do.
4	Edwin Cox	do	May 1, 1867	Nov. 1, 1867	6	17 00	3 50	20 50	123 00	Edwin Cox	Do.
5	William Braithwaite	do	May 1, 1867	Nov. 1, 1867	6	17 00	3 50	20 50	123 00	Wm. Braithwaite	Do.
1	David Shaw	Private	May 1, 1867	Nov. 1, 1867	6	13 00	3 50	16 50	99 00	David Shane	Do.
2	Robert Johnson, jr	do	May 1, 1867	Nov. 1, 1867	6	13 00	3 50	16 50	99 00	Robert Johnston, jr	Do.
3	John Buchannan	do	May 1, 1867	Nov. 1, 1867	6	13 00	3 50	16 50	99 00	John Buchanan	Do.
4	George Braithwaite	do	May 1, 1867	Nov. 1, 1867	6	13 00	3 50	16 50	99 00	George Braithwaite	Do.
5	Elias Dernll	do	May 1, 1867	Nov. 1, 1867	6	13 00	3 50	16 50	99 00	Elias Dirnll	Do.
6	William Funk	do	May 1, 1867	Nov. 1, 1867	6	13 00	3 50	16 50	99 00	Wm. D. Funk	Do.
7	Sanford Forbush, jr	do	May 1, 1867	Nov. 1, 1867	6	13 00	3 50	16 50	99 00	Sanford Forbush	Do.
8	Thomas Boyington	do	May 1, 1867	Nov. 1, 1867	6	13 00	3 50	16 50	99 00	Thomas Boylington	Do.
9	George E. Bench	do	May 1, 1867	Nov. 1, 1867	6	13 00	3 50	16 50	99 00	George E. Bench	Do.
10	Isaac Voorhes	do	May 1, 1867	Nov. 1, 1867	6	13 00	3 50	16 50	99 00	Isaac Voorhees	Do.
11	Elias Crain	do	May 1, 1867	Nov. 1, 1867	6	13 00	3 50	16 50	99 00	Elias Crane	Do.
12	Henry D. Gifford	do	May 1, 1867	Nov. 1, 1867	6	13 00	3 50	16 50	99 00	Henry D. Gifford	Do.
13	Samuel Davenport	do	May 1, 1867	Nov. 1, 1867	6	13 00	3 50	16 50	99 00	Samuel Devenport	Do.
14	Henry Henrickson	do	May 1, 1867	Nov. 1, 1867	6	13 00	3 50	16 50	99 00	Houtroh Honbriksen	Do.
15	John Wilkenson	do	May 1, 1867	Nov. 1, 1867	6	13 00	3 50	16 50	99 00	John Wilkenson	Do.
16	Franklin Spencer	do	May 1, 1867	Nov. 1, 1867	6	13 00	3 50	16 50	99 00	Daniel Spencer	Do.
17	Nathan E. Louis	do	May 1, 1867	Nov. 1, 1867	6	13 00	3 50	16 50	99 00	Nathan E. Lewis	Do.
18	Hyrum Forbush	do	May 1, 1867	Nov. 1, 1867	6	13 00	3 50	16 50	99 00	Hyrom Forbush	Do.
19	John E. Klais	do	May 1, 1867	Nov. 1, 1867	6	13 00	3 50	16 50	99 00	John C. Kjeer	Do.
20	Hance C. Hanson	do	May 1, 1867	Nov. 1, 1867	6	13 00	3 50	16 50	99 00	Hance C. Hanson	Do.

	Name		Mustered in	Mustered out						Name	
21	Henry Parsons	do	May 1, 1867	Nov. 1, 1867	6	13 00	3 50	16 50	99 00	Henry Parsons	Do.
22	James Burton	do	May 1, 1867	Nov. 1, 1867	6	13 00	3 50	16 50	99 03	James Barton	Do.
23	Peter Brown	do	May 1, 1867	Nov. 1, 1867	6	13 00	3 50	16 50	99 00	Peter Brown	Do.
24	George P. Portal	do	May 1, 1867	Nov. 1, 1867	6	13 00	3 50	16 50	99 03	George P. Portal	Do.
25	William M. Marble	do	May 1, 1867	Nov. 1, 1867	6	13 00	3 30	16 30	99 00	William L. Marble	Do.
26	Hyrum Marble	do	May 1, 1867	Nov. 1, 1867	6	13 00	3 30	16 30	99 00	Hiram Marble	Do.
27	William Kilpack	do	May 1, 1867	Nov. 1, 1867	6	13 00	3 50	16 50	93 00	William Kilpack	Do.
28	William Rudd	do	May 1, 1867	Nov. 1, 1867	6	13 00	3 30	16 30	99 00	William Rudd	Do.
29	Harvey Brouns	do	May 1, 1867	Nov. 1, 1867	6	13 00	3 30	16 30	99 00	Harvey Brouns	Do.
30	Nelson Higgins	do	May 1, 1867	Nov. 1, 1867	6	13 00	3 30	16 30	99 00	Nelson Higgins	Do.
31	Nels Christoffersen	do	May 1, 1867	Nov. 1, 1867	6	13 10	3 50	16 50	99 10	Nieh Christoff-rown	Do.
32	Nathaniel Marble	do	May 1, 1867	Nov. 1, 1867	6	13 03	3 50	16 50	99 00	Nathaniel Marbel	Do.
33	Byron Cox	do	May 1, 1867	Nov. 1, 1867	6	13 00	3 50	16 50	99 00	Byron Cox	Do.
34	Lyman Beach	do	May 1, 1867	Nov. 1, 1867	6	13 00	3 50	16 50	99 00	Lyman Beach	Do.
35	Lakey Shoemaker	do	May 1, 1867	Nov. 1, 1867	6	13 03	3 51	16 51	99 00	Lakey Shoemaker	Do.
36	Neils Nelson	do	May 1, 1867	Nov. 1, 1867	6	13 00	3 30	16 30	99 00	Niels Nielsen	Do.
37	Henry Cook	do	May 1, 1867	Nov. 1, 1867	6	13 00	3 50	16 50	99 00	Henry Cook	Do.
38	Ruben Hewitt	do	May 1, 1867	Nov. 1, 1867	6	13 00	3 50	16 51	99 03	Ruben Hewitt	Do.
39	Franklin Snow	do	May 1, 1867	Nov. 1, 1867	6	13 01	3 51	16 51	99 00	Franklin Snow	Do.
40	Vence Larsen	do	May 1, 1867	Nov. 1, 1867	6	13 00	3 30	16 30	99 03	John Larsen	Do.
41	George Peacock jr	do	May 1, 1867	Nov. 1, 1867	6	13 01	3 50	16 50	99 00	Geo. J. Peacock	Do.
42	Ezeriah Tuttle jr	do	May 1, 1867	Nov. 1, 1867	6	13 01	3 30	16 50	99 00	Azariah Tuttle, Jr	Do.
43	Rowland Braithwaite	do	May 1, 1867	Nov. 1, 1867	6	13 01	3 50	16 50	99 00	Rowland Braithwaite	Do.
44	Joseph Braithwaite	do	May 1, 1867	Nov. 1, 1867	6	13 03	3 30	16 30	93 00	Joseph Braithwaite	Do.
45	Ethelbert Barton	do	May 1, 1867	Nov. 1, 1867	6	13 00	3 50	16 50	99 00	Ethelbert Barton	Do.
46	Peter J. Marker	do	May 1, 1867	Nov. 1, 1867	6	13 00	3 50	16 50	99 00	Peter J. Marker	Do.
47	John Hannah	do	May 1, 1867	Nov. 1, 1867	6	13 00	3 50	16 50	99 00	John Hannah	Do.
48	Jerome Kempton	do	May 1, 1867	Nov. 1, 1867	6	13 00	3 51	16 51	99 00	Jerome Kempton	Do.
49	Tennessee Kempton	do	May 1, 1867	Nov. 1, 1867	6	13 00	3 50	16 50	99 00	Teancum Kempton	Do.
50	Watermare Minster	do	May 1, 1867	Nov. 1, 1867	6	13 00	3 50	16 50	99 00	Waldemar yuster	Do.
51	Andrew Larson	do	May 1, 1867	Nov. 1, 1867	6	13 00	3 30	16 30	99 00	Andrew Larson	Do.
52	Cyrus Wingt	do	May 1, 1867	Nov. 1, 1867	6	13 00	3 30	16 53	99 00	Cyrus Wingt	Do.

This company was mustered into service at Manti City, Sanpete County, May 1, 1867, by Brigadier General W. B. Pace, and assigned to duty in the vicinity of said city. They were in active service every day, as guards and patrols in the mountains and valley, until mustered out, November 1, 1867.

I certify that the above account is correct.

H. B. CLAWSON,
Adjutant General Utah Territory Militia.

Pay-roll of Captain Orange Seely's company —— cavalry, Utah Territory militia, employed in the suppression of Indian hostilities in Sanpete County, Utah Territory, from May 1, 1867, to November 1, 1867.

We, the undersigned, acknowledge to have received from James W. Cummings, paymaster Utah Territory militia, the sums set opposite to our names, in full payment for our services for the time specified.

Number	Names	Rank	Commencement	Expiration	Months	Pay per month	Monthly allowance for clothing	Total monthly pay and allowance	40 cts. per day for use and risk of horse and horse equipment	Total pay and allowance	Signatures	Witness
1	Orange Seely	Captain	May 1, 1867	Nov. 1, 1867	6			$129 50	$72 00	$849 00	Orange Seely	W. B. Pace.
1	Levi B. Reynolds	1st lieutenant	May 1, 1867	Nov. 1, 1867	6			112 83	72 00	748 98	Levi B. Reynolds	Do.
2	Squire Reynolds	2d lieutenant	May 1, 1867	Nov. 1, 1867	6			112 83	72 00	748 98	Squire Reynolds	Do.
3	Erick Bartel Erickson	do	May 1, 1867	Nov. 1, 1867	6			112 83	72 00	748 99	Erick Bartel Erickson	Do.
4	William Alma Allred	do	May 1, 1867	Nov. 1, 1867	6			112 83	72 00	748 98	W. A. Allred	Do.
5	Christian Sorenson	do	May 1, 1867	Nov. 1, 1867	6			112 83	72 00	748 98	Christian Sorensen	Do.
6	Peter Morgensen	do	May 1, 1867	Nov. 1, 1867	6			112 83	72 00	748 98	Peter Morgensen	Do.
1	George Catlin	Sergeant	May 1, 1867	Nov. 1, 1867	6	$17 00	$3 50	20 50	72 00	195 00	Geo. Catlin	Do.
2	Hans Poulson	do	May 1, 1867	Nov. 1, 1867	6	17 00	3 50	20 50	72 00	195 00	Hans Poulsen	Do.
3	William Morrison	do	May 1, 1867	Nov. 1, 1867	6	17 00	3 50	20 50	72 00	195 00	Wm. Morrison	Do.
4	Jens Christian Meiling	do	May 1, 1867	Nov. 1, 1867	6	17 00	3 50	20 50	72 00	195 00	Jens C. Meiling	Do.
5	Hans Christian Beck	do	May 1, 1867	Nov. 1, 1867	6	17 00	3 50	20 50	72 00	195 00	Hans C. Beck	Do.
1	James Hanson	Bugler	May 1, 1867	Nov. 1, 1867	6	13 00	3 50	16 50	72 00	171 00	Jens Hansen	Do.
1	John Young	Private	May 1, 1867	Nov. 1, 1867	6	13 00	3 50	16 50	72 00	171 00	John Young	Do.
2	Joseph Gribble	do	May 1, 1867	Nov. 1, 1867	6	13 00	3 50	16 50	72 00	171 00	Joseph Gribble	Do.
3	James Wishaw Meyrick	do	May 1, 1867	Nov. 1, 1867	6	13 00	3 50	16 50	72 00	171 00	James W. Meyrick	Do.
4	Thomas Ivie	do	May 1, 1867	Nov. 1, 1867	6	13 00	3 50	16 50	72 00	171 00	Thomas Ivie	Do.
5	Alphonson Wheelock	do	May 1, 1867	Nov. 1, 1867	6	13 00	3 50	16 50	72 00	171 00	Alphonso Wheelock	Do.
6	Neils Rasmussen	do	May 1, 1867	Nov. 1, 1867	6	13 00	3 50	16 50	72 00	171 00	Niels Rasmussen	Do.
7	George Coats	do	May 1, 1867	Nov. 1, 1867	6	13 00	3 50	16 50	72 00	171 00	George Coats	Do.
8	Mads Jensen	do	May 1, 1867	Nov. 1, 1867	6	13 00	3 50	16 50	72 00	171 00	Mads Jensen	Do.
9	Peter Jensen	do	May 1, 1867	Nov. 1, 1867	6	13 00	3 50	16 50	72 00	171 00	Peder Jensen	Do.
10	James Walker	do	May 1, 1867	Nov. 1, 1867	6	13 00	3 50	16 50	72 00	171 00	James Walker	Do.
11	Andrew J. Snydergaard	do	May 1, 1867	Nov. 1, 1867	6	13 00	3 50	16 50	72 00	171 00	Anders Synderguard	Do.
12	Jens C. Nebellio	do	May 1, 1867	Nov. 1, 1867	6	13 00	3 50	16 50	72 00	171 00	Jens C. Nelliele	Do.
13	Christian Jeson	do	May 1, 1867	Nov. 1, 1867	6	13 00	3 50	16 50	72 00	171 00	Christian Jensen	Do.
14	Andrew Peter Jensen	do	May 1, 1867	Nov. 1, 1867	6	13 00	3 50	16 50	72 00	171 00	Andrew Petter Jensson	Do.
15	Christian Wintergreen	do	May 1, 1867	Nov. 1, 1867	6	13 00	3 50	16 50	72 00	171 00	Christian Widdergreen	Do.
16	Erick Gunderson	do	May 1, 1867	Nov. 1, 1867	6	13 00	3 50	16 50	72 00	171 00	Erik Gunderson	Do.
17	William Coats	do	May 1, 1867	Nov. 1, 1867	6	13 00	3 50	16 50	72 00	171 00	William Coats	Do.
18	Jens Christian Harbro	do	May 1, 1867	Nov. 1, 1867	6	13 00	3 50	16 50	72 00	171 00	Jens C. Hernbro	Do.
19	Morten Rasmussen	do	May 1, 1867	Nov. 1, 1867	6	13 00	3 50	16 50	72 00	171 00	Morten Rasmussen	Do.

No.	Name		Mustered in	Mustered out							Name	
20	William Walurick	do	May 1, 1867	Nov. 1, 1867	6	13 00	3 50	16 50	72 00	171 00	William Walurick	Do.
21	Peter Miller	do	May 1, 1867	Nov. 1, 1867	6	13 00	3 50	16 50	72 00	171 00	Peter Miller	Do.
22	Martin Aldrich	do	May 1, 1867	Nov. 1, 1867	6	13 00	3 50	16 50	72 00	171 00	Martin Aldrich	Do.
23	Caleb Hartley	do	May 1, 1867	Nov. 1, 1867	6	13 00	3 50	16 50	72 00	171 00	Caleb Hartley	Do.
24	W<ford W. Brandon	do	May 1, 1867	Nov. 1, 1867	6	13 00	3 50	16 50	72 00	171 00	W<ford W. Brandon	Do.
25	Martin Miller	do	May 1, 1867	Nov. 1, 1867	6	13 00	3 50	16 50	72 00	171 00	Morten Miller	Do.
26	Augustus Anderson	do	May 1, 1867	Nov. 1, 1867	6	13 00	3 50	16 50	72 00	171 00	Augustus Anderson	Do.
27	Peter Larsen	do	May 1, 1867	Nov. 1, 1867	6	13 00	3 50	16 50	72 00	171 00	Peter Larsen	Do.
28	Bendt Hansen	do	May 1, 1867	Nov. 1, 1867	6	13 00	3 50	16 50	72 00	171 00	Bendt Hansen	Do.
29	Rasmus F. Jorgensen	do	May 1, 1867	Nov. 1, 1867	6	13 00	3 50	16 50	72 00	171 00	Rasmus F. Jergensen	Do.
30	Hyrum Seely	do	May 1, 1867	Nov. 1, 1867	6	13 00	3 50	16 50	72 00	171 00	Hyrum Seely	Do.
31	Comderset Rowe	do	May 1, 1867	Nov. 1, 1867	6	13 00	3 50	16 50	72 00	171 00	Comdercet Rowe	Do.
32	Frederick Peterson	do	May 1, 1867	Nov. 1, 1867	6	13 00	3 50	16 50	72 00	171 00	Frederick Petersen	Do.
33	Peter Frederickson	do	May 1, 1867	Nov. 1, 1867	6	13 00	3 50	16 50	72 00	171 00	Peter Frederikson	Do.
34	Joseph Willcox	do	May 1, 1867	Nov. 1, 1867	6	13 00	3 50	16 50	72 00	171 00	Joseph Willcox	Do.
35	Niels Peter Neilson	do	May 1, 1867	Nov. 1, 1867	6	13 00	3 50	16 50	72 00	171 00	Niels P. Nielsen	Do.
36	Andrew Peterson	do	May 1, 1867	Nov. 1, 1867	6	13 00	3 50	16 50	72 00	171 00	Andrew Peterson	Do.
37	William G. Barton	do	May 1, 1867	Nov. 1, 1867	6	13 00	3 50	16 50	72 00	171 00	William G. Barton	Do.
38	Colnau Joplin	do	May 1, 1867	Nov. 1, 1867	6	13 00	3 50	16 50	72 00	171 00	Colnau Joplin	Do.
39	Christian Peter	do	May 1, 1867	Nov. 1, 1867	6	13 00	3 50	16 50	72 00	171 00	Christian Peter	Do.
40	Rodolphus N. Bennett	do	May 1, 1867	Nov. 1, 1867	6	13 00	3 50	16 50	72 00	171 00	Rodolphus N. Bennett	Do.
41	Jefferson Tidwell	do	May 1, 1867	Nov. 1, 1867	6	13 00	3 50	16 50	72 00	171 00	J. Tidwell	Do.
42	Thomas Fuller	do	May 1, 1867	Nov. 1, 1867	6	13 00	3 50	16 50	72 00	171 00	Thomas Fuller	Do.
43	Bendt Swensen	do	May 1, 1867	Nov. 1, 1867	6	13 00	3 50	16 50	72 00	171 00	Bendt Swensen	Do.
44	Christian Jensen	do	May 1, 1867	Nov. 1, 1867	6	13 00	3 50	16 50	72 00	171 00	Christian Jensen	Do.
45	Peter Johnson	do	May 1, 1867	Nov. 1, 1867	6	13 00	3 50	16 50	72 00	171 00	Peter Johnson	Do.
46	Lyman Peters	do	May 1, 1867	Nov. 1, 1867	6	13 00	3 50	16 50	72 00	171 00	Lyman Peters	Do.
47	George Fransum	do	May 1, 1867	Nov. 1, 1867	6	13 00	3 50	16 50	72 00	171 00	George Fransum	Do.
48	John Carter	do	May 1, 1867	Nov. 1, 1867	6	13 00	3 50	16 50	72 00	171 00		
49	Thomas Coats	do	May 1, 1867	Nov. 1, 1867	6	13 00	3 50	16 50	72 00	171 00	Thomas Coats	Do.
50	Don Carlost Seely	do	May 1, 1867	Nov. 1, 1867	6	13 00	3 50	16 50	72 00	171 00		
51	Christian N. Christiansen	do	May 1, 1867	Nov. 1, 1867	6	13 00	3 50	16 50	72 00	171 00	C. N. Christiansen	Do.

This company was mustered into service at Mount Pleasant, Sanpete County, May 1, 1867, by Brigadier General William B. Pace, and were engaged as scouts and mounted patrols; were also engaged in the battle at Thistle Creek Cañon, June 1, 1867, under command of Lieutenant Colonel John L. Ives, also at the battle at Springtown, August 13, 1867, under command of Colonel R. N. Allred; were mustered out November 1, 1865.

I certify that the above account is correct.

H. B. CLAWSON,
Adjutant General Utah Territory Militia.

Pay-roll of Captain Peder Isackson's company —— infantry, Utah Territory militia, employed in the suppression of Indian hostilities in Sanpete County, Utah Territory, from May 1, 1867, to November 1, 1867.

We, the undersigned, acknowledge to have received from James W. Cummings, paymaster Utah Territory militia, the sums set opposite to our names, in full payment for our services for the time specified.

Number	Names	Rank	Commencement	Expiration	Months	Pay per month	Monthly allowance for clothing	Total monthly pay and allowance	Total pay and allowance	Signatures	Witnesses
1	Peder Isackson	Captain	May 1, 1867	Nov. 1, 1867	6			$118 50	$711 00	Peder Isaacsen	H. F. Petersen.
1	John F. Dorius	1st lieut.	May 1, 1867	Nov. 1, 1867	6			108 50	651 00	John T. Dorius	Do.
1	K. H. Brown	2d lieut.	May 1, 1867	Nov. 1, 1867	6			103 50	621 00	K. H. Brown	Do.
2	Wilhelm Berman	do	May 1, 1867	Nov. 1, 1867	6			103 50	621 00	W. F. O. Behrmann	Do.
3	Lars Anderson Strip	do	May 1, 1867	Nov. 1, 1867	6			103 50	621 00	Lars S. Anderson	Do.
1	Frederick Jensen	Sergeant	May 1, 1867	Nov. 1, 1867	6	$17 00	$3 50	20 50	123 00	Frederich Jensen	Do.
2	Peder Hansen	do	May 1, 1867	Nov. 1, 1867	6	17 00	3 50	20 50	123 00	J. Peter Hansen	Do.
3	N. P. Bartholm	do	May 1, 1867	Nov. 1, 1867	6	17 00	3 50	20 50	123 00	N. P. Bastholm	Do.
1	Peter Westenror	Private	May 1, 1867	Nov. 1, 1867	6	13 00	3 50	16 50	99 00	Peter Westenoor	Do.
2	Hans Westenror	do	May 1, 1867	Nov. 1, 1867	6	13 00	3 50	16 53	96 00	Hans Westenor	Do.
3	Johan C. Jensen	do	May 1, 1867	Nov. 1, 1867	6	13 00	3 50	16 50	99 00	John C. Jenson	Do.
4	John C. Jensen	do	May 1, 1867	Nov. 1, 1867	6	13 00	3 50	16 50	99 00		
5	Thls G. Hansen	do	May 1, 1867	Nov. 1, 1867	6	13 00	3 50	16 50	99 00	T. J. Hansen	Do.
6	Anton Lewilberg	do	May 1, 1867	Nov. 1, 1867	6	13 00	3 50	16 50	99 00		
7	Tues Tensen	do	May 1, 1867	Nov. 1, 1867	6	13 00	3 50	16 50	99 00	Pues Pensen	Do.
8	Peder Neilson	do	May 1, 1867	Nov. 1, 1867	6	13 00	3 50	16 50	99 00	Peter Nielson	Do.
9	Christian Jensen	do	May 1, 1867	Nov. 1, 1867	6	13 00	3 50	16 50	99 00		
10	Chris Thomsen	do	May 1, 1867	Nov. 1, 1867	6	13 00	3 50	16 50	99 00		
11	Christian Christiansen	do	May 1, 1867	Nov. 1, 1867	6	13 00	3 50	16 50	99 00	Christen Christenson	Do.
12	Andrew Neilson	do	May 1, 1867	Nov. 1, 1867	6	13 00	3 50	16 50	99 00		
13	Christian Hansen	do	May 1, 1867	Nov. 1, 1867	6	13 00	3 50	16 50	99 00		
14	N. C. Anderson	do	May 1, 1867	Nov. 1, 1867	6	13 00	3 50	16 50	99 00	N. C. Andersen	Do.
15	Fred Julius	do	May 1, 1867	Nov. 1, 1867	6	13 00	3 50	16 50	99 00	Frederik Julius	Do.
16	Rasmus Anderson	do	May 1, 1867	Nov. 1, 1867	6	13 00	3 50	16 50	99 00	Rasmus Anderson	Do.
17	Tues C. Neilson	do	May 1, 1867	Nov. 1, 1867	6	13 00	3 50	16 50	99 00	Tues C. Nielsen	Do.
18	Bernt Rasmusen	do	May 1, 1867	Nov. 1, 1867	6	13 00	3 50	16 50	99 00	Bernt Rasmussen	Do.
19	Jens Larsen	do	May 1, 1867	Nov. 1, 1867	6	13 00	3 50	16 50	99 00	Jens Larsen	Do.
20	J. C. Gravenstein	do	May 1, 1867	Nov. 1, 1867	6	13 00	3 50	16 50	99 00	J. C. Gravenstein	Do.
21	A. Westerguard	do	May 1, 1867	Nov. 1, 1867	6	13 00	3 50	16 50	99 00	A. Westegard	Do.
22	Hans Boesen	do	May 1, 1867	Nov. 1, 1867	6	13 00	3 50	16 50	99 00	Hans Bosen	Do.
23	Andreas Petersen	do	May 1, 1867	Nov. 1, 1867	6	13 00	3 50	16 50	99 00	Andrew Pedersen	Do.

25	Jens Neilson	do	May 1, 1867	Nov. 1, 1867	6	13 00	3 50	16 50	99 00	Jens Nielsen Engager	Do.
26	Chris Christianson	do	May 1, 1867	Nov. 1, 1867	6	13 00	3 51	16 50	99 00	Chrl Chri-tiansen	Do.
27	Samuel Beal	do	May 1, 1867	Nov. 1, 1867	6	13 00	3 50	16 50	99 00	Samuel Beal	Do.
28	A. F. C. Hansen	do	May 1, 1867	Nov. 1, 1867	6	13 00	3 50	16 50	99 00		Do.
29	Jorgen Nielson	do	May 1, 1867	Nov. 1, 1867	6	13 00	3 50	16 50	99 00	Jowgen Niulxun	Do.
30	Andreas Anderson	do	May 1, 1867	Nov. 1, 1867	6	13 40	3 50	16 51	99 00	Andrew Anderson	Do.
31	P. M. Pederson	do	May 1, 1867	Nov. 1, 1867	6	13 00	3 50	16 50	99 00	P. M. Pederson	Do.
32	Neils Mortensen	do	May 1, 1867	Nov. 1, 1867	6	13 00	3 50	16 50	99 00	Niels Mortensen	Do.
33	A. P. Bastholm	do	May 1, 1867	Nov. 1, 1867	6	13 00	3 50	16 50	99 00	A. P. Bastholm	Do.

This company was mustered into service at Fort Ephraim, Sanpete County, May 1, 1867, by Brigadier General W. B. Pace, and assigned to duty in the vicinity of said city. They were in active service every day, as guards and patrols in the mountains and passes, until mustered out, November 1, 1867.

I certify that the above account is correct.

H. B. CLAWSON,
Adjutant General Utah Territory Militia.

Pay-roll of Captain William Bench's company —— infantry, Utah Territory militia, employed in the suppression of Indian hostilities in Sanpete County, Utah Territory, from May 1, 1867, to November 1, 1867.

We, the undersigned, acknowledge to have received from James W. Cummings, paymaster Utah Territory militia, the sums set opposite to our names, in full payment for our services for the time specified.

Number	Names	Rank	Commencement.	Expiration.	Months.	Pay per month.	Monthly allowance for clubbing.	Total monthly pay and allowance.	Total pay and allowance.	Signatures.	Witness.
1	William Bench	Captain	May 1, 1867	November 1, 1867	6			118 50	$711 00	William Bench, sr	W. T. Reid.
1	William Anderson	1st lieutenant	May 1, 1867	November 1, 1867	6			108 50	651 00	William Anderson	Do.
2	Elisha Edwards	2d lieutenant	May 1, 1867	November 1, 1867	6			103 50	621 00	Elisha Edwards	Do.
3	Azariah Tuttle, sr	do	May 1, 1867	November 1, 1867	6			103 50	621 00	Azariah Tuttle, sr	Do.
4	Gardner Snow	do	May 1, 1867	November 1, 1867	6			103 50	621 00	Gardner Snow	Do.
5	Hans Larsen	do	May 1, 1867	November 1, 1867	6			103 50	621 00	Hans Larsen	Do.
6	John Tutton	Sergeant	May 1, 1867	November 1, 1867	6	$17 00	$3 50	20 50	123 00	John C. Tutton	Do.
1	Jens Hansen	do	May 1, 1867	November 1, 1867	6	17 00	3 50	20 54	123 00	Jens Hansen	Do.
2	Nells P. Domurgaard	do	May 1, 1867	November 1, 1867	6	17 00	3 50	20 50	123 00	Niels P. Domund	Do.
3	Andrew C. Peterson	do	May 1, 1867	November 1, 1867	6	17 00	3 50	20 50	123 00	A. C. Petersen	Do.
4	Andrew Poulson	do	May 1, 1867	November 1, 1867	6	17 00	3 50	20 50	123 00	Andrew Poulson	Do.
5	Jens K. Peterson	do	May 1, 1867	November 1, 1867	6	13 00	3 50	20 50	123 00	Jens K. Petersen	Do.
1	William Beal	Private	May 1, 1867	November 1, 1867	6	13 00	3 50	16 50	99 00	Willonem Beal	Do.
2	Richard Hall	do	May 1, 1867	November 1, 1867	6	13 00	3 50	16 50	99 00	R. Hall	Do.
3	Robert Logan	do	May 1, 1867	November 1, 1867	6	13 00	3 50	16 50	99 00	Robert Logan	Do.
4	Claus Rasmussca	do	May 1, 1867	November 1, 1867	6	13 00	3 50	16 50	99 00	Claus Rasmussen, his + mark	Do.
5	Peter Larsen	do	May 1, 1867	November 1, 1867	6	13 00	3 50	16 50	99 00	Peter Larsen	Do.
6	Jens Jensen	do	May 1, 1867	November 1, 1867	6	13 00	3 50	16 50	99 00	Jens Jensen	Do.
7	Frederick W. Cox, sr	do	May 1, 1867	November 1, 1867	6	13 00	3 50	16 50	99 00	F. W. Cox, sr.	Do.
8	John Williams	do	May 1, 1867	November 1, 1867	6	13 00	3 50	16 50	99 00	John Williams, his + mark	Do.
9	Jens Peter Marker	do	May 1, 1867	November 1, 1867	6	13 00	3 50	16 50	99 00	Jens Peter Marker	Do.
10	Peter Jensen	do	May 1, 1867	November 1, 1867	6	13 00	3 50	16 50	99 00	Peter Jensen	Do.
11	Christian Munk	do	May 1, 1867	November 1, 1867	6	13 00	3 50	16 50	99 00	Christian Munk	Do.
12	Samuel Markey	do	May 1, 1867	November 1, 1867	6	13 33	3 50	16 50	99 00	Samchez Neckoy	Do.
13	Abraham Washburn	do	May 1, 1867	November 1, 1867	6	13 00	3 50	16 50	99 00	Abraham Washburn	Do.
14	Peter C. Nielson	do	May 1, 1867	November 1, 1867	6	13 00	3 50	16 50	99 00	P. C. Nielsen	Do.
15	Jezreel Shoemaker	do	May 1, 1867	November 1, 1867	6	13 00	3 50	16 50	99 00	Jezreel Shoemaker	Do.
16	Albert Smith	do	May 1, 1867	November 1, 1867	6	13 00	3 50	16 50	99 00	Albert Smith	Do.
17	William Follett	do	May 1, 1867	November 1, 1867	6	13 00	3 50	16 50	99 00	W. T. Follett	Do.
18	Soren Pedersen	do	May 1, 1867	November 1, 1867	6	13 00	3 53	16 50	99 00	Soren Pedersen	Do.
19	Nells Madsen	do	May 1, 1867	November 1, 1867	6	13 00	3 50	16 50	99 00	Niels Medsen	Do.
20	Jens Marker	do	May 1, 1867	November 1, 1867	6	13 00	3 50	16 50	99 00	J. J. Marker	Do.

No.	Name									Name	
21	Nathan Lewis	May 1, 1867	November 1, 1867	do	6	13 00	3 50	16 50	99 00	Nathan Lewis, sr	Do.
22	James Cook	May 1, 1867	November 1, 1867	do	6	13 00	3 50	16 50	99 00	James Cook	Do.
23	Frilosen Deraill	May 1, 1867	November 1, 1867	do	6	13 00	3 50	16 50	99 00	Frederra Deraill	Do.
24	Soren Christoffersen	May 1, 1867	November 1, 1867	do	6	13 00	3 50	16 50	99 00	Soren Christoffersen	Do.
25	Matthias Andrew, sr	May 1, 1867	November 1, 1867	do	6	13 00	3 50	16 50	99 00	Matthias Andersen	Do.
26	Ole Pedersen	May 1, 1867	November 1, 1867	do	6	13 00	3 50	16 50	99 00	Ole Pederson	Do.
27	Ole Svindsen	May 1, 1867	November 1, 1867	do	6	13 00	3 50	16 50	99 00	Ole Svindsen, his + mark	Do.
28	Neils Larsen	May 1, 1867	November 1, 1867	do	6	13 00	3 50	16 5.	99 00	Neils Larsen	Do.
29	Rasmus Hongaard	May 1, 1867	November 1, 1867	do	6	13 00	3 50	16 30	99 00	Rasmus Hongerd	Do.
30	Hans Madsen	May 1, 1867	November 1, 1867	do	6	13 00	3 50	16 50	99 00	Hans Madsen	Do.
31	Morten Brown	May 1, 1867	November 1, 1867	do	6	13 00	3 50	16 50	99 00	Morten Brown	Do.
32	Allen Wilkenson	May 1, 1867	November 1, 1867	do	6	13 00	3 50	16 50	99 00	Allen Wilkerson, his + mark	Do.
33	Hans Madsen, 2d	May 1, 1867	November 1, 1867	do	6	13 00	3 30	16 50	99 00	Hans Madsen	Do.
34	Hans Jensen, 2d	May 1, 1867	November 1, 1867	do	6	13 00	3 30	16 50	99 00	Hans Jansen, 2d	Do.
35	Ole Madsen	May 1, 1867	November 1, 1867	do	6	13 00	3 50	16 50	99 00	Ole Medsen	Do.
36	Soren Neilsen	May 1, 1867	November 1, 1867	do	6	13 00	3 50	16 50	99 00	S. Nielsen	Do.
37	Lars A. S. Rontige	May 1, 1867	November 1, 1867	do	6	13 00	3 50	16 50	99 00	L. A. Skonbge	Do.
38	Christian Christiansen	May 1, 1867	November 1, 1867	do	6	13 00	3 50	16 50	99 00	Christen Christiansen	Do.
39	Jens Neimann	May 1, 1867	November 1, 1867	do	6	13 00	3 50	16 50	99 00	Jens Neumann	Do.
40	Christian Neilson	May 1, 1867	November 1, 1867	do	6	13 00	3 50	16 50	99 00	Christian Nelson	Do.
41	John Stearn	May 1, 1867	November 1, 1867	do	6	13 00	3 50	16 5.	99 00	John Shears	Do.
42	Rasmus Jorgensen	May 1, 1867	November 1, 1867	co	6	13 00	3 50	16 50	99 00	Rasmus Jorgensen	Do.
43	Jens Halversen	May 1, 1867	November 1, 1867	do	6	13 00	3 50	16 50	99 00	Jens Julesen	Do.
44	Robert Johnson	May 1, 1867	November 1, 1867	do	6	13 00	3 50	16 5.	99 00	Robert Johnson	Do.
45	Emanuel Pederson	May 1, 1867	November 1, 1867	do	6	13 00	3 50	16 50	99 00	Emanuel Peterson	Do.
46	John Peterson	May 1, 1867	November 1, 1867	do	6	13 00	3 50	16 50	99 00	Johann Peterson	Do.
47	Marcus Troelsen	May 1, 1867	November 1, 1867	do	6	13 00	3 50	16 30	99 00	Marcus Troelsen	Do
48	Andrew Anderson	May 1, 1867	November 1, 1867	do	6	13 00	3 50	16 50	99 00	Andrew Anderson	Do
49	Andrew Neilsen	May 1, 1867	November 1, 1867	do	6	13 0	3 50	16 50	99 00	Anders Nielsen	Do·

This company was mustered into service at Manti City, Sanpete County, by Brigadier General William B. Pace, and assigned to duty in the vicinity of said city, in the mountains and passes. They were actively engaged every day for the time specified above, and mustered out November 1, 1867.

I certify that the above account is correct.

H. B. CLAWSON,
Adjutant General Utah Territory Militia.

Pay-roll of Captain William L. Binder's company —— infantry, Utah Territory militia, employed in the suppression of Indian hostilities in Sanpete County, Utah Territory, from May 21, 1867, to October 21, 1867.

We, the undersigned, acknowledge to have received from James W. Cummings, paymaster Utah Territory militia, the sums set opposite to our names, in full payment for our services for the time specified.

Number	Names	Rank	Commencement	Expiration	Months	Pay per month	Monthly allowance for clothing	Total monthly pay and allowance	Total pay and allowance	Signatures
1	William L. Binder	Captain	May 21, 1867	Oct. 21, 1867	5	$17 00	----	$118 50	$592 50	William L. Binder.
2	Michael Stockdale	1st lieutenant	May 21, 1867	Oct. 21, 1867	5	17 00	----	108 50	542 50	Michael Stockdale.
3	William Traharne	2d lieutenant	May 21, 1867	Oct. 21, 1867	5	17 00	----	103 50	517 50	William Traharne.
4	Thomas Cooper	do	May 21, 1867	Oct. 21, 1867	5	17 00	----	103 50	517 50	Thomas Cooper.
5	Samuel Woolley	do	May 21, 1867	Oct. 21, 1867	5	17 00	----	103 50	517 50	Samuel H. Woolley.
6	Alma W. Babbitt	Sergeant	May 21, 1867	Oct. 21, 1867	5	17 00	$3 50	20 50	102 50	Alma W. Babbitt.
7	Thomas Stevens	do	May 21, 1867	Oct. 21, 1867	5	17 00	3 50	20 50	102 50	Thomas Stevens.
8	George Murray	do	May 21, 1867	Oct. 21, 1867	5	17 00	3 50	20 50	102 50	George Murray.
9	Robert Parker	Private	May 21, 1867	Oct. 21, 1867	5	13 00	3 50	16 50	82 50	Robert Parker.
10	William Cook	do	May 21, 1867	Oct. 21, 1867	5	13 00	3 50	16 50	82 50	William Cook.
11	John Miller	do	May 21, 1867	Oct. 21, 1867	5	13 00	3 50	16 50	82 50	John Miller.
12	George Riser	do	May 21, 1867	Oct. 21, 1867	5	13 00	3 50	16 50	82 50	Geo. C. Riser.
13	James Wood	do	May 21, 1867	Oct. 21, 1867	5	13 00	3 50	16 50	82 50	James Wood.
14	John Dikeman	do	May 21, 1867	Oct. 21, 1867	5	13 00	3 50	16 50	82 50	John Dikeman.
15	Amos Jones	do	May 21, 1867	Oct. 21, 1867	5	13 00	3 50	16 50	82 50	Amos Jones.
16	Christian Sanderson	do	May 21, 1867	Oct. 21, 1867	5	13 00	3 50	16 50	82 50	Christian Sanderson.
17	Lorenzo Sintz	do	May 21, 1867	Oct. 21, 1867	5	13 00	3 50	16 50	82 50	Lorenzo Sintz.
18	Robert Morris	do	May 21, 1867	Oct. 21, 1867	5	13 00	3 50	16 50	82 50	Robert Morris.
19	James Clark	do	May 21, 1867	Oct. 21, 1867	5	13 00	3 50	16 50	82 50	James Clark.
20	John Hay	do	May 21, 1867	Oct. 21, 1867	5	13 00	3 50	16 50	82 50	John Hay.
21	John Noble	do	May 21, 1867	Oct. 21, 1867	5	13 00	3 50	16 50	82 50	John Noble.
22	Charles Cottrell	do	May 21, 1867	Oct. 21, 1867	5	13 00	3 50	16 50	82 50	Charles Crottral.
23	Joseph Beck	do	May 21, 1867	Oct. 21, 1867	5	13 00	3 50	16 50	82 50	Joseph Beck.
24	William Richan	do	May 21, 1867	Oct. 21, 1867	5	13 00	3 50	16 50	82 50	William Richan.
25	Henry Smith	do	May 21, 1867	Oct. 21, 1867	5	13 00	3 50	16 50	82 50	Henry Smith.
26	Robert Widderson	do	May 21, 1867	Oct. 21, 1867	5	13 00	3 50	16 50	82 50	Robert Widderson.
27	John Bernidael	do	May 21, 1867	Oct. 21, 1867	5	13 00	3 50	16 50	82 50	John Bernlubdsel.
28	Joseph Zollig	do	May 21, 1867	Oct. 21, 1867	5	13 00	3 50	16 50	82 50	Joseph Zollig.
29	Paul Olsen	do	May 21, 1867	Oct. 21, 1867	5	13 00	3 50	16 50	82 50	Benj Olsen.
30	Amos Smith	do	May 21, 1867	Oct. 21, 1867	5	13 00	3 50	16 50	82 50	Alma Smith.
31	George Carr	do	May 21, 1867	Oct. 21, 1867	5	13 00	3 50	16 50	82 50	George Carr.
32	Don Carlos Brown	do	May 21, 1867	Oct. 21, 1867	5	13 00	3 50	16 50	82 50	Don C. Brown.

.

Pay-roll of Captain Niels C. Christiansen's company,——infantry, Utah Territory militia, employed in the suppression of Indian hostilities in Sanpete County, Utah Territory, from May 1, 1867, to November 1, 1867.

We, the undersigned, acknowledge to have received from James W. Cummings, paymaster Utah Territory militia, the sums set opposite to our names, in full payment for our services for the time specified.

Number	Names	Rank	Commence-ment	Expiration	Months	Pay per month	Monthly allowance for clothing	Total monthly pay and allowance	Total pay and allowance	Signatures	Witness
	Niels C. Christiansen	Captain	May 1, 1867	Nov. 1, 1867	6	$17 00		$118 50	$711 00	Niels C. Christianson	W. R. Pace.
	Rasmus Olsen	1st lieutenant	May 1, 1867	Nov. 1, 1867	6			108 50	651 00	Rasmus Olson	Do.
	Jens M. Lion	2d lieutenant	May 1, 1867	Nov. 1, 1867	6			103 50	621 00	Jens M. Lyon	Do.
	Jens T. Bella	do	May 1, 1867	Nov. 1, 1867	6			103 50	621 00	Jens Thoumudson Balle	Do.
	Stephen Williams	do	May 1, 1867	Nov. 1, 1867	6			103 50	621 00	Stephen Williams	Do.
	Christian A. Thorum	do	May 1, 1867	Nov. 1, 1867	6			103 50	621 00	Christen A. Thorum	Do.
	Andrew Agreen	do	May 1, 1867	Nov. 1, 1867	6			103 50	621 00	Andrew Aagreen	Do.
	Andrew S. Jensen	do	May 1, 1867	Nov. 1, 1867	6			103 50	621 00	Andrew S. Jensen	Do.
	Soren H. Larsen	Sergeant	May 1, 1867	Nov. 1, 1867	6	$17 00	$3 50	20 50	123 00	Soren Larsen	Do.
	James A. Oveson	do	May 1, 1867	Nov. 1, 1867	6	17 00	3 50	20 50	123 00	J. A. Oveson	Do.
	Hans Hansen	do	May 1, 1867	Nov. 1, 1867	6	17 00	3 50	20 50	123 00	Hans Hansen	Do.
	Hans A. Hanson	do	May 1, 1867	Nov. 1, 1867	6	17 00	3 50	20 50	123 00	Hans A. Hanson	Do.
	Jens P. Anderson	do	May 1, 1867	Nov. 1, 1867	6	17 00	3 50	20 50	123 00	Jens P. Anderson	Do.
	Pehr Pehrson	do	May 1, 1867	Nov. 1, 1867	6	17 00	3 50	20 50	123 00	Pehr Pehrson	Do.
1	Sealer Attwood	Private	May 1, 1867	Nov. 1, 1867	6	13 00	3 50	16 50	99 00		Do.
2	John Larsen	do	May 1, 1867	Nov. 1, 1867	6	13 00	3 50	16 50	99 00		Do.
3	Abraham Hansen	do	May 1, 1867	Nov. 1, 1867	6	13 00	3 50	16 50	99 00	Abraham Hansen	Do.
4	John A. Jensen	do	May 1, 1867	Nov. 1, 1867	6	13 00	3 50	16 50	99 00	John A. Jensen	Do.
5	Jens Rosengreen	do	May 1, 1867	Nov. 1, 1867	6	13 00	3 50	16 50	99 00	Jens Rosengreen	Do.
6	Berthel Buhl	do	May 1, 1867	Nov. 1, 1867	6	13 00	3 50	16 50	99 00		Do.
7	Andrew B. Hansen	do	May 1, 1867	Nov. 1, 1867	6	13 00	3 50	16 50	99 00	Andrew B. Hansen, his + mark	Do.
8	Peter Hansen	do	May 1, 1867	Nov. 1, 1867	6	13 00	3 50	16 50	99 00	Peter Hansen	Do.
9	Nills Johnson	do	May 1, 1867	Nov. 1, 1867	6	13 00	3 50	16 50	99 00	Niels Johanson, his + mark	Do.
10	Peter P. Thomsen	do	May 1, 1867	Nov. 1, 1867	6	13 00	3 50	16 50	99 00	P. P. Thomsen	Do.
11	Ivar Petersen	do	May 1, 1867	Nov. 1, 1867	6	13 00	3 50	16 50	99 00	Iver Petersen	Do.
12	Jens C. Jorgensen	do	May 1, 1867	Nov. 1, 1867	6	13 00	3 50	16 50	99 00	Jens C. Jorgenson, his + mark	Do.
13	Andrew Norensen	do	May 1, 1867	Nov. 1, 1867	6	13 00	3 50	16 50	99 00	Anders Sorensen	Do.
14	Lars Poulsen	do	May 1, 1867	Nov. 1, 1867	6	13 00	3 50	16 50	99 00	Lars Poulsen	Do.
15	Christen Willardsen	do	May 1, 1867	Nov. 1, 1867	6	13 00	3 50	16 50	99 00	Christen Willardsen	Do.
16	Rasmus Larsen	do	May 1, 1867	Nov. 1, 1867	6	13 00	3 50	16 50	99 00	Rasmus Larsen	Do.
17	Niels Sorensen	do	May 1, 1867	Nov. 1, 1867	6	13 00	3 50	16 50	99 00	Niels Sorensen	Do.
18	Peter Hanson	do	May 1, 1867	Nov. 1, 1867	6	13 00	3 50	16 50	99 00	Peter Hansen	Do.
19	Peter Madsen	do	May 1, 1867	Nov. 1, 1867	6	13 00	3 50	16 50	99 00	Peter Madsen	Do.

No.	Name									Name	
20	Niels Clemensen	do.	May 1, 1867	Nov. 1, 1867	6	13 00	3 50	16 50	99 00	Niels Clemmensen	Do.
21	Peter C. Anderson	do.	May 1, 1867	Nov. 1, 1867	6	13 00	3 50	16 50	99 00	Peder C. Anderson	Do.
22	Rasmus Johnson	do.	May 1, 1867	Nov. 1, 1867	6	13 00	3 50	16 50	99 00	Rasmus Johnson	Do.
23	Soren T. Muller	do.	May 1, 1867	Nov. 1, 1867	6	13 00	3 50	16 50	99 00		Do.
24	Andrew S. Frost	do.	May 1, 1867	Nov. 1, 1867	6	13 00	3 50	16 50	99 00	A. S. Frost	Do.
25	Niels T. Peterson	do.	May 1, 1867	Nov. 1, 1867	6	13 00	3 50	16 50	99 00	Niels F. Peterson, +	Do.
26	Hans R. Larsen	do.	May 1, 1867	Nov. 1, 1867	6	13 00	3 50	16 50	99 00	Hans Larsen	Do.
27	Hans C. Jensen	do.	May 1, 1867	Nov. 1, 1867	6	13 00	3 50	16 50	99 00	Hans C. Jenson	Do.
28	Peter Wolff	do.	May 1, 1867	Nov. 1, 1867	6	13 00	3 50	16 50	99 00	Peter Wolff	Do.
29	Ole Peter Larsen	do.	May 1, 1867	Nov. 1, 1867	6	13 00	3 50	16 50	99 00	Ole P. Larsen, +	Do.
30	Niels N. Haagen	do.	May 1, 1867	Nov. 1, 1867	6	13 00	3 50	16 50	99 00	Niels N. Haug'n	Do.
31	John Beal	do.	May 1, 1867	Nov. 1, 1867	6	13 00	3 50	16 50	99 00	John Beal	Do.
32	Lars Anderson	do.	May 1, 1867	Nov. 1, 1867	6	13 00	3 50	16 50	99 00	Lars Anderson	Do.
33	Niels Peterson	do.	May 1, 1867	Nov. 1, 1867	6	13 00	3 50	16 50	99 00	Niels Pedersen	Do.
34	Niels P. Anderson	do.	May 1, 1867	Nov. 1, 1867	6	13 00	3 50	16 50	99 00	N. P. Anderson	Do.
35	Peter H. Sorensen	do.	May 1, 1867	Nov. 1, 1867	6	13 00	3 50	16 50	99 00	Peter H. Sorenson, +	Do.
36	Jens C. Madsen	do.	May 1, 1867	Nov. 1, 1867	6	13 00	3 50	16 50	99 00	Jens Crewalnx Madsen	Do.
37	Gehrt T. C. Jensen	do.	May 1, 1867	Nov. 1, 1867	6	13 00	3 50	16 50	99 00	T. C. Jensen	Do.
38	Soren Rasmussen	do.	May 1, 1867	Nov. 1, 1867	6	13 00	3 50	16 50	99 00	Soren Rasmussen	Do.
39	Jens T. Peterson	do.	May 1, 1867	Nov. 1, 1867	6	13 00	3 50	16 50	99 00	Jens T. Peterson	Do.
40	Christian Nielson	do.	May 1, 1867	Nov. 1, 1867	6	13 00	3 50	16 50	99 00	Christian Neilson	Do.
41	Mads Christiansen	do.	May 1, 1867	Nov. 1, 1867	6	13 00	3 50	16 50	99 00	Mods Christensen +	Do.
42	Christian P. Steek	do.	May 1, 1865	Nov. 1, 1867	6	13 00	3 50	16 50	99 00	Christian P. Steek, +	Do.
43	Samuel Aiken	do.	May 1, 1867	Nov. 1, 1867	6	13 00	3 50	16 50	99 00	Samuel Aiken	Do.
44	Christoffer Olsen	do.	May 1, 1867	Nov. 1, 1867	6	13 00	3 50	16 50	99 00	Christoffer Oleson	Do.
45	Hans Rasmussen	do.	May 1, 1867	Nov. 1, 1867	6	13 00	3 50	16 50	99 00	Hans Rasmussen	Do.
46	Jens Rasmussen	do.	May 1, 1867	Nov. 1, 1867	6	13 00	3 50	16 50	99 00	Jens Rasmussen	Do.
47	Christen Peterson	do.	May 1, 1867	Nov. 1, 1867	6	13 00	3 50	16 50	99 00	Chrisffn Peterson	Do.
48	Niels Solslom	do.	May 1, 1867	Nov. 1, 1867	6	13 00	3 50	16 50	99 00	N. Solom	Do.
49	Frederick Mortensen	do.	May 1, 1867	Nov. 1, 1867	6	13 00	3 50	16 50	99 00	Frederick Mortensen	Do.
50	Soren Anderson	do.	May 1, 1867	Nov. 1, 1867	6	13 00	3 50	16 50	99 00	Soren Anderson	Do.
51	Thomas C. Haddon	do.	May 1, 1867	Nov. 1, 1867	6	13 00	3 50	16 50	99 00	Thos. C. Huddnt	Do.
52	Ole Hugg	do.	May 1, 1867	Nov. 1, 1867	6	13 00	3 50	16 50	99 00	Andru P. Jenson	Do.
53	Andrew P. Jensen	do.	May 1, 1867	Nov. 1, 1867	6	13 00	3 50	16 50	99 00	Andrew P. Nielson, his + mark	Do.
54	Andrew P. Nielson	do.	May 1, 1867	Nov. 1, 1867	6	13 00	3 50	16 50	99 00	Frederik C. Schwalbe, his + mark	Do.
55	Frederick C. Schwalbe	do.	May 1, 1867	Nov. 1, 1867	6	13 00	3 50	16 50	99 00	William Quinm	Do.
56	William Quinn	do.	May 1, 1867	Nov. 1, 1867	6	13 00	3 50	16 50	99 00	Andrew Rosenquist	Do.
57	Andreas Rosenquist	do.	May 1, 1867	Nov. 1, 1867	6	13 00	3 50	16 50	99 00		

This company was mustered into service at Fort Ephraim, Sanpete County, May 1, 1867, by Brigadier General Wm. B. Pace, and assigned to duty by him in the vicinity of said city, for the protection of its inhabitants and stock. They were in active service every day for the time specified above, and mustered out November 1, 1867.

I certify that the above account is correct.

H. B. CLAWSON,
Adjutant General Utah Territory Militia.

Pay-roll of Captain Claus Peter Anderson's company —— infantry, Utah Territory militia, employed in the suppression of Indian hostilities in Sanpete County, Utah Territory, from May 1, 1867, to November 1, 1867.

We, the undersigned, acknowledge to have received from James W. Cummings, paymaster Utah Territory militia, the sums sets opposite to our names, in full payment for our services for the time specified.

Number.	Names.	Rank.	Commencement.	Expiration.	Months.	Pay per month.	Monthly allowance for clothing.	Total monthly pay and allowance.	Total pay and allowance.	Signatures.	Witness.
1	Claus Peter Anderson	Captain	May 1, 1867	Nov. 1, 1867	6			$118 50	$711 00	Claus Peder Anderson	H. P. Peterson.
1	Andrew Hendrickson	1st lieutenant	May 1, 1867	Nov. 1, 1867	6			108 50	651 00	A. Hendriksen	Do.
1	Nick Larsen Christiansen	2d lieutenant	May 1, 1867	Nov. 1, 1867	6			103 50	621 03	N. L. Christenson	Do.
2	James Olsen	do.	May 1, 1867	Nov. 1, 1867	6			103 50	621 00	James Olsen	Do.
3	Mads Peter Nielson	do.	May 1, 1867	Nov. 1, 1867	6			103 50	621 00	M. P. Nielsen	Do.
1	John Johnson	Sergeant	May 1, 1867	Nov. 1, 1867	6	$17 00	$3 50	20 50	123 00	John Johnsen	Do.
2	Christen Oversen	do.	May 1, 1867	Nov. 1, 1867	6	17 00	3 50	20 50	123 00	Christian Oveson	Do.
3	Andrew Overloddy	do.	May 1, 1867	Nov. 1, 1867	6	17 00	3 50	20 50	123 00	Andrew Ovelndø	Do.
2	John Tencum	Private	May 1, 1867	Nov. 1, 1867	6	13 00	3 50	16 50	99 00		Do.
3	Samuel Tencum	do.	May 1, 1867	Nov. 1, 1867	6	13 00	3 50	16 50	99 00		Do.
4	Carl A. Z. Ukerman	do.	May 1, 1867	Nov. 1, 1867	6	13 00	3 50	16 50	99 00	C. A. Z. Uckermann	Do.
5	Andrew Borgist	do.	May 1, 1867	Nov. 1, 1867	6	13 00	3 50	16 50	99 00	Andrew Rokkvist	Do.
6	Swen Malmgreen	do.	May 1, 1867	Nov. 1, 1867	6	13 00	3 50	16 50	99 00	Swen Malmgreen	Do.
7	Jens C. Larsen	do.	May 1, 1867	Nov. 1, 1867	6	13 40	3 50	16 50	99 00	J. C. Larsen	Do.
8	Rasmus Christiansen	do.	May 1, 1867	Nov. 1, 1867	6	13 00	3 50	16 50	90 00	Rasmus Christensen	Do.
9	Soren Togersen	do.	May 1, 1867	Nov. 1, 1867	6	13 00	3 50	16 50	99 00	Sowren Thoegersen	Do.
10	Even Torkersen	do.	May 1, 1867	Nov. 1, 1867	6	13 00	3 50	16 50	99 00	Evea Torgresen	Do.
11	Thomas Borrgard	do.	May 1, 1867	Nov. 1, 1867	6	13 00	3 30	16 50	99 00	Thomas Birrgaard	Do.
12	Andrew Hansen	do.	May 1, 1867	Nov. 1, 1867	6	13 00	3 50	16 50	99 00	Andrew Hansen	Do.
13	Soren Jensen	do.	May 1, 1867	Nov. 1, 1867	6	13 00	3 50	16 50	99 03	Soren Jensen	Do.
14	August Anderson	do.	May 1, 1867	Nov. 1, 1867	6	13 40	3 50	16 50	99 00	Agust Anderson	Do.
15	John N. Nielson	do.	May 1, 1867	Nov. 1, 1867	6	13 00	3 50	16 50	99 00	Johns Nicolais Nielsen	Do.
16	Lars Hansen	do.	May 1, 1867	Nov. 1, 1867	6	13 00	3 50	16 50	99 00	Lars Hansen	Do.
17	Niels C. Hansen	do.	May 1, 1867	Nov. 1, 1867	6	13 00	3 51	16 50	91 00	Niele C. Hansen	Do.
18	Jens Oterstram	do.	May 1, 1867	Nov. 1, 1867	6	13 00	3 50	16 50	99 00	Jens Ote-tatron	Do.
19	Marcus Hansen	do.	May 1, 1867	Nov. 1, 1867	6	13 00	3 59	16 50	99 00	Marcus Hansen	Do.
20	Nick L. Peterson	do.	May 1, 1867	Nov. 1, 1867	6	13 00	3 50	16 50	99 00	N. L. Peterson	Do.
21	Mads Larsen	do.	May 1, 1867	Nov. 1, 1867	6	13 00	3 50	16 50	99 00	Mads Larsen	Do.
22	August Johnson	do.	May 1, 1867	Nov. 1, 1867	6	13 00	3 51	16 50	99 00	August Johansen	Do.
23	Hans Peterson	do.	May 1, 1867	Nov. 1, 1867	6	13 00	3 51	16 50	99 03	Hans Peterson	Do.
24	Morten Neilson	do.	May 1, 1867	Nov. 1, 1867	6	13 00	3 50	16 50	99 00	M. Nilsson	Do.
24	Peter Ahlstrom	do.	May 1, 1867	Nov. 1, 1867	6	13 00	3 50	16 50	99 00	Peter Ahlstrom	Do.

No.	Name		Mustered in	Mustered out						Remarks
25	Andrew C. Nielson	do	May 1, 1867	Nov. 1, 1867	6	13 00	3 50	16 50	99 00	Andrew C. Nielsen	Do.
26	Niels Peter Nielson	do	May 1, 1867	Nov. 1, 1867	6	13 00	3 50	16 50	99 00	Niels P. Nielson	Do.
27	Niels Anderson	do	May 1, 1867	Nov. 1, 1867	6	13 00	3 50	16 50	99 00	N. Andrew Son	Do.
28	Oleif Larsen	do	May 1, 1867	Nov. 1, 1867	6	13 00	3 50	16 50	99 00	Oleif Larsen	Do.
29	Peter Rasmussen	do	May 1, 1867	Nov. 1, 1867	6	13 00	3 50	16 50	99 00	P. Rasmussen	Do.
30	Niels Mortensen	do	May 1, 1867	Nov. 1, 1867	6	13 10	3 50	16 50	99 00	Niels Mortensen	Do.
31	Morton Mortensen	do	May 1, 1867	Nov. 1, 1867	6	13 00	3 50	16 50	99 00	Morton Mortensen	Do.
32	Rasmus Rasmussen	do	May 1, 1867	Nov. 1, 1867	6	13 00	3 50	16 50	99 00	R. Rasmussen	Do.

This company was mustered into service at Fort Ephraim, Sanpete County, May 1, 1867, by Brigadier General Wm. B. Pace, and assigned to duty in squads, as patrols, in the mountains and passes. They were actively engaged every day for the time specified above, and were mustered out November 1, 1867.

I certify that the above account is correct.

H. B. CLAWSON,

Adjutant General Utah Territory Militia.

Pay-roll of Captain Thomas Robertson's company —— infantry, Utah Territory militia, employed in the suppression of Indian hostilities in Sanpete County, Utah Territory, from May 1, 1867, to November 1, 1867.

We, the undersigned, acknowledge to have received from James W. Cummings, paymaster Utah Territory militia, the sums set opposite to our names, in full payment for our services for the time specified.

Number.	Names.	Rank.	Commencement.	Expiration.	Months.	Pay per month.	Monthly allowance for clothing.	Total monthly pay and allowance.	Total pay and allowance.	Signatures.	Witnesses.
1	Thomas Robertson	Captain	May 1, 1867	Nov. 1, 1867	6	$17 00	3 50	$118 50	$711 00	Thomas Robinson	Rees. R. Lewellyn.
2	Peter Oldroyd	1st lieut	May 1, 1867	Nov. 1, 1867	6	17 00	3 50	108 50	651 00	Peter Oldroyd	Do.
3	Thomas J. Caldwell	2d lieut	May 1, 1866	Nov. 1, 1867	6	17 00	3 50	103 50	621 00	Thomas J. Caldwell	Do.
4	Edward Collard	do	May 1, 1867	Nov. 1, 1867	6	17 00	3 50	103 50	621 00	Edward Collard	Do.
5	Cornelius Collard	do	May 1, 1867	Nov. 1, 1867	6	17 00	3 50	103 50	621 00	Cornelius Collard	Do.
6	Roger Openshaw	do	May 1, 1867	Nov. 1, 1867	6	17 00	3 50	103 50	621 00	Roger Openshaw	Samuel Jewkes.
7	William Huegins	do	May 1, 1867	Nov. 1, 1867	6	17 00	3 50	103 50	621 00	William Huergens	Do.
8	Archibald Oldroyd	do	May 1, 1867	Nov. 1, 1867	6	17 00	3 50	103 50	621 00	Archabald Oldroyd	Do.
1	George Horrace	Sergeant	May 1, 1867	Nov. 1, 1867	6	17 00	3 50	20 50	123 00	George Horrac	Do.
2	Thomas Crowther	do	May 1, 1867	Nov. 1, 1867	6	17 00	3 50	20 50	123 00	Thomas Crowther	Do.
3	Ole Sorensen	do	May 1, 1867	Nov. 1, 1867	6	17 00	3 50	20 51	123 01	Ole Sorrensen	Do.
4	Andrus Bertelsen	do	May 1, 1867	Nov. 1, 1867	6	17 00	3 50	20 53	123 01	Andrus Bertelsen	Rees. R. Lewellyn.
5	William Green	do	May 1, 1867	Nov. 1, 1867	6	17 00	3 50	20 50	123 00	William Green	Do.
6	James Darton	do	May 1, 1867	Nov. 1, 1867	6	17 00	3 50	20 50	123 00	James Darton	Do.
1	Martin Land	Private	May 1, 1867	Nov. 1, 1867	6	13 00	3 50	16 50	99 00	Morten Land	Do.
2	Thomas Cahnway	do	May 1, 1867	Nov. 1, 1867	6	13 00	3 50	16 50	99 00	Thomas Cahnway	Samuel Jewkes.
3	George Smith	do	May 1, 1867	Nov. 1, 1867	6	13 00	3 50	16 50	99 00	George Smith	Do.
4	Henry Tuttle	do	May 1, 1867	Nov. 1, 1867	6	13 00	3 50	16 50	99 00	Henry Tuttle	Do.
5	Soren Eskelsen	do	May 1, 1867	Nov. 1, 1867	6	13 00	3 50	16 50	99 00	Soren Eskelson	Do.
6	David Moore	do	May 1, 1867	Nov. 1, 1867	6	13 00	3 50	16 50	99 00	David Moore	Rees. R. Lewellyn.
7	Moroni Degraw	do	May 1, 1867	Nov. 1, 1867	6	13 00	3 50	16 50	99 00	Moroni Degraw	Do.
8	Frederick Williams	do	May 1, 1867	Nov. 1, 1867	6	13 00	3 50	16 50	99 00	Fredrik Williams	Do.
9	Niels Christiansen	do	May 1, 1867	Nov. 1, 1867	6	13 00	3 50	16 50	99 00	Niels Christiansen	Do.
10	William H. Johnson	do	May 1, 1867	Nov. 1, 1867	6	13 00	3 50	16 50	99 00	William H. Johnson	Do.
11	James Collard	do	May 1, 1867	Nov. 1, 1867	6	13 00	3 50	16 50	99 00	James Collard	Do.
12	Richard Crowther	do	May 1, 1867	Nov. 1, 1867	6	13 00	3 50	16 50	99 01	Richard Crowther	Do.
13	Edwin Robertson	do	May 1, 1867	Nov. 1, 1867	6	13 00	3 50	16 50	99 00	Edwin Robertson	Samuel Jewkes.
14	James Woodward	do	May 1, 1867	Nov. 1, 1867	6	13 00	3 50	16 51	99 00	James Woodward	Do.
15	William Coombe	do	May 1, 1867	Nov. 1, 1867	6	13 00	3 50	16 50	99 00	William Coombs	Do.
16	Joshua Coombs	do	May 1, 1867	Nov. 1, 1867	6	13 00	3 50	16 50	99 00	Joshua Coombs	Do.
17	Jans Jacobsen	do	May 1, 1867	Nov. 1, 1867	6	13 00	3 50	16 50	99 00	Jans Jacobsen	Do.
18	John L. Jewkes	do	May 1, 1867	Nov. 1, 1867	6	13 00	3 50	16 50	99 00	T. L. Jewkes	Rees. R. Lewellyn.
19	John Shawcroft	do	May 1, 1867	Nov. 1, 1867	6	13 00	3 50	16 50	99 00	John Shawcroft	Do.

No.	Name		Mustered in	Mustered out	Days				Total	Commanding officer	Remarks
50	George Combs, Jr	do	May 1, 1867	Nov. 1, 1867	6	13 00	3 50	16 50	99 00	George Combs, Jr	Do.
51	Alonzo Nay	do	May 1, 1867	Nov. 1, 1867	6	13 00	3 50	16 50	99 01	Alonzo Nay	Do.
52	Abbey Sherman	do	May 1, 1867	Nov. 1, 1867	6	13 00	3 50	16 50	99 00	Albey L. Sherman	Samuel Jewkes.
53	John Llewellyn	do	May 1, 1867	Nov. 1, 1867	6	13 00	3 50	16 50	99 00	John Lewellyn	Do.
54	Lars Nielsen	do	May 1, 1867	Nov. 1, 1867	6	13 00	3 50	16 50	99 00	Lars Nielson	Do.
55	Soren Christiansen	do	May 1, 1867	Nov. 1, 1867	6	13 00	3 50	16 50	99 00	Soren Christensen	Do.
56	Walter Jones	do	May 1, 1867	Nov. 1, 1867	6	13 00	3 50	16 50	99 00	Walter Jones	Do.
57	Reuben Carter	do	May 1, 1867	Nov. 1, 1867	6	13 00	3 50	16 50	99 00	Reuben Carter	Do.
58	Thomas Morgan	do	May 1, 1867	Nov. 1, 1867	6	13 00	3 50	16 50	99 00	Thomas Morgan	Rees R. Lewellyn.
59	Simon Simonson	do	May 1, 1867	Nov. 1, 1867	6	13 00	3 50	16 50	99 00	Soren Simonsen	Do.
60	Jens Nielson	do	May 1, 1867	Nov. 1, 1867	6	13 00	3 50	16 50	99 00	Jens Nielsen	Do.
61	Jens M. Jensen	do	May 1, 1867	Nov. 1, 1867	6	13 00	3 50	16 50	99 00	J. M. Jensen	Do.
62	Andrew M. Bearnsen	do	May 1, 1867	Nov. 2, 1867	6	13 00	3 30	16 50	99 00	Andru M. Bevontsen	Do.
63	Andrus Anderson	do	May 1, 1867	Nov. 1, 1867	6	13 00	3 50	16 50	99 00	Andrew Andersen	Samuel Jewkes.
64	Andrew Neilson	do	May 1, 1867	Nov. 1, 1867	6	13 00	3 50	16 51	99 00	Andru Nilsson	Do.
65	Samuel Jewks, jr	do	May 1, 1867	Nov. 1, 1867	6	13 00	3 50	16 50	99 00	Samuel Jewkes, junior	Do.
66	Ole Jensen	do	May 1, 1867	Nov. 1, 1867	6	13 00	3 50	16 50	99 00	Ole Jensen	Rees R. Lewellyn.
67	Ephraim Coombs	do	May 1, 1867	Nov. 1, 1867	6	13 00	3 50	16 51	99 00	Ephraim Coombs	Do.
68	Jacob Jacobson	do	May 1, 1867	Nov. 1, 1867	6	13 00	3 50	16 50	99 10	Jacob Jacobson	Do.
69	Soren Hanson	do	May 1, 1867	Nov. 1, 1867	6	13 00	3 50	16 50	99 00	Soren Hanson	Do.
70	Christian Christiansen	do	May 1, 1867	Nov. 1, 1867	6	13 00	3 50	16 50	99 00	Christian Chretenson	Do.
71	Nels Jensen	do	May 1, 1867	Nov. 1, 1867	6	13 00	3 50	16 50	99 00	Nichi Jensen	Do.
72	Robert L. Johnson	do	May 1, 1867	Nov. 1, 1867	6	13 00	3 50	16 50	99 00	Robert L. Johnson	Samuel Jewkes.
73	Andrew Bransen	do	May 1, 1867	Nov. 1, 1867	6	13 00	3 50	16 50	99 00	Andri Brennen	Do.
74	Jens Augard	do	May 1, 1867	Nov. 1, 1867	6	13 00	3 50	16 50	99 00	Jens Augaard	Do.
75	John Harrison	do	May 1, 1867	Nov. 1, 1867	6	13 00	3 50	16 50	99 00	John Harrison	Do.
76	George Powell	do	May 1, 1867	Nov. 1, 1867	6	13 00	3 50	16 50	99 00	George Powell	Rees R. Lewellyn.
77	Wiley P. Allred	do	May 1, 1867	Nov. 1, 1867	6	13 00	3 50	16 50	99 00	Wiley P. Allred	Do.
78	Peter C. Peterson	do	May 1, 1867	Nov. 1, 1867	6	13 00	3 50	16 50	99 00	Peter C. Peterson	Do.
79	Isaac Henning	do	May 1, 1867	Nov. 1, 1867	6	13 00	3 50	16 50	99 10	Isaac Henning	Do.
80	Parley Allred	do	May 1, 1867	Nov. 1, 1867	6	13 00	3 50	16 50	99 00	Parley Allred	Do.
81	Major Killian	do	May 1, 1867	Nov. 1, 1867	6	13 00	3 50	16 50	99 00	Major Allred	Do.
82	James Killian	do	May 1, 1867	Nov. 1, 1867	6	13 00	3 50	16 50	99 00	James Killian	Do.
83	Cyrus Hill	do	May 1, 1867	Nov. 1, 1867	6	13 00	3 50	16 50	99 00	Cyrus Hill	Do.
84	Polk Sampson	do	May 1, 1867	Nov. 1, 1867	6	13 00	3 50	16 53	99 00	Polk Samson	Do.
85	Solomon Case	do	May 1, 1867	Nov. 1, 1867	6	13 00	3 50	16 50	99 10	Salomon Case	Do.
86	Walter Gardner	do	May 1, 1867	Nov. 1, 1867	6	13 00	3 50	16 50	99 10	Walter Gardner	Do.
87	John Gardner	do	May 1, 1867	Nov. 1, 1867	6	13 00	3 50	16 50	99 00	John Gardner	Do.
88	Bernard Snow	do	May 1, 1867	Nov. 1, 1867	6	13 00	3 50	16 50	99 00	Bernard Snow	Do.
89	Lewis Anderson	do	May 1, 1867	Nov. 1, 1867	6	13 00	3 50	16 50	99 00	Lewis Anderson	Do.

This company was mustered into service at Fountain Green, Sanpete County, May 1, 1867, by Brigadier General William B. Pace, and was actively engaged every day for the defense of said city, and performed regular service for the time specified above, and was mustered out November 1, 1867.

I certify that the above account is correct.

H. B. CLAWSON,
Adjutant General Utah Territory Militia.

Pay-roll of field and staff officers commanding the Utah Territory militia, employed in the suppression of Indian hostilitits in Sanpete, Sevier, and Piute counties, Utah Territory, from May 1, 1867, to November 1, 1867.

We, the undersigned, acknowledge to have received from James W. Cummings, paymaster Utah Territory militia, the sums set opposite to our names, in full payment for our services for the time specified.

Number.	Names.	Staff appointment; office.	Rank.	Commencement.	Expiration.	Months.	Pay per month.	Monthly allowance for clothing.	Total monthly pay and allowance.	40 cts. per day for use and risk of horse and horse equipment.	Total pay and allowance.	Signatures.	Witnesses.
	William Byram Pace	Brigade adj't	Brig. general	May 1, 1867	Nov. 1, 1867	6			299 50	$72 00	$1,869 00	Wm. B. Pace	
	John W. Vance	Brigade q. m.	Lt. colonel	May 2, 1867	June 2, 1867	1			187 00	12 00	199 00		
	George W. Bean	Brigade q. m.	do	May 1, 1867	Nov. 1, 1867	6			167 00	72 00	1,194 00	Geo. W. Bean	
	Benjamin W. Driggs	Brigade a. de c	Major	May 1, 1867	Nov. 1, 1867	6			163 00	72 00	1,050 00	B. W. Driggs	
	John D. L. Pearce	Brigade a. de c	Captain	May 1, 1867	Nov. 1, 1867	6			129 50	72 00	849 00	John D. L. Pearce	
	Alexander F. McDonald	Brigade adj't	Lt. colonel	June 8, 1867	July 8, 1867	1			187 00	12 00	199 00	A. F. Macdonald	
	James E. Daniels	Brigade adj't	do	July 9, 1867	Nov. 1, 1867	3		32 2	187 00	44 80	742 93	James E. Daniels	John R. Wuder.
	William H. Gray	Brigade a. de c	Major	May 1, 1867	Nov. 1, 1867	3		32 2	163 00	44 80	653 33	Wm. H Gray	
	Reddick N. Allred		Colonel	May 1, 1867	Nov. 1, 1867	6			211 00	72 00	1,338 00	R. N. Allred	
	John L. Ivie		Lt. colonel	May 1, 1867	Nov. 1, 1867	6			187 00	72 00	1,194 00	John L. Ivie	
	Joseph L. Page	Reg'tal adj't	Major	May 1, 1867	Nov. 1, 1867	6			163 00	72 00	1,050 00	Joseph L. Page	
	Joseph S. Wing	Surgeon	Major	May 1, 1867	Nov. 1, 1867	6			129 53	72 00	819 00	Joseph S. Wing	John R. Winder.
	Reuben W. Allred	Battalion adj't	Major	May 1, 1867	Nov. 1, 1867	6			163 00	72 00	849 00	Reuben W. Allred	Do.
	George Brough		Captain	May 1, 1867	Nov. 1, 1867	6			163 00	72 00	1,050 00	Geo. Brough	W. B. Pace.
	William S. Seeley	Battalion adj't	Major	May 1, 1867	Nov. 1, 1867	6			129 50	72 00	849 00	William S. Seely	Do.
	William N. Tidwell		Captain	May 1, 1867	Nov. 1, 1867	6			163 00	72 00	1,050 00	Wm. N. Tidwell	Do.
	Jens Jorgensen, sr		Major	May 1, 1867	Nov. 1, 1867	6			163 00	72 00	1,050 00	Jens Jorgensen	Do.
	Henry W. Sanderson	Battalion adj't	Captain	May 1, 1867	Nov. 1, 1867	6			129 50	72 00	849 00	Lauritz Larsin	John R. Winder.
	Lyrurgus Wilson	Battalion adj't	Major	May 1, 1867	Nov. 1, 1867	6			163 00	72 00	1,050 00	Henry W. Sanderson	Do.
	Abner Lowry	Battalion adj't	Captain	May 1, 1867	Nov. 1, 1867	6			163 00	72 00	849 00	Lycurgus Wilson	Do.
	Jabez Faux	Battalion adj't	Major	May 1, 1867	Nov. 1, 1867	6			163 00	72 00	1,050 00	Abner Lowry	Do.
	James Guyman	Battalion adj't	Captain	May 1, 1867	Nov. 1, 1867	6			129 53	72 00	849 00	Jabez Faux	W. B. Pace.
	Rees Lewellyn	Battalion adj't	Major	May 1, 1867	Nov. 1, 1867	6			163 00	72 00	1,050 00	James Guynon	Do.
	Nathaniel S. Beach		Captain	May 1, 1867	Nov. 1, 1867	6			163 00	72 00	849 00	Rees. R. Lewellyn	
	Foster R. Kenner		Lt. colonel	May 1, 1867	Nov. 1, 1867	6			211 00	72 00	849 00	N. S. Beach	
	Edward W. Fox	Reg'tal adj't	Colonel	May 1, 1867	Nov. 1, 1867	6			187 00	72 00	1,191 00	F. R. Kenner	
	Ilural M. Rogers	Surgeon	Captain	May 1, 1867	Nov. 1, 1867	6			163 00	72 00	1,051 10	Edward W. Fox	
	George P. Billings	Battalion adj't	Major	May 1, 1867	Nov. 1, 1867	6			163 00	72 00	849 00	Ilural M. Rogers	
	Hans Madsen		Captain	May 1, 1867	Nov. 1, 1867	6			129 50	72 00	1,050 03	George P. Billings	
	William K. Barton	Battalion adj't	Major	May 1, 1867	Nov. 1, 1867	6			129 50	72 00	849 00	Hans Madsew	
	M. D. Hambleton	Battalion adj't	Captain	May 1, 1867	Nov. 1, 1867	6			129 50	72 00	1,050 00	William K. Barton	W. Sr. Snow.
												M. D. Hambleton	

James Wareham	Major	May 1, 1867	Nov. 1, 1867	6		163 00	72 00	1,050 00	James Wareham
H. F. Peterson	Battalion adj't.	May 1, 1867	Nov. 1, 1867	6		129 50	72 00	849 00	H. F. Peterson
Carl C. N. Dorius	Major	May 1, 1867	Nov. 1, 1867	6		163 00	72 00	1,050 00	Charles C.N.Dorell
J. P. Christiansen	Battalion adj't.	May 1, 1867	Nov. 1, 1867	6		129 50	72 00	849 00	J. P. Christensen
Robert G. Frazier	Major	May 1, 1867	Nov. 1, 1867	6		163 00	72 00	1,050 00	Robert G. Frazier
Peter Micklesen	Battalion adj't.	May 1, 1867	Nov. 1, 1867	6		129 50	72 00	849 00	Peter Micklesen
David Candland	do	May 1, 1867	Nov. 1, 1867	6		129 50	72 00	849 00	David Candland
John K. Kirkman	do	May 1, 1867	Nov. 1, 1867	6		129 50	72 00	849 00	John K. Kermes

*Killed in battle by Indians.

The above-named field and staff officers of Utah and Sanpete counties were mustered into service by order of Lieutenant General Daniel H. Wells, and assigned to duty by him in the field. They were in active service every day for the time specified above.

I certify that the above account is correct.

H. B. CLAWSON,
Adjutant General Utah Territory Militia.

Pay-roll of Captain Christian Madson's company —— infantry, Utah Territory militia, employed in the suppression of Indian hostilities in Sanpete County, Utah Territory, from May 1, 1867, to November 1, 1867.

We, the undersigned, acknowledge to have received from James W. Cummings, paymaster Utah Territory, the sums set opposite to our names, in full payment for our services for the time specified.

Number	Names	Rank	Commencement.	Expiration.	Months.	Pay per month.	Monthly allowance for clothing.	Total monthly pay and allowance.	Total pay and allowance.	Signatures.	Witness.
1	Christian Madsen	Captain	May 1, 1867	Nov. 1, 1867	6		$3 50	$118 50	$711 00	Christian Madsen	A. C. Merriam.
1	William M. Fudgreen	1st lieutenant	May 1, 1867	Nov. 1, 1867	6		3 50	108 50	651 00	William McFudgreen	Do.
1	Parland McFarlin	2d lieutenant	May 1, 1867	Nov. 1, 1867	6		3 50	103 50	621 00	Parlin McFarlin	Do.
2	Jens M. Nielsen	do	May 1, 1867	Nov. 1, 1867	6		3 50	103 50	621 00	Jens M. Nielsen	Do.
3	John Pickrt	do	May 1, 1867	Nov. 1, 1867	6		3 50	103 50	621 00	John Pickrtt	Do.
3	Henry Roper	do	May 1, 1867	Nov. 1, 1867	6		3 50	103 50	621 00	Henry Roper	Do.
1	Mads C. Andresen	Sergeant	May 1, 1867	Nov. 1, 1867	6	$17 00	3 50	20 50	123 00	Mads C. Andresen	Do.
3	Lars P. Fichlated	do	May 1, 1867	Nov. 1, 1867	6	17 00	3 50	21 50	123 00	Lars P. Fyeklsted	Do.
3	George Fenn	do	May 1, 1867	Nov. 1, 1867	6	17 00	3 50	21 50	123 00	George Fvan	Do.
4	Soren Sorensen	do	May 1, 1867	Nov. 1, 1867	6	17 00	3 50	20 50	123 00	Soren Sorensen	Do.
1	Jacob Leclander	Private	May 1, 1867	Nov. 1, 1867	6	13 00	3 50	16 50	99 10	Jacob Lalander	Do.
2	Carlas Hales	do	May 1, 1867	Nov. 1, 1867	6	13 00	3 51	16 50	99 00	Carlas Hales	Do.
3	Jens F. Mortensen	do	May 1, 1867	Nov. 1, 1867	6	13 00	3 50	16 50	99 00	Jens F. Mortens'n	Do.
4	Andrew C. Nelson	do	May 1, 1867	Nov. 1, 1867	6	13 00	3 50	16 50	99 00	Andru C. Nielsen	Do.
5	Eick Lemburgh	do	May 1, 1867	Nov. 1, 1867	6	13 00	3 50	16 50	99 00	Erik Lindburgh	Do.
6	Seth Child	do	May 1, 1867	Nov. 1, 1867	6	13 60	3 50	16 50	99 00	Seth Child	Do.
7	Carl Berglund	do	May 1, 1867	Nov. 1, 1867	6	13 00	3 50	16 50	99 00	Carl Berglund	Do.
8	John Swan	do	May 1, 1867	Nov. 1, 1867	6	13 00	3 50	16 50	99 00	John Swain	Do.
9	Martin Mortensen	do	May 1, 1867	Nov. 1, 1867	6	13 00	3 50	16 50	99 00	Marten Mortensen	Do.
10	Mads G. Sorensen	do	May 1, 1867	Nov. 1, 1867	6	13 00	3 50	16 51	99 00	Mads P. Sorensen	Do.
11	John Sorensen	do	May 1, 1867	Nov. 1, 1867	6	13 00	3 50	16 50	99 00	Johanaw Sorvnsen	Do.
12	Peter Sorensen	do	May 1, 1867	Nov. 1, 1867	6	13 00	3 50	16 50	99 00	Peter Sorvnsen	Do.
13	Nick Johnson	do	May 1, 1867	Nov. 1, 1867	6	13 00	3 50	16 50	99 00	Neils Johnasen	Do.
14	John Anderson	do	May 1, 1867	Nov. 1, 1867	6	13 00	3 50	16 50	99 00	John Anderson	Do.
15	Christian Anderson	do	May 1, 1867	Nov. 1, 1867	6	13 00	3 51	16 50	99 00	Christian Andersen	Do.
16	Hans Hanson	do	May 1, 1867	Nov. 1, 1867	6	13 00	3 50	16 50	99 00	Hans Hanson	Do.
17	Carl Olsen	do	May 1, 1867	Nov. 1, 1867	6	13 00	3 30	16 50	99 00	C. Olson	Do.
18	John W. Bowman	do	May 1, 1867	Nov. 1, 1867	6	13 00	3 50	16 50	99 00	John W. Bohman	Do.
19	Lars Jacobson	do	May 1, 1867	Nov. 1, 1867	6	13 00	3 50	16 50	99 00	Lars Jacobson	Do.
20	Peter C. Nielsen	do	May 1, 1867	Nov. 1, 1867	6	13 00	3 50	16 50	99 00	Peter C. Nielsen	Do.
21	Charles Bardsley	do	May 1, 1867	Nov. 1, 1867	6	13 00	3 59	16 50	99 00	Charles Bardsley	Do.
22	William Bardsley	do	May 1, 1867	Nov. 1, 1867	6	13 00	3 50	16 50	99 00	William Bardsley	Do.

23	Hyrum Lablin	do	May 1, 1867	Nov. 1, 1867	6	13 00	3 50	16 50	Herman Lablin	99 00	Do.
24	Robert Newsom	do	May 1, 1867	Nov. 1, 1867	6	13 00	3 50	16 50	Robert Newsom	99 00	Do.
25	Frederick Wadsen	do	May 1, 1867	Nov. 1, 1867	6	13 00	3 50	16 50	Fredrick Wadsen	99 00	Do.
26	John Swamburgh	do	May 1, 1867	Nov. 1, 1867	6	13 00	3 50	16 50	John Swamburic	99 00	Do.
27	Evert Ashworth	do	May 1, 1867	Nov. 1, 1867	6	13 00	3 50	16 50	Evert Ashworth	99 10	Do.
28	Jens Fry-idsted	do	May 1, 1867	Nov. 1, 1867	6	13 00	3 50	16 50	Jens Fryidsted	99 00	Do.
29	John Christenson	do	May 1, 1867	Nov. 1, 1867	6	13 00	3 50	16 50	John Christenson	99 00	Do.
30	Jens Larsen	do	May 1, 1867	Nov. 1, 1867	6	13 00	3 50	16 50	Jens Larsen	99 00	Do.
31	William Childs, Jr	do	May 1, 1867	Nov. 1, 1867	6	13 00	3 50	16 50	William Childs, Jr.	99 00	Do.
32	James C. Brown	do	May 1, 1867	Nov. 1, 1867	6	13 00	3 50	16 50	James C. Brown	99 00	Do.
33	Jens Bergquist	do	May 1, 1867	Nov. 1, 1867	6	13 00	3 50	16 50	Jens Bergquist	99 00	Do.
34	Joseph West	do	May 1, 1867	Nov. 1, 1867	6	13 00	3 50	16 50	Joseph West	99 00	Do.
35	James Kearnes	do	May 1, 1867	Nov. 1, 1867	6	13 00	3 50	16 50	James Kearney	99 00	Do.
36	Hans Eskelund	do	May 1, 1867	Nov. 1, 1867	6	13 00	3 50	16 50	Hans E-klund	99 00	Do.
37	Reuben Nerson	do	May 1, 1867	Nov. 1, 1867	6	13 00	3 50	16 50	Ruben Nerson	99 00	Do.
38	Peter Nelson	do	May 1, 1867	Nov. 1, 1867	6	13 00	3 50	16 50	Peter Nelson	99 00	Do.
39	Soren Jensen	do	May 1, 1867	Nov. 1, 1867	6	13 00	3 50	16 50	Soren Jensen	99 00	Do.
40	John Pine	do	May 1, 1867	Nov. 1, 1867	6	13 00	3 50	16 50	John Pine	99 00	Do.
41	Hamilton Garrick	do	May 1, 1867	Nov. 1, 1867	6	13 00	3 50	16 50	Hamilton Garrick	99 00	Do.

This company was mustered into service at Fort Gunnison, Sanpete County, May 1, 1867, by Brigadier General William B. Pace, and by him assigned to duty in the hills and mountains in the vicinity of said city, for the protection of life and property. They were actively engaged every day, and mustered out November 1, 1867.

I certify that the above account is correct.

H. B. CLAWSON,
Adjutant General Utah Territory Militia.

Pay-roll of Captain Christian Tallerstrup's company —— infantry, Utah Territory militia, employed in the suppression of Indian hostilities in Sanpete County, Utah Territory, from May 1, 1867, to November 1, 1867.

We, the undersigned, acknowledge to have received from James W. Cummings, paymaster Utah Territory militia, the sums set opposite to our names, in full payment for our services for the time specified.

Number.	Names.	Rank.	Period of service. Commencement.	Expiration.	Months.	Pay per month.	Monthly allowance for clothing.	Total monthly pay and allow.	Total pay and allowance.	Signatures.	Witnesses.
1	Christian Tallerstrup	Captain	May 1, 1867	Nov. 1, 1867	6	$17 00		$118 50	$711 00	Christian Tollestrup	A. E. Merrian.
1	Hance Tummeen	1st lieutenant	May 1, 1867	Nov. 1, 1867	6			108 50	651 00	Hans Thunneson	Do.
1	Joseph Bartholomew	2d lieutenant	May 1, 1867	Nov. 1, 1867	6			103 50	621 00	Joseph Bartholomew	Do.
2	Andrew Yorgensen	do	May 1, 1867	Nov. 1, 1867	6			103 50	621 00	Andrew Jorgensen	Do.
3	Lars Petersen	do	May 1, 1867	Nov. 1, 1867	6			103 50	621 00	Lars Petersen	Do.
4	Thomas Hunt	do	May 1, 1867	Nov. 1, 1867	6			103 50	621 00	Thomas Hunt	Do.
	John Bartholomew	Sergeant	May 1, 1867	Nov. 1, 1867	6	$17 00	$3 50	20 50	123 00	John Bartholomew	Do.
	Kenud Jensen	do	May 1, 1867	Nov. 1, 1867	6	17 00	3 50	20 50	123 00	Kenud Jensen	Do.
	Jenee Otteseen	do	May 1, 1867	Nov. 1, 1867	6	17 00	3 50	20 50	123 00	Jens Ottesen	Do.
	Henry Allred	do	May 1, 1867	Nov. 1, 1867	6	17 00	3 50	20 50	123 00	Henry Aldred	Do.
2	William Beal	Private	May 1, 1867	Nov. 1, 1867	6	13 00	3 50	16 50	99 00	William Beal	Do.
3	Henry D. Gifford	do	May 1, 1867	Nov. 1, 1867	6	13 00	3 50	16 50	99 00	Henry D. Gifford	Do.
3	Joseph Booth	do	May 1, 1867	Nov. 1, 1867	6	13 00	3 50	16 50	99 00	Joseph Booth	Do.
	George Bartholomew	do	May 1, 1867	Nov. 1, 1867	6	13 00	3 50	16 50	99 00	George Bartholomew	Do.
5	James Medcalf	do	May 1, 1867	Nov. 1, 1867	6	13 00	3 50	16 50	99 00	Anthony Metcalf	Do.
6	John E. Medcalf, jr.	do	May 1, 1867	Nov. 1, 1867	6	13 00	3 50	16 30	99 00	James Metcalf	Do.
7	Philip Dack	do	May 1, 1867	Nov. 1, 1867	6	13 00	3 50	16 50	99 00	John E. Metcalf, jr.	Do.
8	James Mallor, sr.	do	May 1, 1867	Nov. 1, 1867	6	13 00	3 50	16 50	99 00	Philip Duke	Do.
9	James Mallor, jr.	do	May 1, 1867	Nov. 1, 1867	6	13 00	3 50	16 50	99 00	James Mallor, sr.	Do.
10	William Mallor	do	May 1, 1867	Nov. 1, 1867	6	13 00	3 50	16 50	99 00	James Mallor, jr.	Do.
11	John E. Medcalf, sr.	do	May 1, 1867	Nov. 1, 1867	6	13 00	3 50	16 50	99 00	William Mallor	Do.
12	George Hawley	do	May 1, 1867	Nov. 1, 1867	6	13 00	3 50	16 50	99 00	John E. Metcalf, sr	Do.
13	Mads Jensen	do	May 1, 1867	Nov. 1, 1867	6	13 00	3 50	16 50	99 00	George Howley	Do.
14	Thomas Jones	do	May 1, 1867	Nov. 1, 1867	6	13 00	3 50	16 50	99 00	Mads Jensen	Do.
15	Ivory Hendrickson	do	May 1, 1867	Nov. 1, 1867	6	13 00	3 50	16 50	99 00	Thomas Jones	Do.
16	John Calvin	do	May 1, 1867	Nov. 1, 1867	6	13 00	3 50	16 50	99 00	Ivory Hendrecksen, +	Do.
17	Soren P. Petersen	do	May 1, 1867	Nov. 1, 1867	6	13 00	3 50	16 50	99 00	John Calvinn	Do.
18	Christian Anderson	do	May 1, 1867	Nov. 1, 1867	6	13 00	3 50	16 50	99 00	Soren T. Peterson	Do.
19	John Swinson	do	May 1, 1867	Nov. 1, 1867	6	13 00	3 51	16 50	99 00	Christen Andersen	Do.
20	Samuel Lubler	do	May 1, 1867	Nov. 1, 1867	6	13 00	3 50	16 50	99 00	John Svenson	Do.
21	John Anderson	do	May 1, 1867	Nov. 1, 1867	6	13 00	3 50	16 50	99 00	Samuel Lublin	Do.
22		do	May 1, 1867	Nov. 1, 1867	6	13 00	3 50	16 50	99 00	John Anderson	Do.

No.											
23	Lars Eskelund	do	May 1, 1867	Nov. 1, 1867	6	13 00	3 50	16 50	99 00	Lars Eskelund	Do.
24	William Christiansen	do	May 1, 1867	Nov. 1, 1867	6	13 00	3 50	16 50	99 00	William Christiansen	Do.
25	Harman Christiansen	do	May 1, 1867	Nov. 1, 1867	6	13 00	3 50	16 50	99 00	Thomas Christiansen	Do.
26	Hans N. Toft	do	May 1, 1867	Nov. 1, 1867	6	13 00	3 50	16 50	99 00	Hans N. Toft	Do.
27	Jorgen Peterson	do	May 1, 1867	Nov. 1, 1867	6	13 00	3 50	15 50	99 00	Jorgen Peterson	Do.
28	Christian Hansen	do	May 1, 1867	Nov. 1, 1867	6	13 00	3 50	16 50	99 00	Christen Hansen	Do.
29	John Lemon	do	May 1, 1867	Nov. 1, 1867	6	13 00	3 50	16 50	99 00	John Lemon	Do.
30	William Reebead	do	May 1, 1867	Nov. 1, 1867	6	13 00	3 50	16 50	99 00	William Reebead	Do.
31	Jense Jeppesen	do	May 1, 1867	Nov. 1, 1867	6	13 00	3 50	16 50	99 00	Jense Jeppesen	Do.
32	Christian Christiansen	do	May 1, 1867	Nov. 1, 1867	6	13 00	3 50	16 50	99 00	Christen Christensen	Do.
33	Christian Christiansen, 2d	do	May 1, 1867	Nov. 1, 1867	6	13 00	3 50	16 50	99 00	Christen Christenson, 2d	Do.
34	Abraham Shaw	do	May 1, 1867	Nov. 1, 1867	6	13 00	3 50	16 50	99 00	Abraham Shaw	Do.
35	Marius Nielsen	do	May 1, 1867	Nov. 1, 1867	6	13 00	3 50	16 50	99 00	Marius Nielsen	Do.
36	John Warren	do	May 1, 1867	Nov. 1, 1867	6	13 00	3 50	16 50	99 00	John Warren	Do.
37	Julius Christiansen	do	May 1, 1867	Nov. 1, 1867	6	13 00	3 50	16 50	99 00	Julcus Christensen	Do.
38	Theodore Christiansen	do	May 1, 1867	Nov. 1, 1867	6	13 00	3 50	16 50	99 00	Theodor Christensen	Do.
39	H. H. Kearnes	do	May 1, 1867	Nov. 1, 1867	6	13 00	3 50	16 50	99 00	H. H. Kearnes	Do.
40	Rasmus Jensen	do	May 1, 1867	Nov. 1, 1867	6	13 00	3 50	16 50	99 00	Rasmus Jenson	Do.
41	John Knighton	do	May 1, 1867	Nov. 1, 1867	6	13 00	3 50	16 50	99 00	John Knighton	Do.
42	William Andrew	do	May 1, 1867	Nov. 1, 1867	6	13 00	3 50	16 50	99 00	William Andrew	Do.
43	Andrew Lorenzen	do	May 1, 1867	Nov. 1, 1867	6	13 00	3 50	16 50	99 00	Andru Lorenzen	Do.
44	Johan Anderson	do	May 1, 1867	Nov. 1, 1867	6	13 00	3 50	16 50	99 00	Johan Anderson	Do.

This company was mustered into service at Fort Gunnison, Sanpete County, May 1, 1867, by Brigadier General Wm. B. Pace, and assigned to duty by him in the vicinity of said city for the protection of its inhabitants. They were in active service every day until mustered out, November 1, 1867.

I certify that the above account is correct.

H. B. CLAWSON,
Adjutant General Utah Territory Militia.

www.ingramcontent.com/pod-product-compliance
Lightning Source LLC
Chambersburg PA
CBHW020100030726
47498CB00006B/1875